THE JIKAIDA CYCLE

The Dray Prescot Series

THE JIKAIDA CYCLE

Kenneth Bulmer

writing as
Alan Burt Akers

Published by
Bladud Books

First published in 2009 by Bladud Books

Originally published separately by Daw Books, Inc., as:
A Life for Kregen (1979)
A Sword for Kregen (1979)
A Fortune for Kregen (1979)
A Victory for Kregen (1980)

This first omnibus edition published in 2009 by
Bladud Books, an imprint of Mushroom Publishing,
Bath, BA1 4EB, United Kingdom

www.bladudbooks.com

ISBN 978-1-84319-822-2

Contents

A LIFE FOR KREGEN

On the Jikaida Cycle

A Life for Kregen is the first volume of the Jikaida Cycle chronicling the history of Dray Prescot on the fascinating world of Kregen four hundred light years from Earth. Reared in the inhumanly harsh conditions of Nelson's Navy, he has been transported through the agencies of the Star Lords, the Everoinye, and the Savanti nal Aphrasöe to the terrible yet beautiful world of Kregen under Antares, where he has struggled through disaster and success to make a home.

He is a man above middle height, with brown hair and level brown eyes, brooding and dominating, with enormously broad shoulders and superbly powerful physique. There is about him an abrasive honesty and an indomitable courage. He moves like a savage hunting cat, quiet and deadly. He has acquired a number of titles and estates but now the people of the island empire of Vallia, which has been ripped into shreds by ambitious and mercenary invaders, have called on him to lead them to freedom as their emperor. Reluctant to accept the imperium, he shoulders the burden because, rightly or wrongly, he sees this as the lesser evil.

Dray Prescot is undeniably an enigmatic figure; but on the ferocious and lovely world of Kregen he has found headlong adventure, brilliant life and a deep and lasting love. Whatever lies in store for him—and we are fortunate that I have a fresh supply of the precious cassettes on which he records his narrative—life will continue to be a challenge under the streaming mingled lights of the Suns of Scorpio.

Alan Burt Akers

One

Death Warrants

Signing death warrants is no decent occupation for a man. Yet there was no question in my mind that I, Dray Prescot, Lord of Strombor and Krozair of Zy, should delegate the wretched task.

The day had dawned bright and clear with the promise of a breeze to mellow the heat, and the drifting linking lights of the Suns of Scorpio bathed the early world through the windows in pastel tints of apple green and palest rose. By Zair! but this was a time to be alive. I breathed deeply and sat myself down at the balass desk and pulled the official forms nearer and forced myself to the job.

Nath Nazabhan, stony-faced, looked on. The small room was furnished with books and maps, chairs and the desk, and not much else. It was a room that suited me. But I had to sit there and scrawl Dray Prescot, Emperor of Vallia, in the abbreviated Kregish script, a mere DPEV, at the foot of each warrant, at the foot of what was a tree and a dangling rope and smashed neckbones. The reality sickened me.

"Thirteen this morning, majister."

"Aye, Nath. Thirteen miserable wights to be shuffled off."

"You have pity for them?"

"Perhaps. I can't afford pity for myself."

"Vallia would have been finished without you. As it is we've a task on our hands to tax my mythical namesake." Nath took up the first warrant as I pushed it across, signed. "The factions continue to squabble and the country is drenched in blood. The enemies of Vallia seem to grow stronger every day, by Vox, even though we hold the capital. Vondium is—"

"Vondium will stand!"

I looked up and I know my face held that leem-look of primeval savagery that so displeases me and puts the frights up those unfortunate enough to be loo'ard. Nath fingered his chin and fell silent.

He wore a square-necked tunic of a soft pastel tint, girdled by a thin belt from which swung one of the long thin daggers of Vallia. He wore normal morning dress, as did I, and the spread fingers of his right hand groped for the hilt of an absent sword. My gaze shifted to the arms rack. No one on

Kregen, that marvelous and mystical world of terror and beauty, strays far from a quick snatch at a weapon. It is not healthy.

"Yes, majister." Nath might be a fine limber young fighting man, commanding the Phalanx; he was a terror for strict discipline properly administered and maintained. Yet he could temper justice with mercy, as I well knew, understanding the ways of command. We had fought together to free Vallia from the enemies who had swarmed in to feast on a bleeding corpse, and his loyalty and devotion were unquestioned. The pen scratched as I signed, and then poised, the black ink glittering like an ebon diamond.

"Renko the Murais?" The name leaped out at me, written in that perfect script of Enevon Ob-Eye, my chief stylor. "I know a Renko the Murais. A tearaway, yes, very quick with an ax." I looked at the charge. "But not, I would have thought, the man to slay a Relt stylor."

"The charge was proved, majister."

Very stiff and formal, on a sudden, Nath Nazabhan.

"You are satisfied? Renko said nothing in his defense?"

"The case was tried by Tyr Jando ti Faleravensmot. A hard man, yes; but just."

I nodded. "You did not attend?"

"No, majister. The Second Jodhri was receiving new colors at the time, and I—"

"Yes. We were there together. The management of a city and what we have of an empire, quite apart from the army, takes up too much time." I shuffled the warrant aside. "Have in this Renko the Murais. I'll see him before I sign."

"It may not be the same man."

"Exactly my thought. But I must be sure."

"Quidang, majister!"

The papers lay on my desk and the tiny breeze whiffled in through the open casement and lifted the corners. I pondered. There just was not enough time. But—twelve men and the thirteenth might go free, if there had been a miscarriage of justice and Renko the Murais was the Renko I'd known in Valka. He'd been a Freedom Fighter then, when we'd cleared the island of Valka out and the people had fetched me to be their lord. Time would have to be found. I stared at Nath.

"Have Enevon send me in all the papers on these cases. Delay the executions," I said. "I would like to satisfy myself..."

Without going on, I could see that Nath both fully understood why I did what I did, and despaired of me as an emperor who would have a fellow's head off in a trice.

The blurred shouts as orders were cracked out and repeated and the clink-clank of weapons drifted up from the court below where the guards worked at the drills that might keep them alive in battle. The flick-flick

4

plant on the window-sill twined its long green tendrils hungrily, its orange cone-shaped flowers gaping emptily. Later on a dish of fat flies would have to be brought in to keep the flick-flick happy and lush.

"All the same, majister," said Nath, stroking his chin. "When you fight for your rights men must die. It is a law of nature. Death comes to us all—sooner or later—and—"

I smiled. I smiled at Nath Nazabhan and let the smile linger for a full heart-beat before my face resumed its usual craggy mask. I pushed the papers aside and picked up a fresh batch, details of weapons, stores, conditions of wagons. The paperwork was never-ending.

"You quote proverbs at me, Nath. Well, and so it may be true. But the state of the country demands we push out from Vondium and consolidate the midlands and the northeast. I do not know what rights there may be in this."

"You have been fetched to be Emperor of Vallia."

At my instinctive gesture of displeasure, he went doggedly on.

"Everyone shouts for you and they know why they shout. If we are to re-conquer Vallia—"

I glared up at him, sternly, and this time he paused. Then, without embarrassment, he said: "Yes, majister, I know your words. It is more liberation than conquest. But the facts remain and they cannot be altered. If our country is to find any peace at all we must unite ourselves under one flag. And that means the new flag of Vallia you have shown us."

"You have heard me speak of the Wizard of Loh called Phu-Si-Yantong? Yes, well, he is a damned great villain filled with a maniacal desire to subdue and control and hold in his hand all the lands of Paz. It is an insane dream. But, in Vallia, where he has caused us so much trouble—what is the difference? Why should I take the throne and crown and not Yantong?"

Nath's gasp halted me. His face screwed up into the most ferocious scowl, like a chavonth about to charge.

"Because we've seen how the rast treats those he enslaves! By Vox, majister, as soon consign us all to Cottmer's Caverns as let that cramph Yantong rule us."

"So we consolidate what we have and then bring war and bloodshed and misery to the rest of the country—"

He shook his head, angry at the way I was treating him, for which I couldn't blame him. The truth was, and I think he saw a little of it, that I carried the blood-guilt badly.

"We can move with safety in the Imperial provinces surrounding Vondium. The northeast and all the Hawkwa country stands firm for Jak the Drang, Dray Prescot, as emperor. The midlands will rise for us. The northwest—we must deal with the arch-traitor Layco Jhansi and after that teach the Racters a lesson. They fight each other, for which Opaz be praised."

"The Blue Mountains," I said, mildly, "and the Black Mountains are nearer than Jhansi's province of Vennar."

He shook his head. "Only if we strike more westerly of north. And, majister, do not forget the Ochre Limits bar off Vennar and Falinur."

My glance favored the map hung on the wall. The colors mocked me. The mountain chains and rivers, the canals and forests, the badlands and the lush agricultural heartlands, they all demanded attention. Movement of armies bedevils those who would bring overwhelming force to bear on their enemies.

"That is so, Nath. But the Blue Mountains—"

"The Empress, may Opaz shine the light of his countenance upon her, commands the hearts of all, and none more than those ruffians, the Blue Mountain Boys. I think whoever tried to subdue the Blue Mountains has rued the day."

Again, I smiled. Well, Delia and her Blue Mountain Boys are enough to make any old sweat perspire a trifle.

"I had thought we would use the Great River and hit the northwest by curving in from the east." My pointing finger described an arc in the air, extending those phantom lines of march on the map. "As we came in from the south. I had in mind a man to command that army."

He knew exactly what I meant. And, the stubborn old graint, ignored that with sublime self-confidence.

"Any man would be proud to be appointed Kapt and command any army you entrusted into his hands. And there are many men in the army worthy of the task." He looked at me, his eyebrows drawn down, almost challenging me. "As for me, majister, I command the Phalanx with your blessings and where you march there I march."

I grumped at this. "And have I not explained to you, Kyr Nath, that the Phalanx is not best suited to mountain work?"

"Layco Jhansi, who deserves to be shortened by a head, does not foment his insurrections in a mountainous country. The land up there is ideal for my Phalanx."

"And after you've seen off Jhansi, you'll go haring after those damned racters north of him? Yes, well, they all deserve to be made to see the error of their ways."

The papers before me now detailed the condition of the canal narrow boats I had ordered collected. From the famous canals of Vallia the vener were trudging in, hauling their boats, answering the call. The basins and pools of the capital were filling with the brilliantly painted boats. I needed a fleet, and the canalfolk, always proud and independent and disdainfully removed from the petty party politics of the island empire, had decided that for the sake of peace and prosperity and the movement of trade their star must be linked with the new emperor in Vondium. I was happy about that. I had good friends among the canalfolk. And they would be invaluable in the coming struggles.

The future loomed dark and ominous—as so often it does on Kregen, by Zair—and everyone who would stand with us and strike a blow for freedom, in the cant phrase, was welcome.

I say "in the cant phrase." But for the colossal task facing us more than cant would be needed. If we were to cleanse all Vallia, and the island was frighteningly large with many areas still virtually unpopulated, we must seek to make allies of all whom we could and only in the last resort take up arms against them. This was a view not highly regarded, I knew. But the new Dray Prescot saw the wisdom of it, even if my other persona, that wild leem Jak the Drang, was toughly contemptuous of shilly-shallying.

As though Jak the Drang flared up in me I pushed the papers away pettishly and stood up.

"By Vox! I need some fresh air."

Crossing to the arms rack I took down a solid leather belt with a fine rapier and main gauche already scabbarded, the lockets of plain bronze. The weapons were workmanlike, nothing fancy, with silver-wire wound hilts. A matched pair, they were balanced to perfection. Belting the gear on I half-turned to speak to Nath and saw a shadow move against the map. No shadow could be thrown there by the light from the window.

Nath leaped back and the slender dagger appeared in his fist. His face looked stricken.

"Daggers are useless here, Nath," I said, on a breath, quickly. "I think."

The shadow writhed and thickened and flowed, smoked coiling into the semblance of a man, a hunched man in a black cowl, the hood drawn forward so that only the deep furnace-glow of feral eyes showed, demoniac, peering.

Nath shuddered, a deep hollow revulsion of flesh. The dagger shook.

The thought flamed into my mind: "Thank Zair I had not marked the map with my intentions!"

The projected image of the sorcerer wavered, as though his powers fought to coalesce his immaterial substance within the imperial palace. The whole structure had been sealed by my own Wizard of Loh, Khe-Hi-Bjanching, against such lupal projections; but that had been some time ago. The sealings must be weakening with the passage of time. And Bjanching, along with my other old friends, had been hurled back to his home by the mightier sorcerous powers of Vanti, the guardian of the Sacred Pool of Baptism in far Aphrasöe.

We needed sorcerous help here. But Nath Nazabhan after that first stricken reaction responded as a warrior responds. A streak of light hurtled across the room. The dagger glittered as it flew from his hand. Straight through that insubstantial image it whisked, to clang and chime against the map, gouging out a chunk of Falinur, and so drop harmlessly to the floor.

"Devil's work!" burst out Nath, moving back, going for the arms rack, his fist already raking out for a fresh weapon.

"That will do no good." I stood quietly, feeling the blood in my veins, wondering what Phu-Si-Yantong intended now.

For, quite clearly, this lupal projection was Yantong. An evil emanation, certainly, and a dangerous one. He spied on us and he didn't give a single block of ice from Sicce if we knew or not.

The ruby eyes within the enveloping hood would strike a cold chill into the stoutest heart. Narrowly I surveyed this sorcerous apparition of a hated enemy. A cripple—that was the part Yantong had played during the only time I had met him. And it had not been face to face. Always, he kept himself hidden, shrouded. Perhaps he was in very truth a cripple. Maybe that might explain his crippled ambitions. The shadowy form moved of and within itself, as smoke coils upwards. The colors of the map showed through the image, fragmentarily, their brilliance dimmed.

As always and with everyone, I attempt to see the best side. Always, the remembrance of the frog and the scorpion is with me, that a man no less than a scorpion must act to his nature. But, also, I do not forget that a man can judge the consequences, and although he might not fully comprehend all that will follow, must by the very nature of manhood understand that his actions will inevitably be followed by results. Yantong could not, I thought, be all evil. There had to be some streak of better feeling in him. So I looked at the hunched shadowed shape and I pondered.

Nath remained transfixed by the arms rack, held there, I fancied, no less by my words than by the apparition.

For six heartbeats Phu-si-Yantong's lupal projection hovered in the room. I know, for I counted.

The spell broke as a trumpet pealed outside, high clarion notes against the blue. The outlines of the figure shimmered as though bathed in invisible heat. The hooded head turned. The glitter from those ruby eyes dimmed, sparking feebly, paled. As the form vanished, the last of it to disappear was that pair of demoniac eyes.

I let out a breath.

Nath wiped the back of his hand across his forehead.

For a space neither of us spoke. We did not care to break the spiderweb of silence that fell after those silver trumpet notes.

Then I said, "By Vox! May Opaz rot the fellow. At least, he got nothing out of us."

A fraction unsteadily, Nath walked across to retrieve his dagger. He gestured with the blade.

"Falinur will never be the same."

I warmed to him. The experience through which he had just been would have left many a man gibbering.

"Seg wouldn't know whether to be glad or sorry."

"As to Seg Segutorio, the Kov of Falinur," said Nath, re-sheathing the dagger with a snick. "I know he was a blade comrade of yours; but he is peskily absent from his kovnate when we need all the friends we can muster."

It was not a rebuke. Merely a hard-headed comment.

I chose to say, with a little snap, "Seg is a blade comrade, not was."

Nath half lifted his chin; but he chose not to reply.

"Now, Nath, not a word of this to a living soul."

"Quidang, majister."

"Good. Yantong spies on us with an advantage. We must cloak our designs in shadow, sheath our plans in subterfuge. We hew to the plans I have mentioned—unless unforeseen circumstances force us to alter them. If they do, we will."

The clepsydra on its own shelf told me that the hour was almost up and we were due on Voxyri Drinnik. A small ceremony was to be held there to mark the presentation of medals, 'bobs' the swods in the ranks called them, like phalerae, and the importance of keeping the army happy outweighed much. The matter of Renko the Murais had been dealt with in court by one of the judges appointed to the task. It might be thought that presenting new colors to a Jodhri could not rank as importantly in a humanitarian scheme of government as being present in a court of justice. But a man has only so much time on Earth, or Kregen. No matter that because I had dipped in the Sacred Pool of Baptism I was assured of a thousand years of life, each day still contained only forty-eight burs. So we had been presenting standards when Renko had been sentenced. Now we must present bobs when we had promised. The apparition of Yantong must be pushed into its proper perspective.

And, anyway, what was there I could do about the Wizard of Loh? He worked through human tools. His minions sought to enslave the country. In our turn we must resist them.

Anything else was fantasy.

The days were filled with hard work. There was everything to do. The country was still in turmoil and no one talked of the Time of Troubles being over merely because Vondium was in our hands. Vondium, the proud city, was mostly ruins, with the grandiose rebuilding schemes of Yantong halted in mid-execution because I would not flog on the people to work as slaves, and, also, because they insisted on flocking to join the colors and form fresh regiments to help clear out the rest of the island.

Walking out into the mingled streaming suns shine of Antares, I hoisted up the rapier to sit more comfortably. The chances of assassins, stikitches, still being active and seeking my life, in the pay of any number of cramphs who would as lief snuff me out as they would snuff a last candle, remained high. A man must be ready always on Kregen to fight for his life, just as he is ready to sing or to drink, to eat or to laugh.

9

Many of my new comrades waited. Nath Nazabhan was a relatively new comrade, also, for we had been together since we had trained up the Phalanx in Therminsax ready for that great battle. My choice band waited for me. A right rough and tumble crowd, festooned with weapons, brilliant in a motley of uniforms, they greeted me with a roar. I bellowed back, most affably, banishing the dark schemes of Yantong from my mind. Together we rode for Voxyri Drinnik where the great victory had been gained that gave over Vondium to our hands.

The last of the Hamalese prisoners were being sent off back to their homes in Hamal. This had aroused great controversy and acrimony, men saying why did we not keep the rasts as slaves. I would not execute them, for I knew the Hamalians, knew their army, knew the swods in the ranks. I would not kill or enslave, and so they were sent home to Hamal. We still had a debt outstanding with the Empress Thyllis of Hamal, the despotic ruler of the greatest empire in the southern continent of Havilfar. Yantong had used her to further his own schemes; but Vallia had been invaded by Hamalese, there was the matter of the defective airboats, and, also, there was the island of Pandahem to be liberated.

Every way I turned there was work to my hand.

And, always, the greater menace of the Star Lords hovered over me. At a whim they could dispatch me back to Earth, hurl me four hundred light years through the deeps of space, send me back to the planet of my birth and, perhaps, forget me and let me rot.

Fresh concepts about the Star Lords, the Everoinye, had been plaguing me. I had begun to wonder if their designs were so baffling, after all, for certain events seemed to me to bear of only one interpretation. I will leave the reasoning by which I reached this surprising conclusion until later, contenting myself with the simple remark that, if there was good in every man, might there not be a greater good in the Everoinye, who were so much greater than men?

"Lahal, Majister!" bellowed Cleitar. He had once been Cleitar the Smith, and he bore his wicked war-hammer into action. But now he was generally called Cleitar the Standard, for he carried my own battle flag, that yellow cross on a scarlet field fighting men call Old Superb. He rode a zorca and his uniform was splendid.

I raised my hand in salute as we rode out. Vondium was a shadow of the great city it once had been. The other spirits in my choice band were mostly, at this time, from the provinces, for we had recruited there in our drive to the capital; but they were aware of the despoliation. We would rebuild; but our aim was to rebuild the heart of the country through the people and the agriculture and husbandry. Bricks and stones and mortar must follow that.

Volodu the Lungs, a leathery man if ever there was one whose appetite for ale could never, it seemed, be quenched, blew a stentorian blast on his immense trumpet. And that silver instrument was immense. With it Volodu had crushed in the head of a too froward Hamalese Hikdar, smashing through helmet and bone to the very brains beneath. The blast echoed through the streets and cleared a way for us as though we were a pompous procession of robed priests.

There was no need for lictors or any other street-clearing violence as the Emperor of Vallia rode out.

The ceremony passed off well, brilliant and dashing in the glitter of the Suns. I will not go into detail, save to say the old sweats took their medals with a swagger, and no doubt, like Vikatu the Dodger, would trade shamelessly on their prowess to dodge the column for a few sennights to come. And good luck to them. They had risked their lives and limbs in the battle line.

Like any good Kregen who tells the time of day by the state of his innards, I felt the time was ripe for a meal and so we wended our way back to the palace. I had barely crossed the first of the twin canals straddled by the Bridge of Voxyri with the confused onward shrilling of that great fight ringing in echoing remembrance in my head, and Naghan ti Lodkwara was as usual engaged in a slanging match with Targon the Tapster, when the shadows fleeted in.

A lancer, Naghan Cwonin, reined across. Dorgo the Clis shouted. Cleitar the Standard began to furl up the flag. Naghan ti Lodkwara and Targon the Tapster took mutual breaths and, instead of slanging each other, yelled the alarm.

The airboats floated down as though guided by rails.

There were six of them, and each one was of a capacity to hold a dozen fighting men.

So—we were in for a fight.

The devils had chosen their place well. The troops back on the Drinnik would never be over the Bridge in time to assist us. The streets were filled here with ordinary folk about their business trying to put Vondium back together again. Phu-si-Yantong's spying mission must have told him what he wanted to know, and this was a direct result.

Shades of Rafik Avandil, Lion-man!

I ripped out the clanxer scabbarded to my zorca. He was a fine black, mettlesome, whom I called Snowy out of stupid humor as much as contrariness, and I'd ridden him because he needed the outing. The stables were not too well provided as yet, and discretion had to be used. But the men tumbling out of the airboats almost before they touched down were afoot, and so we, mounted on zorcas, were by that much better off.

Two fliers landed in our rear, cutting off a flight back the way we had come.

Cleitar had the flag furled and stowed away now, and his hammer glittered as he lifted it.

Nath Nazabhan drew his clanxer and called across to me, "Ride, majister—there is an alley mouth there—"

I looked at him.

"Well," he said, huffily, swirling the straight cut and thrust sword about, loosening up his muscles. "It was just an idea."

We numbered about twenty or so, bright rollicking companions of my choice band. We faced about four times our own numbers. Well. Yes, a situation in which I had found myself more than once, and usually through my own block-headedness. I lifted in the stirrups. I'd gone out for a breath of fresh air. I was like, and my companions also, to taste blood as well as air. And the air we tasted might well be let in through our ribs.

"Straight through them!" I bellowed. "Slap bang and no tickles. No man stands for handstrokes. Ride like the agate-winged jutmen of Hodan-Set!"

We clapped in our heels and in a rampaging bunch roared into the forming ranks of our Chulik foemen.

Two

Assassins at the Gate of Voxyri

Oh, yes, they were Chuliks all right. Ferocious, yellow-skinned fighting men with ugly three-inch long tusks jutting cruelly up from the corners of their mouths. This bunch was as well-trained in the martial arts as any Chulik mercenary band on Kregen. Reared from their earliest infancy to the bearing of arms, trained to be cold and merciless killers, Chuliks can handle any variety of weaponry they need, and in that heartless and iron-hard discipline they had forgotten, if ever they had known, the softer virtues of humanity.

They are loyal mercenaries if they are paid and fed. They command higher fees than most, excepting Pachaks and Khibils and a few other, not many, of the vast variety of splendid humans on Kregen. They have always been and continue to be formidable opponents.

But my choice band recked nothing of that. Yelling and cursing they clapped in their heels and went racketing down.

The Chuliks with their oily yellow skins and long dangling pigtails from their shaven heads formed a line swiftly. Their faces remained blank and impassive. They knew exactly what they were doing and they did it well.

Their uniforms were simple tunics of brown cloth over which they wore armor of a scaled form, bronze-studded, highly barbaric and flaunting their power. Their helmets bore black and green feathers, but shorn short, workmanlike, a badge of identity clamping each tuft in place. Black and green. Well, they were colors I knew Yantong had used at least once, and so by their use now he seemed to be openly proclaiming his power and contempt for me.

Truth to tell, in that hectic moment as we belted along, I wondered if we would have done better for Cleitar to let Old Superb float free, a ringing challenge to the power confronting us. But that way lay the hubris, the megalomania, the self-importance I detest so much. I had sworn, as I was called to be Emperor of Vallia, that I would do a good sound workmanlike job. Pride is for the vainglorious, in excess, and its unbounded license has caused great sorrow in two worlds.

And then we were among them and Cleitar's hammer lifted dripping crimson, and so that answered that question.

At my back Korero the Shield bore a single targe, a small parade ornament, but with its yellow and scarlet traceries he fended a sweeping blow and lashed back with the blade gripped in his tail hand. Ferocious, Korero the Shield, a Kildoi whose four arms and handed tail both protect and devastate.

With a jolt and a crack we overbore the first line.

Chuliks sagged back—and when a Chulik sags he is either dead or dying.

The zorcas responded nobly as only those superb four-spindly-legged steeds can, all fire and spirit. Never meant for the charge, they flowed on and over in a fleetness of rhythm that bore us on and up. Like hunters at chase we cleared the first line and slammed into the second. But the Chuliks were ready, well-knowing the business of tackling a zorca-charge. Their weapons glittered. We sliced and drew our blades reeking in crimson as we leaped ahead. But the fray thickened and grew denser and Largo the Astorka was down, a spear through his throat. We yelled and swirled our blades and pressed on. But our progress slackened. The impetus of the charge dwindled.

The noise bellowed up, echoing in rolling confusion under the Gate of Voxyri. Volodu put three distinct dents into his massive silver trumpet, and each time burst out with genuine anguish at that desecration. But three Chuliks dropped as though the trumpet had been a poleaxe.

The third line of yellow-tuskers swayed, and men went down. But they held us. The zorcas drew back, pirouetting from a hedge of steel. Furiously I bellowed it out.

"Reform! Break out over the Bridge!"

We swung the zorcas about, their nimble hooves clicking on the cobbles where blood ran between the time-worn stones. The Chuliks back there were unlimbering crossbows, and this made me frown.

"Heads down!" I yelled and clapped in my heels and Snowy surged on, picking up speed, elegantly avoiding tumbled bodies.

The bolts would have had us but for the Gate. The trajectory intersected the masonry and the bolts chinked and tumbled like chicks disturbed in the nest. In the next mur we were out in the sunshine again and bearing down on the men from the two guarding fliers. It was all nip and tuck. Korero surged ahead, despite my yell, and his little yellow and red shield whipped up.

I urged Snowy to greater efforts. In a bunch we crashed out and the Chuliks rose to meet us.

Naghan Cwonin's lance tip was a clotted red mass. He lowered that steel wedge of death and then he was hurled back off his saddle, trailing blood, yelling, a stux clear through him. The Chulik who had hurled that spear did not hurl another, for a streaking dagger crossed the narrowing space and chinked in most neatly over the brass-coiled rim of his corselet.

That Chulik bore a golden image of a grascent on his breast, suspended by golden chains around his neck. The dagger protruded above the golden image of the risslaca for a heart beat, and then the Chulik walked forward, as a dead man walks, blindly, walked forward three paces, four, and almost a fifth before he tumbled under the hooves of the zorcas.

The weapons flamed. The Suns beat down. The dust lifted. And the blood spurted.

The pandemonium was, for a brief moment, akin to the last dying scenes in a sinking ship where the crew panic. Blades clashed. Korero's shield split asunder and he used the half in his hand to dash a Chulik away. But another leaped for him, his yellow tusks dripping, and my clanxer only just swept down in time in a precision-controlled arc that kissed death across a corded neck.

"My thanks, majister—"

"There's another devil, Korero—"

"Your back, Nath!"

"On, on!"

The shouts racketed as we forced our way on. And then we were through. Before us stretched the Bridge of Voxyri, and the open plain with the distant lines of men coming on swiftly. We could have ridden on. We might simply have nudged the zorcas to a further effort and ridden away.

But, as one man—as one man—we turned.

We turned back, raging, and tore once again into those murderous Chuliks and their yellow tusks and their ferocious military skills.

The mellow stone of the Bridge and the Gate, the coolness of blue shadows and the piercing brilliance of the suns light, the clatter of hooves, a distinctive, brittle, rousing sound, the pants of men in combat and the yells of the wounded, the stink of rawly spilled blood—yes, yes, it struck responsive chords in me. But until we were done with scenes of this ugliness Vallia would never be the peaceful country we all intended her to be.

Well—Nath Nazabhan and a few others might question that assumption—but it was what I intended.

The Chuliks saw their attack had failed. They had killed or wounded a number of us, and they had lost more men than they liked. With that quick appraisal of the situation that had earned them as much contempt—in this case misguided contempt—in the past as praise, they took their airboats aloft. The fliers lifted off, swiftly rising and turning to head toward the north.

North.

That made a kind of sense, although they might have been expected to head for the southwest, where no one seemed to know what was happening. Equally, they might have gone southeast, for the situation there was confused. The truth was they might have headed anywhere in Vallia, for we were ringed.

And, even so, this northward flight might be a mere subterfuge.

We were plagued by the lack of airboats. All the vollers had been confiscated by the victors, and we, late into the fray, had to make do with what sorry remnants we could scrape up. As for aerial patrols, they were carried out by a skeleton force that had no chance to halt any determined aerial attack.

Before the troops from the Drinnik reached us we were off our mounts and tending our wounded.

Those who had already started on their last journey to the Ice Floes of Sicce were Naghan Cwonin, Largo the Astorka, Nath the Flute, Aidan Narfolar ti Therduim, Roban Vander and Nath the Mak, sometimes known as Nath the Waso.

We had another five with wounds, great or small, from which only one, Larghos Shinuim the Fortroi subsequently joined his comrades among the ice floes.

So we were cut down by a half.

Nath's face bore a grave look that I saw was compounded as much of worry as of grief and anger.

I attempted to rouse him.

"You, it was, Nath, who told me that all men must die in their time. Praise Opaz for those who survived."

"Wounded or slain," he said. "A half of us. Some will rally, of course. But it is not good enough."

I was not sure what he meant; but in the nature of the circumstances as the first of the men from the Drinnik reached us, I forbore to inquire. Had

15

I done so I know now he would have given me no answer, or would have evaded the issue. What was planted in his mind then was subsequently made plain. And, I may add, to my own personal pleasure and profound gratitude to my comrades.

Looking up from the sprawled body of Nath the Flute, Dorgo the Clis contorted his scarred face into a grimace of anger. He was cut up by Nath's death, seeing they had been friends from boyhood, and however much of death a man sees in his life, the passing of a friend carries a heavier weight.

"Here they come," growled Dorgo, "making a right hullabaloo and late, too damned late, by Aduim's Belly."

"They ran as fast as they could, Dorgo," said Magin, who philosophically bound up a spear wound in his arm. His son, who had been unable to find the excitement he craved in his native Vallia and had gone to be a paktun, would have found all the nerve-tinglers he wanted now, in Vallia. And we could do with all those brave sprightly young men who had left sea-faring, trading Vallia to be mercenary swods overseas.

The men from the Drinnik came up, puffing a little, for they had run fast, as Magin said. They were Hakkodin, axe and halberd men who flanked the regimented files of the Phalanx, and they were raging that they were too late.

At their head came Barty Vessler, his shining, red, smooth, polished face a scarlet glow. No overemphasis can possibly convey the gorgeous color of Barty's face in these moments. He was infectiously impetuous as usual, and spluttering with mingled joy and rage.

"Jak," he bellowed. "Dray, I mean, majister! You might have been killed. Oh, my aching ribs. Oh for a zorca!"

Everyone laughed. There was no stopping that unleashing of pent-up emotion.

Gravely, I regarded him; gravely, for I was the only one not to laugh. Mean, tight-lipped, yes, if you will. But I looked with great favor on this young man, Barty Vessler, for all his incautious ways and feckless moments. And I knew well enough that if he'd had his zorca between his knees he'd have come bolting in from the rear upon the Chuliks and, for almost a certainty, got himself chopped for his chivalric notions.

His brown Vallian hair flopped wildly as he gesticulated. Young and filled with notions of honor, Barty Vessler, the Strom of Calimbrev, yet a fellow who saw the way that honor led him and unflinchingly followed it even if it led through Cottmer's Caverns.

Bells started up a-ringing and citizens came flocking down. The uproar was worse than the fight. I glanced at Nath and Barty and jerked my head. Volodu picked up the little sign and immediately slapped that silver trumpet to his lips.

Volodu the Lungs blew the Clear.

16

Well, the citizens wouldn't know the calls blown by the Phalanx, of course. But the silver notes cleared a way and having sorted out both the quick and the dead, and seen to the wounded, we trotted our zorcas on into the city. Barty took a spare mount and came with us, for he was of that choice band, without a single doubt.

Barty rode with Nath, and scraps of their conversation reached me. Barty was saying: "...quite agree with you, Nath. It just is not good enough."

And Nath, gravely, answering: "Time something positive was done about it, and done quick, by Vox."

They were up to some deviltry, I fancied, and left them to it. I needed a drink of tea, and that was doing something positive, and the quicker the sooner. So we trotted through ruined Vondium the Proud, and the people gave us a cheer as we passed, and so we crossed the wide kyro before the imperial palace, and passed through the gates where the guards slapped their three-grained staffs across, most smartly, and we let the hostlers take the zorcas in an inner court where purple flowers hung down in a scented profusion. The zorcas had done well, and we patted them affectionately as they were led off.

"Let us meet in the Sapphire Reception Room," I called to them as they prepared to trudge off to their quarters. "That is informal enough and yet formal for what we must decide."

I met their puzzled looks with a benign disregard that made them all the more curious.

Barty and Nath exchanged quick, puzzled looks.

But I shouldered off and into the inner apartments of the palace, looking for a rapid bath to wash off the muck and blood, and then for the tea and a repast that would keep the leems of hunger at bay for a bur or so. It was still too early for wine.

The Sapphire Reception Room and most of the wing which housed that informal chamber for semi-formal gatherings had been spared the fire that had gutted a very great deal of the old palace. Yantong had rebuilt much; but the place sagged as though tired, towers and spires toppled inwards and walls slaked along the entrenchments, so that the skyline that had once lifted so arrogantly now looked like a haphazard collection of tooth-stumped jaws. The imperial palace of Vondium looked rather like a tent with the central pole chopped down. Some essential work still went on so as to house conveniently the people involved in the type of government I intended—if that is not too strong a word for the still bumbling ideas I entertained on running the country—and carpenters and masons and brickies gave a pleasing air of busy activity. No one was slave. The reverberations of that stringent policy to which, despite all opposition, I clung, had made, was making, and would continue to make life unpleasant in silly and petty ways as much as large and ponderable fashions.

A party brought in the uniforms and equipment of the dead Chuliks. They had taken their wounded with them. As I say, Chuliks are fighting men.

Giving instructions for the lot to be dumped in the Sapphire Reception Room and for tea in immense quantities to be prepared, I carried on into the small suite we had managed to make habitable. The rooms were not large; but they possessed walls and ceilings, and the water still ran, pumped up by windmills hastily erected on the roof. If you looked out of the north window you saw the charred stump of the old Wersting Tower where they used to keep kenneled those fearsome hunting animals. Already green growing shoots clambered across the blackened crevices and specks of brilliant color lightened with blooms the sere gauntness of the wrack.

Delia was not to be found in the outer rooms, and her handmaidens told me she was in the bedroom. Like me, Delia kept only a very few personal servants, and if I do not mention them overmuch it is because they were so good that they had become a part of our life. Fiona and Rosala tended Delia, and they were girls formed for the delight of the gods, smiling, bright of eye, brilliant of lip, with natures that decked the world in sunshine. No obstacle would be placed in their path when, as is the way of the world, they would wish to marry the young men of their choice. The same openness applied to Emder, a quiet-spoken, gentle, dextrous and extraordinarily competent man who looked after most of my material wants. If you wish to call him a valet, the description matches perhaps half of his duties. He was a treasure and I valued him as a friend.

"Bedroom?" I said. Then, already stripping off the bloodstained clothing: "The empress is not ill?"

"Oh, no, majis," they chorused, and laughed.

Only in the most deeply felt personal relations could the diminutive majis be substituted for majister. Nath Nazabhan would not allow himself the usage, although the offer had been made.

"Well, then, you pretty shishis—out with it!"

Emder, smiling, gathering the clothing, slinging my crusted clanxer harness over his shoulder, said, "The empress has never been better, praise Opaz. The bath is drawn—"

One of my own rules is that because so many times I have presented myself to Delia in a shocking state, hairy, filthy, bleeding, almost done-for, whenever it is possible for me to bathe and change and look at least halfway respectable I will do so. I took the bath first before discovering what the laughter and the little mystery was all about.

Feeling refreshed and still toweling my hair I went through to the bedroom. A pang struck me as no familiar and horrific form arose to check on everyone daring to enter the room where Delia, the Empress of Vallia, took her ease. Melow the Supple, that horrendous and sweet-natured

Manhound, had been sorcerously sent back to her native Faol and my eldest son Drak was off there now, trying to find her, and with her her son Kardo. By Krun! A few Manhounds in our ranks would do wonders for the discomfiture of those who opposed us.

Inside the doorway with my bare feet sinking into Walfarg weave rugs, the towel dangled over into my face. I could see nothing and gave the towel a swipe out of the way as I walked on. When the yellow toweling whisked away I stood gaping more than a trifle foolishly at Delia.

She looked like a twisted bundle tied up ready for the laundry.

Instinctively, for this was Kregen, I leaped forward and even half-naked straight from the bath a dagger dangled at my side. This I drew.

Delia laughed.

"You silly old fossil. Just stand still and let me get out of this slowly and properly."

"By Zair—"

"Wait."

I waited.

She sat on the rug with her right leg bent over her left, the left foot tucked in and pointed and her left arm stretched down her right foot from knee to ankle. Her upper body twisted right around from the waist, although she sat firmly on the floor, until I thought she could look back over her own shoulders. Her right arm was bent behind her back. And that rounded right knee was jammed tightly up under her left armpit. She looked—well, she looked marvelous, of course, all tied up like that of her own volition— but the power and serenity flowing from her took my breath away.

Carefully, moving with a grace that caught at my throat, she unwound herself.

At last she lay back, her arms at her side, and for all anyone would know she might be laid out ready for her last journey to the Kregen equivalent of the Valley of the Kings.

Then, with a smile, a small, cheeky smile, she sat up and said, "I'm ravenous!"

"There is tea in the Sapphire Reception Room. Shouldn't you wear a leotard for that kind of thing?"

"In my own bedroom? With only a grizzly old graint of a husband to blunder in?"

"Well, you run perilous risks—"

"Not now—I don't. I am for tea and miscils and palines—"

"What was that?"

She told me the Kregish for the Spinal Twist, the equivalent to the Sanskrit Ardha-matsyendrasana.

"That's all a part of the Disciplines of the Sisters of the Rose? We have similar although far less seductive exercises in the Krozairs."

19

"Hardly exercises, Dray. A way of tuning in with Opaz, I think; a way of getting through material worlds to what really matters beyond them."

"I know."

Shaking my head at the marvel of Delia I saw about getting dressed. A simple tunic sufficed me, and Delia wore a soft laypom-colored tunic girded with a narrow belt fashioned from interlinked silver flowers. We both swung daggers from the belts. She looked gorgeous. The dress in its magical way set off the glory of her face and those brown eyes that could be so melting or so imperious, and added a special luster to the chestnut tints in her brown hair. Fit, she looked, radiant. As they say on Kregen, she had the yrium for an empress.

We went together through the hastily refurbished corridors and past blackened and windowless openings in the walls to the Sapphire Reception Room. My people were already there, changed and foaming for the meal. They waited for us, as was decent; but we were not late. We might have been, had Delia not been of so determined a nature.

In the absence of any properly organized palace retinue and court dignitaries, the rump made do as best they could. A major-domo—old Garfon the Staff—hobbled up to me, for he had taken an arrow in his heel and it was slow to heal, and banged the balass, golden-banded staff down on the flags by the door. I stopped his yell at once. If the people in there didn't yet know me, then, by Vox, I was in the wrong business. And, yet, they could know only the outward me, the Dray Prescot who banged and barged about and thumped skulls and got things done. They could know nothing of the Dray Prescot who for long hours agonized over what to do for the best, and hoped he could do it, and trembled in doubt.

"A strange happenstance, majister," old Garfon the Staff boomed. He was a mite put out, as all major-domos are, that he hadn't got around to bellowing out titles. "Two embassies await audience and crave your indulgence."

"Spit it out, Garfon, for my mouth is like the Ochre Limits."

"They await audience in the Second Enrobing Chamber—that was spared except for the northeast corner of the roof—and, well, majister, it is indeed passing strange."

Delia put her hand on my arm. So I just said, "Well?"

"One embassy is from the Racters."

"Those cramphs. Well, they deal legally, or, at least, most of the time. Go on."

"The other is from Layco Jhansi."

A gasp broke from my people who listened.

My brows drew down.

"A deputation from the most powerful political party in Vallia—or, at least, the party that was the most powerful. And a deputation from the old emperor's chief pallan, who betrayed him and tried to assassinate him. This is, good Garfon, exceedingly interesting."

"It does not take a wizard to divine what they want," said Delia.

Barty Vessler bubbled over, half-laughing, half-enraged at what he saw as the effrontery of it.

"Each is prepared to offer you an alliance, majister. That is the gist of it. One against the other, I'll warrant."

"Aye," I said. "Each offers alliance, for they are at each other's throats up there in the northwest."

Delia laughed, a pure tinkle of sound.

I nodded. "And, seeing they are like savage leems, one with the other, you have put both deputations, Garfon the Staff, both of them together in the same chamber."

Three

Two Deputations Amuse Us

The aftermath of that damned vision of the Wizard of Loh, Phu-Si-Yantong, clung unpleasantly. I would not forget what he had attempted against me during the Battle of Voxyri when he had sent me a personal and hideous vision of Delia betrayed by the arch-seducer, Quergey the Murgey. That plot had failed and in nerving me to take a fateful decision had brought Vondium into our hands. That was the battle in which the Phalanx had finally decided it could go up against any kind of army and win, without doubt, against my stern admonishments.

So my anger was still fizzing and undirected, for Yantong could be anywhere in Paz, manipulating his puppets at a distance. I could, for the moment, do nothing against him.

So it behooved me to contain and control anger against the masters of these two deputations. They deserved anger—and the people of Vallia opposed to them would call it righteous anger—but I tried to look into the future. Alliances must be formed, in order to bring to a rapid close the agony that ripped Vallia apart.

Garfon the Staff went scurrying off to separate the two deputations. He went with Barty's raucous comment that he might find the Second Enrobing Chamber a sea of blood if he did not hurry.

One or two voices raised at that, commenting that the event might be a Good Thing, that it would rid the world of a few more rasts.

"Palines," said Delia, with firm practicality, offering me the dish heaped with the succulent yellow berries.

Scooping a handful I cocked an eye at Nath Nazabhan, as, cup in hand, he sauntered across. "Neither of them, majister, for my money."

I chewed. "If we do not have to fight one or t'other, that will free half of our hands."

Korero laughed.

"Mayhap. But an alliance with a traitor or a bunch of political chauvinists is not to my liking." Nath was serious.

"Nor mine, by Vox!" said Barty.

"If you were drowning and an unpleasant villain saw fit to stretch out a hand to save you, would you refuse?"

"That's different!" And: "That's not fair!"

"Nevertheless, we are like to drown under the weight of the military and aerial force the Hamalese and the insurrectionists can bring against us. We hold Vondium, parts of the midlands, and the northeast. The northwest, at the least, is held by Vallians. All the rest—"

"Quite! All the rest is enslaved by this bastard Wizard of Loh, or his minions, or by damned revolutionaries!" Barty was most wroth. His face shone like that famous polished red apple set out at the forefront of the grocer's stall. His brown Vallian eyes popped. He would have gone on, but Delia said, "Barty." He shut his mouth as a trout shuts on a fly.

"I repeat. At the least, these are Vallians."

Now, I said this with some malice. I had sojourned long in Hamal, and knew its ways and people passing well. I had good friends there—admittedly, friends who did not know I was at the time Prince Majister of Vallia. Hamal as the hated enemy had wronged Vallia, that was generally acknowledged. But the Empress Thyllis must answer for much of those crimes. Once this mess was sorted out we must march in friendship with Hamal. Common sanity indicated that. So by stressing the very Vallianness of the compact offered, I sought to open their eyes. Once they agreed, then I could spring the snapper...

Old Archolax the Bones, spare, wiry, dressed somberly in dark gray with a golden and scarron chain about him, spoke up. His face bore deep lines from nose to mouth, and his air of gravitas was heightened by the emphasis of his diction. He had been newly appointed Pallan of the Treasury—for Lykon Crimahan was still away fighting for his estates of Forli and the money situation needed immediate attention—and he took his position seriously.

"If they offer an alliance through their embassies, majister, they are in need of assistance, one against the other. It would be well to seek to know to what degree and amount they are willing to pay for such an alliance. Opaz knows, the treasury is bone dry."

"A shrewd thought, Archolax."

"Anyway," said Barty, a little mollified and once again able to meet Delia's eye. "Let them wait a while." He handed me a plate heaped with sandwiches and with a cup perched on the side. We habitually stood to talk and eat during these sessions, although comfortable seats, brought from all over the ruins of the palace, were available.

I started to eat, and, wolfing down a bamber sandwich, said, "I'll keep 'em waiting just as long as protocol demands."

In the event I gulped down the rest of the meal and wiped my hands on a yellow cloth and went away to the Second Enrobing Chamber, determined to let chance arrange which embassy I saw first. Garfon the Staff had left that from the Racters there, and had shown that from Layco Jhansi to the Samphron Hall's anteroom. The Samphron Hall no longer existed, being a mere maze of foundations, and the anteroom still persisted in smelling of smoke.

The party from the Racters numbered four, and they were led by a man I knew, Strom Luthien.

His thin shrewd face with the bright sharp eyes and the permanently hungry expression did not betray his thoughts as I entered. Guards stood at the door. I wore a rapier, picked up from Emder on the way. We regarded each other for a space.

Finally, with an ironical bow, he said: "Majister." With a sweep of his hand he indicated his companions and named them. Each one wore the black and white favors of the Racters, flaunting those colors here in Vondium from whence all the known Racters had fled.

Luthien was a Strom—that is roughly equivalent to an Earthly count—by title alone, for he no longer owned lands. He was the perfect agent for the Racters, and knew it and acted the part well. His insolence was veiled just enough so that no offense might be taken—at least, not by me, who was not an emperor in the mold of emperors of the past.

The offer was as we had expected. Alliance between our two forces, first against Layco Jhansi, and then against the Hamalese and the mercenaries and all the other vermin who had flooded into Vallia to pillage. He made no mention of the embassy from Jhansi. I forbore to bring up what was clearly a prickly subject. I kept a graven and serious look on my face—not a difficult task, by Krun!—and heard him out.

The clothes these four Racters wore were the usual decent Vallian buff coats and breeches. Their wide Vallian hats with the black and white feathers lay on a side table. They bore no arms. My guards would have seen to that, and relieved them of their rapiers and main gauches long before they were conducted here. I studied the clothes and discreet insignia. Nothing out of the way there.

Memory of the golden image of the grascent, that leaping scaled risslaca with the powerful hind legs and wedge-shaped head of destruction, worn by the Chulik who had attempted to slay us under the Gate of Voxyri, made me wonder if Phu-Si-Yantong had infiltrated the ranks of the Racters. It was most unlikely that he had not. But he would scarcely parade that kind of hidden exercise of power openly.

When that particular Wizard of Loh struck, he struck from the shadows.

Well, of course, they all do. But Yantong's menace held a special brand of cunning and absolute conviction of superiority. I still fancied I could find something in him of admiration to ordinary folk; but I had to acknowledge that it would be damned hard to unearth.

"What answer shall we carry back, majister?"

I let them hang a space before I replied.

"I must ponder on this," I said, at last, keeping a straight face. "It is not a light matter."

"It touches the well-being of all Vallia."

'That is sooth. Tell me, from whom do you come?"

"We represent the Racters."

"That I know. But who sent you? Who is still alive who commands your allegiance among the black and whites?"

"Those whom you met in Natyzha Famphreon's garden, and others. We are a strong and virile party, and—"

"Spare me the boasting. Layco Jhansi will no doubt say the same of his powers."

"That cramph!" burst out Strom Luthien. His narrow face betrayed all the bile in him. "He should be strung up by the heels and left to rot."

'Tell me, Strom Luthien. What does Natyzha Famphreon say to the new emperor? Or did she not give you a private message?"

Luthien allowed his thin dark moustache to lift at one corner. "Aye, she did. I give it to you under the code of heraldry."

I nodded. "Speak."

"When a leem leads a ponsho flock, the chavonths gather. But it is the Werstings who take the flesh."

I did not laugh. The brazen old hussy! At least, she recognized that I was in sober truth comparable to a leem, a powerful and elemental force of destruction imprisoned in human guise and apostrophized as a leem, an eight-legged hunting beast of superabundant energy and incredible ferocity. She knew I was not the fake, the pseudo Hyr-Jikai, the publicity-created Prince of Power without a shred of Jikai about him that so many people in Vallia and other parts still believed me to be.

And, as you will readily perceive, that did not verge on megalomania, on overweening pride, or on puffed-up vanity. No, by Krun! It was all those horrendous things rolled into one and spread out, like a mirror of truth, for me to stare at my own dark reflection and recoil from—if I still had the morality.

But, I sensed dimly that I must distinguish between the sins of evil self-importance and a too-crazed ego-mania, and a sober understanding that to do the things I had set my hand to would demand, must demand, a man prepared to accept the darker destinies of humanity as well as the lighter.

These thoughts were not pleasant, and Strom Luthien moved back a pace, his hand falling to the empty scabbard. He no doubt thought my displeasure had been occasioned by the words of Natyzha he had relayed. Well, he was wrong. But I did not disillusion him.

"Those are the words of San Blarnoi, I believe," I said in that old nutmeg-grating voice. "Very well. Whatever I may decide about this offer of an alliance, there remains this. You may carry back to your masters this word: 'A man pleads with his wife to do something and she refuses on the ground he is giving her orders.'" I glared hotly at the Racters. "You may tell all the Racters that the new emperor in Vondium is the emperor. There is no other. All their puppets have tangled strings. And there are regiments of fighting men with shears to untangle them—finally."

Strom Luthien knew me of old. I do not think he had heard me talk like this before. He had not witnessed the gradual emergence of Jak the Drang.

And, I admit, and with perhaps not enough shame, that I welcomed the chance to let the Racters know the true position.

Luthien swallowed down and got out a few words.

"We will carry your message—majister."

There was no sarcasm in that last word.

I nodded and left them. Before I could face the embassy from Layco Jhansi—and he deserved to swing high, as my men said—I went along to our private rooms. Delia was not there, for which I was thankful. I bathed my face and then found a cup of water and drank that, and spat, and so, pulling my tunic straight, marched off for the anteroom to the Samphron Hall.

This Layco Jhansi... His province was Vennar, immediately to the east of the Black Mountains, a land that gave him an ample income, being lush and fertile in areas which afforded good husbandry and barren in others, where mining brought silver and alkwoin and other valuable minerals to swell his coffers. His colors were Ochre and Silver. He had been the old emperor's chief pallan, his strong right hand, and he had betrayed that trust. He had set Ashti Melekhi to poison the emperor and when that plot had been foiled had seized his chance in the Time of Troubles and struck for the power himself. He had taken over Falinur. He was, without a doubt, still a most powerful foeman. I wondered whom he had sent to talk business with me.

The ashy taste of smoke still clung about the anteroom as I nodded to the guards at the doors and went in.

Jhansi had sent five people to attempt to persuade me to ally with him.

I knew only one, Ralton Dwa-Erentor, the second son of a minor noble, who might style himself Tyr because his father's rank and his own title did not come directly from the hands of the emperor. Had the emperor bestowed the title, Dwa-Erentor would have been Kyr Ralton. I nodded to him, as politeness dictated, for he had proved himself a keen racing man, riding sleeths, a dinosaur-like saddle animal I do not much care for, and I fancied he hewed to Jhansi's party because of his father.

The leader of the deputation rose from the chair to greet me. He rose slowly. I allowed this. I would be patient, understanding, and I would not lose my temper. So I, Dray Prescot, decided.

Ha!

This ambassador introduced himself as Malervo Norgoth, a man whose immediately striking feature was the thinness of his legs and the bulk of his body, which overlapped him on all sides like a loosely-tied haywain. His face bore traces of makeup. I eyed him as he spoke; but he piped up with a bold front, confident that what he had to say was of the utmost importance. Well, it was to him and his master, no doubt.

He wore hard-wearing traveling clothes of buff and gray, and, like his companions, his weapons had been removed. He was a Tarek—a rank of the minor nobility—no doubt created by Kov Layco Jhansi. He was a man whose own importance expanded or receded with the company he kept. And, it was perfectly plain from his bumptious manner, he regarded me as a fake-emperor and someone in whose company he might expand wonderfully.

As he made me the expected offer, I studied his companions. They seemed to me a bizarre lot. One of them, a very tall Rapa whose vulturine head was adorned with green and yellow feathers, and whose clothes hinted at armor beneath, grasped a long steel chain of polished links. The collar was empty, a round of bronze-studded steel. I wondered what manner of feral beast normally occupied that hoop of metal. The ring appeared large enough for a chavonth; probably it was a wersting, half-tamed and savage given half a chance. I doubted it would be a strigicaw.

The fourth personage was a woman, and, to be frank, she was one of the ugliest women I have ever seen. I felt quite sorry for her, for her personal appearance was clean and decent, good clothes, freshly cleansed face, tidy hair and impeccable fingernails. But the cast of her features resembled so much the stern-end of a swordship that I fancied she bore a deep-seated wounded pride under her harsh exterior.

And the last of this deputation—the first, given their respective powers—stood looking at me from under wild tangled brows. His eyes were Vallian brown. But his face was the face of an ascetic, marked by lines of self-inflicted punishment, grooved with masochistic fervor. He wore a hitched-up robe of skins, pelts out. His head was crowned by a rawly yellow skull, the skull of a leem, as I judged, and ornaments and bangles dangled and clanked as he moved. His left hand grasped a morntarch, the crook garnished with brilliants and the shaft embellished with wrapped skins and the legs of small animals and a couple of rast skulls. The smell wafting from this sorcerer, Rovard the Murvish, assured him a wide berth, and the woman kept herself at the far end of the line from him. I wrinkled up my nostrils at his stink; but I gave no sign of the affront I felt he gave me, here in the imperial palace of Vondium. By Vox! I'd been flung down here before the throne in a much worse condition and stinking far higher. He shook the clattering morntarch, softly, as though to remind me of his powers.

Yet, despite those vaunted powers—and how real they were I did not fully know—which he shared as an initiate in the Brotherhood of the Sorcerers of Murcroinim, he wore a gaudy gold and emerald belt from which swung empty scabbards.

Malervo Norgoth, the ambassador, was winding up the preliminary terms of his offer.

Listening, I tried to understand why Jhansi would have sent these particular people and what they could bring to the deputation. Jhansi was a rogue, well enough, and had proved it; but he was shrewd. He liked to work through other people and, as in the case of Ashti Melekhi, when they failed him he would unhesitatingly destroy them.

"Falinur," I interrupted. "How stands Falinur in this?"

Norgoth smirked, very supercilious. "The Falinurese stand with Kov Layco."

That seemed likely. The two provinces marched, the east of Vennar and the west of Falinur sharing a common boundary. The Falinurese had detested their new kov, my staunch comrade, Seg Segutorio, because he had tried to stamp out slavery. The people of Falinur would have been happy to throw in their lot with Jhansi. Well, that plot had failed and the attempt to seize power by force in the descent on the capital had gone awry when Phu-si-Yantong's puppets had appeared on the scene. But the current situation was new and I had to learn what I could. So we talked for a space and then I told them I would consider the matter, as I had told the embassy from the Racters.

Norgoth shook his head.

"That is not good enough! We must carry an answer back today—within the bur, for you have kept us waiting long enough as it is."

I stared at him.

He stood his ground, whereat I was pleased, for that meant I was keeping my temper and my face must appear bland and indifferent.

"There are people—nobles and pallans—with whom the matter must be discussed."

This was not true; but it sounded genuine enough and would be accepted as normal conduct.

Again Norgoth shook his head.

"Not so. You may be a nithing, as all men believe; but I do know you would take this matter into your own hands."

"Believe it. And reck that when I say I will think on this and tell you my answer, that is what I mean."

The woman opened her mouth to speak, and Ralton Dwa-Erentor, that canny sleeth racer, butted in swiftly. He clearly wished to pacify the rising passions here.

"Surely, Tarek Malervo—two burs will not make all that difference?"

Ralton glanced at me as he spoke, so that I understood his genuine desire to help. But his words were wholly wrong.

"Two burs!" shouted Norgoth. 'Two burs! We must have the answer, here and now."

And, of course, Ralton Dwa-Erentor should have seen that I, had I been your ordinary run of emperors, would never have stood still for any kind of time limit. Two burs or instantly. But he tried to help, and that forgave him much. A fleeting thought of Thelda, Seg's wife, the lady kovneva, crossed my mind. She was always trying to help and making a mess of things. She'd been sorcerously flung back to her home in Evir, far in the north of Vallia, and what had happened to her since then Opaz alone knew. I fancied that Seg had gone looking for her. That would explain his absence even though he had been sent off to his home in Erthyrdrin at the northern tip of Loh.

By Zair! What I wouldn't give to have Seg and Inch and Balass and Turko and Oby and all the others with me, here and now, ready to face the perils that lay ahead!

And my family, scattered every which way, each one busy about his or her pursuits—I would really have to talk seriously to Delia and see about rounding them up. Although that would not be the way I'd phrase it, by Vox.

So I looked at Norgoth, this Tarek Malervo Norgoth, and I felt the old blood thumping and I gripped my fists together into the small of my back and ground my jaws down, tightly, so as to keep the proceedings on a half-way decent level of civilized transaction. But it was hard, by Zair, it was hard.

At last I unclenched those old rat-traps of mine and managed to say in a quiet voice: "Here and now, Norgoth? Then you must expect the answer to be no, surely?"

"Aye! That we do expect. I have said so all along."

"But I have not!" burst out Ralton Dwa-Erentor. His young face looked sullen, determined, as though he had built up a charge and now it was coming spilling out. The sullenness was very close to mutiny. "We must stand with honest Vallians against the Racters and the bastards from Hamal and their Opaz-forsaken cramphs of mercenaries."

They tell me that friends and friendship are becoming dirty words in this wonderful new civilization we are building here on Earth. That may be, and may be for the worse. But as I stood watching Ralton as he spoke so vehemently, I felt that in other circumstances we could have been friends. The determination in him to say out what he believed in, against the feelings of the ambassador, warmed me.

I bent my brows on Malervo Norgoth.

"Why does Layco Jhansi choose you to lead the deputation, if you seek only rejection as an answer?"

Ralton fired up at this; but the woman turned her battleship-old-head and he simmered down. But he glowered most handsomely.

"We knew the Racters were sending. That, alone, seemed good enough reason." The contempt in Norgoth stung.

Everyone spied on everyone else. Of course. That was just another of the pretty little ways of life an honest old sea dog had to understand. And, in all this, just how much was the devil's work of Phu-Si-Yantong?

"I still see no value in this mission from Jhansi."

"Will you or will you not stand with us against the Racters?"

"I have said, I will ponder this and give you my answer presently."

A rattle from the sorcerer drew my attention away from Norgoth.

A blank and horrifying whiteness shrouded his eyes so they looked like corpse-eyes, glaring sightlessly upon me. Foam speckled his lips and dripped in white-tinged green streamers upon the unkempt beard. He trembled. He shook as a tree shakes in the tempest. The hard bean-rattle of his morntarch clicked and clattered like the claws of rats. His right arm lifted and extended horizontally. The clenched fist uncurled and the long brown fingernails, rimmed in grime, spread and the forefinger pointed at my breast.

His panting filled the anteroom with opaque beats of sound.

"Now you will see why!" shouted Norgoth. His thin legs carried that gross body sideways, away from the sorcerer, and his face betrayed a glee made manifest in his delight at my coming destruction.

I felt the blast of psychic power.

I felt it. Like a wall of rushing air as one puts one's head over the shield in a flier. Like the blow from an axe against the brim of the helmet. Like the nuzzling embrace of a graint as that great beast seeks to crush ribs and pelvis and skull. All of these sensations flared in the scything attack. I staggered. I took a step backwards.

Norgoth yelled again, urging his sorcerer, this Rovard the Murvish, to greater effort, demanding that he render me incapable and in his power.

So they did not wish to kill me. They had deeper designs. Their object

29

was to place me in hypnosis, a saturated psychic state in which I would obey every command they chose to give me, in which I would be their puppet.

Well, I have been the puppet of the Star Lords, aye, and of the Savanti, too. I have been used by Wizards of Loh in ways that are passing strange, and have fought. And I have been the recipient of favors from Zena Iztar, that superhuman woman who from time to time had appeared to me, exhorting me to courage and to perseverance, and who had enabled the genuine formation of a devoted Order of Brothers, the Kroveres of Iztar. She it was who had extended some measure of protection over me, spreading her aegis. And even the Star Lords had descended from their aloof mistiness to afford me a defense against Phu-Si-Yantong. So I staggered back and then recovered and glared at the sorcerer with a malice that rose fiery and lurid from the depths of my spirit.

Well, poor fool, Dray Prescot. Instantly Rovard the Murvish spun his magical apparatus into wilder swings and sweeps and the reek of him puffed loathsomely into the anteroom. But I stood there, defying him. Poor fool indeed!

For, of course, I should have appeared to succumb. I should have pretended to fall under the hypnotic sway. In a deceit like that I could have carried off easily enough, I fancy, lay the way to learn much.

But I did not. I do not think it was pride, pride that showed itself in my unsought ability to withstand his sorcery. For I have little truck with pride. Rather, it was a sheerly warrior's reaction, an instinct to fight back when attacked.

So, for a space, we stood there, locked in psychic combat.

And then—by Zair!—and then the horrifying numbness began to eat at my brain and the anteroom spun dizzily about me and I staggered, brought low as a tree is brought low when floods eat away its roots.

Four

Rovard the Murvish, Sorcerer of Murcroinim

The stink of smoke clinging in the anteroom mingled with the stench from Rovard. My head felt unscrewed, ready to lift off as a voller lifts off, and spin away and up into the vasty reaches beyond the stars. I had traveled between the stars, carried along by the Star Lords, and the queasy sensation in my guts acted as an unpleasant tonic to afford me an antidote to that drifting, rising, floating sensation of helplessness.

If the Star Lords who held such potent sway over my affairs on Kregen had given me protection, if Zena Iztar to whom I looked for help had spun a dazzling net of defense for me, I needed that help now.

One of the troubles with me, I often feel, is that I am not flesh, fowl or good red herring. I hover and drift between roles and if, as friends have assured me, that is a part of strength, it's a peculiar form of strength when compared with the single-mindedness of those who know exactly what they want and go hell for leather for it and devil take anyone who gets in their way.

Probably that feeling, dredged from the hidden themes fundamental to my nature, is why I take such joy in adopting disguises and assuming different names. My story so far will make much clear; I do know that when Rovard sought to dominate me and thrust his will power down over mine as a man cloaks a beast before he slits its throat, he aroused such a storm of rejection that I have the nasty feeling that even if the Star Lords and Zena Iztar had not pressed the sign of their protection upon me I might have resisted him.

And—I had sworn to myself not to lose my temper.

I staggered and almost fell. The waves of psychic power beat upon me as the tides of Kregen beat upon the rocks of the sea shores. I staggered; but I did not fall.

I glared back. My hand did not grope toward the rapier hilt. I made no physical move save to plant my feet firmly on the rugs. I battled. I used that same will power I had sought to use against the Star Lords and so prevent them from hurling me back to Earth. I struggled. It was done.

Do not ask me how it was done.

I was standing up, tall, wide-shouldered, and Rovard was vomiting all over the rugs, a vile stream as he retched and choked.

Norgoth let out a howl of pure frustration.

And Ralton laughed.

The woman screamed.

The Rapa touched a secret latch and the steel hoop sprang open and then, poor fool, he stood gaping witlessly as nothing sprang foaming and clawed in death toward my throat.

Norgoth glared around, his eyes rolling up as his sorcerer vomited and vomited upon the rugs.

"There is a greater sorcery here," he said. He looked wild, frightened and yet still bolstered by remnants of his own imagined strength. "A Wizard of Loh. There is a Wizard of Loh near and he thwarts all."

I shook my head. I was amused.

"Not so."

As though he took my words as a signal, for they were true as far as I knew, Norgoth acted.

For all the magical powers I believed assisted me, I remained a mortal man still. Maybe there were no sorcerous powers. Maybe my dip in the Pool of Baptism was enough. Perhaps the Savanti nal Aphrasöe had exerted some influence. But, for all that, I was a mere mortal man and could be slain by steel.

On those spindly legs Norgoth leaped.

He did not lack courage. His hand closed on my rapier hilt and I realized with a shock that the sorcerer's attack had left me weak, weak and slow.

My own hand clamped on his before he could draw. He would have done better to have tried for the left-hand dagger. For a space we struggled. He struck me in the face with the brass-studded back of his glove, and I took the blow and felt the sticky wetness and so gave him back the buffet. He sprawled back. His gross body balanced wonderfully upon those thin and ludicrous legs and he did not fall. But he collided with the woman. She pushed him off with a curse and tried to stick her nails into my eyes. I swayed and tripped her and I did not hit her as she went down.

Ralton remained standing, steadfast, unmoving.

The sorcerer now held his guts under the stinking pelts and groaned and gagged and rolled his eyes, which had reappeared from wherever they had been during his demonstration of sorcerous powers. The Rapa kept fiddling with his steel chain and collar and made no move against me.

I hauled the woman up by the collar of her tunic and stood her on her feet and pushed her at Norgoth. The two clung. Well, they were fit partners, I judged.

Then, with a fine swing and panache, the guards threw open the door and the anteroom filled with twinkling steel.

"Hold!" I bellowed. "All is in order. See that the deputation from Layco Jhansi is assisted on its way back. They are returning—now!"

At this, Ralton Dwa-Erentor took a step forward, his face strained, puzzled, and his right hand half extended.

I looked at him, a straight, level, demanding glare.

"My thanks, Ralton Dwa-Erentor. I recall your sleeth—Silverscale, I think—gave my zorca a fine run. But sleeths will never best zorcas. Go back to Jhansi and remember this."

He took my meaning.

"I will, majister."

So I stood aside as the guards, tough, no-nonsense Pachaks, saw the embassy out. The woman favored me with a long look of loathing. The Rapa held the steel collar open, and his vulturine face with the arrogant beak exhibited expected joy at once more beholding his pet, whatever ferocious beast it might be. The sorcerer, Rovard the Murvish, had to be assisted out. Green foam-flecked slime dribbled from his beard. And, I swear it, his eyes were crossed as he left.

The last to leave was Malervo Norgoth.

He said, "I shall carry your words to Kov Layco. But I do not think he will be discomfited by them."

"Words won't hurt you," I said, most cheerfully, "unless a Wizard utters them, and then only if you are credulous. Tell him there is a length of rope waiting for him, with a loop at the end. I fancy it will snug right tightly up under his ear when the time comes."

"When the time comes, Dray Prescot, the rope will be around your neck."

"Oh, I don't doubt I deserve it. But Jhansi will be there first to show me the way."

So they left and there was no Remberees between us, and I was told that they did not observe the fantamyrrh—except Ralton Dwa-Erentor.

Taking myself off to the Sapphire Reception Room I reflected that there was little in this to please. The exhibition to which I had just been treated ruled out the possibility of thinking about the offer of alliance from Jhansi. But then, could the offer have been genuine? My reactions in more or less having the embassy slung out must have been right, instinctively right. And I had promised myself not to flare up into that old intemperate rage. Almost, I had broken that promise. I tried not to feel smug as I went back to the people waiting for the news.

"So, majister," said Nath, somewhat heavily. "Does this mean you ally us with the Racters now that Jhansi is once more foresworn?"

"I don't see why you had to let the kleeshes go!" burst out Barty. He was furious, and, in his eyes, rightly so. "They betrayed their embassy, all their talk of heraldic immunity was a mere base trick. String 'em all up, that's the way of it—or should be."

Delia regarded him, for she favored him as a son-in-law when our daughter Dayra returned to the fold. Barty spluttered and splashed and covered his face drinking a cup of good vydra tea. Oh, yes, a right hellion our Barty Vessler in matters of chivalry and honor.

My people knew our ways well enough by now to talk freely among themselves discussing the offer from the Racters. Also, they knew that while I would take cognizance of what they said, the final decision was down to me. That was what being an emperor was about. I felt inclined to hear what Delia had to say. She was an emperor's daughter. But in all this idle chatter about emperors, I never forgot what I had promised myself on Voxyri Drinnik. The ways of emperors were not for me.

The talk flowed. The tea was quaffed. The food was eaten. We all had busy lives to lead with much to do and the few murs we could spare for this kind of pleasant interlude had already been exceeded. By ones and twos the company began to leave and the clepsydra on the shelf would have collapsed if worried stares carried physical force.

Nath Nazabhan and Barty Vessler were talking to Delia and I crossed to them, having had a few words with Jago De-Ka, a Pachak Jiktar who had come in from Zamra with news. The island was almost clear of the reiving mercenaries and flutsmen, he reported, and the Pachaks who had made a part of the island their home were now more than ever wedded to their new way of life. I expressed myself as satisfied, keeping a grave mien, as was seemly in so important a matter to a Pachak. Pachaks are a race of diffs with whom I delight in doing business.

Barty was still rather high on indignation, and Nath was as grimly ferocious as ever when I joined them.

Archolax the Bones, the deep lines in his face more pronounced than ever, walked across to us with a most determined air about him. I sighed. I could guess.

"...until they dangled for two sennights!" quoth Barty.

"But you have friends up there, do you not?" inquired Delia with that devastating simplicity that snicks in like a rapier between the ribs.

"Friends? Oh, aye, friends. But if they wear the white and black these days, how can they be friends?"

Old Archolax sneezed. With great ceremony he withdrew an enormous square of yellow silk and blew. While the stentorian bellow was still echoing through the room he spoke up, swirling the yellow silk about grandly.

"Majister! The treasury is scraped to the bottom so hard I swear you would not get a single stiver out of the dust in the vaults. The Racters are all the grievous things we know them to be. But, majister! They have money. They are rich. Their estates up there are fabulously wealthy. An alliance there would fill our coffers. We could hire mercenaries and throw the damned mercenaries from Hamal out of Vallia."

He did not finish with: "I have spoken." Had he done so it would have fitted perfectly.

Delia's face bore that knowing, half-mocking, teasing smile.

The way these old buffers use their sneezing and their kerchiefs always amuses me—and causes me some facetious admiration, too, seeing that they thereby cloak their own highly individual designs. Old Evold Scavander, the wisest of the wise men of Valka, could always get that haughty and promising Wizard of Loh, Khe-Hi-Bjanching, going by a few splutters and sneezes and a whisk of bright cloth.

"I hear your words, Pallan Archolax, and they are indeed worthy of note. The embassy from Jhansi revealed their true purpose, and have left, with a zorca hoof up their rump." One of the Kregish ways of saying with a flea in their ear, that charming expression, and the others smiled. "But that does not tilt the balance down in favor of the Racters."

"Their gold tilts the balances."

About to give what I considered a stiff reply, Barty saved me the trouble, saying what was in my mind.

"But honor will tilt the balance back!"

So we wrangled for a space, and I think they could all see already the way my mind tended. Finally, I said, "We have the resources if we plan carefully. Gold to buy mercenaries will not set Vallia free. Our country must be set free by her own efforts. This is a cardinal principle."

Archolax opened his mouth ready to sneeze, saw me watching him, and merely swiped the yellow silk over his nose.

"Your commands, majister," he said. And then he added: "My fingers itch to feel Racter gold. But my heart would not be in it."

"Of course," put in Nath Nazabhan. "We could take the Racter gold, anyway."

"What, Nath!" exclaimed Barty. "Double deal 'em?" He screwed up that incredibly naive face, and one could almost see the wheels whizzing around in his head as he once more confronted the thrill of skullduggery in action.

The idea was intriguing; but it would not do, and we all saw that. Nath's flyer remained unsaddled.

Pallan Myer walked over from the door, and coughed, and stood waiting. He was youngish, stooped over from long hours of reading, with always a book or a scroll tucked under his arm or, to be honest, more often opened as he walked along reading, a constant terror to anyone else who did not look where they were going. I had put him in charge of education, the Pallan of Learning, and I was due to go with him to see about a group of new school buildings being fashioned quickly from materials left over from a slave bagnio, after it had burned, and many of the poor devils inside it, too.

Acknowledging Pallan Myer, I said: "Educating the children of Vallia is more important than wrangling. Nath. Do you go and see Strom Luthien and give him our word. And, Nath. Try to be gentle with the rast."

"Aye, majister. I will try."

Barty chuckled. "That'll be a pleasant surprise for him."

Myer started in eagerly talking away about the plan to give each child in the new building his or her very own desk. That way, he said, they'd do a lot more work without the jostling and larking you always found when the children sat on long benches, all scrunched up. I nodded, agreeing, and figuring out where we could find the artisans and the wood. Barty fell in with us as we went. Delia called across, saying she had work to do, and I smiled at her as we went out.

His face shining like one of those fabulous polished apples of Delphond, Barty Vessler strode along with us out into the suns shine. I saw Delia looking after him as I turned to give her a parting smile. Barty was deeply in love with Dayra and she was off somewhere adventuring on her own account and had been numbered in the ranks of those who opposed us. She had been or was still, for I did not know, a boon companion to Zankov and that crowd of cutthroats. Now that the Hawkwa country had declared for Jak the Drang and I was emperor in Vondium, now that Phu-Si-Yantong had withdrawn from this area, what in a Herrelldrin Hell Zankov was about posed a prickly problem.

Zankov had slain the old emperor. That emperor was Dayra's grandfather. I wondered if she knew that her comrade Zankov had murdered her grandfather.

Attitudes are easy to strike and damned difficult to un-strike.

Barty burbled on about the coming campaign as we mounted our zorcas to ride out to the new schools. We had already traveled a fair bit of the road in freeing all Vallia and we looked forward to riding side by side to finish the task. Every day Barty grew in stature, in wisdom and cunning. Of courage there had never been any doubt. You will perceive, I think, that I was looking with increasing favor on Barty Vessler, the Strom of Calimbrev. I knew practically nothing of my daughter Dayra. Yet the hope, barely formed and certainly not articulated, was that Barty would match up to Dayra, who was also Ros the Claw.

Ros the Claw. The suns slanted their radiance down about us and the day smiled with promise, and I thought of that wicked steel taloned glove she wore on her left hand. Those cruel curved claws could have your eyes out in a twinkling. A real right tiger-girl, Ros the Claw, a she-leem, clad in her black leathers hugging her skin tight, all grace and lithe lissomness and striking feline beauty. And Barty had no idea that Dayra was Ros the Claw.

My own feelings muddled my thinking. I had not been on Kregen when Dayra and her twin brother, Jaidur, had been born, and Delia had shouldered a heavy burden—two heavy burdens. And there were the other children, also. The Everoinye had banished me, then, and I had now firmly made up my mind not to cross them again in any open way. The feelings about Dayra made me itchy, fretful, tearing open tender wounds I had thought long since scabbed over.

No matter where Dayra might be in Vallia, no matter what she was up to, it seemed to me right that I should talk to her in friendship and love. She hated me. I had had proof of that. And, also, I thought I had proof that she did not hate me, for she had drawn back and had not struck me from the instant she understood that I had at last recognized Ros the Claw as my daughter Dayra.

That gave me hope.

Emotions and feelings run all tangled, like disturbed water in a stream choked with fallen rock. We must have reliable news of Dayra soon. We must.

So I rode in the suns shine to see about facilities for educating the young, and I realized with a sober chill that I had few and contemptible qualifications for the task.

Five

Justice

Plots and counter-plots. Masks and disguises. The shadow in the night and the swift glitter of a blade. Well, they are all a part of Kregen, just as much as the pomp and grandeur, the armies, the brilliance of nobility and the shining of courage.

There was the matter of Renko the Murais.

Where I rode I noticed that the members of my choice band, those fighting men who were veterans now although so short a time ago being simple tradesmen or farmers, had strengthened their number by mustering more of the old comrades. They formed a powerful little mounted squadron riding at my back. And, with them, rode a formed and formidable body of upwards of fifty Pachaks. While welcoming this, I was puzzled. I mentioned the matter to Nath as we rode forward along the gutted Avenue of Hope and out into the virtually untouched Kyro of Taniths. This kyro was a particular pride of Vondium, being graceful in architecture, bright with color, a perfect place to take one's ease after the strife and turmoil of the day. The luxurious and headily perfumed trees and bushes growing in a profusion of beauty like a woman's hair and trailing splendor along the tessellated walks and cool colonnades always offered a welcome and a surcease. A man could expand his lungs here, and yet relax, safe and with the feeling he had come home. I smiled at Nath as I asked him, and he merely answered with a casual comment that, by Vox, a man needed friends at his back.

With this sentiment I agreed.

I did not press the matter. In truth, the thought that ferocious and loyal fighting men rode with me, keeping a weather eye open against assassins, stikitches dropping on us from any direction, was mightily comforting.

Each man of this impromptu bodyguard wore a tiny tuft of yellow and red feathers in his helmet, a brave show of color, highly evocative.

The business with the schools happily concluded and an old friend, Anko the Chisel, proving only too happy to place the entire resources of what was left of his workshops at our disposal, the matter of the desks was attended to. With them, also, grave details of ink and pens, of paper and tablets, and the correct clothes the youngsters should wear had all to be attended to with the same strict punctilio I might give to the decisions over the number of shafts an archer should carry in his quiver when we marched out, and how many with the regimental wagons, or the best method of ensuring next season's crop, or of how I might receive a deputation from a province seeking alliance. The work of empire is made up of details, great and small, and who is to mediate between them?

So, with the schools, and a faulty aqueduct to be seen to, and repairs to the walls where battering engines had breached them, and a swift and summary decision between a man and his brother over the rightful possession of a shop their father kept, he now being dead and nothing decided, I at last turned my zorca's head in the direction of the palace and a meal and the inquisition into Renko the Murais.

Well, the meal was a splendid affair, and I shall not spend time on such gourmet delights. Enevon Ob-Eye, Nath, Barty, the responsible officials and whoever else thought they had a hand in the affair all assembled in a relatively undamaged chamber where once music had flowed to delight lazy afternoons. The charred triangles of harps still stood in the corners, and the twisted remnants of many of the exotic musical instruments of Kregen had been hastily swept away into an alcove under the windows. I sat at a long table, with the dignitaries flanking me, and the condemned men were led in under guard.

I knew Renko the Murais. It was the same Renko who had fought with us as a Freedom Fighter in Valka.

I treated him as I treated the other miserable wights, showing no special favor.

"Have the charges and the findings read out."

This was done with due solemnity.

The contrast between the genuine solemnity of these proceedings, despite the deliberate air of informality I had introduced, and the fascial solemnity of the twin embassies from our foes, amused and depressed me. Nath had seen Strom Luthien off, treating him, as he reported hard-faced to me, with all due civility. The Racters, too, had been seen off with a zorca hoof up the rump.

The charges having been read out—a dismal catalogue of rapine and plunder and murder—the findings were studied. Here I welcomed the presence of Nath Nazabhan. His meticulous eye, his keen nose, his habitual and natural aptitude for turning over stones to discover the truth, were wonderfully displayed. The judges had judged fairly, we decided, in all but three cases of the thirteen. And all three had been dealt with in the court of Tyr Jando ti Faleravensmot.

I frowned.

"Is Tyr Jando here?" I spoke very mildly.

Enevon Ob-Eye shook his head. "He has been called away to his estates in Faleravensmot, majister. Some business of a cracked cistern and ruined flour."

"Important enough to warrant his absence, then, in a time of shortage." I pondered. Two of the wights standing in their gray breechclouts, chained, hang-dog before us, had been accused of raping two little Fristle fifis, and their story was that they had been over on the Walls of Opaz the Deliverer, hoisting stones, for they were powerful, hairy apims, with faces that would normally have been frank and open, and were now shattered and frightened and destroyed.

"Majister," said one, Tom the Stones. "False witness was borne against us by Tabshur the Talens—"

Nath, Barty and I listened and weighed the stories. A matter of a debt to this Tabshur the Talens, an inheritance, a squabble between siblings, and a charge of rape to remove Tom the Stones. The inheritance would then by default fall to Tabshur through the sibling. Tabshur the Talens was a moneylender. Well, men must live in the world however they can shift. The unfortunate comrade of Tom the Stones, Nath the Ears—they were, indeed, remarkable— had been caught up in the plot because he was a comrade and could have borne counter-witness. Now we heard it all out and sent a guard of Pachaks to find this Tabshur the Talens and the sibling and hear their stories.

"Stand aside, Tom the Stones and Nath the Ears. Rest easy that justice will be done." How easy to say that! And how damned hard, by Vox, to make sure!

Then it was the turn of Renko the Murais.

He had been so dragged down by his ordeal that he kept his face lowered and his gaze on the floor, and so had not looked up once, being prodded into position by the guards. He wore a gray breechclout and was chained, and although the laws had seen to it that he was clean and deloused, he looked defeated and tattered.

Because he was an old blade comrade I must allow no favor to overbear my judgment.

The Relt that the stylor Renko had been found guilty of murdering had been discovered in the cellar of a ruined pothouse down on the Canal of the Cockroaches. The Relts with their bird-like faces are the more gentle cousins of the warlike Rapas, and are very often employed as clerks and accountants. This particular Relt appeared to be a stranger in Vondium. His satchel was missing and the leather straps had been slashed through. He had been searched, for his tunic had been ripped to shreds exposing the linings and the hems.

"Was the satchel discovered in the possession of Renko?"

Nath's words were pleasantly mild.

Enevon Ob-Eye said, "The records state the satchel was not recovered."

"And no one thought to search, or inquire?"

"The records state that Renko the Murais was discovered crouching over the body, as you have heard. There was a knife in his hand, and there was blood on the blade. The Relt had been stabbed six times in the small of the back. It does seem the proof was plain."

"Plain enough for me, by Opaz," declared Barty.

I said, "Was there blood on the cut straps?"

Renko the Murais jumped.

His shaggy head lifted with a snap. He looked up. He looked at me. An expression—a sunrise, dawn, the flowering of a bloom—shocked across his face. His eyes widened. His mouth abruptly trembled—trembled and then firmed.

"Strom Drak!"

"Aye, Renko, Strom Drak. And a pretty pickle you have got yourself into."

"I did not slay the Relt, strom! I swear it by Opaz the All-Glorious! I found the body and was set on, and so fought for my life, and was knocked on the head and left for dead. And when I woke—"

"You were taken up." I looked at Nath and then at Barty and the others at the table. "The law of Vallia—the new laws of Vallia that the new emperor will see maintained—demand absolute proof of guilt. No one saw this man slay the Relt. You must prove beyond all doubt he did the deed before you pronounce him guilty."

"But he was standing over the body with a bloody knife in his hand!" Barty spluttered, his face perplexed and yet clearly showing the way he struggled with preconceived notions.

"The chavnik knocks over the bowl of cream and the slave girl comes in to set it right and the mistress sees her and has her whipped for stealing and spilling the cream."

"Yes, majister, but—"

"Enevon. Read out the description of the wounds."

Enevon rustled his papers and then read: "Six stab wounds in the small of the back, close together, deep."

I looked at Renko. "You were an axeman, as I recall."

"That I was, strom." Renko, still disoriented, took a grip on remembered pride.

I nodded. "Are the clothes of the dead Relt available?"

They were not. They had been burned.

"Tell me of the men who attacked you."

Renko screwed his leathery face up. He wanted to rub his nose, I could see; but the chains stopped that.

"I saw three of them, strom. But there must have been another one at my back who hit me after I stuck the bastard in front. By Vox, but the whiptail was quick, and I'd have had him, too, but for that crack on my noodle."

I said, sharply: "A Kataki?"

"That's what I said, strom."

He'd said whiptail; but that was the slang term for a Kataki, a nasty member of a nasty race of diffs, slavers, with fierce brow-beating faces, and intemperate dispositions and with long sinuous tails to which they strapped six inches of bladed steel. There were Katakis on Kregen who had no other aim in life but to degut me. The ambition was reciprocated.

"Anything else? Clothes, faces, weapons—?"

"Rapiers, strom, but they kept them scabbarded. They hit me with what felt like the Lenk of Vox. The whiptail had a favor of black and green feathers clipped by a golden grascent—I think, strom, for I was taken by surprise."

For a space a silence fell. Then, to give Barty the due he deserved, he was the one to burst out: "By Vox! Under the Gate of Voxyri—when I came running up—this Renko the Murais speaks the truth. I'll swear it!"

"Aye," said Nath. "The devil's work spreads itself."

After that we prosecuted further inquiries and a garbled story came out that made me itch with worry and with frustration. It seemed clear that the Relt stylor was bringing in a message and had been waylaid and slain and the message stolen. But from whom had the message been sent? The minions of Phu-Si-Yantong had heard of it, and we had not, and they had struck. There was no question now in anyone's mind that Renko the Murais was not guilty. His chains were ordered struck off at once. He expanded after that, and a cup of wine further restored him. But he could add nothing further to the story, being engaged in eking out a living scrounging scraps from the ruins, as so many were. Now there was a happy outcome to the adventure, we could feel thankful he had stumbled on the corpse of the stylor. Although, frustratingly, we knew no more than that there had been a message from someone.

"Anyway, majister—what made you—?" asked Barty.

"The blood. There was no blood on the cut straps. Had Renko stabbed him in the back, that would have been the beginning of the murder—or the end of the Relt—and then he'd have cut the satchel free. No blood meant a clean knife had been used." I smiled—I, Dray Prescot, smiled—across at Barty. "Anyway, Renko is an axeman. He wouldn't have stabbed with such a heavy knife. He'd have sliced the Relt's throat out."

"Yes," said Barty.

"And where stands Jando ti Faleravensmot in this?" demanded Nath.

"His judgments have always been impeccable," offered Enevon, shuffling his papers together. I rather think, as my chief stylor, he had been put out at the murder of a brother in his craft, and was pleased that at least some truth had been revealed.

A stir at the back of the chamber announced the arrival of Tabshur the Talens and the sibling who had won the inheritance, a lean fellow in an apron called Naghan the Tallow. They both looked as guilty as hell. But that must not be allowed to weigh against them. Somehow—and in this I do not boast but rather feel a sense of deflation and defeat—the news that the Emperor of Vallia himself had sent for them and was to look again at their stories, had unnerved them. And, in the case of Tabshur, at least, he was a hard-case, cunning and vicious in his extortions. Naghan the Tallow had been a mere tool in his hands, credulous and willing to be led into infamy.

They broke down and confessed. I think the jingle of chains as the Pachak guard waited added to their misery.

And then Tabshur said: "I paid Tyr Jando twenty golden talens for his judgment. The Fristle fifis was the case he chose. You cannot trust anyone these evil days."

In that he was right—or almost right. There are people I trust on Kregen. Not many; but they do exist.

As you will hear, there were some I should not have trusted, for betrayal touches high and low, friend and foe, and is indeed a foul stink over life.

I said: "Nath. Do you dispatch a guard to request Tyr Jando ti Faleravensmot to return to Vondium. There are questions to which he must give the answers. Oh—and tell the guard commander to make sure the cistern does not spoil any more flour."

"Quidang, majister!" barked Nath, and turned to one of the Pachak Jiktars.

There was no particular cleverness in the investigations we had made leading to the establishment of Renko's innocence. Had the questions been asked at the trial the outcome would surely have been different from what it had been. And people had made certain that Renko had been found guilty. He told us that he had been given no opportunity to speak then.

Another important detail had to be settled.

"Make further investigations into the Fristle fifis. The villain or villains must be brought to justice. Setting the innocent free is a half of the matter."

"Quidang, majister!"

Justice of a sort had been done here. That was cause for partial satisfaction. Jando ti Faleravensmot would have to answer for his conduct. Tabshur the Talens had paid Tyr Jando twenty gold pieces.

I wondered how much the minions of Phu-Si-Yantong had paid him.

Six

Yellow Sun, Silver Moon

When you live on a world as wild and ferocious as Kregen, for all its beauty and splendor, missions of mercy such as rescuing girls in distress or marching to the relief of a besieged city are a natural order of life, given the way of the world. Although I would not go so far as to claim they are of the same order as worrying about the overdraft, or the state of the automobile, or the parlous conditions of employment or where the next meal is coming from on this Earth, the parallels are clear and ominous.

One has to do what one can against the strokes of Fate and, really, that is all there is to it.

We all worked in those days as our plans matured. The crumbling walls of the city occasioned a great deal of worry, and much effort was expended in rebuilding the fortifications. Over the sennights, what began as rumors hardened into facts. Unpalatable facts. Spies and scouts brought in sure word that a host marched on Vondium from the southwest.

All that wedge of Vallia remained locked in mystery since the victories there of the minions of Phu-Si-Yantong. His insane ambition to rule all Paz had received a setback in the island, and he was set, with or without the help of the Empress of Hamal, on imposing his will on us all.

So we labored and set our house in order and sharpened our weapons.

With the new threat from the southwest there could be no thoughts of our marching north. The Racters and Layco Jhansi would still fight each other, no doubt, and the reverberations of that conflict would be felt in Inch's Black Mountains and in Delia's Blue Mountains. East of them across the Great River we held the land. There was, again, no thought of a westerly expansion for the time being.

The imperial provinces around Vondium were now almost wholly in our hands, pockets and enclaves still being held by insurgents and reiving bands of aragorn, slavers. There remained also a number of roving gangs of flutsmen, mercenaries of the skies, who flew their great winged saddle animals in raiding descents wherever they sensed the pickings were easy. Strong detachments of the army had to be posted not only on the borders of the imperial provinces, but in strategic loci from whence they could march out forthwith against the threat wherever it might be found.

The whole island presented a patchwork of warring factions. How we were to bring peace to the whole land exercised our minds wonderfully.

And if you comment that the peace we brought merely represented the rule of me, Dray Prescot, well, then—yes, I suppose you are right. But I had fought that battle with myself and now my course having been set by the acclamation of the people, I could not in honor draw back. And I still devoutly believed that, blood or no blood, Vallia would prosper far more sweetly with my people to handle affairs than under the iron heel of Yantong or ripped apart by bandits and mercenaries and flutsmen who simply reived for their own benefit and no others.

As for Hamal—the Empress Thyllis would have to withdraw her iron legions, and see to her own internal problems. One day, and the quicker the sooner, by Zair, we would shake hands with the Hamalese in friendship. Until that time they were our bitter foes.

And Pandahem—well, the various countries of that island would have to serve as a friendly bridge to Hamal.

After Hamal the rest of the massive southern continent of Havilfar would ally together against our common enemies.

And there was Segesthes, and Turismond, and Loh...

All Paz must stand shoulder to shoulder against the Shanks who raided and destroyed, sailing up over the curve of the world.

By Opaz! It was a task to daunt the stoutest heart. With all this mighty clangor of distant ambitions reverberating in our minds we were forced to deal with the here and now, the relatively minuscule problems of an army marching against our city.

As the reports came in we understood that the problem was by no means minuscule. Given our resources, the odds against us were gigantic.

Mind you, the Star Lords might suddenly decide they had a sticky problem somewhere on Kregen they wished sorted out for them. Then I would find myself hoisted up out of Vondium whirled by the gigantic blue semblance of a Scorpion, thrust down all naked to get on with the job. So, as was my custom, as I planned and directed, I molded men and women to handle the tasks that must be undertaken should I not be there. And, as always, they could not understand.

Only Delia grasped what I was doing, and sorrowed for it.

To the end of leaving everything in as apple pie an order as might be contrived should I be suddenly whisked away I looked carefully at the commanders available to us.

Nath—whose name of Nazabhan came as a courtesy from his father, who was a Nazab, an imperial appointment as governor of a province and equivalent to a kov—resolutely insisted that he wished to continue in command of the Phalanx. He put great store by that cutting instrument of war. I tried to make him see reason on both counts. But he would not leave the Phalanx command, and he would not allow that the Phalanx could be bested by infantry—as for cavalry, they were just a laugh.

Against aerial attack strong forces of archers were incorporated, and the artillery park was built up.

All Vondium and the imperial provinces surrounding the capital city resembled a gigantic beehive, humming with activity. What cheered me most was the demeanor of the people. Almost without exception they were cheerful, sprightly, utterly confident in themselves, their new army and their emperor. Feeling like a cheat and a fraud, and with profound doubts about the new army, but with pleased awareness of the new spirit of the citizens, I sorted out the folk to take over should the necessity arise. This is mere common-sense insurance when your name is Dray Prescot and you are Emperor of Vallia, and the Star Lords remain unsatisfied.

Messages carried swiftly by one of the few fast airboats we possessed assured me that the Lord Farris, the Kov of Vomansoir, prospered in his newly-restored kovnate. His people accepted him back with a warm welcome because he had been associated with Jak the Drang and was remembered and well-liked as a fair, just and generous man.

The airboat which brought him flying swiftly into Vondium bore the gray and yellow of Vomansoir. Alert, active, bronzed, he jumped down and saluted Delia and me as we waited to greet him.

"Lahal and Lahal," he called, smiling, brisk and yet with that sureness of purpose about him that marked him as a man who knew what was what and got on with it. "Majister—it is good to see you again. Majestrix, my eternal loyalty."

I wasted no time but spelled it out, right there and then, as we walked into the shambles of the palace to find refreshment.

"But, majister! Why should you go away again? Now all Vallia awaits your victorious arms."

"You will have Nath to handle the Phalanx—and if we persevere with him I think he will take on a larger command of the army. Barty Vessler will be of help—he is a fine if headstrong aide-de-camp—more than that, really—and there is Enevon to handle all the finicky details of daily administration."

"But—"

"There are pallans appointed to all the departments of government and they can function autonomously with only an occasional eye." We told him of the sad business of Tyr Jando ti Faleravensmot, and of how he had hanged himself rather than return to Vondium. That meant another possible lead to the Wizard of Loh who sought to destroy us had been lost.

"But—"

"You will have Laka Pa-Re to run the mercenaries for you. He is a fine example of the best of the Pachaks. He remained after the nikobi was discharged and I have promoted him Chuktar. You may repose complete confidence in him. And there is Naghan Strandar, and Larghos the Left-Handed, and there are all those ruffianly companions of the choice band. Only if I am called away, Lord Farris, will your services be needed in this. I ask it as a favor."

"But, majister—your sons. Prince Drak, Prince Jaidur—"

He knew that Zeg was away somewhere and had heard us refer to him as the King of Zandikar.

"Drak is off in Faol looking for Kardo and Melow, and Jaidur—well—" I cocked an eye at Delia and she smiled, both radiantly and ruefully.

"The last I heard of that rapscallion son of ours he was seeking the whereabouts of his sister."

My ears pricked up at this. These women and their infernal secret societies are one thing; but now they had inveigled a brash fighting man in the person of Jaidur into their schemes. I saw that, and quickly enough, if you please.

At last I overbore Farris by saying around a goblet of the best Gremivoh, the wine favored by the Vallian Air Service in a voice I made as neutral as possible: "Anyway, I need you here to keep an eye on things and on the Empress Delia also." Farris was a man whose life had been dedicated to the emperor and whose fanatical loyalty to Delia was a part of his makeup.

"An army marches against us from the southwest and I've a mind to go out there and spy them out. Perhaps—"

"Aye, Dray Prescot," quoth Delia, sharply. "Aye! And you've a mind to crack a few of their villainous skulls, too, while you're at it. I know."

"Mayhap, my love," I said, unrepentantly. "Mayhap."

So, the matter being settled, we passed onto a more detailed assessment of the situation, which was pretty fraught as I have explained.

Reports from our scouts indicated that the army had landed in Vallia on the coast of Kaldi to the west of the Island of Wenhartdrin. This gave the invading host a long distance to march, for they might have landed much nearer the capital, and I surmised that they hoped to pick up recruits as they advanced. Just how the honest burghers and farmers of Vallia would react to this hope remained to be seen. Certainly, the southwest had not, to my knowledge, shared the ambitions toward self-determination of the northeast.

In a direct line—as the fluttrell flies as they say in Havilfar—the invaders had six hundred and fifty miles to cover to Vondium. It seemed clear they would not march a direct line. At an average speed of ten miles a day—more or less—at which a spry army can march with its baggage and artillery and followers and all the rest of the baffling impediments that so slow up armies on the march, they would take better than seventy or eighty days. The latest reports gave their position as being at the border between Ovvend and Thadelm. They had come, therefore, roughly halfway.

Estimates of their numbers varied enormously. This was partly due to the inexperience of some of our volunteer scouts and partly to the complexity of an army on the march, where thousands of followers confuse the eye. A sagacious Khibil, a paktun with many battle scars, had told me that he estimated the core of the army—the formed ranks of fighting men and the wings of cavalry—at fifty thousand. This was an army, therefore, of indeterminate strength, not so small as to be contemptible, and not so large as to be truly overpowering.

My reaction to that information had been to cast the net of scouts wider, suspecting another army marching parallel to the first. So far no confirming reports had reached me.

Nath was white with fury at my decision not to take a single brumbyte from the Phalanx. And, because I would not take any pikemen from the files, the Hakkodin, who flanked them, would not be touched, either.

"But majister! We are the army—the heart and sinew and core. If we march out, now, in all our strength, we can crush them—"

"Utterly?"

"By Vox! Yes!"

"I think not."

"But they are just an army—cavalry with zorcas and these white-coated hersanys, and infantry with nothing untoward in the way of weapons or formations. Fifty thousand! We will go through them as a cleaver goes through beef."

"And you're like to strike a bone, in the middle, Kyr Nath."

The invading army flew no colors that had been reported to me. The hersanys present, those shaggy, six-legged, chalky-white riding animals, indicated there were contingents from Pandahem. And Phu-Si-Yantong had set his ferocious seal on the whole island of Pandahem, subjugating all its kings and rulers to his despotic sway. I wished him joy of it. He must be mad, for that seemed to me the only way to explain the ambitions he cherished. As for the good in him, that must lie so deep that Cottmer's Caverns brushed the heavens.

"Well," said Nath, breathing deeply and the whiteness denting the corners of his nostrils. "If I may not march my Phalanx, then, at the least, majister, let me come with you."

With a sorrow tinged with affectionate amusement, I said: "And leave the Phalanx without the leader? Come now, Nath, surely you see I cannot do that?"

He was in a cleft stick and he knew it, and the knowledge made him barge off with a parting Remberee and I did not doubt that his Relianchuns would skip and dance to his tunes and give their brumbytes in the ranks a little stick, also. Well, that is the way of it. He kept his men in fighting trim and I was unsure if I really did want him to hand over control of the Phalanx to somebody else. There were plenty of superb fighting men who could handle that immense and crushingly destructive mass of men with their pikes and shields and deadly onrushing force, naturally; but the sight of Nath commanding had power to instill perfect confidence.

The business of the day being settled for the time being, for alarums and excursions cropped up at any hour, I was free to give thought to what Delia had said about Jaidur. The notion in my mind that there must be more than one army advancing on Vondium had, for the moment, to be pushed aside. I left it with the thought that the mercenaries and the detachments from Hamal who had taken over the southwest had not obstructed the landing of the new army from Pandahem, and this argued they were in league and mutually assisting each other.

But, Jaidur...

As we sat to a private meal in what would be called our withdrawing room, with Delia superb in a long sheer laypom-colored gown, and I lounging in a white wrap, the whole small room limned with gold from the samphron-oil lamps, I found her as reticent on this as I had on other occasions touching the Sisters of the Rose. That secret society of women demanded much of their members, and had a hand in a great deal of what went on in Vallia.

"You know I am under vows, my heart."

47

"I know. At least reassure me that Jaidur is—well—" I gestured helplessly. "That he is not likely to be chopped and eaten at any moment."

Delia laughed. The line of her throat caught at mine.

"No, no, you hairy old graint. You worry too much over the children, and yet—"

"And yet they have been woefully neglected by me, I know. Some people, looking at our family, might well say they have turned out a thoroughly bad lot. Well, not Drak. I except him, of course, and, I suppose, Zeg, seeing he is fully occupied in the Eye of the World being the king of Zandikar."

"A bad lot? We-ell... Lela bides her manners and is so mewed up with the SoR she hasn't been home for—"

"I haven't seen her since I got back—" I choked on my words, and seized up a crystal glass of best Jholaix—for we had unearthed a cellar full of the superb wine in a ruined wing of the palace—and drank it off, scarlet-faced, I have no doubt.

Gravely, Delia regarded me. Her gown slipped demurely from one rounded shoulder. The lamps caught flecks of gold in her brown hair. She looked gorgeous.

"From where, my heart?"

I swallowed down. Sudden, it was, sudden and quick and fierce, like a first love.

"From that world I told you of. That world with only one sun, and only one moon, and only apims."

She caught her breath, and was still. And that was her only reaction.

Then: "You have spoken to me of this strange world which boasts one small yellow sun, and one small silver moon, and lacks any kind of humans save apims, without a single diff to make life interesting. And is it real? And is it—?"

"It is real. It is called Earth. And it is where I was born." I reached over the table and took her fingers. They were warm, alive, trembling only a little. "And, my heart, it is many and many a dwabur away from Kregen, lost among the stars of the heavens."

"Your home—is among the stars..."

"No, Delia, no. My home is here, on Kregen. With you."

Her smile transformed her face, making what was beauty into a radiance so all-encompassing the loveliness dizzied me. I closed my eyes, and opened them, and Delia still smiled on me.

"And this weird crippled world is where you go when you leave me?"

"I am sent there. Against my will. Because I defy those who wield the power. I shall not defy them so stupidly again." We talked then, quick questions and answers, and I told her much. She was fascinated by the idea of Earth, and quite beyond any childish feelings of guilt that the pure religions of Opaz would frown on her or condemn her conduct.

We talked through many burs of the night.

And, when at last we slept, we still had not talked enough to satisfy her curiosity or relieve my mind of those years of guilty secrecy. But, when all was said and done, what difference would this make in our relationship? We were a twinned whole, a twosome that transcended one-ness. She had always been aware that I left her from time to time, without explanation, and always returned. She always waited. No moist-mouthed seducer from Quergey the Murgey could sway her love away from me, as he had so often done with lesser women from their husbands. We remained still Dray and Delia. We were. But I felt a deal easier in my mind now that Delia knew. And, when she did know, I saw all my previous fears as the childish phantasms they were. To be brutally honest, the truth had come out and the whole episode smacked of anti-climax.

And, to be equally truthful, that was exactly how it should be.

The next day I mounted up and rode out at the head of my little band, aiming to get on with the hard business of rebuilding an empire, not for the glory of empire but because it was a task that had been set to my hand by the people of Vallia.

Seven

Jilian

Barty reined up and swung his zorca about to fall in with me.

"They're three ulms away, off beyond that ridge of trees."

He pointed ahead. The trees lined the horizon, barring off forward vision. The clouded sky towered above and, I fancied, when the wind dropped there would be rain. The turf compacted firmly beneath the hooves of the zorcas and nikvoves, the breeze rustled bushes and small trees among the grassland, and we were approaching Dogansmot, which is a lively enough little town in the vadvarate of Thadelm in the southwest of Vallia.

I said to Volodu the Lungs: "Do not lift your trumpet, Volodu. Word of mouth, and quietly. Dismount."

Approaching us walked three zorcas, one of whom had a broken horn, carrying two dead men and two wounded. I looked at them and felt the anger, and repressed it.

"Close, Barty. You did well."

He nodded and was enough of a veteran now to say, merely: "Our patrol was ambushed. They left two dead men, three zorcas. The Pandaheem know we are about."

"Surely." At our backs the long columns were dismounting. "Get the men away into what cover they can find. Spread out. Strict silence." I swung to Targon the Tapster and Naghan ti Lodkwara who rode with Korero the Shield. "Come, and quietly as you value your hides."

The four of us cantered out across the turf, making very little sound. The zorca hooves beat softly. And I would have no truck with junk like jingling accoutrements and flying tassels and nonsense of that sort. Our harness and gear made no sound as we cantered out to scout the enemy.

"Gallop," I said, in a harsh penetrating sort of way, and with a swift look back, which assured me that the troops were finding cover and making themselves and their mounts invisible, clapped in my heels and took off. The others followed.

We reached the line of trees without strain.

The situation was as I had expected.

The enemy general had sent forward a patrol to the line of trees and their distance beyond gave us time to reach the trees first. But only just.

We saw the green and blue uniforms, the brilliance of bronze and silver, as the zorcas broke up the ridge from the far side. There were ten of them, riding hard, and their plumes nodded very bravely.

"Let them get in among the trees," I said, most mildly. "Ten. Well, who-ever gets himself a third man will be right merry and quick." From which, you will perceive, I was in a grim humor that needed a little skull-bashing to relieve the tensions. Vondium had burned and Vallia had been ripped into shreds. Somehow we had to start rebuilding, and here and now was a tiny fracas along the way...

The trees rose tall and heavily foliaged, their roots no doubt drinking deeply of a subterranean stream. The shadows fell bafflingly, and we waited in silence, completely confident.

The ten cavalrymen spread out a trifle as they reached the crest of the ridge and plunged boldly in among the trees, and this made me think they had once been good soldiers but were now by reason of easy marching and the absence of fighting grown somewhat careless. That carelessness cost them their lives.

After the first surprise and sudden onset they fought well. But four of them were down on the instant before they had drawn, and the next four, wheeling their mounts and setting up an outcry, barely had time to clear scabbard. The remaining two, those on the wings, fought their zorcas under control and attempted flight.

I reined in. The brand smoked red in my fist. Targon, Naghan and Korero whooped up their mounts and went flying in and out among the trees, like bats. They caught the last two Pandaheem before they quitted the tree-lined crest, and I did not wish to see who claimed three.

My desperadoes trotted back, looking mightily pleased with themselves.

I was already dismounted, the reins slung over a handy branch, examining the dead men and their equipment. Their zorcas stood by the corpses, which made me think we dealt here with an army of professionals, or hardened mercenary veterans. By this I mean men accustomed to working with zorcas for most of their lives, and not levies scraped up for a quick and cheaply promised conquest. Their carelessness had been a self-confident carelessness, when all was said and done.

"Summon up Karidge's regiment," I told my men, without looking up. One of them would ride with my orders. "Silently. The rest to move up in order to the ridge."

Rising, with what I wanted to know already tucked away, I walked to the far edge of the ridge. Fallen leaves kicked underfoot. The shadows dropped down, and then a chink in the overspreading leaves rained a color-fall of ruby and emerald. The army advancing down there were still two ulms away, that is to say around three thousand yards, and I could make out with the aid of my Kregen spyglass the way they came on.

Well. An army is an army. And there are all kinds, and, as I must have remarked, they are all the same and all different.

This ridge with its awkward traverse would make them trend away, following the easier ride to the north, and already the outriders were swinging. As my scouts had reported, there were no banners displayed. The cavalry screened the infantry. The artillery was mostly small-wheeled varters, drawn by hirvels and quoffas, with just the two big catapults. These were drawn by teams of twenty-four krahniks apiece.

The infantry were predominantly sword and shield men. This made a frown of black fury and exasperation cross my face, whereat Targon said: "Have you the gut ache, then, majister?"

"Sword and shield men," I said, grinding the words out. "From Pandahem."

"They learn," said Korero in his aloof way. A Kildoi, a man of that race of diffs from far Balintol that are little known beside so many other of the brilliant diffs of Kregen, Korero the Shield moved always at my back. His lithe limber physique was that of the master in martial arts of all kinds, with a command of the Disciplines. He had four arms and a tail equipped with a hand, and his handsome face with its golden beard overtopped me by four clear inches. Withdrawn, Korero, yet ready with a quip that would dart to the heart of the situation. Now, with a nod of his head, he finished: "There will be Hamalese drill instructors with that little lot. And a rascally gang of masichieri, too, if I am not mistaken."

"I do not think, Korero the Shield, you are mistaken."

Odd, when you thought about it, how in a world where men swore all the time by gods and spirits and phantom beings dredged from their various racial pools of unconsciousness, Korero hardly ever let fall a good round oath. That, I surmised, was a part of that aloofness bred in him in Balintol.

And when I say he was an adept of the Disciplines, I did not at that time know which particular set had trained and molded him. They were not those of my old comrade—never a blade comrade, of course—Turko the Shield, who was a Khamorro. Nor were they of the Kem-Brysuang of the land of Jeveroinen. We had a fellow from Jeveroinen in the ranks who was an adept of the fifth degree of Kem-Brysuang, and he was a most peculiar fellow indeed. His name was Bengi-Trenoimian and he had been bested in two falls out of three by Korero who had, by mutual arrangement, not employed his tail hand in the bouts.

Now I stared with concern at that army trending away to the north to pass the tree-crowned ridge. Shields were not a common article found in the armories of Pandahem or Vallia and we still had a deal of trouble to persuade men who regarded a shield as a coward's article of equipment to use them. One of the earliest regiments formed in Vondium after we re-captured the capital and filled with eager young volunteers had proved that point. Rank after rank, they had thrown down the shields we had just issued. The shields lay on the grass of the drinnik like pathetic flower-heads slashed down wantonly. Well, as you may imagine, there was a hell of a fuss, and a great hullabaloo and in the end we reached a compromise.

That was one of the many times I regretted the enforced absence through sorcery of Balass the Hawk, for that kyr-kaidur could demonstrate sword and shield work to perfection.

It seemed that the fighting men of Pandahem had heeded the lessons brought to their discomfiture by the iron legions of Hamal. The sword and shield men—we generally called them churgur infantry—marching down there looked as though they were not yet completely sure of their weapons. You can usually tell.

The blocks of color moving all together represented massed regiments, five hundred or so men apiece, swinging along in column. We spied on them from the ridge of trees and marked their progress and the little breeze flicked and flecked the leaves about us and the slanting rays of the suns flickered opaz light upon the world. Kregen—ah, me, Kregen...

"Nearer sixty than fifty," said Korero.

I nodded.

"And a good quarter cavalry."

As though the name cavalry conjured him from the ground Karidge moved up at my side. He breathed only a little more heavily than usual, being a sprightly fellow with a tufty beard that bristled even when he sang. A consummate artist with a zorca, he was turning into a good cavalry commander. His regiment was always impeccable and meticulously turned out. They wore the red and yellow, for they were an imperial regiment, all three hundred and sixty of the jutmen, organized into six squadrons plus ancillaries. Karidge employed a long curved sword, and his dolman and pelisse were marvels of gold and silver lace and embroidery.

"A damned great gang of them, majister, by the Spurs of Lasal the Vakka."

"Aye, Jiktar Karidge."

"We could knock a few feathers out of their tail."

"Aye. We could."

Targon the Tapster grunted. "Then let us mount up and ride."

"Tsleetha-tsleethi," I said. "Let us watch them for a space."

The obvious plan was so obvious my men grumbled and fidgeted as we waited in the shade of the trees and watched the army march past below the ridge.

Easy enough to knock a few feathers out of the tail, to ride down whooping and cut up the long straggling baggage lines and provender wagons. That was the way of the raiding cavalry. But I hungered for more. I hungered for the complete destruction of this damned army that had invaded our country.

And that must wait until they were within easier striking distance and we could bring greater power down on them. I mentioned this to Karidge and to Jiktar Nalgre Randur, the numim commander of the nikvove regiment. They thought about the situation, and then Randur stroked his ferocious lion-man's whiskers and gave his opinion that, as usual, the emperor was right; but that it was hard on a man to show him a mangy gaggle of foemen and then forbid him to unsheathe his sword.

Jiktar Wando Varon ti GrollenDen, commanding the second zorca regiment, left his command strung out to guard our rear and walked through to join us. He wanted to know why we were not mounting up and riding down and, as he put it, letting some good Vallian air into those Opaz-forsaken Pandaheem down there.

Another fiery-tempered, audacious, sword-swinging cavalryman was Wando Varon, who maintained his regiment smartly enough but harped all the time on spear work from the saddle.

Holding these men in check now that they had set eyes on their enemy was like trying to hold an armful of kittens. I sighed.

"Very well. But toward dusk, when the chances favor a swift and determined attack. And, for the sweet sake of Opaz, do not get entangled. Quickly in, quickly out, and avoid taking plunder." I meant what I said. "They have regiments of zorcas down there. We will have to move like the Flame Winds of Father Tolki when you have had your fun."

Following my words there was a quantity of pelisse-swinging and feather ruffling and sword slapping, together with a deal of boot banging and moustache stroking. The cavalrymen swelled their chests. Their faces appeared to fill out, grow larger and firmer, and the brightness of their eyes matched the brilliance of their appearance. Yes, your dyed-in-the-wool jutman, your cavalryman who gallops in with a skirl and a whoop, knows how to ruffle it.

The two regiments of zorcas and the single regiment of nikvoves totaled around a thousand riders. There were fifty or so of my choice band with me, together with the Pachaks. These last two sets of ruffians, and I joke most feebly there, I cautioned off to another duty.

So, and for our mounts in a literal sense champing at the bit, we waited out the long descent of the suns.

Dorgo the Clis, his scar giving him the look of a desperado who would as lief slit your throat as doff his hat, was sent off to Dogansmot with a few riders to find out what the invading army's mischief had been there. This would be the first place they had bivouacked in that we had found and I felt the heaviness of heart that the usual rapine and plunder would have taken place. Dorgo rode circumspectly around toward the south before cutting west. The breeze at last died away and the rain gentled down, lustering all the greenery with a veil of silver.

Dogansmot lies not too far from the eastern border of Thadelm where that vadvarate marches with the imperial province of Vond. Vond was solidly with the new emperor in Vondium, and we had ridden through from town to town and village to village in a kind of triumphal procession. We had left in our wake a determined intention of resistance to the invaders. A good blow here by this small cavalry force, the success of my own plan for the night, and then we could return and set our own army in motion.

And, all the time I schemed, that irritating little itch persisted. There had to be another plot by our foemen afoot. This army below us was in one sense derisory for the sack of a great capital city. There just had to be other forces in the field.

The army was from Pandahem, that seemed clear and would explain the absence of saddle flyers and vollers. We had seen not a single aerial force, and our own couple of air-boats were at a discreet distance, waiting the signal. There was something afoot, something nasty and something that boded ill for Vondium.

When I told Barty that he might ride with the three regiments in command he said in his eager way: "That is very fine of you, Dray. But I'd rather ride with you. I know you're up to some kind of deviltry and that sounds much more interesting than beating up a baggage train and firing tents."

I regarded him stonily. A stout-hearted young man, the Strom of Calimbrev, if a little hasty and not over-inclined to think of consequences. But I could not find it in me to deny his request to join in my little spot of mayhem.

So Jiktar Nath Karidge, as the senior regimental commander, would conduct the cavalry. I gave him strict instructions and we checked sand-glasses, and then I led out my choice band and the Pachaks. The suns were drifting down behind banks of vermilion and emerald clouds, and the rain sifted in as though shaken from a trag's pelt. We rode silently. Ahead of us lay an army preparing to bed down for the night.

"They're pretty free and easy with their lights," observed Barty as we jogged down.

Indeed, there was plenty of light from lanterns and torches, whereat I frowned. What I purposed needed the shrouding cloak of Notor Zan.

"They act," said Targon with all the wisdom of his newly won state as a veteran warrior, "as though they're a friendly host. They didn't even investigate the disappearance of their patrol."

"Whatever the explanation," I said, "it must wait for now. Shastum!" Which is to say, "Silence!"

The sand trickled away and by the last of the light we saw the final grains tumble through. In the growing shadows, flames licked up from the baggage lines and tents began to burn.

No need for further orders. Everyone knew what had to be done and their part in the operation. The expertise we had laboriously acquired during those hectic and wearing times clearing out the Radvakkas and the Hamalese and their mercenaries was once again put to the test. Barty and the others led off, their mounts going quietly through the night, only an occasional stray chink of reflected light striking up from steel or armor.

The sky faded in a dying riot of color. A few stars began to prick out. The tents burned splendidly and already an uproar was beginning that would cloak our designs. Straight for the sumptuous marquee we rode, with its pennons of colors that held no heraldic significance, its pearl lights shining through the cloth, its armed guards, its total air of munificence. This, we were confident, was the marquee of the army commander.

Guards rose to challenge us, cloak-flaring shadows in the night. We rode through or over them and the alarm was up. But we went galloping on, striking down opposition, intent on our target and our tasks.

The thumping onrush of the zorcas, the sound of steel on iron, the shrieks of men, the bluster of wind and the frantic flicker of flames out of the corner of the eye melded to make a bedlam—a familiar bedlam that released inner compulsions together with the blood that coursed around the body, freely, stimulating us all to greater exertions.

Two Chuliks disputed the cloth-of-gold entrance to the marquee. Their comrades were down. Targon and Naghan struck horizontally, lethal sweeping blows. The Chuliks tumbled away; but one was only half-dead, and his flung spear took Naghan in the shoulder. He yelped, more in surprise than pain. That would bite him later.

"Take Naghan," I yelled at Targon. "You too, Korero. Ride on."

In the bedlam about us as men struggled and died they obeyed instantly. I leaped off the zorca and tumbled pell-mell into the cloth-of-gold opening. Lamps burned in mellow blazes and I could see only a Rapa at the far end of the tunnel-like entrance about to loose a shaft. The bow snapped and the arrow sped. My rapier shisked up and the shaft caromed away, to slice through that precious cloth-of-gold. I was up and past the Rapa before he could draw, and left him coughing on the carpets. The inner cloths flung back. I strode through.

This was a tented antechamber. Stout wooden posts had been driven into the ground and beautiful slave girls, practically naked, were chained by their necks to the posts. There were eleven posts and ten girls, and the odd post's iron chain lay like a serpent upon the ground. I walked on past with a stony face and two more Rapas fell away, screeching.

The girls were all screaming and caterwauling away, and I hoped I might release them if I returned this way. But ahead another tented chamber within the marquee revealed other men, sumptuously uniformed, relaxing with chased goblets of wine, and the girl who danced for them. She danced unwillingly, and a greasy slave-master snapped a whip at her buttocks, from time to time, to remind her of her duties.

The men were slow to react to my presence.

They displayed the same casual carelessness we had observed in the cavalry patrol and the general attitude of this army.

Firmly convinced that the solution to the mystery must lie with the commander, I moved on. They saw the rapier in my fist, they saw the slender blade and the crimson stains, and they started to lumber to their feet. Their reactions began with surprise, went through startlement, anger, furious rage—and then went on to dismay and fear and a babbling rush to get away, anywhere away. Those who could escaped. Those who could not, including the slave-master with his whip, remained stretched out in the tented enclosure. I did not think many would sup wine and watch a girl being whipped into dancing for their pleasure again.

"Hai, Jikai," said the girl, very calmly. Her body was lithe and lissome, remarkable, firm and curved, and she swayed with natural grace as she picked up a discarded cloth to cover her nakedness.

I gestured the rapier.

"The commander?"

"Oh, Lango is in there with his painted boys. You will have no trouble with him. Your men will destroy this army with ease."

"Mayhap," I said. I went across to the inner opening which was fastened with more cloth-of-gold. The girl picked up a rapier and by the way she handled the blade it was clear she had used weapons before. She smiled at me.

"But, I think, Jikai, you will let me deal with him."

"He is of concern to me only as an enemy of Vallia."

"So ho! A patriot. I had thought all patriots long since fled. Your name, Jikai?"

"As to that, I have been called Jak the Drang. And you?"

"Lahal, Jak the Drang. You may call me Jilian."

"Lahal, Jilian. Now, for the sweet sake of Opaz, let us get on and do this Lango's business for him."

The close atmosphere with the lamps shining evenly, the long lines of drapes against the tent walls, the gold and silver goblets spilled across the rugs and the wine soaking into the priceless fabrics, the stink of blood, the sprawled bodies of the men, clung about us. Her coolness both amazed and amused me—the amusement a genuine feeling, the amazement stupid in a world where I had already encountered Jikai Vuvushis—Battle Maidens.

I noticed without comment that Jilian selected from among the pile of tumbled clothes a red length of cloth to wrap around herself, ignoring the lustrous golds and silvers, the greens and blues.

She called me Jikai, which in the connotation she used meant great warrior, and understood that I commanded men. She would get a shock, I thought, when she discovered I had merely three cavalry regiments with me. But all that must wait. We moved together toward the inner opening.

Her face was pale. I thought that to be a natural part of her beauty and not brought on by the circumstances. There was color there, a palest tinge of rose along the cheekbones. Her face was artfully formed, low-browed, wide, with deep eyes that appeared in the lamps' glow to burn with the desire to exact revenge. Well, there were red and angry weal marks on her buttocks and thighs, and I did not doubt she felt she had good cause to give back what had been taken out on her body.

Her dark hair reached low over that broad white forehead, adding a luster to the eyes, giving an air of intenseness to her whole face, the features clear and pleasing, the mouth warm and red and mobile. She moved with grace. We stood together by the entrance and from beyond the muffling drapes of cloth-of-gold the sound of light laughter reached us.

Jilian's rapier flickered like the tail of a leem.

"They laugh, those rasts. But now we will smoke them out."

"We must hurry. There is a whole army encamped about us and there will be many guards."

Her dark eyes flayed into me, and I could feel the pressure of her thoughts.

"And do you, Jak the Drang, Jikai, fear an army?"

"Assuredly so—when I have other irons in the fire."

She reached out and ripped away the cloth-of-gold.

"Then let us heat this iron, together, and soon!"

Eight

Kov Colun Mogper of Mursham

Wherever Jilian had sprung from, the people there had taught her sword-play. Also, and this I found highly intriguing, she stopped to pick up the thick black whip the slave-master had wielded. When we burst through into the inner tented enclosure of the army commander, Fat Lango, it was the whip which, cracking out like a striking risslaca tongue, barbed, lashed him into painful movement. He shrieked. The lash coiled and lifted and struck, and again Fat Lango shrieked.

Jilian laughed.

Her teeth were very white and even.

The guards here were apim, slothful, over-dressed and arrogant to the point of stupidity. They did not interfere as Jilian lashed Lango.

And, still, I carried the Krozair longsword scabbarded over my back.

The painted and perfumed boys fled screaming from the wide pillow-strewn bed. Lango was bleeding. He tried to scramble away on all fours, like a dog, and the whip belted chunks of skin from his rump. Again Jilian laughed, drawing her arm up so that her whole body tensed, cracking the whip forward in a long raking slash that sliced all across Lango and made him shriek in agony.

He fell face down, and now the whip rose and fell, rose and fell, and I saw the last of the guards run. I turned back.

"Time to go, Jilian."

"I," she said, panting only a little, magnificent in her barbarism, "have not yet finished."

"Then, lady, I must leave without you."

She looked up, and the whip trailed.

"You would?"

"Believe it."

"I do, Jikai, I do. And, I am ready." With this she struck not, as she had done, in the pain-ways of the whip, but in the death-ways. I have described this vile kind of Kregen whip before, like a Russian knout or a sjambok. A thick, tapering instrument of agony and death. Fat Lango jerked, abruptly, rearing up like a praying mantis; then he slumped and he was dead.

"Now," said Jilian, and she coiled that thick rope of vileness along her white arm. "Now, Jikai, I am ready."

She moved like a stalking chavonth toward the cloth-of-gold entrance. I went the other way, toward the rear, where blue and green striped cottons covered the thicker material of the marquee. She stared after me.

"I go this way."

The bloody rapier licked out and stripped away the cloth, ripped in a lunge and a twisting tear down, and then across and down again. An opening gaped onto the starshot night.

"I," said Jilian, with some amused acerbity, "will go with you, Jak the Drang, Jikai."

"You may call me Jak, Jilian. And I welcome you. You are, I think, a mistress of the Jikai Vuvushis."

"Yes."

Together, shoulder to shoulder, we stepped out. Guy ropes angled, glimmering whitely, to catch unwary feet. The commotion boomed away and the flames were still shooting up, orange and lurid, blurring the luminous stars. I headed directly away from the sumptuous marquee of the commander, the late and unlamented Fat Lango, and I kept my eyes peeled for sight of my men. The uproar was prodigious, and once away from the marquee and only four dead men to betray that anyone had passed, we were able to slow down. But there was no sign of my men.

"Where, Jak, is your army?"

We stood by a line of picketed hersanys, their white coats ghostly in that eerie light. Jilian looked completely composed, the red cloth wrapped about her waist, the rapier in her left hand held negligently, the whip coiled up along the right arm, ready to be shaken down in an instant.

"Why do you think I have an army?"

She smiled. "Men like you always command armies."

"That may be. But my army is not here. We must find mounts and ride."

She threw her head back and laughed. Then, abruptly, her head came forward and her face lowered on me, intense, demanding, challenging. "Yes, Jak. Yes. I think—I think I would ride with you."

I was turning away, ready to free the nearest couple of hersanys, and cursing one that tried to take a bite out of my arm. The six-legged beasts are as intractable as any of the trix family of saddle animals, but thicker in the body and, certainly according to my lion-man comrade, Rees, thicker in the skull. I gave the hersany a pat along the neck, soothing him, and swiftly freed the tether. I handed the rope to Jilian, not doubting that she could ride bareback.

A Fristle guard came running up, yelling, his whiskery cat-face outraged. Jilian felled him with a single slicing blow from her whip. It had sprung from her arm and struck as though impelled by an inner life of its own.

The Fristle fell against my hersany. I took the opportunity to wipe my rapier clean on the fellow's tunic, before I thrust the blade away in its scabbard. And Jilian laughed.

As we mounted up I reflected on her intense and brooding face, almost fierce—not quite fierce, I remark, but intent and concentrated—and compared that with the wild passion of her laughter. This was a girl whose inner spirit held much within her opaque depths. Maybe no man had plumbed her fully yet. Well, that was no job for me. I had not envisaged rescuing a girl, anyway, in this night's work. And that, of course, brought to mind the other girls chained to their posts, terrified and shrieking in their nakedness.

I turned the hersany's head back.

Jilian said: "You may be a Jikai, Jak; but your bump of direction is sadly misplaced."

"Your friends," I said, most mildly. "I think I should see if their chains may be removed."

She stared at me, and, I think for the first time, saw me as other than a hulking warrior.

Silently, she turned her hersany too, and together we trotted back to the marquee.

Many a time I have ridden quietly through a shrieking bedlam, an uproarious furor, and marveled at the maniacal things poor crazed wights will do in times of stress. We saw sights that would have amazed your solid stay-at-home citizen; men yelling and crying, women rushing about with streaming hair oblivious to anything, anything at all, so that they ran all a-crying into blazing tents, animals driven mad with fear and trampling down men too crazed to step out of their way. Other things there were too that it would be kinder not to talk about. Through it all Jilian rode with that intense, lowering look on her face that was not a frown, not quite. We reached the marquee and saw how the guards were.

A windrow lay in blood. Others were reeling and staggering, desolated by wounds. The shambles showed a fight had raged here that must have been terrible in its ferocity. Among the corpses I saw a twisted figure, wearing the brave old red and yellow, and I dismounted and turned him over gently. It was Yallan the Iron-throated, a good comrade, who had ridden with us since the Battle of Sabbator. A spear had penetrated between the hooped plates of his kax tralkish and done for him.

Jilian dismounted and walked across to stand at my side.

"One of your men?"

"Aye. Just the one. The wounded would have been carried off. That is the way my men are."

She said, "There are many dead here. Yet you mourn just the one?"

The flash of feeling I experienced shook me. We had just met and I had thought—and now, how little she knew of me! I knew nothing of her, save that she had courage, and a beauty to set a man's pulses thumping, and a cool appraisal of life that, I suspected, had brought her through many a dangerous turn.

So, just as gently, I said, "I mourn for all men slain in battle or dead in bed. Yet some must, I think in nature, mean more than others. Is that so strange?"

"No. But they look so—so pathetic. Like the offal a butcher throws to the dogs."

I marked her words.

She was right. And, by saying that, she revealed more of herself.

Inside the marquee we found more dead guards, blegs and numims and Fristles, and all the slave girls had gone. The chains had been parted by savage blows, the cut edges of the links bright and glittering. So I knew Barty and the others, looking for me, had taken the time.

"We must leave. My men have saved your friends."

As we mounted up—and the whip chopped two Rapas who would have taken our mounts, as the rapier snicked the life from a third—she said, "I pray you, Jak. Do not call them my friends. They were poor little shishis, slave-girls by nature. I am not as they are."

I restrained my anger.

"No one is a slave by nature unless they are told this. A baby is born and must learn—"

"Slaves are born slaves."

"On this, Jilian, you and I must have words later."

"With you, Jikai, mayhap words will not be enough."

The tip of the rapier snicked up the warrior-cloak from a body, and a flick sent it sailing like a zizil of The Stratemsk toward Jilian, who caught it deftly and wrapped its blue and green check folds about herself. Another blue and green check enfolded my red and yellow. We turned the hersany's heads away from the marquee and the windrows of dead, as soldiers with torches ran across from the bivouac lines, shouting.

Into the shadows we rode, but gently, gently, restraining the impulses of our mounts to gallop in frenzy from the bedlam.

The noise of genuine combat floated up in a clangor of iron from the east and that, therefore, was the way my men had gone and the way I must go, too. I glanced at the girl.

Erect, she sat her steed, bareback, grasping the coarse rope with a slender hand that, I could guess, would have a grip of steel. She looked across at me and the redness of her mouth, purple plum in that light, curved into a smile. And then her eyes widened and she stared across my shoulder.

I switched around on the beast's back and saw riding among torches carried by a body of zorcamen a man in armor who glittered like a golden idol, resplendent, radiant, his sword lifted high as he bellowed orders. The zorcamen surrounding him looked more competent than any of the soldiers I had yet encountered in this army. They rode hard and they trampled down anyone and anything that chanced to get in their way.

It seemed prudent for us to sidle into the shadows of an undamaged tent until this formed body of hardened veterans passed.

Jilian's face screwed up into a fist. The whip snapped free. Her naked heels lifted out. I reached out and grabbed for the rope and her heels kicked in and the hersany leaped.

My clutching fingers missed the rope. The animal bounded away. Jilian made straight for that body of zorcamen and straight for that shining golden figure. The fury in her face was colder than the Ice Floes of Sicce.

"By the disgusting diseased liver and lights of Makki Grodno!" I yelled, clapping in my heels. "Can't you control your temper, girl!"

With Jilian in the lead we hurtled toward the zorcamen.

If the Fates, who play with us poor mortals as children play with insects, inspecting a wing here and a leg there, had a hand in it I do not know. But Jilian's hersany caught a hoof in a guy rope and staggered sideways, twisting, hurling her from his back. The beast went down thrashing and I had time only to haul my own away. I checked him with a vicious tug on the rope and swung down. Jilian lay winded, glaring up with such a look of vindictive hatred as would make a man's innards turn to treacle.

"Kov Colun," she said. She spoke in a whisper. "I have sworn to have his manhood and have it I will—I will make him into a nithing, a mewling spineless ninny, and then perhaps, if it pleases me, will I kill him."

The zorcamen rode on, not seeing us in the shadows, our falling commotion merely a part of the greater confusion.

Jilian stood up with my hand under her armpit. She breathed deeply, magnificently. "The bastard came from that marquee, the unburned one with the golden flags. He has something of mine I would have back."

With that, without a look at me or another word, she started for the marquee. The cloth-of-gold was not as lavish as that festooning the marquee of Fat Lango; but everything spoke of wealth and refinement and a lavish expenditure of money and the labor of slaves. Jilian's whip lashed the life from two Rhaclaw guards, their heads shining, domed and as wide as their shoulders, bursting under the impetuous ferocity of the lash. Jilian ran on past them and entered the marquee, the whip black and cutting striking before her.

Whatever was so important as to warrant this risk was no doubt somewhere in there, if she said so. This Kov Colun had looked a different prospect from the others of this army and I deemed it expedient to stand on guard by the marquee entrance. Jilian would find what she wanted, so I contented myself by a harshly shouted: "Hurry, girl!"

She re-appeared and color stained her cheeks like flame.

"By the Rod of Halron and the Mount of Mampe!" She spoke in a breathy whisper, as though drunk, and yet she moved with a sureness that told me she was vibrantly alive with her own personal triumph. Under her arm she carried a silver-mounted balass box, about eighteen inches long. The rapier in her left hand snouted parallel to the ground and even with the box under her arm I fancied she could give an account of herself. The whip was recoiled up her arm, and her white skin was blotched and stained with blood.

I said: "You are quite ready?"

"More ready than those cramphs within."

"No doubt," I said, handing her across a couple of corpses and a pool of spilled blood. "They are also without."

She laughed.

"Aye! Without much."

The blue and green checks swathing us would serve for a space yet. But the sounds of distant strife wavered on the night air, faded and were gone. A silver trumpet note sounded, tiny and far, signaling the "Recall" and the "Reform." The way the notes trilled told me that was not Volodu the Lungs but one of the trumpeters of Karidge's Regiment. They had done well, for the army encampment was in a leem's mess; but we were left here, alone, and must make shift to get out of this ourselves. In thus pulling his men out, Nath Karidge was strictly obeying my orders. I took Jilian's arm again and we moved silently into the shadows between the tent lines.

"Zorcas, I think," I said.

"With a saddle this time, Jak."

"Aye."

With a bitterness she made no effort to suppress, she said, "You marked that tapo in the golden armor?"

"You called him Kov Colun."

"Yes. A piece of dirt that walks about on two legs. Colun Mogper, Kov of Mursham. Never turn your back on him, never trust him. If you can, try to stamp his face flat in the mud—after I have done with him."

"Mursham," I said. "In Menaham. That explains the difference, for if he is one of the Bloody Menahem then he would be affronted by the sloth of this army."

Her bitter anger had been partly mollified by her success in recovering her property, and my words finally brought her thoughts back into some kind of coherence. "You know Menaham?"

"I have fought the Bloody Menahem before. They are one people of Pandahem we will have trouble with in the future—"

"One! All of the rasts in that Opaz-forsaken island."

"I do not think so."

"You think because this army is a farce they are all like this?"

We passed beyond a smoke pall from burning forage and the Maiden with the Many Smiles shone out, plunging between cloud wrack, the moon shedding down her fuzzy pink light upon scenes of desolation and death. We saw zorcas moving and headed that way, ready.

"No. There is something almighty strange about this little lot—"

"Of course. They are the dregs of the gutters and the Wharves, dressed up as soldiers. The Chulik paktuns they have engaged as drill instructors left en masse, disgusted. There are no Pachaks and a few Khibils in this sorry army. Pandahem breathed easier when these cramphs were shipped out."

These words gave me serious concern—more than concern, an all panic stations alarm. I saw it—not all of it, but a deal of it and the core of it. The plan against Vallia... This army was the decoy, a rabble dressed up in fine fancy uniforms and taught to march together and then let loose into Vallia. They were expendable. They had been provided with a cavalry screen composed of men who had once been soldiers and who had been told off for this duty probably for dire misdeeds, or indiscipline or some fault. There are always these men who take the letter of Vikatu the Dodger and fail to see the spirit of that archetypal old sweat of the armies of mythology. That explained the conduct of the patrol we had ambushed. It explained why the army was as it was. But it did not do one very vital and overmasteringly fearful thing.

This knowledge newly given into my hands did not tell me where the real armies were, where the blow aimed to destroy us all would be struck at Vallia.

Nine

The Whip and the Claw

Jilian kept singing snatches of a silly little song as we jogged along in the suns shine the next day. We had all the world to ourselves, it seemed. The sky stretched emptily and the unending grassland was studded only with small trees and bushes, a wide heath that was, in truth, deceptive, for it extended merely between towns here in eastern Thadelm. The song concerned the comical efforts of a little Och maiden and a strapping young Tlochu youth to sort out the twelve limbs they possessed between them. I found Jilian's song silly but enchanting. It is called The Conundrum of the Hyrshiv. The eventual solution the Och girl and the Tlochu boy worked out for themselves is ironical and funny; it is touching and true, though, for it illustrates that despite difficulties love, what is sometimes ludicrously called "True Love," will find a way around problems of this physical kind.

She broke off singing and with that graceful turn of her head looked across at me and said, "You could, at least, Jak the Drang, Jikai, have found us zorcas."

Her use of Jikai here was entirely sarcastic.

We rode hirvels. Now the hirvel is a perfectly good saddle animal. He is a stubby, four-legged beast looking not unlike a nightmare version of a llama with his tall round neck, cup-shaped ears and shaggy body and twitching snout. But he will carry you along if not as fleetly as a zorca or as powerfully as a nikvove in some comfort and despatch.

I said, "There has been enough killing for one night."

"Deaths don't frighten me."

"I saw that. Can you tell me where you were trained?"

By my phraseology she understood that I was circumspect about the sororities. She laughed.

"There is no secret about where, Jak. That was at Lancival. Oh, a wonderful place, all red roofs and ivied walls and the gentle cooing of doves and the sliding gleam from the water well, that is a long time ago now." She sighed and her laughter died. I judged that to a man with a thousand years of life, as I had awaiting me, her memory of a long time ago might seem as yesterday. Or not, given the terrors and the pains of the intervening period. She flashed her eyes at me. "But as to how, that you may ask and never get an answer."

"I do not think I would choose to ask."

"And you?"

"Here and there about the world—"

"Oh, really, Jak! If we are to be friends, as I sincerely hope, you must do better than that."

"You would wish to be friends with me?"

Her regard on me wavered and she looked away. She shivered. "Better a friend than an enemy."

"Well," I said, trying not to be offended. "And I think if we are to be friends you must do better than that."

"Mayhap I do not wish to be—friends."

"As to that, we must let Opaz guide us."

"Yes."

"So how was it you were slave with the Pandaheem?"

Her face flushed up again in remembered terror and anguish, and, too, recollected anger.

"I served the Sisters well. At least, I think I did. I have some skill. But when the Troubles fell on Vallia, flutsmen came and I was taken. They dropped from the air like stones. We fought but were overborne. They are not—not nice, flutsmen."

"Most, not all," I agreed, equably. "And this Kov Colun?"

"I will say nothing of him save that I shall sink my talons into him, and rip him, and may then, if it pleases me, kill him."

I nodded and the conversation died for a space.

After a time as we rode along and the motion of the hirvels jolted our livers, we regained a more pleasant atmosphere and she told me she was one of six children born to a shopkeeper in Frelensmot. He had been a happy, jolly man, and just rich enough to buy three slaves for the shop, which was, she said with a funny little toss of the head, a Banje store, a place where you could buy candy and sweets and toffee-apples and miscils and all manner of toothsome, mouthwatering trifles. But the shop fell on evil days and her father spilled a vat of boiling treacle on his foot and it never healed and that broke him. She herself was sent at first to the Little Sisters of Opaz, where she learned a great deal of how to be demure and polite and sew a fine stitch. Later she went—and here she hauled herself up in her tale, and regarded me with those eyes of hers slanting on me with the telltale surprise for herself that she had said so much.

"When I went to Lancival I learned what to do with a length of steel somewhat longer than a sewing needle."

She laughed. "And I learned other things, also, and one day Kov Colun will find out how I can rip him up in a twinkling."

Her hand reached back and stroked down the polished balass of the box. A sensuousness in the gesture reminded me of the way a great cat will turn her head and rub a paw down past her ear. Then Jilian laughed again, her head thrown back and the long line of her throat bared and free to the breeze.

"And you are just Jilian?"

"For you, Jak, just Jilian."

"I see." Well, it was no business of mine. Although she wouldn't understand, I did not think we would go up the hill to fetch a pail of water together.

We would have to avoid habitations until we reached Vond, and any other riders we encountered would without doubt be hostile. The rendezvous with Barty and the others lay some way ahead and although I was in a fever of impatience to reach Vondium and attempt to discover where the main threat to the city would come, I had to tread cautiously. So we covered the dwaburs, talking and laughing, and keeping our weapons loose in their scabbards.

A scatter of black-winged warvols rose ahead of us. The scavenging birds would rip a body up, dead or half-dead; but they were a part of nature fulfilling a function and so must be treated on their own merits. We rode up to the mess hunkered by a grassy hillock.

The three zorcas were almost stripped down to the bone. The three jutmen because of their armor were not in so detailed a state of dissolution, although their faces were gone, and only three yellow skulls jutted above the corselet rims. Their weapons were gone, and although two of the arrows had been withdrawn, the third, broken in half, still shafted from the gaping eye socket of a skull. One always, in these circumstances, inspects the fletchings.

There was no sense in grieving over the three zorcamen. By their uniforms and insignia they were of the Second, Jiktar Wando Varon's regiment. Stragglers, they must have been attempting to catch up with the main body, as we were, heading for the rendezvous.

The arrows were fletched with natural gray and brown feathers, and were of the length to be shot from a standard compound bow. "Hamalese?" said Jilian.

"Very likely, or their mercenary allies. We have a ways to go before we reach Vond. The river will set a barrier of some sort between us. Keep your eyes skinned."

And that was an unnecessary injunction, to be sure.

The mercenaries turned out to be masichieri, very cheap and nasty examples of men earning a living hiring out as killers and pretending to be soldiers, and they found us as the twin suns were sinking into banks of bruised clouds and streaming a choked, opaline, smoky light over the grass.

"I make ten of them, Jak."

"Yes."

"Will that be five each, d'you think?"

They were infantry, armored in an assortment of harnesses, bearing a variety of weapons, and their bristly ferocious faces exhibited their joy at thus finding two lonely strangers at this time of the evening. They rose from the bushes and four of them bent bows upon us. They were joking among themselves.

"Best step down nice and easy, horter and hortera," one shouted, very jocose, calling us gentleman and lady.

"Had I a bow—" began Jilian.

I said: "Put your head down, girl!"

I clapped in my heels, the Krozair longsword flamed a single brand of livid light against the sky and I leaped forward.

Three of the arrows were caught and deflected as the masichieri, startled, loosed. The third whistled past out of reach to my rear. Then I was in among them. The Krozair longsword—well, that brand of destruction is indeed a marvel, and this was a true Krozair brand, brought from Valka, the blade and hilt so cunningly wrought that the steel sings of itself as it thrusts and cuts. Four, five and then six were down before they even had time to consider what manner of retribution they had brought on themselves. I kneed the hirvel to the side and the Krozair blade hissed. Back the other way and a thraxter that came down at me abruptly checked, snapped across, and its owner went smashing backwards without a face.

The remaining two were to my rear and I hauled the hirvel up squealing on his haunches and swung him about. His hooves clawed at the sunset. We were down and I was belting back, and saw a sight, by Krun!

One of the masichieri staggered away, his hands to his face, and between his clenching fingers spurted a crimson flood.

The other screamed as the whip coiled around his neck. He was dragged bodily up to Jilian's hirvel. I saw her face. It was drawn and intent. I saw her left hand.

She did not wield a rapier.

As the shrieking wight was dragged in, struggling futilely against the coils of the lash, a steel taloned left hand raked out, glinting in the dying light, slashed all down his face. That cruel, steel curved claw ripped his face off as a mummer takes off a mask. Blood spouted. Jilian reined back and flicked her whip and allowed the body to drop.

She laughed.

Her left hand, gloved with taloned steel, a razor claw of destruction, glimmered darkly as she lifted it to me in triumph.

Ten

What Difference Does an Emperor Make?

"By Vox! I do not know. I've no idea at all."

"Us and Sogandar the Upright," said Nath at Barty's wail of despair.

We stood in that book-lined room glaring in baffled fury at the map of Vallia. The colors mocked us. No scouts reported an invading army, we had had not a whisper from our spies in the occupied territories. We knew nothing. And yet, I was convinced, there had to be the real invasion force from which that ludicrous gaggle of men masquerading as an army under command of Fat Lango had been intended to decoy us away.

"Where among all the Ice Floes are they?" said Barty.

He stood with his hands on his hips and his head thrown back and he looked as though he'd just tried to eat a five-fathom eel lengthways.

"There's only one way to find out." Nath slapped his rapier up and down in the scabbard, fretfully. "And we're doing that right now. Scouts, spies, aerial observation. What else can we do?"

"Wait," I said.

"Aye, majister. Wait. And the men grow lean and hungry although we fill their bellies six times a day."

"The fight will come. We must ensure we fight it where we choose."

Most of my joy at rejoining the force and then of marching back to Vondium had evaporated when I discovered that Delia had taken herself off again about important and secret business of the Sisters of the Rose. Always I felt irritable and half-lost when she was away. This is natural, if foolish, behavior and I do not choose either to defend or curse at it. It just is.

The arrow that had winged past me in that short sharp fight had sliced a chunk out from under Jilian's breast and I'd had a fair old game with her at the end, just before we joined up with the rest of the retreating force. She'd fought her two masichieri well. But she'd become a little delirious and I'd had to strap her down to the hirvel. It was a most undignified young lady who was decanted in Vondium and hustled off by the ladies to their own wing where the doctors could attend more effectively than I had done. Had Seg's wife Thelda been here the to-do would have been much greater, of course.

The trouble was—this meant I could not question Jilian about her steel claw, which was a twin to that worn by Dayra.

Jilian had kept the clawed glove strapped to her hand and wrist after the fight. That had caused some of the bother, for she'd taken it into her head to slash at anyone who came near. Well, that was all over and she was safely asleep festooned with acupuncture needles. When she awoke, poulticed, bandaged, dosed and medicated, she'd be herself again.

So we pondered the dark designs of those who sought to topple Vallia, and, besides wondering where they would strike, wondered who in a Herrelldrin Hell they were.

One thing I could do, and that was make sure the army was up to scratch. We were forming regiments at a fair pace, of course; but it takes time to turn a man into a soldier. I offer no excuses for this conduct in a land where always before in living memory gold had been used instead of warriors. Now we must free ourselves by our own efforts. The response of the Vallians was immediate and generous and we had no difficulty in filling the muster lists of any regiment on the day they were opened. Cavalry, infantry, artillery, we formed fresh bodies and trained them. For air—well, I had found myself one of the wise men of Vallia, who are not to be confused with sorcerers although often termed wizards, and he was busily producing the substances necessary to fill the silver vaol-paol boxes that lift and power fliers. We would build ourselves a fleet of sailing fliers, able to lift into the air but dependent on the breeze for sailing. At the least, they would give us some support, and at the best would help us rout the enemy.

In the great waters of Kregen there are perhaps only the devil Shanks from over the curve of the world who can teach Vallians much about sailing ships. From the fleets of great Vallian galleons would come eager volunteers to sail the ships of the sky.

The map of Vallia, as well as remaining blank as to the intentions of our foes, showed not a single mention of any place called Lancival. I had not

69

commented to Jilian that I did not know it. And she, the minx, had known all along that I could not. No smot, den or village, no province or estate that I could find was called Lancival, and none of the men I questioned had heard of the place, no, by Vox, never!

The Lady Winfree, a charming girl and married to a Chuktar newly appointed to command a brigade, looked right through me when I mentioned the name to her. She excused herself rapidly and made off, her skirts swaying, her head high. So that was that. Lancival was another of these damned secrets the women held so close to them. Well, they were entitled to secrets, of course, that went without a say-so. And, equally of course, there are secrets wives hold that they are not entitled to, just as their husbands hold remembered guilt. I felt the thankfulness in me I had told Delia of Earth, that weird little planet with one tiny yellow sun, one small silver moon and not a diff in sight.

I went to see Jilian in her yellow-sheeted bed with the flowers banked around the suns-filled room. She lay white and lovely and completely unconscious of anyone or anything save what paraded before her in dreams. I sighed.

The doctor said: "Give her another two days, majister."

Long before I left the ladies' quarters, which had been among the first of the palace ruins to be rebuilt, Barty met me bubbling with an enthusiasm and a joyful eagerness I found despite my mood to be wonderfully infectious.

The first thought was that one of the invading armies had been discovered.

But Barty called out: "Dayra!" He waved his arms, his face almost bursting, and fell in beside me to trot along babbling out the news. "She has been seen. It must be her, definitely—the spy was well paid. She rode into Werven with a rascally gang buying supplies. I am sure, Dray, there can be no doubt."

"Werven. That is in Falinur, Seg's kovnate."

"Wherever it is, Dray—I must be off. This is the chance we have been waiting for."

He was right. And the devils of temptation leered and beckoned to me. My daughter, my elfin wayward daughter who wore a steel-taloned claw and slashed men to pieces, Ros the Claw—how could I not rush instantly to find her and how could I not stay in Vondium in her time of trial? What to do?

Barty must have sensed that indecision in me, for he was becoming more and more attuned to the delicacies of personal relationships these days. He cocked an eye at me, and stopped speaking, and for a dozen strides we marched side by side out of the women's quarters. In silence we continued through the Mother of Pearl Court, under the colonnades where purple-flowered ibithses glowed against the limewash, and so over tessellated paving into the cool blue shade of the Goldfish Court where the tanks rippled ghostly flickers of orange-gold like sparks against the milky silver.

"You must go, Barty." I spoke heavily. "And my heart goes with you. But for me, I must stay here."

He understood.

There was no way of telling if he was pleased or sorry I would not be with him, for we had gone through a few hairy moments together, and to do him credit he expressed immediate understanding and determination to talk to Dayra. He was aware of problems. He did not know Dayra was Ros the Claw. I felt it right that he should know before he went, and found little sense in my withholding the information previously.

"By Vox!" he said. "You mean—like that ghastly steel claw your friend Jilian was wearing?"

I nodded.

He shook his head. "What a girl. I've romped with her when we were very young—before I knew you, Dray. I think she must be very—grown up—now."

"Yes." I spoke dryly, and my throat choked up. "Very."

Barty had owned a number of airboats and all the survivors of the troubles had been placed at the disposal of the Vondium Defense Forces, as was proper. The Lord Farris was reluctant to release a single unit from the small forces we had; but he understood from what I did not say and from my demeanor that the need was pressing. Barty was fully supplied with all that a man needs to survive on Kregen and with a party of his own men was sent off in fine style. He called down the Remberees, which were answered with bellows of well wishers, and the flier fleeted up and away into the radiance of the Suns of Scorpio. A fine, headstrong, courageous young man, Barty Vessler, the Strom of Calimbrev.

But, all the same, the thought occurred to me and I could not halt it, that it ought to be me who flew off with such high hopes. And, come to think of it, where the hell was Delia?

The next few days passed most miserably.

There were, at the least, no more ghostly visitations from that infernal Wizard of Loh, spying on us in lupu; but even that would have been a welcome interruption. As it was, and despite the people around me who worked hard and with a will, I felt alone, isolated, cut off from all the things that seemed of worth. So when Nath, who as the commander of the Phalanx was now called a Kapt, a general, wanted me to inspect the new bodies he had formed, I was glad to go.

Now, as you know, a Phalanx consists of two Kerchuris, the two wings, each of five thousand one hundred eighty-four pikemen, the brumbytes.

71

Flanking them are the Hakkodin, the axemen and halberdiers, eight hundred sixty-four strong. Because we now had access to adequate supplies of iron, and Vondium's forges produced first quality carbon-steel, we had incorporated bodies of men equipped with the big two-handed sword. With these fearful weapons they could knock a jutman from his saddle with a single blow, if they did not slice him in half.

In addition, and because of the promised threat from the air, the Phalanx had attached strong forces of archers. These were not, alas, the famed and feared Bowmen of Loh armed with the superb Lohvian longbow. They used the compound reflex bow, powerful, accurate, flat in the loose, and they had been drilled and trained until shooting oozed from their ears. They had been given particular attention. The Vallians were now aware of the danger from the skies.

As for artillery, wheeled varters, the Kregan ballistae, were manufactured and artillerymen drilled and practiced with a keen desire to make their battery the best in the army. The superior Vallian gros-varters, too, were produced. There just was not time to have the wise men go into the problems of design and manufacture of the repeating-varters I had set my heart on. They would have to come later—if Vallia survived.

The two Kerchurivaxes came up to report, massive and brilliant in armor and a profusion of ornamentation. I never stinted on the amount of decoration a fighting man cared to wear, provided always that nothing was allowed to interfere with his efficiency. The long period of waiting was trying, but as the two Kerchuri commanders saluted and I looked beyond them, with a welcoming word, to the massed blocks of the Phalanx, I saw with a lift of elation that the men showed not a sign of boredom or slothfulness. Of course, Nath kept them up to the mark. But, all the same, idleness breeds slackness. We would have to take a little stroll in the suns shine of Antares and give the brumbytes and the Hakkodin a modicum of exercise.

Each Kerchuri contains six Jodhris, and the twelve Jodhrivaxes were wheeled up smartly to me to be received with a Vallian handshake after the formal salute. They were all tough-looking men, sweating a little in their armor; but big, bold, bulky, fit men to stand in rank and file and handle the long deadly pike. Pikemen need bulk as well as muscle. The Hakkodin, as I received their commanders, were lither; but still big men, still men who could swing a halberd and take the legs from under a charging totrix or benhoff.

The archer force attached to this Phalanx was under the command of Log Logashtorio. He was a Bowman of Loh, from Erthyrdrin, Seg's homeland, and he did not know whether to laugh at the antics of his men with the smaller bow or to be proud of their achievements. He was an old professional, a man I had known for some time and who had remained loyal throughout the Time of the Troubles. I had promoted him to the command with the rank of Chodkuvax. A few words quickly revealed his delight in his command and the work involved and his whole-hearted support of his bowmen, despite that they were not Bowmen of Loh and did not pull the fabled Lohvian longbow. I shook hands and said, "Now if Seg Segutorio were here, Chodkuvax Logashtorio..."

And his seamed face split into a massive smile and he beamed and said: "By the Veiled Froyvil, majister! Seg would say never a word of praise; but he would see, he would see!"

And, as you will readily perceive, Log Logashtorio was anxious that Seg should know of his good fortune in gaining a command himself. So with the shouted words of command and the long blam-blam-berram rataplan of the massed drums, the Third Phalanx marched past. Everywhere I went where men spoke to me the "Majister's" flew thicker than swallows in spring. I had grown partly used to it, as the Prince Majister; but now, every now and then, I'd be pulled up sharply as I was addressed as emperor. That was a job I'd not sought, and meant to do and have done with, and shuffle it off onto my splendid son Drak.

This Third Phalanx presented a fine stirring sight. But, as Nath said: "They have not been blooded yet, majister."

"Come the day, Nath, and they'll do as well as we did with the old Phalanx of Therminsax."

"They will, by a Brumbyte's Elbow! They will!"

The next day it was the turn of the churgur infantry, long flexible lines of sword and shield men, splendid in their crimson and yellow. By example and exhortation we were gradually dinning into their heads that shields were not cowards' weapons, and the success of the Phalanx at the Battle of Voxyri had done much to impress all. These men were organized into regiments under a Jiktar, four hundred eighty strong, although some were still short while others contained as many as six hundred in their ranks. This situation I tolerated; time would straighten all that out. And every minute of every live-long day was spent in training these men and drilling them and turning highly individual citizenry who were habituated to working together when profits were involved into that fierce, demoniac, cutting machine of an army that would be vital to our survival.

Also, at this time, members of the Order of Kroveres of Iztar began to trickle in from wild adventurings around the country. I welcomed them with the utmost warmth, for these were the men with whom I sought to change the ways of a world. I shall have much more to say of the KRVI later; but suffice it for now to say that they formed a powerful if small band of devoted comrades, beautifully complementing that choice band who had followed me in the Times of Troubles. And, from time to time, when a man proved himself, fresh candidates were taken in and, slowly, the strength of the KRVI grew.

The Grand Archbold of the Kroveres of Iztar did not put in an appearance in Vondium which saddened me mightily.

So, events were happening thick and fast every day; but the events I hungered for did not happen. Delia did not return. Dayra and Barty did not return. The damned ghost invasion remained invisible. And my friends did not show their faces in Vondium, as I would have wished. As for the rest of my family—enough for them that I wished them well and, indeed, messages had been sent to Zeg, the King of Zandikar.

Jaidur, of course, was prancing around running errands for the women.

The sailing fliers were built with the utmost urgency and the yards turned them out by the handful. Mere clumsy wooden boxes, they seemed, square-ended, blunt, and yet purposeful, designed to do a job and adequate for the demands that would be placed upon them. The silver boxes were readied and installed. The masts were raised and all the complicated rigging of the sealanes was dispensed with; we rigged them, with foremast, main and mizzen, courses, topsails and royals only with spinnaker and jib. I had decided it was scarcely worth the complications to rig masts extending from the sides at right angles, as we had done in the past. With these sailing boxes stuffed with varters and catapults and gros-varters, aswarm with aerial sailors and fighting men, I fancied we would give another nasty shock to the invading armies, as we had trounced the army of Hamal at the Battle of Jholaix.

The silver boxes lifted the skyships only. The lines of force—etheromagnetic force, old San Evold sometimes called them—which crisscrossed the world, were gripped onto and held by the power of the silver boxes, as though a keel was extended. By this means the skyships could tack against the wind, unlike free-flight balloons which are helpless in a breeze.

I went to see Jilian on the day of the departure of part of the army in a fleet of skyships. It was an evolution only, to see how quickly we could transport and disembark a Phalanx into battle. The ships were not all the same, naturally, being the work of individuals; but they were of a size. There were the smaller vessels, sloops of the sky, and the medium sized frigates of the air. And there were the mammoths. These were four and five decks high, with towering superstructures studded with varter ports. Flung together, they were cross-beamed and buttressed, their knees sturdy, their scarphs rudimentary and reinforced with bronze, their planking coarse and heavy. Without the need to combat the hogging and sagging motion to which a ship is subjected in the sea, without the need for fine lines, they could be built cheaply and efficiently as hulking great boxes stuffed with fighting potential.

Each of the larger ships could carry a Jodhri from the Phalanx or two regiments of churgur infantry or a regiment of cavalry. I needed to know how swiftly the whole force could be brought into a concentration, landing and disembarking and the troops forming. This kind of exercise was vital to our planning. We took that Third Phalanx that had looked so fine on parade, two brigades of churgurs, and four regiments of cavalry, two of zorcas, and one each of totrixes and nikvoves.

At the last minute, by design to test the men, I added the Fourth and Sixth Regiments of Totrixes. That, at the least, gave a more equable balance as between infantry and cavalry. With the bedlam going on as the two regiments frantically loaded themselves into their ships, I went to see Jilian.

She looked up from the yellow pillows and she did not smile.

"So, Jak the Drang, Jikai—you are the Emperor of Vallia."

"You are feeling better? The wound has healed?"

Her claw was removed; but the end of the balass box stuck out from under the bed. The scent of roses overpowered in the room. The quietness fell soothingly after the uproar outside.

"Yes. You bound up my wound—and the doctor says you sucked out the poison."

"Yes."

Her hand moved under the yellow sheet, across her breast, and was still. Still she did not smile.

"And—the emperor?"

"What difference does that make?"

"To you—or to me?"

'To either of us."

"Nothing." And then she smiled. "No difference at all."

"When you are fully recovered I want to talk to you about Lancival, and other things." I licked my lips. "About a girl called Ros the Claw—"

She half sat up. Her dark hair shimmered in the light.

"Ros? How do you know her?"

I felt the leap in me. I kept my face composed. "I have met her."

"Well, steer clear of her. She has a leem temper." Jilian lay back, and I could see she was still very weak. "It is something to do with her father. A right cramph, by her account. But she is good with the—" Here Jilian halted herself again, and then said, "With her claw." And so I knew she had nearly told me the secret name these women called that vicious weapon.

"The people here will look after you well. Get strong again. The poison weakened you—"

She saw the way I was clad, the harness, the colors, the weaponry. "You march out to war?"

"No. An exercise only."

She laughed. It was a small, pale laugh; but it reminded me of the way she threw her head back and laughed, fine and full and free, as we rode across the grasslands.

"You look as grim as though you ride out to confront the legions of Hodan-Set."

Eleven

Of Lahals After Battle

Fifty immense sailing skyships lifted out of Vondium and spread their wings and with a good breeze set course southeast. I had a mind to find out what was going on in that corner of Vallia.

Crossing Hyrvond, the imperial province which extends a finger to the south alongside the Great River, we were over friendly territory and the people, looking up in wonder and seeing our flags, waved in greeting. Next came Valhotra, of which Genal Arclay was Vad. Continuing on with the breeze backing a trifle and making us slant our yards to catch the best of it, we crossed the Vadvarate of Procul. Procul, and the Vadvarate of Gremivoh to the southwest of it, lies at the heart of superb wine country. But our thoughts were not on fine wines as we neared the border with Mai Yenizar. This kovnate, which was then fairly large, extending from a wide loop of the Great River southwards to the coast, was firmly in enemy hands.

That enemy, we had reliable reports, consisted of a multiplicity of fortresses set up by the aragorn, lordly slave masters terrorizing the districts under their heels. They descended on weak and undefended places and set up their centers and decimated the countryside. The border had been patrolled by us and defended as best we could with the forces at our disposal, as I have related. I fancied we might drop down on an aragorn fortress or two, near at hand, and give the men a taste of real action. At the least, that operation would relieve some of the pressure.

North of that wide-ranging loop of She of the Fecundity, Vallia's chiefest river, lay the imperial province of Bryvondrin. Over the River again and north and eastward lay lands held by our foes that interposed a buffer between us in the provinces around Vondium and our allies in the northeast. A goodly stroke might be brought about here if we did not become entangled. Always, the fear that mighty hosts converged on us had to be lived with, making my days, at the least, dark with the forebodings of coming disaster.

We in Vondium were like blindfolded men who are attacked from out of the darkness and do not know in which direction to strike, for fear that a blow one way will expose the back to the deadly stab from another.

I had told Jilian this was a mere exercise, and the men believed that, and here was I already planning a miniature campaign in which real blows would be struck and real blood shed. From such shoddy stuff are emperors made.

Nath, who as the Kapt of the Phalanx, had insisted on his right to fly with us, said to me: "We fly well to the east, majister. Aragorn down there."

"Aye, Nath. A visit from us might tone up their muscles."

"Amen to that. But, I would suggest, before the suns set."

"Assuredly. Have the captain signal preparation for descent." I pointed over the rail. "There is a wide swathe of land all set out for us. And the trees are far enough away. There is not a sign of a habitation anywhere." I looked at Nath as I spoke, and he braced up, knowing I summed him up.

"With respect, majister. I would prefer to land nearer the target."

"When you see a damned aragorn fortress, Nath, you may descend. Be prepared to have your men disembark smartly. I am going below. Call me the instant anything happens."

"Quidang, majister!"

As I went down the companionway I reflected that the exercise would reveal faults in the most glaring way. We proposed a disembarkation in sight of the enemy. Interesting. Most.

The deep end is very often a capital way of learning to swim. Not always, though, and so as was to be expected I merely fretted and fumed in the stateroom, and could get scant comfort from a pot of superb Kregen tea.

The hails, floating in with a joyous raucousness, came as a blessed relief. But I waited before going on deck for Nath's report.

When I stepped onto the quarterdeck with the wind blustering the canvas and the busy activity of bringing the ship in to land, I was struck by the similarities and the differences in this sailing ship of the air and all those other ships I have sailed on the seas of two worlds.

"Not so much a fortress, emperor!" sang out Nath, mightily pleased at his discovery. "More a whole stinking town of 'em!"

And, indeed, as I looked over the rail there was a town spread out below, slate-roofed, granite-walled, huddled behind battlements. Smoke rose from the evening meal cooking fires. A bell sounded, faintly, borne away by the wind. We could see flocks of cattle being driven along white roads toward the gates. The smells rose up, some appetizing, some bringing a gushing memory of slaughterhouses. I frowned.

We had determined to drill the men in the evolution of disembarking as speedily as might be contrived. Then I had thought it would be salutary to teach the aragorn the lesson that Vondium still survived. And now Nath was bringing us down onto a town, where a full-scale battle could be expected, and where his beloved Phalanx would be of little use.

I expressed these thoughts to him.

He smiled triumphantly, and pointed past the long gray walls of the town below.

Men rode toward the town. They were aragorn, haughty in their armor, proud with weaponry, and there were many of them. But the miserable crowds of slaves who lurched and staggered on numbered many many more, and we watched the end result of a slave drive here, a successful slave round-up that brought in the miserable wights from a very large area. I nodded, convinced.

"Churgur infantry to the town with a regiment of zorcas," I said. "The Phalanx and the rest of the cavalry to form ready to stop those cramphs down there. Move!"

The signals hoisted away from the yardarms, scraps of colored bunting in true-blue navy style. I had taught my own aerial sailors much. Signaling, even then, was smart and accurate.

The sword and shield infantry ships wheeled away, their canvas swinging free as they slipped sheets, heading down to the gray confusion of the town. The Phalanx ships dropped ponderously to a long sloping meadow. I watched the aragorn.

Their confusion must be expected to be immense. But in a very short space of time they had shaken out into line, formed, their spears all slanting, and their helmets catching the light of the suns. Whoever ran this town was a man who knew what he wanted and made damned sure he got it.

The ships were touching down, massive argosies landing as light as thistledown. The men leaped out, running to form their files on their faxuls, their file leaders, each file of twelve men forming in twelve ranks to give the one hundred forty four brumbytes of the Relianch. The Relianchun stood at the head of the right hand file. As the Relianches formed they joined with others, so that six Relianches formed the Jodhri. Flanking them the Hakkodin fell in, and the archers took up their places in the intervals.

It was all done with a smartness, a panache, a cracking sense of style and occasion. These men had never been in action before—only a few in positions of command—and so that had to be taken into consideration. All the same, they handled themselves well, and the solid bulk of the two Kerchuris was wonderfully reassuring.

I had the oddest feeling that I would have liked Delia to see the Phalanx in operation. Not fighting, but in maneuver.

"Send a totrix regiment back up to the town," I yelled. "Volodu—signal Jiktar Karidge to keep his men back." For that intemperate commander was edging forward and forward, ready to get a good smack at the aragorn before anyone else could get in. Volodu put his silver trumpet to his lips and blew Karidge's Regiment and Hold Fast, and I saw the distant figure astride the zorca, all a glitter of gold and crimson, turn indignantly in the saddle and glare back. And I smiled.

It was quite clear that the aragorn, who are always completely assured of themselves, arrogant past arrogance, did not quite know what to make of this sudden descent from the sky. They were abruptly confronted by a thick body of men forming up into solid masses, and carrying damned great long spears. They were, by Krun, highly perplexed. They could understand the wings of cavalry, and being sensible fighting men would give great care and caution to the movements of our nikvove regiment. But, as for the stolid brumbytes, no. No, they didn't know what to make of them.

One thing the aragorn did understand. If they attacked they won. Or, to be more accurate, those aragorn who had not so far lost had won. I fancied it was the turn of this little lot to experience defeat.

The notion seemed pleasing to me to see what our new archers might do.

Volodu blew Archers Forward and Log Logashtorio led his men out. The new Chodkuvax rode a zorca and gave signals with his very own Lohvian longbow. The bowmen spread out and, at the signal, drew and loosed, sweetly, as they had been taught.

The shafts glinted against the sky like shoals of barracuda. Up and over and down, they plunged, volley following volley. Chodkuvax Logashtorio's Third Phalanx Archers shot five smashing volleys, and then they were running back, haring between the intervals of the Phalanx, pelting out to their new positions on the flanks. As a sheer demonstration of textbook drill and controlled shooting, it was masterful.

But it did not stop the aragorn.

As that avalanche of cavalry smoked down the hill toward the Phalanx it was the turn of the brumbytes. The aragorn rode the usual mix of saddle animals, but they modified speeds and kept together, rank on rank, so I judged they had been fighting drilled troops at some time recently. That was not altogether a marked trait among the aragorn. They liked to raid and slave and pen their captives in barracoons. If they met drilled and disciplined opposition they would decamp and set up shop elsewhere.

I sweated, suddenly.

Had I made a ghastly mistake? The onrushing host of aragorn were almost on the Phalanx now. The Phalanx was composed of green troops. Were these aragorn different from the usual? Were they about to topple my massed brumbytes into bloody ruin? I sat my zorca and I trembled. Pride, pride, what a stupid thing to do—and I had done it. I, Dray Prescot called Jak the Drang, Emperor of Vallia—Emperor of Nothing!

But how splendid the Phalanx looked...

With fierce down-bent heads, their helmets all in line, plumes nodding, the pikes thrust forward into a glittering hedge of steel—yes, yes, the old words, the old words. But, by Zair! How they stood, clamped to the earth, like a primeval cliff face, adamant against the sea. A song rose from their packed ranks, a paean, a soaring battle hymn. The words were the old words, and they set the blood to pulsing. With the front rank pikes firmly bedded in the earth, the next thrust over the first, and the next in two-handed grips, shoulder high, twelve men deep, the Third Vallian Phalanx took the shock. As the rolling thunders of the ocean break in spume and fury against those weathered cliff faces, so the aragorn foamed against the pikes. A welter of uprearing steel, of screaming animals, of blood, of noise and bedlam and then of a receding wash of sound, as the recoiling waves break and flow and surge away, rippling, spreading, so those Opaz-forsaken aragorn, damned slavers to a man, broke and fled.

The trumpets rang out, crashing notes of silver urgency.

The Phalanx formed, became a cohesive whole, surged upright, moved, advanced—charged!

And on the flanks the Hakkodin hacked and slashed and carved a path through the fleeing cavalry.

"Time for our cavalry, Volodu," I said.

Volodu the Lungs blew Cavalry, General Chase.

The Vallian zorcas, totrixes and nikvoves leaped forward.

Spuming down in their turn like the returning tide, they roared on after the fleeing aragorn.

Everything now could be left to Nath. And here came a zorcaman, red-faced, exhilarated, racing down from the town, roaring out that the place was in our hands. I acknowledged him, shouted, "Well done!" and turned my zorca toward the mob of chained slaves crouched in long rows of misery.

As I trotted carefully across I reflected that the aragorn had not known how heavily, man for man, we outnumbered them. The close-packed blocks of the Phalanx tended to conceal the numbers. But, for all that disparity, there had been a sizable crowd of slavers, and their captives stretched in row after row, chained, naked, hairy and filthy, crooning those soul-songs of misery and inwardness that pass beyond mere despair.

The naked bodies sprawled on the dirt in postures of abandonment. Calloused elbows and knees, sores, scars, the brutal signatures of whips, the matted forests of hair in which lice roamed, miniature denizens of miniature jungles, yes, the trademark of the slaver is far-removed from the fictions written and believed by the willfully blinkered. Looking at those bare, bruised and begrimed bodies, exposed in nakedness, I was reminded of Jilian's comments outside the marquee of Fat Lango. And, also, of nakedness I recalled what a dowager, quivering in repulsion and outraged moral rectitude had said, speaking with that plummy voice of conscious refinement. "Going naked," she had said, "is disgusting. Why, if God had intended us to go naked we would have been born like it."

The contrast between these bundles of half-starved naked wretches in their filth and degradation, and the well-fed, smart and sumptuously-clothed men who had rescued them could not have been more marked. Everywhere the movement of crimson and yellow as the troops busied themselves about humanitarian tasks seemed—at least to me—to bring a glow of glory to the field. And my views on glory are well known and hardly repeatable in mixed company. Crimson is the imperial color.

The cavalry attired in scarlet and yellow formed a kind of personal body—not a bodyguard—and the brave old scarlet struck a distinctive spark as Targon took the choice band trotting out.

Karidge's Regiment streamed past heading up to the town to make sure of the place. We knew it from our maps as Yervismot, and I was damned sure Nath knew what he was doing when he'd brought the aerial squadron here.

The totrix regiments and the nikvoves were distant figures under the slanting rays of the suns, dispersing the last of the aragorn. Their uniform colors varied, for according to long tradition the cavalry wore regimental colors distinct from those of the infantry. This practice had been allowed to continue. In the glittering group of riders surrounding me were representatives from all the regiments to act as messengers, in addition to my own aides de camp. So as I rode toward the slaves, where a fresh hullabaloo started up with a deal of chain swinging, I moved in the midst of a tapestry of color in which the scarlet and yellow predominated.

A group of Gons who habitually shave their heads to leave bare and shining skulls were frantically digging out handfuls of mud and plastering it into that bone-white hair of which they are so ashamed. A person's beliefs are a private affair, and who would deride a man for removing his hat when he enters a church, or keeping his hat firmly on his head and removing his shoes?

There were so many slaves chained in their long rows that it seemed to me natural to guide my zorca toward the scene of the commotion. Here a fleeing posse of aragorn had tripped across outstretched chains. Steel against bare hands—well, there were dead bodies here, naked and bleeding; but, also, there were riderless animals and aragorn on the ground being beaten to death. The anger of slaves moves like a choked watercourse, a blocked drain, and when the obstructing filth is removed, the outburst smashes forth, unchecked.

Grimed naked bodies slashed iron chains. Heads burst and limbs broke and ribs caved in. But swords bit deeply in return and I urged my zorca on more smartly. To lose one slave after we had liberated them seemed to me to be offensive to the order of life.

The sword I drew was a Valkan-built weapon, brought by Delia from our arsenal in the stromnate. With master-smiths, and notably Naghan the Gnat, we had designed and built the brand. Owing much to the Havilfarese thraxter and to the Vallian clanxer, it also shared as much as I could contrive of the master-weapon, the Savanti Sword. Men called this new sword the drexer. I swung it forward as I rode, deeming it suitable for employment here, and jumped off the zorca to get in among a clumped group of aragorn who speared and slashed away at slaves who screeched and fell, bloodied and stumped, and could not break through to the slavers.

The men at my back broke out in yells of concern.

81

"Majister! Hold back. Wait for us." And: "Emperor! You endanger your life."

The last of the light flared deceptively as the twin suns speared their emerald and ruby fires erratically through tortured cloud castles. The aragorn were confident against the naked slaves and were busying themselves in collecting riderless animals. Those who caught a steed mounted up and galloped off, although slaves hung onto them and lapped them in chains, and brought some down. It was all a shadowy, bloody, confusing fracas, the kind of nonsense in which a fellow can get knocked on the head and never know he was dead.

Not all the slavers were apim, and I crossed swords with a Rapa, who went down as I jumped past. A bleg beyond him staggered back on his four legs, and a cham tripped him and another slashed his guts out, and I helped knock him down—for their four legs make blegs mightily resistant—and jumped on past to get at an aragorn who lifted a sword against two women, naked, screaming, hugging each other in a last paroxysm of terror.

The aragorn turned to meet me. All about us men and women shrilled in horror, and chains clashed and the spears drove in. My men were still racketing away and coming on, for my last savage lunge astride the zorca had distanced them. The aragorn fancied himself as a swordsman; but I chopped him without finesse and saw another from the corner of my eye, and ducked, and swirled back. A naked figure, with a mass of dark hair and a superb body, leaped on the slaver and hauled a chain around his neck. Entangled like a wild beast trapped in iron nets, the slaver choked back.

He went down and two more came at us, desperate now, determined to break past and get at the totrixes who stood, shivering in terror at the blood and noise. Together, the naked man and I met them. The drexer drank the life from one and the chains crushed the life from the other.

"Majister! Emperor!" The yells lifted and the men of my retinue were there, slashing aside a last frantic attempt by the aragorn. The light shifted, dying in an opaz haze. The dirt ran with blood. Naked flesh stained crimson. The slave with the dark hair and the body of a fighting man slumped, and he collapsed to his knees and I saw he was wounded, a jagged rent across his back.

Half-kneeling, he looked up.

The brilliantly attired soldiers of the new Vallia crowded about me. They were profuse in their expressions of concern. "Majisters" and "emperors" filled the evening air. And I looked at the slave, collapsed there in his blood and filth still gripping the harsh iron chains.

"Majister—the risks you take... Emperor, we are here to protect you..." Oh, yes, majister this and majister that, emperor and emperor...

The slave looked up and spoke.

"Lahal, my old dom," he said. "I might have known you'd get here—given time."

82

He coughed, then, and a spittle of blood trickled down his chin.

It was extraordinarily difficult for me to speak.

The babble of voices at my back, with their continual interlarded majisters and emperors... I straightened my shoulders. I found my voice.

"Lahal, Seg," I said.

Twelve

Jikaida over Vallia

We flew back to Vondium. The odd little thought occurred to me that had I known it was Seg Segutorio struggling all naked with his chains, I would have unlimbered the Krozair longsword and gone in raging like a maniac.

And that was a demeaning thought, to be sure; but it adequately expresses my own confessed confusion in personal relationships.

"By the Veiled Froyvil, my old dom, but that is good," said Seg as he took the goblet from his lips. His mouth shone with fine Gremivoh, and I instantly refilled the goblet for him. We sat in my study, with the books and the maps, and Seg looked more like my old friend than a sodden wrung-out chained-up slave.

The doctors had seen to him and patched him up, declaring he needed rest. His first words after that typical greeting had been: "And Thelda?" Whereat I had shaken my head. "There has been no news of her, none at all."

"I went up to Evir," said Seg, now, as we brought each other up to date with our doings since we had parted on the way to the Sacred Pool of Baptism in Aphrasöe. "I went into that damned pool with Delia and the emperor and the others, and then I was back home in Erthyrdrin." He drank again, and shook his head. "Mightily discomposing, I can tell you."

"I know."

He looked up. "Well, you would, wouldn't you?"

"So you made your way back to Vallia and went to Evir?"

"Yes. If I'd been sorcerously transported home, then Thelda would, too— or so I thought."

"You were right." I told him a little of the power of Vanti, the Guardian of the Pool, enough to allow him to understand that we had been caught up in a wizardly manifestation. He seemed satisfied with my explanation.

"She'd been there. They told me. An uncouth bunch, all right, those Evirese."

"And?"

He moved his left hand emptily.

"I went to Falinur, then. After all, I am supposed to be their damned kov. But, for me, they can keep their kovnate and their mangy ways. I was taken up by flutsmen, and escaped, and then, being a trifle down, was easy prey for the aragorn. We'd been marching for days on end. I think—I'm not sure—I escaped a couple of times. But the lot I was with when you came up were the last."

"You are home now, Seg."

He gripped that empty hand into a fist. A Bowman of Loh, Seg Segutorio, for my money the best bowman on Kregen, and a kov, the Kov of Falinur. Yet he was the truest friend a man can have, and be thankful to all the Gods of Kregen he may call a friend. Now he looked down, shrunken, fearful of the terrors the future must bring.

"Home—yes, Dray, I made Vallia my home. And, now—my wife, my children, where are they?"

"You have returned. They will, too."

"I believe that. I have to believe that. But the whole business has been a nightmare."

He had heard the news, how the emperor's life had been saved by his immersion in the Sacred Pool, of how all those who had taken him there had been sorcerously dispatched to their homes, of how the emperor had at last been slain in the final moments of the Fall of Vondium. He had listened stony-faced as the story of Kov Layco Jhansi's treachery was told, and of how Zankov, the mysterious agitator, had killed the emperor. He heard about Queen Lushfymi of Lome, and expressed no great desire to meet her, despite that she worked hard and devotedly for Vallia. I knew that Seg loved his Thelda very deeply. For all her faults she was a good comrade and I often castigated myself for my treatment of her, for the supposedly funny remarks I made about her. She tried desperately hard to be a good friend to Delia, and Delia loved her, too, in her own way.

And now she was missing and might be anywhere, not only in Vallia, either. Anywhere at all on Kregen...

Seg fetched up a sigh. "Well, Thelda always means well," he said, at which I shot him a hard look. "I just pray Erthyr the Bow has her in his keeping."

"Amen to that, Seg, and Opaz and Zair, too."

The doctors having told me that the Kov of Falinur needed a proper convalescence, which was not at all surprising, I made Seg see sense. In addition to seeking Thelda he wanted to know what had happened to his children, Dray and the twins. From my own bitter experiences of the past, and more recently in attempting to trace Dayra, I knew the wait might well be a long and agonizing one before any news was received. And, all this time, the work of preparing Vondium and the provinces loyal to us to resist the coming attack had to go on.

I said to Seg: "I am particularly pleased that the Grand Archbold of the Kroveres of Iztar is now with us."

Seg showed a flicker of interest.

"The Order has admitted a number of new brothers lately. The work goes on. It seems to me, as a mere member, seemly for the Grand Archbold to welcome the new brothers."

"Yes, my old dom," said Seg, but he spoke heavily. "You are right. I value your words in this. You made me the Grand Archbold—for my sins, I suspect, as you so often say. But I will perform my duty." He brightened. "Anyway, it seems to me a perfectly proper function of the KRVI to search out and rescue ladies in distress."

"Ah!" I said.

If I thought then that this work with the KRVI might help Seg, I feel the thought to be just and proper. If, as I suspect may have been the case, I also thought it would get him out of my hair, the thought was not only unjust and improper—it was despicable. Still, as they say, only Zair knows the cleanliness of a human heart.

Seg did say, with a flash of his old spirit, that, as for the new army, they were a fine, frilled, lavendered bunch of popinjays with their laces and decorations and brilliance of ornamentation. "I mind the days when you and I, Dray, marched out with a couple of rags to clothe us. Provided our weapons were fit for inspection by Erthanfydd the Meticulous, we didn't care what we looked like."

"Ah, but, my old dom," I said, somewhat wickedly, to be sure: "That was before you met Thelda."

Which was, to my damnation, a confounded stupid thing to say.

Seg took himself off to meet the brothers of the Order and discuss plans and, no doubt, take a stoup or two, and I went back to the paperwork. Blue was a color not in favor in Vallia save in the northeast, where it had been adopted in provincial badges and insignia as a kind of silent insult to the south, and in certain seacoast provinces where the ocean gave ample reason for its inclusion. These color-coded badges and banded sleeves and insignia of Vallia can be lumped together under the general name of schturvals, and by the schturval a man wore you could tell his allegiances. Nath Orcantor, known as Nath the Frolus, came to see me, highly indignant, determined that the fine spanking regiment of totrixmen he was raising should wear blue tunics over their armor, and red breeches.

Enevon Ob-Eye and Nath were in the room with me at the time, going over sumptuary lists, and they looked on, more than a little astonished.

"Blue?" said Nath. "In the Vallian Army?"

"And why not, Kapt Nath?" said Nath Orcantor the Frolus. "I am from Ovvend, as you very well know, and our colors were granted in the long ago by the emperor then."

"Oh," said Enevon, and he smiled. "You mean sky-blue."

"Done, Jiktar Orcantor," I said. "Your totrixmen may wear sky-blue tunics and red breeches—but let the red be more a madder, or a maroon, rather than a crimson."

Nath Orcantor the Frolus nodded, well pleased. He was not a whit put out that his regiment could not wear the imperial crimson, for that was an understood part of the hoary traditions of Vallia. The emperor said what was what, and crimson was the imperial color, and Nath the Frolus was raising a private regiment—for which, I add with great emphasis, I was most glad. We needed every man with us in this fight.

And there, in this piddling little frivolous-seeming incident, was another example of the way the imperium was eating away at my brain.

Nath Perrin the Oivon was raising a regiment of light-armed infantry who would act as skirmishers before the main line. When Jiktar Perrin wanted to clothe his regiment in green no one could see any objection. So, neither could I. After all, as I have reiterated, green is a fine color—for some people and in some areas. So Jiktar Nath the Oivon's five hundred drilled in a leaf-green tunic, with minimum armor and armed with stuxes, spears and swords only. They did not carry shields and, for a space, I was willing to allow that.

The army grew.

A regulation had to be promulgated setting the largest size of epaulettes it was permissible to wear. The normal male Vallian's outfit in civilian life is the wide-shouldered buff tunic, with breeches and tall black boots. The size of these wings gives a fine dramatic effect. But now, with the blaze of uniforms to play with, and bronze or steel wings to clamp over the shoulders, the Vallians seemed to have gone mad. I saw a Hikdar with silver epaulettes stretching out a full hand's length beyond his shoulder. A sensible size had to be established, for these enormous shoulder-boards with their fantastic decorations could seriously impede the sword arm, or the spear-wielding sweep, if unchecked. Truth to tell, the wide metallic wings of the soldiers became a kind of trademark of the Vallian army. No one wanted to be without bronze, iron or steel epaulettes, and their use was demonstrated in battle where they saved many a slashing blow from taking off an arm. They complemented the leather, bronze-studded jerkins admirably.

When the fellows of my choice band ceremoniously presented me with a golden pair, I caved in, and wore them when in a certain uniform which they suited. But how I thought of the days when, clad only in the old scarlet breech-clout, I went swinging off to the fight!

The food situation had now eased enormously. This was due in no small measure to the wise precautions we had taken to return agriculture and husbandry to their usual high state of efficiency. The pallans, that is ministers or secretaries, appointed to the various posts of government, functioned well. I had told them what was needed and they had done their best to do the job. In truth, Vallia, or that part of it still owing allegiance to Vondium, had been ruled by decree. Now, in conversations with the Lord Farris and the other pallans and responsible officials, I announced that the Presidio would be reformed.

Farris was delighted.

"That takes a load off my shoulders!"

"Mayhap, Farris. But you are still the imperial Crebent Justicar—when I am away, the responsibility is yours."

"Do you anticipate—?"

Farris could not be told of my real fears. I said, "I am fretful. Everything runs here in Vondium. We remain in the dark. Perhaps I will tour around the frontiers." And, at that, we all felt the pain. Those frontiers were tightly drawn around us now, well inside what had once been a united country. And, again, I could not tell him that some itch in me, an ache in my bones, told me that I would soon have news from Barty.

Two fresh regiments of archers had been formed and their Jiktars besought me to present the standards and to inspect their men. Sitting at my desk—that infernal desk with its never-ending avalanche of papers—I looked up most pleased when Seg came in, smiling.

"You look—look better, Seg."

"Aye. I have been working. I know Thelda will be found."

"Good." I nodded vigorously. "These bowmen this morning, Seg. I have to inspect them. Will you...?"

"Delighted. I shall, of course, say nothing."

"You may say nothing to them or their Jiktars. But to me, you will speak and I shall take heed of your words."

"Well, then, let me go to Loh and recruit Bowmen of Loh."

"No!"

He was surprised at my tone.

"But, Dray—why not? Always Vallia has paid gold for mercenaries. And the Bowmen of Loh are the best archers in the world. Why not?"

"Vallia must free herself by her own efforts."

"If there is not gold enough in the treasury, why—"

"Aye!" I said, and my bitterness shocked Seg. "Aye! If the mercenaries cannot be paid honestly, they may take their pay in loot."

"From your enemies. That has always been the way of it."

"You saw the Phalanx when we met again? Each brumbyte, each Hak-kodin, is a free man of Vallia. They take their silver stivers in pay, and they know if they loot Vallian property they will dance on air for it."

He shook his head. "But it is enemy—"

"Look, Seg. All Vallia is like a gigantic Jikaida board. The drins are set out, the squares colored, the men in action. We fight and struggle for possession of drins and advantageous positions. Men die in the real world, instead of being swept up and replaced in the Jikaida box. This is not a game. And, remember, this enormous Jikaida board is Vallia, all of it, all Vallian. When you destroy a town full of foemen you destroy a Vallian town."

We had played Jikaida the evening before and Seg had lost disastrously. This game, which is just about the most popular board game among most Kregans, can become a disease, taking up all a fellow's time and thoughts, move and counter-move obsessing his every waking moment. It is, in most people's estimation, far superior to Jikalla. And the image it brought to mind, of men marching and counter-marching from square to square, of the player concentrating on every move and trying to outguess his opponent, was an image of our present position in Vallia. We played a real life flesh and blood Jikaida on the giant board of Vallia, and our opponents would have no mercy if we played a false move. And, as you shall hear, I was to play another and altogether more personal game of flesh and blood Jikaida. But, then, that lay in my troubled future.

Seg started to say in his forthright way, "Well, all right, my old dom, I can see that plain enough—" when the door burst open and Jilian ran in, laughing, excited, her pale face flushed with happiness.

"Jak, Jak—the Lady Franci's rark has had puppies and here is—oh!"

She saw Seg, big, handsome, yelling at me, worked up at my stupidity in not hiring a strong force of the finest bowmen in the world, and Jilian halted and the rark puppy wriggled and squirmed against her breast.

Very mildly, I said: "Jilian, you should meet Seg Segutorio, the Kov of Falinur, who is a blade comrade and the truest of friends. Seg, this is Jilian, who is just Jilian and who I am sure would love to shoot a round with you."

Seg stared at her. "A bowgirl?"

"Among other accomplishments."

I had not told Seg about Ros the Claw. His daughter Silda had been mixed up with the wild gang with whom Dayra ran, and I was not sure quite what his reactions would be. He had hauled his daughter out of it; I had not.

They made pappattu and exchanged Llahals and then Lahals.

Seg eyed me.

"So, and pardon me, Jilian, for finishing this subject, you will not, Dray, hire Bowmen of Loh?"

"No."

"And if they are brought against us by our enemies?"

"Then the Archers of Vallia must outshoot them."

"Impossible."

"I know. But it will be done."

88

Jilian watched us, stroking the puppy. She wore a laypom-colored tunic with silver edging, one of Delia's, and the four pin holes made a square punctuation, empty of the brooches usually pinned there.

The moment was broken as the puppy at last broke free and, a lightning-fast ball of ginger fur, led us a dance around the room before we caught him. Jilian gathered him up, crooning to him, stroking his fur. I smiled.

Seg saw the smile.

"These two regiments of these marvelous archers of yours?"

I glanced at the clepsydra.

"Yes. Time to go. You will excuse us, Jilian?"

She put her head on one side, her hair dark and low over that broad white forehead, and all her intent look returned.

"I think, Jak, that I shall raise a regiment of Jikai Vuvushis. We can fight for Vallia."

Seg looked at her, and then at me, and I said: "That would be interesting, anyway. They have Battle Maidens up in the northeast who have declared for our foemen. It would be—both amusing and horrible—to see Jikai Vuvushis in line against one another."

Jilian tossed her head. She laughed. "That will be no new thing."

"Kregen," I said, but to myself. "Kregen..."

As we went out I noticed Jilian's sandals. Light and airy, they were thonged with golden straps to the knee. Those sandals were never Delia's.

Jiktars Stormwill and Brentarch met us on the parade ground and the inspection went off faultlessly. Everyone knew the Kov of Falinur was a Bowman of Loh, and the ranks stiffened up wonderfully. Their shooting was good. It was not excellent, just good, and I knew Seg would be highly dissatisfied. But these were green regiments, and must learn. Their Jiktars would keep them at training, making sure the Hikdars ran their pastangs firmly and fairly, and the Deldars would run along the ranks bellowing and shouting as all Deldars bellow and shout.

The standards were presented, the trumpets blew, and a band from the Second Archers, a seasoned outfit, played stirring marches. By my express wish they played "The Bowmen of Loh." Seg looked at me. Then he looked away. Well, in this life we all have to learn, and it is always the hard way, and painful.

The parade marched off to the strains of "Old Drak Himself," which was by way of being a growing habit, and would soon be a tradition, when a flier circled across the rooftops, obviously searching. Seg had been given a Lohvian longbow by Log and his other comrades, for he felt naked without, and the great bow was out of its scabbard, strung, and an arrow nocked at a speed which would have dizzied the green archers marching off the parade ground.

I saw the schturval painted up on the side of the flier. Gray, red and green, with a black bar.

"Lower your bow, Seg. Those are the colors of Calimbrev. The flier is from Barty Vessler."

Seg lowered the bow; but he only half unbent it and he kept the shaft ready in that casual, superbly competent way of a true Bowman of Loh, the master archers of Kregen.

The men in the voller spotted us. What with Cleitar holding my own flag aloft, and with Ortyg the Tresh lifting the new flag of Vallia, and the blaze of scarlet and gold about, it was pretty clear where stood the Emperor of Vallia.

Targon the Tapster and Naghan ti Lodkwara, who had rejoined after his wound had half-healed, exchanged remarks. The others of my choice band, also, expressed opinions. I sat, looking forward and up, stony-faced. These staunch companions of the choice band and Seg had lived and worked with me in different times, and, it seemed, times centuries apart. Seg was not himself. If anyone questioned me, and no one did, I was prepared to be reasonable on the point. But Seg Segutorio meant a great deal, a very great deal, as you will know. As, to be sure, did every single one of the choice band.

The flier landed and Hikdar Douron jumped down and ran across, saluting as he hauled up before me.

"Majister!"

"Spit it out, Hikdar Douron."

"The strom begs to report," he started off. I killed my smile. That, for a certainty, was not the way Barty had given his message.

"Yes?"

"The—person—he sought has left certain signs so that the Strom is confident he knows where she is. But the strom has been wounded and is mewed up in the fortress of the Stony Korf. He cannot leave our wounded."

I said: "Why did you not all leave in the flier?"

"We have been joined by freedom fighters—we could not bring them all and the strom would not abandon them. Honor—"

Barty's honor! Well, the lad was in the right of it.

I turned to speak and Seg said: "Stony Korf! I know that devil's eyrie. It is in Falinur, that is supposed to be my kovnate, may it rot in the Ice Floes of Sicce."

The decision was made without thinking about it.

Farris was told he was to take over. No attack was imminent, everyone was sure. I would take a pruned down group of the most ferocious desperadoes of my band. Seg would come. We were at last going to find my daughter Dayra. We were going to talk to Ros the Claw.

And about time, too.

Thirteen

A Bowman Topples a Blazing Brand

To be free of the cares of empire! Once more to ride the winds and with a cutthroat band of loyal companions to hurtle across the face of Kregen, speeding beneath the Moons, and sword in hand once more to plunge into headlong adventure. Ah! This was the old Dray Prescot, a fellow with whom I had barely been on nodding acquaintance lately.

We had packed Barty's flier with men and supplies and, Hikdar Douron having assured us we were adequate for the job ahead, I had not pressed Farris to release any more vollers from his small and hard-pressed fleet. Our sailing skyships would be, by days, too slow.

Now in fading light, Douron pointed ahead, where a jagged line of peaks rose against the star-glitter. This was an uncomfortable little corner of Seg's kovnate, a sour, dull place inhabited by sour, dull people. They insisted on keeping slaves and all Seg's attempts had failed to convince them otherwise. I knew that toward the end, before the Time of Troubles, he had been at his wits' end, unwilling to use the force at his disposal against the people of his new kovnate, and yet, sharing my views, desperate to end the blasphemy against human nature that slavery was, in very truth, in our eyes.

"I remember this fortress," said Seg. He wiped his lips and peered ahead. "When I asked its chief, a bent-nosed rascal called Andir the Ornc, to manumit his slaves, he threw my messenger out, a fine young fellow, Naghan Larjester, and sent him back to me with a nose as bent as his own. It was a jest. I was screwing up my mind to march on him with my people and make an example of him, when the emperor was poisoned."

"I think, Seg," I said with some gravity as we flew down, "I really do think you are well out of Falinur. It is a kovnate of which much may be made. But slavery has to be ended. And there has been far too much water under the bridge."

"If you mean, Dray," said the Kov of Falinur, "that you wish to strip my kovnate from me, why, then, I will be the first to throw my hat in the air."

"I will do what you wish. You are still a kov, that is something useful to be in this world, as you know. And a kov must have estates. There is a province ready for you, once—"

"Aye, dom!" he said, his wild blue eyes bright in that mingled light. "I know! Once we have cleared out whatever bunch of rasts is sucking it dry now."

"Aye. And there will be a lot of that, by Krun."

He did not ask where away this new kovnate of his might be and, truth to tell, I was in nowise sure myself. But, I was firmly convinced, unalterably convinced; Seg Segutorio was a kov and would have a kovnate.

He told me something of conditions he had found north of the Mountains of the North when he had gone seeking Thelda in Evir, the northernmost province. A fellow had taken over up there and was calling himself the King of Urn Vallia. He controlled Durheim and Huvadu although running into some trouble from the High Kov of Erstveheim. Venga, of which the hapless Ashti Melekhi had been the vadnicha, had been invaded and her twin brother, the vad, was on the run. It was all a mess up there, and, that was true of the southwest and the southeast and the mountains, also. There was no profit in worrying over those broader problems now when the stone fortress below rushed up toward us as the flier dropped, and we saw the men waving below, waiting for us.

We were in enemy territory here. That was a foul note, to be sure. Enemy territory, in Falinur, one of the heartlands of Vallia!

Almost, we got through unobserved. Almost...

As we skimmed for the stone ramparts a volley of arrows whisked up toward us. Campfires burned in a circle about the fortress of the Stony Korf. A few shafts punched into the flier; but no one was hit. Varter bolts lanced the dusky air. We even saw two catapult stones come arching up, like balls tossed high in sport, and curve over and so fall away. But the arrows persisted. Seg perked up, taking a professional interest.

"Undurkers," said Seg. The fascinating information in his comment was the comparative lack of contempt. I wondered what scrapes he'd pulled out of since we'd parted that might have given him this new outlook. Certainly, he was scathing enough about the short bow, as was I. "Undurkers. Well, my old dom, we've seen them off before."

"And will again, despite that we have no Bowmen of Loh with us, save yourself."

He did not laugh. The voller whooshed air over the crumbled stone battlements and circled once, losing speed, before dropping to a mossy patch of stone at the center of the tower. That was just about all this place was, a tower. Seg said, quietly, as the besieged folk came up: "You may not be a Bowman of Loh; but you'd give most of them a run for their money."

Well, of course, from Seg Segutorio, that was high praise.

Then we were exchanging Lahals and jumping from the flier and I was being led off to where Barty sat under a canvas awning, looking most disgruntled, with an arrow-wound in his shoulder.

The people clustered around, their bearded grimy faces reflecting villainously in the torchlights. They were smiling a little, now, thinking rescue had reached them. The scene was like a witch's coven. Barty waved a hand.

"The emperor and I would speak in private." He had not risen to greet me—and the reason for that was plain enough. His people backed off. My own desperadoes were busily engaged in estimating the defenses and getting an idea of the enemy out there in the darkness that shut down with the last of the suns. It was not a night of Notor Zan; but for a space the star glitter and two of Kregen's smaller moons gave the impression of a night darker than it really was. Seg stood at my shoulder. Barty looked up. His face looked odd; his usual high color had fled, but his pallor was made more leaden by the red stains under the skin, high on each cheekbone. He looked at Seg.

"I said the emperor and I would be alone."

Seg did not move.

I said, "Seg, this handsome young man who has fallen so low is Barty Vessler, the Strom of Calimbrev. And, Barty, you have the honor and pleasure of meeting Seg Segutorio, the Kov of Falinur."

Barty opened his mouth, shut his mouth, extended his hand as the pappattu was made. My new friends had said harsh words about Falinur and its kov. But, as always, I could not be harsh on Barty. So I added, casually, "Seg is with us in this." Here I had to trip daintily around certain subjects. "He is aware of the problem and—"

"Oh, them," said Seg. "My girl Silda wanted to go off and be some kind of Jikai Vuvushi. But Thelda didn't like the idea and I had to bring Silda home." He glanced at me, and, amazingly, laughed. "She is not at all pleased that Drak has gone off adventuring in Faol."

So ho, I said to myself, so the weathervane spins that way, does it...?

Barty's news was both stimulating and depressing. Dayra had most certainly been seen and then the local gang of mercenaries who held the district for Layco Jhansi had mewed him and his men up here, together with the local Freedom Fighters. And, one of these, the guerilla chief, was in a right state over his wife. I said: "Dayra first. Then the others, all of them, as many as we can contrive."

"I agree. But Dayra isn't with this bunch of cramphs trying to burn us out." His words were not idle. Every now and then a varter bolt tied with burning flax would arch up and over and fall into the tower. Sand was flung in strewed winnowed falls to quench the flames.

"Well, young Barty! Where the hell is she, then?"

At this he spread his hands helplessly, and winced, and looked more gray and drawn than I liked.

"My spies got wind of what she came for. That kleesh Zankov has been thoroughly rejected by the Northeast Parties, and so he is seeking an alliance with Jhansi."

Seg ran a hand along his longbow. "It will be interesting to meet this Zankov."

"But now," I said. "Right now!"

"Majister," said Barty, and his voice shook. "I do not know."

"These cramphs are getting troublesome," said Seg, brushing sparks away as a blazing bolt hit and bounced near us.

"Where was she last seen, Barty?"

"Trakon's Pillars. Jhansi was supposed to be meeting her at a summer villa the old kov had there."

"Him," said Seg, and sniffed. "I'd as lief Naghan Furtway had his Opaz-forsaken kovnate back again."

"You know the place, Seg?"

"Yes. Damned degenerate pest hole. Furtway was a great Jikaida player—you know that, Dray—and the whole place was built like a Jikaida board. Most odd. And devilish, too. I can take you there. But our friends outside grow impatient."

A few words soon showed that the mercenaries outside the tower had been reinforced after Hikdar Douron had left for Vondium. We had brought men, yes; but had we brought enough to break through the ring? Barty was all for getting up and bashing on. There were saddle animals stabled in the lower floors. But the Jiktar who ran his guards, a man who could have sat for a por-trait to represent the professional, life-time fighting man, shook his head.

"In my view we are still too few," said Jiktar Noronfer.

"Um," said Seg.

"We must break out!"

Barty sank back on the blankets. He looked in bad case.

Then Jiktar Noronfer, with the infuriating ability of the professional to state a situation as though it was not a matter of life and death affecting him no less than anyone else, said: "They will break in before the flier can return to Vondium for help."

Another iron-headed bolt arched over the ancient stone battlements and hit, bouncing. The flames from the tar and bitumen-soaked flax blazed up. The brand skated across the stones straight for us like a comet on a colli-sion course.

Barty let out a feeble yell. Jiktar Noronfer dived out of the way. The caroming bolt leaped, like a fractious zorca, spat sparks, sizzling with a noise like a cage full of serpents. It roared directly at us.

I leaped for Barty. Seg—the infernal idiot!—seized up Noronfer's dropped spear and swung toward the blazing brand. Even as I got Barty up and scrambled him out of the way so Seg with a beautifully lithe skip and jump got the spear point under the iron head of the bolt and heaved. Then he, too, jumped for safety. His cloak was alight. He landed and rolled and I put Barty down as gently as I could contrive and as the flaming bolt reared up and spilled over the stones at our back I leaped on Seg. With my bare hands I batted at the flames and got his cloak ripped off and tossed aside. I was not burned, thank Zair—well, not much, not enough to notice.

Seg sat up.

"Thanks, my old dom. We've enough light as it is without using me as a living torch."

"You maniacal Erthyr nitwit! Why didn't you jump out of the way?"

"Never thought you'd get the youngster out of it in time. You were damned quick."

"Not as quick as you, you—"

Seg's face drew in with pain. His eyes misted. Torchlight hung shadows along his jaw and his cheeks hollowed.

"Get that tunic off! And the kax! Your wound, when you were slave—"

"Aye, Dray, aye. It's plaguing me, devil take it."

Seg's wound had opened and the bloody mess made me go cold. Barty's needleman was summoned and we kept everyone else away and I made up my mind.

I made up my mind not as the Emperor of Vallia, not as Dayra's father, not as a friend to young Barty. I made up my mind because Seg needed immediate and expert attention which the needleman here was not equipped to give. He could insert his acupuncture needles and dull Seg's pain. But that was not enough. This was just another obstacle and, like all obstacles, must be evaluated and the best course chosen.

Seg protested vehemently. But I would not be swayed.

"And Jiktar Noronfer," I said with emphasis, my face I am sure as hard and merciless as it had ever been. "I see you are a shebov-Jiktar. If you wish to gain the remaining three steps in the Jiktar grade to make zan-Jiktar and, if you are lucky and live, ob-Chuktar, you had best pick up the spear you dropped and fight with us."

"I will fight, majister. I do not seek to excuse my conduct."

"Make it so."

I thought he would come through and fight well, better than well, after the spectacle he had made. But I would keep my eye on him.

Barty and Seg, of course, both of them, kicked up a frightful indignant racket. But I was prepared in this to be high-handed, very high-handed, even going to the ridiculous length of reminding them that I was, for Vox's sake, the Emperor of Vallia. Thankfully, it did not come to that sorry pass and they agreed. I turned on Jiktar Noronfer.

"Wheel me up the leader of the local Freedom Fighters, Jiktar. He ought to know his way around."

"Quidang, majister!" barked Noronfer, very businesslike, and clattered off down the stairs to the lower stories.

Seg looked mighty sullen. Because he, like me, had dipped in the Sacred Pool of Baptism he would live a thousand years and his wounds would heal swiftly and cleanly, leaving no scars. But nature will not always be baulked and his wound had been far more serious than I evidently had realized. He would heal. But that last foolhardy, heroic act had burst the fragile adhesions of the wound's surfaces. He needed proper rest and attention and that, by Krun, was that. As Kregans say, the situation was Queyd-arn-tung! No more need be said on the subject.

Barty, too, as I say, had to have his lines read to him. The two wounded men lay side by side, Seg on his side, and glowered at me. At last Seg said, "That flint-fodder outside. You have a good longbow? Mine—"

"Rest easy and stop chaffering like a loloo over chicks!"

"Thelda—"

"I know. In this short time we've been away there could be news in Vondium. The whole world can change in an instant." By Zair! But wasn't that right! I knew, perhaps none better, how in a twinkling life can make a one-hundred-eighty-degree turn, and stand you on your head, gasping, with nothing ever the same again. "And you can go see if Delia is back, too."

"I will. And getting out of here?"

"The plan calls for us to rush 'em and knife through. It will knock over a dermiflon." Which is a cast-iron guarantee of success. "Now shut your great fanged wine-spout and let yourself be loaded aboard the voller. And, Seg—"

"Yes, my old dom?"

"Take care of yourself. You hear?"

His smile might be a wan ghost of his old reckless fey laugh; but he mustered up a smile for me. "I hear." And then, being Seg Segutorio and the best comrade a man could have on two worlds, he barbed in a cutting: "Majister!"

I winced, and then they came and took Seg and Barty and the other wounded and loaded them into the voller.

As the flier rose into the air I saw a dark hunched shape lift in an embrasure and the thin pencil mark of a great Lohvian longbow being fully drawn. That was Seg Segutorio for you. Despite his lacerated and bleeding back he was up there and ready to cast down a few deadly shafts to help us. The cramphs out there were flint-fodder, no doubt of it, and I crossed to the battlements and looked down. Three dark figures spun away, arms wide, screeching soundlessly as She of the Veils rose through wreathing mists and shed her fuzzy pink and golden light. Now we would have light enough to see by, light enough to kill by—if we were unlucky or unskilled, light enough to die by.

The voller vanished into the night and another besieger toppled with a long Lohvian arrow through him. Four times, Seg had shot. I do not think there was another archer in the whole world who could have loosed three—and hit with every shot.

Losing Seg like this naturally made me think of Inch and Turko and Balass and Oby and the rest. By Krun! Devil take these troubles consuming Vallia. I ought to be out scouring Kregen for my friends.

Going down to the lower stories I found them choked with saddle animals and calsanys. Jiktar Noronfer was just about to climb back up. He looked annoyed.

"Beg to report, majister! The local chief—Lol Polisto ti Sygurd—has just got back." He paused, waiting. I did not amuse him by bursting out with a hot-headed: "Back from where, by Vox!" I looked at him. Noronfer wet his lips, suddenly, and finished in a rush: "His wife has been taken by these rasts and they sent a message. He tried to fight through; but was beaten back."

I said: "Was he wounded?"

"No, majister."

I looked again at Noronfer, and, again, he wet his lips.

I wondered what Barty was coming to. Noronfer was a mercenary, although not yet a paktun despite his rank of Jiktar, and he must have seen the way we were ceasing to employ mercenaries in Vallia. Yes, more than an eye would have to be kept on this one...

Lol Polisto ti Sygurd lay exhausted on a straw pallet, smothered in blood, not his own, and looked savage and wan and distraught and, also, a useful-appearing fighting man. As the leader of the local resistance fighters warring in guerilla fashion against the minions of Layco Jhansi he must have a fair amount of the yrium, the power to move men to actions of which they deem themselves incapable. I did not smile; but I bent down to shake hands, saying: "Lahal, Tyr Lol Polisto. Tell me; their numbers, their strengths—their weaknesses?"

"Cramphs, the lot of them!" He struggled to stand up; but I pushed him down, gently. He whooped in a breath. He was a fit, limber man, with dark hair and he reminded me, with Seg in my mind, very much of that master bowman. Now he got out: "At least two hundred of them, swordsmen and Undurkers. Layco Jhansi is determined to have my head and uses the Lady Thelda as bait. By Opaz the Deliverer! I pray she is still safe, she and the child they took with them, the Opaz-forsaken kleeshes."

My response was instant, particularly as thinking of Seg's Thelda brought the plight of this man more sharply into focus. He was clearly suffering anguish. If Jhansi had taken Lol Polisto's wife Thelda as a hostage, I, for one, had no sanguine hopes for her survival, hers or the child's.

I told Lol Polisto the plan and he expressed the opinion that as a plan it would sieve greens very well, which warmed me to him; but that if we swung our swords right merrily enough we should break through with the warriors I had brought. We had, as yet, no wounded to worry our heads over. The saddle animals were made ready, a mixed bunch, and I was found a zorca who, although his single spiral horn was broken, appeared a spirited-enough beast and anxious to get out of the dark and fetid hole in which he found himself penned. We mounted up and the rest grasped the stirrup leathers. Talk about the 92nd charging on the stirrups of the Scots Greys at Waterloo! The big lenken double doors were thrown open with a smash and golden moonlight splashed in. Then we were out, a dark mass of men and animals, roaring out and slap bang into the surprised mercenaries opposite us. It was all a sheerly onward-surging mass tumbling the foe left and right.

We racketed on, leaping shadows, swarming on, sweeping away in an instant a line of Undurkers who were thrown down and shattered, sent reeling, before they could pull string to chin. We hit the mercenaries and pulped them and then went on, striking fiercely left and right, leaving a trail of bloody corpses bleeding on the churned up dirt.

The drexer proved admirable for this foul work; and, to be sure, I did my share. But I kept both Lol Polisto and Jiktar Noronfer in my sights as we galloped fiercely on.

A quick bellow to Polisto directed him to lead on. I hauled my maddened beast up, his polished hooves striking the air, swung him about. The tail of our company pressed swiftly on and now the mercenary cavalry was reacting. Totrixmen appeared like lumbering phantasms from the golden-fretted shadows.

"Jhansi! Jhansi!" They screeched as they came on. The golden glitter of moonlight ran down their blades.

"You make a man twist to follow you!" exclaimed Korero, hauling his twin shields up. Only a few arrows sported down. Dorgo the Clis reined up beside me, and Naghan and Targon the other side. Others of the choice band clumped. We formed a small but very knobbly afterguard, a nut these cramphs of mercenary totrixmen would find extraordinarily hard to crack.

Dorgo had reported on the blasphemies he had witnessed in Dogansmot. These men we faced tonight were very different from that fatuous army of Fat Lango's, which had sat down and vegetated after the death of its leader; but they shared the same avariciousness for rapine and pillage. We were sharp set for them. On they came, heads bent, weapons glittering, and we faced them, and if I say we were the more vicious and savage and barbaric, well, I think that to be true if understandable, Zair forgive us.

The two lines clashed and there was a moment of tinker-work before we belted them, belted them in true style, hip and thigh. The totrixmen turned and fled. Someone set up a cheer, but I bellowed out intemperately: "Stow your gab! There will be more of 'em. Now, ride. Ride!"

We swung our mounts' heads and gladly galloped off into the golden-tinged darkness.

Fourteen

Lol Polisto ti Sygurd

Having outdistanced the pursuit we eased our mounts. We intended to be long away from this neighborhood by dawn. We had suffered six casualties, and carried with us ten or so who bore wounds, light or serious. Not one, thank Zair, of my choice band had taken so much as a scratch. They were by way of becoming your well-accomplished band of desperadoes, to be sure.

Lol Polisto said with a matter-of-fact simplicity that carried more chill conviction than any amount of loud-mouthed bragging: "The cramphs have my wife Thelda and our child and I am going to get them out."

"Where?" I said to him, just as quietly.

"In a camp they've set up at Trakon's Pillars."

"Ah!"

"You know of the accursed place? Surrounded by bogs, deep and dark and treacherous. And decadent too, once you get there. They were proud and gleeful in their triumph." He held out a bracelet, a heavy silver thing engraved with strigicaws and graints. "This is a trinket I gave to Thelda, in remembrance of our adventures and our love. They flung it into the fortress of the Stony Korf, with a note tied to it. See." The note was obscene. It mentioned Trakon's Pillars. I understood the feelings torturing Lol Polisto.

"We will ride there, Lol. I think we can perhaps pay a call they do not expect."

"Majister!"

"Aye," I said. "Aye. Of all Vallia. A thing I do not easily forget."

We rode hard all the rest of that night and rested up a couple of burs before dawn. The wounded with a strong escort went off to one of the hide-outs the freedom fighters had set up. Among them was a lop-eared rascal with a lewd grin exposing snaggle-teeth, by name Inky the Chops, who, having been born hereabouts laid claim to a working knowledge of the treacherous pathways through the quagmire of Trakon's niksuth, the bog area surrounding Trakon's Pillars. There was no holding Lol, who appealed to me as a fighting man battling for his homeland and his people, and a family man tortured by fears for his wife and child. It was clear that he loved them both deeply, and, I could see, the love was returned. So, in daylight, we pressed on into the bog.

Mists wreathed the pewter-placid waters and green scum floated and laid carpets for our feet that would have pitched us into the stinking depths had we been foolish enough to trust them. Bladderworts burst, it seemed, just as we passed them, in succession like a royal salute on Earth, and the smells clashed and stank. We wrapped scarves around our noses and pressed on along the spongy ways, with lop-eared Inky the Chops loping ahead. He prodded with a long tufa-tree stick he had slashed off, and every now and again he stopped, and sniffed, and picked his nose, and heaved up a gob, and spat, and then started off along a fresh trail. I put my trust in Zair and followed on, letting the zorca sink his feet where he would, knowing he had sense enough in this.

Ashy-trees hovered over the ways, their spectral branches splotched, dripping with green and orange slime, like Spanish moss. Clumps of scraggy rusty-black birds rose, squawking in indignation at our trespass. These last I eyed with exasperation and concern. A watchful sentry could mark our progress by those betrayers. They were, in very truth, not unlike the magbirds of Magdag, inhabitants of the land of betrayal and treachery, as I considered them.

Presently Inky the Chops halted. The way, such as it was, stretched ahead between water-grasses and bulrushes and clumps of floating weeds. The stink offended man and beast alike. Mist wreathed and there was nothing silvery in that oily, greenish-black effluvium.

"Well, Inky?"

"It gets a bit tricky hereabouts," said Inky, flashing his snaggle teeth. "There's risslaca in some of these stretches of open water. Real nasty 'uns."

The risslacas come in a fantastic variety of sizes and shapes, and only some are akin to Earthly dinosaurs. I could see the wriggle of a leepitix as it chased a fish in a pool to our left. Oily mist swirled down on the other side, and a vast and creaking giant of an un-named tree hung over the squelchy trail. I cocked an eye at Inky.

"Do you wish me to lead?"

He had no time to answer before Korero—and Targon and Naghan and Dorgo and Magin—were up and pushing to get to the point position. I let the corner of my mouth twitch.

"Go on, Inky. You will have spears to protect you."

"Spears!" He spat—most accurately, overwhelming a dragonfly. "If'n you get a real big 'un—don't git in my way when I runs!"

"I won't," I promised him. An engaging rascal, Inky the Chops, in the style of Kregen rascals I have known.

We pushed on for a space in this fashion, my men taking it in turns for the dubious honor of leading out. I made good and sure I was up near the head of the column. The beasts did not like it at all, and were growing increasingly restive. What happened, when it did, at last, happen, reflected scant credit on any of us. The labyrinth of boggy pathways and precarious footholds along the compacted dirt gathered between tree roots, mazed in its complexity. Inky seemed to know where he was going. We reached an open space that bore the marks of solid land. Trees bowered it in that green and orange dangling slime, and mist coiled, and no birds sang.

But the risslacas were waiting.

Equally at home on land or in water, they charged us with clawed and webbed feet expanded to give them perfect support on the treacherous boggy surface. Squamous hides gleamed in orange and green, camouflage colors, and bright and glittering eyes measured us for size. Talons raked. In an instant we were battling desperately with spear and sword against talon and fang.

The noise spurted. Ichor smoked as sword strokes opened up reptilian innards. We were fortunate in only one thing; they had attacked head on instead of lying in wait.

With the drexer slicing away and the zorca a live coal between my knees I was forced to pirouette away, and felt the beast sliding dangerously, hock-deep, into slime. With a convulsive heave he was up and out of the muck. On a semblance of dry ground he gathered himself. Lol Polisto had stayed near me throughout this nightmare journey. His zorca collided with mine. Both animals squealed their fears.

As though impelled by the same evil spirit they took to their heels. Heads down, spiral horns thrusting, they bolted.

No effort of sawing on the reins would halt my zorca. He went bald-headed up the trail, brushing past Inky, and I got in a good thwack at a reptilian head, all scales and eyes and fangs, as we racketed past. Lol led. We were both carried on and away and into the shrouding mists and we left the sounds of that desperate combat far in our rear.

As I say, little credit to any of us—and least of all to me.

By the time we had the zorcas under control once more we were well and truly lost.

"Well," said Lol. "I am not giving up."

"Nor me. There is a—girl—who was at Trakon's Pillars. She may have left there by now; but I hope to find someone who saw her, who perhaps knows where she has gone."

"And I will fetch my Thelda and the child out of that filthy den."

"Then let us go forward. This lead looks promising."

We led our mounts for a space, quieting them down, and walked with careful feet along the shuddery trail between quagmires. We walked with naked steel in our fists, and, because I was now afoot, considered it more fitting to unlimber the Krozair longsword. Lol stared.

"I know I am in the best of company with Jak the Drang," he said. His own clanxer glimmered. "Men have heard of the deeds of Jak the Drang."

"And you?"

"I was tending my estate of Sygurd when the Troubles began. I had no truck with politics. But in evil times a man must turn his hand when he can. And then I was able to help my Thelda, and we married and we carried on the fight as guerillas. At times, I think, you could almost call us drikingers."

"I have used bandits, Lol. Properly motivated they are just people—it is those who seek only self-gratification who pose the problems."

"Aye. We have been fighting Layco Jhansi's men for a long time now, and never seem to gain an advantage."

"And the Kov of Falinur? How stands your allegiance?"

"He is dead—" Lol started to say and then he swung about sharply and the clanxer flashed and a tendrilous mass of fleshy pseudopods writhed onto the trail. In the next instant we were fighting together, shoulder to shoulder, almost, to clear the path as bulbous growths, half-flesh, half-plant, descended on us from the dank recesses of the overhanging trees. I say almost shoulder to shoulder. I like to stand with a free space so as to get a good swing with the longsword. So, together, as comrades in arms, we fought, and cleared a passage through for ourselves and our zorcas.

When at last we burst free, Lol drew the back of his hand across his brow, and ichor dripped from the blade of the sword.

"That weapon, Jak the Drang, is incredible."

"It has been called an old bar of iron."

"Would we had a thousand such to face Jhansi and his lurfings."

"We shall deal with Jhansi, if the Racters have not done so first, in due time. What d'you know of this fellow Zankov?"

"Only that he is a devil. He seeks an alliance with Jhansi. There is some foeman they both fear—apart, that is, majister, from you."

"Aye, me. They mock me, I know." I told him about Yantong and his crazy schemes. "If Zankov has fallen out with his Hyr Notor, he is in parlous case and must seek fresh allies."

"They could form a powerful combine across the center of Vallia. If—"

"You said, Lol, you were not a political."

"I said, if you will pardon me, majister, that a man must turn his hand to the business of the moment in evil days."

"And so you did, Lol, so you did. And what is that, striking a hard corner through the mist?"

On the instant we halted and remained perfectly still and silent.

Strands of spiderweb drifted from tree to tree, intertwined bundles of gold-glinting threads like gilded thistledown floating on the breath of the breeze, and at the center of each small aerial maze the darkly red body of the spider, crouched and ready, feeling the currents of the air upon his senses and the trapped thrashings of insects on his hairs. Beyond the drifting spider-silk puffballs and the down-drooped trees, beyond the last curl of orange and green mist, the hard outline of a blockhouse thrust a man-made objection into the running deliquescence of the marsh.

"The first outpost," breathed Lol. I barely heard him. "Now may Opaz be praised."

"Amen to that. D'you know the best place to hit 'em?"

"No. But I guess we should circle around—"

"They'll be wary of that trick, I'd guess. Mantraps, stavrers, spikes. Let's just stroll up to the front door and knock. What say you, Lol?"

His features brightened and took on a fierce look of joy. He moved his sword, freely, liberated from worry over trivialities. "By Vox, majister! I am with you!"

So, as calm as you please, we strolled up to the front door of the block-house, leading our zorcas. Yes, we were an impudent pair, or a foolhardy pair; but we did it.

A Rapa stepped out, a dwa-Deldar, big and vulture-like in his leather and bronze harness. His sword pointed at us.

"Llanitch!" he shouted when we were within a dozen paces. "Llanitch!" Which is by way of being an intemperate order to halt.

We moved on a full four paces before we hauled up and I said: "Llahal, dom. This bog! It is enough to give the Reiver of Souls a touch of the black dog. Layco Jhansi is expecting us." Then, as though that little halt had fully obeyed his order and as though it was the most natural thing in the world, still speaking, I started to move on. "This bog—it tires the sword arm and that is the truth, by Krun!"

The Havilfarese oath must have gone a little way to reassure him, per-haps, even to soothe him, for he lowered his sword and half turned to call back into the blockhouse.

I sprang. I was on him like a leem. He went down, unconscious, gathered under the black cloak of Notor Zan, and Lol and I were into the ominously gaping doorway.

There were four others inside, lolling on bunks, and another two who contested fiercely over Jikalla. We dispatched them all after a short and not very bloody struggle. We did not slay them all. I was pleased at the way Lol worked. Short, efficient strokes, a minimum of fuss, and a neatness about his fighting told me he might have been a peaceful farmer before the Time of Troubles but, like so many Vallians, he had been forced to take up the sword instead of the ploughshare and found in the new occupation an apti-tude that, while it must please him, left him also with that dark and hollow feeling of self-disgust and despair.

We surveyed the interior of the blockhouse, then Lol went out and dragged the Rapa in. The Rapa's big cruel beak of a nose was dented in where he had hit the dirt face-down. It had been his misfortune to find a solid chunk of earth instead of the ubiquitous mud.

"This one is half-conscious," I said, and hauled the fellow up. He was an apim, like us, and wore a fine fancy uniform of leather and bronze with a short and ridiculous cloak of ochre and umbre in checkerboard style.

"Wha—?" he said in immemorial stupid question.

"We did," I said, cheerfully.

"Uh?"

"I assume you were asking who or what hit you?"

It was a little too much for him. He decided to tell us what we wanted to know when Lol, very casually, asked which portion of his anatomy he fan-cied he could best do without.

The trail opened out past the blockhouse, becoming firmer and less treacherous and there were no more risslacas. That, at the least, was good news. The openness was something else again. We put him to sleep, gently, and bound and gagged all those still alive and, going out and bolting the door and wedging it with a half-rotten log covered with woodlice and limpet-like sucking slugs, we took ourselves and our zorcas off along the trail to Trakon's Pillars.

Presently Lol, who had been showing acute symptoms of earnest thought, said: "Why not take a couple of their uniforms? We could pass muster for guards, you and I."

"Aye, Lol. We could. I think you have been a farmer and a guerilla. Those guards back there—their uniforms. They are outpost men, exterior details. If Jhansi is still as slippery as I think, he will have arranged first-rate and differently accoutred guards for inside."

"Oh," said Lol. Then, "I see."

"We'll try the same trick again, and this time say we have been passed on by the outpost guards. It should serve to bring us within range for hand-strokes. I'm loath to shaft 'em without warning."

The wide-eyed and incredulous gape Lol favored me with indicated, truly enough, the flabbiness of this my later self and the unwelcome realization that I would have to stiffen up, brassud! in the near future.

To attempt some limping explanation of my words and thus reveal my hopeless confusion seemed to me an enormous task and one from which I shrank. I was saved further emotional turmoil of that nature by the simple-minded and cunning lie the guard we had questioned had told us, seeking in his professionally loyal way to encompass our downfall. He had said there were no more risslacas.

Quite evidently, the beastie which hopped up out of the bog, dripping slime and stinking like a Rapa barracks the night after, had not heard the guard. He opened his gapers and charged, hissing.

"My Vall!" shouted Lol. He let go of his zorca and swung his sword forward. I stepped up to his shoulder on the narrow trail and held the longsword, two-handed, pointed front and center. There was no room to dodge, no time to run and only a squidgy and slime-sucking death in the swamp on each side. So we had to face the monster.

His clawed and webbed feet slapped like suction pads against the ground. His hisses were boiler-punctures. His fetid breath hit us like a furnace blast from hell. His fangs glinted yellow and green, choked with bits of rotting flesh. Without a coherent thought I took a step forward and swung the Krozair brand.

That magnificent steel bit. It chunked solidly alongside the risslaca's head and then I was knocked lengthwise. The mud sprayed. I near choked on the slime and was on my feet and hacking at the beast's underside. His back was armored with spines a foot long, draped with trailing weeds. Lol had struck and was down and stabbing away from underneath. Green ichor flowed, bubbling. Together we worked on the dinosaur, hacking and spearing, and avoiding the desperate tramplings and slashings of his feet. Luckily—and I mean that fervently—he was a four-footed fellow, and so we did not have that extra or those two extra pairs of death-dealing talons to worry about. He sagged to his chest, and we stood to either side, hacking away as though we chopped down trees in a primeval forest. Lol took a razor slash along his thigh, and cursed, and set to again with a will. We did not shout or rave; just got on with the disgusting job.

By the time the beast decided he had had enough and attempted to evade us, sliding like a parcel of rotten cabbages into the marsh, we, too, had had our fill.

Lol sagged back. His face showed a greenish pallor.

"By Vox! He nearly had us."

"And the zorcas have gone, Drig take it."

"Yes." And Lol Polisto laughed. "Now Thelda will have to walk out. She will not like that, if I know her."

"Well, let us go on. Now we look enough like half-crazed fugitives from the niksuth to make our story watertight."

"Which," observed Lol with another laugh, "is more than that sorry beastie is right now."

As I say, Lol Polisto was quite a character when he got a head of steam up.

We padded on soundlessly with ready weapons as the mist gyrated and swung oily green and orange streamers about us, mingling in confusing gossamers with the trailing slime from arching tree branches. We met no more risslacas. The trail gleamed like a cobbled street after rain. The smells lessened. The mist still clung, dank and miasmic; but the way opened ahead and the next guard was, most unfortunately, a bleg. He and his companions came trotting along in that weird jerky way of the four-legged blegs, and while they were no doubt anxious to traverse the trail through the bog and reach the outpost where they would relieve the guards on duty there, we were as anxious that they should not betray us. The unfortunate circumstance lay in that they were blegs. With their Persian Leaf Bat faces and four legs like Chippendale chairs, they were clad in uniforms that, although we might make shift to don, would never serve to fool another guard. So we fought and passed on, and looked always ahead.

A parcel of slaves lurched lugubriously across a side trail. They were burdened with sacks and staggered as they struggled on under the whips and goads of Och guards. One tends to talk of slaves in this context in terms of parcels; no disrespect is meant by it. The Och guards were disposed of and the slaves, dully incurious, went on their lurching way. We walked on into the mist. A Fristle astride a totrix came lolloping along singing a song, his feet jutting out at arrogant angles. He went whiskers first into the quagmire. Lol stood back and put his hands on his hips.

"I," he said, "just do not believe this."

"You may ride, Lol," I told him. "We're bound to run across a couple of decent uniforms soon."

We found the uniforms stretched across the broad backs of three Chuliks. These diffs were a different proposition, and we had a nice little set to before we could claim their garments for ourselves.

"I see what you meant about the uniforms and gear," observed Lol as we dressed in the fancy ochre and umbre and buckled up the lesten-hide harness. The sleeves were ochre and white—the serving swod's approximation to Layco Jhansi's kovnate colors of ochre and silver—and the accoutrements of the men were of good quality. I nodded and stowed the longsword and longbow and quiver over my shoulder, draping a checkerboard cloak across them.

"We'll penetrate a good long way dressed like this. But do you keep your own sword, also."

"I understand."

When we reached the artificial lake surrounding Trakon's Pillars and surveyed the narrow wooden bridge that connected the pillared stronghold to the land—so-called—we realized what a foolhardy errand we were on. But there was nothing else for it now but to press on as cheerfully as might be. So, singing that silly little ditty about Forbenard and the Rokrell, we pushed on over the bridge. At the far side under the overhanging wooden gateway a Fristle guard awaited us.

"Six of 'em, majister," said Lol, leaning down from the saddle. "I'll rush 'em, and then—"

"Hold, Lol! You may rush 'em, with my blessing. But I shall feather three of them for you as you ride. And, once inside, make for the deepest darkest dirtiest shadow and await me. I shall not be long."

"Majister!" He looked stricken. "I did not mean—"

"I know what you mean, Lol Polisto, and I welcome your thought. Now, as you love Vallia, do as you are bid."

He grunted, and said, softly, "As I love my Thelda and my son." But he waited until I had unlimbered the bow. Then he clapped in his heels and was away and I hauled back the string and snapped three arrows across the gap, whistling past Lol's down-bent head. Three of the Fristles coughed bright blood and collapsed. Lol took two more and the last turned to run. Lol's totrix, tangling his stupid six-legs, stumbled the wrong way. The Fristle, screeching, his whiskers flaring, would escape and arouse the castle—all I could do was call on Seg's Supreme Being, Erthyr the Bow, and cast a last shaft.

It sped true.

Lol spurred on swiftly, as we had agreed, and I ran in after him, hurdling the fallen men, for the Fristles may have cat-faces, but they are men and can prove it. Inside the gateway the wooden walls stretched, and ahead showed shadows under brickwork, arches and galleries. That looked promising and so I ran—fast, you may be sure—expecting an arrow to float silently down any mur and knock my brains out. I reached the brick, gray with age and round-edged, and ducked into the shadows. A totrix snuffled and Lol said, "All clear."

"Well done. Now let us get on."

From previous experience of the uniquely Kregen architecture of palace and castle I expected us to be able to move about with comparative freedom provided no alarm was raised. The alarm was going to be raised in no uncertain fashion the moment the first of the Fristle guards was discovered. So we must tailor our cloth to suit the narrowness of our movements.

This rat's warren of Trakon's Pillars turned out to be something of a surprise, in the end, for we ventured through courts of moldering brick and past colonnades of gilded wood where every motif shrieked of one thing and one thing only.

Jikaida.

Our bedraggled appearance which had served to give us time to fell the Chuliks had vanished with the donning of their guard uniforms provided by Jhansi. We moved smartly, with that unmistakable swagger of the mercenary drawing swift, half-averted glances from serving wenches, free and slave alike. For a space we could proceed unmolested. The totrix was like to be a hindrance but we were loath to part with the steed against his immediate and urgent need in the near future. Past tumbled ruins, past brand-new buildings, freshly lime-washed, we went, seeking always to come to the center. There, we both felt, lay the answers to our dual questions.

We skirted several courts laid out as Jikaida boards of various sizes. Not one was in use this early in the morning. An ob-Deldar moved bulkily out of an arched doorway and bellowed at us, and we ignored him and marched on as though about the kov's business. Later on we were accosted again, this time by a thin-nosed and supercilious Hikdar. His misfortune was that he snapped at us in an alleyway between ochreberry bushes, and so had no protection from inquisitive eyes as we clapped him down in his cape and sat on him. He struggled like a landed fish.

"Dom," I said, very friendly. "Tell us where the captives are stowed away and you may live."

He started to bluster and then to yell as soon as Lol took his clamping hand away. Lol tapped him alongside the skull, gently, put his fist back over the fellow's mouth, and, leaning down with a fierceness that perfectly complemented my apparent gentleness, said, "If you do not instantly tell us what we wish to know, and do so quietly, you will miss—" Well, what he would miss would make him miss a lot of life hereafter. The Hikdar was happy, most happy, to tell Lol what he wanted to know.

Leaving the Hikdar stuffed under the ochreberry bushes we led the totrix through ways advised us until we passed a neat little pavilion reflected in a goldfish pool. Past a tall yew hedge a gravel path led to a small wicket set in a creeper-bowered brick wall. Here the sentry eyed us as Lol, most officiously, said: "We have news for the kov, dom. You had best not keep him waiting."

The guard—one of that nameless band of heroes whose sole function, as I have pointed out before, seems to be to stand all puffed in gold and silver finery, with a spear, and to be knocked on the head—was inclined to argue. He was also incautious enough to open the wicket to make his point with great vehemence. Lol hit him, whereupon he ceased to be an obstacle and we were able to pass inside.

"Now where?"

"We must ask again, and keep asking, until we get the answer we seek."

"You have, majister, I think," said Lol, "done this before."

"On and off," I said. "On and off."

But, the truth is, and will remain, that no two occasions are ever the same. And, every time, the old gut-tightening sensations afflict you and you have to keep a damned sharp lookout behind you. Damned sharp.

The bustle of the place was refreshing after the dolorous dragging down effect of the bogs. Slaves and servants and guards moved about and we were able to make our way forward. A swod with purple and green sleeves told us that he thought, the prisoners were confined in dungeons where the rasts nested and the schrafters sharpened their teeth on the bones of corpses.

"The lady prisoner, cramph!"

The swod rolled his eyes down, trying to focus the dagger pressing into his throat. "In the Lattice House," he squeaked.

So we went to the Lattice House.

This turned out to be a brick-built structure whose bricks were still sharp-cornered, and whose roof was tile rather than wood or thatch. We stopped by the corner of a gravel path, where brilliantly plumaged arboras strutted, and took in the prospects of breaking in. Lol was shaking.

"Easy, Lol. We are almost there."

"Aye. I haven't even thought of getting out."

"One thing at a time."

A dozen guards sweating with effort ran past, and their Deldar bellowed at them to spread out and search the Ladies Quarter. I frowned. "The hunt is up."

"Just let us break in. Then—"

We glared from the shadows of the foliage, and I saw that Lol's shaking had stopped. I rather fancied he would make a good companion, even a member of the KRVI, if we got out of this in one piece apiece, so to say. For the life of me I couldn't take it seriously, and this, I vaguely realized, was because Lol was the kind of fellow to make you do things you wouldn't dream of doing in more staid moments. He was a lot like Seg, and Inch, in that...

"Bluff," I said. "It will work if you believe it will."

With that and giving Lol no time to argue I straightened up, gave the stolen uniform a flick, and marched very arrogantly toward the entrance door. This was of lenken wood with bronze bolt heads, and each side stood an apim swod, brilliant in the ochre and white livery of Layco Jhansi.

"Llahal, doms," I called out. "There are two madmen at large and the kov has sent us to protect the prisoners. Let us in and be quick about it."

The two rankers frowned at us, and their swords twitched up. You couldn't blame them. Now I have been accused, here and there, of saying that a certain man was a fool to draw a sword against me, and this has been alleged against me as proof positive of my overweening self-pride and pompousness. This is not so, as you who have heard my story will know. The truth is rather that I sorrow at his foolishness and take no pride from it whatsoever—how can one man take pride in the exposure of another? These two swods would have fallen into the category of fools, but that Lol stepped in first, feverish with frustrated impatience, and belted them, one, two, and knocked them flying.

"Very pretty," I said. "Now we must drag them in and find someone else to ask where away is your lady wife."

"We will," he growled. As we dragged the guards in through the doorway I reflected that Lol was picking up my ways with a pleasing aptitude.

The lenken door closed with only the wheezingest of groans and as the wood latched shut a posse of Rapa guards ran past, swords and spears at the ready. I cursed them and turned to follow Lol into the interior of the Lattice House.

The place was lushly furnished, carpeted, lit by skylights well out of reach of even my Earthly muscles. We found a Fristle fifi who was eager to tell us where the captives were. Captives. I frowned.

We padded along on the carpets, past statuary of an erotic and convoluted kind, up stairways where candelabra branched, unlighted now, and tall mirrors reflected us as two stikitches, murderous with intent, stalking their prey. I fancied the mirrors did not entirely lie...

This Lattice House contained a distinctive smell compounded of sweat and scent, of heavily perfumed flowers and that sharp aroma that Jilian would call armpit-smell. There were mirrors and statues, paintings and tapestries everywhere. I wondered if Seg had ever been here, and, if he had, why the place still stood.

The Fristle fifi hurried ahead. Her fur was of that sweet honeydew melon color so highly-prized by connoisseurs, most of whom deserve chains themselves. She led us along a purple velvet draped corridor toward a balass door. No guards stood there. Lol pushed on ahead, eagerly, and thrust the door open. The Fristle let out a little squeal of surprise, and half-turned to me. Lol yelped. He vanished. His yelp broke up in a startled bellow, and echoes caught it, twisting and magnifying it into a booming hollowness. I caught the Fristle by her upper arm and held her gently and so looked down into the pit.

The shaft was black and unpolished by a single shard of light save what few rays fell from the lamp over the door. No sound reached me from that ebon pit.

I said, "How far did he fall?"

The Fristle was sobbing and squirming, terrified. At last she got out, "There is straw below. He is not killed."

"You should, fifi, be very thankful for that." I saw that the pit extended from jamb to jamb. "How do we reach the bottom of the pit?"

"You cannot. It is guarded by werstings. The handlers will come later and—"

"Show me the way."

"I cannot! I cannot!"

The scene was not pretty. I said, "I think you can—I think you will, Fristle."

She wailed and sobbed but began to lead me back and along a side corridor covered in pink brocades. I carried the drexer naked in my right fist, and my left hand clamped the fifi's arm. She wore a copper bracelet there, and that should have warned me, onker that I am.

The likelihood was that she was more terrified that I did not rave and shout, and my calmness in a situation she must know was one of frightful horror for me, unnerved her. She led me along the corridors and I sheathed the blade only three times so as to avoid suspicion as we passed people. The girl Fristle made no attempt at raising the alarm at these times and, to my sorrow, I realized she imagined she would be the first to die.

At the next corner of the corridor, where an ivory statue of a talu swirled multiple arms in exotic frozen dance, she hung back. The tears glistered pearl-like on her face.

"Go on, girl."

"There are guards—"

I pushed her back, still holding her, and stuck my head around the corner. Four apim guards lounged outside a door. Clad like the others in ochre and silver, bearing swords and spears, they yet, for all their lounging, looked alert and a cut above the usual run. One revealed the glitter of a silver pakmort at his throat.

"The lady captive," I said to the Fristle fifi. "She is in there?"

"Yes. She and the child."

I pondered.

No harm seemed to have come so far to Thelda Polista and her child. The priority appeared to me to get Lol safely out of that black pit, then rescue his Thelda, and so make our break out. I did not wish to be lumbered with a woman and a baby going down against Werstings. So I hitched my left fist around the girl's arm, very friendly, and said to her a few home truths, whereat she trembled anew, and so started off with a confident swing, my story all ready for the guards.

Well, men grow corn for Zair to sickle.

Somewhere a harp was being played, long muted ripples of sound pouring through the close confines of the corridor where the lavender drapes and the pictures set an incongruous note against the harsh armor and weapons and the passions. For I was wrought up, and the Fristle was half-dead with fear, and the guards to relieve the tedium were mindful for a little fun.

We walked along as sedately as a pair of candidates for the Dunmow Flitch. But these idle-bored-half-witted guards! The antics of people attempting to relieve the tedium by teasing and taking pleasure from baiting others have always repelled me, and, by Krun, always will. These four started the usual nonsense and I walked on with a stony face which, in their ignorance, they failed to observe. The Fristle gasped. When the buffoonery became too coarse, for they halted us with a lazily dropped spear to bar the passage, and the Fristle, shivering with a paroxysm of terror, fell half-swooning, and the guards moved in with more intent purpose, there was nothing else left for that onker of onkers, Dray Prescot, to do but prevent them.

They went to sleep peacefully enough, all four of them.

"The devil take it!" I was wroth. Now, as there had been nothing for it when the guards started to have their idiot nasty fun, so now there was nothing for it but to go in and bring Thelda Polista and her son out. The guards' slumbering bodies would soon be noticed. If we dragged them in and locked the door their absence would soon be noticed. And if we simply left them they would recover and they would soon give notice.

So, in we went.

The revolting behavior of the guards outside should have given me some warning. Of the four, one had been a paktun. Their Hikdar inside the prison chambers was also a paktun, an apim and a damned handsome fellow in his own eyes with his curly brown hair and striking eyes and smooth easy swagger. The woman he held in his arms in an alcove struggled silently with him. He had begun his little antics early. I wondered if Layco Jhansi was aware, and realized instantly that he could not be. Or, he might—and not give a damn. Provided Lol's wife was still alive to act as a bargaining counter, Jhansi wouldn't care what tortures she went through. The two were in partial shadow. I let go of the Fristle, who swooned clean away, and crossed the rugs in half a dozen strides, knocking an ornamental table with spindly legs over on the way. The baby lay in a crib to the side and Thelda's dress was disarranged and I guessed she had been putting the infant to sleep after his morning feed. I felt inclined to put this rast of a Hikdar to sleep, also.

I hit him with a certain force under the ear.

He collapsed, face first, soundlessly, onto the carpets at the woman's feet. Her face blazed up. She swayed. Her hand went to her breast.

"Dray! Oh, Dray—it is you!"

I stared, appalled.

15

I Postpone a Problem

Sometimes a man will leap out of bed after a vile dream with a cry of horror on his lips, and his hand will reach out for the sword scabbarded conveniently on the bedpost.

Well, I could not stop the anguished cry from bursting past my lips. And I already held a sword in my fist.

But I knew I could not awake from this nightmare.

Seg!

"Dray, oh, Dray!" Thelda lurched toward me, her arms out and I could only take her into my arm, and hold her and feel how she trembled, like a hunted beast in a snare. She was trapped, horribly trapped, and she did not know it.

"Thelda," I said, stupidly. Then, "We'll get you out of this. Now, love, brace up."

Her face lifted and she looked at me. Tears spangled her cheeks. She was just as I remembered her, just as beautiful, just as plump and happy, just as self-oriented with all her outward devotion to her friends, like puppy-love. Yes, this was Thelda, whom I have mocked and laughed at, who was a good comrade to Delia and me, and who was Seg's wife and the mother of his children.

I moved a little back in a gentle attempt to free myself from her embrace and swung about a little; but she clung to me, her naked arms about my neck, her tear-stained face reaching up to mine. I did not kiss her. I do not think I ever had. Standing thus so closely-entwined I could feel the warmth of her, the perfume, and I saw the door open with a smash and a man burst in. I started to hurl Thelda away and then there was no need.

Lol Polisto stood there, disheveled, the sword in his fist caked with blood to the hilt and blood splashed most horridly over that smart Chulik uniform. He saw us.

The instinctive and fierce flash of jealousy that burst up like flame into his face was instantly quelled as I spoke.

"Thank Opaz you got out of that pit, Lol. Here is Thelda and safe. The baby too. Now, for the sweet sake of all we hold dear, let us get out of here."

"Yes, yes," cried Thelda. There was no pretense in the way she freed herself from me and flung herself at Lol all blood-caked as he was. I stood there and the brains in my old vosk-skull felt as though they were frizzling. Didn't Thelda know Seg was still alive? And, if knowing, did she care? Then I remembered what Lol had said, off-handedly; that the Kov of Falinur was dead. Thelda must believe that, too. She must...

"Now, my heart," said Lol, holding Thelda close, stroking her back, her hair, soothing her in an old familiar way that spoke eloquently of their intimate relationship. "The emperor and I will get you out of here, and our son, and then—"

Thelda drew back a little, her face flushed; but she still clasped Lol with a fierce and supplicating grasp. "Is the emperor here with an army, then? After all I have done for him and his family that is the least he could do for us."

And, I swear it, I laughed.

Wasn't that Thelda—to the life?

The puzzlement in Lol's tough face added to my amusement.

"Here is the emperor, Thelda, my heart, so do be—polite."

"I do not see him, Lol. What—?"

"Come on, you two," I broke in. "If you must gabble, gabble as we run."

Leaving the unconscious and unharmed Fristle where she lay a-swoon, and the Hikdar, of whose conduct I felt it best not to apprise Lol, draped across the carpets, we went out. Thelda carried the baby on her breast. Lol's protective instincts were now so fully aroused I had not the slightest query to make how he had got out of the pit. As we went quickly along the corridor he told me that he had chopped a couple of werstings, those ferocious hunting dogs of Kregen, and a couple of slave handlers, too, the cramphs. At this I lost my smile. He had arrived here from the other direction, the way the Fristle was leading me, and seeing the guards guessed at once he had arrived at where he needed to be. He had also, he said, breathed a quick prayer to Opaz before flinging the door open and bursting in.

At the first stairway we went up, for Thelda told us there was a small and private flier park on the roof of the Lattice House. This was the means by which she had been brought here. The next flight of stairs was guarded by two Fristles, lounging and yawning, and they yawned in a more ghastly way after Lol was through with them. The stairs were no longer carpeted with lushly decorative patterns, merely a plain ochre weave. Our footsteps remained soundless. Near the top an alcove held a silver lamp shaped in the form of an airboat, its tall single flame unwavering. The quietness struck oddly after the racket below. Thelda paused, and gasped, and half-laughing said: "Give me leave to rest awhile, my love."

At once full of contrition, Lol halted and Thelda sat down in the alcove and began to fuss with the baby. I stood with my back against the wall below and Lol above on the stairs.

Thelda wanted to talk and she asked again about the emperor and his army. I said, "You found yourself in Evir, Thelda. So what then?"

Being Thelda and being faced with something she found incomprehensible, she had simply blotted the incident out as though it had not happened. From the Sacred Pool of Baptism in far Aphrasöe she had been magically transported to her homeland of Evir. She had at once started for Falinur where she was the kovneva and her husband, Seg Segutorio, was the kov, however unwilling a kov he might be. She had arrived just in time to be caught up in the Troubles.

"Oh, it was terrible, Dray! The burning and the looting and—"

I could not help noticing how Lol kept jumping each time Thelda called me by name. Despite all my own views on the idiocy of protocol and such-like fripperies, I do not accept into the circle of those who may call me by my given name everyone who may imagine he or she has the right. So— beware! And for Lol Polisto it was very clear I should be addressed as majister. So, to smooth one difficulty and to skirt another, I said: "Thelda and I are old friends, Lol. And, it is clear she does not know of Jak the Drang."

"Who?" said Thelda.

Lol started to say something, but I went on speaking, asking Thelda to tell us the rest before we pushed on. From below stairs no sounds reached us. And Thelda was still in a state of shock, too abruptly released. And, also, I wanted to scout the roof before we burst out.

She had been through a lot in her kovnate of Falinur, where she had been thoroughly detested. And, in the way of things, Lol Polisto had come along and rescued her from a particularly nasty scrape. And nature had taken its course. She firmly believed Seg was dead. She had been told so by taunting officers of Layco Jhansi before Lol took her away from them.

The inevitable had happened. For, as she said quite simply: "Seg wasn't there when I needed him."

By Zair, he wasn't! He was busy trying to escape the lash and the chains of slavery with a damned great wound in him, that had healed only to be broken again and again, and now this last breaking would be attended to, or my name wasn't Dray Prescot. The machinations of the Savanti nal Aphrasöe through their creature, Vanti of the Pool, ensured that Seg could not be in the same place as Thelda when she needed him, for he had been pitchforked back to his homeland of Erthyrdrin in Loh. Never had fate— and fate had been employed, this time, by the Savanti—played a much dirtier trick.

By the way in which these two looked at each other, the way they touched, by what they said, I could see with limpid clarity they were deeply in love. Well, that was all very fine. I knew that Seg and Thelda had loved each other very deeply, also. Some people aver that it is possible to love more than one person at the same time; love, I mean, in the intimate, sexual union properly belonging to man and wife. Monogamy was the fashion in Vallia, never mind what exotic goings-on occurred in other parts of Kregen. To love more than one person in sequence, that is understandable, else widows and widowers would never escape happily out of their state. But—at the same time? I was not sure. It is a knotty one, and demands scrutiny. Total love, well, by its very nature that cannot be given to more than one at a time. Can it?

Equally, although I had known Lol Polisto for a short time, a very short time, I fancied I had summed him up as a courageous, upright, honest man, who fought for what he loved and believed in. There was nothing here in this new union of the moist-mouthed contemptible underhand way of Quergey the Murgey, the arch-seducer. The obvious way out meant it was all down to Thelda. For the time being I would not, could not, tell her that her husband still lived.

Lol did not know, for he had been out on his fruitless bid to break through the ring of besieging mercenaries when Seg and I had arrived in the fortress of the Stony Korf. So why destroy the happiness of these two now? Anyway, despite his immersion in that milky fluid that gave such tremendous recuperative powers, Seg might still die of that ghastly wound. And we were not out of the wood yet. Lol might die. Thelda might die. We might all die. I pushed away from the wall and, saying, "Bide a space here while I scout the roof," went on up the stairs.

What a situation! Maybe it is not new on two worlds, maybe it seems trite to the blasé, I could feel for my comrade Seg, and feel for Thelda, and, by Vox, I could feel for Lol, also. Emotions twist a fellow's guts up in a positively physical way, putting him off his food, making him lean and irritable. And I was feeling highly wrought up as I shoved the door open and stepped out onto the roof, the naked brand in my fist.

The roof was empty.

A single small flier stood chained down, and a tiny wind blew miasmic odors in from the niksuth.

I went back through the doorway and motioned to them to come up. Thelda carried the baby up first, and Lol guarded the rear. We stood on the roof and looked at the flier.

"That is a single place craft..." Lol stated the obvious.

"Hum," I said, for I had nothing helpful to add.

"It is very clear you must go," said Lol, speaking with a tightness to his lips that, while it warmed me, made me angry, also. "As for us, we will—"

"Thelda and the baby will go, Lol, and you will ride the coaming. That voller will take you both, I know. I have built the things." I walked across, not prepared to have any further argument.

Lol wouldn't have it. "But—" he began.

I took Thelda's arm as she came up and swung around to face Lol. "In with you, Thelda. Careful of the baby. Now, Lol, stretch out here, on the coaming, and we will strap you tightly."

"But there is room for you—"

I shook my head, "The way they build these things is a disgrace. All Vallians know that. But this will be built by Hamalese for Hamalese and so should not fail. But she won't take us all. Now, Lol, get aboard!"

"But you! How will—?"

I lifted Thelda bodily and plumped her into the narrow cockpit of the flier among the flying silks and furs. She held the baby with a care that was completely genuine. I faced Lol.

"Do you wish to argue, Tyr Lol?"

His face betrayed the emotions of rebellion, fear for his wife—for the woman he believed was his wife—and loyalty to Vallia represented by me. I wanted to smile at his confusion; but time was running out. I jerked my head at the voller. "In with you."

"But it isn't right—"

"I am perfectly prepared to knock you over the head," I told him. "But would prefer to say, simply, that your emperor commands you. Would you disobey a lawful command of your emperor?"

"Emperor?" said Thelda, looking up from the child.

"I'd obey any damn command, lawful or unlawful," said Lol, feelingly, on a gust of expelled breath. "But—"

"Go!" I bellowed. "And buckle the straps tightly."

So, still loath but his conscience clear, Lol climbed onto the coaming. The straps were fastened, Thelda took the controls, the baby started crying, and the voller took off.

"Well," I said as the airboat lifted away. "Thank Zair that little nonsense is over. What a to-do!"

But what the to-do would be when Thelda discovered Seg still to be alive was past me. It was all down to her, it would have to be all down to her. No one else could dictate what she should do. I found all my feelings for Thelda rising and tormenting me, for she had been a good companion, as you know.

So, feeling treacherously free of the problem, for I had merely shuffled it off for a space, I went back to the stairs and started to think about getting myself out of this dolorous place.

Sixteen

The Carpeting of Ros the Claw

Before I could do that desired thing there was another task to my hand. I had not failed to ask about Dayra as well as Thelda on the way in; and had received no useful answers. At the time, with Lol along, Thelda had been our main concern, and rightly so, for Dayra was here not as a prisoner but as an embassy, bringing offers of alliance from that bastard Zankov.

It seemed to me perfectly proper to find another guard with a fancy uniform, a pakmort and the rank of Jiktar, take what I wanted from him, clean myself up, and then go looking for my wayward daughter. All this I did, and as a smartly turned out Jiktar, with the silver mortil head on its silken cord at my throat, went through from the slave quarters to the inner recesses of Trakon's Pillars.

This stronghold within its encircling bogs was an open place covering a fair amount of ground. Much of it was on stilts, some on mats, and the hard ground was reserved for the highest of the high. The Pillars from which the place took its name were volcanic extrusions, tall separately trunked obelisks of naked tufa, pitted and worn, rising like unformed Easter Island statues in a clump at the center. They provided a pivot around which the busy stronghold revolved.

In lifting terraces below, the palaces had been built, each one more grand than the last. White columns, pavements and walls blinded in the suns as I climbed leaving the dank mists below. I was not stopped, was not even questioned. A Jiktar is a reasonably exalted rank, and the insignia told observers that I was an ord-Jiktar, having risen eight steps in the grade. The pakmort carried more weight, even, than that, here where gold still bought swords.

Now, just because a Jiktar is a pretty high rank, the holder usually commanding a regiment, the disguise took me through the lower ways up to the palaces. But once there I would have to find a swod's gear; for all Jik-tars would be known and recognized. A party of men marched across and the dwa-Deldar in command saluted me. I returned the compliment. They were archers, and their bows were long and hefty, round staves of a certain length. They were Bowmen of Loh.

Finding one on his own was not easy; but eventually I was buckling up the leather gear of a Bowman of Loh and settling the bronze helmet on my head. I kept my own bow. Then I went boldly into the first palace, a sea-green confection profuse with satyrs and nymphs carved on the walls.

The quondam owner of the archer's gear had told me that the embassy from Zankov was housed in this place, the Palace of the Octopus. So, in I went. In for a zorca, in for a vove.

Layco Jhansi had been the old emperor's chief pallan and had run things in Vondium most tightly. He had subverted the allegiance of the Crimson Bowmen of Loh. So there were plenty of Lohvians with their red hair about, as well as dark-haired archers from Erthyrdrin. My brown hair, being Vallian, did not attract undue attention. Five-handed Eos-Bakchi, that mischievous Vallian spirit of luck and good fortune, favored me unduly. A Deldar spotted me and bellowed and soon I found myself marching in a three-deep column of Bowmen, en route to provide a guard. Well, the ploy got me in well enough.

Five-handed Eos-Bakchi, however, did not see fit to arrange for me actually to attend in the reception for Zankov's embassy. That would have been to ask too much. We were stationed at intervals along the corridors and the tessellated pavements, and I drew a billet at the head of some stairs that led down to what depths I did not know. I stood there, alert, looking the very personification of one of those guards I have detailed as being fancifully dressed, spear-bearing and ripe for knocking on the head.

Now it is perfectly true that most people inhabiting palaces staffed with a plethora of guards barely notice their guards at all. Old rogues like myself who have served their time do notice; but we are in a pitiful minority. No one noticed me. I'm damn sure they'd have noticed had I not been on duty, like a pickled gherkin at my post.

And so my daughter Dayra walked along the corridor and past the stairs, deep in conversation with that foresworn scoundrel, Tyr Malervo Norgoth, him who had once come with an embassy from Jhansi to me and set his sorcerer, Rovard the Murvish, on me. I just stood there, lumpen, my face shadowed by the ornate helmet. Malervo Norgoth with his gross body and spindly legs looked much as I remembered him. He wore loose robes of a sickly green color, with much gold and silver embroidery. But Dayra— Dayra looked magnificent.

She wore a long dress of the imperial style, all in sheerest sensil, that finer silk of Kregen, of a pale oyster color that shimmered as she walked.

Her carriage was that of an empress. There were feathers in the golden circlet around her brown Vallian hair. Her face glowed with conviction and passion as she talked. Her figure was a knock-out. Yes, I well realize the dignity and impudence of that; but it fitted. Fitted perfectly. For I had seen this glowing girl when she had been clad in black leathers, with her long legs flashing, driving wicked steel with her right hand, and her left taloned in those vicious raking claws.

Her jewelry glistered and blinded. She wore far too much. I fancied the massed iridescence of gems was genuine. Just whose gems they were seemed to me—her father—as a matter of moment. But, not for the moment. Why she wore so much jewelry might have been puzzled out by an earthly psychologist, with a glib theory that it reflected rebellion against her mother's elegant and refined taste, which leant more to small and costly items of quality, rather than a massed and vulgar display. I did not think so. This was Kregen. Dayra flaunted the gems so as further to convey the power she represented as embassy from Zankov.

Malervo Norgoth was saying as they walked along: "...doesn't mean a single damn thing, my dear, and it would be best if you did not forget it."

The reply Ros the Claw would make to that insulting comment intrigued me; but she simply said: "Yet Zankov's new allies do mean a damn thing. They mean very much. No one is going to stand before them, you may believe me."

"There are many dwaburs between the east and Vennar."

"They can be crossed. Zankov would cross them in friendship."

"A friendship which he values highly in terms of what he asks in the way of gold..."

They walked on, wrangling, and a few personal guards followed them, whereat I drew up even straighter and angled the helmet to shadow my face even more. Rovard the Murvish trailed along at the rear, emitting his unmistakable effluvium of dead rats and sewers, and shaking his morntarch with a reflective gesture. His furs and bangles and shaggy hair lent him a wild and grotesque appearance. The party moved on and I breathed out and glanced back along the line of guards.

The Deldar was nowhere in sight. Not one of those ramrod guards would move if I walked off. That was a racing certainty. So, shouldering the spear I had taken from the archer, an ornate and highly-polished piece with tufts of white and ochre ribbons, I marched off after Malervo Norgoth, Dayra and the rest.

The search for the two madmen who had broken into Trakon's Pillars from the bogs continued and so I assumed no one had yet discovered the absence of that single-place voller. That pleased me, for it meant no pursuit would take off after Lol and Thelda. So, feeling ready for what might come, I followed the embassy into a cross-corridor where tall windows threw diamonds of brilliance across the carpets and where Norgoth led Dayra into a room through an ochre and silver doorway.

The thought occurred to me that both Zankov and Jhansi were avid for an alliance. Both felt their own weakness and needed additional strength. And both, it was clear, would seek to dominate their partnership. It seemed to me clear-cut that I should do all I could to upset that understanding between them and prevent the alliance. That fitted in with my plans for Dayra. I fancied it was high time that minx answered to her mother and father. That her answers might make the sweetest of sense I have already indicated, and I was fully prepared to take her side in all things, if it came to it, bar, perhaps, a coherent understanding of the man who had slain her grandfather. And, even there, reasons impelled him that were sound, even honorable, to him. I owed him that much. Zankov might not be the black-hearted scoundrel everyone said he was. The odds were against it; but the chance remained.

And, as I walked up with a swagger toward the two Bowmen who guarded the ochre and silver door, I recognized in my thoughts the bias I owed to the condemnation of Zankov that stood in my brain like a light-house in stormy seas. I was prejudiced against him—for good reason—and must attempt in justice to take that into account in my dealings with him.

"Lahal, dom," I sang out to the first guard, scraping up a frozen grimace that might pass muster for a smile, and nodding to his companion. "You're in luck, by the Seven and Two."

"Oh?" spoke up the first worthy, flicking a glance to his comrade. "And, dom, how are we so fortunate?"

"Why, to be sure. Here am I come to stand your watch while you have fun chasing after these madmen who have broken in. I wish you well of it, although I could do with loosing at fair game rather than the butts."

The guard favored me with a hard look. But I had slipped the longsword on its strap down my back so that the checkered cloak covered it, and although the sword of the Bowmen of Loh was usually the Walfargian lynxter, many of them preferred other weapons picked up in their mercenary trade, so that my drexer passed muster. The second guard let a broad and happy smile part his whiskers.

"That is good news. Come, Nath, let us go and feather a few rasts and earn our hire."

"Gladly, Naghan. I am with you."

And, with that jaunty mercenary swing, they marched off with a perfunctory: "Rember!" and a laugh. I stood by the door and breathed out and considered.

To break in would be easy. To slay a few of the cramphs in there probably also not too difficult. But Ros the Claw would fight. She had fought before, although sparing me in the end. I did not wish once more to face my daughter with naked steel between us.

120

A subterfuge of the simple-minded kind was called for.

No food had passed my lips for far too long, a most unhealthy and anti-social attitude that, for Kregen, by Krun, and I had not slept much lately, either. But one must accept the needle. I pushed the door open and slanted my head so that the helmet brim shadowed my face. The small chamber beyond was an anteroom, with doors in three walls, fast closed, and a rumble of voices reached me from the door with a strigicaw head in half-relief above the architrave. I put my ear to the wood and listened.

A rumble of voices in which no words were clear left me, as ever, it seemed of late, no alternative. My hand reached out for the latch fashioned after a pair of entwined totrixes and then I halted, dumbstruck at my own stupidity. My hand withdrew and I looked about swiftly. The next door along, the one with the chavonth head above it. Yes—another alternative had presented itself, and the simple-minded stratagem had become positively imbecile.

The door opened soundlessly. Two young fops, all lace and embroidery, playing Jikaida, looked up with guilt stamped all over their asinine faces. They went to sleep peacefully and I pressed my ear against a grille in the wall adjoining the strigicaw room. The voices spurted, not particularly clear; but I heard enough to make me feel that my daughter was a scheming minx and a half, a worthy daughter to her mother.

"...voves! Nothing will stand before them."

"So you say, Lady Ros. But the distances and the gold speak against you."

"The clans are with us in this. Their hatred of Vovedeer Prescot is as the prairie fire. It rages up fiercely and is all-consuming. Beware lest you and your master are broiled in the blaze."

"Threats?"

Dayra laughed, that ringing, silvery, contemptuous laugh of Ros the Claw. "You have put these chambers at my disposal, good Norgoth. How sits a threat against you here?"

"I am glad you remember this."

Then another voice broke in, a more distant rumble, and scraping sounds indicated the movement of chairs so I took it the conversation was ended. A few strides took me back to the door and I peered through the crack. Norgoth and Rovard and their retinue sailed out like galleons of Vallia, proud and puffed and supremely conscious of their superiority. I waited.

When they had gone I eased across to the door of the strigicaw and tried the totrix-latch. The door was locked. I rapped my knuckles on the wood. How formal one becomes in these moments! The door made clicking sounds of sliding metal and opened a fraction and a young, handsome, boy's face showed, slightly puzzled, perhaps a trifle apprehensive. I pushed up and spoke in a swod's metallic bark.

"Message to be delivered personal to the Lady Ros."

"She does not wish to be disturbed. She will not see anyone save the lord—"

"I think," I said, "she will see me."

The boy jumped, and his face twitched, and he closed the door and went away, whereat I smiled. Presently he returned, the door was opened, and I went in. My right hand rested at my side. The hilt of the drexer angled across most conveniently. If Ros came at me with a rapier or her damned steel claw I'd have to skip and dance a measure, and no mistake...

The room led onto another chamber of some refinement and luxury, with rugs and hangings and golden lamps on chains. A zhantil-skin pelt was strewn artfully across a couch whose strigicaw-head legs rested on ochre and white rugs. Long curtains at the far end parted and Ros walked in. She was in the process of buckling up a war-harness over her black leathers, and her face was tight with annoyance.

"Who demands to see me so intemperately?" She struggled with a bronze buckle which refused to close. "There can be no more messages to which I will listen unless they bring firm promises of gold." She looked up, breathing hard, and saw the Bowman of Loh who stood ramrod straight but submissively before her, as she must have seen so many in her time.

"Voves," I said. "So you bring voves into Vallia."

She jumped as though I had struck her.

Her naked left hand struck up before her face. The fingers extended. She wore no rings. Her nails were trimmed and polished, unpainted, neat. That left hand clawed at the air in reflex so automatic it left her gasping.

"Yes, Ros," I said.

To give her credit she did not gasp: "You!" like some ignoramus of a heroine from one of the operettas of the flea-pits of Vondium. I enjoy operetta. She lowered that lethal left hand, naked of its lethal weapon, and gazed on me and her look passed from astonishment through anger to a brooding puzzlement. Then:

"What am I to do with you?"

"Nothing. It is what I am to do with you. Boy!" I turned to the lad, who was not yet full grown, a dimpled handsome boy wearing a rose-colored tunic and with a pretty little dagger swinging from silver chains at his waist. His brown Vallian hair tumbled in locks about his ears. "Boy! Pull out that carpet—that long wide one with the silken tassels and spread it out on the floor."

She knew at once.

"You would not dare!"

"How much do you hate me, Ros?" I kept to this name of hers, instead of Dayra, out of an instinctive feeling for the moment, where Ros the Claw was at home and Dayra not.

"Hate you? More than you can imagine—more than the whole world can encompass!" She had not moved since that first instinctive gesture. Her face—beautiful, ah, yes, beautiful and passionate, willful, stubborn, marked with a pride I could sigh over, and marked, also, with a vicious sadness I found desolating—her face bore now the high flush of a controlled anger. "Are you not deserving of all the hate and all the contempt of the whole wide world?"

"Yes."

Her hand went to her throat, above the rim of the black leathers. She was surprised. "But—"

"Turn around, Ros the Claw, and I will fasten up your wrists. Stand, boy!" For the lad made to draw his toy dagger.

The footfall at my back was soft. It was not soundless. I should not speak to you had that footstep been soundless. I ducked and turned and the drexer was out and the giant who slashed a giant sword at me staggered on with the violence of his blow. He was quick. Off balance, before I could get back and the drexer into him he swung around, the giant sword sweeping. I hurdled it and landed cat-footed and so faced him.

Well, he was big. He was broad and wide and bulky and he went up and up and up, his thatch of straw-yellow hair overtopping me by seven good inches. He wore a bronze-studded leather kax, and arm-bands of beaten gold, and a war-kilt of ochre and bronze, pteruges which swung to his knees. His sandals would have carried a landing party from ship to shore. And his sword—massive, thick through and wide, with a solid pommel shaped like a zhantil-head—that sword was like no other I had seen on Kregen. I rather fancied it would be slow, even for him, even with his enormous muscles.

Dayra laughed her silver tinkle.

"You have not met Brun before. I think the meeting opportune." She was enjoying this. "Do not slay him Hyr Brun. His mangy hide has a certain value in certain quarters. We will grow fat on his profit."

Despite the gross proportions of that sword, Brun carried it one-handed and the hilt was close, not fashioned for two-handed work, not even for hand-and-a-half. I took three quick backward steps. Brun's cheerful face, open, mellow, clean-shaven and with a few spots on one cheek, broke into a delighted smile. His reactions were those of a cat stalking a mouse. The drexer snapped away into the scabbard. I reached around.

"So, master, you give in?" Brun's voice carried a clarity of sound amazing, until you realized the enormous cathedral-cavity of his lungs. "That is wise of you. The mistress is to be obeyed in all things."

"I don't know where you got him, Ros," I said, as I put my hand on the hilt of the Krozair brand. "But I'd like to make friends with a thousand or so. What a bonny regiment they would make for Vallia!"

"For my Vallia!" she spat at me. "Never yours!"

"Well, my girl, you are going into that carpet, and this Hyr Brun is going to carry you out. You had best reconcile yourself to that." I whipped the longsword out and it sparked a shard of light into that chamber as it swung out into line. "As for you, friend Brun. I shall not slay you, as you would not me. But carry your mistress in the carpet you will."

He boomed a gigantic laugh and rushed.

The fight was not pretty—or extraordinarily pretty—depending on your personal viewpoint.

He had a knack of swinging the huge sword around in his fist as though it was a length of rope so that it wove a circle of light. The trick was effective. Besides demonstrating his strength it confused his opponent. Inch had a similar trick with his long Saxon-pattern axe. Again I do not wish to dwell on the fight. It was interesting. Brun wore a leather strap around his head which confined his thatch of yellow hair. The Krozair brand met the gigantic sword and the metal rang and the jolt belted up my arms and across my shoulders. But the Krozair Disciplines held and the blows slanted and glanced, and, like a striking risslaca, the longsword licked out and sliced neatly through the leather fillet. Not a drop of blood was drawn, the skin was not marked. But the leather fell away and Brun's yellow hair dropped down before his face.

Before he had time to brush it away I stepped in and clouted him over the head with the flat.

He dropped. I do not think there can be many men born of women who will not drop when struck by a Krozair brand.

Before he hit the carpet I had leaped aside and swung the flat around horizontally and the boy was swept away, his toy dagger spinning up like a comet of diamonds in the lights.

Ros leaped for me and she wore her talons.

I ducked, put my shoulder into her stomach, clapped my left arm about her back and hugged her. Horizontally she thrashed her legs wildly. I felt the kiss of the talons against the back of my thighs, and so banged her—gently, gently!—on her bottom with the hilt.

"Stay still, daughter, or I shall tan you, but good."

"You—!"

"Yes."

Presently we were sorted out. Ros, with wrists and ankles fastened with the silken cords from the curtains, lay rolled in the ochre and silver carpet with the silk tassels. Brun said to me: "You would not really slay the boy?" I stood with a dagger at the boy's throat, the rest of my armory scabbarded.

I said, "Do you wish to find out? Pick up your mistress and we will walk out of here, all friendly and nice. Boy, do you walk quietly and not wriggle." I took the dagger from his throat and flapping a corner of the cloak over it, pressed it into the small of his back. "You walk before death."

Well, it was detestable; but he believed me. And, believing, said, "You may kill me, master, if you desire. But I will not betray my mistress."

"Well spoken lad. Your name?"

"I am called Vaxnik."

I was astonished. Vax was the name used by Jaidur in the Eye of the World. And Jaidur was Dayra's twin. I would ask the boy his history when we were safely away. Now, I said, "You have my word as a koter that no harm will befall your mistress. Despite her seeming hatred of me, I love her more deeply than you can understand. I would be cut down before harm should come to her. Now, lead on."

Brun rumbled: "Do you speak sooth, master?"

"Aye, Hyr Brun, I do."

"You are a Jikai, master, that is plain. And we do not do well in this evil place. But—"

"Carry your mistress out of here. All will be revealed."

Cheap and easy words; but they were true, by Vox.

A serving man—for Brun was clearly no slave—carrying an expensive carpet, and an important boy to strut his office, and a dour professional mercenary to guard them, excited no attention in the busy warren. We saw parties of guards searching for those who had broken in. We walked solemnly on and were not challenged all the way down from the Pillars to the beginning of the mists rising and stinking from the niksuth.

Besides the carpet in which was rolled Ros the Claw, Brun carried a leather sack hastily stuffed with portable food, a few bottles of wine, and a curtain stuffed down on the top. He could, I thought, have carried a whole wagon-load of supplies without visible effort. So we walked on and passed parties of guards still searching and began to discern a pattern in the search for the intruders. I fancied we might run into serious trouble at the gates, and Vaxnik led on with an eager step.

Now it appeared to me improbable that the outpost guards would have an expensive carpet delivered to their blockhouse. So we would have to re-arrange ourselves for the next step. I halted us in the shadows of a half-ruined building fronting the open space before the gate Vaxnik had chosen, and stared out as Bowmen and churgur guards moved about, parties coming and going, with Deldars yelling and a group of totrixmen spurring across in a swirl of dust and blown leaves. H'mm...

There was a double enceinte here, where Vaxnik had led us, and I chalked a mark up to him, the cunning little devil.

Waiting until the open space was completely free of guards would take too long. Time pressed. Norgoth as Jhansi's lieutenant would be raging with impatience that the intruders had not been found, and I suspected that some, at least, of those unfortunates who had been knocked on the head had recovered to add further to the alarm. So, once more, there was nothing for it. I settled the longsword more conveniently to hand. The shadows lay blue and bright. The suns shone. And then tendrils of oily mist wafted and the whole scene dulled to a dun mange, and a chill descended.

"March straight, Hyr Brun. And you, too, boy. I have a story for those guards yonder."

A party of diffs wearing the gray slave breechclouts passed in a straggling line. They carried obese pots on their shoulders, no doubt water for the baths of those up in the palaces, if they'd run out of milk. I made a face, and we stepped out.

Two parties of guards approached. That to our right rear was composed mainly of Rapas, with a few apims and Brokelsh. They carried their spears all at the regulation slope and were mercenaries, skilled fighting men. The party advancing through the gate wore the ochre and white, and were armed with a medley of weapons which spoke again of mercenaries, although not the regimented and disciplined kind. I frowned.

Walking along a couple of paces in rear of Brun I readied myself. We attracted no attention from the guards with the spears. They were commanded by their Deldar and would do as he directed. We made a picture that held no menace for him.

A movement caught the corner of my eye and I looked forward again. The open end of the carpet was moving like the trunk of an elephant. How she had done it I do not know. Dayra's head appeared, and an arm ripped free of the binding silks. Her face was flushed and her eyes looked murderous. She saw the guards. She yelled. She yelled good and loud.

"Guards! Guards! Here is the man you seek! Guards, ho!"

Her triumphant face bore on me, bright, vindictive, filled with passion.

Vaxnik squeaked. Brun dropped the carpet.

I saw the guards running on. Their Deldar bellowed and they turned toward us. The other party of guards, attracted by the shouts, also turned toward us. We were trapped between them.

"You're done for, now, you villainous rast!" shouted my daughter at her father.

I ripped the longsword free. Two-handed I gripped the Krozair blade.

"Done for!" shrieked Dayra. "They will not kill you. But you may wish they had."

"I do not hate you," I said, stupidly, spreading my fists along the hilt of the longsword.

"Throw down your sword, cramph! Oh that I could get free and sink my talons in you!" And her left hand at last broke free from the swathing carpet and the suns shone through the drifting mist and glittered most vilely upon that curved and cruel claw.

I saw the spearmen charging toward me. I half-turned and saw the guards from the gate pressing swiftly on, their weapons drawn.

And I said, very gently: "I do not think your guards will take me, Dayra. But it was a nice try."

Seventeen

Disaster

The spearmen ran yelling on their doom.

For a short space only I fronted them with the deadly Krozair longsword singing, and then Targon and Naghan and Dorgo and Korero were there, with the others of my choice band clad in their stolen ochre and white uniforms, and the blades clanged and rang. The spearmen were either cut down or ran. The fight was brief and bloody, swift and savage.

"Well met!" I bellowed. "Now back through the gate and into the swamps before they gather their wits."

"You are safe?" demanded Korero, and blood dripped from his tail hand and the blade he bore.

"Aye! Now—move!"

So we ran.

Brun lifted the carpet and I stuffed Dayra back, whereat she squealed and tried to slash me. I looped the silk around her wrists and drew it tight, tight, and said: "Daughter. Bide you still or earn a father's wrath."

"And what else have I ever had?"

There was nothing I could say to that. Filled with a sudden and blinding sense of infamy, I ran with my comrades out through the gate and past the dead guards sprawled there, and along the causeway and through the other gate where the guards lay naked, and so out and into the bog of Trakon's niksuth.

Well into the slimy stinking labyrinth we slowed down and caught our breaths, and I let them tell me the story as we pressed on. Inky the Chops had vanished when the risslacas attacked. My men had gone on, finding their own way through the boggy maze, half-blinded, choked with the miasmic stinks, but coming at last to this gate and so making their way through determined to rescue Lol and me or burn the place down. I said: "I regret we had no time to do that. It would have been—useful."

"Useful," growled Targon. "Aye, majister, and overdue."

The riding animals were gone and so we must walk. So we did. I reflected that the reasons that had impelled my fellows to choose a double-walled entrance, so that they might obtain uniforms without arousing suspicions inside, and the reasons impelling Vaxnik, that we would have a double chance of being caught, had coincided nicely. My band would have wrought fearful havoc looking for me: chance only had decreed we should meet when we did. Now chance, or fate, decreed we should walk.

We reached an area somewhat less boggy than most and opened the leather bag carried by Brun. Its provender gave us all a slender meal, and then it was done. Ros the Claw was brought out. I told her that she would walk, seeing she was so limber and lithe a lass, and that Hyr Brun would carry Vaxnik. She was amenable to this, having an affection for the boy.

No one knew a certain way out of the bog, and so we walked in as straight a line as we could contrive. We knocked over a few risslacas on the way, and Brun smashed in the head of one ugly monster with a single swipe of that giant sword. We kept alert for sounds of pursuit on the backtrail. We heard none and so got clean away. At last we emerged from the miasmic labyrinths of Trakon's niksuth and breathed in air that tasted like best Jholaix.

"However," said Targon, hitching his belt. "We are as like to be out of the frying pan and into the fire. All this country would as lief chop us as say a cheery Llahal."

"They would find us a prickly mouthful," I said.

That night we made a cheerless camp; but were able to catch up on our sleep. Our sentries reported all's well during the hours of darkness and by dawn we sat up, hungry and thirsty, and contemplated the labors of the day.

I do not propose to give a blow-by-blow account of the shifts we were forced to in the ensuing days. We headed south and we foraged for food and we picked up a few riding animals here and there; but of fliers we saw no sign. During this period I was obsessed with what was going on in Vondium, and cursing myself that I should have been so blind or foolhardy as to leave the center at this moment. That no other invasion armies had been reported now, in retrospect, appeared to me, tortured by guilt, to be totally irrelevant.

Dayra, quite naturally, would say nothing about her plans or the voves. I am a zorca and a vove man, each superb animal supreme in the tasks nature has intended for each. The vove—well, yes, there is the supreme riding animal of Paz, as I understood then. Powerfully built, large, with eight muscle-packed legs, the vove boasts both fangs and horns through his mingled ancestry, and a coat of a glorious russet color. He is exceptionally ferocious to those he does not know. And he will run and run until his heart bursts asunder, for his strength and his loyalty are well-matched; but his devotion is the stronger.

The obvious answer to the problem was an ugly one. Zankov must have gone to Segesthes, the large sprawling eastern continent of the Paz grouping, and there contracted an alliance at best, or a mercenary undertaking as the more probable, with clans hostile to the clans owing allegiance to me as their Zorcander and Vovedeer. Hap Loder, my old blade comrade and the man who stood in my stead with the clans of Felschraung and Longuelm and Viktrik—and any others he had taken over lately—had been with us to the Sacred Pool. He must have been pitchforked back to the Great Plains of Segesthes. Well, I could send a flier to him—when we got back to Vondium, Drig take it—but the logistical problems involved in shipping an army of the massive voves staggered. Phu-Si-Yantong could have done it. The galleons of Vallia could do it. The skyships of Hamal could do it. And, by the disgusting diseased entrails of Makki Grodno, so could the ships of the great enclave city of Zenicce.

That was the answer. And here was I, traipsing about like a loon in the backwoods of Vallia instead of being in Vondium.

It was enough to make a man swear off strong drink for life.

No, I will not go into that journey or into my state of mind.

The occasion is worth a mention when, during the night of storms when the wind blew streamers of screaming fury across the sky and the moons remained hidden so that the world became bathed in darkness like a night of Notor Zan, Hyr Brun, Vaxnik and Dayra escaped. They hardly escaped. They simply staggered off into the darkness, holding on to one another and with Brun like a massive anchor to hold them to the earth. They vanished within a couple of arms' lengths and we did not see them again, or for a very long time thereafter.

In order to bolster my failing sense of direction and to give some semblance of rationality to what I was doing, to counter the absolute loss and waste of my efforts with Dayra, I told myself that this journey had been worthwhile for the rescue of Thelda and my discovery of the misery in store for Seg and Thelda, and for Lol Polisto, too. So I told myself.

In the fullness of time we trailed into Vondium.

We had obtained vollers for the last part of the trip and when I vaulted out on the high landing platform of the palace and searched the faces of those who waited to greet us for just the one, and failed to see her, I felt another and more treacherous feeling of loss. I needed Delia near me now.

And then—well, I looked again at the faces of the crowd.

Glum. Drawn. Haggard. Cast down as though sent reeling by some ghastly catastrophe. Many of the women were mourning. A chill gripped me. And, of course, I already knew. But I did not know the full horror of what had befallen the pride of Vondium, capital of the Empire of Vallia.

Kyr Nath Nazabhan, a good comrade, a fine fighting man, commander of the Phalanx, Kapt, was so cast down in his pride that at first he would not look at me, merely cast himself down in the full incline, trembling, clad in black, contrite, ashamed, grief-stricken—and guilty.

"For the sweet sake of Opaz, Nath! Stand up straight and tell me. Openly and honestly, as we are comrades."

"Majister—majister—the army. My Phalanx..."

"Voves, was it?"

His gray-carved face looked up. "Majister? How could you know that?"

"You forget, the Emperor of Vallia has eyeballs everywhere."

Well, how can one remain unamused and not essay a feeble jest in the face of disaster?

So the story came out, brokenly, the grim, ugly, cold story.

I sat at my desk in that book-lined room with the maps and the weapons, and presently Nath was persuaded to sit across from me. He stabbed the map as he spoke. Lines, arrows, routes of penetration, ambush and surprise, and, at the end, the battle. News had reached Vondium that an army had at last been sighted, an army marching southwest from Vazkardrin on the east coast. I nodded. Vazkardrin lay between the coast and the Kwan Hills which demarcated the borders of Hawkwa country thereabouts. Zankov clearly had inserted his tendrils of power into the vadvarate of Vazkardrin, which had been run by canny old Vad Rhenchon, a numim, who had always kept himself unaligned in the struggles of power politics. Zankov had taken over with his cronies and his renegade Hawkwas and provided a secure base for the arrival of the clans carried in Zeniccean ships from Segesthes. It had to be.

Southward of Vazkardrin lay the imperial province of Jevuldrin. That was flat country, ideal, as Nath said, for the maneuvers of the Phalanx. It was also ideal cavalry country. And there is no cavalry in all of Paz, so I thought, to compare with vove chivalry. The only animal and human thing to stand against a vove charge was another vove charge...

"We shipped out," said Nath. Then he caught himself, and paled, and ground his fists together. "No, majister. I shipped them out. Me. I did it. Every sailing skyship we had. Every last one. We—I—took the First and Second Phalanxes, leaving the Third here. The churgur infantry, the axemen, the spearmen, three quarters of the cavalry of all kinds. And the artillery. We were a brave sight." He swallowed. "A brave sight."

"Yes."

"We landed and formed. And then came a storm, a monstrous storm. The sailing ships of the sky could not stand before it but had to run."

In the skirts of that storm Dayra and her friends had run, too...

"So," I said. "Farris could do nothing with his air?"

"Nothing. The army formed on the second day. Magnificent, magnificent. You should have seen them, majister—"

"I wish," I said, with a note of dryness in my voice I could not withhold. "I wish I had."

Nath understood and he bowed his head.

"We stood as we had been trained. The Phalanx resplendent in crimson and bronze. The paean was chanted and the songs sung. And we advanced. And they rode like an avalanche, like the wind, like the irresistible tides of the ocean. The voves..." For a space he could not go on.

Well, in Vallia they ride the nikvove, the half vove, and that is indeed a fine animal. But he does not have the fangs and the horns, does not have the sheer crushing battering bulk. A vove, it is half believed, could knock down a church steeple. I have ridden in many a vove charge, coursing knee to knee with my clansmen, charging headlong into the massed ranks of the enemy clan. Terrible, a whirlwind of destruction, the vove charge. I did not want to think what had happened to my Phalanxes. But I had to. I was responsible. Not Nath. I had warned him, oft and oft, against fighting unsupported against sword and shield men, the churgur infantry. But he had believed implicitly that the Phalanx could defeat any cavalry charge, any cavalry charge at all.

"There were many casualties?"

He could only nod.

"And the army?" I riffled out well-thumbed papers. "Here are the lists. Take up this pen and strike through the formations that no longer exist."

He did as he was bid. As the pen scratched with a vicious stab across the paper, time after time, I felt the cold clench around my heart. Most of the fine Army of Vondium had been swept away.

People talk of an army being decimated, not knowing what the word means, intending to imply wholesale destruction. We had been far worse than decimated. We had lost far more men than a mere one in ten. The units had been drastically thinned, the ranks devastated. That army had to be written off.

That campaign had been lost. This was not Jikaida. Those men had not been swept up in the cupped hand to be placed back in the velvet-lined box, to be brought out again all fresh for the next game. They were gone forever. They were dead.

"The Third is still here," I said. "With its Hakkodin and three regiments of archers and spearmen. There are two regiments of zorcamen, four of totrixmen and one of nikvove-men. Artillery is thin, but can cover." I looked at Nath. "This army of clansmen from Segesthes was not brought against us by that Opaz-forsaken Wizard of Loh. His ruse is still hanging. We still have him to contend with. This cramph Zankov—he brings the clans against us."

"Nothing has happened in the southwest. Fat Lango's army stagnates. The man you saw, Kov Colun Mogper of Mursham, has disappeared. Had he assumed the command—"

"Thank Opaz he did not. But, Nath, mayhap he has gone to command the real army from Yantong against us."

Nath spread his hands. "We are doomed, it seems."

"No." I rubbed my nose. "No. I do not think so. I remember a man called Filbarrka. He is a great zorca man, the Filbarrka na Filbarrka. He and I have talked about zorcas and voves and his theory is overripe for the testing." I stood up. "You and Farris, and everyone else, must rebuild the army. Work hard and work fast and work well. I am for the Blue Mountains."

"The Blue Mountains? But—"

"Yes. But I fancy Filbarrka has not taken kindly to a damned invasion from anyone. Build up the army. And stay close. If I am wanted, ask in the Blue Mountains."

Eighteen

We Gamble on Filbarrka's Zorcamen

Certain important tasks had to be completed before I could leave. I went to see Barty, who was up and pacing about, rotating his arm and bristling to get back into action. I told him to see about raising fresh regiments. We had lost a doleful number of good men; but there were others, and the spirit of the people, with that stoical and yet fierce Vallian integrity, rose to the crisis. New armies would be formed. He wanted to go off adventuring with me until I convinced him he was more valuable in Vondium. As to Dayra, I told him what had happened, and he blamed the storm again, this time not for wafting away an air fleet leading to the destruction of an army. I wondered. Perhaps I had secretly wanted my daughter to run off again. Perhaps I could not face the meeting between her mother and me and her... Had I wanted to keep her close I could have hobbled her feet and tied up Hyr Brun and Vaxnik.

Then, with a mere continuation of my feelings, I went to see Seg. He mended. That cheered me. Very soon, he told me, he would be back fighting fit. He, too, wanted to come with me. I told him, sternly, to get well first. I could not speak of Thelda. How could I? He did not know. The hateful thought occurred to me that perhaps Lol and Thelda were dead already. They had not flown to Vondium, and had no reason to, since they resisted the occupation of Falinur.

All of life during this period was a pickle. Delia was away, Seg's problems and Barty's problems weighed on me. Jilian cheered me up a little; but she was busy doing just what she had said she would, and I stole a half-bur to watch her Jikai Vuvushis at practice.

"By Vox, Jilian. They frighten me. Opaz knows what they will do to the enemy."

"Not a one of them has been through Lancival and so none wears the— wears the claw. But they come on apace." She looked ravishing, seductive in her black leathers. I thought of Dayra and I could not find a smile. She went on to talk of the disaster to the Army of Vondium, which had taken place near a little village called, ominously, Sicce's Gates, from the eons-old cracks in the earth nearby which led down so deeply into the crust of the planet none had ever ventured to the bottom. The Battle of Sicce's Gates would be recorded in agony and lamenting in the records of those times kept by Enevon Ob-Eye. I bid Jilian farewell and took myself off to the landing platform.

Farris, with a pinched look, had spared me a fast single-place airboat. My mission demanded urgency. I missed the fond preparations made by Delia on these occasions, and shifted for myself in the matter of provisions.

Be sure I took many wicker hampers. My armory remained as it had been, it had served me well so far.

Observing the fantamyrrh with care as I went aboard I called down the Remberees. Barty had come up to wish me all speed with Opaz. I had a hell of a game with Korero and the others. But the voller was a single-place job and that, it seemed to me, was that.

"I will send for you when the Lord Farris can place a sizable voller at our disposal. But the defense of Vondium is vital and our air fleet—well—" I did not go on.

That dratted storm had not only blown the sailing fliers away from Sicce's Gates, it had destroyed the majority of them. Farris was busily rebuilding. And we had cut down forests to build those ships...

It would be infantile and pompously stupid of me to suggest that my brief reappearance in Vondium had made a vastly impressive increase in the recuperation of the people from the debacle. But more than one old sweat had said that, by Vox, now I was back and safe they could get on with drilling the coys and look forward to knocking the daylights out of those zigging vovemen. Off on my travels again, I prayed that Farris and Nath and Barty and all the others—including Seg when he had recovered— would, indeed, recreate the Army of Vondium.

For much of the journey the River of Shining Spears paralleled my course. Once I had taken a roundabout way to the Blue Mountains, by way of Delphond, riding a hired zorca. I felt that Korf Aighos would have dealt very harshly with the invaders of Delia's country. Filbarrka ran the wide plains country at the foot of the Blue Mountains in the fork of the two rivers, and that country, I believed, was the best zorca country in Paz. Now I was going to put to the test the theories Filbarrka held. Despite all the long series of misfortunes, despite what had happened, despite my intense sensation of loneliness, despite the foreboding dread with which I viewed the future in spite of my brave words, I still experienced a profound excitement at what was proposed.

Vallia swirled past below and I ate roast vosk sandwiches and drank superb Kregen tea brewed on the little spirit stove packed within a sturm-wood box. I looked up. Yes, there he was, the Gdoinye, the giant raptor of the Star Lords. A beautiful scarlet and golden bird, glistening in the mingled rays of the Suns of Scorpio, he flew lazily above me, looking down with one beady eye from his sideways cocked head. The Star Lords wanted to know my doings. Well, I felt the uplifting sense that I was far more involved with what I was doing in the here and now, attempting to hold Vallia together, than in the machinations of the Everoinye, who could hurl me back to Earth, four hundred light years away, at a whim.

There appeared to be no sign of the white Savanti dove.

More out of habit than with a positive feeling of enmity, I shook my fist at the Gdoinye. He slanted a wing, and flew away. I went back to my food, and scooped a fistful of palines.

There was a squish pie in the hamper and I thought of Inch, and sighed, and so prepared to finish the long flight and bring the flier to earth. I did not anticipate too much trouble in finding Filbarrka. He would be leading the resistance and, I felt sure, the local people would be solidly on his side, the Vallian side, against the mercenaries and flutsmen and aragorn who had flooded in on the misery of Vallia. A few careful inquiries in out of the way places, and I would be directed to him. I just had to steer clear of the occupation forces.

These things worked out to plan and I caught up with Filbarrka as, big, bluff, red-faced, happily twitching his fingers together, he watched his zorcamen run rings around a hapless party of totrixmen. I landed the flier and walked across, aware of the bows bent against me. But Filbarrka recognized me and bellowed a cheerful greeting.

"Lahal, majister! I am glad to welcome you to the fun. See how the rasts run!"

The totrixmen were remorselessly cut down. I did not particularly relish the sight; but it had to be done if you concede that the freedom and happiness, not to say health, of a country matters more than the lives of its harsh invaders.

The amusing thing here was that Filbarrka did not seem in the least surprised to see me. He talked away, filled with his news, as we jogged along together. In a predominantly grass land I would have thought that guerilla tactics would prove particularly difficult; but Filbarrka would have none of that.

"We ride rings around 'em, majister! And there are the foothills of the Blue Mountains if things get tough."

My flier was stashed away in a wood and the locals would keep an eye on it. The country was pastureland, lush and lovely, well watered and wooded, and zorcas could live here as though grazing in a zorca heaven. I told Filbarrka that as I was the emperor now, and the Blue Mountains and this plains section of it called Filbarrka, the same name for man and country, was the empress's, he, Filbarrka na Filbarrka, was now an imperial Justicar and might style himself Nazab. He was pleased. But titles, I felt, meant little to him beside the thrill of simply riding a zorca.

I told him the problem.

He fired up at once. Eager, alive, filled with a fretting spirit, he tore into the problem.

"Voves. Ah, yes, voves..."

He had seen voves in action, having visited my clans in Segesthes at the invitation of Hap Loder. Now he began to talk in his quick, bubbling way, red-faced, twitching, full of cunning and guile and sound common sense.

"As San Blarnoi says," he observed, "preparation is improved by digestion. Ha! We have a snug little camp in a fold of the hills—pimples to a Blue Mountain Boy, to be sure—where we can eat and drink—and think. But the tactical situation vis-à-vis a zorca and a vove is fascinating, fascinating. And I have had thoughts, by Vox, yes!

"No clansman would dream of riding against voves with zorcas."

He did not say: "But they are only shaggy clansmen," as many a wight would have done in Vallia. For, was not I, Dray Prescot, taken for just such a shaggy graint of a clansman?

He did say with bluff politeness: "We do not have voves to go up against voves with, majister, as they do on the Great Plains."

"Discard all notions that I can magically produce an army of vove cavalry. The damned Hamalese burned most of the galleons. I'd hazard a guess that the shipping from Zenicce has been engaged to transport these voves we're up against. And our own sailing skyships were dispersed and smashed up by the storm at Sicce's Gates. We're on our own, Nazab Filbarrka. It is zorcas for us—"

"What could be better?" He rubbed his hands as we stepped away from the steeds where handlers were already leading them off, talking to them, cajoling them, for every Filbarrkian loves a zorca. We entered the camp area, tents under the trees in a fold in the hills. The weather remained bright; but I fancied it would rain before morning. The food was good, straight from a looted caravan. Filbarrka ate and drank as hugely as he talked. "The zorca is close-coupled, we know that. A good animal can turn on a copper ob. So we can run rings around voves—"

"They charge in an unbroken knee-to-knee mass."

"Naturally. They aim to crush anything in their way."

"They do."

"So, majister, we are not in the way."

I quaffed good Vallian wine and hid my smile.

The problem spread out for Filbarrka spurred him on as he would never spur on a zorca. I had my own ideas which I intended should meld in with his, so as to maintain the pleasant harmony. He shared my view that if an army was really serious about fighting to win and to stay alive, or as many swods as might be who would stay alive, the discipline must be instant and automatic. That demanded high-quality officers, and these, too, must instantly obey the orders of their generals. As to these latter, if Filbarrka himself was to be a Kapt, I fancied I'd take his recommendation on the others to be appointed. He drank his wine and then looked at me, his face large and happy in the lamplight.

"How long do I have, majister? And—numbers?"

"As to numbers, the reports I have indicate the clans brought over at least six divisions."

He nodded, for the calculation was easy. A division consisted of a thousand warriors. The clansmen stuck to the old ways of ranking, so that their Jiktars who commanded the divisions did, in fact, command a thousand.

"By their colors, weapons and harness, it seems, there is more than one clan involved. From what I have been told I have identified the Clan of Rudimwy. The others are unknown to me and must come from north and east of the parts I know."

"Six thousand vove-mounted cavalry, clansmen, renowned and feared." He brisked up. "Life is going to be interesting."

"As to time—yesterday. The army or armies that menace us from the southwest cannot be discounted. The lice that infest Vallia daily suck more blood. And Vondium's army is not yet rebuilt, not ready." A nasty thought occurred to me. "Anyway, it will be interesting to see who can train and provide their force first; the army in Vondium or you here."

That got to him. As I say—nasty.

He drank again and one of his lieutenants—a raffish bunch, these, liberally bedecked with the ritualistic trappings of zorcamen—leaned across and passed the opinion that any zorcaman of Filbarrka, of the Blue Mountains, which was the blessed Delia's province, could do what ten of those fat and callous-arsed citizens of Vondium could do, and in half the time, by Vox!

That made it my turn to hide my face in the wine cup.

Presently I asked about Korf Aighos of the Blue Mountain Boys.

Filbarrka roared out a belly-laugh.

"The old Korf! Why, he's strung up so many damned flutsmen he could build a hedge with them. No mercenary ventures into the Blue Mountains these days."

"Does he send men to assist you down here on the plain?"

"Aye, oh, aye. We strap everything down, then, and chain and padlock it all triple-tight."

Great reivers, the Blue Mountain Boys. Only sharing a common fealty to Delia prevented the Blue Mountain Boys and the Filbarrkians of the plains from being at each other's throats as once they had to their mutual loss and benefit.

"And the Black Mountains? Kov Inch—?"

"Not a word. The Black Mountains remain as impregnable to the invaders as the Blue. But they are hard-pressed by that rast up north of them, Kov Layco Jhansi."

"And east, too," I said. "In Falinur."

"And, over the river, the black and whites, may their eyeballs fall out."

"Amen," I said, companionably, and drank, and we chatted in this polite way a little longer.

At last, judging the moment ripe, I proposed to Nazab Filbarrka that the Blue Mountain Boys be invited to contribute a component of the zorca force he would form. They might be infantry, archers, axemen, to fight in the intervals—anything, in my view, just so long as I could get their ferocious fighting ability put to use in the coming struggle.

"And if we can get word to the Black Mountain Men, them too."

The threat posed by raids by the Racters over the border into the Black Mountains was serious; but the greater menace drew swiftly on us with those infernal Pypor-worshiping cramphs of clansmen and their voves from Segesthes. The Black Mountains must strip much of their own strength away, if we could reach them, to face Zankov. These are the hateful decisions emperors have to make every day before breakfast.

For a brief treacherous moment my thoughts dwelled on Drak and his fortunes in Faol among the Manhounds.

Filbarrka nodded in his enthusiastic fashion. "The great two-handed Sword of War of the Blue Mountains will serve excellently once I have broken up the main mass. I know they regained their pride in the weapon." He cocked an eye at me, a knowing eye. "There was this business of you and the shorgortz, majister, as I recall."

"Aye," I said. "And the Sword of War was blunt."

"Against the Racters and Jhansi, and now these vovemen, the great Swords of War will be sharp."

"By Zim-Zair!" I said. "Yes!"

Filbarrka began to expatiate on the methods and equipment he would use and need. "I am prejudiced toward comfort in the shape of a four-legged animal, and am convinced that in spite of apparent lessons to the contrary, zorca cavalry can successfully fight those mounted on heavier animals." He rubbed his fingers together, happily planning cunning tactics and stratagems. "Weapons will be a slender lance, twelve feet long, for a start, until we see how the men behave and the weapons serve. A number of lead-weighted and feathered throwing darts with broad barbed heads will be kept in a case at the saddle."

"And a striking weapon, Nazab?"

"From a nimble zorca curveting about against an oaf astride a lumbering vove? Oh, a mace. A heavy, flanged head mace. Hit the fellow anywhere with that, and one of the flanges will bite in and do his business for him."

"Very pretty. These weapons can be built for you in Vondium, together with such harness as you require."

"Excellent, excellent!"

"And you will leave sufficient forces here to contain the confounded mercenaries."

"I will. But it will be a task to choose who is to go and who to stay."

"That's why you are a Nazab."

"And you, majister, an emperor."

Just because of that it was possible for me to introduce the subject of shields. Some of Filbarrka's people emitted loud snorting noises of derision at this; but I noticed others who, sitting forward intently, marked what was said.

"Shields?" said Filbarrka. He entwined his fingers and bounced up and down on his seat. "Well, now... Yes. Yes, I have seen shields in action and, if we are to have them, I would favor a long triangular convex-section shield."

Well, argument ensued. In the end we agreed that the suggestions put forward by Filbarrka would be acted on to the best of our ability. The arsenals in Vondium had been instructed in the best way of manufacturing shields, and I guaranteed to supply the articles requested.

As for armor, Filbarrka wanted a light quilted knee and elbow length coat with a steel bar sewn to the outside of the sleeve, steel right forearm guard and shoulder plates. These latter, being the trademark of the Vondium soldier, fitted in perfectly. In all probability what the arsenals produced would be high-quality iron; but we tended to call it steel, as one does. Steel is usually reserved for weapons.

For helmets of the force, it was proposed that a small, round helmet rather like an acorn in shape, be fitted with a mail hood fastening up to the nasal. Mail was not easily come by in Vallia, as you know. The mail of the Eye of the World was effective but crudely heavy in comparison with the superb mesh of the Dawn Lands of Havilfar. The arsenals in Vondium could produce a mesh link that would serve. I had the sneaky suspicion that many a man of Filbarrka's zorca force would ride into action without this mail hood.

"And, in the rear ranks," said Filbarrka with anticipatory satisfaction, "we substitute bows for the lance and darts. The shields must be different, too. Smaller round parrying shields fastened to the lower arm. They should serve capitally."

So it was settled. Settled, that was, in conference. The hard slog of bringing theory into practice must begin now. One supreme advantage Filbarrka did have. He could call on the services of superb zorcamen. That gave him a flying start.

Although pressed to stay and see some more fun—they had a raid against a caravan, of whose route they had been apprised, planned for the next day—I expressed my regrets. Vondium and the raising of a great city to renewed effort called. Satisfied that the mercenaries and aragorn in this part of Vallia were paying dearly for their plunder, I bid the zorcamen of the plains of the Blue Mountains Remberee, and flew fast back to the capital city.

The news that met me, conveyed by Enevon Ob-Eye with an appearance of studied calm, was that Barty Vessler the Strom of Calimbrev, wounded though he was, had stolen an airboat and flown from Vondium in the devil of a hurry and the devil of a state. My chief stylor contrived to appear matter-of-fact, but he was enraged, amused, and downright admiring about the stir.

"Hardly stole, Enevon," said Seg, stretching his arms, as he kept doing to explore the pains in his mending back. "It was his to start with, you know."

"It is gone now, and the Lord Farris is shorter still of air for surveillance."

No message had been left. I could only assume that Barty could contain himself no longer and had gone to carry on the overdue talk with Dayra interrupted by the storm and their escape from us. I did not know how long it had been since he had last seen her. I'd wager a king's treasury against a copper ob that she was never the girl he remembered.

Nothing could be done about that situation. Every effort must be bent to building up the warlike capacity of the city. Seg said: "I have scoured around, Dray, in the taverns and dopa dens and stewpots. I've dug up three hundred men who claim to have been Bowmen of Loh. Some may never have been within a hundred dwaburs of Loh; but I have them sweating over their drills now, under command of Treg Tregutorio, a right old devil but a man with a bow, by Vox. You will find they will stand come the day."

"Good," I said, cheered in a way Seg could not hope to understand. "But, come the day, I shall need you to command the vanguard, as ever. I rely on you, you know."

"That is where Treg will want his men if I know him."

Despite his shortages, Farris kept up observations of the country and the day did come, sooner than we expected. Farris burst into my room without ceremony, looking wild-eyed, a most unusual state for him to be in.

"Majister! That cramph Kov Colun! He is found—aye, and an army with him. A great army of mercenaries from Pandahem and Hamal, marching from the south on Vondium. There is little time left."

So, with what we had, we marched.

We marched to the south.

The host of clansmen mounted on their terrible and terrifying voves pressed in on us from the north. If we were to be the nut in the nutcracker, then we would make sure we broke off one of the jaws, broke and splintered, and sent it shattered back before we turned—with what we had—to strike at the other.

In those dark days for Vondium and for Vallia there were few, and fewer with every day that passed, who believed any more that we would win through. But, still, we would fight. We would fight on, although doomed, fight on without surrendering. For that was the way of it, in those days. Surrender would bring our utter annihilation. Everyone knew that from bitter example. So we would fight on and if we were doomed, why, then, we would go down before Fate and put as brave a set of faces on it as we could muster.

That was the way of the new Vallians.

139

Nineteen

Surprises in the Delphondian Campaign

I had been wrong about Delphond.

Delphond, the Garden of Vallia, a sweet, languorous, easy-going place where the fruit hung heavy on the tree and the fat kine filled lush pasturelands, where men and women laughed easily and ate well and quaffed good Delphondian ale, where life flowed in smooth mellow rhythms and it was good to be alive and rest awhile—Delphond, Delphond—the sword and fire and destruction came to Delphond. And the good people arose in their wrath. Calling on the name of Delia of Delphond, they rose and smote the invaders.

Always I had considered the Delphondi would be too lazy, too good-natured, too easy-going, to resist, even though I had seen evidence of a new awareness and a growing suspicion during that time I had sought news of the mystery of the Black Feathers of the Great Chyyan.*

The distance from Vondium to Delphond is not great. That was the paramount reason why the invasion army under command of Kov Colun Mogper of Mursham had chosen to land there, on the south coast. He might have sailed his fleet up the wide mouth of the Great River; but then he would have faced crippling odds as all the small craft we could muster would have assailed him. He was confident, I'll give the cramph that. Straight across Delphond he marched, in a straight line, through the orchards and the cornfields, over the pastureland, and in his wake he left a broad swathe of destruction.

Also, he left many a man of his regiments hacked to pieces in a ditch where the enraged Delphondi had thrown him.

We marched southwest to get around that curve of the Great River, crossing the imperial province of Vond. We cut well south of the route of that earlier quick and improvised march against the mock army of Fat Lango. The comparative failure of that ruse had not deterred Kov Colun from setting forth on the balance of the ploy. If we did not stop him, he would be in Vondium, and Yantong would have won another round.

Although I had long ago come to the conclusion that bricks and mortar were not worth human lives, there were other considerations in the decision to defend Vondium. The arsenals being there constituted one obvious reason. But for that, by Zair, I'd have let Kov Colun and Zankov fight it out between them.

"By the Veiled Froyvil, my old dom," exclaimed Seg, reining up and shading his eyes. We looked up into the high blue of a Kregen day. "That looks a trifle likely."

---

* see *Secret Scorpio*

Up there, swirling away from the advance guard of our little army, black dots pirouetted across the blue. They appeared to frolic between puffball clouds; but we knew they were not of the frolicsome kind, being aerial cavalry of the army we challenged.

"Mirvols," I said. "So Colun has brought aerial forces with him."

"We've seen them off before, Dray! D'you mind the times in the Hostile Territories—and that scheming woman, Queen Lilah of Hiclantung?"

"Aye, I mind me, Seg. But we have no air to speak of."

"Your Djangs from Valka—"

"If they get here in time."

"Erthyr the Bow will see to it that they do."

Ahead of us stretched the open park-like landscape of Delphond. We had marched fast and light, having information from our spies that Colun tarried for his rearguard to come up. If all went as we planned, we would harass the invaders as far as we were able until we were all formed. That was a grim note—all. There were pitifully few of us left. And the new regiments were not ready.

Karidge's regiment of zorcamen—the First—went cantering past. Because Nath Karidge had caught a small punitive excursion mounted by Farris against a fortress of the aragorn over our borders, he had missed that fight at Sicce's Gates. At the time he had raved. Now he said that Opaz had saved him and the best zorca regiment in the army for greater things—for victory. I had agreed with him. His men were raging to get at the invaders and a deal of the gloom and doom so rampant elsewhere was missing in their ranks. Karidge's wife had recently had twins, and Seg made some remark as to his good fortune, and mentioned Thelda.

Again and again I had struggled with myself, quite unable to decide the best course. In all mercy I ought to tell Seg that Thelda was still alive. That would lead to questions. I could simply say that I had had a report that she had been seen, alive and well. I knew what that would mean. Instantly, Seg would be off hot foot on the trail. And I knew he dared not go with that wound in his back. Now the wound was almost healed, and the doctors of Vondium had expressed their amazement at his recuperative powers. Now, if I spun him some cock and bull story, he would have no reason not to go off. The plight of Vondium ought not to move him. It wouldn't me, if it had been Delia I was chasing. So...

Up until now I could with justice claim I had not told him Thelda was alive so as to save him from killing himself by searching for her with that damned great wound. Now that he was well again—could I in conscience keep the news from him? The half of the news? Sink me! I couldn't tell him about Lol Polisto. And yet, for him to discover the story in some hole-in-the-corner way would be even more frightful.

By the disgusting diseased tripes of Makki-Grodno!

And then a trumpet pealed sweet and silver, hurling notes through the air and sending birds scurrying from the nearby wood as though the notes took wing. A zorca rider burst up over the ridge and bore on toward us, riding hard and low in the saddle.

He was from the forward advance guard and so I knew one of our patrols had come in with news. We might have no aerial scouts; but we kept our patrols probing well ahead. He brought the news for which I had hoped, scarcely thinking such good fortune would fall our way. But Five-Handed Eos-Bakchi had smiled and his knuckle-bones had turned dexter.

"Ha!" said Seg when the rider had finished speaking. "We have the cramph now."

"We have the opportunity," I said, mildly. "We have but to execute the design."

"Execute! Aye, we'll execute Colun and all his villains."

Waiting for his rearguard to come up, Colun was separated from them by a good forty miles. If we could strike into the gap and turn on one force before they linked, we would stand a chance. The forces were ill-balanced. Which should it be?

"Hit Kov Colun," counseled Nath Nazabhan, sturdily. He had left his devoted Phalanx, being infantry, to be with us in the vanguard. Our vanguard was all cavalry or mounted infantry.

"His main body outnumbers us five to one, Nath."

"Maybe," said Seg, screwing up his eyes and with all the shrewd practicality of his race showing through the fey recklessness in him in these matters of operational policy. "Maybe it would be better to chop his tail off first. They are two to one. I'd say he was waiting for stores and equipment. Then he'll be isolated, and if your Phalanx gets here in time, Nath—"

"If? If!"

"Well—when. We will crush him sweetly, like a rotten gregarian."

I said: "I would like to hit Colun immediately. He has at least fifty thousand or so with him, with twenty thousand in the rearguard. We have almost four of cavalry and six of mounted infantry. And, in the rearguard, I fancy as Seg says, will be artillery, stores, battering equipment." I looked at these men with me, loyal, shrewd, experienced. "The rearguard it is!"

Nath sniffed and nodded. "Very well, by Vox. I am with you, majister. But when my Third come up—why, then we hit Colun—"

"We do, Nath. We hit him most severely."

The orders being given, the vanguard stirred into motion again, ten thousand jutmen riding in a jingling, turf-thumping stream of zorcas and totrixes and nikvoves. To the regiments left after the debacle at Sicce's Gates we had added a further regiment each of the three main saddle animals. Seg's Bowmen of Loh rode zorcas and acted as mounted infantry. They wore dark crimson uniform with light bronze-studded leathers and I had great hopes for them, a mere three hundred though they might be. So we rode on through the mingled streaming lights of Antares. As Jiktar Nath Karidge said, breathing hard with his beard all a-tufting: "By the Spurs of Lasal the Vakka, majister! We will tweak this rast's tail for him—aye, yank it out by the roots!"

He then went on to make some disparaging comments about our mounted infantry, typical jutman's talk, and he made great play with his pelisse as he spoke. Some of the mounted men riding in the group of messengers and aides-de-camp with him started to wrangle at this, and a merry little professional ding-dong ensued as we trotted along in the suns shine. We had twelve regiments of infantry mounted up on an amazing assortment of saddle animals, preysanys, hirvels, totrixes, marlques and urvivels among them. We also had, would you believe, a regiment of spearmen mounted on sleeths. Sleeths!

This last regiment had been formed by Tarek Roper Ferdin, a passionate sleeth-racer who still, to the despair of us zorca men, refused to concede the superiority of the zorca. The regiment, being a private one, was clad in a bright bottle green outfit with a quantity of bronze studding. But, troops as green as their uniforms though they were, I had inspected them and fancied they would stand firm on the day of the battle. They were representative of what Vondium had put forth, again, and if they failed then all might fail.

By a series of forced marches we covered the ground and, choosing our time and place well, were able to strike at Colun's rear guard just as they had begun preparations for pitching camp for the night. Give them their due, they were not like Fat Lango's apology for an army. They were tough and hardened. But, all the same, caught with tents half-erected and men out collecting firewood and fetching water and leading the animals to the picket lines, they folded. Pockets fought madly and well; but the cavalry swamped them and the infantry raced in with a whoop and dismounted and finished the job.

It was all over as the last of Zim and Genodras flushed ruby and emerald fires over the land, painting everything in an eerie sea of flame and verdigris.

There were many prisoners and the local Delphondi promised not to slay them all but to keep them penned until they might be ransomed or exchanged. We counted the cost and felt the satisfaction of relief from dire foreboding that our casualties were so few. We were still an army in being, and, into the bargain, an army crowned with success.

"Now," said Nath. "For the main body?"

"We must chivvy them a space, yet. Hit them here and run. Ambush there—and run. We run rings around them and no man will take shame that he runs. When we have them nicely molded to the certainty of their defeat—then we will deal with them."

Certain information reached me that this Kov Colun had been badly shaken by the defeat of a part of his army. He continued his advance; but he advanced cautiously instead of, as we all felt would be the wiser course, making an all-out effort to race through to the capital. His air component, mainly mirvols although he had some fluttrells, would prove uncomfortable in the day of the battle. During this period as we prepared his army for destruction they were chiefly an irritant. They scouted us with insolent ease and at times we were forced to pretty shifts to deceive them.

Seg's contingent of Bowmen set themselves the task of driving off the mirvols, and succeeded remarkably well at most times. But there were many pretty little skirmishes as Bowman and flyer clashed.

In the end Farris spared us a couple of small four-place airboats and these did sterling work. Colun's air was almost all flyer-mounted; of fliers he had a few he kept close and I, with a cynicism born of being an emperor, had no need to be told what those particular vollers were intended to do.

As each day passed and Colun struggled nearer and nearer Vondium, we chipped away at his forces. And, each day, messengers reached me with the latest news. Much of it concerned the preparations we made. The most ominous told me that the clansmen led by Zankov were now moving steadily down toward the city. As a defensible city, Vondium stood in much the same league as a holiday camp. The walls and fortresses had suffered so severely in the Time of Troubles that, as even Yantong had seen when he had been in control there, it would take many seasons to rebuild them. Mind you, by Zair, Vondium would be defended at the end. There was no doubt on that in anybody's mind. None whatsoever.

This discrepancy in the defensive power of the city between the time when we Vallian Freedom Fighters had taken it back, and now when we sought to defend it, lay in the nature of the forces involved. Now the attackers would be clansmen from the Great Plains of Segesthes. The very thought of them sent cold shivers down the backs of civilized men.

The determination to fight on to the end and, if it came to it, die well, carried the men on during this period. They just did not think too far ahead. When the day came to meet the clansmen in battle, well, they'd call on Opaz and go forward and fight. And when it was over and they lay in their windrows of death, what would it matter then?

Seg remained amazingly cheerful, fully occupied, a fiery spirit of defiance and resistance. I could guess at the hurt he thus hid, the agony in him, and still I could not allay that hurt or intensify it by a single word.

Every day the sense of pressure increased. We chivvied and chopped Kov Colun's army, and ran. The clansmen drew nearer the city. The recruits drilled and sweated in Vondium and the adjoining areas. The arsenals worked all day and night producing the new arms and armor we required. Each day twisted another circle in the spiral of the press that closed on us. But we soldiered on.

The progress of Colun's army slowed. It faltered to a stop, clustered about a bend in a tiny river, a mere stream, where once it would have boldly pushed on. Provender had been scarce for that invading army of late. We hemmed them in, and still they substantially outnumbered us.

Nath walked over to where I stood in the shade of a group of missals and his face bore a wide and beaming smile. Seg looked up, and said, "So your Third have come up, then, Nath?"

"Aye, Kov Seg. They have. And a magnificent sight they are, fined down, lean and hard. By Vox! Let me at this rast of a Colun and his cramphs."

The Third with the accompanying churgurs and spearmen and archers had had to march. You could account the Third Phalanx a veteran body, now, after their victory at Yervismot where, thanks be to Opaz, we had found Seg Segutorio again. But most of the infantry were green troops, churgurs and spearmen. As for the archers, Seg pulled a face, and took himself off to make a most careful and intolerant inspection.

Now that the chance for bringing Colun's invading army to battle had come, and the opportunity must be taken on the wing, I was plagued by all those old and hateful doubts. The idea of splendidly attired regiments hurling into the clamor and horror of battle is bad enough. But you must never forget that those bright blocks of moving color beneath the banners and the glitter of weapons are men. Living men. To hurl them into battle must, inevitably, mean that many will be dead men.

So, for the next few days as Colun sought to move his men away from the stream, we chipped away at him. Then, when he did move, it was a question of maneuver and counter-maneuver. The army appeared to have abandoned all ideas of marching on Vondium. They began to move south again, trying to keep in a single compact body and reaching strong places for each night. Patrols reported in regularly. I took a flier and went ahead and scouted the terrain most carefully, at last selecting a likely looking ridge bisecting the expected path of the enemy. The ground sloped just enough to make the Phalanx into a tiered and impregnable wall of steel. The level ground would give the cavalry a capital chance of putting in some real charges. With a heavy heart I gave my orders and the Army of Vondium moved out to secure the ridge and the surrounds.

Many deserters fled the ranks of Colun's army. They were mercenaries, and told us much of conditions; but they were astonished that we refused to hire them. We rounded them up and let the locals escort them to the coast and their ships. The invaders had swept up most of the occupying forces in their march, and, now that our tactics had dragged them to a standstill and then a reversal, the country was just about clean. Once we had disposed of these invading cramphs we could claim this southern section of Vallia back.

A Rapa veteran, his beaked face filled with outrage, was brought to my tent. My men stood looking on. This Rapa wore hard-worn harness, and his weapons were bright.

"You are the emperor?"

"Aye."

"I am told, majister, that you will not hire my men. We relinquished our allegiance to Kov Colun to join you. We are honorable men, paktuns, whose living is by the sword. Tell me, majister, why you do not hire us to fight for you?"

I told him. He either didn't understand or didn't want to understand. He could see that my new policy meant there would be no employment in Vallia for mercenaries in the future.

As he turned to leave, much cast down, he said: "Well majister, at least Colun will not be there to see the defeat of his army."

I quivered alert. I looked at the Rapa, and his vulture-face twitched and he went on quickly: "Kov Colun left the army by voller when we were encamped by that muddy little stream."

I sagged back, both elated and dejected. The army was doomed. Colun had seen that, despite its apparent strength. So, that meant—where had the rast gone to stir up more trouble?

The Rapa did not know. Diligent inquiries elicited no further information. Colun had flown away and left them to their destruction. The question now was: Would the new army commander, Kapt Hangreal, fight? Or would he agree to terms? You may imagine the tenterhooks we were dancing on as we awaited his reply to our message. The reply was short and brutal. Kapt Hangreal was confident that his army could whip us and make a clean escape to the coast. So, to my chagrin, we were committed to a fight.

That was the Battle of Irginian.

Kapt Hangreal completely misjudged the strength of the Phalanx, as the aragorn had done. Formed, compact, a solid mass of crimson and bronze, glittering with steel, the Third Phalanx took the foam-crested shocks of the cavalry charges. When Hangreal flung in his infantry our own churgurs swept in from the flanks. And, all the time, the deadly arrows crisscrossed. His aerial cavalry played a small part, until Seg's Bowmen rode up, dismounted, and shot them out of the sky as they tried to attack in flank. Well, it was a battle. It was not a particularly bad battle. Long before it could develop into a slogging match the Phalanx moved. Surrounded by clouds of churgurs and archers, the Phalanx charged.

The Battle of Irginian was over.

The local people, many of whom were sending their strongest sons to join the new armies of Vallia, cleared up. There was no time to waste. With a single day for recuperation the Army of Vondium started in motion, heading back for the capital. Forces of observation were left to ensure no flare-up occurred as the lines of prisoners marched for the coast. I left Seg and Nath in command and took voller and flew for Vondium. Now it was Zankov's turn. Now, perhaps, we would reach the beginning of the end.

Twenty

The Battle of Kochwold

Drak had not returned so far from Faol. Jaidur had not been released by the Sisters of the Rose from whatever deviltry they were egging him on to. And Zeg had not as yet responded to the call to leave Zandikar where he was king. As for the distaff side of the family, the babies, Velia, and Didi— the daughter of Gafard, the King's Striker, and our daughter Velia—were growing apace but not yet old enough to cause us the kind of pangs their elders were so good at. Lela, presumably with Jaidur, was off adventuring. And Dayra—ah, well! No word had come from Barty telling me how he fared in his renewed search for Dayra, and I fancied that Ros the Claw would lead him a merry dance, by Zair, yes!

And, as you will instantly perceive, Delia had not returned home.

I mumped about the city, and in between brooding over the unkind cuts of Fate got on with rebuilding the army.

There were a few burs to spare for lighter moments and Jilian proved a tough and cunning opponent at Jikaida. She had a most devilish way of cutting in from a flank when you were sure everything on that side was battened down tight. Also, of course, her person was such as to distract the most hardened old misogynist from the board and the marching ranks of model men.

"By Vox, Jak! As Dee-Sheon is my witness something addles your brains. You've let my left-flank Chuktar in—and, see—" and here Jilian did the most diabolical things to my model men. "Do you bare the throat?"

"Aye. Aye, I bare the throat."

We sat on a snug balcony bowered in moon-blooms and with a table handy loaded with silver flagons of wine. The night was cool and refreshing, and She of the Veils smiled down serenely, her fuzz of pink and golden light shedding a mellow roseate glow over the rooftops and battlements of the palace spread out below. Jilian yawned and covered her face with her hand, and then stretched.

"You had your girls hard at it today."

"And every day. But I wish I had been able to lay that cramph Colun by the heels."

"He'll turn up again," I said, comfortably. "That sort of villain always does. The only trouble is—"

"He'll turn up when it's most damned inconvenient, I know!"

Jilian wore one of Delia's loose lounging robes all of white sensil and she shimmered like an ivory flame in the moonlight. During the day she strode about among her girls and although she did not crack and snap her whip, she carried the ugly thing looped up around her arm.

The Enevon walked onto the balcony from the room beyond, rubbing his eyes, bringing fresh problems to be sorted out.

The exact spot at which we would like to meet Zankov and his wild clansmen had been chosen. If Opaz smiled, then the enemy would choose that route. In order to encourage Opaz to make up his mind I'd sent high-speed forces out to cut the bridges of alternative routes and to harass Zankov enough to make him swing, like a bull, to face the fancied threats. If he was prepared to follow the guidelines I had set for him, he would— Opaz willing—pass across the stretch of land known as the Kochwold. If he did, as we prayed, we would be waiting for him. And this waiting came as a vast and unexpected reprieve. Mind you, as a wild and hairy clansman myself I should have anticipated what was occurring up there in Jevuldrin. Clansmen are clansmen, accustomed to the airy sweeps of the Great Plains. When they ride through hamlets and villages, seeing the spires of cities rising before them, they feel all the itchy-fingered avarice of your true reiver. Plunder was retarding the onward march of Zankov's hired army. And, that very plunder was the hire money. I raged and fumed and could not, in all conscience, following the sad example of King Harold, allow the enemy to devastate the country. A policy of scorched earth would have served, perhaps; but the country up there was generally in the hands of that rast Ranjal Yasi, Stromich of Morcray, the twin brother to the strom, Rosil Yasi. Zankov was having either to fight or come to terms with his old ally.

So the Kochwold it was to be. Zankov was clearly aiming to march to the east around the mountains, known as the Mountains of Thirda to some folk, rather than the west of them. That way would force him to make too many river crossings. East about he would have fewer major rivers to bar him. Kochwold extended its sweep of moorland on the southern borders of Jevuldrin and the northern borders of Forli. The last I had heard of Lykon Crimahan, the Kov of Forli, was that he was fighting desperate guerilla actions, with the help of us Valkans as promised, and slowly, painfully slowly, regaining some of his province, the Blessed Forli. Now, all that was, if not irrelevant, then of far less importance than the rampaging invasion of ten thousand wild clansmen.

Oh, yes, ten thousand. A further four thousand had been disembarked. And, again, that explained the disembarkation point still further. The ships from Zenicce were engaged in ferrying men and voves across, and the passage between Zamra to the south and the islands below Vellin to the north afforded relatively sheltered waters. No doubt they were making a third trip even now. So that, starkly, was a most potent reason why our waiting, useful as it was, must be curtailed.

"Come on, Jak! For the sake of Vox's Arm! You look as though your zorca's run off and you've found a dead calsany."

"I was wishing Delia was here."

Jilian smiled. "So do I. From all I know of the empress she would have my girls trimmed up in no time at all."

"Oh, aye. Mind you, I don't think she ever went through Lancival. Although, everything is possible with that lady."

"Everything, Jak. Everything."

She spoke in so knowing a way that my old head snapped up. But Jilian just smiled her smile, her dark hair low over that broad white forehead, and her red mouth arched, so that I knew I was beaten. Jilian was not prepared to let me into her secrets—not just yet, anyway.

While we awaited certain news that Zankov and the clansmen had chosen the route we wanted, we labored hard and long. The army was built up again. The remnants of the force almost destroyed at Sicce's Gates had come in and formed cadres. Nath was fiercely determined on having three full phalanxes, and the veterans of the First and Second were slogging away teaching the newcomers to the files. The brumbytes worked willingly, with the triumphs of the Third to guide them.

Spearmen, archers and churgurs filled the regiments of the infantry, along with axemen and double-handed swordsmen and the rest. The cavalry was not, to their baffled fury, unduly expanded. But they worked hard, damned hard, and I concentrated strength on the armored nikvove regiments. This was obvious sense to anyone who knew what was going on in Filbarrka.

A message had been sent to Filbarrka telling him that instead of six there were now ten Divisions to be dealt with. His reply was typical. I could imagine him entangling his fingers and bouncing up and down as he dictated it to his stylor. "A better target for the dartmen and archers, majister! They'll be so confused, being so many, they won't know which way to run or what is hitting them."

Well, it was comforting to know someone was so confident.

Enevon sought assistance from the army in gathering the third mergem harvest and this was done. Mergem, a capital all-purpose foodstuff, would be vital in the campaigns.

Farris reported that the new ship construction proceeded well, although: "Ships!" He pulled his lip. "Mere rafts."

"Exactly, Farris. And functional."

The production of silver boxes which would lift the new ships was well advanced. So I had said we would simply construct huge raft-like structures, open-sided, railed in and five or six storied. Each one would be propelled by a rig of the utmost simplicity: foresail, mainsail and mizzen. With the silver boxes exerting their lifting power and extending their invisible keels into the lines of force, we could sail and tack and steer a course. When it rained, well, we'd get wet.

But, with these flying chicken-coops we could transport the army.

I may add that there were very few forests left for dwaburs around Vondium.

On three separate occasions I saw the gold and scarlet hunting bird of the Star Lords circling above me. I took no notice. If the Everoinye switched me away to some other part of Kregen now—or, horribly, banished me back to Earth—there would be a struggle and I might win or lose. As of now, as they say, the defense of Vondium and the uniting of all Vallia obsessed me. Every day we heard fresh stories of atrocities committed in those areas occupied by any of the various invaders. We all felt, unshakably, that we had to ensure that the new flag of Vallia floated over a free country.

Trite, chauvinistic, opportunistic—maybe. But it was not me, not Dray Prescot, not even Jak the Drang, who alone held this point of view. Nothing could have been done if the people were not every one fully dedicated and committed.

So, mentally committing the Gdoinye and its masters to the Ice Floes of Sicce, I stuck doggedly to the task at hand.

A regiment of my Valkans flying the superb flutduins eventually reached us, and they were greeted with roars of pleasure. Everyone regarded these splendid flyers with great affection and treated their riders right royally, a very different situation from even a few seasons ago when most Vallians regarded saddle flyers as birds of the devils of Cottmer's Caverns.

Came the day.

At last.

Zankov was reported as definitely taking the route that would lead through to the Kochwold.

Imagine a miles wide area smothered in men and animals all loading aboard vast and creaking five-story rafts, like a bedlam of the Ark in monstrous proportions. Dust, yelling, smells, the neighs and whinnyings of animals, the choleric bellows of Deldars, the snapping of whips, the creaking of wheels. And, over all, the forest of masts and yards. Well, somehow or other the mass was loaded and the ships—the flying chicken-coops—lifted into the air.

Wearing the blazing golden and scarlet Mask of Recognition specially made for me, I stood in the bows of a small voller and watched the departure. The ships rose and spread their wings. The wind zephyred them along. One by one, three by three, squadron by squadron, they took up their stations. Sailing orange boxes flying through thin air. Railed rafts loaded down with men and animals, with artillery and weapons, stores and fodder. They excited enormous sensations of disbelief, and wonder, and sheer jumping excitement.

This excitement thrilled through the air, leaping from man to man, bringing the color up, lending a sparkle to the eye, making every conversation bright and meaningful. Off they sailed, off to war, off to fight the

Kregen-renowned and ferocious clansmen of Segesthes—off to find their destinies.

When the voller landed back at the palace, for there was still work to be done before I could leave—always there was work—Jilian waited for me to wish me Remberee.

She looked stunning. Her black leathers clung to her, molding her figure, and her long legs seemed to go on and on for ever. She carried her bronze-mounted balass box under her left arm, and rapier and main-gauche were scabbarded to her narrow waist. Also, she carried a drexer at my wish. Her hair was covered by a helmet in which crimson feathers tufted bravely. She smiled.

"So it is Remberee, Jak the Drang."

"Aye, Jilian. Remberee."

Her voller was waiting. The mingled streaming lights of the Suns of Scorpio fell about us, drenching us and the landing platform in ruby and emerald fires. The air smelled sweet with that pungent, unique, glorious Kregen sweetness.

And then she surprised me. Still smiling she leaned forward and kissed me. I was stunned. She stepped back, observed the fantamyrrh of her voller and climbed aboard. She lifted her arm in final salute.

"Remberee, Jak. I do not forget what help you have given a poor girl from a Banje shop."

"You mean a wild tiger-girl, do you not? Remberee, Jilian the Claw."

The voller lifted away. I wondered if I would ever see her again.

Work—well, there is always work. The army was commanded by men whom you have met in my narrative, and others I have not so far mentioned. But all, I felt, were competent, brave and loyal. To be anything less in those dark days for Vallia was a species of crime. Nath had taken his three Phalanxes. Farris commanded the air. He would have nothing of remaining in Vondium to be the imperial Crebent-Justicar. The Presidio would run things in Vondium. If we failed, of course, there would be nothing for them to run, except—to run themselves. Seg stood by me and we would fly up together, he to command the vanguard as ever.

Most of my choice band had gone; but about fifty of them remained to escort Seg and me, enough to fill the voller we would use. And, in these last days I had discovered what their secret was. Many a time, when one or the other of them should have been off duty I had stumbled across them on duty at my door or the flap of my tent on campaign. Slowly I realized that after the assassins' attempts on me they had, privately, formed a kind of purely personal bodyguard. This was something I had never encouraged, for palace intrigues can breed in this kind of Praetorian Guard, this Imperial Guard, this Life Guard syndrome. But they insisted, and, to be truthful, I knew every one of them and fancied every one a true comrade.

They called this new bodyguard the Emperor's Sword Watch.

They all wore a yellow scarf tucked in around the corselet rim. Also, I noticed that their crimson trappings tended more to the scarlet...

Left in Vondium were a few regiments so new the armory grease still clung to their weapons and their uniforms were not marked by a spot, and a convalescent regiment of men recovering from sickness or wounds. All the rest flew northeast. We followed and I, at the least, had thoughts of Armageddon plaguing my mind.

The armada was blessed with favoring winds and we lost only two of the sailing chicken-coops, the vast rafts crashing in splinters but not harming the men in them. These last, I know, raved frantically and then set about repairing their ungainly craft. The rest of the army set down safely.

The details of the campaign need not be gone into at length, suffice it to say that by luck and planning we contrived that the army should be drawn up in proper array on the ridge we had chosen, with the Kochwold about us, in good time. Zankov's scouts had reported our presence. The enemy host drew in and concentrated. They possessed such sublime confidence in their own invulnerability that we anticipated a wild and reckless clansman's charge which, they supposed, would settle the issue once and for all.

Filbarrka, brought by a flying collection of rafts and chicken-coops, landed his zorcamen. At once I rode out to inspect them. I rode Snowy, that coal-black zorca, and I was dressed in my usual fashion. The brave old scarlet glowed under the suns. I carried a longbow, a quiver of arrows fletched with the rose-red feathers of the zim-korf of Valka, a Krozair longsword, a drexer and a rapier and main-gauche. Also, strapped to the saddle swung an axe. Not overdressed, not carrying a ridiculous over amount of weaponry, I fancied. This was the Kregen way. Not as many weapons as a man can carry—no. As may weapons as are needed for the job in hand—yes. That is the Kregen way.

Accompanied by aides-de-camp and escorted by the chiefs of the Emperor's Sword Watch, we cantered out to the place where Filbarrka, radiant, immense in armor, had drawn up his brand new zorca force for inspection.

And, indeed, they looked splendid.

"Let 'em bring on their ten thousand," said Filbarrka, twitching his fingers. "We'll dart 'em and feather 'em and then you lot can have a go."

Our sailing rafts had taken the equipment asked for out to the Blue Mountains and so the zorca force was accoutered as I expected and as Filbarrka had suggested. Also, a contingent of the Blue Mountain Boys was present, extraordinarily ferocious and many of them armed with the great Sword of War. Korf Aighos was there and I greeted him as an old friend and kept a wary eye on my own equipment.

"Although," said the Korf. "What is going on in the Blue Mountains now I do not like to think."

"Why, Korf! I'm surprised anything remains for anyone to want to take away."

"You would, majister, be surprised. And we have some Black Mountain Men with us, although not many. They are hard pressed up north."

"All in good time."

He did not mention Delia and so I knew she had not been to her province of the Blue Mountains. She hadn't been in Delphond, either. I remember I said to myself something like where the hell can the pesky woman be? and immediately felt aghast at the thought. What the Sisters of the Rose got up to would make even Korf Aighos scratch his head.

The ground over which the coming battle would be fought was surveyed again most thoroughly. Hundreds of lads were out spreading their caltrops, and the chevaux-de-frise were stacked ready and waiting to be run out onto the flanks as required. That night the sky glowed with the reflections of campfires.

As a general rule I do not believe in Councils of War and I saw no need to make an exception now. We gathered, the Kapts and the chiefs, and there was little talk of what to do on the morrow. Every one knew his task. So we drank in moderation and cracked a few silly jokes and sang and then sought our beds. If they slept I did not inquire. I made the rounds of the campfires and was aware of the hovering shadows of the men of the Sword Watch. One of the songs that was currently popular kept breaking out from this group or that clustered about their fire. "She lived by the Lily Canal" the song was, a sickly sentimental ditty of very little musical worth; but somehow it got to the men, and they warbled it over and over, almost obsessively. Yes, I can never hear that old song now without a powerful pang of remembrance of that night before the Battle of Kochwold, among the campfires of the army, the sizzle of the flames, the smells of animals and dust, the tang of leather and sweat and oil. Well, a battle is a battle, as I have said, and they are all the same and all different—as I have said...

Well before dawn the host was astir and breakfasting mightily. Then we moved forward from the camp area and took up our battle positions. Patrols reported that the clansmen were doing exactly as we anticipated and were moving forward for the confrontation that daylight would bring. Nothing would stop them from putting spurs in and charging. It was our job to stop that charge.

Perhaps one day a full and detailed account of the Battle of Kochwold will be given to you by me, for it was a fascinating battle and deserves commemoration. Enevon committed all the salient facts to paper; but it needs a military historian to sort them out and make sense of them. Very many fine poems were written and there are countless songs marking this or that incident. At the time and to most of us engaged, it was a huge sprawling untidy mess.

153

And, to be sure, the message I received half way through did not make understanding any easier. The initial stages went as we had planned—almost.

The sprawling untidy mess occurred, as in many fights, after the initial movements of each side, being completed, had achieved or failed to achieve their objectives. Our first requirement was to stop that charge. That objective had been required by many a fighting host before us, and most of them were long a-moldering.

But the clansmen of the Great Plains of Segesthes, among whom I am proud to be numbered as a member, although not in my own eyes skilled enough to be dubbed a Clanner, are not your stupid brainless illiterate barbarians. They are not like the Iron Riders, the radvakkas whom the Phalanx had so signally overthrown.

"By Vox!" said Seg, at my side just before he left to take over his position with the vanguard. "The cramphs!"

"Aye, Seg," I said. "Clansmen are clansmen. It will be a bonny fight."

For the tremendous dark mass of the vove cavalry halted, a plains-filling concentration of men and animals, silent, awe-inspiring, totally menacing in their appearance. And forward trotted the archers. These were men who were the occupiers of the land hereabouts, Ranjal Yasi's men, and so I knew the Kataki Stromich had come to terms with his old friend Zankov. Perhaps the sight and sound and stink of ten thousand clansmen and their voves had had a deal to do with that...

Also, of course, in these nation-wide struggles for power, the double-dealing would always go on. No doubt Phu-Si-Yantong kept a close observation on what went on and had advised his lieutenant, Ranjal Yasi, to appear to acquiesce in the rebellious plans of Zankov, who had been disowned by the Wizard of Loh. That, at least, would be in keeping with the character of the participants.

Whatever accommodations had been reached, in addition to the ten divisions of vovemen we faced a host of other cavalry and infantry. They were mercenaries, hired by Yasi to keep the country in subjection, and they had been earning their hire. We men of Vallia vowed to make them rue their wages this day of battle.

"Better clear them away with your cavalry, Seg. But I shall keep the nikvove regiments under my hand for a space."

"Yes, my old dom, and make damned sure they nip in quick when they're needed. By the Veiled Froyvil! I really think this is going to be a battle that will be remembered to the end of time." He walked with me toward the four-place voller he required as a commander and which he would quit for a zorca or nikvove when he reached his battle line. "This is going to be a big one, Dray!"

"Aye. Would to Zair it was not necessary."

In the voller waited his pilot, his trumpeter and his standard bearer, all old friends to whom I spoke a few words. Then Seg Segutorio took off, flying forward into battle. Would I ever clap eyes on my blade comrade again? That kind of thought always occurs to me, always tortures me, and is always a stupid nonsense. When Zair crooks his finger, then up you go, my friend, and nothing will detain you on Kregen...

It was time for me to perform what later generations would call the Public Relations Stunt. Mind you, I do not denigrate the value of thus showing myself, as the commander, and the flags. Mounted on as large a nikvove as we could find, a superb charger called Balassmane, and clad in a brilliant golden armor, emblazoned with scarlet, I rode along the forward face of the army. The blazing Mask of Recognition glittered in the light of the Suns of Scorpio. Scarlet feathers fluttered. I lifted the drexer high in salute.

Following me trotted Cleitar the Standard bearing the flag with the yellow cross on the scarlet field, Old Superb. With him rode Ortyg the Tresh proudly lifting the new red and yellow flag of Vallia. Volodu the Lungs rode to hand and his silver trumpet, much dented, gleamed like a leaping salmon. At my back and on the side nearest the enemy rode Korero the Shield. It would take a very great deal to shift him from that devoted position. Others of my Sword Watch trotted in that imperial cavalcade, glittering with light, colorful with uniforms, proud, eager, nerved to the occasion, men you have met in this my narrative, men I am proud to call comrades.

As we passed down the lines the roar of approbation swelled and the men in the ranks lifted their weapons, a swirling forest of blades, and cheered. The answering shouts from our foes drifted in, thin and attenuated. But, then, all our bellowing would reach them as a mere whisper beside their own war chants.

"By Aduim's Belly!" said Dorgo the Clis.

"I never thought to see a day like this," said Targon the Tapster.

"Nor me," said Naghan ti Lodkwara.

Their words were lost and blown away in the swelling cheers from the army.

By the time that morale-boosting and flag identification exercise was over and we had returned to our positions, the first clashes had taken place. The archers had been sent forward by Zankov to prepare our mass. He must, then, have a great deal of control over the unruly clansmen. But Seg would have none of that and he would not sit on his hands when there was shooting in the wind. His advance guard cavalry swept out, screeching, long lines of glittering figures bounding over the moorland. They tumbled the enemy archers over and Seg's mounted Bowmen roared forward. He had so few Bowmen of Loh to hand that he reserved them for the special occasion, the point d'appui. But the compound reflex bows of our men spat. The range to the enormous mass of clansmen was far too far; but the confused fighting between the two ranked armies slowly sorted itself out, and then the recalls were blown and our men, triumphant, rode back.

Of course, the discomfiture of that ploy of Zankov's would merely make the grim Chuktars of the clansmen say in their savage way that he should not have bothered with all this fancy strategy and tactics. Let the clansmen charge. That would be the end of it.

Our position on that little ridge must have worried Zankov. I had not formed any great opinion of his qualities as a military captain; but something must have alarmed him at the sight of those massed ranks and files of men, silent and motionless in their crimson and bronze. Perhaps he had heard of the fate of the radvakkas against the Phalanx.

Looking about, I'll admit I missed the warm and eager presence of Barty Vessler. Nath Nazabhan cantered over and instantly wanted me to order the advance. I looked at him and he said: "Well, majister, by Vox!"

"Once Filbarrka has been at work for a space, then you may advance, Nath. But you will not move until you have my personal word. Is that clear?"

"It is clear and it makes sense, as we planned. But it is damned hard standing still with a pike in your fist at a time like this."

"Agreed. You saw their bowmen?"

He ducked his head, eager, alive, vehement. "I did. I may have spoken harsh words against the Kov of Falinur in the past, when I did not know him. No one could have cleared our front as well as he has just done."

That, I may say, pleased me enormously.

The clansmen with the failure of their missile men were not as foolish as the knights at Crecy. There was no Comte d'Alençon in their ranks to bay out: "Kill me this rabble! Kill! Kill!" and go spurring down on his mercenary allies. They waited calmly for the outcome of this first encounter and when it went against them they waited for the ground to clear. Again, that made sense, for even a vove in the midst of a charge may stumble over a wounded man or a wounded and terrified zorca or totrix. So we watched them and the ranks held and the suns crawled across the sky and I knew Filbarrka was bringing his torrent of zorcamen up on flanks and rear.

Whether the clansmen charged before or after he hit them, I knew, made little difference to Filbarrka. Except that if they attempted to charge afterwards their onslaught would be a little dinted...

For myself, I would prefer the vove charge to begin and then for Filbarrka to hit them, as they rode bunched, knee to knee.

A certain amount of aerial activity took place. Our flutduin regiment had done splendid work in scouting; but there were too few of them to affect in any greatly material way the outcome of the main battle. But, at least, it was better they fought for us than against us. I saw them swooping down and shooting into the ranks of the vovemen, and presently a mirvol-mounted force of aerial cavalry flew up and tried to chase them off. The aerial evolutions were pretty to watch. But my Valkan flutduinim had been well-trained by Djangs who are past-masters at the art of aerial combat, and they both held off the mirvols and continued to attack the army below.

Those mirvols—they wore gaudy trappings and their riders no less gaudy uniforms. Uniforms, I fancied, I had last seen in Fat Lango's army.

Abruptly, Nath rapped out an oath. "I am for the Phalanx, majister. They move! See! The clansmen move!"

And, indeed, the front ranks of the vovemen were in motion, leading out, beginning to stretch forward into the charge.

So—the moment everyone waited for, hoped for and dreaded, had at last arrived.

"Stand like a rock, Nath!" I bellowed after him, and he half-turned in the saddle and flung up his hand in parting salute.

I could tell to the mur when Nath arrived with the three Phalanxes. From every Jodhri the battle flags unfurled and broke free, thirty-six Old Superbs, to add a special luster to the display of heraldry and defiance flaunting in the breeze.

Cleitar the Standard grunted and shook his own flag, Old Superb, making it ripple and glisten.

"It is a right they have earned, Cleitar."

"Aye, majister. And, anyway, the Jodhri banners are smaller than your own personal standard. As they should be."

And I had to smile.

Where one caltrop will bring a four-legged animal crashing to the ground, a vove with his eight legs will carry on until he is a veritable pincushion with the vile things tangling him. I do not like caltrops or chevaux-de-frise as a cavalryman; as an infantryman they are gifts from the gods. The vovemen moved. They advanced. Their banners fluttered. Their pace increased. Like the irresistible ocean, like the Tides of Kregen themselves, like—like a charge of vovemen!—like nothing else in Creation, they charged.

The drumming hoofbeats battered the ground. The ground shook. The onward surge consumed the senses. On trampled the vovemen. On thundered the sea of steel. Forward they came. Six thousand in that first charge. Six thousand monstrous beasts. Six thousand ferocious warriors. On they rode, onward, ever onward, cantering into a gallop, racing full stretch, pouring resistlessly on, on, roaring down on the grim compact masses of the Phalanx.

How they rode! How they rode, those wild shaggy clansmen of the Great Plains!

Timing their attack to coincide with that great charge, the enemy's vollers crested forward above that sea of tossing heads and flaring pelts, of horns and fangs, of clansmen gone wild. But our own airboats rose, reserved for this stratagem, and soared up and forward to tangle in a wild melee above the onrush below.

And now the clansmen shrilled their warcries. Onward they rushed.

Onward, a torrent of monstrous beasts and savage men, onward in a tempest of steel.

Silent, motionless, solid, the Phalanx awaited the shock.

By Zim-Zair! I admit to it. The fire scorched into my blood. I have ridden in many a vove charge and thrilled to the mad onward rush when all the world blurs into a flowing frieze of color. When you know nothing and no one can stand before you and live. The sheer bulk of the vove beneath you, the solidity of him, the square impact of his eight hooves beating the ground in unison, the smooth flowing onward rush, the steadiness of the lance couched and pointed, its steel head sharp and glittering, bearing on, bearing on!

These vovemen had shattered and destroyed two Phalanxes already. We had rebuilt, and there was the Third. But, but... Oh, yes, by Vox, I sweated apprehension, tension—and fear.

Six thousand in that first wild charge. And the other four thousand? The spyglass confirmed it. They were circling out on the flanks, two Divisions each, like horns, like pincers, raking forward to encircle and crush us.

But a stir was visible in that onrushing riding horde on either flank. The vovemen were in disorder there. And, at the rear of the great main charge a further disturbance attracted the attention of my men.

Filbarrka was in action.

His zorcamen, light-armored, swift, deadly like wasps, darted in and out, maddening, pirouetting, curvetting, slaying. In orderly groups they fought with intelligence and cunning and high courage. Their archery shot coolly and methodically. Their dartmen raced in, flung their barbed weapons, and withdrew. The darts were poor at penetrating armor; but against unarmored parts of men and animals were highly effective and unpleasant. They penetrated deeply and were hard to remove. They caused constant pain as they flopped about in the convulsive movement of the voves, maddening the animals and causing them to disorder the formations still further.

The long slender twelve-foot lance was employed against man or animal. Then the mace—the vicious, heavy-headed mace, unerring—crunched with bone-smashing power. The zorcamen were nearer the ground than the vovemen. Many a clansman felt that stunning smash against his thigh or pelvis, toppling, his armory of weaponry flailing the air over the aggressive zorcaman, falling, being hit again as he fell. Oh, yes, Filbarrka's Lancers and Filbarrka's Archers wreaked enormous havoc and confusion as the vove charge poured across the plain and narrowed the gap.

And that gap itself proved a deadly obstacle to the voves. Liberally we had strewn the ground with caltrops and chevaux-de-frise, with narrow, wedge-shaped ditches. Many voves pitched to the ground, all their eight legs unable to cope with the obstacles. And our own dustrectium flayed them. Shaft after shaft sailed across the narrowing gap. Our archers shot well on that day, thanks be to Opaz. The steel-tipped birds of war thinned the onrushing mass. But still they came on, upborne with pride, with knowledge of their own invincibility, and, by Krun, my heart rode with them, for they were clansmen.

Following them rode the mass of totrix and zorca cavalry put into the field by Zankov and Stromich Ranjal. Their infantry waited in dense masses for the outcome. But the charge, the charge of the voves—that was the battle winner!

Watching, lifting in my stirrups, I saw the way the leading masses roared up the first of the slope to the ridge. Would nothing stop them? On and on they raged, beating on and up, and the pikes all came down as one, and the trumpets pealed, and the crimson and bronze stretched out, taut and thin to my eye, firm and like a rock in a raging sea.

The three Phalanxes had been arranged with the First on the right of the line and the Second on their left and half of the Third, the Fifth Kerchuri, on the left of the line. The Sixth Kerchuri stood fast in reserve to the rear. All the emotion of two worlds concentrated down for me in that impact. I was aware of the flanks surging on and of churgur infantry and spearmen clashing on the wings. I was aware of the ceaseless flights of arrows. I was aware of the cavalry fights taking place all over the plain. But the impact, nearer and nearer, took my attention and I could not tear my eyes away from that enormous collision.

Irresistible and immovable objects? No, by Krun, not quite. For the Phalanx had been bested before by the clansmen, and the clansmen knew nothing of defeat. The impact, when it came, racketed such noise, such clamor, such soul-searing horror, that I felt the salt taste of blood on my lips.

That was where I should be, down there, in the front rank of the files with the faxuls, down there, wielding my pike against that onrushing host. And I sat my nikvove and watched and could only judge the time to send forward the Sixth Kerchuri and order in the churgurs and the spearmen. The Hakkodin were slashing and slicing away, the front swayed, locked, striking in insane fury. Incredible, the ferocity of the charge and sublime, insane, the solidity it met.

The Second swayed.

The Second Phalanx swayed and its front crumbled.

I saw the yellow and red flags go down.

Voves began to pour through a narrow gap that rapidly widened. At my instant order Volodu blew Sixth Kerchuri; but Nath was before me and I saw the Sixth moving up, solid and dense in their masses, the crimson and bronze shouldering forward to plug the gap. The Second recovered. The officers down there were raging and bellowing and the files reformed and the pikes came down again, all in line. But the lines were thinner, now.

The confusion down there tantalized me. The voves recoiled and came on again. The Phalanx held. I saw the rear markers going up, the Bratchlins urging the men on. I saw the swaying movement as though the very sea itself sought to pour on and over a line of rocks. And the zorcamen were in among the voves now, prancing around on their nimble steeds, striking and sliding return blows. The state of flux might continue, or it might break on an instant.

Zankov flung his infantry in, before they had time to decide if the day was lost or won, hurling them on intemperately to support the charge, to get in among the Phalanx. Our own infantry moved to mask the flanks, channeling the attack onto the melee. The Hakkodin now had fresh targets for their axes and halberds and two-handed swords.

This was the crucial moment.

Even when he fights in the melee a clansman is an opponent greatly to be feared. Even when he does not hurl forward in the charge, he is a fighting man of enormous power. The slogging match had begun.

At that instant a troop of zorca riders flew up the long slope to my left side, riding hard, and I saw they were girls, Jikai Vuvushis.

Some of the Emperor's Sword Watch angled out to halt them; but I saw the leader, drooping in the saddle, saw the arrow in her shoulder.

"Let her through!" I bellowed.

Jilian hauled her lathered zorca up before me. Her pale face was so white I fancied she had no blood left at all, and knew that was not so, as the blood stained around the ugly shaft in her shoulder. She tried to smile and the pain gripped her.

"I am sorry to see you in such case, Jilian." I spoke with anger. "I had thought you in the reserve where—"

"Where you ordered my girls, aye, Jak, I know. But I have had another zhantil to saddle. My regiment is in the reserve and will go forward with the victory." She swayed and I leaned down from the nikvove and got a hand under her armpit. "But there is no time. You must fly—" Her gaze flicked to the reserve troop of flutduins who waited beside Karidge's Brigade, in the reserve, under my hand. Her girls were there, brilliant and chattering, and every eye fixed on that titanic fight going on along the face of the ridge. I looked there, alert for any change; but the slogging match continued and the Phalanx had not moved and the clansmen had not retired. Men were dying down there, dying by the hundred.

"The empress..." Jilian swayed and I was off the nikvove and hauled her off her zorca, and held her, looking down, and my face must have appeared like a chunk of granite.

"What of the empress?"

Jilian caught her breath. And I saw she bore an axe wound in her side, gashing and horrible, exposing pink and white ribs.

"That is nothing, Jak. The empress needs assistance—the Sakkora Stones—"

"I know it." I placed her down, gently, for she was a great spirit, and bellowed at my company of brilliant aides. "Send to Seg Segutorio, the Kov of Falinur, commanding the vaward. My compliments. He is now commanding the army." I was running toward the flutduins as I shouted, and each one of the great birds ruffled his feathers, as though asking me to pick him. "Tell the Kov to send in the reserve the moment the line wavers. Not before, not afterwards. He will know."

Then I was hauling the flutduin Jiktar off his bird and mounting up, disdaining the straps of the clerketer. Everyone was yelling. Shouts of consternation broke from the Emperor's Sword Watch. The flutduin troop gaped. I cracked the bird and he rose at once, his wings wide and gorgeous and of immense power. Together we rose into the air.

Below us a tremendous battle raged. Thousands of men were locked in hand-to-hand combat. I barely saw the red horror of it, barely heard the screeching din.

Over the clangor, over the blood, over the agony and death below I flew. I left the battle in the culminating moments of victory and defeat. Headlong, caring for one person and one person only in all of Kregen, I flew like a maniac across the gory battlefield of Kochwold.

Delia...

Twenty-one

A Life for Vallia

Desertion. Infamous conduct. Lack of moral fiber in the face of the enemy. Lack of judgment of issues. Nothing of that mattered. Vallia did not matter, nor Kregen itself.

Only Delia mattered.

I knew the Sakkora Stones.

Like the Kharoi Stones of my island of Hyr Khor in distant Djanduin, it had been raised by the Sunset People who had lived on Kregen before the Star Lords had brought diffs to that beautiful planet to make it the wild and terrible world it is today. Ruined, tumbled into moldering stones, mysterious, unforgettable, the buildings of the Sunset People yet lived in legend and song.

Over the battlefield I flew and mirvols attacked me and I shot and slew them and their riders, and with the long whippy aerial sword strapped to the saddle fought off those who would have stopped me. In a straight line across the front I flew. The Sakkora Stones had been figured into our calculations in picking this site for the battle, and had been reckoned as not having any influence, one way or the other. They stood some ulm or so in rear of the position taken up by Zankov and we expected them to be used as a field hospital or supply dump. They lifted from the moorland, quite plainly, fallen columns, walls and roofs marking a once-vast star-shaped structure whose function remained obscure. As on Earth today, an archaeologist, faced with an artifact whose manner of use he does not know, will say it is a cult object or a ritual object, so we said the Sakkora Stones were a cult object.

Over the rear echelons of Zankov's army I flew and alighted in the grove of drooping trees gaining nourishment from some underground stream in this desolate moorland country. The flutduin immediately lifted off with a massive beat of his pinions and a wicked toss of his head. Magnificent saddle birds, flutduins. He was off back to his master.

I looked about, sternly and yet filled with terror. What in blue blazes Delia had been up to, how Jilian was involved, I did not know. But, by Vox, I would find out!

All the detritus, human, animal and material, in rear of a great army in conflict, lay scattered about. The trees afforded a slight amount of cover and men and animals moved to and fro, with a steady stream of wounded coming back. A party of spearmen, second-line troops no doubt assigned to guard the baggage train, approached the wood to question me. It were better—and more decent—not to relate what happened to them. I did not deign to don one of their uniforms as a disguise. I ran toward the nearest abutment of the Stones.

Anything could be happening in there. Jilian had been in no case to be specific. If she did not die I would be in her debt—if Delia lived. Whether or not I lived seemed to me of scant importance then, which is a strange attitude for me, Dray Prescot, to take, by Zair!

As I ran on with the blood thumping around my body it felt as though that very blood fought against constrictions in my veins. I'd been living very high and mighty, just lately, very high on the vosk, and, now...! This was more like the old Dray Prescot, rushing headlong into danger with a naked sword in his fist. Rushing, like the veritable onker I am, headlong into danger that forethought would avoid. But, then, that is me, Dray Prescot, prince of onkers.

The clansmen started up from their fire on which grilling ponsho

162

smelled sweet. There were four of them and they were not skulkers, each being wounded. They saw my scarlet and gold flummery of dress and they did not hesitate. Out whipped their broadswords and they charged.

Well, it was a merry little ding-dong; but I was frantic with worry and in no mood for a long exchange of handstrokes. The drexer snapped back into the scabbard. The next instant the Krozair longsword flamed. They were skilled clansmen, enormously powerful warriors; but they were not fighting for the life of Delia of Delphond, Delia of the Blue Mountains.

As the last of them sank down, he gasped out: "You fight like a clansman, Vallian."

"Believe it, Clanner," I said, hurdling him and rushing on into the gloom of the stones. "By the Black Chunkrah, believe it!"

Something caught in his eyes as he died.

Headstrong, headlong, and utterly foolish, Dray Prescot. I should have paused to snatch up a clansman's russets and cover my insolent scarlet and gold. But there was no time, no time... Through the gloomy aisles of the leaning columns I raced. And I began to catch a glimpse of the truth. This place had been used as a headquarters. That would have made no difference to us. And what had been wrought here had been wrought with cunning and stealth and high courage. Running on I passed dead clansmen, dead mercenaries of various races of diffs. And, also, I passed dead bodies of Jikai Vuvushis, Battle Maidens. They looked pitiful and twisted in their fighting leathers of russet or black. And on their supple bodies, so lax and ghastly now in the final sleep, the badges of the Sisters of the Rose glowed in mockery.

This was the kind of operation I, the stupid, proud, so inordinately presumptuous Emperor of Vallia, should have mounted. I had not. I had staked all on the impregnability of the Phalanx, the prowess of the warriors of the army and the new Filbarrka zorcamen. I prowled on, understanding what had passed here, and knowing that I would find the answers I sought when I came at last to the operations room of this headquarters and discovered what had chanced between Delia and her Battle Maidens, and Zankov, the slayer of her father.

Entwined clumps of purple-flowered Blooms depended from the shattered columns. Here and there the orange cones of Hyr-flicks congealed spots of deadly color. Their green tendrils snaked this way and that, seeking prey, snatching up the tikos of the cracked masonry, snaring any animal of reasonable size unwary enough to venture here. A Rapa had been caught and engulfed; only his beaked face glared sightlessly from a distended orange cone, and soon that would be gone, digested along with the rest of him.

Many of the Hyr-flicks, gigantic cousins of the flick-flicks that graced the windowsills of Kregen homes, had been slashed through. And yet still their tendrils writhed.

"Sink me!" I burst out as I ran on. "That Delia has put her head into a mighty unsavory pest hole, by Zair!"

The Krozair brand carved me a slimy way through and I understood this way was what could be called the rear entrance. Those four clansmen, hunkering wounded over their roasting ponsho, had been all unwitting of the drama enacted here. They had been of a clan I did not know. But I would know them hereafter, and Hap Loder would be advised.

Thinking sour thoughts like that led me on, as I ran, to a single scarlet speculation of the fate of the battle. The front would still be in flux, for the sounds of combat reached here as a muted hum, as of bees on a sunny summer afternoon, without the devil-boom of gunnery. The Hakkodin would be fully in action, the sword and shield men attempting to smash forward, the reserves being used—I must trust Seg. He must judge the time when to send in the reserves, when to commit our nikvove cavalry. But I pushed on without a pause, for ahead of me in the half-light of the aisled and gloomy Stones a radiance like the eye of the setting Zim, the red sun of Antares, drew me on.

There were diffs there, I remember, men in armor and brandishing weapons, and the manner of their going is something I do not clearly recall. I can still feel the hot wet drops of blood falling from my longsword onto my fists.

I must, I realize, have looked a monstrous sight. I had fathomed out, or thought I had, what had passed here. Delia and her Battle Maidens had struck, and kept their doings close, and somewhere up past that blood-red radiance which vanished from sight ever and anon as I twisted through the labyrinth of columns, up there—yes—Delia? Where was she, what was she doing now? Where her Jikai Vuvushis?

The Sakkora Stones spread over an extensive area, more than I realized; but through smothering vegetation I neared the operations room at the forward edge of the Stones—and Zankov. The battle raged apace, and knowledge of what reserves he could muster would have mightily interested me only a very short time earlier. Now—only reaching Delia obsessed me.

Soon I reached a part of the Stones where recent work had provided roof coverings, imported wooden beams with straw laid across making impromptu roofs. In one chamber a pile of dead lay sprawled in the attitudes of frozen battle. Diffs of various races including Katakis, Jikai Vuvushis at whom I looked with a mingling of quick and useless sympathy and a live and vibrant dread, and clansmen. I passed on and now the sounds of voices raised in anger reached me from beyond a curtaining wall of vegetation. I quickened my steps. I realized with a shock my hands were trembling on the hilt of the Krozair longsword.

The half-lit gloom of the place and the bone-aching sensation of its unfathomable age lent mystery and terror to the Sakkora Stones. I slashed away a tendril that sought to encircle my neck and drag me into an orange gullet, and so put my ear to the green and living wall.

"Keep out of it, mother! It is no concern of yours!"

"You are my daughter and therefore my concern—"

"If Ros pleads for your life, I may grant it."

I knew those three voices. I knew them!

With a vicious and intemperate slash with the longsword I ripped the curtained hangings across. Samphron oil lamps beyond splashed mellow light into a lurid scene. I stepped across the threshold and checked, struggling to focus on what lay beyond.

A further hanging partially obscured my view and, in turn, hid me from those who wrangled so bitterly. Delia—Delia stood there, pale-faced, wrought-up as I could see, unutterably lovely in her russet leathers, bereft of weapons, chained to one of the millennia-old columns of the Sakkora Stones. Facing her—Zankov stood, thin and brittle, alert and alive, his head jutting forward and the sneer of his face like the blow from a whip. At his side, Dayra—Dayra, Delia's daughter and my daughter, Dayra, who would be called Ros the Claw. She wore the wicked steel set of talons now and they glittered in the lampglow. She looked almost bereft of reason, high-colored, frantic, beside herself with a fury she could neither understand nor control.

Delia, Dayra, and Zankov. I stood for perhaps a heart beat, for I saw they did not intend to kill Delia just yet. And the reason for that lay in Delia's spirit, in her refusal to beg or to cringe. She spoke to Dayra as she must have spoken to her in the long ago, when I was banished to Earth.

"Do you know, daughter, who and what this man is? Do you know what he has done?"

"Whatever he has done—he belongs to me!"

"No man and no woman ever belong one to the other, Dayra."

Those words struck through to me with the pain of a white hot iron. I knew Delia spoke the truth; but I could not accept that truth. Perhaps the word "belong" was the wrong word. I could accept another, less final, word...

"My army is now winning a great victory over that onkerish cramph of a husband of yours, majestrix."

So Zankov still spoke to Delia as majestrix. I listened on for a space, wanting the words I hungered for to be spoken.

But Delia just said: "I do not think you will beat him. He is very proud of his new army. He is a man with a stiff neck. I know."

"He is a clansman, is he not? A hairy barbarian savage?" Zankov laughed in his bright, brittle way, most puffed up with his own pride and cleverness. "Then he knows full well the ferocity of the clansmen. They obey me, me! And I am Zankov."

"You call yourself Zankov. But that is not your name. I know who you are, now—"

"Mother!" cried Dayra. She started around, and I saw she trembled.

"Aye, daughter. This man who calls himself Zankov is the son of Nankwi Wellon, the High Kov of Sakwara. And Kov Nankwi has sworn allegiance to the Emperor of Vallia—"

"Son!" shrieked Zankov. "Aye, son. Illegitimate son!"

"So you seek to gain all by slaying all—"

"That is the way of the Hawkwas."

"And if you murder me before the eyes of my daughter, as you murdered her—"

"Enough of this nonsense!" bellowed Zankov and I saw he thus shouted in anger because Dayra did not know he had killed her grandfather. "You will say the words required to pass Ros—Dayra—into my keeping. You will say them, majestrix, if I have to—" Then he paused, and shifted his gaze to Dayra, who stood taut and lovely at his side.

"You had best leave us for a space, Ros. There are things of the bokkertu I must discuss with your mother."

So that was the way of it, then. The mother's agreement and her full acceptance of the bokkertu must be obtained. Even in this, the people of Vallia would not be hoodwinked. So Delia's life was safe for a space yet.

This knowledge did not make me relax as much as the point of a Lohvian arrow. But I did become aware of other people in the partially roofed chamber between the Stones. They stood under a straw-thatched roof supported by twisted beams of raw wood, in a shadowy space, and they watched Zankov and his doings with the bright blood-lusting avidity of a crowd in the Jikhorkdun watching the death-sports of the arena. As I looked at them the whole brilliantly attired group wavered and rippled as though I peered drunkenly at them through a ghostly waterfall. I blinked my eyes. The images slowly refocused and I put my hand up to my neck, just above the rim of the kax, and, lo! an arrow, embedded in the flesh, all unknown to me. I must have got this beauty in one of the fights astride the flutduin.

With a pettish snap I broke it off.

There was no time, now, for shilly-shallying; but my warrior instincts recognized why I had not rushed headlong out into the cleared area. Those cramphs watching so avidly would take a deal of beating. But, beat they had to be, because Dayra was at last leaving the chamber, with a long hungry look back at Zankov, and I knew what lay in store for Delia.

"Do not be long, my love," she said.

"Not so long as the time between an axe and death."

I felt a fist constrict around my heart, and then Dayra, looking back, her eyes brilliant, her form tensed, lifted that vicious steel claw. "I shall do as you ask of me, and my Jikai Vuvushis call. But, Zankov, as you love me, I wish to speak with my mother when I return."

His laugh was high, brittle and, at least to me, artificial. But, I could be wrong. "Of course, Ros. She is, after all, your mother whom you love. It is not your father we ask this bokkertu in all legal formality."

"Him!" spat Dayra. "The betraying rast—I would it was him. Then I would stroke him with my claw."

The scene wavered again before my eyes. For a desperate moment ghastly phantasms of the time I had ridden after my daughter Velia rose to rend and torture me. I shut my eyes, pressed down hard, hard, and struggled to regain my senses. When I looked again, Dayra had gone. Now I saw under that partial roofing there were Battle Maidens there, twisted lesten-hide thongs cruelly constricting their limbs. There were four Katakis in the front rank, arrogant, lofty men, with their bladed whiptails flaunted menacingly. Them first, then...

Next to them the two clansmen... They were Zorcanders. No doubt they were witnesses to this bokkertu, the Vovedeers out conducting the battle. And, the sight of Katakis, here, involved in legalities of Vallia gave eloquent testimony to the kind of country Vallia would be if Zankov had his way.

Very carefully I placed the Krozair longsword hilt-up on the stone flagging, leaning against the column. Next to it went six Lohvian arrows. I bent the great Lohvian longbow. Seg believes I can shoot as well as he, although I am not sure; I think even he might nod a tight approval of that six-shot group.

The four Katakis and the two clansmen were flung back by the smashing power of that tremendous bow. The longsword was in my fists and I was leaping forward and, as though the uproar in the chamber was the signal, other men boiled in from the far side, men and Jikai Vuvushis.

Leaping for Zankov, who sprang away with a high screech of sudden fear, I saw Barty Vessler there, splendid, splendid, hacking his way through the ranks of diffs who sought to drag him down. His personal guard fought at his side. He made for Zankov who, attempting to escape me, scrambled into Barty's path.

Men reared before me and there were handstrokes aplenty. Then I was through them or their remains and the Krozair blade bit cleanly through the iron links of the lapping chain. I took Delia into my arms.

She said: "Dayra—"

"I know. Hush."

"There is no time to hush. Give me a weapon, and—"

"Perhaps she truly loves this Zankov, as he her. Perhaps—"

"No, my heart. It is not like that." She pushed me away and bent to retrieve a fallen rapier. As she straightened, her face, incredibly lovely, tautened, and I whirled, sword up.

Barty was in the act of bringing his drexer down on Zankov. Zankov's rapier angled, the light runneled along the blade, and then the drexer bit into his face. With a demoniac screech he leaped away and the blood poured down that thin and bitter face, painting him like a devil of Cottmer's Caverns.

His face as red with passion as Zankov's was red with blood, Barty bellowed. "Cramph! Seducer! Pray to all your evil gods, for, by Opaz, your time has come!"

I saw it.

Colun Mogper, the Kov of Mursham, sprang up, tall at Barty's back. The dagger in his fist did not glitter, for it was dulled a deep and ominous green. High, Kov Colun raised the poisoned dagger. With a convulsive effort he brought it down and plunged it deeply into Barty's neck.

His life saved by his ally, Zankov did not hesitate. He ran under the roofing and vanished in shadows. I started after him, and found I was barely moving. The stones of the floor surged up and down under me like a swifter in a gale. I was sitting down. I was the Emperor of Vallia. I could not sit down when the country depended on me. Delia bent to me.

"Stay still, my love. The arrow is deep."

"Zankov... Dayra... Barty!"

She pointed.

Through the ferocious hand-to-hand struggle as Barty's men and the Battle Maidens sought to overthrow Zankov's people a man moved with a purpose I recognized. Clad like a Krozair of Zy, he wielded a great Krozair longsword, and he cut down all those opposed to him as the reaper cuts corn. He carved a path to the far side and ran into the shadows after Zankov.

"There goes our son, Jaidur. He has worked well for Vallia!"

"But—Barty!"

She put her hand on my forehead and it felt like ice against my skin. "Barty Vessler is dead."

I could say nothing. Nothing I could say was of any use.

With a roar as of a volcano exploding the roof broke into a thousand shards, dragged up by hooks hauled up by air-boats. Men smashed down, sliding on ropes, men wearing scarlet and yellow, their weapons aflame. I recognized them. The Emperor's Sword Watch. Devoted to the Emperor of Vallia, each one would give his life. They were here to ensure the emperor's safety. And this they would do. But they had come too late for another life...

A life for Vallia had been given, given willingly, but that life was gone, snuffed out, and Barty Vessler would never rush eagerly, honorably and joyously headlong into adventure at my side, not ever again.

"Barty," I said. I just felt stupid. Delia held me.

Korero bellowed at me. "The battle is won! They flee!"

"That," I said. "Is very good, by Zair."

And, as I spoke in a strange stupefied whisper, I saw a glistening red scorpion waddle out contemptuously from under the ancient stones.

A SWORD FOR KREGEN

Dray Prescot

Dray Prescot presents an enigmatic picture of himself; reared in the inhumanly harsh conditions of Nelson's Navy, he has been transported by the Scorpion agencies of the Star Lords, the Everoinye, and the Savanti, the superhuman yet mortal people of Aphrasöe the Swinging City, to the demanding and fulfilling world of Kregen orbiting Antares, four hundred light years from Earth, where he has made his home.

He is a man above middle height, with brown hair and level brown eyes, brooding and dominating, with enormously broad shoulders and superbly powerful physique. There is about him an abrasive honesty and indomitable courage, he moves like a savage hunting cat, quiet and deadly. He has struggled through triumph and disaster and has acquired a number of titles and estates, and now the people of the island of Vallia, which has been ripped apart by ambitious and mercenary invaders, have called on him to lead them to freedom as their emperor.

His story, which he records on cassettes, is arranged so that each volume may be read as complete in itself. There have been many questions about the role of Prescot on Kregen and particularly about the nature and purpose of his antagonists. I am firmly convinced he does see far further ahead than perhaps he is given credit for. His words inspire our belief, particularly in what he has to say about the Star Lords. He implies they are not as malefic as at one time we might have been led to believe.

Whatever the outcome for Dray Prescot, we are aware that he is conscious that he struggles against a far darker and more profound fate than is revealed in anything he has so far told us.

Alan Burt Akers

One

Jaidur is Annoyed

"Do you bare the throat?"

"Aye, my love. I bare the throat."

The brightly painted pieces were swept up and returned to the silver-bound box. I had been comprehensively defeated. The game had been protracted and cunning and fiercely contested, filled with shifts and stratagems on Delia's part that wrecked my cleverest schemes. I leaned over the board awkwardly from the bed and picked up my right-wing Chuktar. He was the only piece of high value my remorseless antagonist had failed to take.

"You held him back too long," she said, decisively, her face half-laughing and yet filled with concern for the instinctive wince I failed to quell as that dratted wound stabbed my neck.

"I did."

He was a marvelously fashioned playing piece, a Chuktar of the Khibil race of diffs, his fox-like face carved with a precision and understanding that revealed the qualities of the Khibils in a way that many a much more famous sculptor might well miss. Delia took the Chuktar from my fingers and placed him carefully in his velvet-lined niche within the box. When you play Jikaida, win or lose, you develop a rapport with the little pieces that, hard to define or even to justify coherently, nevertheless exists.

"You will not play again?" I leaned back on the plumped-up pillows and found that smile that always comes from Delia. "I am mindful to develop a new ploy with the Paktuns—"

"No more games tonight." The tone of voice was practical. There is no arguing with Delia in this mood. "Your wound is troubling you and you need rest. We have won this battle but until you are fit again I shall not rest easy."

"Sink me!" I burst out. "There is so much to do!"

"Yes. And it will not get done if you do not rest."

The invasion of the island of Vallia by the riff-raff of half a world, and the onslaught by the disciplined iron legions of Hamal, Vallia's mortal enemy, had been checked. But only that. We held Vondium the capital and

171

much of the northeast and midlands; from the rest of the empire our enemies pressed in on us. I'd collapsed after this last battle in which we had successfully held that wild charge of the vove-mounted clansmen—I'm no superman but just a mere mortal man who tries to do the best he can. Now Delia looked on me, the lamps' gleam limning her hair with those gorgeous chestnut tints, her face wonderfully soft and concerned, leaning over me. I swallowed.

"You rest now. Tomorrow we can strike camp and fly back to Vondium—"

"Rather, fly after the clansmen and try to—"

"The wind is foul for the northeast."

"Is there no arguing with you?"

"Rather seek to argue with Whetti-Orbium, of Opaz."

I made a face. Whetti-Orbium, as the manifestation of Opaz responsible for the weather and under the beneficent hand of that all-glorious godhood, the giver of wind and rain, had not been treating us kindly of late. The Lord Farris's aerial armada had played little part in the battle, the wind being dead foul, and only his powered airboats had got themselves into the action.

"Then the cavalry must—" I began.

"Seg has that all under control."

Good old Seg Segutorio. But— "And there is—"

"Hush!"

And then I smiled, a gently mocking, sympathetically triumphant smile, as with a stir and a rattle of accoutrements, the curtains of the tent parted and Prince Jaidur entered.

He saw only Delia in the lamplit interior with its canvas walls devoid of garish ornament, with the weapons strapped to the posts, the strewn rugs, the small camp tables, the traveling chests. Delia turned and rose, smooth, lovely, inexpressibly beautiful.

"Mother," said Jaidur. He sounded savage. "That rast found himself some flying beast and escaped."

Jaidur, young and lithe and his face filled with the passions of youth and eagerness, took off his helmet and slung it on the floor. Through the carpets the iron rang against the beaten earth.

"Mirvols, I think they were. Flying beasts that cawed down most mockingly at us as they rose. I shot—but the shafts fell short." His fingers were busily unbuckling his harness as he spoke, and the silver-chased cuirass dropped with a mellower chime upon the floor. Armed and accoutred like a Krozair of Zy, Pur Jaidur, Prince of Vallia. He scowled as Delia handed him a plain goblet of wine, a bracing dry Tardalvoh, tart and invigorating. Taking it, he nodded his thanks perfunctorily, and raised the goblet to his lips.

"Prince Jaidur," I said in my old gravel-shifting voice. "Is this the way you treat your mother? Like a petulant child? Or a boor from the stews of Drak's City?"

He jumped so that the yellow wine leaped, glinting over the silver.

"You—"

"You chased after Kov Colun and Zankov. Did they both escape?"

His brown fingers gripped the goblet.

"Both."

"Then," I said, and I gentled my voice. "They will run upon their judgment later, all in Opaz's good time."

"I did not know you were here—"

"Evidently."

My pleasure at his arrival, because it meant I could go on taking an interest in affairs instead of going to sleep at Delia's orders, was severely tempered by this news. There was a blood debt, now, between Kov Colun and my friends. For a space I could not think of Barty Vessler. Barty— so bright and chivalrous, so ingenuous and courageous—had been struck down by Kov Colun. And Zankov, his companion in evil, had murdered the emperor, Delia's father. But, all the same, vengeance was a road I would not willingly follow. The welfare of Delia, of my family, and of my friends and of Vallia—they were the priorities.

"I will leave you," said Jaidur with a stiffness he cloaked in formality. He bent to retrieve his harness. He made no move to don the cuirass and the helmet dangled by its straps. "Tomorrow—"

"Tomorrow!" The surprise and scorn in my voice braced him up, and sent the dark blood into his face. "Tomorrow! I recall when you were Vax Neemusjid. What harm has the night done you that you scorn to use it?"

Delia put her hand on my arm. Her touch scorched.

Jaidur swung around toward the tent opening.

"You are the Emperor of Vallia, and may command me. I shall take a saddle-bird. You will not see me again, I swear, until Kov Colun and Zankov are—"

"Wait!" I spat the word out. "Do not make so weighty a promise so lightly. As for Kov Colun, there is Jilian to be considered. You would do her no favor by that promise."

He looked surprised. "She still lives?"

"Thanks to Zair and to Nath the Needle."

"I am glad, and give thanks to Zair and Opaz."

"Also, I would like you to tell me of your doings since you returned from the Eye of the World."

"I see you humor me, for whenever have you bothered over my doings?"

"Jaidur!" said Delia.

"Let the boy speak. I knew him as Vax, and took the measure of his mettle.

173

I own to a foolish pride." Here Delia turned sharply to look at me, and I had to make myself go on. "Jaidur is a Krozair of Zy, a Prince of Vallia. I do not think there can be much else to better those felicities." I deliberately did not mention the Kroveres of Iztar, for good reasons. "His life is his own, his life which we gave to him. I, Jaidur, command you in nothing, save one thing. And I do not think I need even say what that thing is, for it touches your mother, Delia, Empress of Vallia."

"You do not. I would give my life, gladly—"

I said the words, and they cut deeply.

"Aye, Prince Jaidur. You and a host of men."

The color rushed back to his bronzed cheeks. With a gesture as much to break the thrall of his own black thoughts as to slake his thirst, he reached for the silver goblet and took a long draught.

"Aye. You are right. And that, by Vox, is as it should be."

Delia wanted to say something; but I ploughed on.

"Go after Kov Colun and after Zankov. Both are bitter foes to Vallia. But do not be too reckless. They are cunning rogues, vicious and cruel." My voice trailed away. On Earth we talk about teaching our grandmothers to suck eggs. On Kregen we talk about teaching a wizard to catch a fly. And here was I, prattling on about dangers and cunning adversaries to a Krozair of Zy.

Jaidur saw something of that belittling thought in me, for his brows drew down in a look I recognized and with recognition the same familiar ache. How Delia puts up with me and three hulking sons is a miracle beyond question. And, thinking these useless thoughts, the tent spun about me, going around and around, ghostly and transparent. I fell back on the bed, all the stuffing knocked out of me.

"That Opaz-forsaken arrow," said Delia, leaning across, wiping my face with a scented towel. I felt the coolness. I must be in fever. My throat hurt; but not enough to stop me from speaking; but the weakness made the tent surge up and down and corkscrew like a swifter in a storm.

"I—shall—be—all—right," I said.

"I will fetch Nath the Needle." With that Jaidur ran from the tent, dropping his gear and casting the wine goblet from him.

"All this fuss—for a pesky arrow."

"It drove deeply, my heart. Now—lie still!"

I lay still.

Fruitless to detail the rest of that night's doings. Nath the Needle, looking as he always did, fussing and yet steadily sure with his acupuncture needles and his herbal preparations, fixed up my aches and pains in the physical sense. But my brain was afire with schemes, stratagems I must set afoot at once, so as further to discomfort the damned invading clansmen. Our enemies pressed us sorely, and they must be dealt with as opportunity offered. The chances of success here must be balanced against defeat there. The campaign against Zankov's imported clansmen had been waged with fierceness. But it was all to do. I, a clansman by adoption myself, knew that no single battle would decide the issue.

The Clansmen of Segesthes are among the most ferocious and terrible of fighting men of Kregen. That we had put a check on their advance must have hit them hard, hit them with shock. But they were clansmen. They would retire, regroup, and then they'd be back, thirsting for vengeance.

And here I lay, lolling in bed like a drunkard in the stews.

There were able captains among the Army of Vallia. Many of them bore names not unfamiliar to you, many there were who have not so far been mentioned in this narrative. Delia told me, with a firmness made decisive by the crimp in those seductive lips, that I must leave it to Seg and the others. For now, she told me severely, they could handle any emergencies.

So, because Delia of Delphond, Delia of the Blue Mountains, who was now Delia, Empress of Vallia, willed it, I was immured. The fate of the island empire was, for that space, taken from my hands.

Phu-Si-Yantong, one of the chief architects of the misery in which Vallia now found herself, would not rest, either. His schemes had for a time been thwarted. But he held the southwest and unknown areas of the southeast and many of the islands. His partnership— and then I paused. Yantong was too egomaniacal a figure ever to acknowledge anyone his peer or to admit them to an equality suggested by a partnership. Yantong wished to rule the roost, the whole roost, and he wished to rule alone.

First things first. Our tenuous hold on the link through the eastern midlands between Vondium and the imperial provinces around the capital and the Hawkwa Country of the northeast had to be strengthened. We must attempt to relieve the pressure on the western mountains where people devoted to Delia, as to myself, still grimly held out. And there was always the far north, Evir and the other provinces beyond the Mountains of the North, where his self-styled King of North Vallia held sway. The north had to be forgotten for now. First things first.

As soon as I was deemed fit to travel Delia had me carted back to Vondium.

During that period there were many visitors, representatives of the churches, the state, the army, the air service and the imperial provinces. The navy and merchant service also showed up; but they were dealing now almost entirely with flying ships of the air. The once-mighty fleet of galleons of Vallia was being rebuilt; but slowly, slowly.

These men and women who came to see me spoke all in soft voices, even the gruff old Chuktars of the army mellowed their habitual gruff barks. Always I was conscious of the presence of Delia, hovering protectively, and I guessed she had given strict injunctions on the correct sick-room behavior. And, by Zair, when Delia spoke it behooved everyone to heed, and heed but good.

So, as you will see, I must have been much sicker than I realized.

Seg Segutorio, that master Bowman of Loh, kept his reckless face composed as he sat at the bedside to tell me of the fortunes of the army. I had peremptorily thrust command on him at the height of the battle—that engagement men called the Battle of Kochwold—when Jilian had reported in the news of the desperate affray involving Delia at the Sakkora Stones. We had brought her safely out of there, from that miasmal place of ages-old decay and present evil. But our daughter Dayra, she who flaunted her steel talons as Ros the Claw, had once more disappeared. I did not know if she was with Zankov, who had slain her grandfather. Truth to tell, I did not know how to view that situation, just as I did not know how to contain within myself the ghastly news of Seg's wife, Thelda. I made myself agreeable to Seg, which is not a difficult task, and did not summon up the courage to tell him that his wife, whom he thought dead and sorrowed for, believed him dead, also, and had married another upright and honest man, Lol Polisto. So we talked of the army.

"The clansmen fight hard, and, by the Veiled Froyvil, my old friends, they led us a merry chase. They regroup now up past Infathon in Vazkardrin. We chivvy 'em and give 'em no rest. Nath is foaming to get at them with his Phalanx, but—"

"They may be amenable to an attack in their rear from the Stackwamors." I pondered this. "Certainly we must keep them off balance. But reports indicate we may need the Phalanx elsewhere."

Seg fired up at this. All the fey and reckless nature of his fiery race suddenly burst out, subduing the shrewd practicality.

"Where, my old dom? We will march—the men are in wonderful heart—"

"I am sure," I said, somewhat drily. "With a victory under their belts."

These audiences—if that is not too pompous a word to use of these discussions between the Emperor of Vallia and his ministers and generals—were conducted in a neat little withdrawing room off the old wing once inhabited by Delia and myself in the imperial palace of Vondium. There was a bed, in which I spent far too much time, tables and chairs and wine and food, with a bookcase stuffed with the life of Vallia. And, also, many maps adorned the walls. As a matter of course and scarce worth remarking, an arms rack stood handy. Handiest of all was the great Krozair longsword, scabbarded to the bedpost. Now I pointed at the map which showed the southwest of Vallia.

"There, Seg, again. The army which Fat Lango brought has been seen off. But others are landing. It seems that some countries of Pandahem are still desirous of carving a helping of good Vallian gold for themselves."

"Vallia has something they deserve and which they will receive," quoth

176

Seg, without flourish. "Something that will last them through all the Ice Floes of Sicce."

He referred, quite clearly, to the six feet of Vallian soil each one of her invaders would be dumped into. I smiled. Very dear to my heart is my blade comrade, Seg Segutorio. He and I have battled our way through some hairy scrapes since he first hurled a forkful of dungy straw in my face. And, by Zair, that seemed a long long time ago.

With that old memory in mind I said, and my voice, weak as it was, sounded altogether too much like a sigh: "If only Inch was here. Inch and all the others—"

Seg looked swiftly at me. He was not reassured by what he saw. He put a spread of fingers up under his ear and scratched his jaw. A very tough and craggy jaw, that jaw of Seg Segutorio's.

"Aye, Dray, aye. But I think Inch will not forget Vallia, or that he is the Kov of the Black Mountains. His taboos—for my money Inch has been eating too much squish pie."

That made me smile.

"When we were all slung back to our homelands by that sorcerous Vanti," Seg went on, half-musing, his eyes bright on me, his hand rubbing his jaw. "I felt no doubt that every single one of us would make every effort to get back to Valka or Vallia as soon as humanly possible." His voice betrayed nothing of the agony he must still suffer over his belief in the death of Thelda. I had pondered that problem. For all the news we had, Thelda and Lol Polisto might be dead by now. They were leading a precarious existence fighting our foes as guerillas. They could so easily be dead. Until Thelda was proved still to be alive, why torture Seg with a fresh burden that was so different and yet so much the same as his belief his wife was truly dead?

"My son Drak is still down there in Faol trying to find Melow the Supple." I spoke fretfully, for I wanted Drak back here in Vallia, with me, so that he could take over this business of being Emperor of Vallia. "But I think you have something else on your mind?"

"Aye. You have found a new marvel in Korero. He is indeed remarkable with his shields. So..."

"You don't think I haven't wondered what I'm going to say to Turko?"

His rubbing hand stilled. "What will you say?"

That was another poser for my poor aching head. The yellow bandage around my throat seemed to constrict in to choke me with problems. Turko the Shield stood always at my back with his great shield uplifted in the heat of battle. But, now, Korero the Shield, with his four arms and handed tail, stood always at my back with his shields upraised in the heat of battle...

I said sourly, "I'll make Turko a damned Kov and find him a province and get him married to raise stout sons for Vallia and beautiful daughters to grace the world. That's what I'll do."

"He, I think, would prefer to stand at your back with his shield."

"D'you think I don't know that!"

"Hum, my old friend, a very large and ponderable hum."

That was Seg Segutorio for you, able to cut away all the nonsense with a word. But he was smiling. By Vox! What it is to have comrades through life!

We talked for a space then about our comrades and wished them with us, and eventually returned to the subject of the army to be sent to the southwest and the knotty problem of choosing a commander.

Seg said, "I still have a rapier to sharpen with those rasts of clansmen. And, yes, before you ask me, I can spare a Phalanx, although preferring not to. Filbarrka's zorcamen make life a misery for them. And I am slowly becoming of the opinion that perhaps, one day, I shall manage to make bowmen of the fellows I have under training."

Well, if Seg Segutorio, in my opinion the finest archer of all Kregen, couldn't fashion a battle-winning missile force, then no one could.

We looked at the maps and pondered the likeliest routes the invading armies from Pandahem might choose. I would have to delegate responsibility in that area of the southwest, and make up my mind as to the numbers and composition of the army we would send. That would be the Army of the Southwest.

Presently I placed my hand on the silver-bound balass box.

Seg shook his head.

"Much as I would love to rank Deldars against you, my old friend, and thrash you utterly, I have another zhantil to saddle."

"There is never enough time," I said. And added, under my breath, "In two worlds."

"Anyway," he said, standing up and shifting his sword around more comfortably. "Delia tells me you have been playing Master Hork."

"Aye. Katrin Rashumin recommended him, although he has been famous as a master gamesman in Vondium for many seasons."

Once, I had interrupted a proposed lesson that Katrin was to have taken from Master Hork. He had returned to the capital city, and had, I knew, played his part in our victory. As for Katrin, the Kovneva of Rahartdrin, Opaz alone knew what had happened to her. Her island kovnate was situated far to the southwest and messengers we had sent had not returned. Perhaps our new Army of the Southwest might succeed in gaining news of her and her people.

"Master Hork has a great command of the Chuktar's right-flank attack," said Seg. "Personally, I incline to the left wing."

"Mayhap that is because an archer must have something of a squint—"

"Fambly!"

"And Seg, do you take great care. Your back is healed, well and good; but I don't want you—"

"I know, my old dom. May Erthyr the Bow have you in his keeping, along with Zair and Opaz and Djan." Then Seg, turning to go, paused and swung back. "And, I think, may the lady Zena Iztar also approve of our ventures. The Kroveres of Iztar do little, to my great frustration; but we try—"

"There is a great work set to our hands with the Kroveres." That sounded fustian; but it was true. "We must continue as we are, recruiting choice spirits, and remain steadfast. As the Grand Archbold, you have a double duty."

So I bid farewell to Seg and ached to see him go, and presently in came Master Hork with his own bronze-bound box of playing pieces and we set the board, ranked our Deldars, and opened the play.

Master Hork held within himself that remote and yet alive inner sense of being that marks the Jikaidast. A Jikaidast is a man or woman who plays Jikaida on a professional level. Because of the enormous popularity of the game on Kregen such a person can make a handsome living and receive the respect that is due. I was most polite with Master Hork, a slender, well-mannered man with brown Vallian hair and eyes, and a face that one felt ought to be lined and wrinkled and which was smooth and untrammeled. His movements were neat and precise. He wasted not a single scrap of energy. But he could play Jikaida, by Krun!

There was no point in my attempting to play an ordinary game against his mastery, so we went through the moves of a famous game played five hundred seasons or so ago. Outstanding games are usually recorded for posterity, and many books of Jikaida lore exist. The notations are simple and easily read.

This game was that remarkable example of high-level Jikaida played between Master Chuan-lui-Hong, a Jikaidast then in his hundred and twentieth year, and Queen Hathshi of Murn-Chem, a once-powerful country of Loh.

A Jikaidast will not deliberately lose a game, not even against so awesome a personage as a fabled Queen of Pain of Loh. But Chuan-lui-Hong had had to play with extraordinary skill, for Queen Hathshi might, had she not been a queen, have been a Jikaidast herself.

From the impeccable written record on the thick pages of Master Hork's ponderous leather-bound tome we re-created that famous game. It was, indeed, a marvel. The queen swept all before her, using her swods and Deldars to push on and deploying her more powerful pieces with artistry. At the end, Master Chuan-lui-Hong had played the masterstroke. By using a swiftly developed file of his own pieces, by placing a swod, that is, the Kregan pawn, into the gap between his own file and that of the queen's and so closing the gap, he was able to vault his left-flank Chuktar over the conjoined files into a threatening position that offered check. Check in jikaidish is kaida.

That spectacular vaulting move is unique to Jikaida. A piece may travel over a line of other pieces, either orthogonally or diagonally, using them as stepping-stones, and alight at the far end. The jikaidish word for vault is zeunt. The Chuktar moves in a similar fashion to the Queen of our Earthly chess. Master Hork read out the next move.

"A beautiful response." I felt the pleasure inherent in a neat move. "Hathshi avoids the Chuktar's attack and places her Queen on the only square the Chuktar cannot reach."

Although Vallians call the piece a King, many countries use the names Rokveil, Aeilssa, Princess, and in Loh, much as you would expect, the piece is called a Queen. The object of the game is to place this piece in such a position that it cannot avoid capture. In the jikaidish, this entrapment is called hyrkaida.

"And if the Chuktar moves to place the Queen in check, he will be immediately snapped up by her Hikdars or Paktuns. Although," I said a little doubtfully, "her position is a trifle cramped."

A Jikaidast lives his games, and lives vicariously through the games of his long-dead peers. Master Hork allowed a small and satisfied smile to stretch his lips. Deliberately, he closed the heavy leather cover of the book. The pages made a soft sighing sound and the smell of old paper wafted. I looked at Master Hork across the board where the pieces stood in their frozen march.

"See, majister," he said, and reached far back into Chuan-lui-Hong's Neemu drin.

His slender fingers closed on the Pallan.

The Pallan is the most powerful piece on the board. He combines in himself moves that include those of the chess Queen and Knight, plus other purely Jikaidish possibilities. Chuan-lui-Hong was playing Yellow.

His Pallan stood in such a position that he could be moved up to the end of the long file of yellow and blue pieces—and vault.

The instant Master Hork touched the Pallan I saw it.

"Yes," I said, and my damned throat hurt with that confounded arrow wound. "Oh, yes indeed!"

For the Pallan vaulted that long file and came down on the square occupied by his own Chuktar.

The Pallan has the power to take a friendly piece—excepting the Queen, of course.

Chuan-lui-Hong used his Pallan to remove his Chuktar from the game. Now the Pallan stood there, an imposing and glittering figure, and with the moves at his disposal he trapped, snared, detained, entombed Queen Hathshi's own Queen.

"Hyrkaida!" said Master Hork. And, then, as Chuan-lui-Hong must have done all those dusty seasons ago, he said: "Do you bare the throat?"

"I fancy Hathshi bared her throat with good grace, Master Hork; for it is a pretty ploy."

"Pretty, yes. But obvious, and one that she should have foreseen three moves ago when Hong's Pallan made the crucial move to place him on the correct square within the correct drin." Master Hork screwed his eyes up and surveyed me. "As majister, you should have seen, also."

With Seg, I said, "Hum."

Casually, Master Hork said, "Jikaida players say I am the master of the right-wing Chuktar's attack. This is so. But in my last ten important games, against Jikaidasts of great repute, I have not employed that stratagem. Not in the opening, the middle or the end game. There is a lesson there, majister."

I was perfectly prepared—happy—to be instructed by a master of his craft. But what Master Hork was saying was basic to cunning attack. Be where you are not expected.

"You are right, Master Hork. More wine—may I press this Tawny Jholaix?" From this you will see the truly high regard in which we of Kregen hold Jikaidasts, for Jholaix is among the finest and most expensive wines to be obtained. As Master Hork indicated his appreciation, I went on: "I have likened all Vallia to a Jikaida board. But how you would denominate the Phalanx I do not know for sure, for where they are they are, and there they stand."

"I saw the Phalanx, majister, at the Battle of Voxyri." He drank, quickly at his memories, too quickly for Jholaix, which should be savored. But I understood. When the Phalanx sent up their paean and charged at Voxyri it was, I truly think, a sight that would send either the shuddering horrors or the sublimest of emotions through a man until the day he died.

We talked on, mostly about Jikaida, and it was fascinating talk, filled with the lore of the game. As ever, when in contact with a Jikaidast, my memories flew back to Gafard, the King's Striker, Sea Zhantil. Well, he was dead now, following our beloved Velia, and, I know, happy to go where she led, now and for ever.

"Many a great Jikaidast," Master Hork was saying, "set store by the larger games, Jikshiv Jikaida and the rest. But I tend to think that there is a concentration of skill required in the use of the smaller boards. Poron Jikaida demands an artistry quite different in style."

"Each size of board brings its own joys and problems," I said, sententiously, I fear. But my head was ringing with sounds as though phantom bells tolled in my skull. I felt the weakness stealing over me, and growing, and pulling at me.

Master Hork started up. "Majister!"

There was a blurred impression of the Jikaida board spilling the bright pieces to the floor. That resplendent Pallan toppled and tumbled into a fold of the bedclothes. Master Hork made no attempt to save the scattering pieces. He turned, his face distraught, and ran for the door, yelling for the doctors.

His voice reached me as a thin and ghostly whisper, faint with the dust of years.

That Opaz-forsaken arrow wound! That was my immediate thought. By the unspeakably foul left armpit of Makki-Grodno! There was much to do, and all I could turn my hand to, it seemed, was playing Jikaida and lolling in bed.

And then...

And then I saw a shimmer of insubstantial blueness.

The radiance broadened and deepened.

So I knew.

Once again I was to be snatched away from all I held dear and at the behest of the Star Lords who had brought me to Kregen from Earth be flung headlong into some strange and foreign land. The injustice of this fate that doomed me rang and clangored in my head with the distant sounds as of mighty bellows panting. And the blueness grew and brightened and took on the form I knew and loathed.

Towering over me the lambent blue form of a gigantic Scorpion beckoned.

Once again the Scorpion of the Star Lords called...

Two

The Star Lords Disagree

Around me the blueness swirled and I knew no doctors or Kregan science could save me for I was in the grip of superhuman forces that made of human aspirations a mere mockery. Yet I had thought the Star Lords possessed a superhumanity in keeping with their superhumanness. Maybe I was wrong. Maybe they were entirely inimical. Still, as the gigantic Scorpion leered on me, blue and shimmering with all the remembered menacing power, I saw the betraying flicker of greenness suffusing through the blue.

That Star Lord whose name was Ahrinye and who was evilly at odds with the rest of the Everoinye had his hand in this. He it was who summoned me now.

He was the one who wanted to run me hard, to run me as I had never been run before. I made a shrewd assessment of what that would mean. My life, over which I had been gradually assuming some kind of partial control, would never again belong to me. Ahrinye would have me continually at his beck and call.

"You are called to a great task, mortal!" The voice was as I remembered it, thin and acrid, biting. In those syllables the power of ages commanded both resentment and obedience.

"Fool!" I shouted, and my voice brayed soundlessly in that bedchamber. "Onker! Do you not—"

"Beware lest I smite you down, mortal. I am not as the other Everoinye."

"That is very clear." My bravado felt and sounded hollow, false, a mere mewling infant's bleatings against the storms of fate. "They would soon see in what case I am."

The idea that the Star Lords couldn't actually see me when they summoned me was not worth entertaining.

The blueness sharpened with acid green. The green hurt my eyes, and that, by Vox, is far from the soothing balm that true greenness affords.

"You are wounded, mortal. That is of no matter. I speak to you. That is something that you cannot grasp, for the Everoinye speak to few."

"Aye," I bellowed in that soundless foolish whisper. "And I'd as lief you didn't speak to me."

The shape of the Scorpion wavered. I knew that for this moment out of time no one could see what I saw, that no one could hear what I heard. Master Hork would, for all he knew, run out to fetch the doctors. When he returned he would find an empty bed and I would be banished to some distant part of Kregen to sort out whatever problem this Ahrinye wished decided in his favor.

That was, and I realized this with a sudden and chilling shock of despair, if he did not smash me back contemptuously to Earth, four hundred light years away. I must keep a civil tongue in my head.

Yet, for all that, I was involved in some kind of dialogue with this Star Lord. Many a time I had engaged in a slanging match with the gorgeous bird who was the spy and messenger of the Everoinye. But that scarlet and golden bird, the Gdoinye, was merely a messenger, and we rubbed along, scathing each other with insults. But this was far different. Never before, I fancied, had I thus talked to a Star Lord and, too, never before—perhaps— had a Star Lord been thus spoken to by a mere mortal.

"Your wound is not serious and you merely sulk in bed and play at Jikaida."

"That is what I say, and not what the doctors say."

Was it possible to argue with a Star Lord? Was it perhaps conceivable that one might be swayed by what I said?

That had hitherto seemed a nonsense to me.

The Everoinye did what they did out of reasons far beyond the comprehension of a man. They had brought the fantastic array of diffs and strange animals to Kregen, upsetting the order established by the Savanti, who had lived here millennia ago. Why they had done this I did not know.

But, clearly there was a reason.

"You cannot refuse my will, mortal."

"I do not accept that." As the blueness shimmered like shot silk waved against a fire, I went on quickly: "I cannot obey your orders if I cannot fight—for that, I take it, is what I must do for you?" And then, from somewhere, the words sprang out, barbed and sarcastic. "For I assume you Star Lords are incapable of fighting your own battles on Kregen?"

"Whether we can or cannot is of no concern of yours. We choose to use mortal tools—"

A voice broke in, a thin, incisive voice that yet swelled with power. "Ahrinye! You have been warned. This man is not to be run by you, young and impetuous though you may be."

I felt the draining sense of relief. When one Star Lord called another young he probably meant the Everoinye was only four or five million years old. A wash of deep crimson fire spread against the blueness. The Scorpion remained; but I sensed he was removed in that insubstantial dimension inhabited by these superhuman beings.

"I have a damned great arrow wound in my neck," I shouted without sound. "And a fever. And bed sores, too, I shouldn't wonder. Let me get on with my tasks in Vallia, that you, Star Lords, promised me I might undertake. Of what use am I to you now?"

"Your wound," the penetrating voice said, "is of no consequence. You may remove your bandage, for your neck is whole once more and your fever dissipated."

And, as the words were spoken, damned if the aching nag in my neck didn't vanish and my whole sense of well-being shot up wonderfully. I ripped the bandage free and explored my neck. The skin felt smooth and without blemish where a jagged hole had been left when they'd taken out the arrowhead.

"My thanks, Star Lord." And, if I meant that, or if I spoke in savage sarcasm, I could not truly say.

"We are aware of the emotion called gratitude. It has its uses."

"By Vox," I said. "D'you have ice water in your veins?"

Even as I spoke I wondered if they had veins at all. I was not unmindful of the enormous risks I ran. These were the beings who had brought me here and who could banish me back to Earth. They had done so before now, to punish me, and on one occasion I had spent twenty-one miserable years on Earth. I was not likely to forget that.

The next words shocked me, shocked me profoundly—although they should not have done.

"We," said the Star Lord, "were once as human as you."

Well, now...

This bizarre conversation with superhuman beings had lulled me into a false idea of my position. With genuine and I may add fervent interest I asked the question that had long burned in me, gradually losing its intensity in my realization that the Everoinye, being superhuman, had no need to care over my welfare.

"Why, Star Lords? Why have you summoned me? Why have you demanded I save certain people? Where is the sense in it all?"

With lightning-strokes of rippling crimson bursting through the blue radiance, I was rapidly reminded of my true position and disabused of the notion that I might speak with impunity to the Everoinye.

"What we do we do. Our reasons are beyond your understanding. The Gdoinye carries our orders. We speak with you only because you have served faithfully and well. There is another task set to your hand. We will apprise you nearer the time. The warning you now receive is in earnest of our benign intentions toward you."

If I say I found it extraordinarily difficult to swallow I think you will understand me.

Yet I could not in all caution make the kind of impudent and insulting reply I would surely have hurled at the Gdoinye as he whirled about me on flashing wings, all scarlet and gold, superb, a hunting bird of the air. So, instead, I took a different tack.

"Very well, Star Lords. You seem to be implying a compact between us and one I will honor if you honor it also. I will do your bidding and rescue the people you wish saved. Although," I added, and not without resentment, "I might take exception to your habit of plunking me down naked and unarmed—"

"This we do for reasons beyond—"

"Yes. As a mere mortal I cannot be expected to understand."

Then I hauled myself up to standing. Softly softly! I dare not infuriate these unknown powers or I would find myself banished back to Earth. And Vallia called. And—Delia...

What had happened to Ahrinye I never knew nor cared. But the greenness withered and died, and the blueness of the Scorpion faded. The crimson washed all over my vision, there in the sickroom, and I looked in vain for the mellow flood of pure yellow light that would herald the presence of Zena Iztar. That the Star Lords respected her powers I knew. Just what the relationship was I did not know. But Zena Iztar, I fervently believed, worked for other ends than those sought by either the Star Lords or the Savanti, and they were ends, I fancied, that we Kroveres would find most congenial.

There in that close room the sense of the infinite moving about me dizzied my senses anew. The thin whispering voice attenuated as though withdrawing across the vasty gulfs of space itself.

"Go about your business in Vallia, mortal. But when you receive our call—be ready!"

With an abruptness that left me sprawling blinking and still dizzied on the bed, the blueness returned, the crimson vanished, the Scorpion faded and, with a final swirl as of the wings of fate closing, the blueness dimmed and was gone.

Despite my feeling of physical well-being I felt like a stranded flatfish.

Momentous events had passed, of that I felt sure. Never before had such a conversation been held between the Star Lords and myself and, guessing they did nothing without good reason, I wondered what the reason could be. It would take a little time before I got over this little lot.

Then the door burst open and Nath the Needle and Master Hork were there. And, with them, Delia, her face strained and worried, hurried in ready to fuss over me as only she can.

Despite all my protestations Nath insisted on a full examination, and when he pronounced me fit and well and the wound healed, I, for one, was heartily glad to be rid of the sickroom aroma.

"I have work to do, and work I will do!"

"But, my heart—so soon?"

"Not soon enough."

"The wound has healed with remarkable rapidity," said Doctor Nath. He shook his head. "Your powers of recuperation, majister, are indeed phenomenal, as I have observed before."

Well, he did not know that I, along with Delia and our friends, had bathed in the Sacred Pool of Baptism of the River Zelph in far Aphrasöe. That little dip, besides giving us a thousand years of life, also conferred great recuperative powers. But that would by itself not account for the complete disappearance of all traces of the arrow wound. The Everoinye had accomplished that.

I said, "There is work to do. I am going to do that work and you, good Doctor Nath, have my thanks for your care and attention. As for you, Master Hork, I do not think I shall have the pleasure of your instruction in the more arcane aspects of Jikaida from now on." I stretched, feeling the blood beginning to find its way around my body and go poking into long disused corners. "And for that I am truly sorry. But with Vallia as the Jikaida board, well..."

"My help is always at your command, majister."

"And valued." I bellowed then, a real fruity old-time bellow in my best foretop hailing voice. "Emder!"

When Emder came in, smiling at my recovery, he very quickly organized the essentials. A most valuable and self-effacing man, Emder, what you might call a valet and butler and personal attendant—I disliked to call him a servant—a man whom I valued as a friend.

Enevon Ob-Eye and his corps of stylors were soon hard at work writing out the orders. The Pallans were seen and their doings checked up on. The Presidio met and agreed on much, and disagreed on a number of points, also, which was healthy.

It is not my intention to go into details of all the work that had to be done, and that was done, by Vox. But being an emperor, even an emperor of so small an empire as I then was, takes up more time than Opaz hands out between sunrise and sunrise.

The news from Seg was that he was keeping the clansmen in play, baiting them with Filbarrka's zorcamen. The zorcas, being so close-coupled and nimble, could ride rings around the more massive voves with their eight legs; but I felt that itchy feeling anyone must when he tangles with vove-mounted clansmen. Seg had started the Second Phalanx on their way back to Vondium and the Lord Farris was ferrying them in a detached part of his fleet of sailing skyships.

When the Second flew in, Kyr Nath Nazabhan flew with them.

Delia and I and a group of officers went out to meet him as his sailing flier touched down on Voxyri Drinnik. The wide open space outside the walls beyond the Gate of Voxyri blew with dust, the suns shone and streamed their mingled lights of ruby and jade, and the air smelled sweet with a Kregan dawn.

Here, on this hallowed ground, the Freedom Fighters and the Phalanx had won their victory against the Hamalese and brought Vondium the Proud back once more into Vallian hands.

Nath Nazabhan jumped down and walked most smartly toward us. He wore war harness, dulled with use, and his fresh and open face showed tiny signs of the care that had been wearing at him. But he was his usual alert, cheerful self, and a man I valued as a friend and a commander. Mind you, he never forgave himself for the debacle at the Gates of Sicce where a Phalanx had been overturned by the clansmen. But he had more than made up for that.

We had not seen each other since the Battle of Kochwold.

"Majestrix! Majister!" He thumped the iron kax encasing his ribcage, its gold and silver chasings dulled. "Lahal and Lahal!"

We greeted him, Delia first, and the Lahals were warm and filled with feeling. In a little group we mounted the zorcas and rode into the city. There was much to be said.

He told me he had instituted a thorough inquiry into the reasons for the temporary breaking of the Second Phalanx. This amused me. The idea that anyone should inquire why men should be broken by a vove-mounted clansmen's charge was in itself ludicrous; but Nath was enormously jealous of the reputation and prowess of his Phalanx. And, of course, now that they had won so convincingly, nothing would change their minds and they remained convinced that the Phalanx and the Hakkodin could best any fighting force in the world.

The men of the Phalanx might be convinced; I still did not share that conviction.

But there was no reasoning with Nath.

As we rode through the busy streets where the people gave us a cheer and then got on with their tasks, the grim men of the Emperor's Sword Watch surrounded us. No need for their swords to be unsheathed against the people of Vondium. The ever-present threat of assassination had receded; but there were foemen in Kregen who would willingly pay red gold to see me dead.

As I have remarked, that sentiment was returned.

We all congregated in the Sapphire Reception Room where fragrant Kregan tea and sweets were served. For those who needed further sustenance, the second breakfast was provided. I looked at Kyr Nath Nazabhan.

His father, Nazab Nalgre na Therminsax, was an imperial Justicar, the governor of a province, and Nath took his name from his father. I felt it opportune to improve on that, not in any denial of filial respect but out of approval and recognition of Nath's own qualities, of his service and achievements.

When I broached the subject he looked glum.

"Truth to tell, majister, I have become used to being called Nazabhan—"

"But a man cannot live on his father's name."

"True, but—"

"Our son Drak," said Delia, radiant in a long gown, her hair sheening in the early radiance. "Before he went off to Havilfar—"

What Delia would have said was lost, for the doors opened and Garfon the Staff, that major-domo whose arrow wound in the heel still produced a little limp, banged his gold-bound balass staff upon the marble floor. They relish that, do these major-domos and chamberlains. He produced a sudden silence with his clackety-clack.

Then he bellowed.

"Vodun Alloran, Kov of Kaldi!"

More than one person present in the Sapphire Reception Room gasped. It was easy to understand why. The kovnate of Kaldi, a lozenge-shaped province in the extreme southwest of the island, had long been cut off from communication with the capital and the lands hewing to the old Vallian inheritance. Down there Phu-si-Yantong's minions held sway.

It was in Kaldi that the invading armies from Pandahem and Hamal had landed.

The stir in the room brought a bright flush to the kov's face as he marched sturdily across the floor. I did not fail to notice the discreet little group of the Sword Watch who escorted him and his entourage. A tenseness persisted there, a feeling of waiting passions, ready to break out. I placed my cup on the table and composed my face.

Naghan ti Lodkwara, Targon the Tapster and Cleitar the Standard happened to be the officers of the Sword Watch on duty that day. Their scarlet and yellow blazed in the room as they wheeled their men up. The men and women with the Kov of Kaldi kept together. They looked lost, not so much bewildered and bedraggled as approaching those states and not much caring for the experience. They must have gone through some highly unpleasant times, getting out of Kaldi.

"Majister!" burst out this Kov Vodun, and he went into the full incline, prostrating himself on the rugs of the marble floor.

"Get up, kov," I said, displeased. "We no longer admit of that flummery here in Vondium in these latter days."

Before he rose he turned his face up and looked at me.

A man of middle years, with a shrewd, weather-beaten face in which those brown Vallian eyes were partially hidden by heavy, down-drooping lids, he was a man with depths to his being, a man of gravitas. His clothes were of first quality, being the usual buff Vallian coat and breeches with the tall black boots. His broad-brimmed hat with those two slots cut in the front brim he held in his left hand. He stood up.

He, naturally, wore no weapons. My Sword Watch would not tolerate strangers, even if they claimed to be kovs, the Kregan equivalent to dukes, carrying weapons into the presence of the Emperor and Empress of Vallia. That was a new and unwelcome custom, over which I had sighed and allowed, for as you will know we in Vallia are more used to carrying our weapons as a sign of our independence. But times change. Weapons were a part and parcel of life now, and we would soon be back to the old days, I hoped.

Kov Vodun's retainers wore banded sleeves in maroon and gray, the colors of Kaldi. Their badges, sewn in drawn wire and in sculpted gold for the kov, represented a leaping sea-barynth, that long and sinuous sea monster of Kregen. I looked closely, for by the colors and badges a man wears may he be recognized again.

You can, also, tell his allegiances. There were no other colors—no black and white of the racters, for example—and from what I knew of Kaldi I believed the province to be out of the main stream of power politics. There were many provinces of the old Vallia whose hierarchy preferred to keep aloof from intrigues.

I considered. Then: "Lahal, Kov Vodun. You are welcome."

He did not smile; but a muscle jumped in his cheek.

"Lahal, majister. I praise Opaz the All Glorious I have arrived safely."

As you will see, I had cut through the Llahals straight to the Lahals. A small point; but I fancied this man needed encouragement.

"You will take refreshment?" I indicated the loaded tables and, instantly, a cup of tea was brought forward, for it was far too early for wine. "There is parclear and sazz if you would prefer."

"Tea, majister, and I thank you. Those devils from Pandahem drain the country dry. We are fortunate to be alive."

He was laboring under some powerful emotion that made the cup shake upon the saucer. I assumed what he had gone through had left an indelible mark. He told me his father, the old kov, had been slain by the enemies of Vallia, and that all the country down there was firmly in the hands of Rosil Yasi, the Strom of Morcray. At this name I sucked in my breath. I knew that rast of old. A Kataki, one of that whiptailed race who are slavemasters par excellence, the Kataki Strom and I were old antagonists and I knew him as a man who bore me undying enmity. He was, also, a tool of Phu-si-Yantong's, and he had worked in his time for Vad Garnath of Hamal, a man who had his come-uppance waiting for him if ever we met again.

His retainers were taken care of and the other people in the Sapphire Reception Room were soon engaged in general conversation with him, trying to learn all there was to know of the situation. News, as always, was eagerly sought after.

Introductions were made as necessary and when the cordialities had been completed and he had described graphically how he and his people had fought from the hills until all their supplies had gone, and they were ragged and starving, so that they had at last stolen an airboat and made good their escape, Nath Nazabhan drew me privily aside.

Seeing that Nath had something he wished to get off his chest I moved quietly with him to a curtained alcove. I had been watching one of Kov Vodun's people with a puzzled interest. This man—if it was a man, for in the enveloping green cloak and hood the figure could as easily have been a woman—moved with a slow stately upright stance. He (or she) carried his (or her) hands thrust deeply into the wide sleeves of the robe, crossed upon the chest. The waist was cinctured by a narrow golden chain from which the lockets for rapier and dagger swung emptily. There was merely black shadow within the hood, and a fugitive gleam of eye.

Upon the breast of the swathing green cloak, and very small, appeared the maroon and gray and the leaping Sea-Barynth. So I turned away, guessing this personage to be an adviser to Kov Vodun. If he (or she) turned out to be a Kataki in disguise, or some other evil-minded rast, my people would soon find out.

Nath said: "I suppose he is genuine? I mean, the real kov? He could be a spy, still working for Yantong."

"He could be genuine and the real kov and still be working for Yantong."

"By Vox, yes!"

One of the clever tricks an emperor has to know how to perform is judging character. So many people judge character by a person's relations with society or established social orders; to perform the difficult task properly you have to judge if a person is being true to his own basic beliefs. This is fundamental. What goes even beyond that, penetrating into the unknown depths beyond the fundament—if, truly, that be possible—is to judge not only a person's adherence to his own beliefs and therefore his own qualities of character; but to judge if those beliefs match up to what you yourself believe. If the two square—fine. If they do not—beware!

A part of the puzzle was solved for us almost at once. The least important part, to be sure.

A Jiktar walked across to Kov Vodun and he moved a little diffidently, I thought. He wore a smart uniform of sky-blue tunic and madder-red breeches, and because he was Nath Orcantor, known as Nath the Frolus, and a well-liked regimental commander, he wore his rapier and main gauche as a matter of uniform dress.

He had raised a regiment of totrixmen for the defense of Vondium, and because he was from Ovvend he had insisted on clothing his regiment in blue tunics and red breeches, a combination unusual for Vallia. Now he halted before the kov and was introduced by Chuktar Ty-Je Efervon, a wily Pachak who was Nath the Frolus's Brigade commander.

"Orcantor," said Kov Vodun. "Of course. Your family is well known in Ovvend—shipping, I think."

"That is so, kov. And I remember you when you visited Ovvend with your father. I am saddened at his loss, for he was a fine man and a great kov."

"His death shall be avenged," said Vodun, and he spoke between his teeth. All who watched him saw the flash of insensate rage. "I shall not rest until the devils are brought to justice." His left hand dropped to his belt and groped, and found no familiar rapier hilt. But we all understood the message. Justice, from Vodun Alloran, the Kov of Kaldi, would be meted out with the sword.

"So he is the real kov," said Nath.

"It would seem so. I think it is high time Naghan Vanki earned his hire." Naghan Vanki had come in from his estates and was prepared to resume his position as the emperor's chief spy-master. We had crossed swords in the past, and come to rapprochements. Now, with Delia to smooth the way, Naghan Vanki, Vad of Nav-Sorfall, was prepared to work with me. "He must sniff out all he can of this Kov Vodun."

"Agreed. Vodun has a way with him, a presence. The ladies are quite smitten."

And, by Krun, that was true, for the ladies were clustered around Kov Vodun now and were hanging on his words. Vodun had a story to tell, of hair-breadth escapes and disguises and swift flights in the lights of the Moons of Kregen. That flash of rage we had seen in him had struck like a lightning bolt, and had as quickly vanished. But Vodun would not rest until his father had been avenged.

"Well, Nath, I cannot shilly-shally about like this all day. I have a new flour mill to inspect, and then, I fancy you may feel it incumbent on me to take a look at the Second. Is this in your mind?"

He laughed.

"They are in good heart, now. It is only miserable skulking sorts of formations that do not relish showing off for their emperor."

We had barely touched on that awful moment when the Second had recoiled. They had broken at the junction of Kerchuri and Kerchuri, the two wings of the Phalanx. They had been forced back on their rear ranks, a seething sea of bronze and crimson and many of the pikes had gone up. A pikeman whose pike stabs air is of little use in the front ranks. But the Third's Sixth Kerchuri had swung up and held the torrent of voves, and the Second had closed up, reformed, and held.

That, as I pointed out to Nath, was the achievement.

After the break, they had taken a fresh grasp on courage, had breathed in, and then smashed back, file by file, and the pikes had come down all in line, and they had driven the clansmen recoiling back.

"There are many bobs to be distributed, majister."

"We shall make of the ceremony something special." The men had earned their medals, and if they called them bobs in fine free-and-easy fashion, they valued them nonetheless.

Making my excuses to the company—which had thinned now as the people went about their work—I slipped away without ceremony. The Sword Watch were there. Delia gave me a smile and I said: "I must talk to you this evening, my heart." Whereat her face grew grave and she understood that I did not talk thus lightly. But I went out and mounted up on a fine fresh zorca, Grumbleknees, a gray, and took myself off to the flour mill.

The original mill had burned in the Time of Troubles and the new structure incorporated refinements the wise men said would increase production as well as milling a finer flour.

If I do not dwell on this flour mill it is precisely because this inspection was typical of so many that had to be undertaken. Everyone wanted to shine in the sight of the emperor, and although I could, had I wished, regard that as petty crawling lick-spittling behavior, I did not. We all worked for Vondium and for Vallia and my job was to make sure we all did the best we could.

The streaming mingled lights of the Suns of Scorpio flooded down as the waterwheel groaned and heaved and turned over as the sluice gates opened and the white water poured through. I looked up. Feeding the people would be by the measure of this mill that much easier. So I looked up, and with a hissing thud a long Lohvian arrow sprouted abruptly from the wood, a hand's breadth from my head.

Three

Of a Meeting with Nath the Knife, Aleygyn of the Stikitches

"Hold fast!" My bellow ripped into the air. The bows of the Sword Watch, lifted, arrows nocked, drawn back, poised. Those sinewy fingers did not release the pull on the bowstrings by a fraction.

"There he goes!" shouted Cleitar, furious.

We could all see the bowman who had loosed at me clambering up the outside staircase of a half-ruined building across the canal. He wore a drab gray half-cape, and his legs were bare. He carried the long Lohvian bow in his left hand, and the quiver over his shoulder was stuffed with shafts. Like the arrow that still quivered in the wood by my head, each one was fletched with feathers of somber purple.

"A damned stikitche!" raved Cleitar. "Majister—you allow him to escape. Let us—"

"Lower your bows."

The archers in the detachment of the Sword Watch obeyed.

Targon the Tapster, his face scowling, his brilliance of uniform which lent him, like them all, a barbaric magnificence, aflame under the suns, heeled his zorca across.

"Assassins, majister. They should be put down—"

These officers of the Sword Watch had not always been fighting men. I think it true to say their military experience had all been gained in contact with me. We had fought together in clearing Vallia. Cleitar the Standard, a big bulky man with bitterness in his soul, had been Cleitar the Smith until the Iron Riders had sundered him forever from his family and home. Targon the Tapster and Naghan ti Lodkwara had met over the matter of strayed or stolen ponshos. Now they formed a body of close comrades I came to value more and more as the seasons and the campaigns passed over.

"You are right. But that stikitche, had he wished to assassinate me, would not have missed. Bring me the shaft."

The arrow was brought and I unwrapped the letter attached.

The message was addressed: "Dray Prescot, Emperor of Vallia." The salutation, in the correct grammatical form, read: "Llahal-pattu. Majister."

I sighed and looked quickly down for the signature.

The scrawl, in a different hand from the body of the letter, was just decipherable. It read: "Nath Trerhagen, Aleygyn."

This assassin and I had met before, just the once. He was Nath Trerhagen, the Aleygyn, Hyr Stikitche, Pallan of the Stikitche Khand of Vondium.

This brought up painful memories of Barty Vessler and so looking at the writing I forced unwelcome thoughts away and concentrated on the here and now. Nath the Knife, the chief assassin was called. He wanted to meet me. There was an important matter that had come up. The phraseology was all in the mock legal, written by his pet lawyer he kept tucked up in some lair in Drak's City, the Old City of Vondium, where, so far, the writ of the emperor's law did not run.

"We should go in there and burn the place out," quoth Larghos Manifer, a Vondian who had been newly recruited into the Sword Watch. His round face fairly bristled. His words met with general approval.

"Yet the people of Drak's City held out the longest against the damned Hamalese," I pointed out.

"They could fight all the imps of Sicce from there, majister." Larghos Manifer, because he had been born in Vondium the Proud City, and knew what he knew, held a natural resentment against Drak's City. "For one who is not a thief or a forger or a stikitche or an Opaz-forsaken criminal of one kind or another it is death to venture in."

"Nath the Knife wishes to meet me in the shadow of the Gate of Skulls. That, I think, indicates a willingness to come forward. We are, in theory, on neutral ground there."

So, later on that morning and before we were due to return to eat, we wended our way through the crowded streets toward the moldering pile of old houses clustered behind the old walls that was the site of the very first settlements here, long before Vondium became the capital of Vallia.

Targon, Naghan and Cleitar sidled their zorcas close to one another and after a brief conversation, Naghan went haring off. I had a shrewd suspicion about where he was going and what he was up to, and when we rode quietly up to the Gate of Skulls my guess was confirmed.

The usual hectic activity around and through the gate was stilled. The striped awnings over stalls had been taken down. People kept away. The space this side of the gate and the Kyro of Lost Souls beyond were deserted. In a double line ranked two hundred paces back from the gate waited the Sword Watch. This was the handiwork of Naghan and the others. Bowman and lancer alternating, the men sat their zorcas silently. The scarlet and yellow, the gleaming helmets, the feathers, the brilliance of weapons, all made a fine show. I rather fancied Nath the Knife might have a similar if less splendidly outfitted array on his side of the wall.

And—he had Bowmen of Loh among his scurvy lot. My men were armed with the compound reflex bow of Vallia, a flat trajectory weapon of great power but not a patch on the great Lohvian longbow.

As a matter of interest as I waited for the chief assassin I made a cursory count of the Sword Watch. I was astonished. There were better than five hundred of them. This was news to me. The rascally members of my original Choice Band, with whom I had campaigned and caroused and fought over Vallia, had been busy recruiting. Well, that could be looked into. Now, Nath the Knife made his presence known.

Four hefty fellows walked into the shadows under the Gate of Skulls carrying a heavy lenken table. This they placed down at the midway point between the inner and outer portals. They were followed by four more who carried a carved chair of fascinating design, a chair that breathed authority, a chair that, by Krun, was as like a throne as made no difference.

In the shadows beyond table and chair waited a line of men, indistinct, true; but the long jut of the bows in their fists was not to be mistaken. A bugle pealed.

"They make a mockery of it, majister," growled Cleitar. He gripped the pole of my personal flag, Old Superb, and he scowled upon the Gate of Skulls. On my other side Ortyg the Tresh upheld the new union flag of Vallia. Close to hand Volodu the Lungs, leathery and thirsty, waited with his silver trumpet resting on his knee. At my back, as always, rode Korero the Shield, that splendid Kildoi with the four arms and tailhand, his golden beard glinting in the light of the suns, his white teeth just visible as his half-smile at the panorama before us matched my own feelings.

The Sword Watch had been reorganized. Now they were clearly arranged in order, the companies each with its own trumpeter and standard and commander. Those commanders I recognized from many a long day's campaigning. The small body of men who had appointed themselves as my personal bodyguard—which at the time I had deplored but acceded to at the sense of urgency these men shared—waited close. There were Magin, Wando the Squint, Uthnior Chavonthjid, Nath the Doorn and his boon comrade Nath the Xanko. There were, of course, Targon the Tapster, Naghan ti Lodkwara and Dorgo the Clis, his scar livid along his face.

As we waited for the ponderous arrival of Nath the Knife, Hyr Stikitche, what intrigued me was the apparent lack of a leader of the Sword Watch. Clearly those men I have named ran things. When they gave an order the zorcamen jumped. And they appeared to work together, with a consensus, each one supporting the next. I hoped that state of affairs resulted from the time we had spent campaigning together. There was no mistaking the smooth way things got done in the Emperor's Sword Watch.

The strange fancy struck me, as we sat our zorcas and waited, that we were arrayed as we would be when we waited in battle for the outcome, so as to go hurtling down to defeat or victory. With the flags waving in the slight breeze, with the trumpets ready to peal the calls, with the weapons bright and our uniforms immaculate, we looked just as we looked in battle. We were the emperor's personal reserve, a powerful striking force under his hand. I may say it was most odd, by Vox, to remember that I was that emperor.

Just as a stir made itself apparent in the shadows of the Gate of Skulls I was thinking that the quicker Drak got home from Faol the better.

Alone, walking steadily and without haste, Nath Trerhagen, the Aleygyn, made his way to the table and passed around it and so sat himself down in that throne-like chair.

I smiled.

"The impudent rast!" said Cleitar.

"It is clear," offered Naghan ti Lodkwara. "He will sit. And there is no chair for you, majister."

"Let me shaft the wretch!" suggested Dorgo the Clis.

He would have done so, instanter. But I nodded to the line of bowmen in the shadows.

"They are Bowmen of Loh. Each one would feather four of you before you could reach them. Hold fast!"

I rode out a half a dozen paces before my men and turned and lifted in the stirrups and faced them.

"I ride alone. Not one of you moves. My life is forfeit." Then, to ram the order home, I said quietly to Volodu the Lungs, "Blow the Stand, Volodu."

The silver trumpet with the significant dents was raised to those leathery lips.

Grumbleknees turned again and walked sedately across the open dusty space toward the Gate of Skulls. His single spiral horn caught the mingled light of the suns and glittered.

So it was and all unplanned, that the Emperor of Vallia rode toward this meeting with the pealing silver trumpet notes playing about his ears.

The villains of Drak's City would not know what the call portended. They would probably think it was some kind of pompous fanfare that was sounded whenever the emperor rode out or did anything at all or even wished to blow his nose. I rode on, and I felt the amusement strong in me at the conceit.

There was one thing of which I was pretty sure. I was not going to stand up while this stikitche lolled on his throne.

"By the Black Chunkrah!" I said to myself. "Nath the Knife must think again."

No personal vanity was involved. This was a matter of policy and, of course, of will.

Nath the Knife wore ordinary Vallian clothes, that is to say, the buff tunic, breeches and tall black boots. On his breast the badge of the three purple feathers was pinned with a golden clasp. His face was covered by a dulled steel mask. When he spoke his voice was like breaking iron.

"Majister."

I looked down on him from the back of the zorca. I debated. Then, carefully, I said, "Aleygyn."

The steel mask moved as he nodded, as though under the steel he smiled, satisfied.

"Dismount, emperor, so that we may talk."

"You might have killed me before this. I do not think you wish to talk without reason. Spit it out, Nath the Knife. There is much work to be done in Vondium these days."

He sat up straighter. The power he wielded within the Old City was commensurate with the power I wielded in Vondium.

"There is a matter of bokkertu to be decided."

"Once before you said that. You asked me to pay you gold so that I would not be a kitchew." A kitchew, the target for assassination, usually has a very brief allotment left of life. But that matter had been settled with the death of the stikitche paid to do the job. That, I had thought, was finalized.

Nath the Knife moved his hand. "No. It is not that." He paused. There was about him a strange air of indecisiveness and I wished I could see his face beneath the mask so as to weigh him up better. "No. We had a bad time of it when those rasts of Hamalese captured Vondium."

I said, "I heard how you held out in Drak's City. You deserve congratulations for that. It has been in my mind to offer you masons and brickies, carpenters, so that you may rebuild and clean away some of the destruction."

His head went up. "You are serious?"

It is damned hard to read a man wearing a mask.

"Yes. Perfectly serious."

There seemed little point in adding that I wanted some of the mess in Drak's City cleared up so as to lessen the risk of infection to the rest of the City. They policed themselves in the Old City; but I did not think they were too well-served by needlemen and once an epidemic got hold we would all be in trouble.

"You are not as other emperors—"

"No, by Vox!"

"And would you find men willing to enter here? Would not their tools be stolen, their throats cut?"

"Under proper safeguards and assurances, men would come in here and rebuild."

"Because you told them to?"

I wondered what he was getting at.

"Not because I told them to. Because they understand the reasons. Anyway, I would pay them—pay them well—for the work will not be pleasant."

"I think, Dray Prescot, they would do it for you."

"They are not slaves. We do not have slaves anymore."

Sitting the zorca, feeling the old itch down my back, darkly aware of that line of bowmen, I was all the time ready to get my foolish head down and make a run for it. But the trick of remaining mounted had given me just a little back of a hold on the situation. Nath the Knife waved his hand again.

He wore gauntleted leather gloves; but a ring glowed in ronil fire upon his finger outside the glove.

He came straight to the point, now, putting it to me.

"We have received a contract for you, emperor. Do not ask from whom, for that is our affair, in honor. I run perilously close to breaking the stikitche honor in this. But we stikitches remember the Hamalese and the aragorn and the flutsmen. We were cruelly oppressed. We rose when you and your armies broke into the city. Aye! We of Drak's City hung many a damned Hamalese by his heels. We have seen what you have wrought in Vondium." He pushed a paper that lay on the table. "The contract calls for immediate execution and the price is exceedingly large."

I took a breath.

"And you wish me to pay you the price?"

Before he could answer, I went on: "You will recall what I told you when that was mentioned before—"

"No, emperor! By Jhalak! I know you to be a stiff-necked tapo; but will you not listen?"

I nodded and he went on speaking, and, I thought with a twinge of amusement, a little huffily. It seemed he could hardly understand just what he was saying, or why he was doing what he did. But he ploughed on, natheless.

The gist of it was that the folk of Drak's City felt it would be to their advantage if I was alive and running Vondium. In this I fancied they did not put a great deal of store by the considerable army now at the disposal of the government. Their confidence in their own tumbledown city had been shaken by their defeat and enslavement by the Hamalese. What the chief assassin told me, quite simply, was that they intended to repudiate the contract, they would not accept it, and they wanted me to know. But—

"There is a chance that the client will bring in stikitches from outside Vondium. We frown on that; but it is known. I assure you, emperor, on the honor of a Hyr-Stikitche, that we will prevent that if it is in our power."

What was odd about that was not the talk of assassins' honor, which is just as real to them as any form of honor code to any other group of people, but the suggestion that in stikitche matters the khand of Vondium might not have the power to do what it willed.

"You have my thanks, Aleygyn. Vallia is sundered and torn, and our enemies press in on us from all sides. I think it is a task laid on all of us to resume peaceful ways. But that will not be possible until these invaders have been driven away—"

He did not so much surprise me as reveal that he, too, was a Vallian.

"Until they are all buried six feet deep and sent to rot in the Ice Floes of Sicce!"

"Agreed." I chanced a shaft. "There are many fine young men in Drak's

City, men who have proved they can fight. They would be welcomed in the ranks of the new Vallian Army."

The eyes within the slits of the mask glittered on me. The suns were shifting around and that mingled opaz radiance crept under the arch of the Gate and drove back the shadows.

"I will talk to the Presidio," he said, whereat I smiled. The folk of Drak's City aped Vondium and the whole of Vallia in holding their own Presidio, their governing body. It was a charming conceit. "There are men here who would form regiments that would show you soft townsfolk how to fight."

"I await them in the ranks."

"Not," he said, a tang in his voice, "in the Phalanx."

"No, I agree. As light infantry, skirmishers."

"We have paktuns here—"

"I do not employ mercenaries. Many paktuns have become Vallian citizens. We are a people's army. You are Vallians. Your young men will be paid the same as any other Vallians in our ranks."

He digested that. And then we spoke of the practical side of the matter for a time until I felt I was getting altogether too chummy with a damned assassin, even if he was mindful of the welfare of the country. I twitched Grumbleknees' reins.

"I bid you Remberee, Aleygyn. I shall send a Pallan to talk with you about the rebuilding I promised. I am serious. As serious as I hope you are in sending men to join the army. The quicker Vallia is back to her old peaceful ways the better. Remberee."

"Remberee, Dray Prescot."

But the old warrior did not stand up to say good-bye.

Four

Delia Thinks Ahead

"And you really had a long conversation with a stikitche! My heart—suppose—"

"But it didn't."

"All the same, you are just as feckless as ever you were. I wish Seg and Inch were here—"

"They're just as bad."

"True." She sighed and then laughed. "You're all as bad as one another, a pack of rascals and rogues!"

199

"There is a matter I must talk to you about and yet have not the courage to—"

"Dray! Oh—my dear. You are going away again!"

I nodded.

"Back to your silly little world with its one yellow sun and one silver moon and no diffs?"

"By Zim-Zair! I hope not!"

I told her a little of what had passed between me and the Star Lords, and then added: "And it is mighty fine of them to warn me. They do not often do that. But, my heart, rest assured. As soon as whatever must be done is done I shall fly back here just as fast as I can."

"You make it all sound so—so—"

"I know."

The warm gleam of the oil lamps shed a cozy glow in our snug and private little room. We had both spent a busy day. We were surrounded now by the good things of gracious living, or as many of them as our straightened circumstances would allow, and we relished this time when we could relax and talk of the doings of the day and of our plans for the morrow. To change the conversation, I said: "What do you make of Vodun Alloran, the Kov of Kaldi?"

Delia made a sweet little moue and tucked her feet up more comfortably on the divan. She wore a lounging robe, as did I, and we joyed one in the other. "Well, he is bright and forthright and, I am sure, a fine fighting man. What he is like as a kov I do not know. But, somehow, I must have more time to plumb him properly."

I glanced at her. Delia usually knows her own mind.

"He strikes me as a useful man to have in the army. He will fight like a leem to get his kovnate back."

"I am sure. He is a fighter, of that there is no doubt."

Again, I sensed that deliberate withdrawal.

"I am minded to give him command of a brigade—as a kov he will never accept less. It is a pity he has no men of his own to form a regiment. But with the expansion, promotion will prove no problem." I yawned. "I'll be glad when we can finish with all this fighting and get back to decent living again."

"So, Dray Prescot, you imagine you are well acquainted with decent living?"

She teased me; but it stung. I had been a wanderer, a soldier, a sailor, an airman, a fellow who struggled and fought and brawled until, it seemed, he could not possibly understand that life was not meant to be lived thus. But, the knotty problem there was, quite simply, that all this took place on Kregen. What a world Kregen is, by Zair! Wonderful, unutterably lovely, unspeakably ghastly, at times it is all things to all men. And yet I would not willingly be parted from that world four hundred light years from the planet of my birth or from the woman who meant more than anything else. I had been a slave and now I was an emperor—well, an emperor of sorts.

"The quicker—" I began.

"Yes. I have had word from Drak. Queen Lush is bringing him home."

I gaped.

Then: "Drak? Queen Lush—bringing him?"

"He is not hurt," she said, quickly. "Well, not much. He has rescued Melow and Kardo. The message simply says that we should expect them." Her eyebrows drew down. "Queen Lush is—well—"

"Queen Lush is Queen Lush," I said. "She has changed wonderfully from what she was when Phu-Si-Yantong sent her to entrap your father. Then she did as she was told, for all she was a queen with great wealth and power—"

"And beauty."

"Oh, aye, she looks well, does Queen Lush. And Drak?"

"There is no doubt, at least in my mind. Queen Lush means to marry Drak."

"She set her heart on being Empress of Vallia. Well, it seems she will have her way, seeing she knows very well that I shall hand over to Drak. She has heard me say so often enough."

"Mayhap you do her an injustice."

"I would like to think so. Yes, perhaps I do. I know she was much taken with Drak. Well—any girl with any sense would be. And that brings up Seg's daughter, Silda."

"I like Silda."

"That settles that, then. When she went against Thelda's wishes and joined in the Sisters of the Rose—"

"Hush."

But I had already hushed myself. One did not speak lightly of these female secret Orders. And, too, mention of Seg and Thelda brought up a sharp agony I just could not face then. So I went on: "Silda is a charming girl and I would welcome her as a daughter-in-law. And Seg would be overjoyed. But—what says Drak in all this?"

"I think," said the Empress of Vallia, "you would have to ask Queen Lush-fymi of Lome the answer to that."

We did not play Jikaida that night, for there was a mountain of paperwork Enevon Ob-Eye, the chief stylor, had landed us with. With the morning and a new day in which to work we set doggedly to that work. Rebuilding and healing a shattered city and people demand strenuous and unending efforts. All the time I felt the relief that Drak was safe. He was the stern and sober one of my sons, and yet he could be wild enough on occasion. He had taken over in Valka, as the strom, when I had been snatched back to Earth. He had known me when he had been young, unlike his brothers, for Zeg had been rather too young, and Jaidur had not known me at all. But these were not the reasons I felt he would prove to be a splendid emperor. It seemed to me that he had been born to the imperium. I was just a rough-hewn sailor from a distant planet, schooled by the wildly ferocious clansmen of Segesthes, picking up bits of lore and scraps of knowledge from here and there on Kregen. But Drak was an emperor to his fingertips. I confess I joyed in that.

Mind you, I did not forget that I was the King of Djanduin. But Djanduin was dwaburs away in Havilfar, and my friends could run affairs there perfectly. The moment I could snatch the time from Vallia, it would be Djanduin for me. Even, perhaps, before Strombor. As the Lord of Strombor I reposed absolute faith and confidence in Gloag, who was a good comrade and the one handling everything there. That I had some still remaining links with Hamal, the hated enemy of Vallia, remained true. I was, in Hamal, Hamun ham Farthytu, the Amak of Paline Valley. Nulty was the one in charge there. But that seemed to me distant and vague and blurred; one day I would return to Paline Valley. As Hamun ham Farthytu I would seek out my good comrades, Rees and Chido. Good comrades, and also Hamalese and therefore foemen to Vallians.

What a nonsense all that was!

The plans I hoped to see come to fruition demanded that Vallia and Hamal join hands in friendship, and with the nations of the island of Pandahem begin to form that grand alliance we must forge so as to combat the vicious shanks who raided from over the curve of the world. All these things went around in my head continually as we worked on the immediate problems of clearing Vallia of her invaders.

The news from Seg reaffirmed his skill in keeping the clansmen off our necks until we were able to defeat them once and for all. Patrols of observation in the southwest reported little movement from the invaders there; but that part of the island had been under the heel of foreign lords with their mercenaries for long enough for us to watch and ward the borders and build our strength for the counterstroke.

The Presidio now met regularly in the sumptuous Villa of Vennar, situated on one of the exclusive hills of Vondium. The place had been abandoned since its lord, Kov Layco Jhansi, had proved himself a double dyed villain and a traitor. The deren* of the Presidio had been burned to the ground. We would not waste resources on rebuilding that, not until Vallia was free, and particularly when there were abandoned villas with enormous chambers suitable for the purposes of the Presidio lying empty.

In the Presidio Kov Vodun na Kaldi proved a volatile and persuasive speaker. Constantly he sought to encourage us to action. His hatred for the Hamalese and the Pandaheem was implacable. With his reiterated calls

---

* deren: palace

for the utter destruction of the invaders he reminded me of Cato and his never-ending Carthago delenda est.

Various conversations with him from time to time revealed him as a man with a history. Fretful at being the son of a kov who might have to wait years before he came into the title, the lands and power, and the responsibility, he went abroad and became a mercenary. Because Vallia had not kept a standing army, being mainly a trading maritime nation, many of her young men took themselves overseas to become mercenaries. Many had become famous paktuns. Kov Vodun was one such, entitled to wear the pakmort, the silver mortil-head on its silk cord at his throat. He did not wear it at home for, as he said, that would be too flamboyant.

So, he did understand something of soldiering.

He mentioned various places in Loh, where most of his service had been spent, and, as I summed him up, he grew in my estimation. We needed men like this, tough, no-nonsense professionals to put the polish on the crowds of eager but raw recruits who flocked to the standards.

When I offered him a brigade, somewhat diffidently, I must admit, expecting him to refuse, he accepted.

"Give me the brigade, majister. You will soon see my men will form the best brigade in the army."

The appointment was warmly endorsed by the Presidio.

Thinking myself foolish for offering a command to a man half expecting him to refuse—a very poor way of going on—I wondered if Delia's attitude had contributed to that feeling of inexplicable hesitancy. Naghan Vanki, the emperor's chief spymaster, reported that everything Kov Vodun had said was true. Vanki gave him a clean bill of health, and my spirits lifted at that. Asked about the mysterious green-cloaked figure, Vanki gave his thin smile.

"He is merely an adviser to the kov, majister. He is one of the Wizards of Fruningen, a small sect but with some claim to serious consideration. They regard Opaz, I am told, as a single entity and not, as indeed they truly are, the Invisible Twins, one and indissolubly twins."

I raised my eyebrows at this, for Vanki expressed an extreme view. Most people regarded Opaz as the spirit of the Invisible Twins made manifest. And I knew of the island of Fruningen, a small rocky scrap jutting out of the sea northwest of the island of Tezpor. Reports, amplified by Kov Vodun, told us that the Vad of Tezpor, Larghos the Lame, had been hanged upside down from his own rooftree by flutsmen. And, Tezpor lay due north of the large island of Rahartdrin. There was nothing simple I could do for Katrin Rashumin save pray to all the gods she was safe.

"So far I have not met a Wizard of Fruningen," I said to Naghan Vanki. "They are clearly not to be compared to the Wizards of Loh." At this Vanki let his thin smile indicate the idiocy of the remark. I went on: "But how stand they in relation to the Sorcerers of Murcroinim?"

"If one were to engage the other in wizardly combat, Majister, I fear they would both disappear in puffs of smoke."

"At least that argues real powers."

"Yes."

Naghan Vanki had dealt with a few real powers in his time, powers of steel and gold; I did not think a sorcerer would discompose him overmuch. A tough, wily old bird, Naghan Vanki, always impeccable in his silver and black.

So Kov Vodun got his brigade and began smartening them up and putting a snap in their step and iron into their backbones.

Then, although it spelled misery and desolation for the unfortunate people involved, an event occurred which gave me a capital opportunity to delegate responsibilities in Vondium to the Crebent-Justicar, the Lord Farris, and the Presidio, and take off for action.

"So you are off again, then, husband," said Delia as I strapped on my harness in our rooms and wondered just what selection of weaponry to take. "This time I think I shall go with you, for the folk of Bryvondrin have suffered much and yet they have taken in and cared for the people of the occupied provinces east of the Great River. And they are our people."

What she meant was plain. Bryvondrin, situated in one of the tremendous loops of the Great River, the enormous central waterway of Vallia, was an imperial province.

"True. But what concerns me is that the enemy have got over the Great River. We regarded that as a first-class natural barrier. And, my heart, it is only seventy dwaburs away from Vondium."

"Too close for comfort."

"But that does not mean you will fly with me—"

"You would prevent me?"

I sighed.

"I would if I thought it would do any good. You know how I joy to have you with me—but if there, rather, as there is to be fighting—"

"Fighting!"

I felt suitably chastened. Truly, Delia of Delphond has served in her quota of battles, to my own dread despair.

Her handmaidens, Floria and Rosala came in all chattering and laughing, rosy, gorgeous girls. They brought stands of clothing over which, I felt sure, they would all giggle and try against themselves and spend hours deciding exactly what to wear.

Aghast, I said: "You are not bringing them?"

"Are you taking Emder?"

"Well— to be honest, no."

"Then it will be as it was in the old days."

So that was decided. As usual, the decision seemed to have arrived of its own accord.

Naghan Vanki reported that the invasion over the Great River was not in overmuch force. His spies had the composition confirmed by cavalry patrols from our small forces there.

There were some fifteen thousand fighting men, ten of infantry and five of cavalry, mainly totrixes with some zorcas. These men were formed and disciplined, professional mercenaries, and although they were not in great force they were formidable. Their object, as I saw it, was to create a secure bridgehead for their further encroachments on our country. Certainly, they held all the land from the Great River to the east coast.

"We must fly out in sufficient force to make very sure of the victory," I told my assembled chiefs when, dressed in war harness and with Delia at my side, I rode out to see the army off. We were constrained to leave strong forces in Vondium, for obvious reasons, and I had had to pick and choose the units to go. Everyone wanted to be in on the act, and there were some long faces decorating those hardy warriors I had to leave behind.

Firstly, the Phalanx. Nath insisted on accompanying me and he would bring the Third Kerchuri of the Second Phalanx. With foot soldiers, Hakkodin and the attached archers, the Third Kerchuri amounted to some eight thousand men.

Secondly, three brigades of infantry, the sword and shield men. One of the brigades, the Nineteenth, was that commanded by Kov Vodun. These three brigades amounted to some four thousand five hundred men.

Thirdly, two brigades of archers, around three thousand.

And, fourthly, a brigade of the skirmishers.

That formed the infantry corps, and a fine body they looked as they marched out with a swing to board the sailing fliers. The weird constructions, more flying rafts, we had been forced to use before had now given place, with the time and the rebuilding program, to more sensible flying ships. These possessed hulls with real wooden walls, so that the men would have shelter during the flight. Their sail plan was deliberately kept simple; a fore, main and mizzen with jib and headsails. We rigged courses and topsails, not caring to go further into the fascinating ramifications of the typical Vallian galleon's sail plan. They would fly, and with their silver boxes upholding them in thin air and extending invisible keels into the lines of ethero-magnetic force, they could tack and make boards against the wind. They were sailing ships of the sky, and subject to the vagaries of the weather, quite unlike the vollers of the Hamalese.

For cavalry we took a division of totrix archers and lancers, just over two thousand jutmen, attached to the Phalanx. One division of totrix heavy cavalry, two thousand strong, and one division of zorcas, two thousand one hundred and sixty in number, were joined by a regiment of the superb heavy nikvove cavalry, five hundred big men on five hundred great-hearted nikvoves.

Our tail consisted of engineers, supply wagons, medical and veterinary components, and a goodly force of varters.

Also, I took the whole of the Sword Watch, leaving merely a small cadre at my officer's pleas to carry on with their program of recruitment and training.

In all we were nearly thirty thousand strong. The plan called for us to land, debouch, deploy and then thrash these upstart invaders and send them packing. That was the plan.

Five

Of the Theatre, a Gale and a Surprise

On the evening before we left we visited the theatre. The idea of pomp or pageantry in a simple visit by the emperor to relax for an evening's enjoyment at the play was anathema to me, so Delia and I and a few companions went quietly to our seats in the Half Moon, an old theatre of Vondium and one in which many famous actors and actresses had trod the boards and spoken their lines.

The building was mainly of brick and stone and only the roof had burned in the Time of Troubles. The seats were arranged in a horseshoe fashion, tiered one above the other, and the acoustics and vision were alike first class. As I sat down on the fleece-stuffed cushions and looked about at the black and ugly burn marks high on the walls, and the licks of fresh paint, and saw the stars glittering high and remote, I reflected that the times of troubles were not over yet, by Vox.

An awning had been erected over the stage. During the performance a light rain began. The performers were shielded, and as they were the important part of the night's proceedings, we in the auditorium perforce sat and got wet. Only a handful of people left. Watching the play absorbed us, and a little rain was nothing.

The play was a new one, recently completed by Master Belzur the Aphorist, called The Scarron Necklace. Although my mind was filled with Army Lists, and the problems of supply and transportation, and the natural concern for the morrow, I found I was held by the action of the play. Of one thing I was pleasantly sure: there were still playwrights left in Vallia.

As was often the case, a purely entertaining middle section had been incorporated, in which choirs sang the old songs of Kregen. On this night a new touch had been added. I sat up, and I heard Delia's delighted laugh at my side.

For, onto the stage pranced files of half-naked girls clad in wisps of crimson and wearing fluffed out felt helmets that might, if you did not look too closely, pass as the bronze-fitted vosk-skull helmets of the Phalanx. The girls all carried wands—and then I realized they were intended to represent the pikes of the pikemen. They were only some five feet long; but the girls made great play with them, marching and countermarching and singing a foolish, lilting, heart-lifting ditty. The words were something to do with a soldier being always able to command the vagaries of a girl's wayward heart. This was the song that was afterward called the "Soldier's Love Potion."

"They march well, majister," said Nath, leaning across and not taking his gaze from the spectacle. "I could do with a few of them in the Phalanx, by Vox!" And he laughed.

The girls weaved patterns across the stage, their wands circling and rising and falling, and thrusting. I found it extraordinarily difficult to laugh. By Zair! I approved of this flummery, for it did a power of good for morale—but in the reflected radiance of the mineral oil lamps limning those slender girls out there I seemed to see the clumped and solid ranks and files of the Phalanx and heard the awful clangor of battle. Playacting, make believe, a light-hearted evening's entertainment—why should I make such heavy weather of it and refuse to take the joy? Why this continual questioning of my motives, when I had made up my mind, grimly, and intended to unite Vallia once again and then hand all over to Drak? Why? Why torture myself with regrets? Life is life, and it whirls along and we all get dragged with it willy-nilly no matter how desperately we cling to the deceptively substantial acts of everyday.

I half-expected to see that damned Gdoinye come sticking his arrogant scarlet-feathered head out over the proscenium arch and summon me off to jump about for the Star Lords. By Krun! But that would stir the old blood up.

Delia sensed my mood, half-desperate, half-defiant, and she pressed my hand, and so I turned my fingers over and gripped hers.

"We sail in the morning."

"I think I shall be glad to shake the dust of Vondium out of my head." I felt her fingers in mine, warm and trembling slightly. "I wish Drak were here."

"He will come home with Queen Lush," she said, and I caught the amused puzzlement in her voice. "I have invited Silda to visit us. Her work—well, she will have news of Lela."

"When that young lady deigns to return home to give a Lahal to her father, I shall have a few words to say—"

"Now, then, you grizzly old graint!"

Then the mock-soldiers on the stage, their crimson draperies swirling and their bodies gleaming splendidly, performed their final triumphant charge, and vanished into the wings, and the rest of The Scarron Necklace began.

So, here we were, a little army flying off with the wind across Vallia toward Bryvondrin to meet these upstart foemen who would not leave us alone.

The wind held fair and we bowled along. Standing on the quarterdeck I looked around on the empty spaces of the sky. How odd, how weird, thus to see an armada of sailing ships billowing grandly through the air! Their sails did not gleam, for they were patched brown and pale blue, dappled with camouflage. But the sight of massive ships upheld in the air, bowling along with all sails spread... incredible.

A sniff at the air and a closer look at the cloud formations ahead gave me unwelcome news. The captain came over at my call and he agreed that we were in for a change in the weather.

"In for a blow, majister—and the breeze will back, I think."

"Aye, captain. I am not as sanguine as I was that we will reach Kanarsmot before the gale strikes."

"We can but pile on all canvas and trust in Opaz, majister."

"Aye."

The plan had been to land near Kanarsmot, a town on the Great River situated where, on the southeastern bank of the river, the boundaries of Mai Makanar to the north and Mai Yenizar to the south marched. By this stratagem we would array our forces in rear of the invaders, cut their supply lines, free the town, and then be in a position to hit them in flank and rear and dispose of them with little hope of escape.

But the wind gusted and freshened. And, as we feared, it backed.

Well, weather is sent by the Hyr-Pallan Whetti-Orbium, the meteorological manifestation of Opaz, and we must do what we could. We battened down. There were no seas to come leaping and crashing in over the bulwarks; but as the breeze blew with ever greater strength and backed around the compass, our yards were hauled farther and farther around. Soon we were facing a stiff easterly. The rushing roar of the wind stuffed our mouths and nostrils and half-blinded us. On the ships staggered, lurching as their invisible keels gripped into the lines of force. At last, when we were within only three dwaburs of the town, it was apparent that we could make no further headway.

The twin suns were sinking, flooding the land below with their mingled streaming lights. The jade and ruby cast long tinted shadows. The country here was tufty, cut up by small hills and gullies, scrub country and yet being well-watered festooned with traceries of forests. The clouds sent racing shadows leapfrogging across the grass.

"Down, captain," I shouted, my words blown away. I pointed down and stabbed my hand urgently. If we continued aloft we'd be blown miles off course.

So, in the last of the light, we made our landfall.

We came down fifteen miles short of Kanarsmot and we knew the enemy was in force somewhere between us and the town.

Thus are the grandiose plans of captains and kings foiled by the invisible breeze.

A pretty bedlam ensued as the reluctant animals were herded from the capacious interiors of the ships. The men disembarked and set about bivouacking. The wind tore at cloaks and banners. We pitched a dry bivouac, no fires being lighted. Cavalry patrols, zorcamen, were sent out immediately.

When I gave firm orders that the flutduins, those marvelous saddle birds of Djanduin, were not to be disembarked, Tyr Naghan Elfurnil ti Vandayha stomped across to me, raving.

His flying leathers were swirled about his legs by the breeze. He had one hand gripping his sword and the other outstretched, palm up, as though he was begging for alms.

"Majister! My flyers can scout that Opaz-forsaken—"

"Come now, Naghan—look at the weather!"

"My flutduins can fly through the Mists of Sicce itself."

"I don't doubt," I said, dryly. "However, I shall need your aerial cavalry for the morrow. The breeze will drop by then."

Naghan Elfurnil was a Valkan, and he had been trained up by expert flyers from Djanduin. An aerial detachment was with us; but I was not going to throw them away in weather like this.

"The jutmen will be our eyes tonight, Naghan."

"They'll be outscouted, you mark my words."

"It would perhaps be best if Jiktar Karidge did not hear you say that, Naghan. He has a temper—"

"Oh, aye, majister. Karidge is a fine zorcaman, I'll give you that." Naghan gave a huge sniff that was instantly whipped away by the wind. "But I'll never live to see the day when zorcas can outscout flutduins."

I forbore to suggest that, perhaps, this night, he had lived that long.

"Those oafs we will fight tomorrow have flying fluttrells. Not many. But you'll need to look sharp to drive 'em off."

"And, strom, since when has a fluttrell had a chance in hell of matching a flutduin?"

Well, by Vox, that was sooth, and we both knew it.

So the pandemonium continued, and slowly and in the end surprisingly, order and quietness came out of chaos. The army bivouacked and the sentries were posted and the patrols went out. If we were not outscouted, we could set down all fair and square. I did not think we would outscout our opponents, for they had the advantage of the terrain. And, as the night progressed and the reports flowed in we understood that on the morrow we would advance to battle with a good idea of the strength and location of the enemy, and that they in their turn would know of our strengths and positions.

There were some cavalry clashes during that night. The army was up and breakfasting and on the move early. The wind had dropped; but we judged three burs or so would have to pass before the weather was fit for aerial cavalry. In that time we formed and marched forward.

The commander of the local forces came in with a remnant of exhausted totrixmen. They had been pushed back by the first onslaught over the Great River and had subsequently harried the invaders as best they could.

"The whole situation was completely quiet," the commander told me. He was a waso-Chuktar, Orlon Turnil, and he looked worn out. "But they will not expect so quick a reaction, majister. Truly, the flying ships are marvels."

That was the trouble with the current mess in Vallia. Our enemies pressed in on all sides and we had to leap from here to there to repel each attack. It was strange to think that not so far away we had friendly forces quite cut off from us by enemy occupied territory. We had to build our strength so as to be able to field enough armies of sufficient power to handle each trouble spot. That was taking the time, and, by Zair, it was tiring me out.

"You had best take your men and see them bedded down," I said.

Chuktar Turnil looked at me.

"I think, majister, I did not hear you. We shall, of course, ride with you this day and fight in the line."

I did not smile. "I think, Chuktar Turnil, you did not hear me aright." And then I added: "You are right welcome. May Opaz ride with you."

As he cantered off to rejoin his men, the six legs of his totrix going floppily in all directions, I gave orders that his little force should ride with the cavalry reserve.

During a regulation break in the line of march we spread the maps and studied the tactical situation. Up until now it had been strategy and operations. Now we got down to the sharp end of planning.

"At the moment," said Karidge, thumping the map, "they must at least have reached this line of trees." His headgear glittered with gold thread, his feathers bristled. He was a light cavalryman from the tips of those feathers to the stirrup-marked boots. I had chosen his zorca brigade and joyed in the choosing.

"And is this river fordable?" I pointed.

"Aye. The men will get wet bellies; but they can cross."

"By the time we reach there, the enemy will have set down less than an ulm off. I think that will do."

Nath scratched his nose.

"You mean to fight with a river at our backs?"

"A fordable river, Nath. You and the Third Kerchuri. The churgurs and archers will come in from the right flank. The woods there will screen their initial moves and by the time they are out in the open—"

"By Rorvreng the Vakka!" broke in Chuktar Tabex, commanding the heavy cavalry. "Then I will put in such a charge as will sweep them away!"

"I would prefer," I said mildly, "for Nath to chew them up a trifle before that, Chuktar Tabex."

"Aye, majister. But, I pray you, do not keep us under your hand too long!"

The regulation halt was up and the men were stirring and falling in. A bunch of slingers from Gremivoh were yelling back insults at the Deldars who were bawling them up. Undisciplined and unruly, slingers; but fine fighting men. The suns were lifting into the sky and the breeze was dropping away. The long files formed and the men shouldered their weapons and marched off.

They made a splendid sight and I forced the ugly truths from my mind and concentrated on thinking as an army commander. There would be many dead men and weeping women before Vallia could breathe freely again.

There was time for a last look at the map. A rounded hill was shown beyond the little river and it was my guess the enemy would station their cavalry there so as to get a good run in for their charge. The flanks would be more cavalry, with the infantry positioned in solid blocks interspersed with connecting lines. That seemed a reasonable guess; but you never can tell in dealing with paktuns who have years of campaigning under their belts. Even if the enemy formation was entirely different, I felt we had set down in such a way as to be able to meet them with the force we chose at the spot we chose. There seemed to me no chance that they would refuse battle. Our object was to get forward as quickly as possible and by hitting them in the flank, roll them up onto the pikes of the Phalanx. After that I could let slip the heavies with Chuktar Tabex in the van.

Delia had not insisted on bringing any of those ferocious Jikai Vuvushis, Battle Maidens, that I now knew to be a real part of her secret life. Jilian was still recovering from her wounds, and I had not seen much of her, to my own sorrow. Now Delia spurred up as I mounted and called across.

"I shall ride with you, at your side, Dray."

I nodded, and lifted into the saddle. Korero was there, a golden shadow at my back. I half-turned and opened my mouth, and the Kildoi said, "It is understood, majister."

I felt the quick flush of pleasure. By Vox! What it is to have great-hearted blade-comrades!

And here came Nath, another blade-comrade, and his face froze me.

"Majister!" he called as he galloped. Karidge was belting along to catch him, lathering his zorca, which made me understand with a shiver of dread that the news was bad.

"Those Opaz-forsaken louts!" Nath shouted. He hauled his zorca around and the animal's four spindly legs flashed nimbly as he turned. "They have sucked us in!"

"Aye," said Karidge, reining up, his face a single huge scowl. "By Lasal the Vakka! I trust in Opaz we have not scouted them too late."

"Spit it out!"

Scouts had come in, and their latest reports contradicted what we had hitherto believed. We had thought there were fifteen thousand foemen. There were more than twenty-eight thousand—infantry and cavalry. A reinforcement had reached them from Opaz-knew-where. I felt my face congeal. Doggedly, I heard out the report, beginning to refigure the entire coming contest.

I said, "We are near enough thirty. So the odds are even—weighed in our favor still. The plans stand. We go forward and attack. We cannot shilly-shally about now."

Then it was a question of listening to reports of the composition of the new forces arrayed against us.

"Masichieri, majister. Damned thieving no-good vicious riff-raff, masquerading as mercenaries. But they can fight, and there are fully six thousand of them."

Well, masichieri—bonny masichieri, I have known them called—yes, they are the scum of mercenaries. But in a battle they are fighting men and their rapaciousness drives them on with the lure of gold and plunder and women just as much as the ideal of patriotism drives on other men.

"And? The cavalry?"

"Aragorn, majister. Slavers, come to inspect their wares, aye, and fight for them, too." Karidge drew his gauntleted hand over his luxuriant moustaches. "There are Katakis among 'em, may they rot in Cottmer's Caverns."

"It seems we will be honored by foemen worthy to die by the rope rather than steel," I said, conscious of the turgidity of the words, but conscious, also, that they were true for all that.

"Also," said Karidge, and he looked disgusted, "there are at least four regiments of sleeths."

Nath banged a fist against his pommel. "Sleeths! Two-legged risslacas* suitable for—for—" He paused, and gazed about as though seeking the suitable word. It was a nicely calculated performance. One or two men among the aides-de-camp laughed. For, indeed, to a zorcaman the sleeth is something of a joke. Despite that, they can run and they can give a zorca a run for his money. And four regiments, if the usual regimental organization was followed, meant fifteen hundred or so.

---

* risslaca: dinosaur

"Is that all?"

"Dermiflons and swarths."

The dermiflon is blue-skinned, ten-legged, very fat and ungainly, and is armed with a sinuous and massively barbed and spiked tail. He has an idiot's head. The expression "to knock over a dermiflon" is a cast-iron guarantee of success. They'd have howdahs fixed to their backs and half a dozen men or so would be up there, shooting with bows and hurling pikes. I said: "How many swarths?"

"Around a thousand, three regiments, weak regiments."

I let out my breath. The swarth is your four-legged risslaca with the cruel wedge-shaped head and the jaws, with the scaled body and the clawed feet. He is not very fast. But he has a muscular bulk and he can carry his rider well and, a jutman must admit, is a nasty proposition to go up against. They were relatively rare in Vallia and Pandahem; but I had been told that the Lohvian armies put much store by them. And that stupidly mad and imperious Thyllis, Empress of Hamal, had been busily recruiting swarth regiments for her armies of conquest.

"We will keep a weather eye open for the three swarth regiments. I think our nikvoves will knock them over."

"That is something that old Vikatu the Dodger would be well clear of," said Karidge.

"Indisputably. And the dermiflons?"

"Ten of them. But I think, majister," said Nath, "we will be able to handle them with our javelin men. When they get a shower of pikes about them they'll panic and run. At least, that is the theory."

I rather liked that airy confidence.

"We will put the theory into practice. But you said twenty-eight thousand. There remain two and a half you have not accounted for."

"Irregulars," said Karidge. "Spearmen, half-naked and barefoot. They can be whipped away."

"Be careful there, Karidge. Irregular spearmen can be a nasty thorn in the heel if they scent blood that is not theirs. We cannot just ignore them, like some levies."

"True. But the aragorn and the swarths are what must exercise our muscles."

"And our minds."

Not for the first time I contemplated the large number of men locked up in the Phalanx. Perhaps as foot soldiers they might be spread to cover more ground and thus present a wider frontage. I set great store by the sword and shield men, and wished to increase their numbers, creating a powerful central force of super heavy infantry. But there was no gainsaying the might of the Phalanx. Once the pikes went down and the soldiers charged there was little that would stand before them.

213

A half dozen saddle-birds lined out, curving against the blue sky where the last clouds we would see this day were wafting away with the breeze. They slanted in steeply, their wings stiff against the air, and made perfect landings. Tyr Naghan Elfurnil ti Vandayha unstrapped his harness and jumped down with an affectionate pat for his bird. He walked across to me.

"You have had the report of the reinforcements, majister?"

"Aye, Naghan."

"If my saddle-birds could have been allowed to fly last night—"

"Little difference, Naghan. What do you see now?"

"They have positioned themselves before that low rounded hill, as you said they would. Here are the dispositions." He handed me the paper with the scrawled squares and the scribbled notations. I studied it. Just where each enemy formation was located was important, for it was vital to place suitable forces opposite those they could handle. Cavalry in the center, cavalry on the wings, the infantry lined out. Yes. By rapidly executed flank marches the enemy commander, whoever he might be, could compress or extend his front, and swing cavalry or infantry across to plug gaps at will. I thought for a moment or two and then nodded to the waiting aides-de-camp. Quickly, they took their orders, saluted, and galloped off. As our army marched up to the stream and woods they would be marshaled so as to deploy according to my instructions.

By Zair! I just hoped that what I was doing was correct. The whole situation was likely to slide out of hand. Once the fronts locked in combat and all hell broke loose it would all be down to those initial dispositions and the sheer fighting ability of the men in the ranks.

The orders were to go on. We would appear and attack. There would be no waiting. This was no defensive fight. This was onslaught, guerre a l'outrance, and look at the mess that has caused, by Krun!

The brilliant golden Mask of Recognition was affixed over my face. Cleitar the Standard and Ortyg the Tresh shook out their banners. Volodu the Lungs closed up and Korero, as always, hovered a golden shield at my back. Delia rode close, and Korero knew his duty there.

In a little group we rode forward and so came to the last stand of trees. The sheen of the suns lay across the grass, the little stream and the rounded hill beyond.

Ranked before us, line on line, mass on mass, the waiting formations of the enemy seemed to fill all the space and overflow in a blinding brilliance of color and steel.

Taking out my sword I lifted it high and then slashed it down in a vehement gesture, the point aimed at the heart of the foemen.

Silently, the leading ranks of our men plunged into the stream.

Six

The Battle of First Kanarsmot

Thus began First Kanarsmot.

The feel of the zorca between my knees and the close confinement of the helmet and the Mask of Recognition, the itch of war harness on my shoulders, the brilliance of the splashing water drops as we forded across the stream—all these sensations in one form or another must have been felt by all the men in that little army. All, except the Mask of Recognition. The thing served a purpose, although I doubted if it would stop even a short-bow's shaft. As we came up on the far bank a sudden and sweet scent of white shansili filled our nostrils. The familiar scent must have brought aching-memories of familiar homes and dear faces to the men for those lovely flowers are often grown in trellises over the doors of Vallian homes.

In advance ran the kreutzin, lithe limber young men, raffish and wayward; but thirsting to get their javelins and arrows into play. Half naked, some of them, fleet of foot and agile, they raced forward to be first in action.

Scrambling my zorca—who was faithful old Grumbleknees—up on the opposite bank I rode forward far enough to allow space for the Sword Watch to form at my back.

The enemy were already moving. Their masses came on steadily, and I looked to see who would make first contact.

From the enemy's right they were drawn up thusly: the swarth force of a thousand; two dense masses of paktuns, five thousand each arrayed one behind the other; the central body of totrix and zorca cavalry, five thousand strong; the irregulars a little in advance and already beginning to race onward; the six thousand masichieri, who hung a little back; and, finally, on the left wing, the two thousand zorca-mounted aragorn. Ordered in two sections of five each, and out in front, the dermiflons lifted their stupid heads and brayed. The glitter of the suns smote back from the weapons of the men in their armored howdahs—armored castle-like structures the warriors of Kregen call calsaxes—and the dermiflon handlers ran yelling and pushing around the enormous beasts as they sought to force them into their clumsy stumbling run.

The main strength of the enemy, therefore, lay in his right wing. I did not discount the aragorn; but they and the masichieri would fight only for as long as they could see slaves and plunder coming their way.

Already our bowmen were loosing at the dermiflons.

Once we had seen them off, the real fight could begin.

Equally, massive and impressive striding citadels of war though dermiflons truly are, they must not attract all a commander's attention and he must not allow them to deflect him into wasting too many of his precious resources on them.

From the left we were arrayed thusly: the totrix cavalry division attached to the Phalanx; the Phalanx itself; the Tenth Brigade of Archers; the First Cavalry Brigade of zorcas with the Fourth slightly to their right. I lifted in the stirrups and looked across to the right toward the woods that masked the backward-curving bend of the river. There was no sign of movement among the trees.

With great whoops from the drivers and riders and a veritable Niagara of fountaining splashes, the artillery crossed the stream. A number of different draught animals hauled the equipment, and they galloped on through the intervals and unlimbered to our front. At once they were in action, shooting their cruel iron-tipped darts. Within the space of ten murs they had shot two of the dermiflons out of it, the ungainly beasts turning around on their ten legs, braying angrily, lumbering back for all their handlers shrieked and beat at them with goads.

The forward movement of our men continued. They were not yet charging—they tramped on steadily, rank on rank, file on file, and the pikes lifted, thick as bristles on a wild vosk's back.

The twin suns slanted their rays onto the battlefield from our right flank. Again I looked. Still no movement within the trees flanking the curve of the stream.

Delia said: "The paktuns are coming perilously close."

"Let the bowmen and the spear men play a little longer on the dermiflons."

As I spoke another gigantic beast decided that he no longer wished to go in the direction from which these nasty stinging barbs were coming; braying, he turned about and with his ten legs all going up and down like pistons, he lumbered off.

There were twenty-eight thousand of the enemy. I had spoken lightly of our near thirty thousand—but in that I lied or boasted. Of men we could put in fighting line we had sixteen thousand seven hundred infantry and seven thousand three hundred and twenty cavalry, plus the artillery. And, already, some of our bowmen were down, caught by the deceptive arrow, tiny bundles on the grass, lying still or, more awfully, kicking in the last spasms.

The balance of our thirty thousand was made up of logistics people, medics, vets. Some of the wagoners would fight if it came to it—but I hoped profoundly it would not come to that.

The swarths were moving, the scaled mounts advancing directly with the aim of crunching into the left flank of the Phalanx.

Chuktar De-Ye Mafon, a Pachak with great experience in command of the Tenth Cavalry Division attached to the Phalanx, countered the move. His division consisted of a brigade of three regiments of zorca archers and a brigade of three regiments of totrix lancers. Now he launched the zorcas at the oncoming swarths. The nimble animals swirled in evolutions practiced a thousand times, lined out, and their riders shot and shot as they swooped past the right flank of the enemy mass.

Disordered, the swarths angled to their left and, at that moment, Chuktar De-Ye Mafon led his totrix lancers into them.

The outcome of that fight had, for the moment, to be awaited as the enemy commander pushed through in the center.

The Phalanx had been aimed at the enemy's center, his ten thousand infantry and his five thousand cavalry, mercenaries all, tough, professional, the hard core of his army. With that swerving recoil of the swarths pressing in on the massed infantry, the enemy general had ordered one of the tactical moves he had left open to himself. The ordered ranks of the paktuns inclined to their left. They broke into a fast trot, their banners and plumes waving, their weapons glinting.

They would lap around the right flank of the Phalanx and I was about to give the order for Karidge's Brigade to move up in support, when the last of the dermiflons on this side of the field broke. They fled back, immense engines of destruction, festooned with darts—one with a varter dart pinning three of his starboard legs together—and they crashed headlong into those smart and professional paktuns.

The paktuns were professionals. They opened ranks; but in the incline that proved not quite so easy as it sounded. We were afforded enough space for the Phalanx to go smashing into them, the pikes down and level, the helmets thrust forward, the shields positioned, rank by rank, to serve each the best purpose. The noise blossomed into the sky. The yells and shrieks and the mad tinker-clatter of steel on iron, of steel on bronze, and the crazed dust-whirling advance encompassed by the raw stink of spilled blood brought a horror that underlay any thoughts of glory. On drove the Phalanx. On and with blood-smeared pikes thrust the paktuns aside.

Now was the time for the enemy Kapt to hurl in his five thousand cavalry—and our Hakkodin, our halberd and axe and two-handed sword men, knew it.

The Hakkodin flank the Phalanx and they take enormous pride in the protection they afford and their ability to ensure that no lurking daggerman, no cavalryman, can smite away at the undefended flanks of the Phalanx. And the soldiers, hefting their pikes, know that and relish the feel of solid Hakkodin at their flanks and rear.

Although, mind you, in rear of the Third Kerchuri as it advanced lay only strewn and mangled corpses of paktuns.

The enemy shafts had been deflected by the uplifted shields of the Phalanx,

217

the field of red roses in the popular imagery, the field of crimson flowers, and now our own archers of the Tenth Brigade stepped forward to assist the bowmen of the Phalanx. It was going to be touch and go. The second massed formation of paktuns was advancing in steady fashion and their incline, avoiding the tumultuous upsets of the disaster with the dermiflons, would place them astride the shoulder of the Phalanx. Engaged as the Kerchuri was, it could not toss pikes and turn half-right. That kind of evolution is very pretty on the parade ground; in the midst of battle with the red blood flowing and the screams and yells and the dust boiling everywhere—no, you grip your pike and you go on, and on, when it comes to push of pike.

A zorcaman came galloping up to me, his feathers flying, his equipment flying—he hardly seemed to touch the ground. I knew who he was, right enough.

"Majister!" He bellowed out as Cleitar the Standard had to back his zorca a trifle. "Jiktar Karidge's compliments—will you loose him now—please!"

Deliberately I lifted in the stirrups. I looked not toward the furious turmoil in the center of the field. Deliberately, I looked to the right. The six thousand masichieri were on the move. The two thousand aragorn flanking them were trotting on, splendid in the lights of the suns. The noise everywhere dinned on and on, and those fresh bodies of troops would go slap bang into the flank of our army when Karidge and the other brigade of the light cavalry division charged.

"Give me ten murs more, Elten Frondalsur." The galloper's face shone scarlet with sweat and exertion. He gentled his zorca as the excited animal curveted. "Just that, no more."

"As you say, majister!"

Elten Frondalsur, even in that moment of high tension, had the sense not to argue or plead. Karidge would understand. I just looked steadily at the galloper, and so with a salute he flicked his zorca's head around and took off back to Karidge. Also, I knew that in ten murs, and exactly ten murs, Karidge would set his brigade into a skirling charge. That was the way he would interpret the message the Elten brought.

Calling over the galloper attached to my staff from the light cavalry division, I sent him off to convey the same message to the officer in command. He, cunning old Larghos the Spear, would find himself commanding only the Fourth Brigade when the charge went in. But everyone in the army understood the impetuous ways of Karidge, aye, and loved him for it—well, most of the time.

In six murs the movement I had been fretfully waiting from the trees over by the bend in the stream heralded the arrival of our flank force. And, by Vox, only just in time!

In one sense, they were late, for the paktuns were now at handstrokes with the Hakkodin. The mingled cavalry swirled around ready to complete the impending destruction of the Phalanx, as they imagined. And the aragorn and the masichieri came swiftly on.

From the trees erupted the archers of the Ninth Brigade. Following them and pounding on in their armor, strong, powerfully built men, the front line of the three brigades of sword and shield men burst onto the battlefield. Out to their right and flanking them, galloping swiftly on, roared the Heavy Cavalry Division, two thousand totrixmen formed, clad in armor, bearing swiftly on with lances couched. When those lances shivered they would haul out short one-handed axes, and stout swords, and they'd go through the zorca-mounted aragorn like the enemy had fancied he would go through our ranks.

That marked the beginning of the end.

The commander over there must have looked with despair upon that battlefield. He saw his vaunted swarths mightily discomfited and driven off. He had seen a powerful force of mercenaries, containing Rapas and Fristles, Khibils and blegs, shattered, and a second about to be overwhelmed. The masichieri and the aragorn were hauling up, their ranks disordered and in turmoil. It took little imagination to picture what they were doing, to hear what they were shrieking as they saw this new menace rushing up to smash into the flank. And, with his dermiflons gone, the enemy commander saw his fancied force of cavalry recoil from the center of the field as the Light Division hit them full force.

I do not like letting slip zorcas in a charge; but Karidge and Larghos the Spear had no doubts.

In moments the face of the battle changed.

Everywhere the enemy were in retreat.

That was the end of First Kanarsmot.

Seven

An Axeman Drops In

"It would perhaps have made better sense," said Delia as we sat in the tent and looked at the maps, the casualty returns ugly and horrible on the table, the sounds of an army at rest all about us in the mellow evening. "Perhaps, to have sent the Light Cavalry instead of the Heavies in the flank force."

"As it turned out, it would have been. But they were late." I yawned. "Mind you, my heart, by this time a man should have learned to expect delay in any plans he makes."

"And a woman, also."

"And what plans are you fomenting?"

"For the present situation, why, that we must take Kanarsmot as quickly as possible. Drak should be back by now and I want to go home to Vondium."

"And I." I looked at her, and I smiled. "You could always go—"

She did not say anything; but before I could go on she took off her slipper and threw it at me. I caught it. It was warm and soft.

"Very well. You won't go home by yourself."

"You could go. Nath can handle affairs here."

"That is true. But I feel responsible. I want to clear the area this side of the Great River. After all, the villains to the east seem to have settled down in our country. If they respect the line of the river it will prove valuable."

"You are, Dray Prescot, as cunning as a newborn infant."

"Ah, but," I said. "There is no one more fitted by nature to work cunning than a baby."

She smiled at this, and I knew her memories mingled with mine, and the warmness enveloped us.

Presently we had to get back to work. The army had not suffered the ghastly scale of casualties I had at one time envisioned. But we had not got off scatheless. The final nikvove charge, slap bang through the middle and to hell with anything that got in the way, had relieved a lot of pressure. Karidge and his zorcamen had behaved splendidly. The cavalry was pursuing; but the enemy were not a fleeing force for they had withdrawn onto a further considerable body of reinforcements and then presented a front. They were still in play. The cavalry harried them, and parried their cavalry probes. We had not been worried by their flying machines but in the successful accomplishment of that our small saddlebird force had been fully stretched, so that no aerial cavalry had played a part in the battle.

Nath was most wrought up about the late arrival of the flank force. When I pointed out to him that if they had been too early they would not have had an exposed flank to charge into, he sniffed, and agreed, and said with devastating logic: "But had they been on time, as you ordered, majister, the flank would have been there and we would not have been so hard-pressed."

We had not grown hard and callous over casualties. We mourned good men gone. But more and more the truth, unpleasant at first glance and then, with greater acquaintance, acceptable with a kind of glow of abnegation, was borne in on us that for what we sought to do even death had its part to play. These murky philosophical waters led us on, inexorably, to a continuation of the heady and almost intoxicated feelings the people of Vondium had felt during the protracted Time of Troubles and later, when we were penned up in the city. No one wants to die in the ordinary course of things, but if death comes to us all then a fighting man may choose his going over into the care of the gray ones on a battlefield. That, surely, is his right. And, do not forget, we were an all-volunteer army.

The arguments against this kind of thinking, involving manic pressure and self-hypnotism and twisted logic that goes against the grain of life-enhancement, were well known to the sages of Kregen. There is no proprietary right to life-thinking. But we all felt that our lives were well spent in the attempt to provide a free land for our children.

So I was able to read the casualty returns and see the familiar names leap out at me from the long lists with a calmness that no longer surprised me. No, we of Vallia are not callous in these matters.

Nath said as I lowered the last list: "We lost Yolan Vanoimen, I am sorry to say." Yolan Vanoimen was—had been—Jodhrivax of the Second Jodhri of the Kerchuri. "A stinking Rapa bit his throat out."

Nath looked down at his hands. I said nothing.

After a space he went on: "The Rapa was brave, you have to say that. He went down with four pike heads piercing him and a Hakkodin axe severing his wattled neck."

"I am sorry that Yolan Vanoimen has gone," I said at last. "He was in line for Kerchurivax of the Eighth. We have to pay a heavy price for what we believe in."

The mineral oil lamps glowed and the camp tent was crowded with our familiar belongings. But I felt the chill. I tried to shake it off. The Eighth Kerchuri would have to find a new commander. We were forming a new Phalanx in Vondium, the Fourth. The Kerchuris were numbered throughout the whole Phalanx force. The Jodhris were numbered through their Phalanx, the First to the Sixth and the Seventh to the Twelfth. The Relianches, the basic formations of a hundred and forty-four brumbytes and twenty-four Hakkodin, were numbered through their Kerchuri, the First to the Thirty-Sixth. Later we made adjustments to this numbering.

The aftermath of battle is not kind. Useless to dwell on that. We gave the army a breather of four days during which time the additional units I had summoned from Vondium flew in. After that we pursued the campaign. From information received from the local people, who rallied wonderfully after the battle, we learned that the commander of the enemy army was one Ranjarsi the Strigicaw. He was a Rapa, one of those beaked and vulturine diffs of Kregen, and he showed great skill in fending us off and leading us a dance. But, in the end, with our enhanced forces, we pinned him against the Great River.

The Fourth Kerchuri of the Second Phalanx had joined us, so we had a full phalanx in action. More bowmen and archers and cavalry swelled our ranks. Second Kanarsmot was a fearful debacle for the invaders and Kapt Ranjarsi the Strigicaw was lucky to escape across the river with the remnants. The waters of She of the Fecundity rolled red.

We did not pursue across the river, and we trusted the invaders got the message. Larghos the Left-Handed, a spry, clever, completely loyal Pallan, came up from Vondium to take over the command in the area. I trusted him, along with his comrade, Naghan Strandar, to deal with many of the higher details of the government, the army and the law. They worked with the Lord Farris and made a capital team.

Leaving sufficient forces to ensure that any fresh attempts to invade across the river would be crushed swiftly, we turned toward Kanarsmot itself. This still held out against the small screening forces so far pitted against it, the garrison, of mercenaries, commanded by a Fristle called Fonarmon the Catlenter. He had dubbed himself, no doubt with Ranjarsi's blessing, the Strom of Kanarsmot.

We disabused him of that idea.

The plan I outlined was to take the place by a coup de main. I had no desire whatsoever to sit down to a protracted siege. So, on the night chosen, when for a space only two of the smaller moons of Kregen rushed across the dark sky, we set off. Infiltrators within the walls overpowered the guard at the West Gate and we poured in, a silent host, and set about securing the town, house by house.

Other forces went in over the walls. After that the garrison awoke to their peril and we came to handstrokes.

Over the southeastern walls of the town the citadel had been built with its footings in the waters of the river. The mercenaries fought well, earning their hire, and slowly withdrew to the citadel. The massive gates closed with a couple of ranks of our bowmen trapped inside. We knew we had seen the last of them. Other bowmen dropped with yells into the moat or withdrew from the hail of arrows that sprouted from the battlements. By that narrow margin had we failed to take the citadel.

I said: "I regret the men we lost there. But as for the citadel, well, the cramphs are mewed up inside and we can leave them to rot. I will not lose more good men in unnecessary attacks."

That seemed sound common sense, by Vox.

Dawn was breaking and illuminating the clouds with fringes of gold and ruby, orange and jade. Someone let out a high excited yell. We all looked up.

High against that paling sky the rope arched. It curved like a whip. It fell all quivering down the wall and its length dangled an invitation at the end of the bridge which the mercenaries had been unable to draw up. The next moment helmets tufted with the maroon and white of the churgurs of the Fiftieth Regiment of the Nineteenth Brigade appeared on the left-flank gate tower.

Kov Vodun shouted by my side.

"Those are my men up there." He threw off his cloak.

In the next instant as he started forward across the bridge I was flinging my leg over the zorca to dismount.

Delia's voice, warningly, said: "Dray."

Korero, whose shields were uplifted against the occasional arrow, said, "Majister..."

"You can't expect me to sit here and watch!"

Then a whole bunch of men ran over the bridge, yelling, and with Kov Vodun in the lead they began climbing the rope.

"By Zair!" I shouted. And I was running, too, running like a fool over the planks of the bridge where arrows stood thickly, and taking my turn to grip the rope and so go hand over hand up like a monkey. Korero, with four arms and a tailhand, had no difficulty in swarming up the rope after me, carrying his shields and giving me an assist from time to time. We tumbled over the battlements into a scene of confusion.

Those two ranks had done their job, and there could not have been above fourteen men between the two sections, in jamming the winding mechanism of the bridge and of clambering up the stairs of the left-flank gate tower. They had been unable to prevent the closing of the gates. But their dropped rope gave us an alternative ingress.

The tower top blazed with action, as swords clashed and spears flew. The paktuns, a mixed bunch of diffs with Fristles predominating, fought savagely to hold us back from the battlements. Our way down the gate tower was blocked; but once along the ramparts we could expand. The way into the citadel would lie open. The garrison knew that and fought like leems to hurl us back over the walls to shattered destruction on the ground below.

Very few of our men had climbed the rope with their shields. Vallians still had not fully mastered the art of shield play and had not slung the crimson flowers over their backs. I ripped out my drexer, the straight—or almost straight—cut and thrust sword, and plunged into the fray.

Over the clangor everyone heard the fearsome yells from the tower, dwindling. For a paralyzed instant the action froze... The soggy thumps sounded eerily loud.

"The rope has broken!" bellowed a hulking Deldar from the nearest group who had just climbed up. "We are on our own!"

"Not for long!" I fairly shrieked over the fresh hubbub. "Into them! We must open the gates!"

This was the red hurly-burly of action very far removed from sitting a zorca in the rear and methodically working out which way a battle should be run. We were up at the sharp end and if our wits and our sword arms failed us we were done for.

The party of mercenaries blocking the stairway resisted our efforts. They were fighting men. Many of them showed the gleam of the pakmort at throat, or looped into the shoulder of the war harness. We charged into them and were thrust back, struggling desperately.

Our numbers were thinning. Flung stuxes, those thick and heavy throwing spears with the small cross quillons set back from the head, flew into our ranks. Men shrieked and died, blowing bloody froth, vomiting. I hurdled a sprawled bleg, three of his legs missing, and launched myself at the mercenaries. Their swords flamed. It was all a mad business of cut and hack, of duck, of thrust, of parry, and recover.

I do not think, I seriously do not think, we could have done it. Looking back at that scene of carnage it seems to me the enemy were slowly overmastering us. We fought; but we were few and they continually fed reinforcements up from the garrison so that we faced what appeared to be an unending stream of foemen.

And then...

And then!

By Zair! But to think of it brings that excruciating tingle in the blood, sets the pulses jumping, shows it all again in splendor.

A shadow dropped down over us, a twinned shadow from the twin suns. An airboat hovered, for she could not settle with that seething mass of struggling men below without squashing friend and foe alike. From the voller leaped men. I saw them. Over the coamings they jumped, roaring into action. I saw their yellow hair flying free, for the Maiden with the Many Smiles was not in the sky. I saw the height of them, seven foot, each fighting man. I saw their weapons, those long single-bladed Saxon-pattern axes. Oh, yes, I saw them as they smashed into the mercenaries and the axes whirled in that old familiar way, ripping arcs of silver and red.

Warriors of Ng'groga, they were, tall sinewy axemen, and there was about their work the fierce controlled power of the typhoon.

At their head, urging them on, slashing with cunning skill, opening a path through the enemy—at their head, in the lead, roared on that tall familiar figure that meant so much to me.

"By Zair!" I said. "If only Seg were here now!"

With that and with renewed heart we swept the enemy from before the stairway. They were sent screaming to topple over the battlements of the tower. The stairway was cleared and men raced down, yelling, striking this way and that with lethal axes. The gate was opened.

After that—why, the army poured in and in next to no time the citadel of Kanarsmot was in our hands.

Delia found me as I walked out of the open gate and over the bridge. Walking was not easy for the arrows and the corpses. The Sword Watch were busily engaged in the citadel in rounding up prisoners and discovering what portable property there might be worthy the consideration of a guardsman of the Emperor's Sword Watch.

"Oh, Dray! When you climbed the rope—"

"Did you see him?"

She smiled and the world of Kregen took on a roseate light. "Yes. I saw

him. And here he is, walking up just as though nothing had happened."
She was looking past me and as I turned so Delia ran by and threw herself
at that tall, yellow-haired, grimly ferocious axeman. He clasped her in his
long arms.

"Inch!"

He looked at me over Delia's brown hair and I swear he had to swallow
before he spoke.

"As a comrade of ours would say, Dray—Lahal, my old dom."

"Lahal and Lahal a thousand times, Inch."

And I strode forward to clasp his hand. He had had to swallow before
speaking. Damned if I didn't, too...

Eight

Vondium Dances

Inch's adventures would fill a book of their own. We left affairs in the capable hands of Larghos the Left-Handed and prepared to return to the capital.
Inch kept on looking about and uttering exclamations of surprise—at the
flying sailers so different from those with which we had fought the Battle of Jholaix, at the Phalanx, and this and that. He was delighted to be
back, and when, in an odd moment, we found him solemnly standing on
his head, reciting the Kregish alphabet backwards and at the end of each
recital clapping his heels smartly together, we smiled fondly. Inch and his
taboos! If he fell over when he clapped his heels together, he'd have to start
all over again.

We did not ask him which particular taboo he had broken. When you
got to know Inch of Ng'groga, the Kov of the Black Mountains, you did not
bother to question his taboos and simply took delight in his presence.

He told us that after he had been sorcerously flung back from the Pool of
Baptism to his native Ng'groga, in southeastern Loh, he had been forced to
spend some time atoning for all the mass of broken taboos he felt sure he
had left strewn in his wake. Then, with due ritual and protocol and a mass
of taboo-legitimized formalities he had wed his Sasha.

Delia clapped her hands.

"Wonderful, Inch, delightful. Congratulations. Is she with you?"

"Yes. I left her in Vondium—"

"Oh?" I said.

He looked at me—by this time he was sitting at a table in a decent chair and we had forbidden squish pie to be brought any closer than an ulm—and he smiled.

"I know you think I am a clever fellow, Dray. But it would take Ngrangi Himself to have known you were here at Kanarsmot. No, the moment we heard in Ng'groga of the troubles in Vallia I set off." Across in the continent of Loh they had few if any airboats and travel would be slow and news hardly come by. "I took the liberty of going via Djanduin. I found the people wonderfully hospitable when they discovered I was acquainted with their king."

"Acquainted," I said.

Inch laughed at that. "Oh, yes, Ortyg Fellin Coper and Kytun Kholin Dom are great fellows. They greeted me right royally and gave me splendid fliers."

"Fliers..."

"Well, of course. By Ngroyzan the Axe! You didn't think I'd come empty-handed? I enlisted a parcel of likely rogues, all friends of mine, or friends of friends, and we look forward to a rollicking time, I can tell you."

"How many?"

Five hundred or so—of course fifty of 'em are mindyfingling about somewhere in Pandahem, probably. One of the fliers broke down. And I sent half of 'em up to the Black Mountains under command of my second cousin, Brince, to sniff around and sort out any mischief up there."

Delia glanced at me. Kov of the Black Mountains, our comrade Inch, with responsibilities there he took most seriously. Yet—he had flown first to Vondium...

All the same, the situation had to be explained to him, that same situation that had so puzzled and infuriated Seg.

Also, there was about Inch a new and refreshing air of determination, of a positive approach. He was still the same gangling affable fellow; but clearly discernible in his talk and his movements this new positive attitude to life marked off a change that had taken place in him, also.

I said, "We no longer employ mercenaries in Vallia." I saw his face. "Oh, there are still many paktuns in employ, of course, they have not all packed up and gone home. But as a part of the new imperial policy, Vallia is going to be liberated by Vallians."

If he had stood up, flouncing, and shouted, before he stalked out, I could not have blamed him. This sounded like the basest ingratitude on my part. But Inch just stared at me, and scratched his nose, and pulled a long lock of that yellow hair.

"Yes. They told me something of the sort in Djanduin. If you've managed to persuade Kytun that he must not bring a horde of your ferocious Djang warriors to Vallia—well, the reasons must be cogent, most cogent indeed." He gave a little laugh. "But, by Vox! What a sight that would be!"

"Aye," I said. "It would indeed."

There was a great deal to be talked about and histories to be filled in. Larghos the Left-Handed came in to finalize his orders and the position as we saw it then. He had known Inch as the Kov of the Black Mountains before the death of the emperor, Delia's father. But when Nath came in, fresh from organizing the movements of the Phalanx, I braced myself up. Nath had not easily accepted Seg Segutorio. The last thing I wanted was friction between my comrades and my trusted lieutenants. Some emperors and dictators use antipathies between their subordinates to divide and rule; to me that is inefficient and, to boot, indicative of a society I have no wish to be a part of.

When the formalities were made, Inch, very gravely, said, "It was my misfortune not to have been with you, Kyr Nath, when you led the first Phalanx that the emperor has spoken of. I grieve that I missed so much. But I am here now and my axemen are under your command for the rest of this campaign."

He cocked an eye at me and I wondered if he was bracing himself to break a few of his taboos for which he would have to do remarkable penances later. "I understand we no longer employ mercenaries. But these fellows are not paktuns. They are friends of mine, out for what rascally fun they can find and a little loot if that comes their way. We shall be going up to the Black Mountains before long."

How difficult to judge when men and women talk in apparently open and frank ways just how much of the truth they are telling! Deeply thinking people do not rush into confidences the moment acquaintance is made with strangers. But I felt I knew Inch. He was a blade comrade. His words rang with truth, at least to me, and I knew that Delia also heard that truth.

Nath smiled.

"You are most welcome, kov. Like Kov Seg, you have been much spoken of in your absence. The Hakkodin will marvel at your axes."

"They will that," I said. And then I added, warningly, "But I think it takes a native Ng'grogan to swing that axe in just that way. We continue with our Vallian axes, Nath—do you not agree?"

"Assuredly, majister. And, anyway, I fancy some of my axemen could give Kov Inch's men a gallop for their zorcas."

The conversation eased after that. I was not fool enough to imagine that perfect comradely harmony would exist between Inch and Nath immediately and without a little time for rubbing off the sharp corners. But, at the least, a start had been made.

There remained the last parades and the music and the marching and the distribution of bobs, and then we took off for Vondium. News came in from Seg that he had inflicted a minor defeat on the enemies facing him, that the clansmen were arguing among themselves over what to do, and that given a little more time he rather fancied his chances at driving them into the sea. Nath read the message and said, at once and without preamble: "Let me go up there right away, majister, and join Kov Seg. We have the strength now—"

Farris looked troubled.

"My sailing fliers can—"

"Of course, Kov Farris!" broke in Nath, eagerly. "And we can drop right on them and discomfort them utterly."

I'd heard this before. I pointed at the map, indicating the southwest.

Nath said: "I know, majister. But the Fourth is coming along nicely, we have fresh regiments of churgurs and archers. And, above all, the southwest is quiet now."

"Quiet. But what are they up to down there?"

"I," said Inch, "would greatly like to see Seg again."

There were a few other pallans in my rooms and each gave his opinion, honestly, for what it was worth, and all knowing I would have to make the final decision.

The notion that Vallia was some gigantic Jikaida board returned to me. One moved the pieces here and there and sought to contain strengths and to camouflage weaknesses. If you wonder why I hesitated to take the obvious step and rush up with all the forces at my disposal and smash the clansmen back into the sea, one reason was the ever-present threat from the south. Also the northwest remained a vague area of conflict in which racters fought Layco Jhansi's people, and where Inch would soon plunge with his axemen into the Black Mountains. No—the reason lay in that recent conversation with the Star Lords. I had been snatched summarily from Vallia before. This time I waited. I knew I was to be called by the Everoinye. It was absolutely vital that Vallian affairs remained in honest and capable hands. Seg and Inch, Nath and Farris, all the others, would shoulder their burdens while I was away.

If this was a doom laid on me then I waited for the stroke as I had waited in the dungeons of the Hanitchik.

The happy sounds of laughter outside and the clanging crash as the three-grained staffs of the guardsmen of the Sword Watch presented, heralded the joyous arrival of Delia, smiling, with Sasha, who looked radiant.

"The plans are all prepared and everything is going to be wonderful!" cried Delia.

I, I must confess, gaped.

"And the first dance is to be a mandanillo," said Sasha. "And you, Inch, are to lead off with me."

So I remembered. Tonight all Vondium celebrated. The palace was to see a great ball and the lanterns would bloom colors to the night sky and the tables would groan with food and everyone would dance and sing and laugh as the moons cavorted through the sky between the stars, until the twin suns, Zim and Genodras, awoke to send us all to sleep at last.

"Let us dance the night away," I said. "And in the morning, with Opaz, we will decide."

The dances of Kregen are spectacles that would drive the gods to tripping a measure. Everything conduced to laughter and pleasure. Every girl was beautiful. Every man was a hero. We sang and danced and drank and ate, and we kept it up as the Maiden with the Many Smiles cast down her fuzzy pinkish light, and She of the Veils added her more golden glow, as the Twins endlessly revolved above. The stars blazed. The torches and the lanterns filled the air with motes of color. The orchestras played nonstop, all the exotic instruments of Kregen combining to provide the right music for each dance.

And the dances!

Useless for me to attempt to describe them all. They delighted the senses and they fed the soul.

The sounds of plunking announced the mandanillo and Inch and Sasha led off in that gliding, dreamlike dance. This was followed by more of the stately dances, in which the lines of men and women interlink and revolve and weave their magical patterns that woo the very blood in the body to the rhythms. As the night wore on so the dances grew wilder. Your Kregan loves a riotous rollicking dance, full of blazing passion and jumping and kicking and high jinks. In groups, in couples, the brilliantly attired revelers gyrated through the palace and into the grounds. In the avenues and boulevards the people danced and sang. The kyros filled with the rhythms, and the patterns of the dances cast kaleidoscopes of brilliance against the arcades and colonnades. The vener pranced in their boats along the cuts and the canal water glittered back in blinding reflections.

Oh, yes, we had a ball that night in Vondium.

The dance called the Wend carried people in swaying undulating lines through every corridor in the palace, it seemed, in a procession far removed from the solemn chanting religious festivals where the worshippers all chanted "Oolie Opaz, Oolie Opaz" over and over again. The Wend carried them singing the currently popular songs around and around: "Lucili the Radiant," "The Empty Wine Jar," "My Love is like a Moon Bloom," and dozens more.

As you will realize, they sang "She Lived by the Lily Canal," and "The Soldier's Love Potion," over and over.

Presently Delia drew me into the rose-bordered courtyard where Inch and Sasha and many and many another good friend laughed and waited, for we were to dance the Measure of the Princesses, often called the Jikaida Dance.

The ladies all wore their sherissas, those filmy, gauzy, tantalizing veils that float and drift dreamlike in the dance. The men wore masks, dominoes of silver and gold. The courtyard, massed in its banks of roses, was laid out as a Jikaida board, three drins by four, giving an area of eighteen by twenty-four squares. We all formed up, laughing and fooling, and the orchestra struck up the Jikaida Introduction and the choir started to sing.

Well, now. As the song unfolds the story, you have to suit your actions to the words. We were in the yellow party and we waved yellow favors. The blues, at the far end, waved their blue favors and taunted us, all laughing and joking, and every time some unfortunate made a mistake they were summarily ejected. We pranced around the board, hopping the blue and yellow squares, going through the contortions. No one cheated. There was no point in dancing else.

All too soon I missed a cue and forgot to wave my yellow favor aloft when I should have, and the marshals, killing themselves with laughter, attired in their white regalia, turfed me off the board.

"Dray! You empty-head!"

"It is all too clever for me, my love—but go on, go on—the blues gain on us."

For, indeed, there were far too many yellows gathered in the shadow of the roses, chattering and scoffing and doing their best to upset the blues still in the dance.

What a picture it all made! The gleam of the lanterns, the impression of the shadows of the trees above, the scent of the Moon Blooms, the music twining into our very beings—yes, Kregans know how to enjoy themselves. Be very sure the wheeled trolleys containing their racked amphorae were everywhere to hand.

In the end the yellows just pipped the blues, and Delia smiled and gestured to Sasha, who accepted the golden flower of triumph. We clapped, for Sasha was rapidly proving a popular figure among us.

After that we had the Spear Dance, full of leaping and twisting and jumping the flashing spear blades. The Yekter followed and then there were more dances in which the participants enacted the stories of the songs.

Then, I walked to the orchestra I had spent a few burs with, doing my best to introduce them to the rhythms of the waltz. During my sojourns on Earth I had become addicted to the music of the waltzes that grew every year in popularity. The breadth and humanity of vision of the newest waltzes were a far cry from the early Ländler and I carried the tunes in my head. This is possible, and by repeated practice the orchestra chosen could reproduce the music most wonderfully. It had proved an altogether different kettle of fish with Beethoven; but even in this I persevered. So, now, to those evocative strains, Delia and I led out in the Grand Waltz of Vondium.

Soon the whole company were gliding and swaying and the music rose and a great sense of well-being filled me that was tinged with the sadness of coming parting.

We danced out from the lantern-lit areas and lightly followed the avenues of rose bushes, dancing under the Moons of Kregen. The feel of Delia in my arms, the scents of the flowers, the intoxicating strains of the music, the sense of a whole city enjoying itself, released the pressures and tensions of the times. And then Delia looked up and gasped.

"Dray—an airboat!"

Instantly my right hand darted to the rapier, for, dance or no dance, no Kregan goes abroad at night unarmed unless he has to.

The airboat landed on a wide terrace before the palace where the dancers and carousers scattered away for her. We heard the startled exclamations and then the laughter and the cheering. We stood, together, close. We saw.

From the voller leaped a tall, powerful, dominating man. He landed lightly and instantly turned to assist a woman to step down, a woman who wore a tiered headdress of intertwined silver flowers that caught the lights and glittered. A monstrous shape rose up from the voller. The watching crowds stopped their laughter and cheering, and they fell back. The monstrous shape leaped to the ground with the liquid lethal grace of a giant hunting beast. Instantly a second appeared and leaped to stand, ferocious, beside the first.

Delia gasped. I held her and then she broke free.

She ran.

She ran along the rose-bowered walk, shouting.

"Drak! Drak! Melow! Kardo!"

She ran to greet her son and I smiled and felt the enormous weight lift from my shoulders.

Those two savage Manhounds of Antares, Melow the Supple and her son, Kardo, had been saved and brought back to Vondium by Drak, Prince Drak of Vallia, Krzy, and I felt the proper pride of a father.

And then I smiled a little smile. For Delia had not called the name of the woman who stood so close to Drak. She had not cried out in welcome to Queen Lushfymi of Lome.

But she would do that, I knew; for in Delia there is no room for pettiness. So I slapped the rapier back into the scabbard and hitched up my belt and started off between the roses to greet my son.

Now affairs in Vondium could take a different turn. Farris would be overjoyed to hand over the burden to Drak so that he could get on with his Air Service. I could take the army and see about winning a few battles secure in the knowledge that Drak was here. The moment we had Vallia in good shape he was going to take over as emperor. My heart was set on that. To hand over now, with all the problems still with us, would not be seemly. But, soon now, soon.

The blueness was at first merely a drifting mist that brushed irritatingly in my eyes.

In a summoning flutter of scarlet and gold, wings beating against the blueness, the Gdoinye flew down. The spy and messenger of the Star Lords cocked his head on one side, his beak insolently agape.

"It is time, Dray Prescot. The Star Lords summon you."

I felt my body would burst.

"Fool—" I managed to say.

"It is you who is the fool. You have been warned. See how considerate are the Everoinye, how tender of you—we have spoken aforetime—"

"Aye! And I have bidden you begone, bird of ill omen."

The blueness closed in, thick and choking. The Gdoinye uttered a last mocking squawk. The shape of the phantom Scorpion coalesced, huge and menacing. I caught a last parting fragrance of the Moon Blooms. The ground whirled away. I was falling. The coldness lashed in. The blueness, the swirling movement, the cold—and then the blackness.

Nine

Pompino

A hard abrasive surface scratched at my stomach and legs. The blueness and the Scorpion of the Star Lords had hurled me somewhere. My arms dangled. I opened my eyes. Light—a familiar opaline wash of radiance—reassured me instantly; the idea that I might have been transported back to Earth had tortured me, held me in a stasis that this simple opening of the eyes dissipated.

I was lying full length on the knobbly branch of a tree, my arms dangling into space, and bright green fronds tumbled about me as I moved. Swinging my legs over I sat up. The tree was not overlarge, and the leaves were very pleasant; but the bark was like emery paper.

How far the woods went on I could not see for trees.

About to jump down to the ground a glint of light off metal caught my eye and I waited, still, scarce breathing. In the direction which, by reason of the moss on the tree trunks, I took to be north, that wink of metal blinked twice more and then vanished. I was wrong about the direction being north, as I subsequently discovered. I waited for five heartbeats and, again, prepared to jump down.

A man walked out from under the trees opposite.

Like me, he was stark naked. Unlike me, apim, he was a diff, a Khibil. His shrewd fierce foxy face turned this way and that. His body was compactly muscled and he bore the white glistening traceries of old scars. A bronzed, fit, tough man, this Khibil, with reddish hair and whiskers, and alert contemptuous eyes. He bent and picked up a stout length of wood, a branch as thick as his arm, which he tested for strength before he would accept it into his armory.

At this I frowned.

He looked all about him and then padded off between the trees, going silently and swiftly like a stalking chavonth.

My business, I thought, could not concern him. He was in no immediate danger and, anyway, apart from being naked and weaponless, looked as though he could defend himself.

A cry spurted up from the trees to my rear and I swiveled about. Just beyond the end of the branch on which I sat bowered in leaves, and running to fall on the grass, a young Fristle fifi yelled and blubbered. The Fristle who was hitting her with a slender length of switch wore a brown overall-like garment, and his whiskers jutted stiffly. His gray-furred arm lifted and fell and the switch bit into the fifi's gray fur.

The branch bore my weight almost to the end. Then it broke with a loud crack. I jumped. I fell full on the Fristle. We both collapsed onto the grass.

He came at me raging, slicing his switch. I took it away and clipped him beside the ear and he fell down. He lay sprawled, and his whiskers drooped most forlornly.

Instantly the little Fristle fifi was on her knees at his side, wailing and crying.

"Father! Father! Speak to me!" She shook him, and pulled him to her. Then she sprang to her feet. Like a flying tarantula she was on me, striking and scratching, shrieking.

"You beast! You rast! My poor father—a great naked hairy apim—monster! Beast!"

I held her off. I felt foolish.

"Your father?"

She was sobbing in my grasp.

"We are poor wood cutters. I broke the jar with poor father's tea." She tried to bite my finger. "It was ron* sengjin tea. He beat me for it."

"Tea," I said. I shook my head. "Ron sengjin. A broken jar and a father's chastisement."

She broke free, for I could not bear to hold her, and she dropped to her knees and took her father's head into her hands, crooning over him. Presently he opened his eyes and stared vacantly upward. I put down my hand and hauled him to his feet. He stood, groggily, shaking his head. I feel sure the Bells of Beng Kishi were clanging in there well enough.

---

* ron: red

233

"You fell on me from the sky, apim."

"I owe you an apology—but the switch was too severe a punishment for the crime."

"You fell on me." His eyes rolled. "From the sky."

A blaze of scarlet and gold flew down between us. The Gdoinye passed right before the staring eyes of the Fristle and his daughter. The cat-faced man and girl saw nothing of that impudent bird. He perched on a tree and he squawked at me.

"From the sky," said the Fristle. He swallowed. "A great naked hairy apim. Fell on me."

The Gdoinye squawked again and ruffled a wing.

Knowing when to make myself scarce I left the Fristles to it. The father might have lost his tea; I fancied he had learned a little lesson, also.

"Remberee," I shouted back. And I plunged into the blue shadows of the trees.

With that curious little incident, over which many a man would have grown rosy red in the remembrance, to point me on to my duty for the Star Lords, I ran out from under the far trees and so looked down on my real work here.

And yet, even as I plunged on down the slope, I could not feel fully convinced. The horizon lifted mellowly from a patchwork of fields and woods, threaded by watercourses, and the glittering roofs and spires of a town showed less than a dwabur off. The air held that fragrant freshness of Kregen. I breathed deeply as I skipped down the slope into action. The length of wood I had snatched up would serve to crack a few skulls.

And yet, as I say, I was not fully convinced.

An ornate blue and gold carriage drawn by six krahniks was being besieged by a band of Ochs. The offside front wheel of the carriage jutted awkwardly from under the swingle tree, indication that the axle had broken. The krahniks stood, russet red and placid in their harness, chewing at the grass. Half a dozen Ochs were busily attempting to cut the traces and make off with the animals.

Half a dozen more were banging spears on the wooden panels of the carriage and yelling. A big Rapa was running about, his beaked vulturine face desperate, trying to fend the Ochs off. Another Rapa lay in the grass. He was not dead, for his crest kept quivering as he tried to haul himself up, only for an Och to give him a sly thwack and so stretch him out again. Now Ochs are small folk little above four feet tall with lemon-shaped heads with puffy jaws and lolling chops. They have six limbs and use the central pair indiscriminately as arms or legs. Usually, they prefer to work in as large a body as they can, numbers giving them strength.

234

The rest of the group, about ten or so, were all yelling and jumping about and trying to attack the naked Khibil. He was laying about with his length of wood, knocking Ochs over, sending them flying, whirling them away. It was all a crazy little pandemonium. I ran down, debating.

Often I have had to make up my mind just who the Star Lords wanted rescued. Was this Khibil in need of assistance? Or was he the aggressor and the Ochs required for the mysterious purposes of the Everoinye?

The Gdoinye, who had acted in so strange a manner, left me in no doubt.

He flew on before me and swooped at the Ochs banging on the coach. They could not see him. So I ran on down and stretched that group of Ochs out and turned to give the Khibil a hand.

There were only three left by then and they ran off as I turned on them. The rest left the krahniks and ran off, also, squeaking, their spindly legs flashing.

The Khibil swelled his massive chest and regarded me.

He held his length of wood cocked over his right shoulder. Deliberately, I allowed my length of wood to drop.

"Llahal, dom," I said cheerfully.

For a moment he hesitated, and I fancied he was fighting the inherent feelings of superiority some Khibils never master. Then: "Llahal, apim. You were just in time to assist me in seeing this rabble of Ochs off—they are not worth pursuit."

"Probably."

A noise echoed inside the carriage and I heard a whisper, quick and fervent. I moved slowly sideways so as to get a view of Khibil and coach together. The Khibil lowered his length of wood. Whatever the obi might be hereabouts it evidently did not include the immediate giving and receiving of a challenge it held in other parts of Kregen. I, of course, had no idea where I was. That I was on Kregen was the extent of my knowledge. The two suns were in the sky, and they were high in the meridian, and they did not jibe with my moss-and-tree deduction of the direction of north.

The Khibil shared my curiosity.

He said, "Tell me, dom, where are we?"

Before I could answer, a sharp female voice from the coach window spat out: "Why, you knave, in Kov Pastic's province, of course, and if you don't put your clothes on at once I will have the kov's guard arrest you the moment we reach Gertinlad."

The Khibil and I stared at each other for a space. His reddish whiskers twitched. I thought of the Fristle on whom I had dropped from the sky. I thought of the occasion when I had given a helping hand to Marta Renberg, the Kovneva of Aduimbrev, with her luxurious coach that fell by the way. And, too, I thought of an earlier occasion when I had been transmitted to

Kregen by the Star Lords to assist Djang girls against Och slavers. The two instances were strangely mingled here. Again that sense of machination troubled me, and by machination I mean wheels within wheels and not the ordinary interference in my life by the Everoinye. So the Khibil's whiskers twitched. The woman in the coach was still screaming about our nakedness and her friend the kov. The Khibil was the first to laugh.

And I, Dray Prescot, who had learned to laugh muchly of late in odd ways, I, too, laughed. The Khibil recovered first.

With the length of wood held just so, he approached the carriage. He spoke up; but the note in his voice was of a fine free scorn tempered by social observance.

"Llahal, lady. We have no clothes. They were stolen by these rascally Ochs. But we have saved your life."

The woman was hidden from me by the jut of window; I could see her hand, thin and white, on which at least five rings glittered. Her voice continued in its shrill shriek.

"Onron! Give these two paktuns clothes! Bratch!"

The Rapa who had been running about, the one with the red feathers in whirlicues about his eyes and beak, went to the trunk fastened to the back of the coach and, presently, the Khibil and I were arrayed in gray trousers and blue shirts. I was beginning to have an idea of where I was, and not caring for it over much.

"See to the wheel," said the lady, and the window shutter went up with a clatter. A mumble of conversation began within the coach.

I looked at the Khibil, prepared to get on with fixing the axle, for I conceived that the Everoinye wished this hoity-toity madam in the coach preserved for posterity. If she was anything like the couple I had saved in the inner sea she might pup a son who would topple empires.

The Khibil said: "Lahal, apim. I am Pompino, Scauro Pompino ti Tuscursmot. When I saw the Gdoinye leading you on I realized you were a kregoinye." He sniffed. "Although why the Everoinye should imagine I would need help against miserable little Ochs, I do not know, by Horato the Potent."

I felt the solid ground of Kregen lurch beneath me.

A man, another mortal man, was talking of the Gdoinye, of the Star Lords! He knew! He called me and by implication himself a kregoinye. I swallowed. I spoke up.

"Lahal, Scauro Pompino. I am Jak."

If I was where I thought I was the name of Dray Prescot would have that villain hog-tied and subject to an agonizing death.

About to go on to amplify the single name of Jak with some descriptive appellation—and it would not have been Jak the Drang for news travels where there are vollers—this Scauro Pompino ti Tuscursmot interrupted.

"You call me Pompino. On occasion it pleases me to be called Pompino the Iarvin."

"Pompino."

"Now we had best fix this shrewish lady's axle and then see her safely into the town, which I take to be Gertinlad."

"I agree. We are in Hamal, I think."

He shook his head as we began on the axle. The lady made no offer to get out of the coach, and the Rapas gathered themselves to help.

"No. I am not sure; but not Hamal."

Well, I thought, if you're right, dom, thank Vox for that.

The Rapa called Onron scowled. "Hamal? You are from Hamal?" His fist gripped his sword, a thraxter, and he half-drew.

"No, Knave," snapped Pompino. "We are not from Hamal."

"The Hamalese," quoth the Rapa, "should be tied up in their own guts and left to rot, by Rhapaporgolam the Reiver of Souls!"

"Quidang to that," said Pompino.

A soft clump of hoofs drew our attention as a party of men riding totrixes rode up. There were ten of them and their six-legged mounts were lathered. Their weapons glittered in their hands, apim and diff alike. Pompino grabbed his piece of wood and prepared to fight; but Onron shrilled a silly cackle and said: "Peace, Knave. These are the lady Yasuri's men, my comrades. They were decoyed away by other Ochs, may they rot in Cottmer's Caverns."

With the increment in our numbers we were able to repair the wheel and axle and so the coach started creakingly on its way to Gertinlad. Pompino and I rode perched on the roof, with Onron and his partner driving, and the totrix men resuming their function as escorts. We rolled through the mellow countryside and under the archway of the town and so into the familiar sights and stinks of a bustling market town and to an inn called the Green Attar. This was a high class hostelry such as would be patronized by a lady of gentle birth. The commander of her escort, a surly Rapa called Rordan the Negus, would have seen us off with a few curt words. He and his men wore half-armor, and were well armed with spear and bow, sword and shield. Pompino would have started an argument in his high-handed way; but Onron, who had carried the personal satchels from the coach into the inn, came out and yelled that the lady Yasuri would speak with us, and Bratch was the word.

So we jumped and obeyed on the run, which is what a serving man does when Bratch! is yelled at him.

As we went in Pompino said: "I think the Everoinye wish us to continue to take care of this lady. I admit it is not an assignment I relish, but the ways of the Everoinye are not for mortal man to understand."

I just nodded and so we went into the Green Attar and the smell of cooking and rich wines and stood before the table at which sat the lady Yasuri. The inn looked to be clean and comfortable, with much polished brass and dark upholstered chairs of sturmwood, with a wooden floor strewn with rugs of a weave new to me. We stood respectfully.

"You did well to drive off those rascally Ochs," said the lady in her high voice. "You will be rewarded."

She presented an outré picture, for she was tiny, and lined of face, with shapeless clothes that swaddled her in much black material like bombazine, shiny and hard, with a blaze of diamonds and sapphires, and with fine ivory lace at throat and wrist. She was apim, and her face looked like a wrinkled nut, with yet a little juice remaining. Her nose was sharp. She wore a wig of a frightful blond color. The rings on her fingers caught the oil lamps' gleam and struck brilliants into our eyes.

Pompino said: "We thank you, lady."

She glared at him as though he had offered her violence.

"I am for LionardDen. The kov there is my friend; but he is away in the north helping in the fight against those Havil-forsaken rasts of Hamal. The land is hungry for fighting men. You are mercenaries. I offer you employment to see me safely through to Jikaida City."

Pompino took a breath.

Before he could speak, the lady rattled on: "I can offer you better pay than usual. A silver strebe a day will buy a mercenary here. I offer you eight per sennight."

With a dignity that set well with him, Pompino pointed out, "One does not buy a paktun. One pays him for services rendered." As he spoke I received the impression that he was a paktun, probably a hyr-paktun and entitled to wear the golden pakzhan at his throat. "But, lady—are the silver strebes broad or short?"

She cocked up her sharp chin at this.

This was, indeed, a matter of moment. Coinage varies all over Kregen, of course, just as it does on Earth; but the common language imposed, so I thought, by the Star Lords, and the wild entanglement of peoples and animals and plants mean a creeping universality makes of Kregen a place unique by virtue of its very commonality. A short strebe, the silver coin known over most of the Dawn Lands, is worth far less than a broad strebe, and every honest citizen knows very well how to value the two in the scales. They may carry the very same head of whatever king or potentate has issued them, and the reverse may show the same magniloquent declarations of power or current advertisement of political policy; but the short and the broad will not buy the same quantity of goods in the markets—no, by Krun, not by a long chalk.

Now the Dawn Lands of Havilfar form a crazy patchwork of countries, and they bear no resemblance to the ordered checkers of the Jikaida board. They are a confusing conglomeration of kingdoms and princedoms and kovnates and republics, and a map-maker's nightmare. The lady Yasuri hailed from one kingdom and while she was gone her king might be deposed, or her country invaded, so that when she returned she would have to vow fealty to a new sovereign—that was if her vadvarate still belonged to her. The Dawn Lands, viewed from some lofty perch in space, must resemble a stewpot forever on the boil.

Watching the lady Yasuri I saw how she used her shiny black bombazine to armor herself against the world. She was more accustomed, I guessed, to soft sensil and languorous dresses in the privacy of her own quarters, and she'd probably doff that hideous wig. She presented a hard and shrewish front to the world out of fear or the desire to intimidate. She screwed up her eyes, and her white hand toyed with her glass. She made a great show of thinking deeply. Then:

"Broad."

Pompino nodded, still grave, still engaged in the negotiation of hiring out as a mercenary. But he did not attempt to increase the offer on account of his being, as I supposed, a hyr-paktun. He said: "But I am a Khibil. It would be nine for me."

"Done," said the lady Yasuri, promptly. "Nine for you, Khibil, and eight for the apim."

I was too amused to argue.

Most places of Kregen use the six-day week, which I, rather contrarily, call a sennight. So our pay would be useful. A Pachak here would receive at least twelve broad strebes, possibly fourteen. A Chulik would get the same. You would rarely find a Kataki as a mercenary although there were renowned races of that slavemaster people whose second method of earning a living was hiring out as mercenaries; and they would grump until they got their twelve. As for the Ochs, four or five at the most. Rapas and Fristles and the like would get the standard one strebe a day.

If they didn't argue it out, they'd get short strebes, too.

Pay is relative, of course, and I guessed that in these lands profoundly affected by the war with Hamal up north the price of commodities would have shot up. Perhaps this pay was not as excellent as at first sight it appeared. All the same, I contrasted these rates with those paid to the bowmen and archers of home, where a silver stiver was regarded as the small fortune paid to a Relianchun and where the bronze krad, a denomination of coin newly introduced by the Presidio, figured largely in the imaginations of the men come pay day. The krad, with, I hesitate to observe, an unspeakable likeness of the Emperor of Vallia on the obverse and resounding and inspiring slogans on the reverse, was regarded as fair and just. But, then, my men there in Vallia served their country and not for pay.

Even so, I did not think that the old Crimson Bowmen of Loh, who had formed the old emperor's bodyguard, had received a silver stiver a day. Their Jiktars and Chuktar had taken away their golden talens; of that I was very sure.

When Pompino and I, having made our respects to the lady Yasuri and the hiring being completed, returned to the courtyard of the Green Attar we became immediately aware of an offensive abomination going on there. The sights and sounds were sickening. A number of nobles put up here, for the place was renowned, and one of the members of a noble's entourage was being flogged.

The fellow had been triced up into the flogging triangle in a corner where sweet-scented flowers, brilliant and lovely, depended over the wall, forming a silent mockery of the obscenity going on in their shade. A thick leather gag had been forced between his teeth and secured by thongs around his head. He was flaxen-haired, strongly-built, and his tunic had been stripped down to his waist.

He hung in the leather thongs binding his wrists and ankles to the wood of the triangle. He hung limply, as though accepting what was happening, and then he would jerk, every muscle standing out ridged, and so collapse into that limp huddle again. So he hung and jerked, shuddering, and hung again, and then convulsed once more as the other lash slashed across his bloody wreck of a back.

A left-handed Brokelsh stood at his right side and a right-handed Rapa stood at his left. They took turns to slice the lashes down, black and whistling with stranded thongs.

"By Black Chunguj!" swore Pompino. "I never did like to see a man flogged jikaider."

For the Rapa and the Brokelsh between them were dicing the man's back up into a checkerboard of blood.

A Deldar, a heavy and thick-set man with the weight of years in the grade with no hope of ever making zan-Deldar and then Hikdar about him, spat and swore. "Hangi should have left the wine alone. It's doing him no good, no, nor us, neither."

The noble's guards standing and looking on glumly as their comrade was flogged jikaider—a cruel and inhuman punishment, even to me who had seen men flogged round the Fleet—wore harness much studded with bronze bosses, and with pale blue and black favors. They looked a hard-bitten lot.

Pompino made some remark, and the Deldar hawked up again.

"The notor is strict—aye, may Havandua the Green Wonder mete him his just desserts—strict. You can say that again about the notor, Erclan the Critchoith. Keep at it!" He swung away to bellow at the Rapa and Brokelsh who had desisted in their efforts to flay Hangi's back. "You know the score! Ten times six and six more! Stylor!" to the shaking Relt who stood with slate and chalk marking the strokes. "Keep a strict account!"

240

"Quidang, quidang," stammered the Relt, his weak beaked face betraying by its frizzle of feathers the state he was in.

The lashes thwunked down again, and Hangi jerked, and was still. There is no real mystery why such a beastly practice should be given a name that associates it, however remotely, with the supreme board of Kregen. The contrast, it is said, explains the paradox.

"Stole Risslaca Ichor, did Hangi," the Deldar told us, his face with the veins breaking around the nose sweating and empurpled. "A whole amphora. The notor's favorite, is Risslaca Ichor, always keeps a special supply, and Hangi found it, and Hangi drank it, and there's Hangi now, for all to see."

"Risslaca Ichor." Pompino sniffed. "A mere common rosé adulterated with dopa—"

"Fortified, dom, fortified!"

"So they say."

Then a profound change overcame the Deldar. He grew, if it were possible, even bulkier and more purple. The sweat sprang out in great pearly drops. "Keep at it, you hulus! Hit hard!"

So we looked up to the flower-banked balcony, and there stood the notor, this Kov Erclan Rodiflor. Square and hard and ablaze with gems, he stood braced on wide-planted feet, his hands clamped on his hips, his chin with his strip of black beard upthrust, and his square lowering face brooded on the scene below. Returning to Jikaida City, was Kov Erclan. A man who exuded authority and power, he possessed a dark inner core that gave him the yrium he would have taken had he been a gang leader and not a kov.

Like his men, he wore the pale blue and black favors, arranged in checkerboard fashion. Well, he looked down and we looked up and he saw neither Pompino nor myself in the shadows; his dark eyes were all for the flogging. I thought merely that I had met many men like that, and so we walked on, stony-faced past the guards, and when I next met Kov Erclan— well, that you will hear, all in due time.

Pompino and I thus became, for each of us once more, paktuns, hired mercenaries, bodyguards, men who rented out their skill with arms and laid their lives at risk to earn their daily crust.

Events moved with speed after that. The life of a paktun is mostly boring, and shot through with sudden and brief flashes of scarlet action. Often they are the last things that happen to him. We were outfitted, for it was all found, and donned bronze-studded leather jerkins, with gray trousers and calf-high boots. The weapons were thraxter, the straight cut and thrust sword of Hamal, stuxes, oval shields and a dagger apiece. The green tunic I was handed bore a rusty stain low on the left side, and a rip neatly sewn together, a rip about the size to admit a spear-blade. The trousers had been laundered clean, however, for which I was grateful.

Pompino made a face. "Dead men's clothes."

The helmets were of iron, and not bronze, iron pots thonged under the chin and with ear and back flaps. Holders at the crown bore tufts of green, black and blue feathers.

So equipped and astride totrixes Pompino and I rode out the next morning as part of the escort to Yasuri Lucrina, the Vadni of Cremorra, en route for LionardDen, Jikaida City.

From the rich lands around Gertinlad the way led us across rivers and through forests into country that grew impressively wild and menacingly forbidding. We were in the Dawn Lands of Havilfar. Here, in the ancient countries around The Shrouded Sea, were situated those parts of the great southern continent that had been first settled when men arrived here in the beginning of history—so went the old stories. Both Pompino and I were firmly convinced that the Star Lords had sent us to ensure the safety of Yasuri. The whole operation, at least for me, was so markedly different from what had happened before that I deemed it prudent to follow events and to do my best to avoid the wrath of the Star Lords.

Of one thing I was profoundly grateful. Because of the differences this time, and the warning, there was no extra bitterness in me at the parting from Delia. Of course I grieved for the sundering, and vowed to return as soon as I could, echoing in the old way and the old days, I will return to my Delia, my Delia of Delphond, my Delia of the Blue Mountains. But, this time, she was apprised of my disappearance, and she knew, now, what that fate was that dogged me. No moist-mouthed slimy minions of Quergey the Murgey could affront her now; she would send that lot packing with a zorca hoof up their rumps. Sorrow touched me that I had not welcomed Drak and clasped hands with him. As with Melow the Supple and Kardo. But I felt the warm glow of satisfaction at the thought that Drak, Prince of Vallia, Krzy, was now there, in Vondium, and, Opaz willing, ready to take up the reins. Suppose he refused? Suppose he contumed the task of standing in for the Emperor of Vallia? He had told us that he would not become emperor while we lived, Delia and I, and I had brushed that aside as sentiment. I felt that Drak, who of all my sons was the strong, sober, industrious one, with that wild Prescot streak in him, too, was best fitted to run Vallia. Had I thought Zeg, who was now King in Zandikar, or Jaidur, who was swashbuckling about in connivance with the Sisters of the Rose, could handle the job better, then primogeniture, too, would have been kicked out with a zorca hoof up its rump. Primogeniture obtains on Kregen; but it is not an unbreakable rule. A man must fight for what he wants there, and it is what a man is and the spirit and heart of him that counts, not what his father is.

Or his mother, either... For the ladies of Kregen are people in their own right, and fully aware of that, with minds that are their own. The ladies of

Kregen count, as this Yasuri, Vadni of Cremorra, so sharply reminded us. Some of the women of Kregen there are who hate all men because they are men, as foolish a stance as to hate all calsanys because they are calsanys, or all roses because they are roses. But, then, some women do not deserve to be ladies of Kregen, anyway...

There was little satisfaction to be gained in the situation where I was a puppet of the Star Lords; but it is useless to kick against the pricks when there is nothing one can do about that particular situation. I had slowly and cautiously been attempting to build a kind of structure of deceit against the Star Lords, and had intemperately gone against my own plans and been banished to Earth for twenty-one cruel years. Now I was trying a new tack. But, in the end, obedience to the Everoinye must dominate my actions. They were superhuman. Their powers were far beyond those of mortals, beyond those of the Wizards of Loh, beyond the Savanti. I trembled to dare to think that perhaps Zena Iztar might possess powers to match them.

As we rode, I studied, to learn what I could from what Pompino could tell me. He was of South Pandahem, a land of which I then knew little. He was married with two sets of twins and from what he did not say I gathered that he rubbed along with his wife, in a kind of habit-formed pattern, rather than taking any active joy from the marriage state. Well, two worlds are full of marriages like that. He was not at all displeased to be called out to serve the Everoinye. He talked well as we jogged along through the land that increasingly grew more ominous, with rocky defiles and overhanging crags leading on to wide plains where the sere grass blew. The country was pock-marked with tracts of badlands, and we were due to spend the night at a fortified posting house at the ford of Gilma. Gilma is a water sprite found in the legends of Prince Larghos and the Demons. Pompino told me that he did not like the Hamalese, a sentiment I could well understand from Hamal's ruthless conquest of Pandahem. But he could tell me little of the Star Lords.

He received his orders from the Gdoinye. When I introduced a casual remark about scorpions, he dismissed them as unpleasant but rarely seen creatures of Havil.

I told him I was from Huringa in Hyrklana. This city I knew well from my days as a kaidur in the Jikhorkdun there, and so could fabricate substantial accounts to bolster my story. He eyed me at that.

"Queen Fahia grows too fat, so men say—and I mean you no disrespect, Jak. But men say she cannot live long."

I nodded. "So it is said."

Pompino clicked his tongue at his totrix. We were passing a stand of withered trees and the branches reached out like gray wraiths.

"Men say that the tragedy of Princess Lilah cast a shadow over the kingdom."

Princess Lilah of Hyrklana! I had sent spies to seek news of her whereabouts and all had reported failure.

"It is indeed a tragedy. I would dearly love to know where she is now, By Kru—by Havil."

The slip passed unnoticed.

Much of what we said I will report when the time is due; suffice it that Pompino, for all he was one of those Khibils who consider themselves a cut above ordinary mortals, proved a stalwart companion, and in the manner of Khibils, brave and resourceful and loyal. A task had been set to his hands and he would fulfill that task with his dying breath.

He did grumble: "What the confounded woman wants to go all this dolorous way to play Jikaida for is a conundrum I would not burden Hoko the Amusingly Malicious with."

There were so many burning questions I had to ask that mention of Jikaida passed me by then... But Pompino knew only that he took his orders from a great scarlet and gold bird, that he was paid handsomely for his trouble in real gold, and that should he disobey he would be punished with exceedingly unpleasant penalties. We did not go into their nature.

"Why, Pompino? Why?"

He looked puzzled. "The gods are passing strange in their ways, Jak. Passing strange. But to serve the gods, to serve the Everoinye, is not that a great pride and does it not confer stature upon a man? Is it not, Jak, a High Jikai?"

I had never looked on rushing about pulling the Star Lords' chestnuts out of the fire as a High Jikai. That great word, that supreme notion of high chivalry and courage and self-sacrifice, seemed to me sacred to deeds writ in gold. As I did not answer he scowled. "Well?"

"Yes," I said. "Assuredly."

Because he had been the first to pelt down all naked into action and drive the Ochs away he had quite naturally assumed the leadership of our twin mission. I did not bother my head over that. Let him imagine he carried the burden. Truth to tell, I was happy to allow it—and, equally, I liked him.

The posting house at the ford of Gilma was merely a single story house and surrounding wall all built of the gray stones carried down from the frowning hills. We did not change the totrixes or the krahniks, for we had not been pushing them and they were beasts of price. We set off early the next day and so came down the long valley into Songaslad, a town of thieves.

Over the border some sixty dwaburs off lay the country of Aidrin in which lay the capital, the city called Jikaida City. The journey was fraught with peril. It lay over badlands of an exceedingly bad badness. In Songaslad, the town of thieves, caravans were formed for mutual protection on the journey. The lady Yasuri sent her Rapa Jiktar to haggle for the price of a caravan's protection. Perforce, we waited, and set a doubled guard over our possessions.

We lost only a good saddle, richly inlaid, a carpet of high price, and a set of golden candlesticks whose theft almost gave the lady a fainting fit. Her companions, her handmaids in the coach with her, used burned twigs of Sweet Ibroi to revive her. We concluded a deal with hawk-faced Ineldar the Kaktu, the caravan master, forthwith.

So, a long straggling procession of carriages and wagons and riders and people trudging afoot, we wended out of Songaslad, the town of thieves, to cross the Desolate Wastes, and so win our way to Aidrin, and the rich country around LionardDen, Jikaida City.

Ten

Into the Desolate Waste

Many times have I journeyed in caravans across country inhospitable by reason of nature or man, and on each occasion I vow never again, and know even as I vow that the lure of the adventure will always drag me on. Each occasion is different. Kregen is a world of so many startling contrasts that the beauty and terror mingle and fill the spirit with wild eagerness or desolation, with burning ambition to win against all or a calm and joyous acceptance of the stupendous.

Nights under the stars! Ah—they are never to be forgotten.

The Caravan labored along, crossing rivers and winding down long defiles, gaining the far slopes and so rising to emerge onto the vasty plains where the mist lifted blue and eerie, like lantern smoke against snow.

The totrix of the lady Yasuri's given into my charge and whom I rode across the Desolate Wastes was a skewbald called Munky. I was careful of him. Accustomed as I may be to walking barefoot across the awful places of Kregen, I was now far more of a mind to ride rather than walk.

Oh, yes, despite all my deeper concerns, I enjoyed that caravan across the Desolate Wastes to Jikaida City. And, if the truth be told, the land was not all desolate. Grass grew and the animals fed. There was water in swift silver streams. Every now and then we crossed stony deserts, or sandy deserts; but we prepared for them. The various places along the way were infested with drikingers and these bandits attacked us, as was their custom. We fought them off.

Here we saw why the Star Lords had provided two men—two krego-inye, I must now call them—to escort the person they had chosen to save for posterity. The Rapa escort fought well and earned their hire along with all the other caravan guards. But, one by one, they went down, by arrow or spear, sword or javelin. Soon my companion Pompino was given the escort command, with the rank of Jiktar, whereat he smiled at me, and I warmed to him, realizing how much and how little he valued these titles. But we saved the skin of the lady Yasuri.

It is not my intention to give a blow-by-blow account of that journey, much though the prospect tempts me, for this was a kind of holiday. It is with some of the people of the caravan that my interest lies, and therefore yours.

The lady Yasuri herself was going to Jikaida City to play Jikaida, and most of the other folk in the caravan were doing likewise, to play, to participate, to gamble or merely to make a profit on the game.

As is the way with such caravans, people tend to fall into clumps, who jog along together, for company, good fellowship and mutual protection. A deal of this can be put down to the speed of progress. The lady Yasuri's coach matched the speed of an ornate, top-heavy creation of the carriage-builder's art, in blue and yellow, that swayed along next in line. This conveyance was drawn by six krahniks. In the caravan were so many of the various marvelous animals of Kregen it were vain to name them all; but there were Quoffas, calsanys, plain asses, hirvels, totrixes, and the like. There were few zorcas. Of course, being Havilfar, there were no voves. This blue and yellow coach with the black and white checkerboard along the sides contained Master Scatulo. In Master Scatulo's terms, to speak his name was enough.

Master Scatulo—he trumpeted a host of names all attesting to his enormous prowess as a Jikaidast—permitted the lady Yasuri the graciousness of his company when we halted for meals. Yasuri hung on this young fellow's words—for Scatulo was young, brash, supremely self-confident and, by the reckoning of anyone you cared to ask, a remarkable player of Jikaida, a true Jikaidast.

His face was of a sallow cast, sharp and edgy, with deep furrows between his eyebrows, and eyes of a piercing quality that Sishi, the lady Yasuri's least important hand maiden told me with a laugh, he painted with blue-kohl to enhance their impression of brooding intelligence. I believed this. It is known. Pompino guffawed and passed a most demeaning remark.

"He's real clever, is Master Scatulo!" protested Sishi. She, herself, was apim and a little beauty with dark hair and a rosy glowing face and ways that were still artless, despite the way of the world. I waggled a finger at her.

"Now then, mistress Sishi. Beware of clever men like this Scatulo. Just because he says he is Havil's gift to the world, that he is a genius, doesn't mean he can—"

"I know what you're saying, Jak!"

"Just as well you do, Sishi," said Pompino. "For Jak speaks sooth. This Scatulo will get you—"

Her face was scarlet. Sishi burst out, "You're horrible!"

That, by Vox, was true enough; but had little to do with the subject in question.

There were other Jikaidasts in the caravan; not many. I gathered from sly remarks that a Jikaidast must be in the very topmost flight of his profession to be preferred in Jikaida City. Trouble was, Pompino and I could not flaunt our ignorance; everyone understood so well the significance of Jikaida City that significant details were taken for granted. We agreed to keep our ears open and learn.

The other person who jogged along with us and shared our fire and engaged in conversation was a Wizard of Loh.

Yes. Oh, yes, I well realize the surprise anyone must feel in so cavalier a treatment of a representative of one of the most powerful groups of wizards on Kregen. But Deb-Lu-Quienyin was a pleasant old buffer whose red Lohvian hair was much thinned by perplexed rubbing and whose lined face expressed a perennial surprise at the state of the world. But, for all that, he was a Wizard of Loh. He wore plain robes, with their dark blue only moderately embellished with silver and he wore a stout shortsword, which made me look in wonder.

"Aye, young man, a sword and a Wizard of Loh. Parlous are the days, and grievous the evil thereof."

"Aye, san," I said, giving him the correct honorific of san—sage or dominie. "You speak sooth."

He tilted his lopsided turban-like headdress to one side so as to rub his hair. Strings of pearls and diamonds decorated the folds of blue cloth; but he assured me they were imitation only. "For I have fallen on hard days, young man, and Things Are Not What They Were."

He rode a preysany, the superior form of calsany used for riding, and that indicated a slender purse. Munky jogged alongside the preysany well enough, for a few emphatic kicks indicated to him he had best mind his manners. Preysanys, like calsanys, do offensive things when they are frightened. Deb-Lu-Quienyin wanted to talk. I did not think he suffered from that hideous disease, chivrel, that wastes a man or woman into premature old age; but he was without doubt unlike any Wizard of Loh I had previously encountered. During the days of the journey across the Desolate Waste I heard a deal of his history.

He had been a powerful sorcerer, come from Loh as a young man into Havilfar, and set fair to making his fortune. He had been variously court wizard to kings and kovs in the Dawn Lands, and had spent a time in Hyrklana, whereat we reminisced for a space. Then he had become aware that his powers were failing. He talked to me like this, frankly, I believe, out of the misery in him. He maintained a dignified mien to the people of the caravan and they, being prudent, gave him a wide berth.

Some spark struck between us. I realized he told me much more than he perhaps knew, and I put that confidence down to the journey and the circumstances of the caravan and our traveling together through dangerous country. In the event, we got along capitally. He kept no famulus, for, as he said: "The last one grew too clever, and taunted me, and so left to set up for himself. And I do not have the wherewithal to pay an assistant."

He had a little tame Och slave who tended his clothes and cooked his meals and chattered away to himself, a scrawny bundle in an old blanket coat who walked, for Deb-Lu-Quienyin's purse could not stretch to a second saddle animal. His calsany was loaded with mysterious bundles, bowed under the weight, and there was no room for the Och, Ionno the Ladle. The Wizard of Loh cast glances of mingled covetousness and scorn at the Jikaidast, Master Scatulo, and sighed.

"Look at him, young man, Puffed With the Pride of the Masterful. Once I, too, must have been like that. And see his slave, the muscles, the strength— why, he could carry his master on his back all the way to Jikaida City if he had to."

Truly, Scatulo's personal slave was a powerfully built diff, a Brukaj with immense rounded shoulders and a hunched-forward head with a forceful face with more than a passing resemblance to that of a bulldog. The Brukajin possess legs rather on the short side, it is true; but they are determined, dogged, and I had been pleased to have them serve in any of the armies I had commanded on Kregen. As is to be expected from their natures they are superb in the defense. They are as dissimilar as one could imagine from the Tryfants, who attack with enormous élan, and in retreat merely rout, running every which way. The Brukajin are not to be confused with the Brokelsh, whose thick mat of coarse body hair complements their generally coarse ways of carrying on. I have good friends among the Brokelsh, and I was intrigued to notice the protocol that existed between the Brokelsh in the caravan and this slave of Scatulo's, this powerful but docile Brukaj, who was called Bevon.

Not for Bevon the Brukaj, as a slave, the privilege of a descriptive appendage to his name; Deb-Lu-Quienyin's slave chattering to himself in his brown blanket coat was crowingly conscious of his descriptive name, the Ladle. The Wizard of Loh was good-natured enough to be pleased at this.

"Since my accident, young man," he confided to me as we jogged along under the Suns of Scorpio, tasting the sweetness of the air, watching the ominous countryside. "I have not been the man I was. Time has Entrapped me in Her Coils."

I gathered that the accident, the exact nature of which he did not specify, although it sounded as though he had tried some magic too powerful to be contained, had deprived him of enough of his wizardly powers as seriously to jeopardize his life style. He could not, for instance, go into lupu and spy out events and people at a distance. There were other powers he had lost. He was resigned to them in a bittersweet way, talking of his misfortunes and of life in capital letters. He was a humorous old boy, not strong, proud as are all Wizards of Loh, and yet much on the defensive after the accident.

After a trifling brush with drikingers who drew off after the caravan guards shot their leader, we found we had water trouble. The bandits had shot deliberately at the water barrels fixed to the wagon. The amphorae they smashed with ease. The wooden staves of the barrels resisted; but enough were pierced through to cause Ineldar the Kaktu, the caravan master, to put us all on quarter rations until the next water hole.

This caused trouble.

Two days later we were all hot, dusty, dry—and thirsty.

And an event occurred that brought me vividly face to face with the Meaning of Life.

Eleven

Prince Mefto the Kazzur

"By Horato the Potent!" exclaimed Pompino. "I am drier than a corpse's shinbone."

I said nothing but sucked on my pebble.

The caravan wended along, a brightly colored succession of carriages and wagons, with clumps of people, apim and diff, trudging along in the dust, and the outriders flanking us, their weapons ready. Ineldar the Kaktu had been wroth with his caravan guards, although, in all honesty, they had fought well and driven the drikingers off. But we all guessed we had not seen the last of those skulking rasts. Before we reached the water-hole they would attack again—with a new leader in command, no doubt.

When a straggling line of black dots showed in the southern sky I felt the muscles beside my eyes tighten. At bellowed commands the caravan halted at once. Dust hung about us, slowly dissipating. Everyone stared aloft, to the south, away from the twin suns. Those flyers there must be flutsmen, out reiving, and if they attacked us we'd be caught between two foes. But, and I do not think the flutsmen missed seeing us, the big birds wheeled away in the air and soon vanished. Probably they were in insufficient strength to attack our caravan, which was clearly large and well protected.

This being Havilfar, one would expect many flyers to be seen. That group was the only one we saw on the journey. The exigencies of the war being waged against mad Empress Thyllis of Hamal demanded hordes of flyers and the land here was almost denuded. The same was true of vollers and we saw not one. Some of the countries of the Dawn Lands manufacture their own fliers, and these were in constant demand and short supply. Hamal, as I knew to my bitter cost, had a stranglehold on that particular industry.

We were traveling generally westward toward the rugged chains of mountains running through the heart of Havilfar. These were the same mountains that in their northern reaches the Hamalese call the Mountains of the West, and against which nestles Paline Valley. But that was around four hundred and fifty dwaburs north. We were about halfway between the River Os north of us and the Shrouded Sea to the south. In their southern extremities the mountains swing somewhat to the west and beyond them lie broad rivers and wide lakes, all terra incognito to me. The folk in the caravan called the mountains there—for they have a plethora of names, as common sense must indicate by reason of their extent—the Snowy Mountains.

We were within a day or so of the water hole and the drikingers had not attacked us again.

A group of brilliantly attired riders went past the caravan at a good clip, apparently reckless of our short water supply situation. They had ridden out in defiance when the flutsmen vanished. I had asked Sishi about them and their leader soon after the caravan had started on its journey.

There was no gainsaying their splendid appearance. There were some twenty of them, clustered about their leader. They were diff and apim; the leader was a Kildoi. He reminded me so much of Korero that I had started up the first time I espied him as he cantered past on his swarth. He had the same beautiful physique, the same four hands and handtail, the same golden beard, glinting in the light of the suns. His eyes were lighter than Korero's and, when I got a good look at them, held a lurking distaste in their depths I recoiled from in instinctive antipathy. In this, he was poles apart from Korero.

The swarths they rode were powerful beasts but two or three hands less in height than those we had fought at First Kanarsmot. Their scales were of a more greenish-purple than the swarths we had defeated, which were of a more reddish-brown. The swarths' wedge-shaped heads which protruded from their bodies on necks that were extensions of body and head, diminishing in diameter from body to head, all in a smooth curved line, so that of neck, really, they had nothing, were decorated barbarically with metals and jewels. Their trappings blazed. From the front a swarth presents a picture of a massive humped mass with that wedge-shaped head thrusting down and forward, the jaws sharp and pointed, the teeth bared and serrated like razor-edged saws.

The Kildoi who led this brilliant and barbaric group wore link-mesh of that superb quality that is manufactured in the Dawn Lands of Havilfar. He affected a gilt-iron helmet. He wore a short slashed robe of white liberally encrusted with cloth of gold. His cape was short and flared spectacularly when he galloped. It was a bright hard yellow in color, edged in gold and silver. His feathers blew in white and yellow, fixed into a golden holding crest.

Yes, he looked magnificent, proud, barbaric, blazing with light under the suns.

"Who," I had said to Sishi, "is that man?"

Sishi knew all the gossip of the caravan, and the scandals, too. She had looked and her color mounted.

"Is he not splendid? So brave, so bold and handsome—"

"Who is he?"

"Why, everyone must know! He is Prince Mefto—Prince Mefto A'Shanofero, Prince of Shanodrin!"

As she continued to stare after the Kildoi and his companions I shook my head. Shanodrin was a country situated in the heart of the Dawn Lands, west of Khorundur. It was a full rich land with great wealth to be won from the rocks and rivers.

Then Sishi heaved up a great sigh.

"Oh," she said. "I do so love a prince!"

"And why not?" I said, I fear somewhat drily.

If there was one thing certain sure about Prince Mefto, he liked to show off. He and his swarthmen would gallop around the caravan like gulls circling a ship, affording visible proof to the people of their presence and the sharpness of their weapons.

And then Sishi, still enraptured with the dazzlement of the prince, said: "Prince Mefto—he is the best swordsman in the world."

Well, for all I knew, he could be. I will have no truck with this nonsense of proclaiming boasts about the best swordsman of two worlds. I have expounded some of my philosophy anent the perils of swordplay and the doom by edge or point that lurks—if expound is not too pompous a word. So I made some light quip, whereat Sishi flounced around, blushing, and tried to hit me with the length of sausages she happened to be carrying for the lady Yasuri's midday snack. With that deeply philosophic reminder, I went off to see about my duties as a paktun earning his hire.

The rich personages in their carriages had taken the obvious and sensible

251

precaution of providing a supply of water for their own personal use. We knew Yasuri had her amphorae stacked in her coach, which we louts of her escort were not permitted to enter. Ineldar the Kaktu was cognizant of this trick, of course, and he did his best to share out the water on an equal basis. But, as Master Scatulo was not slow to point out with his sharp Jikaidast's wit, the caravan water was paid for and for the use of all. What he, Master Scatulo, happened to have in his coach was by way of an extra and, by the Paktun's Swod's Gambit! was none of anyone else's damn business.

These sentiments were shared by the lady Yasuri and the other upper crusties of the caravan.

Poor old Deb-Lu-Quienyin, for all he was an apparently dried up old stick, seemed to be in need of water, and I had fallen into the habit of sharing my ration with him. I am often wholeheartedly glad that I can scratch along with little to drink, although preferring unending cups of tea, and when it comes to push of pike and there is a serious shortage of drink—I can manage, somehow.

We had passed the stage where he would say how kind I was, and that people who assisted a Wizard of Loh usually wanted something in return, and now we would sip the water companionably and talk while our mouths were moist.

"Do you notice that our famous Master Scatulo usually talks in terms of Jikaida?"

"I had noticed."

"An affectation. He plays all day. He plays against his slave, Bevon the Brukaj, and always he wins."

"Well, he is a Jikaidast. They are professionals. They have to win to eat."

"True. But watch Bevon. He is a skilled player. I believe he makes stupid moves deliberately so as to lose."

"Scatulo would see that at once!" I protested.

"Maybe. Maybe he is too puffed up with pride."

It was not exactly true to say Scatulo played all day. The board would come out the moment we halted and the Deldars would be Ranked; during traveling periods he read from the many books of Jikaida lore he carried with him in his coach.

I had fallen into friendly conversation with Bevon the Brukaj and had learned some of his history. His gentleness seemed to me to sit strangely with his evident craggy toughness. He carried no sword, although he confided to me that he could use a blade, and as a slave was equipped with a stout stave to defend his master. I knew Scatulo had a sword in his coach that Bevon might use if pressed. The Jikaidast's orders to Bevon resounded with the ugly word "Grak!" It was grak this and grak that all day. Grak means jump, move, obey or your skin will be flayed off your back or you must work until you drop dead. It is, indeed, an ugly word.

I said to Bevon one day: "Are you a Jikaidast, Bevon?"

"No, Jak." He fetched up a sigh. "I might have been back home but for my tragedy." He looked mournful as he spoke. Well, his story was soon told, and ugly in the telling thereof. He had been accused of a cowp, and, as you know, a cowp is a particularly beastly and horrible kind of murder, in which sadism and mutilation form part. The people had cried out against him and he had been locked away and would have been slain in lawful retribution. "Had I been guilty, Jak, I think I would have stayed and let them kill me. But I was innocent, so I escaped."

"I can't see how anyone could think you would commit murder, Bevon."

"The man who died had made advances to a girl with whom I was friendly. I do not know, but I think she slew him. But I was blamed. So I ran away to be a soldier and was taken up as a slave. I do not really mind, for my heart is not in life—"

"By Havil!" I said, incensed. "Now that is just not good enough. So you are slave. Why not escape when we reach Jikaida City—?"

"You know little of that place, I fear."

"I know nothing."

"They play Kazz-Jikaida there." Kazz is Kregish for blood.

That did explain a great deal. It also explained a little of Prince Mefto's vaunted nickname, for he was traveling to Jikaida City to play in the games, and his sobriquet was Mefto the Kazzur.

That splendid prince was pirouetting his swarth about a little to the side of the space where the caravan had halted. I looked at him, and grew tired of his antics, and resumed our conversation. Whenever Bevon found the time away from his master's Jikaida board we would talk, and he joined Deb-Lu-Quienyin and me at night around our fire. The Wizard of Loh regarded the Brukaj not as he did his own slave but rather as a potential Jikaidast who had temporarily fallen on evil times.

Often Pompino would join us, and, to tell the truth, we played Jikaida as well as Jikalla and the Game of Moons. This latter is near mindless; but it amuses many folk whose brains for whatever reason are not able to grapple with Jikaida or any of the other superior games.

So, as we neared the water hole and the drikingers had not put in an appearance and we were hot and thirsty and fatigued, I fancied that we might find the damned bandits waiting for us at the water, mocking us, taunting us to try to reach the water hole against their opposition. Ineldar shared the thought, too, for he hoarded our water meanly. The caravan guards stood watch like hawks.

During a halt when the suns burned down we drank little if at all, for the sweat would waste the precious fluid. That last night before the water hole, with the stars fat in the sky and the cooking fires burning with eye-aching brilliance, we took our water rations thankfully. What happened happened in a kind of copybook way, as though this were the moment I had been waiting for many seasons to arrive. When it did, I found I could not identify my emotions with any accuracy.

It turned out this way... At our fire the lady Yasuri and Master Scatulo finished their meals and retired to their coaches. Bevon, Pompino, Quienyin and myself lingered for a space, for we had hoarded a little water and were about to share it out between ourselves. It was legal water; that is, it was ours issued to us by Ineldar the Kaktu. Sishi slipped past her mistress's coach to join us, giggling, for she had a little sazz with which to sweeten the water. She had probably stolen it from Yasuri, a procedure I regarded with both disfavor and applause. In return for the sazz, which would freshen the water and make of it a pleasant drink, Sishi was to receive her share. We would split the sazz five ways.

Ionno the Ladle might come in for a few mouthfuls, also. To get the sequence right is not easy. In the starlight with the Twins just vaulting over the horizon and the flare of the fire we crouched around like conspirators. The rattle of a window shutter announced Master Scatulo's peevish voice.

"Grak, Bevon! Grak, you idle, shiftless rast! Bring some water—Pallan's Hikdar's Swod to Pallan's Hikdar's sixth! Bratch! You useless cloddish lumop, Grak!"

With a sigh, Bevon stood up, a massive bent shape against the starlight. Quienyin murmured that he was not enamored of Scatulo's notation. The fire struck sparks from a glinting figure that appeared, striding along between the caravan and the fires. I saw this was Prince Mefto. Bevon took up his goblet and started for Scatulo's carriage. Prince Mefto, leading his swarth, approached.

There was nothing any of us could say to halt Bevon and to persuade him that the water ration was his. His master had demanded it and Bevon was slave.

A fellow who had been slave a long time and grown cunning in slavish ways would have gulped the sazz down instantly and then whined that there was no water—and if he got a beating for it would regard that as quits doubled, once for drinking the water himself and second for depriving his master of it. But Bevon was gentle and unschooled in the devious ways of the world. And, too, there is every chance that he really felt his master required the sazz—oh, yes, absolutely. Something like that must surely have been in his mind in view of what occurred.

Mefto was swigging from a bottle. He resealed this and moving to the side of his swarth thrust the bottle away. He patted the swarth's greenish-purple scaled head. He saw Bevon.

"Hai, slave! Kraitch-ambur,* my swarth, is thirsty. Give me that water."

Bevon halted.

---

* Kraitch-ambur: Thunder

254

Better he should have run into the darkness.

Prince Mefto frowned. We could see his resplendent figure reflecting our firelight. His lower right hand fell to one of his sword hilts.

"Slave, the water! Grak!"

"Master," stammered Bevon. "It is for my master—"

"To a Herrelldrin Hell with your master! I shall not tell you again, slave. The water!"

Bevon just stood, his dogged face perplexed, his massive shoulders hunched, it seemed, protectively over the goblet. Scatulo yelled again and Bevon jumped and Mefto reached forward to snatch the water and the goblet fell and the sazz-flavored water spread into the dirt.

"You onker! You stupid yetch!"

Prince Mefto was incensed. He whipped out the sword he gripped and with another hand patted his swarth affectionately. "My poor Kraitch-ambur! There is no water for you. But the slave will be punished!"

With that Mefto the Kazzur began hitting Bevon with the flat of his sword.

Desperately attempting to protect himself with upraised arms, the Brukaj was knocked over onto the ground. The Kildoi went on hitting him sadistically with the flat.

I stood up.

Pompino rose at my side and put a hand on my arm.

"No, Jak. He will take it amiss if you interfere."

"Had I my powers," sighed Quienyin, and took a sip of his drink.

Sishi was gasping and her hands were pressed fiercely to her breast, her face shining in the firelight.

Now Bevon was beginning to yell, the first cries of pain that had passed his lips. The sword rose and fell with wet soggy sounds. Bevon rolled this way and that, a huddled quivering mass, defenseless.

"No, Jak!" Pompino pulled me.

I shook him off and walked across to this gallant Prince Mefto the Kazzur.

"Jak! He will slaughter you!"

The prince paused in the beating to look across Bevon's prostrate and groaning form. His golden eyebrows drew down menacingly. His upper right hand dropped to the second sword hilt.

"Well, rast?"

I said, "Prince. You chastise this man unjustly—"

I got no further. Soft words were not the currency of Mefto the Kazzur. He simply said, "Yetch, you presume to your death!"

He leaped Bevon and charged full at me, two swords whistling. Both were thraxters.

I drew my thraxter and parried the first blows. I gave ground, circling, already realizing I was in for a fight. To be forced to kill this fellow would lead to most unpleasant consequences, for he was a prince and I a hired paktun.

It seemed to me in the first few moments of the fight that I dare not slay him and must therefore seek to stretch him out senseless. He would have to be tackled as I tackle a Djang, with the added complication of his tail-hand. He was rather like a Djang with his four arms and a Kataki with his tail rolled into one. I have fought Djangs and Katakis, and one Djang can dispose of—well, of a lot of Katakis.

This unpleasant cramph was a Kildoi.

Nine inches of daggered steel whipped up in his tail-hand and twinkled between his legs at me.

With a skip and jump I got out of the way. I did not slash the tail off. As we fought I fancied I had not sliced his tail off because that was the beginning of more trouble, that he had to be knocked out. As we fought I realized that he had not let me slice his tail off.

He was a marvel.

We fought. The blades flashed and rang with that sliding screech. Oh, yes, he had three blades against my one; but that was not it, not it at all. I knew and he knew, after a space.

He drew back. He was smiling. He looked pleased.

"Whoever you are, paktun, I have never met a better swordsman. But I think you must number your days now."

The best swordsman in the world, Sishi had called him.

I didn't know if he was that. But I did know that I had, at last, met my match.

Twelve

The Fight Beside the Caravan

Every swordsman must be aware that one day he may meet his match and so enter his last fight.

One reads so often of our intrepid hero who is so vastly superior as a swordsman, fighting other wights, and toying with them, cutting them up, with the outcome never in doubt. As you know I had always entered each fight with the knowledge that this could be the time I met my master. Oh, yes, I have cut up opponents, as I have related. One reads of the way in which the hero goes about his task. But now, here under the fatly glowing stars of Kregen, with the Moons rising and the crimson firelight playing upon the halted caravan, I was in nowise being gently admonished and taught a lesson, rather I was being sadistically tortured before the end.

With a convulsive snatch I managed to get my dagger out and into play. That made two blades against three. But this Kildoi was a master bladesman. The swords wove their deceptive patterns of steel. He knew every trick I essayed. He showed me three or four I'd never come across and only by desperate efforts I managed to escape, and even then I believe he let me, for the fun of it. Once a swordsman sees a trick he knows it—as I have said—otherwise he is dead.

I learned.

But I knew that he knew more than I did. And, all the time, his two left arms poised prettily and the hands hung gracefully. If he wished, he could bring two more blades into the fight.

Well, to take some ludicrous credit, after a space he hauled out a short sword with his upper left hand, and pressed me. I knew now I was fighting for my life and any thought of merely hitting him over the head was long flown. I rallied and fought back, and the swords clashed and clanged, and then, and I saw the fact as proof of something and as a final death warrant, his lower left fist pulled out a long dagger. So now he had five weapons against my two, and some of the smile was gone from his handsome face with the golden beard blowing.

Could Korero, I wondered, fight like this?

I'd have to see when I got back to Vallia.

And then... The truth was I wasn't going to get back to Vallia... Not after Prince Mefto the Kazzur had finished with me.

As some fighting men do, he talked as he battled.

"You are good, paktun, very good. I would love to talk to you about your victories, your instructors. But I am a prince and I do not tolerate your kind of conduct."

He cut me about the left shoulder and I swirled away and then used a risky attack to land a hit on his left shoulder. I saw the blood there, a smear in the light. We both wore light tunics, having doffed our armor. His face went mean.

"You think, you rast, you can better me? Me, Mefto the Kazzur, who fought his way to a princedom over the bodies of his foes? Fool!"

Well, yes, I was a fool, right enough.

I hit him again, a glancing blow across his face and severed a chunk of his beard.

Those two hits were the only ones I scored.

He pinked me again and I slid two of his blades and a third and fourth chunked a gouge out of my right side.

He was beginning to enjoy himself.

He didn't like the cut on his face. I hoped it left an ugly scar, the rast.

Swordsmen have their little foibles. He had me in his toils, right enough. But as we fought and I tried the old trick of dismembering him piecemeal, being unable to finish him with a body thrust, I began to pick up hints as to his favored techniques. The trouble was, it was not just that he had five blades, or that his technique was well-nigh perfect, but that he was just supremely good. He was not quite as fast as me; had he been I'd have been stretched lifeless by now.

So I began to work out a last desperate gamble that would break all the rules and would make or break. Truth to tell, I had little real hope. The moment I began the passage I fancied he would detect instantly the attack and know the correct counter. But desperate situations demand desperate remedies. I was bleeding profusely now; but all the cuts were shallow and I knew he but toyed with me.

He was chattering away as we fought.

"I joy in this contest, paktun! By the Blade of Kurin! You are indeed a master bladesman."

Maybe—but I was like to be a dead bladesman, master or not...

With a sudden and ferocious passade he began an attack aimed at slicing off my left ear—I think. I defended desperately, and gave ground, and faintly I heard screams and guessed Sishi and Pompino were riveted by this spectacle.

Time for the last great gamble... I positioned myself and a long arrow abruptly sprouted from Mefto's right shoulder, between those cunningly swiveled double joints.

He screamed.

He fell back, screeching, and he dropped all his weapons.

Another arrow hissed past my head and went thwunk into the painted wood of Scatulo's carriage. Without a thought I dropped flat and dived under the coach.

Well—yes.

The drikingers had played us and now they drove in to finish us completely and steal all we had.

Logic indicated they had chosen their time well. We were at rest, we were short of water, we were tired and apprehensive, and we ought all to have been asleep but for the sentries, and they, poor devils, would no doubt be sprawled with slit throats. The fight had given the bandits pause and some intemperate hothead had loosed at us and so the alarm was raised.

The drikingers were blessed by me, then, I can tell you.

And, to be honest and all the same—that second arrow would have pinned me but for the instinctive move I'd made when the first one shafted Mefto. Speed—that was all I had as advantage over Mefto, and it was speed of reaction that in the end had saved me.

The caravan roused and the paktuns turned out and Bevon took up his sword from Master Scatulo's carriage and we fought.

The fight was savage and unpleasant with much carving up of leathery hides and stripping of bright feathers; but at last we drove the drikingers off and collapsed, exhausted.

These skirling events were just those I had been missing as emperor in Vallia... How far removed this brisk little encounter was from the ordered and planned evolutions of the Phalanx!

But, death attended both in equal measure.

In the morning we buried our dead or cremated those whose religious convictions demanded that ingress to the Ice Floes of Sicce. Various gods were apostrophized for good fortune for the ibs of the departed. As for the drikingers, we found only three of them, twisted in death by the wagon wheels, and these, too, we buried. They had been lean hardy men, apims, with leathery skins and ferocious bunches of hair dyed purple, and with scraps of armor looted from previous caravans. Of the other bandit dead, they had been all carried off by their comrades.

So, groaning and protesting, the caravan moved off and safely reached the water hole and from then on the journey across the Desolate Waste proceeded as such a journey should—filled with alarums and excursions but with a happy arrival at the end.

The country opened out and grew fat and rich once we crossed the River of Purple Rushes. There was a ford and a strong fort and parties of warriors of Aidrin to escort us in. They greeted us in jocular mood, making light of our problems, telling us of the troubles that previous unfortunate caravans had endured. There were caravans that set out from Songaslad, the town of thieves, that never reached the River of Purple Rushes. White and yellow bones scattered over the Desolate Waste marked their endings.

From the fort by the ford, Prince Mefto was carried swiftly ahead of us, with his men, to Jikaida City. He left the caravan. He had not spoken to me and was reputed badly injured—and at the time I suspected that an arrow in the cunning double-joint had done more harm than it would do to a fellow with only two arms to fight with. I had kept a strict watch for revenge; but nothing transpired. What honor code he followed, if any, I did not know. But I had the strongest—and nastiest—suspicion that I had not heard the last of Prince Mefto the Kazzur.

If I do not dwell overmuch on my reactions to that fight I think you will respect that. I had had a shock, all right; and, too, I had grown in under-standing. In future, fights would not be quite the same again; but I fancied I knew enough of Dray Prescot to guess what he would do. One is as one is, and like the Scorpion, must hew to nature's path.

The Wizard of Loh, Deb-Lu Quienyin, was overjoyed to have reached his destination safely.

"I shall seek out San Orien at once. He, I feel sure, I hope, will be able to cure me—to retrieve my powers."

Saying remberee to him I brought up the subject I had been harboring for long. "I am confident he will do everything he can to aid you, San. Tell me, do you know of a Wizard of Loh called Phu-Si-Yantong?"

"Dear San Yantong! I have not heard of him for ages."

Well, now...

How Wizards of Loh kept in touch was a subject not for ordinary men. But old Deb-Lu-Quienyin burbled on happily about Yantong, the biggest villain unhanged, and I wondered if there could be two Wizards of Loh with the same name. But now, Quienyin would have none of that. He had not heard of Yantong for many seasons, and when last he had been in contact Yantong had been building up a useful practice in Loh. "Of course, I always felt he was marked for great things. There was an aura about him, despite his difficulty. I do hope he prospers."

There was no point in arguing about that; but I did pick up one or two useful hints from Quienyin. He was reticent about this "difficulty" of Yantong's, and would not be drawn, and I wondered if Phu-Si-Yantong was indeed the cripple he had pretended to be and that was his difficulty.

We watched Master Scatulo's coach trundling off to the superior inn where the Jikaidast would stay until, as Bevon put it: "He has established his credentials."

LionardDen, Jikaida City, was given over to one thing in life. Jikaida. The game consumed the people. Of course, they lived by it and it paid them handsome dividends. Their country of Aidrin was rich in worldly goods, the fields and mines and rivers yielded a bountiful harvest. People flocked from all over to play Kazz-Jikaida. There were enormous fortunes to be made. There were reputations to be made.

Standing saying remberee to the Wizard of Loh, Pompino said to me, "I do not fancy staying here overmuch. But it seems we may have to."

Quienyin nodded. "When a caravan returns across the Desolate Waste, I think. It is suicide to attempt the crossing alone or in small numbers. And all west of here across the lakes is dreadful, so I am told by those who know—leem hunters and the like."

I said: "D'you fancy the life of a leem-hunter, Pompino?"

Quienyin laughed and my fellow kregoinye made a face. "By Horato the Potent, Jak. No!"

"You could take employment in the games."

"How so, San?"

"Why, stout fighting men are always wanted. I, myself, do not care for Kazz-Jikaida. But it has its attractions."

"We will, I think, find out a little more first," Pompino told me, whereat, feeling my wounds still a little sore, I nodded agreement.

Jikaida City certainly was beautiful, with airy kyros and broad avenues and with houses that were graceful and colonnaded against the heat and thick-walled against the cold. The climate, by reason of the lakes, was not too extreme this deeply in the center of the continent. Everywhere the checkerboard was used as decoration. One could grow tired of the continual repetition. Even the soldiers' cloaks were checkered black and white.

Quienyin shook his head. "If you go as a warrior you will be expected, as part of your duties, to act in the games. That is understood."

"I have no wish to be a soldier," said Pompino. Truth to tell, we two kregoinye were stranded here.

And there was not a single sight of a golden and scarlet raptor circling arrogantly above us, mocking us with his squawk.

The lady Yasuri paid us off, and she had the grace to thank us for our services. But paid off we were, and so were at a loose end. I said to Pompino: "I am for going back across the Desolate Waste. I have urgent business that will not wait."

"No business," he said sententiously, "is more important than that of the Everoinye."

One could not argue with that sentiment. But I was serious.

"If we can buy or steal a couple of fluttrells—"

"They are more precious than gold. And how many have you seen since we arrived?"

"None." There were volroks and other flying men abroad on the streets of the city; but we saw no aerial cavalry. That there must be some seemed to me probable. I'd have a saddle-bird, I promised myself; but in the interim until I gained one we had to find something to do. So, as we had known, the games drew us.

"Anyway," I said as we hitched up our belts and went off to find a suitable tavern, "Ineldar the Kaktu will be taking a caravan back across the Desolate Wastes. We have only to sign on with him as caravan guards."

Thirteen

In Jikaida City

Before we patronized a tavern there was a duty Pompino and I must do vital to any good Kregan. We retained the shirts and trousers given to us by the lady Yasuri; but all else had been returned. We could feel the golden deldys wrapped in scraps of rag and tucked into our belts. Our first port of call was the armorers.

The fashion of rapier and main gauche imported from Vallia and Zenicce into Hamal had not yet reached this far south into Havilfar. We chose good serviceable thraxters, and swished the cut and thrust swords about in the dim shop with its racks of weapons and armor. The proprietor was a Fristle. He stroked his whiskers as we pawed over his goods.

"Nothing better in Jikaida City, doms. Friendly Fodo—that's me—can set you up with an arsenal for the finest caravan across the Desolate Waste."

"Just a sword and dagger," I said, pleasantly. "And a brigandine, I think?" with an inquiring look at Pompino.

"I have this beautiful kax," said Friendly Fodo, giving the breast and back a vigorous polish. It was iron, with scrollwork around the edges. We did not even bother to inquire the price as we refused. We had to make our pay spin out until we found fresh employment.

The reason I had chosen a brigandine, in which the metal plates are riveted through the material, instead of an English jack, where the plates are stitched and threaded, was simply that even a cursory inspection of the workmanship of the jack Friendly Fodo displayed showed it was Krasny work, inferior. Pompino chose a brigandine and then he touched the forte of his thraxter. Neatly incised in the metal was that familiar magical pattern of figure nines interlocked.

"You're in luck, dom," said Friendly Fodo. "A high-class weapon. Came from a Chulik who died of a fever."

Examination of the thraxter I eventually chose for its feel and balance revealed a tiny punched mark in the form of the Brudstern, that open-flower shaped form whose magic is whispered rather than spoken. I nodded, amused, and paid over the gold required.

Pompino bought solid boots and, after a moment's hesitation, I bought softer, lower-cut bootees. Walking barefoot is no hardship for me, an old sailorman, within reason.

Then, after a few other necessary purchases in the Arcade of Freshness, we placed our new belongings into a small satchel and rolled off to the tavern to begin the next important duty laid on a good Kregan.

Truly, Beng Dikkane, the patron saint of all the ale drinkers of Paz, smiled on Jikaida City.

We had a whole new city and its inhabitants to explore, a happy situation, and after the rigors of the journey Pompino certainly, and I, I confess a little wryly, without too many reservations, set about easing the dust from our throats and seeing what there was to be seen and generally winding down. The wounds I had taken, although superficial, itched nonetheless, and the soreness persisted. Pompino did remark with a twitch of his foxy face that, perhaps, that rast Mefto the Kazzur used poisoned blades. But that is unusual on Kregen.

Very soberly I said, "He has no need of that kind of trick. He is the best swordsman I have ever met." I drank a long swigging draught, for by this time we were on our second and the alehouse was filling up with mid-morning customers. "But he is a rast, more's the pity. All his prowess and skill has not taught him humility."

"He's a yetch who ought to be—"

"Quite. He is the best swordsman. But he is not the greatest."

"Yet, Jak, if I had his skill with the sword would I feel humble?" Pompino pondered that. "I do not think so."

"If you had been picked by the gods to be favored with a great gift, as Mefto surely has, would you feel arrogance over that? Or would you feel awe—and a little fear?"

Pompino stared at me over the pewter rim of his goblet.

"Jak—we are kregoinye. We have been marked!"

"By Havil!" I said, and I sat back, astounded.

After a space in which sylvie glided over to refill our goblets and Pompino spilled out a couple of copper coins, I said, "All the same. It is not the same—if you see what I mean. Mefto's gift and our tasks cannot stand comparison."

Pompino was staring after the sylvie and licking his lips.

"I'm surprised a place like this can afford to hire a sylvie—slave or not. They tend to—to distract a fellow."

That was true.

"We should, I think," I said, "find Ineldar the Kaktu and make sure he will hire us for the return journey. We must know when he is starting." I looked around and lowered my voice. "I begin to think we will not find a fluttrell or mirvol to steal in this city."

"Agreed. But another stoup first, Jak."

By the time we left to explore the city, Pompino was very merry. We quickly discovered that Jikaida City was not one but two. Twinned cities under the twin suns flourish all over Kregen, of course. The extensive shallow depression between low and rolling hills cupped the twin cities in a figure-eight shape. Between them rose edifices of enormous extent whose function was to house the games. We strolled along in the sunshine, admiring the sights, and Pompino kept breaking into little snatches of song, half to himself, half to any passersby who took his fancy. Despite myself, I did not pretend I was not with him. After all, he had proved a comrade.

Many of the more important avenues radiated away from the central mass of the Jikaidaderen and the buildings reflected the architectural tastes of many nations and races. In one avenue we saw a low-walled structure over the gate of which hung a banner, flapping gently in the light breeze, which read: NATH EN SCREETZIM.

Underneath, in letters only slightly less loud, was the Kregish for: "Patronized by the leading Jikaidasts."

Pompino ogled the sign owlishly. "Are you a leading Jikaidast, Jak? I can rank my Deldars and—and reach the first drin. But after that—" He paused to bow deeply to a couple of passing matrons, who eyed him as though the flat stones of Havilfar had yawned and yielded up their denizens. "After that, dom, why—it all gets confusing."

"Stick to Jikalla."

"No, no. The Game of Moons for me. Then the dice decide."

For some perverse reason I defended the Game of Moons. "And skill, also, Pompino. You can't deny that."

He staggered three paces to larboard, smiled, and lurched four paces to starboard.

"Deny it? I love it!"

"Come on. They'll have you inside with a sword in your fist before you can call on Horato the Potent."

He nodded his head with great solemnity, his face glazed, his mouth slowly opening and then closing with a snap, only once more to drop open. I took his arm and steered him along the avenue away from Nath the Swordsman's premises.

Nath's place was not the only establishment we saw where the arts and skills and disciplines of fighting were taught. After my contretemps with Mefto I wondered—and not altogether in the abstract—whether or not I might benefit from a fresh course of instruction. One fact seemed clear to me from what I had pieced together of Mefto's career. As a Kildoi he was by nature possessed of formidable advantages in the fighting business. He had left his native Balintol seasons ago and had ruffled and swaggered his way through the Dawn Lands as a mercenary, rapidly rising through pak-tun to be hyr-paktun and privileged to wear the golden pakzhan at his throat. Then, with all the raffish and bloody accompaniments to revolution, he had taken command of a band of near-masichieri and with their help overthrown the old prince of Shanodrin and taken over the country, the titles, the wealth and the power. His legal acceptance had soon followed. By all the laws of Kregen, he was now Prince of Shanodrin. The revolution by itself would not have been enough—in law—to give him the right. The bokkertu had to be made. Then Mefto the Kazzur became Prince Mefto and could take the name of A'Shanofero as his own.

From what little I knew of the man I wondered why he had chosen a principality and not a kingdom. But, probably, he had his avaricious gaze already fixed on his next victim.

Looked at completely dispassionately, Mefto the Kazzur had merely done what I, myself, had done.

All the same, the idea of Mefto lording it as Emperor of Vallia sent a little shudder up my backbone.

"You ill, Jak?"

"Not as much as you, you old soak, Pompino."

"Don't get away from the wife enough, that's my trouble."

"Then may Havil the Green smile on us, and the Everoinye set another task to our hands."

"Amen to that, by the pot belly of Beng Dikkane!"

The twin Suns of Scorpio, the red and the green, are not called Zim and Genodras in Havilfar, but Far and Havil. Usually on Kregen, Jikaida boards are checkered in blue and yellow or white and black. There are places where the red and green are used; Jikaida City was not, as far as I knew, one of them.

As we neared the imposing pile of the Jikaidaderen the walls assumed something of their true stature, and we saw the palace was large, perfectly capable of accommodating many laid-out Kazz-Jikaida boards. The place was a maze of inner buildings, a vast complex not, I suppose, unlike the Jikhorkduns surrounding the amphitheatres and the arenas of Hamal and Hyrklana and other places. We strolled along, and Pompino was singing a charming if foolish ditty about a Pandaheem who kissed the baker's wife and went floury white to see the sweep's wife, whereat he became sooty black. The song is called "Black is White and White is Black" and I will not repeat it.

The city within Jikaida City in which we thus swaggered along was bedecked with yellow. The other city claimed the blue. They had names, long rigmaroles of high boasting; but folk usually called them just Yellow City or Blue City. I had to stop myself from joining in some of Pompino's songs. And, I wondered how long it would be before the Watch employed by the Nine Guardians would heave up to arrest us.

Each city was run by its own Masked Nine, and they had no kings or queens here. They did have a nobility, and from this aristocracy were drawn the Guardians of the Masked Nine. The system employed was a democratic one that extended only to these nobles and their families; but within that limitation they voted for office and did not fight for it. Jikaida drew the fires of the blood, so it was said.

As a secret ballot was used, the successful candidates remained anonymous, masked, inducted into office by their peers. This system had, so far, proved effective in preventing unrest from developing into revolution. The army and the Watch obeyed the orders of the Masked Nine Guardians and enforced their edicts. We had heard of punishments for disobedience that would give nightmares to a seasoned paktun. All was balance, force countering force, and, over all, the games of Jikaida dominated the twin cities of Jikaida City.

The truth would not be served in saying the inhabitants of Blue City and Yellow City hated one another. They were rivals, at times deadly rivals; but all their hostility was played out on the Jikaida boards. Yellow against Blue. Blue against Yellow. Their loyalties to their color city and their partisanship were alike intense. They were dedicated. The forces aloof from this rivalry, the religious orders, the army—and very few others, by Krun!—were still infected by the Jikaida fever and wore black and white checkerboarded insignia. Havil the Green was a noted deity here, with his temples and priests; but there were others, plenty of them in apparently equal prominence. On the surface there appeared no sign of Lem the Silver Leem, for which I was thankful, although I kept my eyes open on that score.

Managing to drag Pompino off without further problems and keeping the Watch well in the offing, I found a suitable hostelry in the middle-sections of Yellow City called The Pallan's Swod. Here, after due payment, I was able to deposit Pompino in a bed and close the door on his snores.

Useless to detail my doings after that; they boiled down to confirmation of the absence of flyers, the vowed testimony from seasoned leem-hunters that only death by suicide awaited across the lakes, and that Ineldar the Kaktu would be returning when a caravan had been assembled and when that would be, by Havil, he had no idea. In the meantime he was going to drink up and visit the public games and have himself a good time and that was what Pompino and I should do. He'd be pleased to hire us as caravan guards when the time was ripe.

Then he lowered his flagon and laid a long brown finger against his nose. The uproar in the tavern around us masked our words from all but ourselves. He winked.

"That run in you had with Mefto the Kazzur. You are lucky to be alive. He is a marvel with his swords."

"Aye."

"You bear him no rancor?"

"Not for beating me. But, as to himself, as a man—"

"Agreed. Listen. Go to see Konec na Brugheim. He puts up at the Blue Rokveil. Speak of the king korf. Do not mention my name." He drew his finger down his nose and reached for his flagon. He looked at me, once, a shrewd hard glance, and then away. "I have spoken."

"Thank you," I said, not completely sure of what I should thank him for, but detecting his intention to help. He drank noisily and then bellowed for more wine, for the suns were declining. I joined him in a flagon of Yellow Unction, and then hied myself back to The Pallan's Swod to find Pompino not holding his head and groaning, but cursingly trying to pull his boots back on and thirsting for more singing and amphorae of wine.

I draw the veil on that night's doings. But Pompino rolled back to the tavern with his head flung back and his mouth wide open, yodeling to the Moons of Kregen.

In the morning I took myself off to find this Konec na Brugheim at the sign of the Blue Rokveil, and to discover what secrets would be unlocked at the mention of the king korf.

Fourteen

Of the Fate of Spies

As the Zairians of the Eye of the World say: "Only Zair knows the cleanliness of a human heart." I had said I held no rancor against Mefto, and I believed that. But, humanly fallible as I am, perhaps a lingering resentment impelled me to watch my back with a sharper scrutiny even than usual as I walked gently along in the early morning opaline radiance of the Suns of Scorpio. That vigilance which may have been caused by bitterness and suppressed longings for revenge served me well on that morning I walked in Jikaida City to talk about the king korf to a man I did not know.

They picked me up a couple of streets from the hostelry and they paced me, fifty paces or so to my rear. They kept to the shadowed side of the street. There were four of them and they wore swords and were dressed in inconspicuous gray and blue, as was I, save that their favors were of a hard bright yellow. There were two apims, a Rapa and a Brokelsh. I walked on, placidly, and pondered the indisputable fact that no man or woman born of Opaz knows all the secrets of Imrien.

The decision I reached seemed to me common sense. With a succession of alterations in course and speed, and with a swift vanishing into the mouth of a side alley where a stall loaded with appetizing roasted chingleberries smoked in the early light, I lost them. I kept up a good pace, but not too obtrusive a bustle in the morning activity, and so circled the Jikaidaderen and came into Blue City. Would those rasts with their yellow favors follow here?

Finding the Blue Rokveil was simplicity itself; the first person I asked looked as though I was a loon and jerked his thumb, marked with ink, for he was a stylor, to a broad avenue lined by impressive buildings. The place was there, clearly signposted, and looked to be an establishment more properly called a hotel than a hostelry. Only persons of standing and wealth would gain admittance as guests. I walked calmly to a side gate where Fristle slaves were trundling amphorae and shrilling orders at one another, and went in. The yard led by way of odoriferous stables to a long gray wall, mellow in the light, clothed with moon blooms, their outer petals extended and the inner tightly folded. From over the wall came a familiar sound—the ring and chingle of steel on steel and the quick panting for breath, the scrape and stamp of feet seeking secure purchases. A wicket gate showed me men at sword practice. I half-turned, prepared to move on.

Hung on a wooden post just within the gate, and already burnished to a shining brilliance, a silvered iron breastplate was being lovingly polished up by a little Och slave. He had three of his upper limbs busily polishing away and with the fourth he was surreptitiously stuffing a piece of bread into his mouth between those puffy jaws. And good luck to you, my old dom, I was saying to myself as, being an old fighting man, my eye was caught by the sudden and splendid attack one of the energetic and sweating combatants within the courtyard essayed against his opponent in this early morning practice session.

The opponent, a strongly built Fristle, gave ground. The assailant, an apim with strands of extraordinarily long yellow hair swirling, leaped in, roaring his pleasure, his good nature blazingly evident on his round, cheerful, pugnacious face. The men at practice in there all wore breechclouts and sandals. The apim whirled his sword in a silvered pattern of deceptive cunning and the Fristle, ducking and retreating, must have felt that steel net whistling about his whiskers perilously close.

"Ha, Fropo! I have you now!"

"Hold off! Hold off! I'll slice your hair!"

"You dare!"

And with the speed of a striking chavonth the big apim, his yellow hair coruscating about his head in the light, leaped and struck—and the sword hovered an inch from the Fristle's throat.

"D'you bare the throat?"

"Aye, may Numi-Hyrjiv the Golden Splendor pardon me, Dav. I bare the throat."

With a great bellow of good-natured laughter the apim whipped his sword away and clapped a meaty hand around the Fristle's golden-furred shoulders. "You let me best you, Fropo, by thinking of my hair. It never gets in my eyes—ever."

Now they were at rest the two looked an oddly assorted couple, the Fristle and the apim. The apim, this Dav, was a splendidly built man, bulging with muscle; but I fancied his beginnings of an ale-gut might slow him down in a season or so if he did not temper his homage to Beng Dikkane.

So looking at these two as they snatched up towels to wipe the sweat away I saw reflections in the brilliant polish of the breastplate. The Och had dropped his piece of bread and bent to retrieve it. In the polished kax I saw four distorted figures. One was Rapa, one Brokelsh, and two were apims.

The Rapa lifted his hand and light splintered.

Even as I turned sharply away prepared to duck in the right direction, the big apim called Dav poised his sword and threw. It hissed through the air. It buried its point in the Rapa's breast, smashing through his leather jerkin, crunching into his bones, spouting blood.

In the next instant I had drawn and was running upon the Brokelsh and his apim comrades. With a clang the blades crossed. I was aware of the Fristle, Fropo, and the apim, Dav, running up. Somewhere, someone had shouted: "'Ware your back, dom!"

268

The Rapa was done for, the dagger spilled into the dust. His viciously beaked face lay against the earth. But as my sword felt the savage blows of these would-be stikitches, I felt a new and wholly unexpected sensation— an unwelcome and treacherously deadly emotion.

I recalled that last fight with Mefto, and the way he had bested me. My blade faltered. The apims had sized me up and were pressing hard and somehow and, I think of its own volition, my thraxter leaped to parry their blows. But I saw again those five lethal blades of Mefto flashing before my eyes.

My throat was dry. I leaped and slashed the blade about and caught the Brokelsh in the side. The Brokelsh are a squat-bodied race of diffs, and he staggered and recovered and came for me again. Then Fropo's sword switched in and took the Brokelsh in play, Dav took one of the apims, and I was left to face the last. Whatever my emotions had been, however the feelings had scorched through my brain, I felt the old secrets flowing along my arm and through my wrist and into my hand. I turned the sword over and beat and twitched and so lunged, and stepped back.

Fropo and Dav were standing looking at me. The Brokelsh and the other apim were coughing their guts out.

"You were a mite slow, dom," said Dav, in his affable way. "You need to sharpen up."

"Yes," I said. I took a breath. "My thanks—"

"Against them? The apim I took I know. Naghan the Sly, he was called. Look." Dav bent and ripped away the big blue favor. Under it the hard yellow showed. "They tried to cowp you from the back, the yetches. Well, they'll never report back to Mefto the Kazzur, may he rot in Cottmer's Caverns."

I said, "My thanks again. But I do not think they could have known you—who know them—would be here. They would not have been so bold."

"Right, dom. They would not. And..." Here his big smile burst out. He wore a little tufty beard bisecting his chin, and he was burly, no doubt of that, genial. "And no Lahal between us. I am Dav Olmes. Lahal. This is Fropo the Curved."

"I am Jak. Lahal, Dav Olmes. Lahal, Fropo the Curved."

"And now I need three stoups of best ale, one after t'other," quoth Dav. "Instanter, by the Blade of Kurin."

So I knew he was a swordsman, and we went into the courtyard and found the ale and washed the dust away down our throats. And, for me, Dray Prescot known as Jak, the dust went down bitter with unease.

No need to ask where the sword with which Dav had made such pretty play had come from. The little Och was wailing away and scrabbling around picking up the scattered items of the harness that Dav had ripped to pieces from its hangings on the post. The beautifully polished kax had fallen with a crash. The gilt helmet with the brave blue feathers still rolled about, like a balancing act. Now Dav threw the sword at the Och, who caught it with the unthinking skill of the man who spends his life with weapons, free or slave.

"Thank you, notor, thank you," chattered the Och.

"That," said Fropo, "was the kov's own blade."

"Aye. And very fine, too. Now where is this ale?"

"The Och called you notor," I said. Notor is the usual Hamalian way of saying lord. We say jen in Vallia.

Before Dav had recovered from his gutsy laugh at my words, Fropo, with sudden seriousness, said: "Aye. This is Dav Olmes, the Vad of Bilsley."

A vad is a high rank of nobility indeed, and they had mentioned a kov. I said, "And the kov?"

Fropo sucked through his teeth. "Konec Yadivro, the Kov of Brugheim." Ineldar the Kaktu could have told me I was going to see a kov, by Krun!

Dav had found the ale and after he had demolished the first stoup in two swallows, he said: "The kov and I do not parade our ranks here in Jikaida City. We have work to do that—" Here he took the opportunity of destroying the second stoup. Then: "By this little fracas I take it you have run afoul of Prince Mefto the Kazzur the yetch?"

"Aye." I told them I had fought Mefto, and lost, and had been saved by the drikingers. They expressed the opinion that I must be somewhat of a bladesman after all, not to have been slain in the first pass or two. And, I knew, I had stood like a loon, shaking, when I had crossed swords with these stikitches. Kov Konec and his comrades had reached Jikaida City a few days earlier in a caravan whose master was Inarartu the Dokor, the twin brother of Ineldar the Kaktu, and this explained Ineldar's knowledge, I thought.

The kov turned out to be a strong, frank-faced man with charming manners. I formed the opinion that he placed great reliance on the opinions and advice from Dav. Their estates, those of Brugheim and Bilsley, lay in Mandua, a country immediately to the west of Mefto's Shanodrin. At once I realized the rivalry existing, and determined that it had nothing to do with me. Mefto could go hang; Vallia counted for me, and nowhere else. I was wrong there, of course.

However, I did take the opportunity in conversation of remarking that I knew a Bowman of Loh who swore that shafts fletched with the blue feathers of the king korf were superior to any other. I thought it tactful not to mention that Seg had also revised his opinion and had been heard to admit that the rose-red feathers of the zim-korf of Valka were as good. He wouldn't admit, as many a bowman felt, that they were superior.

"You know about the king korf, then, Jak?"

"A little. Not enough, kov."

"You call me Konec, Jak, here in Jikaida City."

"Konec."

"You have no love for Mefto?"

"He bested me. It was a fair fight—"

"A man with four arms and a tail?"

It rankled; but I had to say it, if only to show myself that I was not blinded by self-esteem. "It was not that, Konec. He is just simply superb. I think, perhaps, with other weapons he might... But it would be a brave man who would go up against him, man to man."

"Aye," said Fropo, and he riffled his whiskers.

"His ambitions are overweening. He must be stopped before he brings ruin to all the Dawn Lands. It is here in Jikaida City that we stand the best chance, paradoxical though that may appear."

Dav chipped in to say, "If you are with us, Jak—"

I said, "There is the story in the old legends, true or false who can say after thousands of seasons? The legend of Lian Brewis and his enchanted brush. He was the artist for the gods, he could draw and paint so beautifully that his creations came alive, and peopled the world, and what the gods spoke of, Lian Brewis created out of paint."

"The story is known over Kregen and is very beautiful," said Dav. "So—?"

"So when the evil gods grew jealous in their wrath they took up Lian Brewis. He was cut off in full flower, a plump, jolly, wonderful person. And the gods for whom he had created so much beauty arose likewise in their just wrath and placed Lian Brewis as that constellation of stars that adorns the Heavens of Kregen. He can never be forgotten." I looked at them, at their serious faces, and understood the intensity of their determination to halt Prince Mefto in his career of conquest. "Be sure the gods do not—"

"They will not," said Konec, and he spoke with power. "You may rest assured on that."

There was always the chance that the Rapa, the Brokelsh and the two apims had been sacrificed by their master just so that he might infiltrate a spy into the enemy camp. The trick is known. So I was not accepted whole-heartedly all at once, and of course my hesitation in dealing with my opponent added to the suspicion. But Dav was genuine and genial and my mention of the king korf, which was by way of being a secret signal, allayed much of the natural suspicion. They did not think that Mefto had penetrated that far into their schemes.

As for myself, I pondered just why I was here; how could these folk help me back to Vallia?

In the succeeding days I came to know them better and Pompino made the pappattu as my partner. We shifted quarters and Konec placed a room in the hotel of the Blue Rokveil at our disposal alongside the others. We spent the time practicing at swordplay, and, by Zair, I felt I mightily needed that sharpening up. The remembrance of Mefto's five blades seemed to have mesmerized me.

This party from Mandua were here ostensibly to play Jikaida, and Konec was a player of repute. Their intrigues against Mefto were kept very quiet; but if assassination formed part of them, it stood little chance. Mefto was surrounded continually by his brilliant retinue of followers. He lay abed, recovering from his arrow wound. So Dav insisted we go with him to watch a well-touted game of Kazz-Jikaida. It was to be between rival factions of the twin cities, and was the usual Kazz game and not the Death game, that is, the pieces did not face certain death if they lost.

We went along to take our seats in the public galleries of one of the game courts of the Jikaidaderen and I watched the Kazz game—and I was not enthralled. There was a powerful fascination in Kazz-Jikaida, an appeal to deeply hidden emotions and a dark pull on the blood; but I kept seeing the magical blades and the scornful and triumphant face of Prince Mefto the Kazzur before my eyes.

Fifteen

How Bevon Struck a Blow

The game turned out to be the Pallan's Kapt's Gambit Declined. That was how the encounter began. Because this was Kazz-Jikaida, the precise and elegantly contrived moves broke down after a time when a piece refused to be taken. The game proceeded interestingly enough, despite that. One swod, a Chulik whose fierce upthrust tusks were banded in silver, fought very well, defeating two Deldars sent against him successively. This upset the right hand drins of the game as far as Yellow was concerned, and pretty soon Blue was sweeping through the center with a line of Deldar-supported swods and pieces. When the two Kapts were brought into play they swept aside a Chuktar and a Hikdar and, but for an interesting contest between a Hyr-Paktun and the Aeilssa's Swordsman, the game was over.

Here in democratic-aristocratic Jikaida City the piece around whose capture the game revolved was called not King or Rokveil but Aeilssa, Princess. Well, I liked the romantic ring of that, and having married a princess and having others of that ilk as daughters, I could not in all conscience find fault.

When the game was done, the sand already being raked neatly back into the blue and yellow squares ready for the next game—there being time for two encounters in that afternoon—Dav and I shouldered up to leave. Being Dav, his first thought was to discover the nearest alehouse.

With a flagon in his fist and his elbow on the counter, he said, "The pieces fight differently when it is a Death game."

I nodded, and drank. I was thirsty.

"How often do they—?"

"Very seldom for the public contests. Death-Jikaida is expensive. The inner courts. They are the places for the highest stakes and the most bloody of encounters."

"I have heard it said," I remarked, quoting Deb-Lu-Quienyin as we had talked around our caravan fire under the stars of the Desolate Waste, "that there is no skill in Jikaida where the outcome of carefully planned moves can be upset by mere brainless warriors fighting."

"So they say." Dav supped companionably. "But Konec says there is skill, albeit of a different kind. There is the skill of sizing up your opponent's powers and of arranging within the moves to place your best fighters to bear on the weakest of your opponent's, and of protecting your own lesser pieces."

"That Chulik swod with the silver-banded tusks—"

"In the next game he will be a Deldar, you mark my words."

"Chuliks are ferocious fighters. He'll be a Pallan yet."

"On the Jikaida board only, though! By Spag the Junct! The blue and yellow sand will drink much blood before they put him away in the balass box."

Pompino found us then and wanted to catch up with the flagons, and some of Konec's people arrived, and the alehouse began to liven up. We'd all put in some time in the practice court, and we lived and messed shoulder by shoulder, for Konec paid for everything in the Blue Rokveil with funds provided by contributions from Mandua against Mefto, and I'd practiced in a kind of daze. Dav regarded me as a better than middling swordsman. Pompino he rated much higher. I felt, in the turmoil that I couldn't plumb, that maybe he was right.

Now, with the flagons being refilled by Fristle fifis, who squealed as they did their work, well-knowing that the customers liked that, Dav broached the question. He opened up the reasons behind what had been going on.

"You are a fighting man, Jak. You are good. You could be better, I feel, if—but then, if we all knew that if, we'd all be Mefto the Bastards, eh?"

"I suppose so."

"Cheer up, you miserable fambly! I'm offering you a task you should joy in—we fight for Konec in Kazz-Jikaida. Will you join us?"

Pompino, who had just lifted a fresh flagon to his lips, blew a head of froth a clear six feet and into the cleavage of a fifi. She yelped. She put her finger down and wiped—and then she licked the finger, making a face. But she didn't deceive us. We laughed—even I laughed.

"All right," I said.

"We-ell," said Pompino.

"It depends on the size of the game we get into," Dav said, speaking to Pompino with intent to induce him. "Konec has brought first-class fighters; but we may need many more to make up the pieces. What say you? You know the pay is good, and the inducements offered by the Nine Masked Guardians add up to a handsome sum."

In Poron Jikaida, which is the smallest size reckoned to be worth the playing, there are thirty-six pieces a side. In Lamdu Jikaida there are ninety pieces a side.

In the end Pompino gave his assent; a qualified assent which, as he said, depended on getting the hell out of this city. We were both of the opinion that the Everoinye, having used our services, would not bother us again for a space and therefore we must use our own efforts to escape. For we regarded it as an escape. "There is no chance I shall stay once Ineldar the Kaktu begins to form his caravan," said Pompino, and he meant it.

"By Spag the Junct!" burst out Dav. "You eat Konec's food and sleep under his roof—"

"I shall pay," said Pompino, and his foxy face bristled. "I shall pay—you will see."

"Very well. We shall hire swods from the academies. The higher pieces are named. I think you two may be Deldars—"

"What?" Pompino was outraged. "I am a paktun—"

"We have hyr-paktuns with us in this, with the pakzhan."

Pompino stared furiously at me. I hate to see friends wrangling. "If you could at least give Pompino a decent harness it would—"

"The weapons and the armor are prescribed by law. It is all in the Jikaidish."

Well, by Vox, that was true. Each piece on the board was represented on the blue and yellow sands of Kazz-Jikaida by a fighting man. Each piece was equipped according to the laws of Jikaida as prescribed in the Jikaidish Lore—that is, in this sense of the Kregish word, the hyr-lif written in the Jikaidish. Swods wore a breechclout and held a small shield and were armed with a five-foot spear. The Deldars wore a leather jerkin and carried a more effective shield. Mind you, the Jikaidish Lore provided for an amazing variety of equipments. One of the most important facts to remember about Jikaida is that the ramifications, combinations, extensions and sheer prolific variety of the game demand that before any game begins each player is aware of the exact rules under which the game is to be played. This is cardinal. Much blood has been shed because players were too stupid or lazy to make sure they agreed on the rules they were going to use before they started playing.

Pompino rubbed his whiskers.

"Arrange for me to have a sword, and, maybe—"

"It is difficult." Dav screwed up his face and then reached for the flagon. "It may not be possible to arrange the bokkertu for Screetz-Jikaida. But I will speak to Konec."

"Do so."

"Who is Konec playing?" I said to attempt to bring the conversation down a few degrees. It had been growing too warm.

"Some old biddy called Yasuri."

"Ha!" snapped Pompino. "I might have guessed."

"She didn't hire us to fight for her—she must be using the academies."

Dav nodded sagely. "I am told they train 'em here to fight in ways adjusted to the Jikaida board. It is cramped."

"Wise old lady Yasuri," sneered Pompino.

"Don't tell me the name of her Jikaidast, Dav," I said. "Let me guess. One Master Scatulo, yes?"

Dav shook his head. "No."

I was surprised.

"She put great store by him. Fawned on him."

"If he arrived with you then he wouldn't have had time to Establish his Credentials."

"Bevon the Brukaj mentioned that," said Pompino.

We learned what that meant. Jikaidasts could earn fortunes here in Jikaida City. The great ones who could afford to come here and pay for the privilege of playing Kazz-Jikaida would all be devoted to the game, that went without saying; but they might not be quite as good players as they imagined. It was customary for each player to employ a Jikaidast to be at his or her elbow and to advise. A very conspicuous and ornate clepsydra marked off the time allowed for each move, and when the time was up the water-clock beat a resounding stroke upon a great brazen gong. In some games if a player had not made the move by then he was required to forfeit a piece. As for the Establishment of Credentials, this took place in the Hall of Jikaidasts.

The Hall was long and narrow. Along each side was ranged a column of Jikaida boards. The newcomer seated himself at the end board and played Jikaida against his opponent. If he won he moved up a board. There was a constant stream of Jikaidasts moving up or down—down and out to await their turn to begin the ascent of the ladder again, or up to the topmost table where they would have established their credentials and could then seek employment as advisers to wealthy players.

Master Scatulo, I fancied, would go up the ladder like a dose of salts.

As to my own chances of improving in the Jikaida pieces' hierarchy, I was not so sanguine. It was clear that the party with Konec, including Dav and Fropo, regarded me as a reasonably expert swordsman—they found it difficult to believe I had lasted even a couple of passes with Mefto—but were less than confident about letting me take the part of a superior piece. The Pallan, as the most important piece on the board, wore a full harness of that superb mesh steel. If he came up against a half-naked swod with a spear, the outcome would not be in doubt.

When I questioned the sanity of men prepared to fight as swods, the explanations I was given ranged from blind passionate partisanship for the Blues or Yellow, simple greed, a desire to get on in Jikaida, fear of retribution for a crime—there are many foibles and quirks of human nature that Opaz has given us and that remain dark and shrouded in our inmost beings.

Also, archers ringed the stands. If any piece, including a Pallan, shirked a fight and attempted to run, he would be shafted instantly at the signal from the representative of the Nine Masked Guardians who presided at every game.

As the archers posted up there were Bowmen of Loh; everyone knew they would not miss.

Some games of Kazz-Jikaida employed the rule that to make the powers of the superior pieces more representative of those the pieces really had on the board, more than one warrior took the part of a piece. Chuktars and Kapts might be represented by two fighting men, a Pallan by three. On other occasions all the pieces were armed in the same fashion. Once the stranger realized that Kazz-Jikaida was not quite like the Jikaida he had played as a boy against his father, or as a girl against her mother, then the anomalies were seen in their true perspective.

In the board game a piece landing on the square of a hostile piece captures. In Kazz-Jikaida the square is contested in blood.

To the death in Death-Jikaida.

In most games, but not all, the Jikaidish Lore states that when an attacking piece wins he may be substituted by a fresh fighter of the same force. If a defending piece wins he must remain where he is, on the square for which he has fought so valiantly—bleeding, dying, it makes no matter. Thus a successful defense, which is contrary to board Jikaida, is penalized. The Substitutes lined along the benches wait to go in.

Because like our Earthly game—coming possibly from chaturanga, shatranj—Jikaida has matured over the centuries and, also, because different folk play different rules in different parts of Kregen, there are many similarities and many divergences. The swods—the pawns—move one square diagonally or orthogonally ahead, and take on the forward diagonal. If a Deldar stands on a square adjacent to a swod, then that swod, of the

Deldar's color, cannot be taken by an opposing swod. This leads to fascinating situations which abruptly erupt into furious action.

This rule unique to Jikaida with its possibilities of Deldar-supported chains, is generally believed to have given rise to the traditional opening challenge of Jikaida: "Rank your Deldars!"

The jikaidish for this particular protection is propt, and as we left the alehouse to set off for our quarters and an enormous meal, Dav said, "When the propts collapse the blood will fly, by Spag the Junct!"

Because the prospect was both exhilarating and forbidding, making our fingers tingle, we swaggered and strutted, I can tell you, on our way to one of the six or eight square meals a day any Kregen likes to fuel the inner man. Pompino was more than a little put out by the unspoken imputations. His red whiskers bristled. But he was in the right of it. Our business was not taking part in blood games; it was in getting out of here.

As we walked along he kept rotating his head, looking, as I alone knew, for that magnificent scarlet and golden raptor of the Star Lords. He regarded the Everoinye with none of the scorn and hatred I had once shown them; they had treated him well and fairly and he repaid them in loyal service. In addition, he was possessed of a species of religious rapture at the idea that he was so closely involved with the doings of the gods.

Everybody in the twin cities talked in terms of the game, of course, and someone made a remark as we crossed into Blue City, that we had crossed a front. The Jikaida board is divided up into drins. Drin means land. Or, if you will, a number of drins are joined together to make the board. In general games a drin consists of a checkered board of six squares a side, making thirty-six in all. Six of these drins make up the board for Poron Jikaida, two by three. At the meeting of drins the line is painted in thicker markings. Some pieces have the power of crossing from drin to drin across a front on their move; most must halt at the front and wait until the next turn to cross.*

On the day appointed, Konec led us to the Jikaidaderen where we were to play. The lady Yasuri had hired herself a Jikaidast off the top of the tree. Konec, in his turn, had taken into employment for this game an intense, brooding, nervous Jikaidast called Master Urlando, who wore a blue gown with yellow checked border. For the professionals blue or yellow meant only the angles of the game, for the opening move was decided by chance and not by tradition.

The game was an ordinary one and open to the public and the benches

---

* It is not necessary to understand how to play Jikaida to appreciate what follows. Dray Prescot relates in detail the description and rules of the game. A brief description of Jikaida is given at the end of this volume as Appendix A, together with sufficient rules for Poron Jikaida as to enable anyone to play an enjoyable game. A.B.A.

and covered arcades were filled. In the event Pompino gave in as much to his own estimation of himself as a fighting man as to outside pressures and took up his position as a Deldar. As I had expected, I was to act the part of a swod.

The game was not distinguished. We ranked our Deldars after the impressive opening ritual, where prayers were spoken and the choirs sang suitable hymns and the incense was burned and the sacrifice made. The ib of Five-handed Eos-Bakchi here in Havilfar was represented by the ib of Himindur the Three-eyed. For the first time I realized, with a pang, that five-handed really did have a strong and terrible meaning. So, with due propitiation made and the fortunes of Luck and Chance called upon, we took our places upon the blue and yellow sanded squares.

For a considerable period of the game I stood with a Deldar on an adjacent square and a swod—a Pachak with a brisk professional air about him, determined to get on—on the square to my left diagonal. He could not attack me by reason of the Deldar. We fell into an interesting conversation, although this was against the tenets of the game, and I learned of his history. I like Pachaks with their two left arms and their absolute loyalty in their nikobi to their oaths. Luckily for both of us we did not fight, the main action sweeping up the left hand side of the board and then, as Konec plunged, angling directly to the center and the Yellow Princess. Konec was a bold player, ruthless when he had to be. Dav was acting as Pallan. He was thrust forward, crossing a front, plunging into a direct confrontation with the Yellow Pallan. The fight was absorbingly interesting; Dav won, the right wing Kapt and Chuktar swept in and, with a Hikdar angling for the last kaida, the triumphant hyrkaida was made by Dav, sliding smoothly in and, challenged by the Yellow Princess's Swordsman, defeating him in a stiff but brief battle.

The various shouts of acclaim went up, the Blue prianum, the shrine where the victory tallies were kept, notched up another win, and it was all over. I had neither struck nor received a blow. I bid a shaky remberee to the Pachak swod and we all went back to the hotel.

Anticlimax—no. For I had seen what went on in Kazz-Jikaida, and was not much enamored of it.

Konec said, "In two days' time I meet a fellow from Ystilbur. You will be a Deldar, Jak."

I nodded. There was little I felt I could say.

Pompino, who had had to beat a swod, told me he was not going to act again. We were standing in the shade of a missal tree growing by the wall of the courtyard and the shadows from the walls crept over the sand. The sounds of the twin cities came muted. The air smelled extraordinarily fresh and good.

"Ineldar is forming his caravan. I shall be one of his guards. You, Jak?"

"Yes, I think so."

"Excellent. By Horato the Potent! I cannot wait to get out into the Desolate Waste!"

A shadow moved among the shadows.

Our thraxters were out in a twinkling.

A voice said, "Jak? Pompino?"

Pompino pointed his sword. "Step you forward so that we may see you. And move exceeding carefully."

A dark form lumbered out into the last of the mingled light. Jade and ruby radiance fell about him. His hunched shoulders, his bulldog face, all the gentle power of him was as we remembered from the nights under the stars.

There was blood on his right hand.

Bevon the Brukaj said, "I have run away from my master. He abused me cruelly. And I struck a guard—I do not think I killed him; but his nose bled most wonderfully, to my shame."

"Well, by the Blade of Kurin..." whispered Pompino.

"Will you help me? Will you take me in?"

The sound of loud voices rose from the street, approaching, and with them the heavy tramp of footsteps and the clank of weapons, the chingle of chains.

"Inside, Bevon. Pompino, find Dav. Explain. We cannot allow them to take Bevon."

"But—"

"Do it!"

Pompino took Bevon's arm and guided him into the inner doorway. Fixing a blank look on my face and sheathing my sword, I turned to the gate and stood, lolling there and picking my teeth.

Sixteen

Kazz-Jikaida

Over the seasons I have taken much enjoyment and indulged in merry mockery and silly sarcasm from that fuzzy look of blank idiocy I can plaster all across my weather-beaten old beakhead. But as the guards and the Watch strode up, clanking, I felt the pang of a realization that, perhaps, this stupid expression was truly me, after all.

"Hey, fellow! A slave, a damned runaway slave. Have you seen him?"

I picked my teeth. "Was he a little Relt with a big wart alongside his hooter?"

"No, you fambly—"

"I haven't seen anyone like that."

"A hulking stupid great oaf of a Brukaj—"

"Best look along by the Avenue of Bangles—they're all notors in here." I screwed my eyes up. "D'you have the price of a stoup of ale, doms? I'm main thirsty—"

But, angry and waving their poles from which the lanterns hung, flickering golden light, they went off, shouting, raising a hullabaloo. The black and white checkers vanished along the way and I, still picking my teeth, went back into the rear quarters of the hotel. They had given me no copper ob for a drink. They had cursed me for a fool, unpleasantly, and had there been time they'd have drubbed me for fun. Not nice people. I would not like Bevon to fall into their clutches.

After a quantity of shouting and arm-waving we persuaded Dav that Bevon wouldn't murder us all in our beds. As a runaway slave he was a highly dangerous person to have on the premises; but Dav's good nature surfaced. He was a man who knew his own mind, and he summed Bevon up shrewdly. Runaway slaves are not tolerated in slave-owning society for the bad examples they set. It was left to Bevon to say the words that got us all off the hook.

"Here in Jikaida City," he said in his pleasant voice, having got his breath and composure back and washed off the guard's nose bleed, "I am told that a slave may gain his freedom by taking part in the games."

"That is true, Bevon. But he has to act the part of a swod and he must survive a set number of games. It has been known—but is rare, by the Blade of Kurin."

"Enter me in the next game, and I shall be safe from Master Scatulo. My blood-price will be paid by the Nine Masked Guardians, for they always welcome anyone willing to take part in Kazz-Jikaida as a swod. You know that. I cannot be touched by the law until I am free or dead. That is the law."

Kov Konec, when consulted, agreed to Dav's proposals, and it was settled. I own I felt relief. Bevon seemed to me to be far too gentle a fellow actually to take up sword and fight; but as he said himself, rather that than being slave any longer.

The day of the game against the player from Ystilbur was set as Bevon's introduction to Kazz-Jikaida, and the authorities were notified. Also, this day coincided with the decision about the caravan out of here. Pompino was in no doubt.

"If we do not give our undertaking to Ineldar by tonight and conclude the bokkertu, he will have to employ other guards." Pompino stood with me watching as Dav stood facing a table on which a huge ale barrel was upended. The spout gushed ale into an enormous flagon. Dav stood there, hands on hips, his head thrust forward, licking his lips, and, I am sure, feeling the tortures of the damned. There was no ale for Dav on the day of Kazz-Jikaida.

Rather, there was no ale until we had won.

"I have promised to fight—" I said.

"Well, I shall not. They have been good friends to us, yes, I agree. But our duty lies elsewhere."

"I thought you said you didn't get enough time away from your wife?"

"True. But I've had enough time, now, by Horato the Potent!"

By just about any of the honor codes of Kregen there could not really be any faulting of Pompino's logic. I said, "I'll just play in this game for them and then I'll come with you to sign on with Ineldar."

"You might get chopped."

"Then the problem wouldn't arise."

Dav rolled across, wiping the back of his hand across his mouth just as though he'd demolished a whole stoup, and told us that the cramph from Ystilbur had hired the best the academies could offer. "Those rasts up there have gone in with the Hamalese, may Krun rot their eyeballs."

Very carefully, I said: "They are a small nation. They were overrun by the cramphs of Hamal, just like the folk of Clef Pesquadrin. D'you know what happens when a country is subjected like that, Dav? Put in chains?"

"Aye. And not pretty, either. But this Coner is half Hamalese, I'm told. There is a plot in this, and I don't like it." He frowned and shook his shoulders. "I've tried to warn Konec; but he sees this as merely another step in the games."

The many games of Jikaida all served to enhance or not the prestige of the various participants. There were league tables. This was the Two Thousand Five Hundred and Ninety-Eighth Game, and they played a Game a season, so that shows you. The champions went away from Jikaida City far wealthier than when they arrived; but also they took with them the intangible aura of the victor.

The twin cities lived and breathed Jikaida. That cannot be emphasized enough. Everywhere, in the taverns, along the boulevards, in the parks, people sat all day playing. Those who could visited the public games of Kazz. The highest nobility of Havilfar and anywhere else who were apprized kept strictly to their own private games, where Death Jikaida ruled. These were the games in which the highest honors were conferred. Everyone gambled, of course. I had heard stories of whole kingdoms being staked on the outcome of a single game. People bet on the results, on just which pieces would survive, how long it would be before certain positions were reached, how many pieces would be wounded or slain. They bet on anything.

Pompino said, "Plot or no, Dav, I'd put ten golden deldys on you; but no one will give me reasonable odds."

Dav said, "I've been lucky so far." The truth was, he was a fine fighting man, clever and quick with his blade, and the betting public had seen that and he commanded odds to gamblers.

Remembering how I had met a flutsman of Ystilbur in peculiar circumstances, a Brokelsh height Hakko Bolg ti Bregal known as Hakko Volrokjid, I reflected that the Hamalese had all Ystilbur in their power. Perhaps some of the schemes of Konec also were known to them? Certain sure it was that the Hamalese, despite recent setbacks in the Dawn Lands, were intent on further conquest there.

So Konec led us off to play Kazz-Jikaida against Coner, and Pompino got himself a seat in the stands to watch. The day was fair. The preliminaries were gone through as before, with the rituals and the choirs chanting and the sacrifices and the libations, and mightily impressive it all was. Konec and Coner seated themselves on the playing thrones, one at either end, and we pieces marched out to take up our places on the board.

As a Deldar in this game I carried a shield of wicker and a five-foot spear. I had a leather jerkin. Dav, massive in his mesh, gave me a cheery word. Fropo the Curved, acting as a Kapt, strained his bulk against his lorica. Each piece was equipped according to the rules prescribed in the hyr-lif known as the Jikaidish Lore. I settled myself. Extremely beautiful girls, clad wispily in draperies of white and purple, danced about the board to carry the commands of the players to their pieces. Up on the throne dais each player had his Jikaidast at his side. The feeling of ages-old ritual, that this was the way the game should be played, the way it should be run, held everyone fixed in complete absorption. The fascination was there, like a drug, a dark compelling pull drawing on the deep tides of the blood.

Golden trumpets blew. The banners broke free. The first move was made.

Well, I will not go into it. It was a shambles.

We ranked Deldars and started off in fine style, and then we ran into disastrous trouble as a whole rank of swods was swept away. Red-clad slaves with litters and stretchers carried off the casualties. Other slaves raked the blue and yellow sand neatly back into the squares, and fresh sand was sprinkled over the blood. But Yellow surged on and on, triumphant, and we were pressed back, losing men like flies in winter.

The fighting men trained in the academies had been taught all the tricks of fighting in the admittedly limited space of the Jikaida squares. If a warrior stepped outside the square he was adjudged the loser, of course. If he stepped out too smartly, without giving of his utmost, if he shirked and sought that way out of the horror, then black-clad men ran onto the board. What they did ensured that pieces would fight, grimly and with thought only of victory.

Three swods I fought and dealt with them. Each little conflict took place on two squares, by virtue of the fact that the attacker and the defender occupied adjacent squares and the whole of these two squares could be used. Then a Hikdar came at me, whirling his axe, and I had a sharp set-to before I got my spear between his ribs.

Konec swung the play across to the other wing then and I had time for a breather. The game had rapidly degenerated from the classical simplicity of the Aeilssa's Swod's Opening into a blood bath. Well, we Blues fought.

With consummate skill Konec made a space for fresh development in the center and a diagonal of pieces formed leading to Yellow's Right Home Drin. That would be Blue's Far Left Drin. Every drin has its name; everything has a name; I was concentrating on what I could see coming up. At the far end of the diagonal of pieces stood a Yellow Chuktar. The Yellow Pallan had been busy and was absent; the Yellow Aeilssa stood, just for the moment, vulnerable. But the Chuktar barred the way. An enchanting little Fristle fifi danced across from the Blue Stylor. He was positioned level with the board and beneath the player's throne to pass on the move orders. Konec moved a Blue swod onto the end of the diagonal line of pieces, and into the square diagonally off from me. So that meant I was sure what was going to happen.

Yellow made his move, a nasty threatener down the right wing, and then the fifi, who had been given my orders all ready, for Konec was a shrewd player, said to me: "Deldar to vault and take Chuktar."

I hitched up my belt and put my spear into my left hand. I spat into my right, not having an orange handy, and then took up the spear. Calmly, I started to walk along beside the diagonal line of men. This simulated the vault. What a sight it must all have been! The twin Suns of Scorpio blazing down into the sprawled representation of a Jikaida board, the blue and yellow squares a bright checkered dazzlement, the brilliantly attired figures of the pieces, the color, the vividness, the raw stink of spilled blood—and the tension, the indrawn breaths, the hunching forward of the spectators. The passions were being unleashed here. I walked gently along, and I held my shield just so, and the spear just so, for the moment I put my foot into the square occupied by the Chuktar we would fight.

Because I was coming down off the end of a vault, having leaped over a line of pieces, there was no empty starting square. I would come down slap bang on top of the Chuktar. We would contest the square in its own narrow confines.

The man representing the Chuktar was a Kataki. Unusual to find a member of that unpleasant race of diffs doing much else besides slaving, for they are slavemasters above all and know little of humanity—although Rukker had given certain glimmerings of humanity, to be sure—and this fellow was clearly in Kazz-Jikaida because of some ill deed. He was licking his lips as I approached. He wore an iron-studded kax and vambraces, and carried a good-quality cylindrical shield. His thraxter caught the light of the suns. I walked up to the right of the diagonal line of pieces, which surprised him, for any shielded man likes to get his left side around.

One thing was in my favor: that hyr-lif the Jikaidish Lore specifies what weapons may be used; the Kataki was not allowed to strap six inches of bladed steel to his tail. His lowering brows, flaring nostrils and snaggly-toothed gape-jawed mouth complemented his wide-spaced eyes. They were narrow and cold. His thick black hair which would be oiled and curled was stuffed up under his iron helmet. Formidable fighting men, Katakis, known and detested—and steered clear of.

As I marched up with my wicker shield and the spear, wearing a leather jerkin and helmetless, to face this armored man with his professional sword and shield, I reflected with some amazement that I must be very like a wild barbarian facing an iron legionary of Rome. So—act like a barbarian...

When I got within three squares of him I launched myself forward in a bursting run, wild and savage. I went straight in, the spear out thrust, the shield well up. I saw his ugly face go rigid with shock and the thraxter begin to flick into line. But I was pretty desperate and I had to banish a phantom image of Mefto the Kazzur that sprouted shockingly before my eyes. Straight at him I sprang.

His sword clicked against the wicker and a chunk flew off, sprouting strands of painted wood. The spear went straight on, over the rim of the iron-studded breastplate, punched into his squat neck. He tried to shriek; but could not make a sound with sharp metal severing all his vocal cords. He flopped sideways and I hauled the spear out and lunged again and he went on down and stayed down.

We were playing Kazz-Jikaida, the ordinary game and not the Death Jikaida—we might as well have been for that Kataki.

The stands broke into a bedlam of noise and stamping; but I had not attacked until my foot was inside the square. And he had struck first—a last unavailing blow.

What Yellow's move was I have no idea. He made a desperate scrabbling attempt to get a piece back to defend. But on Konec's next move Fropo the Curved, as a Kapt, vaulted over the same diagonal and then pounced on the Princess. The Aeilssa's Swordsman stepped out to challenge, as was his right, and Fropo finished him off and—amazingly—Blue had won.

In the racket going on all about us, as the young girl who had taken the part of Yellow's Princess stood there with the tears pouring down her face, Fropo wiped his sword on the yellow cloak of the Swordsman and spoke cheerfully to me.

"I never thought you'd do it, Jak. A bonny fight. I was able to vault right home. Konec will be pleased."

"I doubt it, Fropo. We have lost a lot of good men."

At once the Fristle's cat face sobered. "You are right. Now may Farilafristle have them in his care. Good men, gone."

The final rituals were gone through and the Blue notched up another win in the prianum. Our player, Konec, also moved up in the league tables. We marched off. But it was hard. There were many gaps in the ordered ranks. Kov Konec's people had been drastically thinned. And that, I reasoned as we trailed off to our hotel, was the core of the plot against us.

The captured Yellow Princess was brought along in our midst; but she did not make up for all the good men lost.

Seventeen

I Learn of a Plan

We held a Noumjiksirn, which is by way of being a wake, an uproarious and yet serious evening in which we mourned our vanished comrades. There was huge drinking and singing of wild songs and much boasting and leaping about and the odd clash of blade. Those who knew something of the history of the slain stood forth and cried it out, clear and bravely, and we applauded and drank to them, and called on all the gods for a safe passage through the Ice Floes of Sicce. The Yellow Princess sat enthroned on a dais in our midst, stripped of her yellow robes and chained. But this was tradition only; the days when the captured Aeilssa belonged to the victorious side were long gone, for that kind of boorish behavior smacked too much of the uncouth. She would be ransomed by her losing player, of course, and Konec would distribute a donative and pocket a tidy sum himself. This was just one of the perks accruing to a winning side.

The girl who had acted as our Blue Princess was the daughter of Nath Resdurm, a splendid numim who was a strom at the hands of Kov Konec. His lion-man's face bristled with pride as his daughter, Resti, danced the victory dance, taking a turn with every one of us pieces who had survived. The drink flowed. Dav took on a load. He danced and pranced with Resti, who laughed, her golden hair flowing, mingling with Dav's as they swirled across the floor and the orchestra Konec had paid for scraped and strummed and banged away.

Strom Nath Resdurm had acted as the other Kapt, with Fropo. We had lost all our Hikdars, our Paktuns and Hyr-Paktuns, all good fighting men laid to rest. Truly, the lion-girl Resti would not dance breathless with the survivors.

When Dav laughingly yielded her to a Deldar, who pranced her off across the floor, Dav bellowed his way across to the ale table and seized up a foaming stoup. He spied me.

"Aye, Jak," he said, and drank thirstily. "Aye—it takes strength to grasp a spear in that fashion—or skill."

"It did for the Kataki."

"But that bastard Coner has done for us. We are too few, now. And who else will fight for us?"

"Konec has only to hire pieces from the nearest academy—"

"Onker!"

I allowed that to pass. He was by way of becoming a friend, and in the passionate despair at plans gone wrong he knew more than he said and so cried out against fate. Or, so I thought.

"Yes, Jak," he said, after moment, with the uproar going on all about us. "Yes, you are right. We will hire pieces to fight for us. But Mefto—Mefto—" He drank and was swept up by a mob who shouted him into a song, which he sang right boldly, "King Naghan his Fall and Rise." The songs lifted, after a space, "The Lay of Faerly the Ponsho Farmer's Daughter," "Eregoin's Promise." We did not sing that rollicking ditty that ends in "No idea at all, at all, no idea at all." The mood was not right. And that perturbed me. So I started in my bullfrog voice to roar out "In the Fair Arms of Thyllis."

After the first couple of lines when they'd digested the tune and the name of Thyllis, Konec stepped forward, his face black.

"We sing no damned Hamalian songs here, Jak!"

"Aye!" went up an ominous chorus.

"Wait, wait, friends! Listen to the words carefully."

And I went on singing about Thyllis. That song is well known in Hamal, and is beloved of the Empress Thyllis, as it refers in glowing terms to the marvelous deeds of the goddess from whom she took her name and her scatty ideas. One day back home in Esser Rarioch, my fortress palace of Valkanium, Erithor who is a bard and song-maker held in the very highest esteem throughout Vallia, being half-stewed, concocted fresh words about Thyllis the Munificent. The words were scurrilous, extraordinarily melodic, quite unrepeatable and extremely funny.

By the time I was halfway through the second stanza the people of Mandua were rolling about and holding their sides. I do not think Erithor ever had a better audience for one of his great songs. At least, of that kind...

When I had done they made me sing it again, stanza by stanza, and so picked it up and warbled it all through, again, four times.

Feeling that my contribution to the evening had been some slight success I went off to find a fresh wet for my dry throat. Kov Konec joined me, with Dav and Fropo and Strom Nath Resdurm. We all wore the loose comfortable evening attire of Paz; lounging robes in a variety of colors. Konec, for once wearing a blaze of jewelry, looked a kov.

"You do not care overmuch for the Hamalese?"

"Not much."

How to explain my tangled feelings about the Empire of Hamal? I had friends there, good friends, and yet our countries were at war. As for Thyllis, I felt sorry for her and detested all she stood for, and yet often and often I had pondered the enigma that she saw me in the same light as I saw her. Truly, the gods make mock of us when they set political and class barriers between the hearts of humans.

Of course, anyone of the many countries attacked and invaded by the iron legions of Hamal dedicated to obeying the commands of their empress, anyone suffering from oppression and conquest, would not see a single redeeming feature in Thyllis. That seemed only natural. Now Konec began speaking in a way new in our relationship. After all, I was merely a paktun, in employ, and he was a kov, conscious of his power and yet charmingly accessible.

"Mefto the Kazzur, who calls himself a prince. He is hated in Shanodrin by the people he claims as his. Only his bully boys sustain him against the people. Masichieri—scum."

"He never rode with less than twenty," I said. "But there were more in the caravan, that he uses in Kazz-Jikaida. When I fought him he had been visiting a shishi. I know, for Sishi told me. But when we fought I know there were others of his men in the shadows, laughing at my discomfiture." I went on, briskly. "That saved us from the drikingers."

"So assassination is difficult. Very. Stikitches have been sent—Oh, aye, Jak," at my raised eyebrows. "Honor is long gone from desperate men. And we of the countries of the Central Dawn Lands are desperate."

"Against a single prince hated by his people, dependent on hired swords?"

"No. You do well to question thus. Against Hamal."

"But—"

"Mefto is the key. Through him Hamal can extend her power where now she must fight."

I shook my head. "I believe you, Konec, for I have found you an honorable man. But I have been told that Mefto is a real and regal prince, splendid in gold, beloved in Shanodrin—"

"Stupid stories of shifs, brainless giggling serving wenches."

There ensued a pause in this fierce half-whispered conversation then as we all drank, thinking our separate thoughts.

"A great one is coming from Hamal. A kov, or even a prince. He and Mefto meet in Jikaida City under the cloak of Jikaida. It will arouse no suspicion. Our spies have the story sure."

In the world of intrigue secure meeting places are valuable. Jikaida would explain even a meeting between a Grodnim and a Zairian. But as I listened to Konec talking, I began to see more than I had bargained for.

287

A pot-bellied ceramic jar of Neagromian ware sprouting wildly with the drooping tendrils of heasmons stood in its alcove and Kov Konec bent to partake of the fragrant aroma of the violet-yellow flowers. He swiveled his eyes to regard me, and I saw that he, like his men, was not a conspirator born.

"By Havandua the Green Wonder!" said Konec, standing up from the sweet-smelling plants, his face revealing all the passions struggling for utterance. "Mefto must be stopped! If his schemes and this rast's from Hamal succeed—well—" He paused, and his fists clenched. He had sworn by Havandua the Green Wonder. Well, you know my opinion of the color green; I enjoy its serenity, and it is the finest color for Rifle Regiments, and racing cars and Robin Hood and railway engines and passenger rolling stock; but it seemed my fate on Kregen had thrown me into opposition with green, through no will of my own. Men said that the sky colors were always in conflict. The red of Zim, or Far, and the green of Genodras, or Havil. Truly, I confess, the feeling of fighting for the Blue against the Yellow had come on me strangely and strongly; I would take yellow in Jikaida if I could.

"You are with us in this, Jak?" demanded Konec.

"You have not confided any plan as yet," I reminded him, gently.

If they still harbored any lingering doubts that I was a spy this was a good way to get a sword through my guts.

"Plan!" broke in Fropo, twirling his whiskers. "We are plain fighting men. We have our swords—"

"Aye," said Dav, with all the fervor in him.

The numim, Strom Nath, bristled up his golden whiskers in complete agreement. Then he said, "But there is a plan. That is why we are here."

"Ah," I said, and waited.

Useless to sigh and think back to the brave old days when I was newly arrived on Kregen and would as lief bash a few skulls in as listen. Being an emperor—even a king or a prince or a strom—shackled the old responsibilities on a fellow. But I missed the skirling days of yore. That explained, I fancied, my acceptance of this enforced absence from Vallia. I needed to get the cobwebs of intrigue out of my head and the blood thumping around a body bashing into fights. Mind you, the last time that had been an unmitigated disaster, and I was not likely to forget Mefto the Kazzur in a hurry. Maybe I was getting slothful, complacent, too ready to take the easy way out.

I said, "If you have a scheme to do a mischief to Mefto and the Hamalese, I think I might be your man. If you trust me."

From what they said, and not only to me, I gained the impression, the reassuring impression, that they did trust me. They saw things in their own lights, of course; they had no real reason apart from our first meeting to suspect me. And Dav and the others, for all their geniality, would keep an eye on me, and cut me down, too, if I played them false.

The rest of the story made me feel again that sense of destiny taking me by the throat and choking all the sense out of my stupid head.

"By Makki Grodno's diseased left armpit!" I said, in a pause. "I am with you, a thousand times over!"

For what they said boiled down to this—Konec pulled his lip as he said, "The Hamalese are in trouble in Vallia, some island or other far north of here over the equator. I feel comradely sorrow for them. The Hamalese have withdrawn from their insanely ambitious attempts toward the west. Only a horrible death awaits any honest man there. Ifilion between the mouths of the River Os stands aloof." He eyed me. "And they have not struck at Hyrklana—"

They believed me to hail from Hyrklana. I said, "The island is relatively large and is wealthy. We have many troops. She would find it a toughnut, this bitch Thyllis."

"So—it is we here in the Dawn Lands and Vallia. Thyllis seeks to conclude a treaty with certain countries here who tremble at her name, with Mefto acting for her. By this means she will gain the alliance of powerful states. She will have at her disposal thousands of fresh men, professionals, paktuns, mercenaries, regulars. She will be able to advance against us, who await her coming, and free many strong armies to launch afresh against Vallia."

So I said what I said.

"Yes, Jak. The states will follow the strongest lead. Prince Mefto is the coming man, powerful, glittering, his charisma bright. If he can be taken out of the game, thrown back into the velvet-lined balass box, Mandua can take the lead. We stand firm against Hamal. The balance can be tipped."

"Jikaida—?"

"Precisely," said Dav Olmes, and he smiled, and quaffed.

They told me their plan.

Assassination had proved unreliable and a costly failure. Mefto went everywhere he was known with his bodyguard of swarth riders. They did indicate that they wished the gods had directed my sword between his ribs when we'd fought by the caravan; but, as they pointed out with the fatalism I recognized in them, no man could best Prince Mefto the Kazzur in single combat. So they would play in these Kazz-Jikaida games. And when it was the turn of Konec and his people of Mandua to meet Mefto and his people of Shanodrin, why, then, they would simply move their pieces up the board, and consigning the strict rules of Jikaida to a Herrelldrin Hell, charge him in a body and before his pieces could react butcher him and have done.

That was their plan.

I said, after I closed my mouth and swallowed and so opened my crusty old lips again: "The Bowmen of Loh will not tolerate so flagrant a breach of the rules. They will shaft you all."

"Of course," said Strom Nath. "But Mefto will be gone and our country will face the future with hope."

"And you would all give your lives—?"

"If there was more we could give, that, too, we would willingly pay," said Konec, and there was no mocking his dignity as he spoke—although I wanted to mock this so-called plan. By Zair! What a lot! And what I had got myself into!

They were standing, all looking at me with a hard bright regard. Konec said, "You look— You are not willing to give your life to save your country?"

"Only if there is no other way. But I have as tender a regard for my own neck as I have for my country."

At that they would have grown angry; but I said: "Let me think. There has to be another way."

"You disappoint me, Jak," said Dav. And, in truth, he looked cast down. "I had thought you a man among men."

The time was not suitable for me to make the classic rejoinder to that one: "I'd sooner be a man among women." But, by Vox, there had to be another way!

Then I saw Bevon the Brukaj, drinking quietly to himself in a corner. He had acquitted himself well today and proved himself a fine swordsman, for that, he had said, was his weapon.

"Bevon," I said. "He was by way of becoming a Jikaidast. Let me speak to him. He has a head on his shoulders."

The arguments went on a long time; but they were tired and wrung out, and the drink was working on them, and, truth to tell, although I did not doubt for a single instant their burning determination to give their lives, they would welcome another and better way in which they did not face certain death. So we parted, amicably, with my promise that if we could not discover a method of dealing with Mefto, I would join their party and take part in their suicidal plan.

The clincher came when I said, "Your force has been reduced. You are too few to get at Mefto in a body and fight off his men; and they will fight, mark it well."

"D'you think we don't know that!" said Dav, and the agony in him twisted in me, too, for him... "And there is no one here we may ask or trust—save you, Jak the Nameless."

"And yet you would still have gone on?"

"Aye!"

After we left the Noumjiksirn with the bokkertu of the ransom of the

Yellow Princess duly finalized, I met Pompino. He came into the room we shared looking the worse for wear. He threw himself on the bed, and yawned, and said, "By Horato the Potent! If I had a golden deldy for each copper ob I spent tonight I would be a rich man."

"Lucky you."

He regarded me, sharply enough, and sat up. "I have to see Ineldar the Kaktu first thing. He has kept open two places, but he will not hold them past the Bur of Fretch." That was two burs after the suns rose. "We must be up betimes."

"I shall not be taking a place in Ineldar's caravan guard."

"What?" He scowled at me as though I'd sprouted a Kataki tail. "You don't mean that? What of the Everoinye—"

"There is a task I must do—"

"You said you were desperate to go home—back to Hyrklana."

"I was. But now—"

"You are going to act as a piece in Kazz-Jikaida!"

"Yes."

"Fambly! Onker! You'll be chopped. What in Panachreem can?"

"There is a duty I owe which must be honored. A task has been set to my hands and I must do it."

"Ah!" He suddenly understood, or thought he did. "The Gdoinye has visited you. You have a service for the Everoinye—?"

"No. What I do is not for the Star Lords."

He looked shocked. "There is nothing in Kregen more important than laboring for the Star Lords!"

"Yes," I said. "There is."

Eighteen

Of an Encounter in an Armory

Pompino shared my view that the Star Lords had acted in a way far different from their usual abrupt course when they had set us the task of protecting the lady Yasuri. For one thing; we had both been aware that the threat of the Ochs was more apparent than real. I had been warned of the impending mission in a new way, although Pompino told me that he usually received some prior notice. We felt that the Ochs had been laid on in some way so as to introduce us to the lady Yasuri and secure our employment with her.

"Her escort under that rascal Rordan the Negus returned in time. We did a good job, but—"

"Yes, the escort would have just been in time. So the Star Lords set that up for us. Not like most of the times I have been dumped down unceremoniously right in the thick of it."

Pompino was intrigued. I told him a little of some of the occasions when I had done the Star Lord's bidding, and he expressed astonishment. We were up early and making his preparations to leave. I would be sorry to see him go, and I felt he shared that opinion of me; but nothing he said could make me change my mind. We drank early-morning ale companionably together as we watched the suns rise.

"So you actually arrive when the action has begun?"

'Too right. Usually I have to scout around pretty sharpish for a weapon."

He shook his head, his foxy face surprised.

"When I am called the Everoinye place me carefully, and I can size up the situation and take the best course."

"Ha!" This, of course, merely confirmed my own early opinion of the Star Lords that had been changing over the seasons. "If I don't get stuck in pretty sharpish I'd be done for." Then, to be fair, I added: "Well, most of the time."

We talked around this puzzling fact—puzzling to Pompino although to me merely a part and parcel of my life on Kregen—and then he came out with a sober observation that shook me.

"I had a comrade once, a fine man, a Stroxal from a town near us in South Pandahem. We never went on a task together; but we talked. One day he just disappeared and never showed up again. He was, I feel sure, slain on a task for the Everoinye." Pompino looked shrewdly at me. "I think, Jak, that sometimes the Star Lords send a kregoinye to work for them and he fails. He is slain and does not do their bidding. Then, it is an emergency. They have to throw someone in as a last desperate attempt—"

"By Zair!" I burst out. "So I am the forlorn hope!"

"When all else fails they put you into the ring of blood."

I felt the seething anger boiling away and I held it down. After all, wasn't this just another reminder of my powerlessness? And then a thought occurred. "Hold on a mur, Pompino—the Star Lords have thrown me back in time, into a time loop, so that means they can choose the moment to put me into the action."

"I think that after the action has begun they cannot affect the course of time—I, too, have been through a time loop."

"Well, that is possible."

And, too, I had felt this so-called powerlessness ebbing of late. There was the rebel Star Lord Ahrinye to be taken into consideration. The Star Lords were not infallible, as I knew from my arrival in Djanduin. If what

Pompino said was true, and it made good sense, I had another weapon against them.

"Well, Jak, time to be off."

He gathered up his gear and hitched his belt. He smiled at me, his fox-like face suddenly looking remarkably friendly.

"I have greatly enjoyed your company, Jak, by Horato the Potent. I grieve we will not travel the Desolate Waste together. Will you not come? There is still time..."

"I thank you, Pompino, and I have enjoyed our time together. You are a good comrade. But my allegiance is with—is with another area that—"

"Hyrklana?"

I smiled. "Think it, dom, and do not fret."

Companionably we went out and through the crowded streets and past the boulevard tables where folk were already hard at Jikaida, the ranked armies of miniature warriors marching and counter-marching in frozen brilliance, and so came through the Kyro of Calsanys to the dusty drinnik where the caravans formed. The pandemonium was splendid. The colors, the brilliance, the movements, the stinks, the shouting and bawling—Kregen, ah, Kregen!

Ineldar had a go at making me change my mind; but he was in a hurry to get his motley assemblage into sufficient order for them to move off. There'd be confusion for a couple of days yet before he got them drilled. The Quoffas lumbered off, rolling, their patient enormous faces calmly considering the state of their insides, probably, indifferent to the pains of the journey before them. The calsanys were given a wide berth and their drivers wore bright scarves wrapped around their faces. The carriages and the wagons, the vakkas riding a wide variety of the magnificent saddle animals of Kregen, the swarms of people afoot, all moved along, jostling to find a good spot in the procession. A slave brought up Pompino's totrix and strapped his gear aboard. I shook hands. Pompino mounted up and stuck the lance into the boot. He shouted.

"Remberee, Jak! Come and visit me in Tuscursmot. I shall make you a great bargain from my armory."

"Aye, Pompino the Iarvin. I shall look forward to that." I waved. "Remberee!"

"Remberee!"

And Scauro Pompino ti Tuscursmot, known as Pompino the Iarvin, cantered off to take his place among the caravan guards.

With a deep breath that some folk might dub a sigh I turned away and swung off through the departing crowds. The dust hung. The stinks prevailed. Well, a little wet and then a trifle of business with Friendly Fodo...

People were looking up. Pointing fingers strained skyward. I looked up.

An airboat fleeted in over the twin cities. She was a large craft with a high

293

upflung poop and fighting castles amidships and for'ard; but she was not as large an airboat as the enormous skyships of Hamal. But she was from that nation. Her purple and gold flags flew proudly, and in the Kregan custom she flew as many flags as she could cram flagstaffs in along her length.

So I knew who had arrived—not who, as far as name and rank and dignity went—but who in the sense that this was the great one of Hamal who came to talk the Dawn Lands into destruction with Mefto the Kazzur—and, with them, Vallia.

Some faint spark of the old Dray Prescot flared up then. Something that made me say, Dray Prescot, Lord of Strombor and Krozair of Zy. There was now a voller in Jikaida City. So, perhaps, if I was lucky and bold enough and lived long enough, I had me my means of conveyance back home to Vallia.

Feeling ridiculously cheerful I slaked my thirst and then saw Friendly Fodo. I showed him the thraxter I had bought from him. The rivets of the hilt had frayed through the bindings. He made a face and stroked his shiny whiskers.

"Oh, a trifle, dom, a mere trifle, why that can be fixed for you in the shake of a leem's tail."

"No doubt. But I have a little more gold now—"

"Ah!"

The cupidity of him was transparent. Well, he had a living to make, and I had a weapon to buy on which my life would depend.

For a hoary old fighting man this dickering over weapons is always a pleasant business, and Friendly Fodo, assured of my gold, entered into the spirit of the occasion. A table was brought and laid with a purple cloth, and tea, ale, miscils and palines appeared, brought in by a slave Xaffer, distant and remote; but willing enough. I sat in the chair and partook of the goodies as Friendly Fodo paraded his wares.

No thought entered my head other than that I would buy a new thraxter. Fantasies are for fairy stories, sometimes for grim businessmen of the world, occasionally for poets. The thraxter, your hefty cut and thruster of Havilfar, is adapted to do its work. It is superior, even Vallians will tell you, to the Vallian clanxer. The drexer we had developed in Valka is far superior. I looked at the glittering and lovingly polished blades on the counter. I said, "You are cut off from the world, here in Jikaida City, behind the Desolate Waste—"

"Oh, yes, cut off. But the caravans bring in many strange articles from Havil knows where."

"There is a new fashion in Hamal," I said, and immediately added, "That pestiferous rast-nest. They have taken up fighting with a longer, more slender blade—perhaps—?"

He nodded, interested in talking shop.

"Aye, I have heard from the brethren in my craft. Rapiers, they call 'em. Whether they be as quick as they say—" He lifted his shoulders. "But I have not seen one, so cannot say."

"A pity."

We talked on, and I ate palines and examined the weapons. The Kregish for sword is screetz. I seldom use it in this narrative, for, like the Kregish for sea and water, it is not adapted to terrestrial ears. The same goes for princess. There are other Kregish words I do not use here for the same reason.

At last, seeing I was determined, Friendly Fodo brought out his better wares, blades he valued. These stood in a different class—and their price accordingly. But a fighting man does not care to set a price on the weapons of his trade; how to value your own life in terms of gold?

The best—that is the cardinal rule—the best you can afford.

In the end I selected a thraxter with a finer blade than most. The fittings were plain. There were secret marks on the blade, and Friendly Fodo claimed it had belonged to a kov slain in Death-Jikaida, although he did not offer any explanation of how it had come into his possession. The shop pressed in about me, hung with weapons and armor and glinting with steel and iron and bronze. The air hung heavy with the scent of the violet-yellow heasmon flowers. I took another paline, savoring the rich fruity flavor. The Xaffer brought forward a sturmwood box containing a blade; but a single gentle twirl told me the balance was untrue. This is, despite all, a weakness of the Havilfarese thraxter. When I say the blade of the example I chose was finer, I mean the lines were slightly more slender, the fullering that much more exact. I made up my mind.

"Fodo, can you have this blade fined down a trifle—I can draw you the lines. The curve of the cutting edge, so—" I traced a thumbnail down the blade.

He nodded, twitching his whiskers. "I can have that done in my workshop which is, as everyone knows, the finest in all Jikaida City."

"Good. If you will bring paper and pen I will draw it out."

Following my usual custom I had turned the chair as I sat down so that I faced the door. This is a habit, as you know. A shadow moved beyond the panels, and the brass bell chimed. I caught a glimpse of a hard bright yellow tuft of feathers vibrating ahead of the helmet beneath them, and I was out of the chair and back into the shadows of the shop past the counter, pressing up against a reekingly oily kax wrapped about a stray dummy.

The two Shanodrinese swaggered in, throwing their short capes back, laughing, making great play with the rings on their fingers. They wore armor. They guffawed, between themselves, talking of their prince in terms that betrayed respect and obedience but little affection. The two were masichieri, well enough, little better than bandits masquerading as paktuns.

"Hai, Fodo, you lumop! Where is the dagger you repair for me, eh? You useless rast!"

Not, as you will instantly perceive, a pleasant way to talk.

Fodo's Xaffer bustled forward in that indifferent way that strange race of diffs have, and produced the dagger. It was minutely scrutinized and reluctantly passed as serviceable. It would not have surprised me if these two specimens of Mefto's guard refused to pay, and broke Fodo's nose for him if he objected. But they rustled out the coins and made a great show of it, and then turned to leave.

I heaved out a sigh of relief. Oh, yes, I, Dray Prescot, hid and ached for these cramphs to begone. You will easily see why. Dav Olmes had cleared up the mess after the death of the four would-be stikitches and nothing further had transpired; but Mefto's men would still be wondering what had happened to their comrades. They had followed me, and therefore were obeying orders; but Mefto's men could not know I served Konec, at least, not yet, not until we met.

So they turned to leave and then one of them, the apim with the black moustaches and the lines disfiguring his mouth, saw the spread table, and the miscils crumbled on their plate and the dish of palines. He halted and, idly as I thought, picked up a paline and, as one does, popped it into his mouth.

His companion was a Moltingur, one of that race of diffs who, of the size of and not unlike apims, yet are diffs with a horny carapace across their shoulders—atrophied relic of wings, so it is believed. Their faces would be looked on as hideous on Earth, with an eating proboscis and feelers, and faceted eyes that loom large and blank and frighteningly ferocious. His tunnel mouth opened to reveal its rows of needle-like teeth that tore his food for the proboscis to masticate and swallow down. His words were hissed, as all Moltingurs seem to hiss whatever they speak, chillingly.

"You have a customer, Fodo. An honored customer, I think."

"Aye," said the apim. "By Barflut the Razor-Feathered, you are right, Trinko." So by these words I knew he had been a flutsman in his time.

"Just a customer—" began Fodo.

Now it was plain these two thought highly of themselves, as members of the entourage of Prince Mefto of Shanodrin. The clear evidence of the rapid departure of Fodo's customer must either have puzzled them and aroused their suspicious nature or piqued them because of the fancied slight. Either way, with gentlemen of that kidney, it did not matter. They were insistent on meeting this mysterious customer.

If I say, again, in the old way: I, Dray Prescot, Lord of Strombor and Krozair of Zy, I would add only that I would say those great words with a kind of sob, a despairing feeling of emptiness. Oh, yes, Dray Prescot could leap out and with drawn sword confront these two cramphs. Dray Prescot would have done that. The Dray Prescot who had not, as Jak the Nameless, fought Prince Mefto the Kazzur—and lost.

The naked thraxter shook in my fist. The blade had not been paid for yet. And the magniloquent thoughts clashed. The piece of paper and the pen lay to hand. What dreams I had had of getting Fodo to fashion this sword into a more perfect instrument of death—and how insubstantial and meaningless they appeared when I could not even leap forward into action and use that new blade!

"Sink me!" I burst out—but silently, to myself.

What might have happened Zair alone knows. I do not. I do remember that the thraxter was no longer shaking, and that I took a half step forward. The world was fined down to the shadows around me and the brilliant figures of those two men in their armor, tall and bright, and the hard yellow favors and feathers.

What might have happened... The apim reached for more palines and he tossed one to Trinko, the Moltingur.

With a gulp that echoed, Fodo said: "It is a lady of reputation, come to buy a dagger for her husband. Her lover and his men await. It would be—" He hesitated.

The apim laughed.

Trinko hissed, "Passion and daggers and lovers. It is no business of ours, Ortyg." He flapped his yellow cape around and hitched his sword. Well, that familiar gesture can mean many things. But Ortyg, the apim, read his Moltingur comrade aright, and he laughed, and said, "So perish all blind husbands, may Quergey take them up. You are right, Trinko. Anyway," and he popped the last paline, "if there are men waiting..."

"By Gursrnigur!" said Trinko. "You have the right of it."

So, their fists on their sword hilts, they swaggered out.

A space passed over before I emerged from the shadows. I did not ask Friendly Fodo the reason for his words. Perhaps he just did not like Mefto's men. Perhaps. Perhaps he had seen something in my sudden flight that revealed much to his shrewd Fristle eyes.

Nineteen

"Vallia is not Sunk into the sea."

Events moved rapidly in the ensuing days although in ways that surprised me and, by Vox! that mightily discomposed Konec and Dav. My own emotions remained opaque and murky in relation to my feelings about myself. Eventually I had emerged from my hiding place and with no word of the two Shanodrinese between us had completed my business with Friendly

Fodo. He would produce the finer lines in the thraxter blade and he would charge me well.

We heard reports that Mefto the Kazzur was recovered of his wound. His animal-like powers of recuperation aided in this sense of that certain possession of the yrium that aided him in his control of his people. But I wondered. Certainly, had one of my clansmen, or Djangs, been wounded in a wing, as Mefto had, he would not have dropped all his weapons. Those on the wounded side, yes, perhaps; but not all of them.

The day on which Konec's entourage visited the Jikaidaderen to watch Mefto and his people play a game comes back to me now as a day of suppressed passion and seething anger. We took our seats in the public galleries and settled down to study the play. The crowd was of the opinion that the prince would win, and resoundingly. This he did. We studied the way his men fought, their swordplay and techniques, tried to detect any weaknesses, and marked the men to whom he assigned the posts of most danger. On that occasion Mefto took part in only a single encounter. He and his Jikaidast worked the play admirably, and Mefto was able to put himself in as a substitute and deal with the opposing Princess's Swordsman. This man was a Rapa, beaked, proud, fierce and an accomplished bladesman. He had made a name for himself. But against Mefto the Kazzur he just did not stand a chance. As I watched the glittering blades and the dazzling, nerve-flicking passes, I stared hungrily, desperately searching for a flaw in Mefto's art. He appeared to me perfect at every point. When it was over the crowd applauded. At Konec's fierce urgings we clapped, too.

As the games were played and the positions on the league tables changed leading to the final tournament, the patterns of the final opponents emerged. We were at last advised of the day on which we would meet Mefto, for both he and ourselves had fought through successfully. The lady Yasuri, too, was well positioned with a handful of nobles and royalty from various countries. The play-offs would sort out the final positions. The wealth at stake in this session of games was breathtaking. As Konec remarked, dourly, "Let them keep their gold. We fight here for higher motives."

Yes. Yes, I know that sounds banal, juvenile almost, but if you had seen the burning determination of these people of Konec's and understood what they were prepared to sacrifice for what they believed in, I do not think you would mock.

One of the questions to be decided before a game could begin was the notation to be used. A simple grid-reference, or the English notation where squares are named from their superior pieces, were in use, as was the typically Kregan system in which each drin, having its own name, gives drin co-ordinates. Well. As you may imagine, Mefto in the preliminary planning stages insisted on using his system. Konec, who in other times might well have argued with the authority of a stiff-necked kov, gravely assented.

We didn't give the chances of an arbora feather in the Furnace Fires of Inshurfraz what rules were used, just so we could get our swords at the cramph. But Dav screwed his eyes up.

"Do not agree too hastily to everything, Konec. The rast will suspect. I have the nastiest of itches that tells me he guesses we harbor plots against him—"

"You say so?"

"I do not say so. Just that I have this itch."

By this time I had formed enough of an opinion of Dav Olmes to respect his itches of intuition.

During this period when we all fenced consistently in the sanded enclosure at the rear of the Blue Rokveil I took much delight in bouts with Bevon. We used the wooden swords, the weight and feel nicely balanced to simulate the real article. With the rudis Bevon and I dealt each other many a shrewd buffet. He was a strong swordsman, blunt and workmanlike. His skill improved daily as he learned the tricks, his dogged face clamped with effort, the grip-jawed look lowering and determined.

Some of his history, clearly, he had not revealed, although he did mention that his uncle had been a paktun. I caught a glimpse of many a warm summer evening when uncle and nephew would steal away down to the bottom pasture and then go at it, hammer and tongs with their wooden swords; and, later, of the tall stories the scarred old mercenary would tell the boy. But, all the same, Bevon's main interest then and now lay in Jikaida, the purity of the game, the disciplined concentration that drove out every other thought, the sheer intellectual challenge.

"You hit a man shrewdly, Jak," he said once, after we desisted from a session and sought ale, wiping our foreheads with the yellow towels. "By Spag the Junct," he said, having picked up that beauty from Dav. "I swear your sword obeys your inmost spirit without thought. I never saw the last passage at all."

"It is a pretty one." I sliced the wooden sword about. "Look, like this. And, as to the sword and the spirit being one, yes, you have the right of it. Thought is too slow."

Although, I said to myself, I had thought when fighting Mefto the Kazzur. Aye, and the thought never put into practice...

Bevon looked troubled as we drank. "This so-called plan. It is suicide, and that I do not like. Yet it seems I can see no other sure course."

"Well, there has to be. Or, as some of my friends would say: We must saddle a leem to catch a ponsho."

He eyed me. "Aye. And I have noticed that Kov Konec and Vad Dav Olmes speak with you in a way they do not with others. Me, they expect miracles from in Jikaida. But you, I think they see in you something that perhaps—" He paused, and drank.

I made no direct response. But it was true. For the simple paktun I

299

appeared to be, these powerful men handled me with great attention. I know Konec listened to Dav. Perhaps they, at the least, could see something in this Jak the Paktun that was a faint and far off echo of Dray Prescot, Krozair of Zy.

I prayed Zair that this was so.

Some of the party from Mandua went to see Execution Jikaida. Most of us stayed away. When criminals were sentenced to death, as opposed to being sentenced to take part in Kazz-Jikaida, there still remained a chance. They took the part of pieces on the board. When they were taken, their execution happened, there and then, the taking piece striking them down. The Bowmen of Loh maintained order. And there was the chance that they might not be taken in a game. They could go onto the board, with many a wary glance to the position they had drawn, and hope. After all, many a game has been settled in just a few dramatic moves...

One aspect of Execution Jikaida most unlikely ever to be found in Kazz-Jikaida was that, despite the blood-letting, real games of Jikaida still could be played. And one aspect of Kazz-Jikaida most unlikely to be found in Execution Jikaida—although sometimes this, too, was enforced—was the sight of the player taking his place on the board. Usually he or she would take the part of the Pallan, sometimes of the Princess. Mefto had taken part, gleefully, as we had seen.

When the player stood upon the board his professional adviser must be near him for consultation. So the Jikaidast was carried about the board in a gherimcal, a dinky little palanquin with a hood and padded seat and carrying poles. Too much ornamentation was generally considered vulgar; but there were examples finely decorated in precious metals and ivory and silks. Each would contain a conveniently slanted board with holes in the squares and pegged pieces for play so that the Jikaidast might keep track of what plans were afoot. Also there would be reference books, and, most important, shelves for food and drink. Slaves carried the gherimcal about the board, always keeping in close contact with the player and the pretty girls who carried the orders for the moves to the pieces.

In the game for which so much anticipatory apprehension was felt by the people from Mandua, there was no question but that Konec would play and act on the board. He would take the Pallan's part and Dav and Fropo would be Kapts. There was still some uncertainty as to the size game we would be playing, and Strom Nath might, if the game was a large variety, be a Kapt also; otherwise, he would be a Chuktar. They told me I would have to be a Chuktar, and I said that, by Havil, that was rapid promotion in any man's army, whereat they laughed.

Our nerves were fine drawn during this period. Men would suddenly laugh, and clap a fist to sword hilt, and so guffaw again, for nothing, and then turn away, and be very quiet.

Nothing was heard of the man the flier from Hamal had brought in; but Konec told us that he was confident that unless Mefto was stopped the alliance would go through and the countries of the Central Dawn Lands would fall like ripe shonages. I was not a party to the quarrel that occurred between Mefto and Konec when they met to finalize the bokkertu for the game; but the upshot was that Konec returned to tell us that it had been agreed the game would be Screetz Jikaida.

We pondered the implications.

On balance, we felt little had changed. We would have to hire men from the academies to take the places of our pieces, and they would be trained to the sword. In Screetz Jikaida all the pieces are armed with sword and shield alone, as the name suggests, and are naked but for a breechclout. There would be no spears or axes or different shields. Screetz Jikaida holds its own charm, as different and as bloody as Kazz Jikaida of the usual run.

Bevon was pleased. "Swords," he said. "Aye, that will serve."

But, all the same, we had deciphered no other plan in the mists ahead than the one which would encompass all our deaths.

In the last sennight before the game was scheduled zorca riders came in with news that the caravan that had arrived at the fort on the River of Purple Rushes would soon reach the city. One messenger rode straight to the Blue Rokveil and was closeted with Kov Konec.

When we met that evening for our usual lavish meal and general good-natured horseplay, Konec's mood was at once jovial and grim, as though he must plunge his hand into scalding water to snatch out a bag of gold.

"I have had word, certain word. Our spies have done well. If Mefto can be placed back in the velvet-lined balass box all Shanodrin will rise and expel his puppets and followers. The country is held in an iron grip; but with the threat of Mefto removed, the people will strike. Then Khorundur and Mandua will breathe easier, and the smaller states, the kovnates of Bellendur and Glyfandrin. We here, in Jikaida City, hold the key."

"We hold the sword, Konec!" growled Dav.

"Aye!" they chorused.

This news from the outside world affected me in a way different from these men of Mandua. I hungered to know what was happening in Vallia. I had not fretted over this absence, for there were good men there to run things, and Drak had returned. But, all the same, I wanted to know what was going on. There was a chance, a slender one, true, that some news of that distant island empire might have filtered down here, particularly as the people of the Dawn Lands must be aware that Vallia, far away in the north, stood shoulder to shoulder with them in the struggle against Thyllis.

Dazzling schemes of a great combination of forces marching from north and south on Hamal and crushing that empire until the pips squeaked rose in my mind. But they were dreams, dreams...

Dreams, yes. But, one day, all of Paz, this whole island and continental grouping, must unite. It must. That was the task that, more and more clearly, I saw set to my hands—and as I often thought, with the blessing of the Star Lords and the Savanti. There must be a reason why I had been brought to Kregen. Oh, of course—the Star Lords employed me as a useful tool to pull their hot chestnuts out of the fire; but they had other kregoinye I had now learned. And the Savanti, those aloof and superhuman but mortal men and women of Aphrasöe, the Swinging City, had first summoned me to Kregen for their purposes to civilize the world. And, because I had not done as they wished, I had been thrown out of Paradise—well, that was no Paradise for me now nor had been these many seasons. But, I felt with a conviction I could not justify in view of what had happened and yet clung to with stubborn will, I was here on this marvelous and terrible world of Kregen for a purpose. I had to be. If not, then it was all a sham, all of it, save Delia and the family with whom I seemed to be at such odds, them and my friends.

And then, well, they say don't dice with a four-armed fellow.

The lady Yasuri had changed her accommodation to a better class of hotel called The Star of Laybrites. The name tells you it was situated in Yellow City. There had been some business of a Rapa attempting one of her handmaids. If it had been Sishi I fancy the Rapa was nursing a dented beak right now. Happening to be taking a short cut through Yellow City—and when I say happened, I found, when I was there, I wasn't quite sure why I should be—I passed the hotel and gave a quick glance for the circlets of yellow painted stars along the arcade above. Why I had come here was made immediately plain to me.

People were passing along the avenue and giving me no attention, for I found I was wearing a blue favor. A figure staggered suddenly from a side alleyway that led to the rear of the hotel. He was stark naked. He was smothered in dust and unpleasant refuse, and straw stuck out of his hair. I recognized him at once. With a huge guffaw, and a quick snatch at the cords of my cape, I slung it off and swung it about his broad shoulders.

"By Horato the Potent! Of all the infernal—! Jak!" He grabbed the cape and pulled it about his nakedness and, at that, it only just hung down enough to be decent—just about. I still laughed. I knew exactly what he was thinking and the furious sense of frustration seething in that sharp foxy face.

And then, well, it was strange to experience this with someone else who experienced it, also.

A gorgeous scarlet and gold bird flew down the avenue and with wide spread wings cut in over the heads of the people who walked stolidly on with not so much as a single glance at the Gdoinye. Well, why not? They couldn't see this supernatural messenger and spy of the Star Lords.

Pompino the Iarvin looked up, and his face slackened off wonderfully, so that all the fury lines vanished, to be replaced by an expression of obedient wonderment.

"Pompino! Pompino!" called the bird, perching with a great feather rustling on one of the circlets of yellow stars. "You have been given no leave to abandon the Everoinye."

"But—" began Pompino.

"You know your task. You must hew to your path—"

"You stupid great onker!" I bellowed up at the bird. "What are we waiting on that stupid woman for? Let us depart from here—give us a fight, if necessary—you brainless bird!"

Pompino said something like: "Awwkk!" And he looked at me as though expecting me to be struck down in a blaze of blue fire.

Well, I might have been. But the way the Star Lords had been treating me and my recent thoughts on all the pressing work that needed to be done on Kregen braced me up powerfully.

"Dray Prescot! You onker of onkers! Hearken to your fate and submit—"

"Ask Ahrinye about that, fambly!"

"He is young and without caution, as you are. You fret on your Vallia. Rest easy on that score—"

"Rest easy! There is work to do there."

"And it is being done. Your cause prospers. But the Star Lords will not be baulked and they call upon you for a higher service."

Pompino was goggling away at me and at the Gdoinye. He'd been flung back here, just as I had been flung back to the scenes of my labors for the Star Lords when I had taken myself off. He must be annoyed; yet he could only goggle away at me as though staring at a demon from Cottmer's Caverns.

"Tell me about Vallia, you bird of ill omen."

"Why do you struggle against the Star Lords when they seek only your good? They have treated you with great kindness and you repay them with abuse and you miscall me most devilishly. Yes, your Vallia is safe as you left it. Nothing has gone wrong—"

"Has anything gone right?"

"Of course. Do you think you are irreplaceable?"

"No."

Pompino put a hand to his eyes. He was swallowing nonstop.

"Do the business here and ensure the safety of the lady Yasuri. The business of Mefto is yours alone." The scarlet feathers riffled. People were walking past all the time and no one cast so much as a glance in our direction. The Gdoinye lifted into the air. His wings beat strongly. As he had so often done he squawked down at me most rudely. And then he screeched out: "Dray Prescot, get onker, onker of onkers."

Well, we shared that, at the least. We'd established that kind of comradely insult between us, and I pondered his words.

Pompino gathered himself together. He pulled the cape more tightly about himself. It was green, I noticed, with yellow checkered borders. He stopped swallowing. He straightened his shoulders. The Gdoinye lifted high, flirted a wing, swung away and vanished over the rooftops across the avenue.

"The damned great fambly," I said.

"Jak." Pompino stopped shaking. "Jak—to talk to the Gdoinye like that— I've never heard—you might have been—I do not know..." He shook his head, goggling at me. Then: "But, Jak, he was talking about someone called Prescot. It seems to me I have heard that name—"

"Some other fellow," I said. "More likely, two other fellows. And the Gdoinye and I have an understanding. We rub along. But, one day, I'll singe his feathers for him, so help me Zair."

There, you see... Stupid intemperate boasting again.

We sauntered away and Pompino looked halfway respectable. He said, "How did you come to be so close when I was brought back?"

"Thank the Star Lords for that. I had no intention of walking this way; but I am here. And the cape; it is not mine."

He shook his head and I marveled at how quickly he had once again reconciled himself to the Star Lords' demands.

"This lady Yasuri," he said, pondering. "What is so special about her that she is so cherished?"

"She may be an old biddy, but she's not too old to have children if she wills it."

"I'm not sure—?"

"I once rescued a young loving couple out on a spree and they had a child who overturned cities and nations. He is dead now, thankfully, along with many others." How Gafard, the King's Striker, a Master Jikaidast, would have joyed to be here! And how I would welcome him, by Zair!

When Pompino heard of the Sword Jikaida coming up with Mefto he put a lean finger up and rubbed his foxy face. He looked wary.

"I do not think this thing touches my honor."

"Agreed."

He stamped his foot. "You are infuriating! What in Panachreem—?"

"Look, Pompino; you must carry out the duties of a kregoinye and that does not include being chopped. The Gdoinye gave me leave to deal with Mefto, if it is possible. That can only mean the Star Lords have an eye in that direction. But your duty lies toward the lady Yasuri."

"Duty to her! Ha!"

"She looks like a little wrinkled nut, true. But if she took off that stupid wig and let her hair loose, and washed her face with cleansing cream, and wore shapely clothes, why, many a man would delight in proving his duty to her."

"With a nose and a tongue as sharp as hers?"

"They could both be blunted, given love."

"Well, if that is what the Everoinye plan, we are in for a long and tedious wait!"

So, half-cross and half-laughing, we strolled back to the Blue Rokveil.

"As San Blarnoi says," observed Pompino as we went in to find Dav and ale. "The heart leads where the eyes follow."

The incoming caravan was due to arrive the day before the game and, expressing a wish to go down and see the entrance, I was joined by Bevon and Pompino. The others all declined. I pressed Dav; but he excused himself. He had a girl to attend to. Well, that was Dav Olmes for you, big and burly and fond of ale and women and fighting. A combination of great worth on Kregen.

The scene when we arrived presented just such a spectacle of color and noise and confusion as delights the heart. Many cities of Paz boast a Wayfarer's Drinnik, a wide expanse where the caravans form up or disperse, and we stood under a black and white checkered awning and sipped ale as we watched. The Quoffas rolled patiently along, the calsanys and ungars drew up in their long loaded strings, men dismounted from totrixes and urvivels and zorcas, all thirsty, all glowing with their safe arrival. The wagons rolled in. A group of Khibils dismounted from their freymuls, that pleasant riding animal that is often called the poor man's zorca, a bright chocolate in color with vivid streaks of yellow beneath. Willing, is a freymul, and as a mount serves well within his abilities. Pompino eyed the Khibils and then strolled off to pick up what news there was. The dust rose and the glory of the suns shot through, turning motes of gold spinning, streaming in the mingled lights of Zim and Genodras. I sipped ale and watched, and at last saw a man I fancied might be useful.

He was apim, like me, limber and tough, and as he dismounted and gave his zorca a gentle pat I caught the fiery wink of gold from the pakzhan at his throat. He was a hyr-paktun. His lance bore red and blue tufts. I rolled across carrying a spare flagon.

"Llahal, dom. Ale for news of the world." He eyed me. He licked his lips. His weapons were bright and oiled. He stood sparingly against the light of the suns.

"Llahal, dom. You are welcome." He took the flagon and drank and wiped his lips. "Now may Beng Dikkane be praised!"

"The news?"

He told me a little of what I hungered to hear. Yes, he had a third cousin who had returned from up north. Told him that paktuns were being kicked out of Vallia. He'd never been there—fought in Pandahem, though, by Armipand's gross belly, nasty stuff all jungles and swamps down to the south. Yes, Vallia was, as far as he knew, still there and hadn't sunk into the sea. They'd had revolutions, like anywhere else, and a new emperor, and there had been whispers of new and frightful secret weapons. But he knew little. His third cousin had been hit behind the ear by a steel-headed weapon he'd claimed was as long as four spears. Clearly, he was bereft of his sense, makib, for that was laughably impossible.

"Surely," I said. "My thanks, dom. Remberee."

This third-cousinly confirmation of what the Gdoinye had told me had to suffice for my comfort. Bevon and Pompino reappeared and we prepared to leave Wayfarer's Drinnik. And then the slaves toiled in.

Well. The slaves had struggled over the Desolate Waste on foot. They wore the gray slave breechclout or were naked. They were yoked and haltered. They stank. They collapsed into long limp straggles on the dust and their heads bowed and that ghastly wailing rose from them. The sound of "Grak!" smashed into the air continuously, with the crack of whips. The slavemasters were Katakis. We caught a glimpse of this dolorous arrival of the slaves and then a protruding corner of the ale booth shut off the sight.

"No," said Bevon, and there was sweat on his pug face. "No."

Pompino and I knew what he meant.

"I had news from home," said Pompino. "Well, almost home, from a town ten dwaburs away and they'd heard nothing so it must all be all right."

Such is the hunger for news of home that even the negation of news is regarded as confirmation of all rightness. We did not hurry back and stopped for a wet here and there and admired the sights. We wore swords, of course, and our brigandines, and if Bevon tended to swagger a little in imitation of Pompino, who is there who would blame him over much?

The avenue on which stood the Blue Rokveil was blocked by a line of cavalrymen, their totrixes schooled to obedience, their black and white checks hard in the brilliance of the suns. People were being held back, and a buzzing murmur of speculation rose. We pushed forward, puzzled.

"Llanitch!" bellowed a bulky Deldar, sweating. At his order to halt we stopped, looking at him inquiringly. He shouldered across and people skipped out of his way. Just beyond the line of cavalrymen the hotel lifted, its ranks of windows bright, its blue flags fluttering. People craned to see. The Deldar eased back to his men, keeping them face front. We moved to a vantage point and so looked on disaster.

They say Trip the Thwarter, who is a minor spirit of deviltry, takes delight in upsetting the best-laid plans. We saw the dismounted vakkas hauling out their prisoners. There were many swords and spears in evidence, and no chances were being taken, for these men being taken up into custody were notorious and possessed of fearful reputations. We saw Kov Konec being prodded out, dignified, calm, his hands bound. We saw Dav turn on a swod and try to kick him, snarling his hatred, and so being thumped back into line. The swods ringed in the important people of Mandua, Fropo the

Curved, Strom Nath Resdurm, Nath the Fortroi and others. Only the lesser folk were not taken up.

We stared, appalled.

"Treason against the Nine Masked Guardians," a man in the crowd told us.

"A plot to murder them all in their beds," amplified his wife, a plump, jolly person carrying a wicker basket filled with squishes in moist green leaves.

"Lucky for us Prince Mefto discovered the plot in time to warn the Masked Nine. By Havil! I'd send 'em all to the Execution Jikaida, aye, and put them all in the center drin!"

We stood as though frozen by the baleful eyes of the Gengulas of legend. Konec saw us.

With a single contemptuous jerk he snapped the thongs binding his wrists. He stuck both arms out sideways, level with his ears. Then he drew them in and thrust them out again level with his hips. He brought his hand around to the base of his spine and swept it in a wide circling arc up over his head. The pantomime was quite clear. Then—then he drew his forefinger across his throat, forcefully, viciously.

I remained absolutely still.

The guards leaped on him then; but he did not resist as they tied his hands again. He had delivered his message, a chilling and demanding message. His eyes blazed on me.

Between files of the totrix cavalry Konec and his people were led away to imprisonment.

The plot against Mefto the Kazzur was stillborn.

"What—?" said Bevon. He looked bewildered.

"It is all down to you, Jak," said Pompino.

We were alone and friendless in Jikaida City, and it was all down to me to halt this glittering Prince Mefto the Kazzur in his ambitions and to prevent the total destruction of Vallia. As this thought struck in so shrewdly there rose up before my eyes the phantom vision of Mefto, brandishing his five swords and beating down in irresistible triumph.

Twenty

Death Jikaida

"You must be a fambly, of a surety," said Nath the Swordsman, screwing up his scarred face in hopeless wonderment. "But if you wish to act against

Mefto, that is suitable for me. I do not give the lady Yasuri more than one chance in ten."

"You are finding the pieces for the lady Yasuri. Put me down on the list."

"And me," said Bevon, at my side.

Pompino had disappeared. I harbored no grudge; this was no affair of his and he was mightily conscious of his duty for the Star Lords. We stood in Nath the Swordsman's room that looked out upon the inner square of his rambling premises. Men and women were being put through their paces out there, and the quick flitter and flutter of sword blades filled the dusty area. The room was plainly furnished and contained as its centerpiece a finely executed picture of Kurin, delineated as some long-dead artist of Jikaida City had visualized him, blade in hand, in the guard position and, as this was Havilfar, covering himself with a shield. The picture served as the focus of a kind of shrine, with flowers and atras and incense burning, which exuded a stink into the room.

"The lady Yasuri was fortunate in the misfortune of Konec," said Nath. His gaze seldom left the people practicing out there, and he would suddenly leap up and go striding out, yelling, to reprimand some poor wight whose clumsy technique had aroused Nath's displeasure. The women out there were all strapping girls, of course, for they fight hard in Vuvushi Jikaida.

"Yes," said Bevon.

The league tables led up to the final tournament and Yasuri had placed third, because she had already lost to Konec. That was her only defeat. With the absence of Konec, who was due to play Mefto in the final, Yasuri had been switched in. We were here to act as two of her pieces. Neither of us could see any other way of getting to Prince Mefto.

I had, in my old intemperate way, started to make a sally toward his hotel and had fought a few of his folk trying to get through. I had not succeeded and the darker the veil drawn over that chapter of misfortunes the better. I had had the sense to wear a mask. Now we presented ourselves at Nath en Screetzim's premises and he welcomed us like water in the Ochre Limits.

Once we had been accepted, the formalities went through like sausages on a greased plate and very quickly we found ourselves joining the lumpen gaggle Yasuri had been able to find. We waited in a long, wide, tall hall with arrow-slits for windows far higher than a man could jump. We were in the heart of the Jikaidaderen. The game was to be a private one. The public would be able to see most of the other tournament games; but they would not be permitted here to see the final. That they were prepared to accept this indicates something of the obedience rife in Jikaida City. We rubbed shoulders with criminals, with men who had been delegated this duty, slaves fighting for their freedom and few, very few, men who fought for the lady Yasuri.

The atmosphere in that anteroom to the games clogged on the palate, the stink of sweat, the stink of fear—and the silly bravado men put on in times like these to mask their deeper feelings. Well, Bevon and I endured. We studied the Jikaida pieces waiting to go on. We tried to pick the stout from the weak, the brave from those who would be unable to perform adequately through fear—everyone knew the penalty for running. I said to Bevon: "One or two will run, I think, and welcome a Lohvian shaft through them rather than a chopped-up death at the hands of Mefto's bully boys."

"Yet some look capable. That Chulik, he's here for slitting the throat of a Rapa. And that group of Fristles, and see those Khibils? They will fight."

Rumors and buzzes swept through the men. There was weak ale to drink and no wine. There was ample food. We understood that the lady Yasuri had obtained the services of a lady Jikaidasta whose name, we gathered, was Ling-li-Lwingling, or something like that. Bevon listened to the swift gabble of a Fristle, and turned to me. I did not know if he was laughing or cursing.

"Who do you think Mefto has as his Jikaidast?"

"Oh," I said. "Well, Bevon, now you have a personal grudge in it doubled."

"Aye."

Och slaves at last brought in the equipment. These formalities differed markedly for us from our previous experiences. Then we had been part of a noble's entourage, playing for his honor and glory; now we were assembled from the academies of the sword and from the prisons and stews. The bagnios supplied their freight. The lady Yasuri apparently relied entirely on the resources of Jikaida City for her pieces, for we saw none of the small bodyguard she kept up. As for the equipment, that was simple. A blue breechclout, a thraxter and a shield. Plus a headband decked with varying numbers of blue feathers and, for some of the superior pieces, blue favors on sashes. Bevon and I each received a reed-laurium* with two blue feathers. This marked us as Deldars.

The swords were thraxters and Bevon and I, by arrangement as volunteers, received our own weapons. The shields were laminated wood, bronze rimmed but not faced, and were smaller than the regulation Havilfarese swod's shield, being something like twenty-seven inches high by sixteen inches wide, and were rectangular.

The shields were painted solid blue with white rank markings as appropriate, and a fellow would take the shield fitting his position as a piece when he left the substitutes bench.

The lady Yasuri had been obliged to play blue, as she was filling in and, no doubt, overjoyed at her own good fortune. She was a Yellow adherent, I knew; but the glory and profit of winning meant more to her, and it is

---

* reed: headband; laurium: rank.

proper that a Jikaida player should take either color for the experience of the different diagonals of play.

Wrapping the blue breechclout about me and drawing the end up between my legs and fastening it off with the blue cord provided reminded me, with a pang, of the times I had gone through this first stage of dressing with the brave old scarlet. But now there would be no mesh steel, no kax, no leather jerkin; now the blue breechclout was all. Well, by Zair! And wasn't this what was required? Wasn't it high time I went swinging into action wearing just a breechclout and with a sword in my fist?

"By the Black Chunkrah!" I said. "I think Mefto—" But I did not finish the thought. Black and white checks filled the room and we were being herded out. The smell of fear stank on the air, and, also, the sweat of men determined to fight before they died.

We all received a goblet of wine—a thick, heavy, red variety like the deep purple wine of Hamal called Malab's Blood. I do not care for it; but, by Krun! it went down sweetly enough then, I can tell you.

The preliminary ceremonies went as usual, with the prayers and the chanted hymns and the sacrifices. When we came out of the long stone tunnel from the gloom onto the brilliance of the board, the brightness of the light smote our eyes. Ruby and jade radiance drenched the playing board. This was a very select, very refined Jikaida board. There was no noisy hum from an excited crowd of plebs. Around the board and raised on a plinth extended a broad terrace, shielded by black and white checkered awnings. The thrones facing each other at either end were ornate. On the terrace were set small tables and reclining couches, and the high ones of LionardDen lolled there, waited on by slaves, sipping their drinks and daintily picking at light delicacies. They had chairs which could be carried around the terrace by slaves so that they might watch the play from the best positions. No action would begin until the representative of the Nine Masked Guardians was satisfied that all the spectators were in position for the finest view.

"By the Resplendent Bridzilkelsh!" growled a Brokelsh near us. "Why don't they get on with it."

"There is all the time in the world to die, as Rhapaporgolam the Reiver of Souls knows full well," a Rapa told him.

The Brokelsh spat, which heartened me.

A Pachak hefted his shield in his two left hands. "I have given the lady Yasuri my nikobi," he said in that serious way of Pachaks. "And by Papachak the All-Powerful! I shall honor my pledge. But I think this is like to be the last fight for us."

The Chulik slid his sword neatly under his left arm and then polished up his tusks with a spittled thumb. "By Likshu the Treacherous!" he said. "I shall take many of them down to the Ice Floes of Sicce with me."

"Numi the Hyrjiv fights with us," said one of the Fristles. "But I wish I had my scimitar instead of this thraxter."

So, as we waited to march out with our backs as straight as we could contrive and take our places on the board, we called upon our gods and our guardian spirits. This is human nature. And how the exotic variety of Kregen can respond! Truly is it said, on Kregen are joys for all men's hearts.

As we marched out we presented a spectacle at which, I suppose, many a person of limited intellect would scoff, dubbing us a collection of menagerie-men. Yet we were all men, all human beings, and we marched out to fight for our lives.

Even the Chulik shared some reflection of those feelings.

And, there was among our number a single Kataki.

"By the Triple Tails of Targ the Untouchable!" The Kataki swished his bladeless tail about like a leem in a temper. "Would that Takroti would slit all their gizzards!"

"Careful with your tail," snapped one of the Fristles. "By Odifor, you nearly tripped me."

The guards stepped in with upraised bludgeons to separate out the violently brawling combatants in the ensuing melee. Truly, we presented a horrifying and a pathetic spectacle as we marched out.

As we stepped onto the board we saw that the Princess's square was already occupied. The woman standing waiting wore a long white gown of sensil, lavishly embroidered with blue and yellow and black and white checkers. An enormous crowning plume of blue feathers rose above her head, surrounded by tufts of blue. She glittered with gems. As I passed her, and the carrying chair for her Jikaidasta, I saw her face. Most of the lines were gone, her flesh filled out, and I guessed many of those lines had been caused by apprehension for the journey across the Desolate Waste. Her hair was a dark brown, curled, and I caught its perfume. Her shape in the white sensil was a world away from the shape in the shiny black bombazine and lace.

She saw me and a muscle twitched in her cheek. But she made no movement and ignored me. That suited me. I was not here to fight for the lady Yasuri, but to fight against her opponent.

The eight slave girls who carried the Jikaidasta's chair were Gonells. The male Gons habitually shave off their white hair, believing it shames them. But some peoples of the Gon race take a proper pride in the silver hair of their females, and these eight Gonells were splendid girls, well-formed, clad in wispy blue, and their silver hair shone lustrously, sweeping in deep waves to their waists.

The occupant of the carrying chair was invisible to me and the gherimcal rested on its four legs, carved like prychans. We marched past and so fanned out to take up our positions.

As the trumpets blew and the Suns of Scorpio shone down on us, we Ranked our Deldars.

The game opened with Mefto taking the first move and soon his pieces were extending down the board toward us, like rivers of lava from a volcano. Our own lines extended toward Yellow. Truly, Mefto's pieces looked splendid in their yellow breechclouts and with tufty masses of yellow feathers. Their shields formed a field of daffodils. He had picked his best men, no doubt of that; they were brawny, tough, adept. Like us, they were a mixture of diff and apim, and they were confident of victory.

The beautiful girls in their wisps of clothing ran about the board carrying the orders to the pieces. Men moved in obedience and soon the opening clashes began. Swords flashed and blood flowed.

We played Death Jikaida.

It chanced that I was formed into a diagonal line with a swod each side, and there I remained. Mefto had not put in an appearance on the board. I could just see him in the Yellow throne, giving his orders and the stylor below repeating them to the girls who ran so fleetly, their limbs rosy and glowing, or brown or black and splendid in the light. The lines formed and pieces fought and were taken or took, to be tossed back into the velvet-lined balass box or to be replaced from the substitutes' bench. The opening proved to be the Princess's Kapt's Gambit Accepted, and my diagonal remained fast, the action taking place on the right wing.

The young swod by me licked his lips. He was apim, a lithely built lad, without the bulky toughness of the fighting man who has campaigned for seasons on end. Despite the regulations, we talked, as the pieces did. What could the representative of the Nine Masked Guardians do about that now? Have us all shafted?

There were things he could order and which the black-clad men would carry out; but this infringement of the rules was minor.

"I only borrowed the chicken," said this lad, by name Tobi the Knees. "Mother was starving and Father—well, I do not know what happened to him. I would have given the next chicken back, as I always do."

So he had been taken up by the Watch and condemned, and sent to the academy to be trained for Kazz-Jikaida. He came from the teeming sections of the city in which many poor folk eked out a precarious living. There were too many of these poor quarters. The contrast between their squalor, and the lavishness of Yellow or Blue City, condemned the Nine Guardians— at least, in my eyes. As for the Foreign Quarters, where visitors who were impartial as to color stayed, they were as palatial in their hotels as the palaces of the City nobility. Tobi the Knees was not alone in his misery.

"I was going to be a wheelwright—always get work as a wheelwright. And I can shape the wood perfectly. But, mother was ill and I lost my job, and—"

"You borrowed a chicken."

"They got the feathers back!"

"I see."

"And they showed me this sword and this shield and I can make a pass or two. But I still don't understand it all."

"Keep the shield up and keep sticking the sword out, Tobi. You'll make a bladesman yet."

"But I—" He swallowed. He was keeping up a brave front and smiling and swishing his thraxter about; but he was scared, frightened clear through to his ib.

A flash of legs and a wisp of purple drapery and a girl's clear voice saying: "Swod to vault to Prychan D Four."

Prychan Drin was the third drin toward Yellow on the left of the board. Dermiflon was the home drin on that side, and then Strigicaw Drin. These drins do not appear in Poron Jikaida. Tobi the Knees looked. He gripped his sword. Then, without a word to me or the girl he walked up along the diagonal line. Prychan D Four was unoccupied. Tobi came down off the end of the zeunt and stood on the square and looked around. He was right out in the front of the Blues.

I just hoped Yasuri and her lady Jikaidasta knew what they were doing.

D Four is a blue square.

Over on the right of the board Mefto made a bold advance, vaulting a Hikdar down through Neemu Drin to the end of Wersting Drin, and as Yasuri brought a Hikdar across to Boloth Drin to cover, so Mefto advanced a Chuktar. I began to think the crucial action would take place over there, on the front between Wersting and Boloth Drins. I hoped so. I didn't give a damn who won this silly game; I owed Konec and his comrades from Mandua and I owed Vallia to make sure of Mefto when he appeared on the board.

The charming little girls with their blue or yellow feathers who carry the orders are equipped with long light wands of red-painted wood wrapped in blue or yellow streamers. With these they tap the pieces on the shoulders if, as so often happens, the men are staring in sick fascination at the fighting. So I felt the tap, and turned, and the girl said: "Deldar to Prychan E Three."

I vaulted. This placed me diagonally ahead of Tobi. He greeted me as though we'd met on an Ice Floe in You Know Where.

The next instant Yellow's orders were carried out. A fellow wearing the Yellow favors and feathers stalked across the squares from Krulch Drin toward me. Mefto had decided to put an end to this advance.

I recognized the Yellow piece at once. He was acting the part of a Chuktar; but I had last seen him eating palines in Friendly Fodo's Weapons Shop. He halted for a moment on E Two, for as a Chuktar he had come straight on, and then, instantly, flung himself on me.

As his sword beat down on my upraised shield I fancied I'd stir him up a little.

"Why, Llahal, Trinko. Fancy meeting you here."

His muscular body shielded with that shiny carapace across his back bore on, and his Moltingur face, all eating proboscis and feelers and terrifying faceted eyes, showed shock. I thumped forward with the shield, let the thraxter snout to the side and below. The resistance was soggy, and then the blade slid in. I stepped back.

He toppled over and his tunnel mouth emitted a long hissing wheeze.

The slaves in their red tunics ran out with a stretcher and carted him away. Other slaves raked the blood and sprinkled fresh blue sand. There was no lifting uproar from the refined onlookers lounging in their chairs along the terrace. Yasuri made her move.

The red wand touched me again and the blue streamers tickled my face.

"Deldar to take Hikdar on Prychan C Three."

This fellow, a Rapa, had watched the previous contest with his blue-feathered beak stuck high in the air. The yellow feathers in his reed-laurium outweighed his racial feathers. I stalked across and we set to.

He was good—all Mefto's men were good—and the shields gonged like pale echoes of the Bells of Beng Kishi before I slid him and so stretched him out on the blue sand.

The red-clad slaves bore him off. Still there was no sound from the terrace and I did not expect any. They were connoisseurs up there, lolling in their fancy chairs and sipping their wines.

Yasuri, as was her privilege because I was the attacking piece, recalled me then. I trailed off to the substitutes bench with a word for Tobi as I went.

"That's how it's done, Tobi. Keep your chin tucked in and your shield up. Jikai!"

"It is to you the Jikai, Jak."

What could I say? I gave him a hard nod of encouragement and walked slowly back across the blue and yellows.

Up to this point the game had been reasonably equal, for Yasuri's scratch team had fought like wild leems when it came to push of pike. But the tension would increase with each succeeding move, as the pieces drew closer together and the skillful maneuvering gave way to the blood bath.

The palanquin of the lady Jikaidasta rested quietly near Yasuri, who, as the Aeilssa, had not so far been forced to move. As I walked back Yasuri looked at me. "Well done, Jak. I give you the Jikai." Only lower and upper case initial letters can attempt to indicate the quality of meaning in the same word here.

"Watch his center, lady. I recall Scatulo favored a thrust—"

A voice spoke from the palanquin. The golden cords of the carrying-chair's curtains loosened. The voice said: "Go to the substitutes' bench, tikshim, and do not presume." And the curtains at the side parted and a woman's face looked out.

Red hair, she had, a glowing rippling auburn mass piled atop a small face, a pale face with the sheen of ivory of Chem. Her eyes were blue, and direct and challenging. Small her mouth, and scarlet, and pursed above a firm rounded chin. Beautiful? Yes, beautiful, like a stalking chavonth, lissom and slender and feline. Even then I did not liken her to a leem.

I halted stock-still at once. I was very near her chair. The silver-haired Gonells waited, stupidly transfixed by the blood and violence—and, at that, not stupidly. It was we who partook of the blood and violence who were the truly stupid. So I stood, not going to the bench as she had so impolitely ordered me, using that word tikshim that so infuriates those to whom it is addressed, being considerably worse than the condescending "my man" of Earth.

"I was talking to the lady Yasuri." I spoke softly.

The Jikaidasta's face resembled a mask at first sight; the sheen of ivory of Chem, the delineation of line of lip and jaw and nose, the flesh firm and compact as though carved from that smoothest and mellowest of ivories. But, as I stood there, a trifle lumpen and boorish, a faint mottling of color appeared on her cheekbones. She had a most perfect bone structure, fine-drawn, distinct, and in no single place could be seen any sagging of flesh. The effort with which she controlled herself was quite admirable, quite; here was a lady used to having her own way, and highly conscious of her own worth.

"Do not allow the blood to rule your head just because you have won two encounters. This is a game to win."

"You think you will win it—against Mefto?"

"If the creatures we have to fight for us do as well as you then perhaps. Nothing else will do."

I felt the pang in me. What I had done—would that be any use against Mefto the Kazzur?

And then, well, I was a trifle wrought up. So I said, "You are the Jikaidasta they call Ling-li-Lwingling. You are from Loh."

Three men in black appeared on the board heading in our direction. I will not describe the instruments they bore.

Yasuri said: "Be off with you, Jak."

"Aye, my lady." And then, before I went, I said: "We shall win today, by fair means or foul."

Ling-li-Lwingling, of Loh, let the side curtains fall back into place and I trotted off to the substitutes bench. I think, if the three men in black had followed me and attempted to use their instruments I would have dealt with them, not recking the consequences; but they looked malevolently, and then turned away.

The man chosen to replace the piece I had acted on the blue square was a Khibil. Yasuri was bringing her left flank into play with a nicely cal-culated precision of timing that, had this been other than Death Jikaida, would have placed Mefto's pieces in a cramped and unfavorable position. I fancied the lady Jikaidasta's hand was in this strategy. But this was Death Jikaida. Mefto sent a hulking swaggerer of a fellow, acting as a swod, to deal with the Khibil Deldar. The Khibil was carted away, dripping blood on the sand. The victor bore ghastly wounds and Mefto would quite clearly replace him. Yasuri responded by switching her attack, hoping to get our Chulik into action, and then—and at last, at long last—a response was elic-ited from those languid watchers on the terrace.

With the accompaniment of a long sigh susurrating around him, Prince Mefto the Kazzur strode onto the board.

Useless for me to race toward him. I had almost the length of the board to go, and long before I reached the rast I'd be shafted by those vigilant Bowmen of Loh. No, I had to be on a square and near the cramph before I could break all the rules and leap for his throat. He stood on his square and looked about. He preened himself. Well, he was a master bladesman and I would not deny him that. While I would admit I did not know his full character and guessed there was good in him, somewhere, he did seem to me to vaunt his prowess, to take a dark pride from his own gift that, some-how, repulsed me. This is subjective. May Zair forgive me if I swagger in the same way. I do not think I do.

And, this was strange. The great swordsmen I have known usually revere their gift, assessing it humbly as a gift of the gods, however much sweat they distribute in training and understanding the Disciplines. Perhaps I was still sore and vengeful, still filled with resentment. I sat down, and watched as Mefto went to work.

Tobi the Knees stood next in line. Mefto declared his move and pounced. He did not slay Tobi in a simple quick passage as he could have done. He toyed with him, and feigned alarm that he was under pressure, and poor Tobi thus drawn on pressed hard, and was cut, and then cut again, and so, all bewildered and uncomprehending, was sliced into pieces.

I suppose the old intemperate Dray Prescot would have leaped up and gone hurling forward. He'd have swatted the flying arrows away in the old fashion as the Krozairs of Zy do. But I do not think that maniac of a fight-ing man would have lived to reach Mefto the Kazzur, let alone have had time to cross swords with him.

The Dray Prescot that was me sat lumpen on the bench. But a change did come over me. As the remains of Tobi were carried away and the blue and yellow sand was sprinkled I felt I would not wait too long. And the game went badly for us. Our Kataki came up against Mefto, and his tail sliced this way and that, emptily, and Mefto laughed and his own tailhand gripped the Kataki's bladeless tail as he sank his thraxter into his belly.

But our Chulik fought well, and dispatched his men, and Yasuri recalled him. We were being pressed back now, and over the lines of blue and yellow men the yellow of Mefto's pieces vaulted long into our home drins. That unique vaulting move in Jikaidish is zeunt, and the Yellows were zeunting in on us with a vengeance.

The carrying chair pressed close to Yasuri, and the two ladies argued long and fiercely over their next move, and the water dripped in the clepsydra and time fleeted away. The Blues out there began to cast anxious eyes toward the water-clock. The water dripped. The ladies conferred. Some of the pieces began to beat their swords against their shields. The hollow drumroll made no difference to the ladies. Still they talked. And the water dripped.

We all saw the long lenken arm of the gong lift ready to descend with a resonant boom against the brazen gong. Then a purple wisp of gossamer and a flash of spritely legs and a girl was off to order the move. It was made before the gong struck. But even as the Chuktar ordered to move complied, the gong crashed out—too late.

"Well," said Bevon next to me. "I do not wish to be on the board if the ladies do that again."

"Nor me, by Odifor!" quoth the Fristle next to us on the bench. Sweat stank on the air, and both ladies used perfume bottles. Move followed move, and it was clear that Mefto had sized up the play and was ruthlessly pushing everything forward, not caring for finesse, just using the superior skills of his fighting men. Our ranks thinned. It was soon perfectly clear that we were going to lose, for a set-up was approaching in which the Yellow Pallan could sweep down in a long zeunt and coming off the vault turn sharply and so pin the Princess. Yasuri saw it and was helpless. Her every move was beaten by superior swordplay.

Yes, I know—this was an example of the futility of Kazz-Jikaida, and a confirmation of the pure Jikaida player's views.

But, do not forget, this was Death Jikaida. As the final move in Mefto's play was made, a long and satisfied sigh rippled up from the terrace. The men and women up there, sipping their delicate wines, perfumed lace at their noses, appreciated what they were seeing.

Prince Mefto, acting as the Yellow Pallan, made the last zeunt in person. He came off the vault opposite the Princess and his next move would capture her. She threw in our Chulik. He did well, he fought bravely; but he died. He died on Mefto's blade.

Now it was Yellow's move. As the winning defender, Mefto could not replace himself; but everyone present knew he had no intention of doing that. He was unmarked. Glitteringly in the sunshine he stood there, a golden figure of superb poise and accomplishment. He made his move.

In a loud, ringing voice, he called: "Pallan captures Aeilssa. Hyrkaida! Do you bare the throat?"

Yasuri drew herself up, a diminutive figure yet shining and oddly impressive in her long white gown with the tall blue feathers nodding over her head.

"I do not bare the throat! En Screetzim nalen Aeilssa!"

The Princess's Swordsman!

Her prerogative, available only in Kazz-Jikaida, and she had taken it—as, indeed, she must. Mefto knew that. He smiled. We all saw that smile, small and tight and filled with genuine pleasure. Mefto was a bladesman who loved to fight, who enjoyed his work, and who had never met his master.

The man who had been waiting all this time as the Princess's Swordsman started up. His face was green. He was apim. His eyes protruded grotesquely, and glistened like gouged-out eyes on a fishmonger's slab. With a shriek he threw his shield away and ran. He had no idea where he was running. He just fled from horror.

In a blundering crazed gallop he ran over the blue and yellows and the long Lohvian shaft skewered him through the back and another pierced him through the throat and as he fell a third punctured into and through one of those ghastly staring eyes.

His shield still rocked on its face in the mingled sunlight.

Bevon stood up.

"I think I shall see what I may do against this—"

I pulled him by his blue breechclout.

"Stay, Bevon the Reckless!"

So it was I, Dray Prescot, Prince of Onkers, who stepped forward and picked up the fallen shield with its proud marks of the Princess's Swordsman and walked straight and purposefully onto the blue and yellow squares of the board of Death Jikaida to face a man I knew had the beating of me in swordplay.

Twenty-one

The Princess's Swordsman

Traditionally in Kazz-Jikaida whenever the Princess called on her Swordsman to fight for her the drums rolled. Black and white checkered tabards, black and white checkered drum cloths, all rippled and flowed as the drummers plied their drumsticks. The rataplan hammered out. Long thunderous rolls and flourishes, repeated and repeated, roared and boomed over the Jikaida board. And I walked forward, almost in a dream, feeling the blood in my head and the weight of the shield and the heft of the sword and the grip of the sand beneath my naked feet.

These were physical feelings. They bore in on me. They were tangible and real, like the sweat that beaded my forehead and trickled down my face from under the reed-laurium, like the taste of blood and sweat on the air. Physical, material impressions: the glitter of burnished steel, the gloating faces of the privileged onlookers as they crowded from their chairs to catch a closer look at this climactic butchery, the waft of a tiny breeze on my heat-soaked face—how refreshing that breeze, how vividly it brought back pungent memories of other days, of the quarterdeck of a seventy-four, of the scrap of decking of a swifter, a swordship, and the wind in my face and all the seas of two worlds! But I was pent in this stone-walled enclosure, this amphitheatre of death, and I recalled the Jikhorkdun of Huringa, and felt again the concussion of blows given and taken, and the leem's tail and the blood, and all the time as these jangling memories sparked through my head so I walked quietly and steadily out over the blue and yellows to take up my position beside the lady Yasuri.

"En Screetzim nalen Aeilssa! Bratch!" She called again, briskly, for she had not taken her gaze off Mefto, and did not turn, and she waited for her champion to stand at her side.

"I am here, lady," I said, and she turned, and saw me.

"Jak. Fight well. Fight well to the death—"

"Aye, lady, I shall fight as well as I am able and as Zair strengthens my sinews and gives cunning to my fist. And to the death, as it seems. But, lady, I do not fight for you."

She flinched. What she had thought I do not know. But she flinched back, and a look of pain crossed her face.

"This is a game to you, lady. A mere pastime, lady. So that you may wear the diadem of triumph, lady. But the drums roll and blood will be spilled and men will die, and not for your sake, lady."

The curtains of the carrying-chair rustled back. The ivory white face looked out and the glory of the suns caught in the red Lohvian hair. "Still your tongue, tikshim. You are condemned to fight, so fight and do not chatter."

I regarded her as I stood there, waiting for the drumroll to end. I did not look at Mefto—not yet. Ling-li-Lwingling put a hand as white as her face, as slender as a missal, to the golden cord and her fingers toyed with the golden tassel. I knew who she was, now—rather, I knew what she was. The drums rolled. And I said: "Ling-li-Lwingling. By the Seven Arcades, woman, you are a Witch of Loh!"

"Yes, Jak the Condemned. I am a Witch of Loh, and better for you to—"

"Save your pretty threats, Witch. I would give you the Sana; but other and more pressing matters await."

319

Her red red mouth widened. I did not think she knew how to smile.

"Your fears for Vallia are well-founded—you will fight for the lady Yasuri—and you will fight for me!"

I felt the whole enormous expanse of the Jikaida board tilt beneath me, and coalesce into the single square upon which I stood. I noticed it was a yellow square. Ling-li's smile slowly died and her face resumed that fixed foreboding expression as though expertly carved from solid ivory of Chem.

The long-drawn drumroll ended.

Absolute silence engulfed the Kazz-Jikaida board.

And I looked squarely upon Prince Mefto the Kazzur.

Arrogance and power and pride, yes, of course, they were all there, stamped upon him indelibly by his own prowess. I tried to see more. Men and women are more than mere bundles of flesh and blood hung on bones and walking the world in the light and darkness; this Mefto was a man, a five-handed Kildoi, and yet a human being. His presence smote me as a shell, a hard and shiny yellow carapace concealing the humanity within.

The vivid sensory impressions bombarding me as the drumroll rattled to silence contained all of the physical world; I dare not seek to pry into the world of feeling, of emotion, of fear or courage. I was here. Was not that enough?

Yet feeling decided all. Physical sensations were colored by the emotions, so I tried to look past the blue and yellow and the waiting silence and the spectators and the Jikaida pieces, past Yasuri and Ling-li and Mefto, tried to peer into the darkest depths beneath myself.

To find oneself... In that moment even the central core of existence sought its meaning. I was a Krozair of Zy. Did that matter so much?

Mefto's voice lifted, high and hard and challenging.

"I know you, apim!"

I said nothing.

Perhaps, had the question been put to me, I could not have said anything.

But, at the very end of that somber tunnel there might be a light. It was just possible. All I had to remember was one single fact in all the universe: I was Dray Prescot.

That was all.

I am Dray Prescot.

Mefto twirled his sword with great dexterity, shoved up his shield and with a jovial bladesman's bellow, charged.

We fought.

Useless to try to peer past the physical—the feelings must come of their own accord. Our blades met and scraped and clung and parted. The power in his muscles was a dynamic force. It was sword and shield against sword and shield. Oh, yes, he had two left hands to grip his shield and thus afford a superior leverage; but as we fought and circled, and sought the openings, and thrust and recovered to the gong-notes of steel on shield, so I accepted my fate. My only advantage, I thought, lay in that belief I had that I was a shade faster than he was. That was all. But he was a marvel. Often and often have I said that about swordsmen I have fought; but this Mefto the Kazzur was a marvel among marvels.

This marvel went about cutting me up as he went about cutting up all his victims, as he had chopped Tobi the Knees. But I resisted. The thraxters flamed in the mingled streaming lights of the Suns of Scorpio. The sand beneath our feet spurted blue dust; for we fought for the square on which the Blue Princess had taken her stand, the Princess's Square, and this would be hyrkaida when I lost.

For I felt I would lose.

The feeling appeared to me like a strange object in some precious golden-bound balass chest, to be taken out and examined and pondered over. A new experience. A thrilling vibration along nerves and sinews, a dark space in the mind...

Although I took no notice of her, I knew that Yasuri, who had moved back from her square, would be watching this combat with glowing eyes, her lip caught between her teeth, and, probably, her hands clenched over her breast. What the Witch of Loh, Ling-li-Lwingling, was doing I did not know, nor cared; setting out the pieces for a new game, probably.

Mefto the Kazzur sliced me along the right bicep; not deeply enough to hurt, just to draw blood, just to open the scoring. I had not touched him. He cut me again, and I found his thraxter a leaping silver flame, torturing, dazzling, infuriating. I kept myself inwardly, holding in to myself. We circled again, seeking the advantage that was not there, for the circumscribed lines of the blue square hemmed us in with honor. The technique—more a trick, really—I had pondered during the fight by the caravan might serve. But Mefto must be primed before I could use that last desperate throw.

Thinking clogged reactions; the sword must live with the body and become a part of the living being, free and uncontaminated by lethargic thought. But Mefto's reactions and skill negated the usual unthinking skill I exerted. Where he had been trained and who his masters had been intrigued me and I would one day visit Balintol myself. But, then, that was foolish, a child's dream of an impossible future, for I was due to die here, on the blue sand, chopped and bloody and done for.

As the combat went on and time stretched out and I was cut and cut again, a distant howling sound drifted in fitfully. The lethargic watchers on the terrace were responding, and losing all their languid affectation. The blood-sport caught them up in its choking coils.

With an infinite patience I accepted this punishment and worked on him. I found certain weaknesses I do not think he suspected existed. Certainly, I became sharply aware of several glaring deficiencies in my own technique. He feinted a thrust and as my shield flicked to cover and I went the other way, he allowed the almost imperceptible tremor of his body to force my instant unthinking reaction to drive me back. My own skill recognized that body tremor, and reacted to it, and so his original thrust slid in past my shield and sliced a ribbon of flesh from my ribs.

The next time he tried a variation of that I did not react as he expected, and his thrust missed and I leaned in and nicked him on his lower right arm. He sprang back, furiously.

"So you think to best me, Prince Mefto the Kazzur, apim! I have thrashed you before and this time—"

Well, sometimes I have a merry little spot of chit-chat when I fight. I did not reply, then, to his taunts.

The swords clashed again and I felt the power as he sought to overbear me and I resisted and, for a half-dozen heartbeats, we struggled directly together, body against body.

His strength was a live ferocious force. He compelled my sword arm down, and down. And I resisted, and so thrust him back, and slid his blade and sliced at him as he flinched and dodged backwards. I chopped only a strand of his hair. His face, which had been jolly and filled with good humor at indulging in the sport he liked best, lowered on a sudden, and his brows drew down. If this pantomime was meant to frighten me, well— by Zair, I will not lie.

For he bore in now with a more deadly intent.

Useless to attempt to describe the passages of that fight in detail, but it was talked about for season after season as the greatest encounter seen on the Kazz-Jikaida board.

He had taken a gouging chunk out of my shield and the wood splintered away from the bronze framing. Now his blade smashed down on the rim and wrenched the bronze into a distorted ribbon. With a few skillful blows as I defended myself he chopped half the shield away. His own yellow shield bore the marks of my sword; but it remained intact.

And, all the time, he kept up his chatter, taunting me, threatening me, deriding my efforts, sometimes patronizingly praising a last-minute defense that barely kept his sword from my guts.

"You fight well, for an apim. Truly, I admire your skill."

I grunted with the effort of parrying with the dangling remnant of shield. I would not throw it away yet, for it still served in a pitiful fashion, and if I hurled it at him he would merely duck, and laugh.

As he talked on, leaping and swirling and attacking and springing back and so coming in again, I remained silent.

My body was now a single shining sheet of blood. I felt no pain, for a

Krozair of Zy, no less than a Clansman or a Djang, must refuse to acknowledge pain that will hamper his fighting ability. But I was weaker. I could feel that. Nothing could disguise the sluggishness in my limbs, no pushing away of pain and denial of torment could conceal my growing feebleness.

This Kildoi was a rara avis among fighting men, no doubt of that. So I must put in the last throw before it was too late.

With a sudden and shattering series of blows, with a wild smashing onslaught, Mefto came for me and I saw that this time he meant to finish me. I defended. I ducked and weaved and dangled the sorry scrap of shield before him and I flailed his blade away. Somehow I resisted and held my position in the blue square and he drew back, baffled. But my weakness was now on me. I was near the end.

So, positioning myself, I tried to remember who I was, that I was plain Dray Prescot.

He was talking again, not quite so jovially, clearly annoyed that he had not finished me in that passage.

"I said you were a fighter, apim. You have a little skill. I have joyed in our contest; but now—"

And then I spoke. For the first time.

I said: "I, too, have enjoyed this little swordplay. You have tried and you have failed. I have sounded you out." My voice was thick and my throat felt as though it was filled with all the sand of the arena. "But, now, Mefto the Kleesh, it is my turn."

And, instantly, I swept through the dazzlement of the attack I had long pondered, and thrust.

I'd have had him. I would have. But I was weak, too weak. The blows I had taken had punished me, and the blood that leached away took with it my strength.

He just managed to drag his shield across. His Kildoi face, handsome, handsome, with its golden beard and clear-cut features, drew down in shock. He knew he had been caught. He reacted with a primitive violence.

He dashed in on me and his shield collided with my own scraps of wood and twisted bronze. His bulk forced me on and over. I was down. Down on one knee, the dangling shield remnants held aloft in my left fist. For a space, a single heartbeat, I put my right hand and the sword flat on the sand, supporting myself, getting my wind, seeing the world revolving in black stars and icy comets.

He towered over me. He laughed. His thraxter slashed down. Somehow the remnants of my shield slid into the sword's path, and he lifted to strike again, and I forced up my right arm and gripped my sword and took the blows, refusing to go down.

"Die, you rast!" he screamed. "Die!"

The attempt to rise and stand on my own two feet was too much for me.

I was on one knee, the shield held up and the sword feebly pointing, and I gasped and wheezed and fought to clear the black demons in my head and see through the leaping whorls of light and shadow encompassing me. His passion controlled him now, and he struck and struck as though hewing wood. He had had a scare and he could not understand the emotions that corroded within him like poisons—so I guessed, seeing that never had he met his master. But, for all that, I was nearly done for. The pathetic bits of shield still held together and kept out his thraxter; but that was all.

So I tried to stand up. I made a last convulsive effort.

He saw that. He saw the way I lurched and recovered and struggled my foot under me and so started to rise.

"Rast! Yetch! Die!"

Toppling, swaying, I struggled with a despairing savagery to stand up. And I knew I could not. Mefto saw the way I moved, saw my body begin to rise, and it was clear he imagined I was about to stand up. Zair knows what kind of demon he thought I must be, after the way he had chopped me, and the blood, and the punishment, and the state I was in. He thought I was going to stand up. That golden face contorted into a look of bestial unbelieving fury. He took three slow steps back, right to the very edge of the blue square, and then with a howl he launched himself at me.

And, then, Prince Mefto the Kazzur made his mistake.

The blows from his thraxter smashed down viciously on the chunk of shield I held aloft, twisted so that a remnant of bronze framing held against the blows. Mefto was a Kildoi. A Kildoi has been blessed by the gods with a tail hand. Mefto in his blind fury reached out with his tail hand and seized the rim of this infuriating frustrating chunk of shield, ready to tear it away and so leave me open for the last blow.

That hard brown hand gripped onto the bronze before my eyes. I saw the nails, trimmed and polished, the thin bristle of golden hair, the whiteness of constricting violence between the knuckles. The hand gripped and pulled. The shield moved.

With a final lurch I lifted halfway up, reached out with the sword, cut off that tail hand.

Prince Mefto the Kazzur screamed.

His golden body convulsed away, and he shrieked, a high howling screech of agony and fury, of humiliation and despair.

Somehow, do not ask me, for I cannot say, I was crouched over his body as he twitched and convulsed on the blue blood-spattered sand. He held the gory stump of his tail in all his four hands, and he screamed and slobbered and cried.

I said, "Mefto the Kleesh. I have cut Kataki tails off before this, and those yetches did not cry like you do."

All that effort of speaking, of boasting, when I was bleeding to death, exhausted me, such is the stupidity of pride. There was little time. I lifted the thraxter, and it trembled. Mefto was wrapped up in his own horror and was not aware, not aware at all that the steel point hovered above his throat.

He was a master swordsman, he could hand out the punishment with a laugh; but he could not endure punishment. He was the best swordsman I had so far encountered; he was not the greatest by a very long way.

I raised the sword a last inch, grasping the hilt in both blood-stained hands. I took a ragged breath. I started to bring the sword down, to plunge it through Mefto's throat and on to bury the point deeply in the blue sand— and hands grasped my shoulders and the thraxter was taken away as a nurse takes away a baby's bottle and I was placed flat on the sand and there was noise and confusion and a needleman with his acupuncture needles and miles and miles of yellow bandages.

"Why—?" I tried to say.

Yasuri bent over me.

"Mefto's people resigned the game to save his life."

"Then," I gasped out, "Then I have failed!"

A stupid game, and its rules, had saved the rast to bring horror to the Dawn Lands and to Vallia, when a straight and simple fight outside the rules of Kazz-Jikaida—why had I listened to brave Konec and Dav? I should have—I should have—but the words went away and there was blackness like the blackness of Notor Zan. I awoke to see Yasuri looking down on me with the strangest of expressions on her face.

I felt light-headed and empty and very very thirsty. She told a slave girl to fill a goblet with water, and this I drank straight down. Someone with a reedy voice said: "No more for now. He is weak but will mend with care."

"I shall care for him," said the lady Yasuri, and I could see no lines on her face at all.

A shadow moved at her side and the lady Jikaidasta stood there in what must be a private room in Yasuri's suite at her hotel, The Star of Laybrites. Ling-li's pale face glowed in the reflected radiance and her blue eyes were very bright upon me.

"I must leave Jikaida City now. I did not aid you in the fight—Jak." She paused on the name. Then: "The Nine Masked Guardians maintain San Orien, who is a Wizard of Loh of great repute, to warn them of any sorcery practiced in the games. You fought your own fight—and won."

I could not shake my head, for it would probably have fallen off; but I wondered if it was possible for me to agree with her, that she might be right. Had I won? The crucial factor was, it didn't matter if I had won that fight or not.

Then there was a deeper rumble of voices, and shadows, and presently

Kov Konec and Vad Dav Olmes stood by the bed. They were smiling with great broad smiles of triumph, for Prince Mefto the Kazzur had left Jikaida City, his stump tail bandaged, left it the very day after the fight, which was a sennight ago, and because there was no evidence against the people from Mandua they had been freed, and with an apology, too.

The words croaked from my throat. "And the rast from Hamal?"

"He remains. He plays in the Mediary Games, for there are always games of Jikaida going on in Jikaida City."

He smiled down on me, and Dav, with a finger to his nose, said, "Yes, the Mediary Games begin, and the lady Yasuri is the Champion, reigning Champion."

"And now the people of the Dawn Lands will take their own destiny into their hands." Konec's fist rested on his sword hilt. "The alliance between Hamal and Shanodrin never took place. I think, I hope, I pray, Prince Mefto is finished."

Maybe I did not know what the Star Lords wanted with the lady Yasuri. But I did know that, for me, the work I had had to do in Jikaida City was finished. There was nothing to keep me here now. Vallia called. If the Star Lords brought me back here, then I would have to think again. But the Witch of Loh, Ling-li-Lwingling, also, knew more than she allowed. This was all tied up together; but I had fought a fight, and, by Krun! I knew I had been in a fight. I lay back on the yellow pillows.

My way home to Vallia still remained in Jikaida City.

As soon as I could move I would be off.

The Hamalese flier would speed me across the continent and take me home. Home to Delia.

"Let us praise Dromo the Benevolent," said Konec. "We have won. It is all over now. The game is finished."

As I drifted off to sleep I said to myself: "For you it may be finished. But the game is not finished for me, for plain Dray Prescot who happens to be the Emperor of Vallia."

326

Appendix

Jikaida

The smallest form of Jikaida, known as Poron Jikaida, is here described. I should like to acknowledge the advice and interest of John Gollon of Geneva in the preparation of these rules for publication. I must also thank my son for his enthusiasm and expertise in playing Jikaida. He has helped to clarify game situations and contributed to the strategical shape of Poron Jikaida. As a matter of convenience the terminology of terrestrial chess is used when practical.

The board consists of six drins, arranged two by three, each drin containing thirty-six squares, arranged six by six. The dividing line between drins is called a front and is painted in more heavily than the other lines to facilitate demarcation.

The squares are almost always either black and white or blue and yellow, although other colors are known. On Kregen red and green are seldom used. The players have a yellow square on the right of the first rank.

Blue is usually north and Yellow south. Each player has two drins before him, his home drins, and the two wild drins in the center. From Yellow's point of view each drin is lettered A to F from left to right, and numbered one to six from south to north. Each drin has a name.

In Poron Jikaida the six drins are named and arranged:

Wersting	Chavonth
Neemu	Leem
Mortil	Zhantil

By using the drin name followed by the coordinates any square is readily identifiable, and this system has been found to be quick, simple and efficient.

It is possible to place artificial features on the board—rivers, hills, woods, etc.—by prior arrangement between the players. Most often these are not employed, Jikaida purists contending that they interfere with the orthodox developments and powers of pieces in combination on the open board.

The object of the game is to capture the opposing King. This piece is variously called Princess, Aeilssa, Rokveil, and in Loh, Queen. When any piece is in a position enabling it to take the King the player calls: "Kaida." When the King cannot evade capture, "Hyrkaida." At any time he thinks he is in a winning position, a player may ask his opponent: "Do you bare the throat?" If his opponent does, he resigns.

Each player has thirty-six pieces, arrayed in his first three ranks. The pieces are: one King, one Pallan, two Kapts, two Chuktars, two Jiktars, two Hikdars, two Paktuns, twelve Deldars, twelve swods.

The King moves as in Terran chess. Notation: K.

The Pallan moves as Terran Queen plus Knight and may pass from one drin to the next, once only, during his move. The Pallan has the power of taking any friendly piece except the King. Notation: P.

The Kapt moves as Pallan, but may not take a friendly piece. When crossing drin front, must continue direction of travel. Notation: Ka.

The Chuktar moves as Terran Queen. May cross drin front once per move continuing direction of travel. Notation: C.

The Jiktar moves as Terran rook. Must halt at drin front and cross on next move. Notation: J.

The Hikdar moves as Terran Bishop. Must halt at drin front and cross on next move. Notation: H.

The Paktun moves as Terran Knight. Notation: Pk.

The Deldar moves and captures one or two squares in any direction, orthogonal or diagonal. A two square move may not involve a change of direction and is not a leap. Notation: D.

The swod moves one square, straight forward or to the two forward diagonals and captures only to the forward diagonals. Notation: S.

The Paktun may leap twice on his first move. The Deldar may move twice on his first move, being able to move one, two, three or four squares, but changing direction only after the second square. The swod may advance or capture one, two or three squares on his initial move.

In these initial moves of Paktun, Deldar or swod, and in the case of the two-square move of the Deldar under normal circumstances, the move of such a piece ends when he makes a capture. The Paktun, for example, cannot on his initial move leap and capture, then leap again.

After his initial move, the swod moves and captures one square only.

In some areas of Kregen, Dray Prescot notes, players contend that the Deldar may only move and capture for a two-square move. Other areas allow a single square move without capture. These variations are considered interesting, and frustrating, as the piece's power cannot then extend to adjacent squares and would be limited to eight Squares at a straight two-square range diagonally and orthogonally.

The Paktun crosses drin fronts in the normal course of his move. The Jiktar, Hikdar, Deldar and swod must halt at a front and cross on the next move. If the Deldar's normal two-square move is halted by a front after one square, he must halt and wait until a subsequent move to cross. The Chuktar and Kapt may cross a front once only during their move and must continue on in the same line of travel. The Pallan has this privilege; but also he may change direction at the front (like light through the surface of water.) When a Pallan comes up to a front orthogonally he may continue straight on or take either of the two diagonals ahead. If the square adjoining the front is yellow on the hither side of the front, the two diagonals he may follow will also be yellow. If the square is blue, the diagonals will be blue. If the Pallan comes up to a drin front diagonally he may continue on the same diagonal or take either of the two orthogonals enclosing the diagonal. One of these orthogonals will always lie alongside the front. He cannot turn at right angles to his line of advance. The paktun-leap of the Pallan is his move and cannot be taken as well as another move.

A move through an interior drin corner would allow the player to move into any one of the other three drins.

Unless halted by a piece in the way, the Jiktar and Hikdar may move the full distance of a drin up to the front. The Pallan, Kapt and Chuktar, unless halted by a piece, may move the full distance of one drin and the full distance of the next. To cross a front, all pieces with the exception of those with trans-front movement and the Paktun must stand on a square adjacent to the front in order to cross.

There is no en passant capture in Jikaida.

There is no castling as such in Jikaida, but a near-equivalent is employed. If the King is not under attack and the square on which he will land is not under attack, and if the King and the other piece involved are on their original squares (whether or not they have previously moved) once only during the game a player may switch the place of the King with that of a Kapt or a Chuktar. The King would then be moved to the square of the Kapt or Chuktar, and the other piece moved to the King's square. It does not matter if there are, or are not, pieces in the way, nor if the intervening squares are under attack. This move is known as the King's Fluttember. Because of zeunting, this rule is strategically less vital in Jikaida than the castling rule in chess, but nevertheless can be important tactically.

The use of drins and the power of pieces to vault make Jikaida unique. The Kregish word for vault is zeunt.

Any piece (some variations exclude the King) may move from one end of a straight unbroken line of pieces to the other end. The line may be diagonal or orthogonal and be of any length. The piece vaulting must stand on the square immediately adjacent to the end of the line, diagonally if a diagonal line and orthogonally if an orthogonal line, may move along the line and come to earth on the immediately adjacent square at the far end, diagonally if a diagonal line and orthogonally if an orthogonal line. Exceptions will be noted below.

A line for vaulting must consist of three or more pieces.

The pieces in the line may be blue or yellow or a mixture.

If there is a break in a line the vaulting piece must land there and finish his move. A piece may land on an opposing piece and capture anywhere along the line, providing he has already vaulted over at least three pieces, and he is not a swod landing on an opposing swod propt by a Deldar (see below).

Whenever a vaulting piece touches down, to capture an enemy, at the end of the line, or in a break, his move is ended.

The Pallan who may capture a friendly piece may do so in the normal course of a vault.

Any piece may vault across one or more drin fronts providing the line to be vaulted extends unbroken across those fronts. Pieces which would normally have to halt at a drin front when moving do not have to do so when vaulting. However, if a piece moves to a square abutting on a front and the line to be vaulted begins on the other side of the front he must wait until the next or subsequent move to vault.

Vaulting instead of moving normally counts as the player's turn.

Swods vault forward orthogonally or diagonally only.

If a line to be vaulted ends at a front the piece vaulting may touch down in the adjacent square as noted, or capture, over the drin front.

It should be noted that a vault may change a Hikdar's color.

In Poron Jikaida as usually played the Pallan is the only piece with the power of using two other features of the vault. The Pallan may, in his turn, move legally as specified in the rules, to the end of a line and in the same turn vault. The Pallan may make one change of direction when vaulting, but must follow a continuous line of pieces of three or more from one end to the other with a single bend in the line.

The Pallan may move diagonally to the end of an orthogonal line and vault, and vice versa. The change of direction can follow any single bend in the line.

A player wins by either checkmating (hyrkaida) or stalemating (tikaida) his opponent, or by baring his opponent's king, unless the opponent then immediately (on the move) bares player's king also, in which case the game is drawn.

If a Deldar stands next to a swod of the same color an opponent swod cannot capture that swod. Adjacency, to afford this protection, may be orthogonal or diagonal. In the Kregish, this protection is called propt. One Deldar may propt as many swods as he is adjacent to.

Dray Prescot points out that the idea of a rank of Deldars standing against an advance of swods, thus forcing heavier pieces into action, probably gave rise to the traditional opening challenge of the game: "Rank your Deldars!"

When a swod reaches the last rank of the board he may promote to any rank, including Pallan but excepting King, regardless of the number of pieces of the chosen rank already on the board.

The initial array of Yellow pieces from Yellow's point of view is: First rank: from left to right: Chuktar, Jiktar, Hikdar, Paktun, Kapt, Pallan, King,

Kapt, Hikdar, Jiktar, Chuktar. Second rank: twelve Deldars. Third rank: twelve swods.

The initial array of Blue pieces from Blue's point of view is: First rank, from left to right: Chuktar, Jiktar, Hikdar, Paktun, Paktun, Kapt, King, Pallan, Kapt, Hikdar, Jiktar, Chuktar. Second rank: twelve Deldars. Third rank: twelve swods.

Kings stand on squares of their own color.

First move is by agreement, either color may open the game.

Variations

Whatever rules or variations of rules are used, it is essential that players are aware of them and agree before play starts. It is particularly important that the rules governing vaulting should be completely agreed upon.

These variations are similar to differences in chess rules on Earth before advances in communication and transportation allowed standardization. Poron Jikaida is the smallest form of Jikaida. Jikalla will form the subject of an appendix in a subsequent volume in the Saga of Dray Prescot. There are other sizes of board and numbers of pieces employed. Great Jikaida is the largest. Many forms employ aerial cavalry.

Jikshiv Jikaida is played on a board six drins by four drins.

Hyrshiv Jikaida is played on a board three drins by four drins. The Lamdu version of Hyrshiv Jikaida employs ninety pieces a side.

In the larger games with more pieces the power of the superior pieces increases with the additions, the Jiktar taking on the powers of the Chuktar for example. Some additional pieces are: the Hyrpaktun, who moves in an elongated Paktun's move, three squares instead of two before the sideways move. The Flutsman, who moves four spaces, diagonally or orthogonally, over intervening pieces, must touch down on an unoccupied square, and then move or capture one square orthogonally or diagonally. This simulates the flutsman's flight to his target and then the attack on foot. There are other aerial moves of similar character.

In some areas of Kregen the Hyrpaktun is allowed a single square move, like the King, to facilitate color changing.

The Archer moves one square diagonally and then as a rook. The Crossbowman moves one square orthogonally and then as a bishop. Trans-drin restrictions with the missile pieces vary. Vaulting rules vary considerably and have been the cause of great controversy. With the larger games the Pallan has the power of more than one change of direction during a zeunt, and may come down off the vault and continue moving. Sometimes the Kapts have the power of moving to a vaulting line. The pieces with a knight-like leap may come down off the vault to one side or the other, as though continuing their leap. This confers a very great power to these

331

pieces, as they would then cover the entire sides of the vaulting line from three pieces away.

Trans-drin restrictions also vary, as, for instance, the Kapt being allowed to change direction at a front, and the Jiktars and Hikdars being allowed trans-drin movement. The Pallan may be allowed to cross two drin fronts, and this is particularly important during diagonal moves near the center of the board or where fronts meet. On the larger boards increased freedom of movement has been found to be essential, but this is often restricted to the home and central drins, and does not extend to the opponent's home drins.

The powers of the swods and Deldars also vary by agreement, and it is a pleasant game to play Poron Jikaida with two ranks of swods each. In Porondwa Jikaida there are two ranks of Deldars. The larger boards build on the basis of the Poron board, the additional drins of the Hyrshiv Board are as follows... From Yellow's point of view: The right-hand home drin is Krulch. The drins above that are Prychan and Strigicaw. Blue's home drins are Boloth, Graint, Dermiflon.

In notation it is usual to give only the initial letter of the drin, followed by the letter and number of the coordinates.

Prescot says an interesting variation developed in Vallia where the swods were called brumbytes and the Deldars were called Hakkodin; but he gives no details of the play, except a mention of the brumbytes being arrayed initially in three ranks of eight, and provided they are on adjacent squares being allowed to be moved three at a time. One assumes this privilege would end by at least the front of the opponent's home drins.

The above description is necessarily brief; but enough information has been given to enable the game to be played and enjoyed and some of the ramifications and developments to be explored. The construction of a board is a simple matter. It is suggested chess pieces are used where applicable, and the new pieces represented by model soldiers of a suitable scale and color. It is possible that a range of figures from the Saga of Dray Prescot will soon be available.

Finally, it is left to me to say, on behalf of Dray Prescot, enjoy your Jikaida and—Rank your Deldars!

Alan Burt Akers

A FORTUNE FOR KREGEN

A Note on Dray Prescot

Dray Prescot is a man above middle height, with brown hair and level brown eyes, brooding and dominating, an enigmatic man with enormously broad shoulders and superbly powerful physique. There is about him an abrasive honesty and indomitable courage. He moves like a savage hunting cat, quiet and deadly. Reared in the inhumanly harsh conditions of Nelson's Navy, he has been transported by the Scorpion agencies of the Star Lords, the Everoinye, and the Savanti of Aphrasöe, the Swinging City, to the unforgiving yet rewarding world of Kregen, four hundred light years from Earth, under the Suns of Antares.

Here he has made his home and has struggled through triumph and disaster, acquiring titles and estates on the way, which he views with a cool irony. Determined to relinquish the burden of being Emperor of Vallia when that island empire is once more united and at peace, he plans to hand all over to his son, Drak. Now the Star Lords have set to his hands a task in the exotic southern continent of Havilfar, but, as usual, the meaning of the mission is veiled from him. To prevent a league headed by Vallia's bitter foe, the Empire of Hamal, from succeeding, Prescot has played in the deadly game of Death Jikaida. He has been sorely wounded.

Prescot records his story for us on cassettes and each book is arranged to be read as complete in itself. Now the future lies before him as he determines to return home to Vallia, and to Delia and his family and friends. But Kregen is not like this Earth.

Hurled once more into headlong adventure, Prescot must battle for his life—and sanity—but, this time, his struggles do not take place in the streaming mingled lights of the Suns of Scorpio, nor even in the fuzzy pink and golden radiance of the Seven Moons of Kregen...

Alan Burt Akers

One

On a Roof in Jikaida City

There are more ways than one hundred and one of stealing an airboat and this was going to be way Number One. Just walk up to the craft, step aboard, and take off—first making sure she was not tethered down.

That was the theory.

The guard stepped from a shadowed doorway on the first landing and stuck a glittering great cleaver under my nose.

"Stand where you are, dom, or your head will go bouncing down those stairs you've just walked up."

Light from the lamp held in the hand of a bronze cupid at the head of the stairs struck sparks from his eyes. All he could see of me must be a silhouette. The muffling mask of gray cloth over my face and head and the dull baggy clothes were unrecognizable.

"Why, dom," I said. "You're making a mistake—"

No doubt he understood me to be attempting exculpation. When I lowered him gently to the carpet with my left hand gripped in the fancy front of his uniform, and, my right hand tingling just a little, took away that murderous cleaver, he slumbered peacefully—but he'd wake up understanding the mistake I had pointed out to him well enough.

Stepping carefully over him I went on up the next flight of stairs. This hotel, a veritable palace in the Foreign Quarter of Jikaida City, was occupied by the great ones of the world who came here to play Jikaida without affiliation to the Blue or the Yellow. On the roof rested the only flying boat in the city. That airboat was my ticket out of here and, because it was owned by a man from Hamal, and Hamal was at war with my own country of Vallia, it was morally quite proper for me to steal the craft.

Well—morals take the devil of a beating when there's a war on. There are, to be sure, far too many wars and battles on the world of Kregen, but I was sincerely doing what I could to lessen the number.

The time was just on halfway between midnight and dawn. The hotel remained quiet. The carpets muffled my tread. There must be a few more guards about and, sentry duty being what it is, there were bound to be one or two having a quiet yarn up on the roof, one eye on the airboat.

The quicker I got out of Jikaida City and, if the Star Lords permitted, back to Vallia, the better. A caravan across the Desolate Waste to the east would be far too slow for me in my mood. Vallia was in good hands, that I knew; but I still felt the need to get home. Also, knowing the way fate—which is a poor second best in any confrontation with the Star Lords—has the nasty habit of hurling me headlong into adventures that are none of my seeking, I fancied I had a few sprightly moments in front of me before I reached home. Well, by Vox, that was true.

As I stole up the next flight of stairs sounds floated down from above. I frowned. There was laughter, and high shrieks, and a tinny banging. A small orchestra was playing and trying to make its music heard over the din. I went on and came out onto the top landing. In the corner the small door that led onto the roof was unguarded. I had only to cross the stretch of thick pile carpet, open the door, close it carefully after me, and creep up the stairs, my sword in my fist...

More confounded theories.

A door opened and a man staggered out. He wore only a blue shirt and he was highly excited, his arms draped over the shoulders of a couple of sylvies half-dressed in tinsels. He roared, his head thrown back, warbling out a song whose words were unintelligible and whose tune was unrecognizable.

The wall at my back felt flat and hard. I pressed in as though trying to burrow through into the room beyond.

Beyond that suddenly opened door the lamplight glowed, spilling out and casting shadows over me. The noise in there racketed away and now the orchestra, no doubt having made up its mind to be heard, howled and shrilled and scraped. Men and women shrieked with laughter and shouted over the music, determined to be heard. The clink of bottles and the crash of overturning glasses added a genial blend of bibulous accompaniment. The man and the girls staggered past, screaming with laughter, to disappear into a darkened room along the corridor.

Lamplight fell across the carpet in a butter-yellow lozenge.

To reach the door leading onto the roof it was necessary to pass that lozenge of light.

The orchestra and the people—all grimly determined to be heard—redoubled their efforts. The racket coruscated. The door remained open and people passed and repassed—or staggered and restaggered—from side to side. Another man came out. He crawled on hands and knees. A slinky little Fristle fifi rode his back, alternately hitting him with a slipper and giving him sips of wine from a glass. Most of the wine—it was a light straw color—soaked into the carpet. They were both yelling their heads off. I shoved another inch or two into the wall.

Somebody else reeled out of the door, tripped over the man on his knees and the fifi, and collapsed, howling with laughter. His wine went all over them. He had been drinking a deep red wine, and the color blazed up in the lamplight.

A voice yelled over the din.

"Hey, Nath! C'mere, for the sake of Havandua—these Hamalese have me—" The rest was lost in a gurgle.

The fellow who was being ridden by the girl stood up. He reeled. The girl clung to him, her naked legs wrapped about him. Making no effort to throw her off he went barging back, and the chap who had fallen over him lurched up, shaking his head from side to side and chuckling foolishly.

He looked at his empty glass, made a solemn clucking noise, and wandered off toward the open door. He hit the wall beside the door, bounced, shook his head, took a grip on himself and navigated back into the room.

Somebody shut the door.

Oh, yes, by Krun. They were all Somebodies in there...

Letting out my breath I eased from the shadows and started for the door. My hand was on the latch. I was pushing the door open—when the light sprang into being again at my back.

A girl's voice, all giggles and hiccoughs, said, "Leaving already? You Hamalese are too solemn! Come and have a drink."

Without turning, I said in as light a voice as I could muster, "You should try telling that to a Bladesman in the Sacred Quarter of Ruathytu."

A man's voice, heavier than most, said, "Hamalese? I don't—"

There was nothing else for it.

I went through the opened doorway, slammed the wood at my back, and shot the bolt across. No time to catch a breath. It was up the stairs hell for leather and out onto the roof under the stars of Kregen.

The airboat was there—tethered down, of course!—and with a canvas cover thrown across her slim lines.

The first chain ripped free. The second chain was in my fingers. The scrape at my back sounded clearly. In an explosion of movement I dived sideways, recovered, hauled out my sword.

The two guards were in nowise chagrined that they had failed to surprise me. She of the Veils floated free of cloud wrack then and showed them to me—as the moon showed me to them.

A banging started below as the party-goers hammered on the door I had bolted.

The guards bore in, their swords held in the professional fighting man's grip. They wore the fancy uniform of employees of this establishment, a riot of ruffles and bronze-bound armor, the whole outlined in black and yellow checkers. They knew what they were about. They anticipated no real trouble from me. The gray cloth mask over my face would hearten them rather than not, for they would take this as a sign of one who wished to remain unknown in the shadows, and unwilling to face a fight.

And, by Zair, they were right!

The wounds I had taken in that last fight on the Jikaida board were nowhere near properly healed. I was still weak. Yes, I could wield a blade and give some account of myself. But to engage in protracted swordplay, I knew, was beyond my present powers. This night's doings had been intended as a quick and furtive entry, a fast snatch of the airboat, and a remarkably smart getaway.

These two hulking guards had no intention of allowing me to carry on my plans for another moment.

As I say—so much for theory.

With the nerve-tingling scrape of steel on steel, the blades crossed.

Now—now these two were fair swordsmen. They earned their hire by standing guard. And, also, it was perfectly clear they would kill me as a mere part of earning that hire. That was their job. There was no great panache in it, not a sign of lip-licking enjoyment in their work. They just went about the business determined to prevent me, a masked thief, from stealing the airboat they were paid to protect.

As I say, they were fair swordsmen. After a few passes I knew, weak as I was, that I had the mastering of them both.

The blades screeched and rang as I fended them off, and pressed, and retreated, luring them on to the final passage that would settle this thing. But—but they were just men earning their daily bread. They were doing what they did for purely economic reasons. Their morality encompassed my death as a thief so that they might earn their daily bread, in the same way that my morality encompassed stealing this airboat in order to fly back to Vallia.

I could have slain them both; run them through in a twinkling.

Many a superior swordsman of the darker persuasion would have done so and thought nothing of it. There is enough misery in two worlds without adding villainy to it and calling it heroism. These two guards went to sleep after a flurry of blades and a rapid double thump—one, two—from the hilt.

The delay they had caused, slight though it was, had undone my plans and earned their hire.

Men boiled out from the stairway onto the roof, so I knew they had broken down the lower door. Some of them wore shirts, some of them wore trousers or breechclouts, and although very few were possessed of all items of clothing, they all possessed swords. They set up a howl as they saw me, a dark, masked, mysterious figure just stepping back from two unconscious guards. They charged, screeching.

I recognized the tone, the mood, the feeling of their yells.

Anger, of course—but, chiefly, a high delirious excitement, a sudden passion for the chase, the game, the feeling that in a spot of action would come the highlight of the evening's entertainments.

The chains tethering the flier remained fast locked.

Now there was no time to act as I have acted in other places and other times in circumstances not too dissimilar.

I ran.

The roofs of the hotel presented a bewildering jumble—a jungle of tiles and cornices and chimneys and spires.

Away we all went in a rout, and they were hallooing and yelling and prancing about back there, waving their swords, their naked legs flashing in the fuzzy golden and pinkish light of She of the Veils. Kregen's largest moon, the Maiden with the Many Smiles, lifted over the edge of the world and shone pink and rose down through shredding clouds. There would be plenty of light. As I ran and skipped from roof to roof I reflected that, by Vox, there would be far too much light.

This quiet, cautious, carefully planned exercise had turned into a right old shambles.

The fellows chasing me back there were not all apims, not all Homo sapiens like me. Among them the wonderful variety of diffs of Kregen was well represented. A loose slate which made me slither down a prickly roof almost did for me; with a convulsive lunge I hooked my fingers around the guttering and managed to hang on. Below me the gulf yawned. Far below, far and far below, light spilled across a cobbled courtyard as a door was opened. A voice bellowed up.

"What in the name of Vilaha's Tripes is going on up there?"

The pack yelled and caroled and they were creeping out along the roof ridge toward the spot where I had slipped. They looked like a ghostly dance of death up there, silhouetted against the moon radiance, for some of them pranced out balancing as though they walked a tightrope. Others got down on their hands and knees and shuffled along. Only one had the hardihood—or foolhardiness—to slither down the tiles.

He came down rather too fast.

He started to scream as he picked up speed, sliding down the roof. His flailing hands sought for a grip, and scrabbled against the tiles, and slipped. He hit the guttering and it broke away with a groan, and dipped down. Only a bracket near me held the end of the guttering. It hung down like the snapped yardarm of a swifter, smashed in the shock of ramming.

The fellow was screaming now, clutching desperately to the angled guttering, and slowly—slowly and horribly—he was sliding down the guttering toward its splintered end.

In a few moments he would slip off the end, make a desperate and unavailing snatch at the guttering, and fall to the cobbles beneath. He'd go splat.

His death meant nothing to me, of course.

I got my other hand up to the secured guttering and hooked a knee. I looked up. His comrades were still yelling up there and most of them did not even know he had fallen. They were running on to get to the end of the slate walkway along the ridge. There was not much time.

The leather belt around my waist was thick and supple; it came off in a trice and I gripped the end and threw the buckle end around in an arc. It swung like a pendulum.

"Grab the belt, dom!" I shouted.

His white face looked like the head of a moth, in the moon-dappled shadows. I could see his mouth open; but he was too far gone to scream. His eyes were like holes burned in linen.

He made a grab for the belt on the next swing, and missed, and jerked back as the guttering groaned and inched down.

"This time, dom," I shouted. "You will not miss."

The brass belt buckle glittered once and then vanished into the shadows. He made an effort, the humping, thrusting strain of a too-heavy horse attempting to leap a too-high barrier. The brass belt buckle was grabbed; just how good a grip he had I did not know. My own pains were beginning to make me think I might not be able to hold him when his weight came on the line. There was only one way to find out.

The guttering screeched, rivets pinged away, and the guttering fell.

The man swung, like a plumb-bob, dangling on the end of the belt.

Scarlet pain flowed over my body, from my arm and shoulder where Mefto's sword had cut me again and again, and down into my very guts. I shut my eyes for a moment—and held on.

With a clanging roar like fourteen hundred dustbins going over a cliff, the guttering hit the cobbles.

The man swung and dangled.

Presently I started to haul him in. He came up, gasping, his face like the ashy contents of those fourteen hundred dustbins, his eyes black and bruised in the fleeting pink light.

"Get your knee—over—the damned guttering."

He wore a gray shirt. His knee was skinned raw. But he got it over. Better a bloody knee than the squash on the cobbles.

With his weight half on the guttering alongside me I transferred my grip to his shoulder and half-pulled half-twisted him to safety. He lay there panting. His body heaved up and down with the violence of his breathing.

The yells of his friends receded. Only three were left up there on the slate walkway. I ignored them.

"You're safe now," I told him. I spoke sharply, to brace him up. "Brassud!" I said. "Get a grip on yourself."

"You—" He gasped it out, shaking now, looking down at the gulf and that distant rectangle of light from the open door, and back to me. "You—why?"

"I'm not an assassin. Get your breath back."

340

"By Krun!" he said, which told me he was Hamalese. "I'd never believe it—not even if—"

"Believe. And give me my belt back. Unlike you, I wish to retain my trousers."

And he laughed.

The night breeze played along the roof. The man below yelled again, coming back out the door with a lantern. The men up on the roof answered him, shouting down. There was a deal of confused yelling.

"Can you make your own way along the guttering? You'll be safe when you reach the gable end—the ornamentation there is profuse, if in bad taste."

He stared at me. He was a young fellow, with dark hair cut long and curled, and with a nose rather shorter than longer, and with eyes—whose color was imponderable in that light—which, it seemed to me, stared out with forthright candor. He had a belt fashioned from silver links in the shape of leaping chavonths, and a small jeweled dagger; he had lost his sword. He regained control of his breathing.

"I think so." He screwed his face up. "And you?"

"I—" I started to say.

"Stay here. I shall make my way to that zany lot and tell them nothing of your presence. Then, when we have gone, you may get away."

"You would truly do this?"

"Yes. And I give you my thanks. Lahal and Lahal—I am called Lobur the Dagger." He laughed again, and I saw he had recovered himself and was much taken with this night's adventure, now that it had, miraculously, turned out all right and not with his untimely death. "I do not expect you to make the pappattu—"

"I think not. In the circumstances."

"By Havil, no!"

The noise from his comrades had passed over and the three who had remained on the slate walkway above our heads had gone. The man and his lantern below were visible, just, at the far end of the building. The jut of a dormer window obscured him. We were alone under the Moons of Kregen, sitting on the gutter of a roof, talking as though we shared tea and miscils in some fashionable hostelry in the Sacred Quarter.

"There were three of your friends on the roof above—they are gone now—but I think they saw you did not fall."

"Friends? Oh, yes, friends."

He was clearly getting his wind back and setting himself for the scramble along the gutter. I am sure the thought stood in his mind, as it stood in mine, that there was every chance another section of guttering would give way under his weight.

There was no point in urging him to hurry. I fancied the hunt would bay along the next roof and courtyard. But, all the same, I had no desire to sit here all night.

The opportunity to gather information ought not to be overlooked and he might well be in the frame of mind to say more than in other circumstances he would allow himself.

"You are Hamalese. I hope you have enjoyed your Jikaida here. Do you return home soon?"

We were sitting side by side on the edge now, dangling our feet over emptiness. He laughed again.

"Jikaida! No—I have no head for the game. I wager on—on other things. As to going home, that rests on the decision of Prince Nedfar, and he is, with all due respect, besotted on Jikaida."

"Most people are, here in Jikaida City."

"And live well on it, too—" He cocked his head on one side, and added, "Gray Mask." He laughed, delighted at the conceit. "That is what I shall call you, Gray Mask. And the people here know well how to take our money. The whole city is full of sharps and tricksters."

"So, Lobur the Dagger, you believe I am not of the city?"

He looked surprised. "Of course not! Didn't think it for a moment. Who, here, would know aught of the Sacred Quarter of Ruathytu?"

So either he had heard my quick remark to the unseen girl at my back, or had been told. So, he must think I was Hamalese like himself, perhaps a wandering paktun, a mercenary. This could be awkward or could be useful.

I spoke with more than a grain of truth as I said, "Ah, yes. What I would give to be able, at this very moment, to be sitting on the roof of that sweet tavern of Tempting Forgetfulness in Ruathytu instead of here, on The Montilla's Head." And then I thought to prove myself a very cunning, very clever fellow indeed. I added, most casually, "But the commands of the Empress Thyllis are not to be denied."

He drew a quick breath. He cocked an eye at me. "Prince Nedfar—who is the Empress's second cousin—is here on state business. This is known. But a second embassy?" He sucked in his cheeks. "I do not think the prince knows—or would be pleased if he did know."

Well, that wouldn't worry me. Any confusion I could sow in the minds of the nobles of Hamal I would do and glee in the doing. If this Prince Nedfar, who had come here to talk of alliance with Prince Mefto, grew angry at the thought he was being spied on at the commands of the empress then I would have struck a blow, a small and near-insignificant blow it is true, against mad Empress Thyllis.

So, quickly, I said, "The Empress is to be obeyed in all things. That many of these things are such that an honorable man must recoil cannot affect their consummation. I have no grudge against the prince."

"But you sought to steal his airboat." He shifted at this and looked hard

342

at me. "And by Krun, Gray Mask! That would have stranded me here in this dolorous city!"

"Mayhap, Lobur, you would have come to a delight in Jikaida."

"Hah!"

The time had run out and I began to entertain a suspicion that he kept me here talking so as to detain me for his friends. They'd be back, soon, hunting over the back trail. Yet I fancied I might sow a little more discontent and, into the bargain, reap more information, for which I was starved. The risk was worth taking.

So I said, again in that casual way, "Many men murmur at the empress. You must have heard of plots against her. And, anyway, things go badly for Hamal in Vallia, do they not?"

He hitched around and as the guttering gave an ominous groan, stilled immediately. His pride would not allow him to take any notice of that menacing creak from the rivets and brackets.

"Aye, I have heard of plots." This was good news—by Vox! Excellent news! He went on, "And we do not prosper in Vallia. They are devils up there—I have heard stories that are scarcely credible. They have a new emperor now, the great devil Dray Prescot, who was once paraded through Ruathytu at the tail of a calsany—"

"You saw that?"

"Yes. By Krun—the man is evil all through and yet, and yet, I felt a little—" He paused and hawked up and spat. We did not hear the splat on the cobbles far below. "Enough of that maudlin nonsense. If I could get my dagger into him I would become the most famous man in all Hamal."

"Indubitably."

"But the chance is hardly likely to come my way."

"No. And I think it is time we moved off. Much as I am enjoying this conversation—"

"Yes, Gray Mask, you are right. I owe you my life. I shall not forget." He looked at me. "You will not give me your name?"

"If you were to call me Drax, I would answer."

"Drax?"

"Aye."

"Hardly a Hamalese name—"

"What did you expect?"

"No. No, of course, Drax, Gray Mask, you are right."

We had been sitting thus and talking companionably for a time, and he was sitting on the side nearest the broken guttering and farthest from the gable end that was our goal. He inched back and leaned against the tiles, making ready to pass behind me. I got myself two very secure grips. As he eased himself sideways he could easily give me a sudden and treacherous kick and so spin me out into the void.

343

He saw that instinctive movement as I secured myself. When he reached the other side he stopped.

"You thought, perhaps, I might push you over?"

"The thought was in my mind."

In the pinkish glow of the moons his face darkened. "You impugn my honor! D'you think I would—"

"No."

"I owe you my life." He suddenly trembled, and I saw the tremor pass through him as a rashoon shudders over the waters of the inner sea, the Eye of the World. "By Krun! When I was slipping down that damned gutter—sliding to the end to fall and squash—I tell you, Drax, Gray Mask, it was awful, awful. I thought—and then—"

"If we ever meet again we will drink a stoup or three together."

"Aye! That we will."

We spoke a few more parting words, and then we gave the remberees, and he edged his way cautiously along the gutter, making each step a careful probe for weak spots, until he reached the gable end. He vanished in the shadows of sculpted gargoyles and zhyans and mythical beasts. A macabre, a weird, little meeting, this conversation on a roof. But I had learned a little and I hoped I had sown a few seeds of doubt.

Damn the Hamalese! And double damn mad Empress Thyllis. But for her and her megalomaniacal schemes we'd have had Vallia back, smiling and happy, after the Time of Troubles by now.

The moment Lobur the Dagger disappeared into the twisted shadows I started along after him. There was no point in waiting. If he intended to betray me then the quicker I got in among them the better. Hauling him in had taken its toll of my feeble strength. Yes, yes, I had been a stupid onker in thus chancing all when I was not physically ready; but I needed that airboat on the roof. The voller that belonged to Prince Nedfar.

Looking down over the next courtyard from the concealment of that garish profusion of sculpture I could see no sign of Lobur or his cronies. The shadows lay thickly. The moons shafted ghostly pink light down and painted a pale rose patina across the lower roofs and walls. Around me LionardDen, the city of Jikaida, lay sleeping.

Very well.

Despite my physical weakness, despite all that had happened—was not this the moment to strike?

On that I started to climb up the gable end, handing myself up from stone beast to stone beast, working my way back to the slate walkway along the ridge.

Once up there I would retrace my steps to the roof where the airboat lay.

Maybe I would again be unsuccessful. Maybe there would be so many guards, so many obstacles, that I just would not be able to overcome them all. But that made no matter. I do not subscribe to the more stupidly florid of these notions of honor, particularly of rampantly displayed honor. But, here and now, there was a deal of that juvenile and exhibitionistic emotion mingled with the shrewdly practical idea that they'd be off guard up there. This was a chance.

Climbing along the roof back the way I had come, I knew the chance had to be taken.

Two

Gray Mask Vanishes

The kennel containing the two stavrers I had passed in something of a hurry showed up ahead in the moonlight as I leaped—not too nimbly—up onto the coping. The stavrers had been aroused by the uproar. They stretched out to the full extent of the chains fixed to collars about their necks. Chunky, are stavrers, fierce and loyal watchdogs, with savage wolf-heads and eight legs, the rear six articulated the same way, and they can charge with throat-ripping speed. After a distance they flag; but that stavrer charge, bolting all fangs ready to rip and rend, is quite enough to protect an honest man's house.

Now these two set up a fearful howling.

Two helmeted heads popped up over a nearby roof ridge among that jungle of roofs. Two arrows were loosed at me. They were not Bowmen of Loh shooting at me—chances are that I would not be here talking had they been—and I went flying down into a leaded gulley between tiled slopes and so scrabbled along like a fish in a stream trap.

This was all beginning to get out of hand. A guard jumped down from a chimney pot and tried to take my head off with his axe, and I ducked and got a boot into his midriff, and he went yowling away, holding his guts. The axe clattered down over blue slates and vanished into emptiness.

Other men were shouting, there was the shrilling sound of whistles, and more barking, from stavrers and other kinds of domestic animals nicely designed to rip the seat out of your pants, or to rip off other more important parts of your anatomy. Feeling incredibly like a fool, and beginning, also, to feel the humor of the situation breaking down all the silly anger, I went charging down a roof slope, came around a chimney corner and saw the uplifted coping of the roof whereon rested the airboat.

Any hope of stealing the voller vanished instantly.

She lay there bathed in the light of many lanterns. The men had turned out—some still without shirts or trousers, but all with swords. There was one young fellow there, with wide black moustaches, turned out as though for Chuktar's Parade—fully accoutered in harness and with shield and thraxter at the ready. His helmet shone under the lights of the moons.

So I debated. The debate was very short.

The stavrers were baying at my heels, the guards were massed in front, the moons were casting down more and more light as they rose—the Twins, the two Moons of Kregen eternally orbiting each other—had been early this night, and The Maiden with the Many Smiles and She of the Veils were late. The light would strengthen in rose and gold until the first shards of light from the twin suns, Zim and Genodras, illuminated the horizon. Then this exotic world of Kregen would be revealed in radiance of jade and ruby and the light would increase and burn and any fellows foolish enough to be hopping around on the roofs of high-class hotels would get all they deserved.

Home—rather, back to the tavern at which I was lodging for the moment—seemed to me the order of the day—or night, seeing that the day's orders would be so uncomfortable.

Mind you, if in retrospect I make it seem all light-hearted and if, truly, I did feel that light-headedness then, do not misunderstand me. I was raging with anger and frustration. Oh, yes, my island empire of Vallia, cruelly beset by predatory foemen, was in good and capable hands. I could go gallivanting about having adventures for as long as I wished; but I felt the deep tide drawing me back home. I had to get back to Vallia and make sure, make absolutely sure, that all was well. That I intended to hand it all over to my lad Drak as soon as possible was merely another reason for return. He was there, in Vallia, and I had not the slightest inkling what he was up to.

And, too, my half-healed wounds must have contributed to that feeling of light-headedness, as though this was all one gigantic jest.

So, bitterly angry, and stifling my laughter, I hopped off the roof down onto the next one and scuttled like an ancient crab along the ridge and slid down a drainpipe to the courtyard with its arbora trees. They are called this because their flowers look much like arbora feathers. If I thought I was on ground level I was seriously mistaken.

I remember I was thinking that I'd just let all this fuss blow over, and rest up a bit and get my strength back, and then I'd be back here to The Montilla's Head and this time I'd really lay my avaricious paws on Prince Nedfar's airboat. But really.

A door made from sturmwood and the bottoms of old bottles ahead looked promising, the roseate moonlight catching in the bottles and whirling hypnotically. I eased across with a quick glance aloft and then the door opened and disaster walked out—rather, disaster reeled out, shrieking and yelling.

The girl—she was a kitchen maid—was not apim but one of those charming diffs with the faces of apim infants, all soft rounded curves and chuckles and dimples, permanent baby-faces, naive and simple and delightful. The men folk have harder faces, it is true, but they, too, carry that hint of undeveloped childishness about them. For all that, the men have tough, muscle-hard, brawny bodies. The womenfolk have been blessed with female bodies that are marvels of curve and symmetry, sensuous, fascinating, endlessly alluring, intoxicating to any man—whether apim or diff—who shares our common heritage. This race of diffs—I once used to miscall diffs beast-men or men-beasts, halflings, not understanding—are often given the name Syblians; although the name they give themselves, not wishing to be confused with Sylvies, is Ennschafften.

The drunken lout chasing the girl was calling, in between hiccoughing and belching, yelling to her to stop.

"Mindy, miundy," he called, staggering out of the door, his shirt tangled around his waist, his face enflamed with drink and passion, his eyes fairly starting out of his head. "Miundy, Mindy—wait for me, you little—come back—or I'll—" And he staggered against the doorjamb, and bounced up, reaching out after the shrieking girl.

Now in these and similar situations a fellow had best keep out of the way until he knows exactly what is going on. Many an upright citizen stepping in to rescue a maiden in distress has been turned on by what seemed victim and attacker, both contuming him with insults for coming between a family squabble of man and wife. So I waited quietly in the shade of the arbora tree. The scent was delicious, and I breathed in—thankful, I may add, for the rest.

The Sybli caught her foot in a gray old root of the tree and she stumbled forward three or four paces, off balance, her arms spread out to try to save herself. She wore a tattered old blue and yellow checkered dress, badly torn as to bodice and skirt, and her feet were bare. She almost saved herself, and then she lost her balance and fell.

The man laughed and staggered forward. He was apim, a big, husky, full-fleshed fellow who knew what he wanted—and took it.

The girl Mindy tried to rise and gave a gasp as her ankle twisted under her. Her face showed babyish terror. The man leaped forward and she kicked out. I felt like giving a cheer as he yelped and reeled back, cursing.

"Never, you beast, never!" she cried. Her body was shaking.

"You will or I'll—"

She bit him as he came in again, sinking her sharp teeth into his hand. He let out a fearsome yell. It was quite clear that this secluded courtyard was soundproof and that with all the hullabaloo on the other side of the hotel this fellow was perfectly confident that the girl's cries would not be heard.

She bit hard. He managed to drag his hand back and he stuck it in his mouth. He did not look so drunk or so amorous now.

In the confusing lights of the moons reaching ghostly pink and gold fingers into the courtyard the girl tried again to draw away. Her baby-face glistened with terror.

"You leave off, Granoj, you hear! You keep away—"

Granoj shook his head, took his hand out of his mouth and leaped on her. She kicked and struggled and screamed and I slowly straightened up from leaning against the tree. He wore a sword, a thraxter, the straight cut and thruster of Havilfar, and he was probably a soldier off duty, judging by the belt and his boots.

And then, so swiftly I was almost too late, his mood changed. He saw, clearly, that the girl Mindy was not going to do as he wished, and he turned ugly. And, too, she had hurt him. She had kicked him shrewdly.

"I'll show you, you stupid Sybli! You can't make a fool out of me—"

He ripped his sword free and swung it up. That he was going to strike her with the blade was crystal clear.

I stepped out, with a sigh, and caught his arm.

"This has gone far enough," I said, and I tried to put the old snap into my voice.

But I felt that treacherous light-headedness, I felt the weakness, and with an oath he stepped back, having not the slightest difficulty in breaking my grip on his arm.

"You rast! You first—and then the girl!"

With that, he charged full at me, the sword upraised.

My own thraxter cleared the scabbard with what seemed to me agonizing slowness.

He was bull-strong, enraged, the drink lending him a reckless passion. He swung and chopped and hacked, and I had to dance a right merry little jig evading his savage attacks. The girl stopped screaming. The swords rang and clashed. He forced me back, and I felt the tree at my back, and I could not retreat any farther. And he laughed and taunted me most vilely, and rushed in. His words boiled around, his sword flickered cleverly, and he used a swordsman's trick that is well-known in fighting circles, and he would have had me had I not known the trick.

Without thought—for thought was too laggard now—my own sword arm did what a sword arm must do if it wishes to retain a body from which to hang, and this Granoj staggered back, suddenly, and as he staggered back so he pulled free of my blade. That steel glimmered darkly wet. He put a hand to his side, and he looked down, and lifted the hand, and the blood dripped, dripped...

So Granoj fell.

Whether or not he was dead I did not know. I felt the weakness on me, and I staggered and the Sybli was at my side and I thought she would berate me, and attack me for the deed. She put her hand around my waist, and held me, and said, "You must hurry, Jikai! You must go away from here, quickly, and go with the thanks of Mindy the Ennschafftena. Hurry!"

The walls of the courtyard wavered like curtains in a breeze. The whirlicue stump ends of the bottles of the door gyrated at me. I choked up phlegm. I fancied my wounds had opened and were bleeding again.

"Yes—must go—you are—all right—"

All the frivolity of the night's proceedings had turned nasty and ugly.

Death beat his black wings—as the quondam poets say—and I was feeling like one of the warmed-over corpses served up fresh from the Ice Floes of Sicce. If I did not get away, and me with a gray cloth mask over my head, I'd be done for.

"I am all right, Jikai—hurry, hurry—there is a wicket and stairs—the Street of Candles—there will be no one there now—my thanks—"

Staggering, sword in fist, hardly seeing, I was steered toward the little wicket in the corner. She threw open the gate and the slimy stairs led down, little used. I started at the top and the next moment I was at the bottom and with a pain there, too. I clawed up to my hands and knees and looked back. I could just see her outline.

"Remberee, Jikai—again my thanks—hurry!"

The wicket shut with a flat slap, like curtailed applause.

An arched opening gave egress onto the Street of Candles. No one was about, as Mindy the Sybli had promised. The shuttered doorways and windows added a ghostly note of desolation. A stray gyp went whining along, his brown and white coat wavering through the shadows. First things first. I wiped the sword on the gray cloth mask and then carefully folded it, bloodstains inward, and thrust it into my shirt. Clues... clues...

Then, sword scabbarded, all of Jikaida City going up and down and corkscrewing around me, I lurched off. By the time I had reached an avenue I recognized and could take my bearings the city was coming alive and the thin radiance of Zim and Genodras pulsed warmly in the sky to the east.

Three

I Hear of Moderdrin

"Now you've done slallyfanting around, Jak," said Pompino, crossly making his most cunning move in the Game of Moons, "perhaps we can get down to some serious thinking about getting out of Jikaida City."

"Oh, aye," I said. "I've done slallyfanting around for a time."

The bed with its yellow sheets was cool and wide and the loomin flowers and the flick-flick on the windowsill splashed bright color into our room. Pompino's move received my expected counter. He still disdained Jikaida and Jikalla, and was most wary of Vajikry, which, as people who play it thoughtlessly discover, is an unforgiving game. He would have indulged in King's Hand, but we were one die short and you cannot play good games of King's Hand with only four dice. As for Skull and Crossbones, you can enjoy so fearsome a mental bloodletting in that unholy game that I had cried off as being too weak.

We were settled into a reasonably priced and comfortable tavern in the Foreign Quarter. At the lady Yasuri's expense, I might add. I mended. She had pursed up her lips and told us that if we stayed at The Plume and Quill we would attract less attention than if we baited at her Star of Laybrites. As The Plume and Quill catered to the superior tradesmen of foreign parts who visited Jikaida City to do business, I didn't quite follow her reasoning; but she was paying. The lady Yasuri was the reigning Champion, and the Mediary Games had begun, and day by day they played Blood Jikaida, and, every now and then, Death Jikaida.

Pompino, who was, like me, an agent of the Star Lords, had berated me silly for getting mixed up in the schemes of other people, when we should be bending all our energies to doing what the Star Lords wanted. I didn't argue. I was as weak as a kitten, and the wounds had opened and the doctor, a shriveled little needleman with a brusque way with him, had cautioned me to stay in bed—or else. With a sniff he packed up his bag and his balass box of acupuncture needles and took himself off. His bill, too, would be paid by the lady Yasuri.

He had said, this Doctor Larghos the Needle, "I did not have the felicity of seeing the Death Jikaida in which you fought, young man. But I have heard of marvels." He shook his head. "It was said no man in all the world could best Prince Mefto the Kazzur at swordplay."

"I did not best him—"

"I know, I know. But he is minus his tail hand now, and there are only two places in Kregen that I know of where he may have a new hand graft. And he may not know of them."

"I hope the cramph doesn't!" said Pompino, most menacingly.

"Would you tell me of them?" I was thinking of Duhrra.

"No. Idle questions deserve sharp reprimands—"

"It was not an idle question."

He glanced at me, still stuffing his medical kit away, a glance that said eloquently that, as I had not lost a hand I had no need of the information. He probably thought I was making conversation. "The nearest is in the Dawn Lands and is rumored to exist in the country of Florilzun." He snorted. "But try to find that country on any map—try to find it. Hah!"

So I was left to look at the loomin flowers and get well.

Pompino was wearing a smart pale blue lounging robe and he took from a pocket a small brush and started to preen his Khibil whiskers. His sharp foxy face was engrossed. Because he was a Khibil, a member of that race of fox-faced diffs who are keen and smart and superb fighting men, he rather fancied himself. I did not mind. He was a good comrade although setting too much store by his understood duty to the damned Star Lords, the Everoinye, whom he thought of as gods.

To me they were just a pain, superhuman entities who eddied me about Kregen on a whim, and who might, if I rebelled, hurl me back four hundred light years to Earth.

"Had you stolen the Hamalese airboat and taken off, Jak, do you think the Everoinye would have allowed you to depart?"

"I do not know."

"But you had to try?"

"Yes."

"And you will try again as soon as you are well?"

"If that cramph Prince Nedfar has not quitted the city by then."

I had told him just enough about my escapade to answer the most obvious inquiries. I had not mentioned Lobur the Dagger. Pompino, who was a shrewd fellow, imagined I hailed from Hyrklana, a large island off the eastern coast of the enormous southern continent of Havilfar. I had been a kaidur in the arena in Huringa, the capital of Hyrklana, and could pass myself off as a member of that nation without trouble. But Pompino would wonder why a Hamalese—even one whose life I had just saved—had made no greater demurral about letting me away scot free.

Pompino himself, who came from South Pandahem, hated all Hamalese with the vigor of any man who has seen his country overrun and despoiled.

In the quiet backwater of The Plume and Quill I lay abed and mended. Being situated in the Foreign Quarter the tavern was outside the hurly-burly that continually bustled in the twin cities, Blue City and Yellow City. Jikaida dominated all. Jikaida, that greatest of board games of Kregen, was here played with fighting men, played in blood and death. To be of the Blue or to be of the Yellow, to win—and not to think of losing—these were the vital facts of life here.

"I," said Pompino, who like Lobur the Dagger had no head for Jikaida, "am thoroughly sick and tired of this city and Jikaida! By Horato the Potent! What in all Kregen has that stupid woman Yasuri got that we must protect her at the orders of the Star Lords?"

Maliciously, I said, "You question orders from the Star Lords, Pompino?"

He jumped. His foxy face bristled. "No! Of course not. Who said so?"

And I laughed.

Slowly, I mended. Slowly, my strength came back. Truth to tell, I recovered full health and strength far more quickly than anyone could who had not bathed in the Sacred Pool of Baptism in the River Zelph of far Aphrasöe. All the time I lay there, uselessly, I fretted over Vallia, and over Delia, Delia, Empress of Vallia. Was our son Drak doing the right things? Was Delia well? Oh yes, I fretted. But I had had an assurance from the Star Lords, delivered by their spy and messenger, the gorgeous scarlet and gold raptor called the Gdoinye, that Vallia did not succumb to her enemies and that Delia thrived and was well. This, I had to believe.

To do anything else would not only make me go off my head, make a lesser man of me—it would destroy me.

One day when I had demolished a whole vosk steak, a heaping pile of momolams, an equally heaping pile of steamed cabbage, had wolfed down a handsome squish pie—with a mental genuflection to Inch standing on his head—and was popping palines into my mouth, Pompino bustled in. And, I may add, that was the third such meal of the day and the time only just gone the bur of mid. He started without preamble: "Jak, tell me what you know of Moderdrin, the Humped Land."

"The Humped Land? Never heard of it—wait a minute." I chewed a paline, savoring the flavor, feeling the goodness refreshing every part. "I heard a couple of rat-faced fellows—they were gauffrers—arguing in a tavern about going to a place that might have been Moderdrin. I paid them no attention, minding my ale, for Dav was yelling for his stoup—"

"Yes, yes. But you know nothing of the Land of the Fifth Note? Moderdrin?"

"No. What of it?"

"Gold, Jak, that's what of it."

I sniffed, and popped another paline. The yellow berry tasted just as good as the last. Never satiated on palines, no one ever can be, an impossibility. Palines had sustained me on my very first visit to Kregen. They tasted just as good now.

"You may scoff. Gold, jewels, treasure—unimagined treasure—"

"Just lying around for you to stroll along and pick it up?"

His foxy face twisted up in fury at my obtuseness and his whiskers quivered.

'There is more. More than gold and treasure—there are magic arts to be won—secrets that wizards would give their ibs for—sorceries that will transform your life—"

"So?"

His eagerness switched into a comical surprise.

"So—what?"

"So—when do you start?"

"Who says I am going? There is danger—well, there must be danger, else everyone here would be rolling in wealth and all be as clever sorcerers as any Wizard of Loh."

"The point is, Pompino, my fine friend. You have two counts against you. One is you want me to go with you. And, two, you don't know if those onkers of Everoinye will let you go."

His concern was genuine.

"Jak! Jak! How many more times? I pray you, do not contume the Star Lords so! If they punish you—"

"Yes, you are right."

His punishment would be of and on Kregen. My punishment would be off Kregen and back to Earth as quick as a gigantic blue Scorpion could whisk me across the interstellar gulf.

"So you had best tell me all about it."

The telling was brief. All he really knew was that the Humped Land lay to the south and west of LionardDen, that brave men and bold might pluck its treasures, and he was meeting a man who would tell him more later that night at a tavern of ill repute on the edge of the Foreign Quarter. The tavern was called Nath Chavonthjid, after a mythical hero, and was situated very close to a poor quarter of the city where nightly riots brought out the watch with thwacking staves, and sharp swords, too, on many occasions.

"And are you fit enough to come with me?"

"Aye," I said, giving a deep groan. "I suppose so."

"It could make our fortunes and give us magical powers—"

"Or leave us rotting in a ditch with a dagger in our backs."

"I think you scoff too much, Jak the Nameless!"

"You are right, Scauro Pompino the Iarvin!"

The long green tendrils of the flick-flick plant on the windowsill licked out and scooped up a couple of fat flies which had been buzzing about, and slipped them neatly into the waiting and open orange cones of the flowers. All Kregans are aware of the symbolism inherent in the flick-flick.

Pompino laughed.

"Yes, I am right. And tonight you must not scoff. This fellow—he calls himself Nathjairn the Rorvard—is mighty prickly and only lets us into his plans—"

"For red gold, Pompino?" At the Khibil's abruptly upflung head, and the quick stab of his hand, I nodded. "Aye! He will take your gold for this great secret—and what will you get out of it?"

"I have asked questions—" He was mighty stiff about the imputations to his shrewd practicality. "Such a land exists. Expeditions do go there."

"Do they return?"

"You have heard of this famous sorcerer of Jikaida City, Naghan Relfin the Eye? Where did his powers come from, seeing he was but a poor saddler five seasons ago?"

There was truth in the remark. This sorcerer, Naghan the Eye, lived sumptuously, performed magics for large sums of money, and did have real, if indefinable, powers.

"You suggest Naghan the Eye obtained his necromantic powers from somewhere in Moderdrin, the Humped Land?"

"And there is the rich merchant on Silk Street who was ready to enlist to play Death Jikaida when he vanished from the city. He returned with a caravan of wealth—from the south and not the east, over the Desolate Waste."

"No doubt he went with a rascally gang of drikingers, common bandits who robbed honest men—"

"Not from the south and west."

I looked at Pompino. Maybe he had another reason for this folderol about magics and treasures to be picked up. "You suggest, do you not, my Pompino, that instead of attempting to steal the airboat, instead of going with a caravan across the Desolate Lands to the East, we strike southwest in order to put this city behind us? Is this not so?"

"You are too clever for me, Jak. Yes and no. We cannot move if the Star Lords do not permit it. And there is magic and there is gold to be won in Moderdrin. I believe it. Yes, we could do far worse."

If we went far enough to the southwest, got over the Blue Snowy River, and continued on we'd come eventually to Migladrin. I had friends in Migladrin. And, of course, if we turned west and carried on, we'd come to Djanduin. I never forget I am King of Djanduin, although, and deliberately with the troubles in Vallia, I had allowed the fragrant memory of Djanduin to attenuate and grow frail. There was no denying the warm feeling that shook me as I thought of Djanduin, and the rip-roaring welcome that awaited me there, the times we could have...

The superb four-armed fighting Djangs and the clever gerbil-faced Djangs of Djanduin would not forget me, their king, and this I knew with a humility that came fresh each time. Inch had passed on the messages. King of Djanduin I was, and I would be remiss in my duty if I did not visit that wonderful land very soon.

But, now, until the Star Lords discharged us from our duty to this tiresome lady Yasuri, I was going nowhere. And, truth to tell, Yasuri was not so tiresome, not after what she had been through and was now reigning Champion, Queen of the Kazz-Jikaida board of Jikaida City.

I said, "We will see this Nathjairn the Rorvard tonight, Pompino, your new friend, and we will measure his words."

The upshot was that all Pompino's avaricious dreams of quick wealth and superhuman powers vanished like smoke in a gale.

Dressing ourselves with some thought—for we were going into a shadowy borderline where the Watch would venture in strength and not at all if they didn't have to—we donned simple drab-colored clothes, of which we had a supply, and strapped up our brigandines, and hitched on our weapons. The feel of steel about me came with not so much a shock as a kind of surprise; I had skulked abed too long.

The twin suns were just sinking as we walked quietly along the avenues and headed for the poor quarter where the inn was situated. Far and Havil, they call the red and the green suns in the continent of Havilfar. It is a point well worth remembering. The Jikaida players were packing up their boards in the sidewalk restaurants and taverns as we went by. The brightly painted and intricately carved pieces were being laid tenderly away in the velvet-lined balass boxes. Pompino looked at me, and his foxy face bristled brilliant and russet in the last of the light.

There was no need to ask him what he was thinking.

Perhaps, this night, we two would be laid to rest in the velvet-lined balass box.

The inn called Nath Chavonthjid leaned against the evening, and the leaded windows spilled yellow light upon the rutted path. A miscellany of animals was tied to the hitching rail. We walked in. I know my hand rested on my thraxter hilt. The fumes of wine reached us and, mixed with them, the stink of dopa, that fiery liquor of Kregen guaranteed to drive a fellow fighting mad. Nobody with any sense has any truck with dopa, as nobody who values life touches kaff, the virulent Kregan drug that wafts to a heaven and a hell.

"Nathjairn?" said the portly Rapa behind the bar, his beak twisted askew from an old fight. He wiped a flagon on his apron and nodded to where men in leather aprons were hauling something toward the rear door. "There he goes, may Havil take him into his care."

We walked across.

Nathjairn the Rovard was being carried out, sightless, his throat a single crimson wound from which the blood dripped thickly.

Four

I Refuse to Fight in Kazz-Jikaida

Pompino switched his wooden sword about and thunked me prettily on the shoulder. I nodded to him, saluted and disengaged. The flagon of ale invited from the table and I drained it all down thirstily. In these practice bouts I had hitherto always attempted the difficult task of fighting with the object of losing with superior skill, that is, of seeming to give of my utmost and yet contriving to let the other fellow win. This is, as I have remarked, difficult.

Pompino took a swingeing draught of his own ale, and wiping his reddish whiskers where the foam clung, said, "I don't see how you lasted half a mur against Mefto the Kazzur, Jak. I really do not."

"He is the best swordsman I have ever met, Pompino. But, I repeat, he is nowhere near the greatest."

"You make the distinction?"

I threw the rudis onto the bed and pulled a chair forward into the space we had cleared for the practice bout. Fighting men must practice their art. If they do not, and grow slack, the fierce clangor of battle is no time to find out they are out of practice.

"Oh, yes. Swordplay is more a matter of the spirit."

"Horato the Potent is my witness you speak the truth. But how may a man attain to greatness without this spiritual quality?"

"He cannot. Witness Prince Mefto—"

"I could wish it in my heart you had slain him."

I did not wish to pursue a sore subject. "I shall make another attempt on Prince Nedfar's airboat."

He nodded. "I shall come with you—"

"And, my Pompino, you have heard no more of the Humped Land?"

He swore, a resounding oath that rattled the rafters.

"No. Men talk about it, slyly. But Nathjairn was prepared to take an expedition out. Now another one may be seasons—"

"We could always strike out southwestward ourselves."

"All men warn against such foolishness."

"The dangers are not so great as across the river and among the great lakes."

"True. Unless we go with an expedition, it is foolish to think of it. We go by caravan across the Desolate Waste, or we take the voller—and that may be the best answer."

LionardDen, called Jikaida City, was cut off from the rest of the continent of Havilfar. Vallia always called me, that beautiful island always would, and I missed Delia badly; but she had her own life to lead with the Sisters of the Rose. I confess Pompino's wild talk of treasure and sorcery intrigued. And that brought up another question.

I gave him a look as he refilled his flagon.

"You were all for going home to Tuscursmot in South Pandahem. You had, you said, spent enough time parted from your wife—"

"True." He drank and wiped his whiskers. "But the old girl will survive without me. We rub along. And while there is gold and wizardly powers—why, dom—just think of it—"

"Having heard of the Humped Land, now we must wait until someone puts an expedition together—is that it?"

"You mean—you'd go?"

I twirled the rudis. The heavy wood was dented and splintered from the force of our blows. The flick-flick plant satisfied another small segment of its appetite, and a fly vanished from the ken of men. "I may—I do not know. I am in more than two minds. But all is mere conjecture while we must care for the lady Yasuri, under the orders of the Star Lords."

"True. Damned true."

If a weathervane may be blown by the winds of heaven in any direction, then I was a weathervane, right enough.

"Y'know, Jak," said Pompino, carrying on a thread of thought begun by our remarks. "It is strange the Everoinye, if they are so tender for the welfare of the lady Yasuri, allow us to stay here, instead of at her hotel, the Star of Laybrites."

"The Star Lords are a bunch of onkers, of get onkers, and deserve to be stewed in their own juices." At his stricken face, I added, hurriedly, "Yes, yes, my Pompino, I know. But they have understood me, over the seasons. They know what I think of them. Until they prove themselves as being as good as humans, I cannot take them seriously as gods."

"You—" His reddish whiskers bristled, his dark eyes stood out, he looked as though he would choke. "Jak, Jak! They'll strike you down."

"Not them. That's not their damned way."

"Their ways pass the understanding of mortal men."

"If a being, an entity, cannot show the same decent qualities one expects of a fellow human being, why should any man be expected to worship and give praise to such a being?"

"I do not know. No one knows."

A knock at the door heralded the chambermaid, a little Fristle fifi with brown fur and a delightful smile, who told us the landlord had a visitor for us.

"Show him up," said Pompino, and we laid aside the wooden swords and took into our fists steel thraxters.

But it was only Onron, the lady Yasuri's Rapa coachman and chamberlain, decked out in a fine new livery, who told us with some condescension that the lady wished us to accompany her to the play this evening.

"The play?" said Pompino, laying aside his thraxter. "Since when has the lady ever wanted us to go with her to Jikaida?"

"The play, I said, you imbecilic Khibil!" The Rapa fluffed up his red tribal feathers, his beak polished and shining.

Pompino started up, bristling, but we sorted it out.

Between some members of some races of diffs there does exist an immediate, top of the head, instinctive antipathy, varying in intensity from diff to diff, that has over the seasons become formularized and lacking any intensity of conviction. The slanging becomes mawkish or merry, not taken seriously, a peg to hang a mental hat on, a way of release from other tensions, a little banter to lighten up the day.

In that spirit the Rapa Onron could say with a spit, "They should send you both to Execution Jikaida. That would make you skip about, believe me."

"I," said Pompino, "have no wish to hear another word about Execution Jikaida. We don't admit foul smells in here."

Before he could add the obvious and, perhaps, liken Onron to some particular stink, I butted in and got the details, as Pompino would have done after a little more enjoyable wrangling.

As popular entertainment, the theatre lagged a long way after Jikaida in Jikaida City. But there were playgoers in the city who demanded and obtained the best plays, and tonight's offering at Dottles Playhouse was to be given by a traveling company who had just come in with a caravan across the Desolate Waste. Pompino and I prepared for the evening, at the lady Yasuri's instructions wearing brigandines under our lounging robes, and with thraxters belted to our waists—well, they went outside the robes, for no sensible Kregan willingly parts with his sword unless he knows that the company he will keep and the haunts he will frequent will prove friendly.

The play was to be a great and famous old favorite of all those Kregans who love true theater and not the mindless singsong baubles dished up on the popular stage. We were to see *Jögen*, Part One, which comes from the fifth book of *The Vicissitudes of Panadian the Ibreiver*, the sublime cycle of plays by Nalgre ti Liancesmot. I was looking forward to it, and even Pompino, whose tastes were attuned more to the mass media—to use that oft-abused much later descriptive—gave his opinion that *Jögen* was always worth seeing and that he hoped this newly arrived company were of some quality.

There was the obvious aphorism to quote him—from Panadian, to be sure, "The empty grave proves the armor's worth." To which, it is interesting to remember, a later playwright, En Prado, adds the rider: "The gallows dangle proves the armor's faults."

There is debate over the latter, and as we went with the jostle of the crowd toward the theatre, Pompino was attempting to sway me to the school of thought which says that En Prado really wrote armorer's faults and not armor's faults. Either way, as we went in under the mineral-oil lamps' flare to find the lady Yasuri, either way makes sense. It is a pretty point of a particularly fascinating and useless kind of academic lore.

The fellow who tried to slip a dagger into my ribs so that he might more easily steal my purse was jabbed away with a fist in his mouth and then a boot in his guts. The crowd parted around him, and only two women squealed. Pompino wanted to put a knife between his ribs.

"Leave him be, good Pompino. He but practices his trade—and poor pickings he will get tonight, with a broken tooth and a bruised mouth marking him for a brawler."

The would-be thief picked himself up. His clothes were neat as they must be for his trade here. "By Diproo the Nimble-fingered," he spat out, spraying blood. "You are damned quick."

"Schtump!" shouted Pompino angrily. "Clear off!"

He went away, then, as the theater's hired guards stalked across to sort out the disturbance. I noticed the thief walked with a limp, and felt sorry for him, and then we pressed on into the lighted area where people waited and we saw the lady Yasuri.

She saw us too, and her little body drew itself up. Her lined old nutcracker face had mellowed wonderfully of late; but her nose and her tongue were as long and sharp as ever.

"You are late, you famblys."

She wore a deep-maroon cloak over a severe black bombazine dress, as we had first seen her. Her small body was decked with gems so that she glittered like a stalagmite. She was continually being looked at and pointed out as the reigning Jikaida champion, and she lapped up the fame and the applause. I shook my head. She had cared for me wonderfully after the final game in which she had taken the championship; but it had only been because I'd fought a crazy man's fight that she had won. It was clear that she owed me. It was also clear to me that she was now more wealthy than ever. And, with equal clarity, it was borne in on me that I could no longer tolerate the acceptance of charity in lieu of payment.

Pompino started to bumble about being held up on the way.

I said, "We are not late, lady, for the play has not yet begun." Then, as she flinched back, I added, "I am pleased you are keeping so well. What business do you have with us?"

But she was not a great lady for nothing. She was a Vadni, which is very high up the rank tables of Kregan nobility, and after that first surprised flinch, she flared up. Her tiny face screwed up wrathfully. Her sharp nose stuck up toward us like the beak of a swifter. Blood suffused her thin cheeks.

"I should have you whipped jikaider! Insolence—who is paying for you to lie abed in idle luxury?"

"If it is gold you want, lady, gold you may have."

She sneered at this. "And where would you two brave buckos put your hands on gold enough."

"Mod—" began Pompino. I trod on his foot and said, "We can hire out to someone else, lady. Do not forget, you discharged us, turned us off in the city, and when I fought I did not fight for you."

That had rattled her. She waited until a chattering pack of empty-headed girls fluttered past, all silks and draperies, and then she said: "No. No, Jak, you told me that. Who, then, were you fighting for?"

"Better ask the Witch of Loh, Ling-li-Lwingling."

She gave a petty gesture, annoyed. "She has left the city."

"To be truthful with you, lady, I do not know what she knows. But she hinted that she knew much—"

"Oh, that is the way of a Witch of Loh. If they do not know they will always pretend they do."

"So you summoned us here tonight. Here we are. Again—what is the business you have with us? If it is to demand we pay you back for your—"

"No, no, you great lumop! Only your last fight with Prince Mefto—it was wonderful and awful and frightening—only that—but I am champion and, indeed, I never expected it, did not dare to dream—" She pulled a scrap of lace, so that the threads snapped. "But I am champion and must play again, soon, in the Mediary Games. Will you—?"

"No."

"But—"

"I will not fight again in Death Jikaida."

"Jak—"

Pompino was breathing extraordinarily hard at my ear. He'd refused to act as a piece on the board when they played Kazz-Jikaida, Blood Jikaida, and had cogent reasons for that. The plan in which I had become embroiled had succeeded, against all expectations. I wanted nothing more of stepping out onto the blue and yellow checkered sand and of fighting at the whim of a player, fighting for my life for nothing.

"As the reigning Champion you cannot have any difficulty in finding men anxious to act as your pieces."

"True. But I want you as my Princess's Swordsman—"

"No."

A brazen gong note signaled that the play was due to begin. A few late-comers hurried past, heads down. We went toward the curtains which slaves held open for us.

"I have not finished with you, Jak!"

Through the curtains the waiting tiers of seats, the stage in its magic semicircle below, the lamps, the smell of theater, the muted hum and sway—we entered the magic world and, for those moments, could forget the world of Kregen as it was now and revel in the spiritual thoughts and the acts of passion and foolishness, of cowardice and heroism, springing from the mind of a man long dead.

This traveling company of players turned out to be top quality, and the audience sat enthralled. *Jögen* was given a splendid performance. As for the eponymous hero of the piece, Jögen himself, well, what can one say? Yes, he should have known better. He should not have trusted the woman.

But human nature is human nature, and we are supposed to progress through life and learn by our mistakes. Poor Jögen! We all laughed at the right places, and the women cried—some of them, not including the lady Yasuri—at the appropriate moments. At the first interval the wide stone-flagged taverna area, softly lit by shaded lights, filled with the talk of playgoers discussing the play.

I saw Lobur the Dagger, laughing, brilliant in evening dress, talking animatedly to a lovely girl with dark hair, all in shimmering green, and they were oblivious to anything else.

In that group of Hamalese stood a man with a shock of dark hair much like the girl's in color, with a craggy and yet noble face which was the male counterpart to her vivid femaleness, so I guessed they were father and daughter. By this man's dress, impeccable and with a minimum of jewelry, by the deference shown him by his compatriots, and by his own superb poise and sense of being, I took him to be Prince Nedfar. He wore a rapier and main gauche, whereat my brows drew down.

A scheme that was not as foolish as it appeared at first sight occurred to me; but I pushed it away. It was audacious, and that was a merit; it was also chancy, and while I have taken some pretty long chances in my time, here and now it seemed to me was not the time or place. I'd steal the fellow's flier, and curse him for a Hamalese as I flew away.

In many playhouses of Kregen the slaves beat three gongs at the end of the intervals. The first is to tell you to order your last drink; the second is to tell you to sup up and put your glass down; and the last is to say that you have only a few murs to reach your seat and if you are not there in time, then, by Beng Lomier the Blessed, patron saint of every strolling player, the slaves will bar the curtains on you.

The first gong note clashed out over the taverna.

"A Stuvan for me," quoth Pompino.

"A light yellow, Jak," said the lady Yasuri.

I fetched the drinks. The flagged area emptied as the people returned to their seats, anxious to be settled in time and miss nothing, and the second gong had not struck. The Hamalese were arguing about just who had ordered what, as tiresome people do in bars.

The curtains over the doorless opening to the entrance parted and four men walked in. They did not look, even at a cursory glance, like devotees of the stage. They wore dark clothes, dust-stained, and furry caps under which, I was prepared to wager, they had iron skulls. Their faces were grainy, hard, with lips thinned with purpose. Pompino looked, and said: "Hai!" and eased himself back from the little table at which he and Yasuri sat.

Do not forget, Pompino the Iarvin was a Khibil. What is more important—he had been chosen by the Star Lords to be a kregoinye and act in moments of emergency for them.

361

The newcomers looked around, orienting themselves. They saw the Hamalese, who were still squabbling about the drink order. A group of locals went out, and the place looked very empty, and the four men turned their slate-gray eyes on us.

One said something to his companions. He was bigger than the others, bulky with power, and his gloved hands made quick, hard gestures. He advanced toward us.

He bowed. His words were perfectly civil: but he did not smile as he spoke. Nor did he remove his hat, which is a mark of respect not quite as common on Kregen as on Earth, but which would have been perfectly proper in the circumstances.

"You are the lady Yasuri, Yasuri Lucrina, Vadni of Cremorra?"

Yasuri put her hand to her lips. "Yes..."

"Then I have to tell you that the king is dead, that the kingdom is over-run, that your vadvarate is gone—"

Yasuri let out a high shriek at the words. She fell back against the chair. Her face was stricken. Pompino looked at her in alarm.

The hard-faced man went on speaking, and as he spoke he moved like a scuttling tiklo of the desert.

"The king is dead, and King Ortyg the Splendid reigns in glory. He commands instant obedience, lady—and he commands your death!"

The messenger of this ill news sprang even as he spoke.

His sword cleared scabbard and, twinkling like a bar of light, slashed down at Yasuri's unprotected head.

My own thraxter was there, the two blades clashed, and thrummed with the vibration of the blow. My blade turned and his slid along and so I turned with the coming thrust and he leaped away, yelling in anger, and the point fell short.

There was no time to give him room to get set. His three comrades were rushing upon us, bared steel aflame. I leaped the table that had impeded my thrust, and crossed swords with the fellow, forcing him back, angling him away from Yasuri.

He fought viciously and well, shocked to find opposition preventing him from carrying out a mission that had seemed so easy of accomplishment. He shouted insults as he fought, and I saw the first of his bully-blade comrades hurling on, and so I was quick.

They both went down, skewered, and the third was engaged even as Pompino roared in at my side to take the fourth.

We were rather sharp with them. Pompino stepped back, his blade held up. With his left hand he smoothed his whiskers.

"What rubbish they choose to send," he said.

"They nearly did it." I bent to wipe the thraxter on the clothes of the first. "Had they just done the deed instead of parlaying around..."

362

Yasuri put her hand on my arm. She was shaking. "King Ortyg," she whispered. "I am lost, lost—he hates my family dreadfully. They but gloated on my misery—"

"And they paid the price," Pompino said, and snicked his blade away.

"You wish to continue with *Jögen*?" I said as the gong sounded.

She shook her head. "No—no, I cannot—"

Then Prince Nedfar and the other Hamalese with him was there. He was smiling. He held out his hand. "Let me shake the hands of two brave men who know how to protect a lady. Cramphs like this deserve to die a thousand deaths." He bent his stare upon Yasuri. "You are well, lady?"

"Yes—yes, thank you."

He introduced himself, and the chief personages of his retinue. In that number he included his daughter, the Princess Thefi, but not, I was intrigued to notice, Lobur the Dagger.

"I am a connoisseur of swordplay. I have seldom seen two Bladesmen do their work so finely. You must visit me—"

Pompino's face began to stain red and his foxy features bristled up uglily. He was going to burst out with shatteringly rude and impolitic remarks about rasts of Hamal and stinking Hamalese—and so I stepped in quickly and said all the right things, and thanked this damned condescending prince for his kind words on our swordplay, and smirked and smiled, and so got us out of it with the promise to visit him on the following day at The Montilla's Head.

Yasuri was almost overcome.

"Now you see, Jak," Pompino whispered as we escorted her back to The Star of Laybrites. "Now we can see the hand of the Star Lords clearly!"

"Oh, aye. We were sent here tonight to save Yasuri's life. And it is useless to question why the Star Lords want her hide saved. She isn't a bad old biddy; just the result of bad breeding. Let us hope we can retire gracefully now."

We saw her safely home and then went back to our inn.

"And, Jak, if you think I'm going to see that rast of a Hamalese tomorrow, then you can think again."

"I have no love for the folk of Hamal while they continue to obey mad Empress Thyllis. But they are not evil of themselves." I yawned. "Anyway, think of the chance! Now we can get into the hotel without skulking there at night. Now we can smile and act graciously, and get up on the roof, and then—"

Pompino looked up. He nodded.

"To steal their voller I will act like a craven. One must dare all things in service to the Everoinye."

I did not confide to him my feelings on that score.

Five

We Meet Drogo the Kildoi in the Jolly Vosk

"We are off to see Execution Jikaida this afternoon, Jak, Pompino. You will join us?"

Lobur the Dagger spoke cheerfully, because Kov Thrangulf stood with the group smiling and nodding. No one cared much for Kov Thrangulf; but he performed some mysterious function in Prince Nedfar's entourage. Also he was a kov, which is by way of being a terrestrial duke, and so was a man of power of himself.

"I think not, Lobur; but thank you all the same."

Lobur had not recognized me as Drax, Gray Mask—well, by Zair! had he done so I would have been mortally chagrined.

We had taken to visiting the group around the prince and we sensed that they were glad of company, being isolated in this city where, although LionardDen was neutral in the wars Hamal was waging within the Dawn Lands, there were many who hated Hamal and all things Hamalian with blind hostility. We spent time here, and joked and laughed around; but we had not had a single chance to get up on the roof and steal the voller. The airboat was kept under heavy guard, and we had not, so far, been able to get away from our new-found friends. Of course, the slightest suspicion that we were interested in the voller with the view to her purloining would bring disaster. We had to take it easy, tsleetha-tsleethi, and await our opportunity.

As for Prince Nedfar, after the debacle of the alliance with Prince Mefto, he had remained here to indulge himself in Jikaida. So he said. I began to entertain uneasy suspicions that he had ulterior motives. The treaty that was supposed to have released many powerful armies to fight against Vallia might still be concluded—with some pawn other than Prince Mefto.

This business of going to witness Execution Jikaida was a nuisance. The so-called game was ordinary Jikaida, played to the rules, and with living men and women as pieces—just as they do in Kazz-Jikaida. But these pieces were condemned criminals. The moves were made and the piece being taken would be cut down, there and then, on the spot, and the game proceed. This was not my idea of fun.

It was not Lobur's, either, as I could see, and the prince himself had made an excuse. This fat, hard-breathing, smelly Kov Thrangulf was the one panting to go. And Lobur, perforce, as a mere aide to the prince, had to acquiesce.

The oldest families of Hamal hold especial pride in their lineal descent from the ancients, and mark this by including the name ham in their own names. Thus I was, as you know, in all honor Hamun ham Farthytu in Hamal. Paline Valley and Nulty and those skirling times seemed long and long ago now; but such is the accumulation of tradition and the weight of incumbence, that I knew if I turned up at Paline Valley now I would be received as the rightful Amak. Unless, of course, a usurper had managed to arrange the bokkertu and through legal means taken the title and the estates. Then, the cramph, he'd have another fight on his hands.

Lobur the Dagger was a mere Horter of Hamal, a simple gentleman. He was in the prince's service and joyed in that. But I discovered his name. This was Lobur ham Hufadet, and his family were honored citizens of Trefimlad. He was madly, overwhelmingly, besottedly in love with the prince's daughter, the Princess Thefi. A match did not seem in their stars, by reason of their station. But on Kregen all things are possible as, by Zair, had I not shown? This fat and unpleasant Kov Thrangulf did not have the honor of placing the ham in his name. He was a kov, a powerful and wealthy man; but he did not own to the ham. Yes, you will say—a common, a conventional, situation. Agreed. From it all manner of devilments and schemes might spring. And—they did. But, as is my wont, I will hew to the path of chronology and relate to you what happened between Lobur the Dagger and the Princess Thefi and Kov Thrangulf, when what happened impinged upon this my own story. Suffice it for the moment, there in Jikaida City, I had my heart set on that voller. Failing the voller, then I might have to walk out. Either way, I had no wish to linger in LionardDen.

Pompino said, "I trust you enjoy yourselves this afternoon. I am for the merezo where they are racing for high stakes."

As we walked off, shouting the remberees, I knew Pompino lied. He was serious, deadly serious, on a sudden.

"I have had no chance to tell you before, Jak—we are altogether too chummy with these yetches of Hamalese. But—I have had a communication from the Star Lords."

"The Gdoinye spoke to you?"

"Yes. We are quits of our work with Yasuri—"

"We are!"

"Aye. If that assassination attempt was all it was about, well and good. What matters now is we will not be prevented from leaving."

Whatever the situation might appear to be on the surface, I knew well enough that the Star Lords planned long and darkly into the future. What they did they did with fell purpose. Yasuri was important in ways we could not comprehend. But, we were quit of her. I joyed in that, and spared a thought for Yasuri and wondered what she would do now. But that was her business—aye, hers and the Star Lords', no doubt.

"Most of that lot from Hamal are watching Execution Jikaida," I said. I spoke lightly as we walked along in the streaming mingled lights of the Suns of Scorpio. "We are known in the hotel now. Why should we not—?"

"Capital. I am with you."

So we turned around and retraced our steps.

Well, now... If the old blood thumps a little faster around the body, and the sweat starts out on the brow, and the palms grow damp and the throat dry—at memory, mere memory? We were not working for the Everoinye now, we were working for ourselves and for all the help we had ever had from the Star Lords that made not the slightest difference, or so I thought. I recall as we walked along in the suns shine that I contemplated hiring out as a caravan guard and trekking back over the Desolate Waste, as we had planned. But the idea of the voller obsessed us. The speed of a flier is phenomenal compared to a saddle animal.

The caravans continued to ply, one had only just arrived today, and the last had brought in the company of strolling players and the four stikitches who had so signally failed to earn their hire.

Pompino hitched his sword belt.

"Let us have a wet first—in honor of Dav Olmes, for example, or Konec, or—"

"Let us take a drink, anyway, you procrastinating fambly!"

I wanted to give the Hamalese time to get to the Jikaida deren, those massive central blocks where the bloody games of Jikaida were played, before we raided the hotel.

Any hostelry would do, provided it was of the better sort, and not a mere dopa den. The jade and ruby brilliance fell about us. The sweet scents of Kregen intoxicated us with life. Ah, Kregen, Kregen—well, we found a tavern and were about to enter when a man came flying through air and almost brought us both down. And, as far as I know, they don't play exactly that kind of Rugby on Kregen. The fellow hauled himself up. He was a Brokelsh, squat and hairy and gibbering with rage. He shook his fist at the tavern and then lurched off, rumbling and cursing, swearing about a Havil-forsaken Kildoi.

I chilled.

We went in. I am well aware how foolish, how superficial, it is to say, "I chilled." But, by Vox, that is exactly right. I felt the cold clamp around me. I did chill, and you may cavil all you wish at the expression. It is apt and it is right...

The Kildoi was instantly visible, surrounded by a gang of roughs. They were not attacking him, but they were not friendly. Now Prince Mefto the Kazzur was a Kildoi. He had bested me in swordplay—oh, yes, I had cut off his tail hand at the last—but he had proved the superior swordsman. Kildoi have four arms and a powerful tail with a hand. Korero, my comrade who carried his shields at my back in battle, was a Kildoi. They are marvels—and this specimen, although sporting a beard darker than the golden blaze of Korero or Mefto, was just such a one, bronzed, powerful, superb in physique, cunning and most proficient with his five hands.

"We don't want your sort in here," shouted one of the roughs, a cloth around his neck stained greasily with sweat.

"Prince Mefto was a great man!" declared another, a runt of an Och slopping ale.

"Aye," said another. "Prince Mefto may have lost our wagers, because his side thought he would be chopped. But you can't say things about him here. He'll be back to win again—"

Sweat rag chimed in. "You'd better clear off, schtump, five hands or no, before we blatter you."

"You misunderstand me, my friends—" began the Kildoi.

"No we don't. You're asking questions about Mefto the Kazzur and we're all his friends here, and you bear him no good will."

A flung dagger streaked from the gloom of the counter. The Kildoi put up a hand and deflected the dagger. The action was instinctive and unthinking, and I recognized the superb Disciplines that gave Korero such wonderful command of his shields.

"I see you are not friendly," said the Kildoi. "So I will retire—"

A blackjack swung for his head, and he leaned and moved and the blackjack spun away, harmlessly. The very contempt of his actions, innate in their display of consummate skill, incensed these fellows. Mefto had always been a favorite, and these people did not know the full story. In the next instant, summoning their courage, they leaped upon the Kildoi.

I started in to help, intrigued by all this, and, after a pause, Pompino joined me. There was a deal of shoving and banging, and swearing, and a collection of black eyes and bloody noses before the three of us burst from the door of the tavern. On a wooden bracket the inflated skin of a vosk swung in the wind, and the inn was called The Jolly Vosk.

"Whoever you are," said the Kildoi, with a jerk of the thumb of his upper right hand, "my thanks. The sign over the tavern proclaims the denizens within."

We walked off along the sidewalk, and we began to laugh. Snatches of the bizarre flying acrobatics of the fellows in there as the Kildoi threw them hither and yon recurred to us, and we laughed.

"Lahal, I am Drogo, and a Kildoi, as you see."

We made the pappattu, me as Jak and Pompino with his full name. Then Pompino burst out with: "And, Drogo, this is the same Jak who cut off the tail hand of that bastard Mefto."

Drogo stopped dead. He turned that magnificent head to study me more closely. I looked back.

His eyes carried that peculiar green-flecked grayness of uneasy seas, of light shining through rain-slashed window panes—the images are easy but they convey only a little of the sense of inner strength and compulsion, of dedication and awareness, the eyes of this Kildoi, Drogo, revealed.

Presently he took a breath. His arms hung limply at his sides. I noticed that one end of his moustaches was shorter than the other. His teeth were white, even, and showed top and bottom when he smiled.

He smiled now, a bleak smile like snow on the moors.

"I am surprised you are still alive."

"That's what we all say," burbled on Pompino.

"Mefto was foolish," I said, deliberately turning along the flagstones and walking on, forcing them to keep pace.

"Any man who faces Mefto in swordplay is foolish."

"Aye," I said, and with feeling. "Aye, by Zair!"

As is generally the case on Kregen no one pays much attention to the strange gods and spirits by whom a man swears; it is only when they give away your country of origin when you do not want that information revealed that they attract attention.

Pompino laughed, a little too high.

"We never did get that wet."

"I see I was the unwitting cause of your thirst—"

"No, no, horter, not so." Pompino, I felt sure, was now uneasy, had come to a slower appreciation of smoldering passions in this man. He kept walking on, a little too swaggeringly, and laughing. "Oh, no—"

I said, "You were not the cause of the thirst. You merely prevented our quenching it."

He gave me another expressionless look that, with those eyes and that face, could never be truly expressionless. I thought he was trying to sum me up, and running into difficulty.

"I am remiss," he said, and the note of ritual was strong in his voice. "Let me buy you both a drink. I insist. It is all I can do, at the least, to express my thanks."

So we went into the next inn, a jolly place where they served a capital ale, and we hoisted stoups. We went to a window seat and sat down just as though we were old comrades. I fretted. I was shilly-shallying over this business of the voller.

Now, in other times I would have gone raging up to the roof, a scarlet breechclout wrapped about me and a sword flaming in my fist, and down to the Ice Floes of Sicce for any damned Hamalese who got in the way. But, now, I was taking my time, making excuses, seizing every opportunity to prevaricate.

Many times on Kregen I have noticed that when I shilly-shally for no apparent reason, when things do not work out with the old peremptory promptness, there is usually an underlying cause. Often to have rushed on headlong would have been to rush headlong into disaster. And, Zair knows, that has happened, often and often...

But the voller beckoned, and I hesitated and did not know why.

The Star Lords had discharged us from our immediate duty, the Gdoinye had so informed Pompino.

Then why hesitate?

But it was pleasant to sit in the window seat of a comfortable inn in the grateful afternoon radiance of the Suns of Scorpio, with a cool flagon of best ale on the clean-scrubbed table... And, believe me, doing just that is just as important a part of life on Kregen as dashing about with flashing swords.

My thoughts had taken me away a trifle from the conversation. I heard Pompino talking and the words: "...a capital voller..." leaped out at me.

I listened. This Drogo was clearly seeking Mefto—and it was no great guess that he was seeking with no good will. He could be a bounty hunter. He could be a wronged husband. He could be a stikitche. But Pompino must have told him that Prince Mefto had returned to Shanodrin, the land the Kazzur had won for himself in blood and death. Now Drogo wished to get out of Jikaida City as fast as he could—and a caravan, besides being slow, was also not on the schedule for departure for some time.

"An airboat? Aye," said Drogo, and drank.

"It is a great chance—" Pompino was not such a fool, after all.

To have this Kildoi with us when we essayed the airboat would make success much more certain.

I pushed aside the startled inner reflection that this was not how I would have thought and acted only a few years ago. There were wheels within wheels here, and I was canny enough by now to let the wheels run themselves for a space.

Drogo said, "If you will have me, I will join you—"

"Agreed!" said Pompino, and he sat back and quaffed his ale.

I sat back, also, but I did not drink.

Drogo did not look at me. He made rings with his flagon on the scrubbed wood.

"And you, Jak?"

"Why, Horter Drogo, is it that you Kildoi always seem to have only one name?"

His smile was again like those damned ice floes of the far north.

"But we do not. We do not parade our names, that is all."

"Point taken—and, as for your joining us, why, yes, and right heartily." I put warmth into my voice. Foolish, I felt, to antagonize him for no reason.

"Then no harm is done."

What he meant by that I was not sure. I did know that the old intemperate Dray Prescot might well have challenged him to speak plain, blast his eyes.

He went on, "We are of Balintol, as you know, and we keep ourselves to ourselves. There are not many of us. All the first families know one another. The use of family names is felt to be—to be—"

"Drink up, Horter Drogo," I said, "and let me get you the other half."

That, at the time, seemed as good a way as any of ending that conversation.

Once again I promised myself I'd have a good long talk with Korero when I got back to Vallia. My comrade who carried his enormous shields at my back was a man of a mysterious people, that was for sure.

It was, naturally, left to Pompino, when I returned with the drinks, to say, "And you are chasing this rast Mefto to—"

"One of us will kill the other." Drogo took his flagon into his lower left hand. The other three hands visible clenched into fists. "I shall not face him with swords. So he may die. I devoutly hope so."

Like Korero, this Drogo did not habitually swear by gods and demons as do most folk of Kregen.

"You are no swordsman yourself?"

He glanced across at me, and his fists unclenched, and he took a pull of ale.

"Oh, yes, I own to some skill. But my masters suggested I would be better served by taking up some other weapon—"

"And?" interrupted Pompino.

Drogo made himself laugh. His teeth were white and even, and his tongue was very red.

"I manage with an axe, polearms, the bow, a knife—"

I said, "All at once, no doubt." As I spoke I heard the sour note of envy in my voice.

"When necessary."

By Vox! But I had walked into that one with my chin!

"You have met Katakis?"

Offhandedly, he answered obliquely. "The little streams run into the great river."

I nodded. "And Djangs?"

He frowned. "No—I do not know of them."

"Oh," I said. "I just wondered."

I stood up.

"If we intend to take this confounded voller, then let us be about our business."

Six

Concerning a Shortcut

Most men are not mere walking bundles of reflexes. Most men have deeper layers of thought and emotions below the superficialities of life. Among the many people a man bumps into on his way through life there must be some, a few, for whom he feels enough interest to be fascinated by those deeper levels.

And this really has little to do with friendship, which is by way of being an altogether different idea.

As we walked along in the radiance from the twin suns of Antares, I pondered the enigma of this Drogo the Kildoi.

Pompino was prattling on about Jikaida and his own honest conviction that he did not have a head for the game, and Drogo was nodding civilly and saying that, yes, he quite enjoyed the Game of Moons, if he was in the mood, and that he found Vajikry surprisingly challenging for what appeared so simple a game although the version they played in Balintol, his homeland, was markedly different from that played here in the continent of Havilfar. I wondered how he had got here and his adventures on the way. Korero never spoke of himself. Balintol is a shrouded land and a fit birthplace for the men it breeds.

Onron, the lady Yasuri's coachman, caught up with us as we passed through the colonnades surrounding the Kyro of the Gambits. His bright yellow favor glistened. We were about to cross into the Foreign Quarter, where the Blue and the Yellow held no favor one above the other.

"I've been looking for you all over, you pair of hulus," he puffed out. He was riding a freymul, the poor man's zorca, with a chocolate-colored back and streaks of yellow beneath, and Onron had ridden the animal hard. Clots of foam fluffed back from his patient mouth. Sweat stained all down his neck, matting the fine brown hairs.

"Hai, Beaky!" greeted Pompino, jovially.

"May your whiskers shrivel, you—" Onron threw the reins over the freymul's head and stood to face us. "My lady demands your presence—at once. The word she used was Bratch."

"Why should we jump for her any more?"

The Kildoi, Drogo, had disappeared into the shadows. Onron scratched his beak. He was not used to this kind of address respecting his lady.

"You had better go at once," he warned.

Pompino glanced at me, and his bright eye told me that the Star Lords had relieved him of a burden. The case appeared to me, suddenly, and I confess somewhat startlingly, as being different. A tug at his sleeve pulled him a little apart.

"The Everoinye have discharged you of the obligation to Yasuri, Pompino. The Gdoinye spoke to you. But not to me..."

His foxy face took on a shrewd, calculating expression, and yet, I was grateful to see, a sympathetic look also.

"You could be right. The Gdoinye did not speak to you."

"Hurry, you famblys!" called Onron.

"Yet, the voller—"

"Drogo will turn up when Onron is gone. I shall go to the lady Yasuri and see what she requires. If you and Drogo can manage the flier, you will command the air. You can pick me up later at the inn."

"Yes." He stroked his whiskers. "Yes, Jak. You have my word as a kregoinye. I will return for you."

"Good—then we must both hurry."

He turned away at once and started off along the colonnade, his lithe form flickering in light and shade past the columns. He heard Onron's indignant yells right enough; he just ignored them. I turned to the Rapa.

"I will come, Onron—so stop your caterwauling."

He stuck his beak into the air, offended, and climbed back on the freymul. There was no question of my riding, so, perforce, I walked smartly off for the Star of Laybrites.

The thought crossed my mind that more stikitches, assassins, had come in with the caravan that had brought Drogo, and Yasuri's life was again in peril. But that did not make sense. For one thing, this King Ortyg would not know his men had failed. And, for another, had there been assassins there would have been no time for Yasuri to dispatch Onron in this fashion.

One objection to the first point could be that the new King Ortyg of Yasuri's country employed a Wizard of Loh to go into lupu and spy out for him what was happening here. That was possible. I quickened my steps, although recognizing the validity of the second point.

The Rapa coachman took off on the freymul, yelling back that he would tell the lady that I was obeying her and convey to her the news of Pompino's ingratitude and treachery. Onron shot off along the avenue among the crowds, and I took a shortcut.

There are shortcuts in life and there are shortcuts. This one took me through a poor quarter where they spent their time in tiny workshops making tawdry souvenirs of Jikaida for the visitors to pay through the nose for in the souks. And, this shortcut was a shortcut to disaster. The Watch was out, backed up by soldiers in their armor and hard black and white checkered cloaks, helmets shining.

A yelling mob rushed through the narrow alleyway, sweeping away stalls and awnings in their panic. I could see the soldiers riding them down, laying about them with the flats of their swords. Two men almost knocked me flying. I ducked into a doorway with the stink of days-old vegetables wafting out. The rout rushed past. Then—well, I suppose I should not have done what I did—but, being me, I did.

A woman carrying a baby fell onto the slimy cobbles.

The pursuing totrixes hammered their six hooves into the ground, prancing on, and the woman would be run down.

Darting out, with only the most cursory of looks, I scooped her up, baby and all, and started back for my doorway.

A totrix, rearing up, shouldered me away. I spun about, staggering, clutching the woman. A Watchman hit me over the head with his bludgeon. He was shouting, excited, frantic.

"Here's one of the rasts—" And he hit me again.

That was it, for a space.

The blackness remained, the blackness of Notor Zan, and I did not open my eyes. The place where they had thrown me stank. A dismal moaning and groaning filled the air. And, in my aching head the famous old Bells of Beng Kishi clashed and clanged. I winced. Cautiously, I opened one eye.

The place was arched with ribbed brick, slimy and malodorous, and a few smoky torches sputtered along the walls. The place was a dungeon, a chundrog, and the prison would extend about us with iron bars and stone walls and many guards.

Water dripped from that arched ceiling and splashed upon us, green and slimy, stinking. Rivulets of the water trickled down to open drains along the center. The people were crammed in. They were poor. They were tattered and half of them were starving. They moaned in long dismal monotones. And the air stifled with fear.

Gradually I pulled myself together and sorted out what had happened.

Criminals had been sought, and the Watch had scooped up a ripe bunch, and anyone who got in the way was taken up also. It is a dreadfully familiar story. The Nine Masked Guardians who ran LionardDen were fanatical about the order of the city. Many visitors stayed here, and the reputation of the city rested on reports of conditions. Who would journey to a city of thieves, or a city of revolution—even to play Death Jikaida?

There was no sign in this tangled company of the woman and her baby and I just hoped they were all right. The people looked like a field of old rags ready for the incinerators. I have said that the Star Lords never lifted a finger to help me, and although this is not strictly accurate, for they once enabled me to overhear a conversation to my advantage in the island of Faol of North Havilfar, it was precisely in the kind of situation in which I found myself now that no help could be expected from the Everoinye. I expected none.

A group of ruffians near me, all gleaming eye and broken teeth and rags, were discussing future possibilities.

"It is Death Jikaida, you may be sure."

"No—they want fighting men for that."

"We can fight—aye, and will fight, if they put spears into our hands."

"Kazz-Jikaida," said another, shaking. "Blood Jikaida. My brother was cut down in that, two seasons ago."

A man with lop ears and a broken nose, very villainous, stilled them all as he spoke. "It will not be that." He spoke heavily, with a wheeze. "It is Execution Jikaida—"

373

"No! No!" The shouts of horror were as much protestations as outbursts of terror. "Why, Nath, why?"

"They had a blood-letting yesterday, did they not? And the great ones demand another game—I know, may they all rot in the Ice Floes of Sicce forever and ever."

The uproar told me that these ill-used people put store by the words of this Nath. It seemed he possessed enough of the yrium, that mysterious force that demands from other men respect and obedience, to command them.

Lop-eared Nath, he was called, and he looked a right villain.

We were fed a thin gruel and most of it was dilse, that profuse plant that pretends to nourish, and fills a man's belly for a time and then leaves him more hungry than before. We drank abominable water. This chundrog was Spartan, a dungeon from which it would be well-nigh impossible to escape except in death. I began to think along those lines. A feigned death...

Engaging in conversation with the nearest group, I soon discovered that plan was a bubble-dream.

"Anyone who pretends death is stuck through with a spear, to make sure." Lop-eared Nath appeared to relish his words. "Listen, dom, we only get out of here one way. We go to act as pieces in Execution Jikaida."

"But there is a chance in that. All the pieces will not be taken, not all killed."

"Aye. A chance."

A man with a snaggle of black teeth and one eye chuckled. He was half off his head already.

"It depends who we get to act as player."

"May Havil shine his mercy upon us," said a woman, and she made the secret sign of Havil the Green.

We spent three days and nights in the hell-hole. At one point a man in resplendent clothes and a blue and yellow checkered mask over his face appeared. Lanterns illuminated his figure as he stood upon a dais beside the lenken door. The people babbled to a stupefied silence.

"You are all given a trial, and the evidence is against you and you are all condemned." This man, the representative of the Nine Masked Guardians, spoke in a booming, confident voice. He lifted a ring-clustered hand. "The trial was fair and just, according to the laws of the republic. You are all appointed to act as pieces in Execution Jikaida—"

He got no further. The yells and shrieks, the imploring screams, all smashed and racketed to that slimed brick roof. He turned away, disgusted with the animal-like behavior of the mob beneath him, and walked out with a measured, pompous, confident tread. We were left to face our fate.

What the devil had happened to Pompino and Drogo? Had they taken the voller? What ailed Yasuri? These questions flew up in my head, and I saw them as the petty concerns they were.

On the morrow I faced Execution Jikaida, and, by Krun, that was a concern that shook a fellow right down to his boots.

Execution Jikaida may be conducted in a number of different ways, and I guessed we'd get the stickiest.

Guards shepherded us along the next afternoon—we could judge the time because the afternoon was the time for this particularly nasty form of the game—and we shuffled out, loaded with chains manacled and fettered to our hands and legs. Screams and sobs echoed about that dolorous procession.

At a wooden door we were each given a large drink of raw dopa.

I drank the dopa.

Some of the people calmed down, others slobbered, some fell fainting. The guards dealt with them all faithfully.

At last we were marched down a long stone corridor. At the far end double doors arched, and these, we guessed, led out onto the board. A Jiktar, smart in his soldier's uniform, stood by the door, backed by a squad of men. His face, although grim, betrayed a feeling that in my heightened state I hardly recognized as pity.

"Take heart!" he bellowed. "Not all of you will die. It depends on the game. Some will live. Pray to your gods that you will be among the fortunate."

Lop-eared Nath shouted up, truculent, fierce. "And who is to act as our player?"

"You?"

Nath shrank back. "Not me!"

I said, "Jiktar, how can the player be harmed?"

He looked hard at me.

"You are a foreigner? Yes, I see. Then you were foolish to commit a crime in our city. The object of the game is to take the Princess, is this not so? To place her in hyrkaida? Well, then, her Pallan is the player in Execution Jikaida."

I saw it all.

The Pallan is the most powerful piece on the board, and, also, as a consequence, the piece the opposing player most wishes to dispose of.

The smells of this dismal place rose about me. The water dripped. And the people with their bellies afire with dopa moaned softly, given over to their own destruction.

"Thank you, Jiktar," I said, and shuffled off back into the amorphous mass of people.

"Wait!"

The word hit me like a leaden bullet slung by a slinger. "Yes."

"You, dom, will be the player."

The eyes of the people about me showed white. Some started to caterwaul their fears, others cried out, some shrieked.

"But—"

"Shastum!" The Jiktar roared out, instantly halting the growing noise. "Silence. Move out!"

I did not move.

Into that cowed silence I said, "And who acts as player when I am slain?"

"The next in line. There is no interruption in play. Move out! Grak!"

It all made sense. Any fumble-wit might make the moves. The poorer the player—the more the deaths.

The double doors were thrown open. Mingled streaming light poured in, the glorious radiance of the Suns of Scorpio, illuminating a stairway of brilliance out to horror.

Seven

Execution Jikaida

We played black.

Each one of us wore a grimy black breechclout and a tattered favor marking the rank of the piece we represented—and that was all.

Almost all the black breechclouts carried rusted stains—dark and dreadful mementoes of past games.

The brilliance of the day outside smote in with pain. We walked out, for we hardly marched, and so were shepherded willy-nilly to our places on the yellow and blue sanded squares. The terraces were packed. The spectators craned forward. The rituals with their incantations and sacrifices and prayers were all passed. We marched out to a hush, a long hollow waiting silence.

Up there against the brightness of the day the ranks of Bowmen of Loh brooded down, tall and spare; but they were there on this day to perform a slightly different function from their usual task of shafting any wight foolish enough to run. Now they were insurance, in case the men in black were too slow.

One young lad—his face was so contorted with fear it took a moment to realize he was apim—when he was positioned by the marshals upon his square in the front rank, simply ran. He did not know where he was running. Head down, screaming, he fled from horror—and ran into the arms of the men in black, into the arms of horror upon horror.

What the men in black and their instruments did to the young man rooted every other piece wearing the black to the square on which he stood. Rooted him there as though he had grown into the solid ground beneath.

The trumpets blew. The banners waved. The crowd craned forward as the white pieces emerged.

So we understood what kind of Execution Jikaida we played. I stood on my square, feeling—well, feeling that I had had some ups and downs in my life upon Kregen, sudden and dizzy swoops from greatness to disaster. And I had clawed my way back, only once more to be thrust down. The situation was no novelty in that respect; but this was like to be the last time I was so cast down. This time was the casting down and out.

The white pieces were not men condemned to execution. They were soldiers, in garish fancy-dress uniforms, with white favors everywhere. They carried weapons. They were off duty, performing a part of their agreement entered into when they signed on, and earning themselves a tidy bonus apiece.

When they took a piece from the black side they would kill him, chop him—or her—down without thought. When a black piece took one of them, he would simply walk quietly off the board, most probably to sit on the substitutes bench to watch the remainder of the game.

As the Pallan I stood next to the Princess.

She stood there, drooping, pale, and I saw she was the woman I had so uselessly attempted to rescue from the trampling hooves of the totrixes. She wore a black breechclout and, because she was the Princess, a forlorn black crown of drooping feathers.

I looked again. In her arms she cradled the baby.

The bastards had even wrapped a scrap of black cloth about the baby's skeletal ribs. I felt sick.

If I lost the game, then hyrkaida would not be a mere civilized checkmate —it would be the swift and lethal swordblow finishing this woman—and her child.

"What is your name, doma?"

She jerked as though I had assaulted her. Her eyes shifted sideways. She colored. She shook her head.

"They don't mind if we talk a little, quietly."

"Yes... I am Liana whom men once called the Sprite."

"Lahal, Liana the Sprite. I am Jak."

"Lahal, Jak—will it be very—very terrible?"

"For some of the swods and Deldars, and some of the superior pieces, yes, it will be terrible. But you will be safe—"

"Unless you lose!"

"Yes."

Up there lolling on the terraces, ensconced on their comfortable seats, the audience stared down avidly. It seemed to me outrageous that anyone could take pleasure from all this. Although I detested Kazz-Jikaida, where the pieces fought for the squares on which they stood, at least then there was some chance. But here, just to stand and wait to be butchered! And it was useless running. The men in black and their ghastly instruments hovered.

The throng murmured with excitement. They were sick, all of them, sick to their twisted minds.

And perhaps the sickest of all was the white player.

He—or she—would have paid an enormous sum for the privilege of playing Execution Jikaida. I looked at the white throne, at the far end, and the tiny glittering figure there.

An immediate advantage was conferred by that position, the usual one that overlooked the board. From my level place it was going to be difficult to see all the board and appreciate what pieces stood on what squares.

But, then, that was all a part of the fun of the game to these sickening blood-batteners watching.

These wealthy people whose obsession with Jikaida led them to make the difficult journey here and play in Blood and Death Jikaida employed a Jikaidast to advise them in their games. A Jikaidast, a professional who played the game for a living as well as for the absorbed joy of it, would sit at their side and the moves would be seriously discussed. The massive clep-sydra would drip its water, drop by drop, as the move was pondered, and a brazen gong would signal that time had run out. What normally happened then would happen here as a matter of course—just another poor devil would be chopped.

The marshals were finishing pushing and prodding the black pieces. The whites were set and ready. The chief marshal, perspiring, rosy of face, a tri-fle flummoxed, came up to me.

"You ready, lad?"

"Tell me, who is the player yonder? Who the Jikaidast?"

"Why bother your head over—"

"Who?"

He blinked and wiped the sweat away. He was in a hurry to get back to his quarters and a stoup of ale.

"Kov Loriman the Hunter. The Jikaidast is Master Scatulo."

I smiled.

The grimace must have had some effect on the marshal, for he took him-self off very smartly.

Master Scatulo! Well, Bevon the Brukaj, who had been Scatulo's slave, had told me pertinent things of Scatulo's play. Here was the first ray of sun-shine through the clouds.

"Jak..." Liana's quavering voice brought my attention back to the immedi-ate proceedings. "I think they begin..."

"Trust in Havil the Green," I said. How incongruous that remark would have been only a few seasons ago!

"Rather in Havandua the Green Wonder."

"If you will."

Quite naturally white took first move. This was not from any similar tradition to that in the chess of our Earth; simply that we blacks were here to be chopped.

Now—many a Pallan playing for black, I gathered, had desperately sought never to put himself in a position where he might be taken. After all, the object of the game from white's point of view was to win and enhance his prestige in the league tables. Just because black's pieces were slain did not affect the play. This was real Jikaida, not Death Jikaida.

The proper rules were observed and play would have to be skilled. So a Pallan might seek to screen himself. I fancied, with a quick stab of gratitude to Bevon, that Master Scatulo might be in for a surprise.

So the game began, the call of "Rank your Deldars" rang out, and we set to.

It was very far from pretty.

The lines began to form, cunning diagonals of swods propped by Deldars, reaching out to the far drins.*

Scatulo chose the Princess's Kapt's swod's opening. I replied cautiously, opening up just one line. I zeunted—that is, vaulted over a line of pieces—fairly early so as to retain a better grip on the center. The zeunt was to enable the board to be clearer in my mind, as well as to place me in a good position. The first swod was taken by the whites. I could not prevent that.

The soldier with his white favors gleaming lifted his sword, the wretch with the scrap of black cloth around him threw up his arms and screamed, and the blade sliced down.

The men in red ran onto the board and carted him away.

The game proceeded.

The orders for the moves were carried by beautiful girls wearing black or white favors, and with their red-velvet-covered wands of office. Their draperies swirled. We lost more men.

Gradually I gleaned an understanding of just what Scatulo was up to. I do not pretend to be a master player; but I have some skill. And, by Zair, I needed it then!

The disadvantage of standing on the board, with the disorienting perspectives reaching out and the pieces all on a level, was greatly offset by the ability to hold the positions in my head. Blindfold Jikaida and multi-game Jikaida are capital teaching methods.

Pointless to go through the game move by move—or blow by blow.

---

* It is not necessary to go into a full explanation of Jikaida to understand the course of this game. The rules and a description of Poron Jikaida were published as an Appendix to *A Sword for Kregen*, the second volume in the Jikaida Cycle of the Saga of Dray Prescot. A.B.A.

Every time white took a black piece, a man or woman died. It was necessary, it was vital, that I concentrate on the game and not allow the horror of the situation to unnerve me.

Those words to Liana the Sprite had been hollow. I did not think I had much chance of winning, and when I lost she would die.

The shaming thought drilled into my brain—suppose, just suppose, it was my Delia who stood there! Suppose it was Delia of Delphond, Delia of the Blue Mountains, who stood there, straight and supple, wearing that stained black breechclout? Or, just suppose it was my wayward daughter Dayra, who was called Ros the Claw? Or that other daughter of mine, Lela, whom I had not seen for long and long? Why should my reactions then be any different? Were they not all women, like Liana the Sprite? Was not my duty to them all?

As the game progressed and I sniffed out Scatulo's play I think some near sublime passion overcame me, so that Liana and Delia and all the beautiful and helpless women of two worlds were represented by that single shrinking form.

But why only the beautiful? Why exclude those women who have not been favored of the gods with divine faces and forms? Were not they all women? Some women are very devils, as I know; but they are not the helpless of two worlds. And, would it be right to exclude them, just because of that?

Scatulo essayed a clever move down the right-hand side and I countered with the correct answer, as I had played with Master Hork in Vondium. The tiered stands buzzed afresh with appreciation. To the Ice Floes of Sicce with you all, I felt like shouting up at them and their smug knowingness.

Now Scatulo knew he was in a game. I think this Kov Loriman the Hunter, who had engaged Scatulo for the game, must have fancied himself and over-ridden the Jikaidast, for some odd moves were made from time to time. Trying to be quick I seized the opportunity of one such move and zeunted a Kapt over with a good chance of reaching the Princess in two moves.

The Kapt could not, for the moment, be taken. Scatulo moved a piece across which, although blocking his nearest Kapt, threatened on the next move but one to take my Kapt.

I looked at the situation in my head, for it was down at the far end of the board. The blue and yellows zigzagged their way across the board, the black pieces stood, apathetic, frenzied, shaking—but all standing faithfully on their ordered squares through fear of the instruments of the men in black. The white pieces were lounging there, earning a bonus. The stands were quiet, sensing a stroke.

Master Hork had discussed many famous old games with me. I remembered one in particular. In my head I looked at the situation and made the necessary move. If Scatulo did not respond with the single correct move available to him—I had him.

This, I may add, came as a surprise.

As I stood, waiting for Scatulo—or his employer—to make his move, the strangest sensation swept over me. Scatulo had seen the danger, for it had raced in with speed, and his own developing attack was abandoned. I felt— I realized that I had become engrossed in the game. This was needful—by Zair! but it was needful. It had given me this chance. The strange sensation was like coming up out of a deep cave into the light, and remembering that an outside world existed, that daylight smiled over the land, that the whole world was not confined by walls and darkness.

And this burgeoning feeling was not because we blacks might win. It was a realization that my first thought that I had been callous to become engrossed in a game where men died was not the truth. That absorption in the game, despite the blood and the screams, had been necessary. I had to believe that.

Now, facing me, was the final enormity.

Had I not realized my absorption, had I been still engrossed in the game as a contest of skills, divorced from the blood and death, there would have been no problem until the aftermath.

For, you see, my move, the winning move, demanded that the Pallan vault the line of pieces and alight at the end on the one square that would place the white Princess in hyrkaida.

That single crucial square was occupied by a black piece, who did not have the Pallan's powers and could not attack the Princess and end the game.

And a Pallan may capture a piece of his own color.

As we waited and the water dripped in the clepsydra and the time passed I found I hoped, almost hoped, that Scatulo would see the danger, and make the only move that would save him.

And then, angrily, I pushed the betraying thought away.

If I did not do what had to be done, the game would go on and many more of the black pieces would die. Many more.

For my attack had borne the hallmarks of frenzy, which was a part of the gambit which had already sacrificed a Hikdar—who was a man, shaking and trembling, cut down in blood—and to abandon it now would be worse, far worse.

The clepsydra was nearly on its time, the lenken arm of the hammer lifted to crash down resoundingly on the gong—Scatulo made his move and the lissom girl dashed off. The moment I saw the direction in which she sped, I knew the game was in my hand. Scatulo's move was good, exceeding good; but, then, so had been the move of Queen Hathshi of Murn-Chem in that long ago game against the Jikaidast Master Chuan-lui-Hong.

Without hesitation, my moment of doubt passed, I started to walk up the long line of pieces. As I went I lifted up my voice in that old foretop hailing bellow.

"Do you bare the throat?"

That was pure panache, pure exhibitionism, pure self-indulgence.

But, by the Black Chunkrah! Didn't we condemned criminals wearing the black deserve a trifle of flamboyance now—now that we had won?

And then—by Zair; but it hit me shrewdly. It rocked me back. There was I, strutting, marching up along the line of pieces, black and white mingled, simulating that vaulting move unique to Jikaida of Kregen, zeunting in to place the white Princess in hyrkaida. There I was, stupidly proud, scarcely crediting I had pulled it off, puffed up with self-pride—knowing what I had to do to win.

So I halted at the end of the line and looked on the square containing the black piece, and it was Lop-eared Nath.

He stared at me, quite clearly imagining I was zeunting over him to a good attacking position beyond.

His lop-ears, his broken nose, the hairs on his chest, the shadowed cage of his ribs, his thin arms and legs, the piece of black cloth hitched around him, his hair all wild and disarranged and jumping alive-oh, too—there he stood, this Lop-eared Nath.

I could see the way his stomach sagged and tautened as he breathed under the jut of his ribs. He was sweating. But, then, so were we all.

He cracked his lips open as I marched up. He was a stringy old bird, as tough as they come.

"How's it going then, dom? By the Green Entrails of Beng Teaubu! We're up the sharp end here."

"Lop-eared Nath."

I was still staring in a stricken fashion at him and the black and white pieces leading up to him were all staring at me. The soldiers in their fancy white favors and stupidly garish holiday uniforms were interested. The black pieces looked sick with fear.

"Go on, then, dom—get onto the square!"

I shook my head. It was an effort.

In only heartbeats the move must be declared, for I had started off without the usual declamation and I was fearful I would be penalized.

"You being the Pallan and all, and up here right near the Princess—that has to be good, don't it?" He shivered and looked around warily. "Are we going to win? I don't care if we win or lose, so long's I come out alive—course, I feel sorry for Liana and her baby and all. But a fellow's got to live—and I have a quarter to run—"

"D'you play Jikaida, Nath?"

"Me? No—the Game of Moons. What're you waiting for?"

A buzzing and a murmuring began in the tiers and the marshals began to stir themselves.

"A Pallan, Lop-eared Nath, may capture a piece of his own color—not the Princess, not the Aeilssa, of course."

382

"Yeah? You'd better get onto your square, dom, else those bastards in black'll have your guts out with their pinchers."

"Lop-eared Nath—you are on my square."

He didn't understand, not at first.

"Can't be—I'm on it, aren't I?"

"Yes. But I am acting the Pallan."

Then he saw.

"You wouldn't—me! You bastard! You're not one of us—you're a damned foreigner! By the Slimy Eyeball of Beng Teaubu! If I was in the quarter—"

"A lot of other people will die, Nath, if you live, here—and there is nothing to say you will not die anyway."

The marshals approached ready to sort out what this little contretemps might be, and the men in black hefted their instruments with a sharp and pungent professional interest.

The world is made up of people like Lop-eared Nath—oh, not in his profession or appearance or interests or way of speech—but in his inherent inwardness. Or so it is comforting to believe. He saw it. He saw the whole picture, and his part in it. I thought, for a stupid instant, that he would leap on me.

A drop of sweat dripped off the end of his nose. He squinted up in the streaming mingled radiance of Zim and Genodras, and I knew he was partaking of the sunshine for the last time.

"Yeh, I slit the old fool's throat, and took his money—and I spent it, too. So I suppose it all adds up in the end... And—I'm glad for Liana. Use to call her the Sprite, afore her man ran off."

Suddenly, Lop-eared Nath lifted up his arms and laughed.

"Ended up here, most like. But I'm glad for her, and the baby—now, stranger—tell them to get on with it."

So it was done, and Lop-eared Nath paid his dues, and I called "Hyrka-ida" and whites conceded and it was over.

Slaves ran out with rakes and buckets of fresh sand, blue and yellow, to cover the bloodstains. The next game would start after an interval for refreshments.

We condemned marched back into the cells.

Liana the Sprite, holding her baby carefully, contrived to walk at my side.

So we went back into the place of imprisonment, leaving the place of horror. I was under the impression that we would be called out again; but Liana said, "No, Jak. We won—thanks to Havandua the Green Wonder. We will be spared. We will not be driven out to another Execution Jikaida." Her thin face turned to me, and she looked relaxed and at ease, the terror gone.

"Oh, no, they are harsh but just. We will not be killed. They will sell us as slaves."

Eight

Hunch, Nodgen and I Are Auctioned Off

Hunch, the Tryfant slave who with Nodgen the Brokelsh and me cared for our master's animals, was a very devil for roast chicken. Now he came flying back over the prostrate forms of the exhausted slaves in the retinue, stepping on outflung arms and legs, thumping on narrow stomachs, almost tripping, yet miraculously keeping his balance, the roast chicken clasped fiercely in his fist.

"Come back here! By Llunyush the Juice! I'll have you!"

Fat Ringo, the master's chief cook, pursued Hunch with a carving knife in one hand and a meat cleaver in the other. Fat Ringo was uttering the most blood-curdling threats as he ran, fat and purple and perspiring.

The first moon of the night, She of the Veils, was just lifting over the flat grazing land to the east, and lighting in gold and rose the faces of the mountains ahead. The night blazed with the stars of Kregen. Nodgen pulled his tattered rags out of the way of the hunt. His chains clanked. I rolled over and sat up and, seeing what was toward, gave a groan and started to jostle a calsany or two in the way.

Everybody on Kregen knows what calsanys do when they are upset or frightened. Hunch saw that swaying movement. He darted for the herd, shoving the animals this way and that, hurtling past with a quickly whispered, "My thanks, Jak!"

The calsanys started up.

Everywhere on the ground the slaves rolled over and sat up and a chorus of protestations and curses began—then the slaves were hauling their tattered rags around themselves and moving off as fast as they could.

"I'll fritter your tripes and season with garlic and serve 'em up, you hulu!" shrieked Fat Ringo.

He danced around, purple, gasping, shaking the knife and the cleaver. But he made no attempt to push in among the calsanys.

With another groan—for I had been beaten mercilessly twice the day before—I lifted my aching bones and shuffled off out of the way.

The iron chains festooning my emaciated body hampered my movements. I dragged along like a half-crushed beetle. But no one was going to sleep near a bunch of calsanys in that condition.

This whole ludicrous scene was hilarious in a kind of skull and crossbones way. Once Hunch was off by himself he'd wolf the chicken down and scatter the bones, and then no one could say, for sure, that a chicken had ever existed. Fat Ringo knew that. He backed off from the calsanys, shaking his kitchen implements and foaming.

"I'll have you—so help me Llunyush the Juice!—I'll have you!"

Hunch was too sly to answer. He was beyond the calsanys and no doubt was well started on the first leg. He wouldn't save any for me, and I did not fault him for that. The evidence had to be annihilated utterly—as Hunch would say.

The slaves were rolling up again and cursing rasts who disturbed their sleep. Sleep, to a slave, is the most precious of balms. Fat Ringo shook his cleaver, and breathed deeply, and started back to his fire. He was an apim—almost all superior cooks are apim—and when he saw me he aimed a kick at my backside as he lumbered past.

"I know who it was!" he brayed.

I rolled away and found a comfortable depression in the ground and hauled my rags about me. "Yeah? Well, try to prove it then." And I closed my eyes and sought sleep.

On the morrow the caravan would start off again early and march most of the day, with a suitable pause for refreshment. In our case that would be a heel of bread and an onion, if we were lucky. In the evening we would each receive our bowl of porridge and four palines—three if Fat Ringo was in a bad mood. Our lord and master would sit grandly in his tent, with all the appurtenances of gracious living brought with him on the expedition— folding table and chairs, folding washstand, chests and storage jars filled with the goodies that made his rich life the richer. Fat Ringo's choicest delicacies would be brought on golden platters to the great man.

Strom Phrutius was his name, a damned strom from one of the mingled kingdoms of the Dawn Lands, immensely wealthy and yet only a strom, which is equivalent to an Earthly count, and covetously desirous of making himself a kov—or, at the least, a vad. I guessed the old buzzard would make himself a king if he had half a chance.

So that was why he was on the expedition.

He'd bought me and a gaggle of slaves to make his journey comfortable, and so here I was. Four separate attempts at escape I'd made, and four separate times I'd been caught and dragged back by the heels. They had been desperate, frenzied, chaotic bursts of ill planning and stupid execution. I'd reverted, in many ways, to the Dray Prescot who had first been brought to Kregen. But the lash and the chains had made me realize that I must retain my hold on the deeper—if only by a hairsbreadth deeper—realization that there are other ways of gaining one's end than by thumping a few skulls.

The caravan consisted of a vast quantity of animals, many wagons and coaches, lines of folk trudging on foot, and our aim was to be through the passes of the mountains before the snow choked them. Once over that massif, we would be fair set for our goal. Well, the goal of the masters, not of the slaves. Their goal was food and sleep.

Being chained up and confined to the animals with Strom Phrutius, I was totally unaware of the names and quality of the other great ones who undertook this expedition. Every now and then a gaily attired party would ride past, their zorcas pretty and cavorting in the suns' light, their every action indicating the joy of the hunt and of life.

I'd go back to the curry comb, and ponder—had Pompino and Drogo seized the airboat and were they safe? Was Yasuri still alive? And—was Vallia still afloat?

All that had to wait—all that was part of another life. I was slave. I ministered to the animals. I was slave.

Day by day as we marched the mountains neared. We trudged across the high pass before the snow trapped us. On we went over a barren land where men thirsted. The dust powdered us and the grit beneath our feet lacerated our flesh.

Hunch was not fettered. Many of the slaves were not chained. Nodgen the Brokelsh, surly, marched in nik-fetters.

I was chained.

Me they regarded as a wild leem, a monstrous beast of savagery and malice.

And I worked. The animals looked sleek and cared for and I knew every one in the remuda, every one who hauled a cart. The six krahniks who pulled Strom Phrutius's coach were strong, dedicated animals, and I knew each one, and called it by its name.

And my chains remained, and I was slave.

Five-handed Eos Bakchi, the Vallian spirit of good luck, had turned away from me. Equally, his counterpart in Havilfar, Himindur the Three-eyed, had closed each and every eyeball against me.

Those mountains were a relatively small and local grouping and the passes led onto a land that, while it was not true desert, was, all the same, highly unpleasant to travelers short of water and food. We were supplied with ample quantities of both. By the time we reached streams and fields of green grass and pretty stands of trees we had traveled a goodly distance and we had passed no habitations, seen no people, had appeared to travel through an empty land.

A slave, unless he particularly cares, does not see much of the way or know a great deal of what is going on. In order to save my skin I had buckled down to the task of caring for the animals. One calculation—the distance we had traveled—was either easy to make or impossible, depending on whose estimates of speeds, progress made and time spent the slaves accepted.

We measured time by the passage of the suns, by the water dole and by the time of sleeping. If I say the desert was not real desert and we had plenty of water, and yet say also that men thirsted—these statements are not incompatible.

Everyone, including the animals, drank before us slaves.

So that when we reached the first stream, tinkling away between crumbly banks under letha trees, we slaves broke in ragged stumbling runs, tripped by our chains, our mouths furnaces of fire, and fell full length to gulp the water. Oh, yes, we were whipped back by the slave masters. But we drank, by Krun!

Hunch licked his lips. "That cramph Fat Ringo taunted me, said we are to be sold off in the city. Us expendables."

"An expensive way of utilizing manpower—"

"No. Phrutius needed insurance across the mountains and desert. If I wasn't so scared..." He was a Tryfant, and you know I am neutral concerning them. But he was usually a cheerful sort, not much over four foot six tall, and with a lopsided expression that conveyed all the guile of a six-year-old scenting ice cream in the offing. "I escaped once—and when I was caught—" He did not go on. There was no need to go on. He told me he came from the little kovnate of Covinglee in the Dawn Lands and his father had been a brass founder but had fallen on evil times. "He was overly fond of playing Vajikry and spent all his time and money on the game. We were turned out penniless and I ended up slave."

Next to Jikaida, the supreme board game of Kregen, stand Jikalla and Vajikry. Hunch had turned to the Game of Moons out of desperate resentment.

The next day when a city came into sight along a straight ride between trees we knew our fate loomed close. We all wore dirty gray breechclouts, were filthy and covered with sores and wounds, and our hair swirled like bargain-priced Medusae. We were refuse of humanity.

"Perhaps here is where we make a run for it, Hunch."

"As Tryflor is my witness! My legs are too tired to run, dom."

The city, whose name none of us knew, possessed a number of fine bagnios, all stone walls and iron bars and whipping posts, and in one of these we were quartered for the night. We were given no food or water and we all had a whipping, gratis and for nothing. Guards in jerkins of leather and brass patrolled with barbed spears, their whiskered faces sullen, and the watch fires burned in the towers.

Toward morning we were roused by kicks and blows and we shuffled out to stand in dazed lines. Fires burned in open hearths. We were all male slaves, and of many races. We waited as patient slaves always wait, forcing themselves to be incurious about what is going on for fear of the knowledge and the horror it will bring too early, before the horror arrives. Buckets of water were produced and we were instructed to get to work sluicing the water over ourselves and cleaning the muck off. Guards in jerkins produced sharp knives.

Some of us started to yell, then, at the horror here; but—

"Quiet down, you onkers! Quiet!" The slave masters bellowed. They shoved and pushed keeping us in line; they did not hit us with their whips or bludgeons.

And the sharp knives were used to slice off great handfuls of our hair, to trim our beards, to make us look less like fearsome monsters of the jungle.

Then we ate. We ate mergem—which is one of the marvels of Kregen, being a leguminous plant which, dried, will last for years and may then be reconstituted and is fortifying and nourishing—and it was mixed with milk and not water, and spiced with orange honey. We ate to stupefaction.

Our bodies were smeared with oil. Some of us were corked. Our sores were treated and many were painted over, although that practice should not fool even a purblind slave buyer.

Then we were herded out to be auctioned off.

If I do not go into the business it is because I find it degrading—degrading to the sellers and the buyers, not to the slaves. In this they stand apart as mere things, and this does not demean them but removes them from the orbit of creatures who buy and sell slaves.

The slave block built of dusty brick rose head high over the wide court-yard where trees drooped in the heat. Men and women filled this space, most with attendants to minister to their wants. The auctioneers took it turn by turn to shout the wares and display the good points of the mer-chandise before they sloped off to slake their thirsts. We waited in line. We were all numbered and the personal ownership of Strom Phrutius was attested on the chip of painted wood we carried. Lose that, slave, and you have an ear off!

Other groups with their chips of wood bearing their owners' titles waited in line.

Hunch said, "We are not all here."

"No. The masters are bound to keep some slaves—those they had before they bought us. You told me, we were bought for the journey. Expendable. How many of us died on the way?"

"A lot, by Tryflor, a lot!"

Those slaves who had survived Execution Jikaida with me formed a small grouping of our own. But we would all be sold off.

Looking back at the pathetic and brutal scene, I suppose I should not wonder that there was trouble.

After all, although I was slave, I was also Dray Prescot.

And he, as you know, is an onker of onkers, thick skulled as a vosk.

Nodgen, surly and red-eyed, Hunch, apprehensive, and I stood together. We had struck up a companionship in our sufferings.

To speed sales up we were being sold in lots. The auctioneer waiting for us, rivulets of sweat running over his fat cheeks, the brilliance of his clothes stained with dust, bellowed out: "Grak! Grak! You bunch of useless rasts."

He snatched Hunch's wood chip and read off the details.

"Zorcahandlers. Experts at the management of animals. What am I bid for this prime purchase of skilled men?" He lifted Hunch's arm and half-turned him. "Not a mark on him, in his prime—" He looked at me. "C'mere, slave!" He grabbed.

The slave handlers started to run onto the auction block from the sides. People in the cleared area began to yell. The auctioneer lay on the dusty ground with a bloody nose. I looked about, dazed—it had been quick, by Vox!

What would have happened then is anybody's guess. I do not think they would have killed me straight away. Rather, they would have netted me, chained me up, and then wreaked their vengeance.

A voice, a penetrating, bull voice smashed from the crowd.

"Hold!"

A man stepped front and center. I saw him clearly and yet he meant nothing. He wore black clothes and he did not sweat. His weapons glittered. He stood, tall, straight-backed, dominating. He bellowed again, and he made a bid. It was a good bid. The auctioneer, holding his streaming nose, scuttled back to the block and, business as ever sustaining him, started to raise the price by those famous auctioneers' tricks.

He took two bids off the wall before the tall fellow in black shouted menacingly, and then he knocked us down to him.

I will not tell you the price. The gold was paid. The man in the black armor took up the end of the chain binding us.

When he had dragged our little coffle out of the press and got us beyond the wall into a kyro where animals lolloped along and the trees drooped and the white-painted walls glowed in the lights of the suns, he halted us.

He frowned. The black bar of his eyebrows met over his nose.

"If you," he said to me, "or any of you, try to treat me or my people as you served that fat auctioneer—" He drew his sword. It glittered. "Your heads will be off so fast you'll still be licking your lips when they hit the ground!"

Nine

Into the Humped Land

"Better for us if we were still owned by that rast Phrutius," said Hunch, and he shivered. The other slaves in the tiny mud-walled compound agreed, with many and varicolored oaths.

Our new master in his black armor was Tarkshur—known as Tarkshur the Lash.

His face lowered in pride and power, a fierce face with a gape-jawed mouth over snaggly teeth, with wide-spaced eyes that gazed in contempt upon the world, narrow and cold, with thick black hair carefully oiled and curled over a low brow. His nostrils flared that contempt. He was accustomed to command. And as he spoke to us so his long whiplike tail flicked back and forth over one shoulder or the other, and to the tip of that sinuous tail was strapped six inches of daggered steel.

This stinking little compound with its crumbling mud walls wouldn't hold an agile man for long. But our chains had been fastened to stout wooden posts driven deep into the earth. We were effectively hobbled. Escape was just not on—at least, not for the moment.

When you are slave to a Kataki slavemaster, escape is usually not on—not forever, for most folk. Katakis—they are loathed and detested by those unfortunates who fall into their clutches.

A little Och, a small representative of that race of diffs who usually stand six inches shorter than a Tryfant, was clearly ill. He had been corked. His face screwed up with inward pain, and his thick dun-colored hair was gray rather than black at the tips. His master, the Kataki Tarkshur the Lash gave the Och a cursory glance and then jerked his tail at the overseer of his small group of retainers.

This man, another Kataki, stepped in and with a single thrust dispatched the little Och.

The body was dragged away.

Tarkshur surveyed us.

"We are going on an expedition where you will earn your keep. Any man who fails will die. There will be much bread and mergem for you, and palines. If you—" Katakis rarely smile. They do know how to, for I have seen that phenomenon. He finished, "But then, if you fail you know your reward."

When he had gone we were too tired and dispirited to discuss his words. But Nodgen, a Brokelsh with some spirit left, growled out, "Expedition? By the Resplendent Bridzilkelsh! I'd like to have his throat between my fists."

"Aye," said Hunch. "And his tail slicing around to rip out your guts."

"Katakis!" spat the Brokelsh, and he shivered up all his coarse bristle of hair. "I hate 'em!"

Over the next few days animals were brought into the small encampment set up just outside the city walls. The Kataki had flown here with his private retinue of just six mercenaries and was preparing his expedition. His voller had been placed in the city-maintained park, with others, and was to all intents and purposes to us slaves as far off as though it were on the Maiden with the Many Smiles. He had much gold, and he spent it procuring supplies. He came, so the slaves whispered, from Klardimoin, and where away that was no one had the slightest idea.

Hunch and I were given the task of caring for the beasts. There were other encampments outside the city walls and it was clear they all prepared themselves as we were doing. The city, all white walls and rounded domes and shadowed kyros within the blaze of the suns, was Astrashum, and we learned here and there that it was the city from which men ventured into the Humped Land.

When I learned this I instantly thought of Pompino and his dreams of wealth and magic, and much was made clear to me.

It seemed that, willy-nilly, I was to be taken into the mysterious land of Moderdrin, the Land of the Fifth Note. What might befall me there, I thought, could hardly be worse than what was happening now...

Well, illusions beget illusions.

The expedition as a whole was well-planned and the animals and slaves formed a long winding procession as we set off. We slaves had simply been given our orders that morning and off we went without any fanfare. What the great ones had been doing in the matter of eve-of-departure parties was best summed up by the way they kept to their coaches as the long procession wended through the cultivated land to the wastes beyond.

And then I stared.

Each chief member of the expedition moved surrounded by his or her people, so that we formed separate clumps like beads on a string. There, visible as the long lines turned to parallel a river before the last ford, I saw a preysany walking sedately along, with a loaded calsany following, and a little Och walking beside the pack animal. And, flopping about on the preysany's back, a figure in a respectable although shabby dark-blue gown, besprinkled with arcane symbols in silver thread, a figure with a massive lopsided turban garlanded with strings of pearls and diamonds—all of them phoney, I knew—a figure of a man with red Lohvian hair, and with a short sword girded to his plump middle.

"Deb-Lu-Quienyin!" I said, aloud, astonished.

He was a Wizard of Loh who had lost his powers and, fallen on hard times, had journeyed to Jikaida City to recoup both his fortunes and his wizardry. Why should he, of all people, hazard the expedition on which we now entered?

His little Och slave was Ionno the Ladle, walking now on two legs, now on four as he brought his two middle appendages into action to help him keep up. Once I had treated Ochs as fearsome monsters; now they had lessened in frightfulness as other and more hideous monsters of Kregen had been encountered.

And a little Och crone had once ministered to me in the foul clutches of the Phokaym.

"You know him?"

"Aye, Hunch. He is—" I hesitated. I had been about to say he was a Wizard of Loh. But all men share the awe of those famous sorcerers, and so, knowing Deb-Lu-Quienyin was touchy on the subject of his lost powers although carrying it off very well, I said, "He traveled with me to Jikaida City."

"There is that rast Phrutius," said Hunch, nodding to another part of the caravan.

"Aye," I said, looking carefully as we turned again to ford the river. "And there is a bunch of Hamalese—and I am not mistaken." The carriages and wagons and saddle animals splashed across and I saw, quite clearly, the upright form of Prince Nedfar, with his close retinue, crossing over. With him rode Lobur the Dagger and the Prince's daughter, Princess Thefi.

"Sink me!" I burst out. "If I can but get to speak with any of them—"

But the chance was not offered. Katakis are man managers. We slaves were chained close.

The caravan continued and the way became hard and the land thin and attenuated. We still ate well, as Tarkshur had promised. He wanted us fit and strong, and it was easy to surmise that the reasons for that would not make pleasant hearing.

The days and nights passed over, as they must do, and we worked on our chains with bits of rock. But stone takes a long long time to wear away iron, and the Katakis were up to the tricks of chained slaves.

We plodded on and, I own, I was intrigued. The ample food sustained us. There was the opportunity to think of other things than merely the best way to find something to eat. The city of Astrashum, it seemed to me, catered for expeditions out into the Humped Lands. Perhaps the inhabitants knew better than to go themselves? Perhaps some had gone, and never returned?

Gold and magic, was it, awaiting us out here?

In the streaming mingled lights of Antares as we trudged on over that hostile land where the ground cracked in the heat and noisome vapors gushed forth, and in the roseate radiance of the seven moons of Kregen as they passed in procession night by night among the stars, there was opportunity for me to observe the other components of the expedition. I could not call any of them friends, in the real sense, although the old Wizard of Loh and I had warmed, one to the other, in our days in another caravan.

One night I crawled in my chains, carrying them silently, and hit a Kataki guard over the head, and dumped his unconscious body outside the ring of chain slaves. But that was as far as I reached, for the Jiktar of the retinue, Galid the Krevarr, chose that moment to rumble a deep-throated question in the shadows and then to stroll across, annoyed that the guard had not replied.

With Jiktar Galid came the ominous form of Tarkshur.

Now, I paused. Again and again I ponder—did I do right?

There was a slender chance. I could have dealt with these two, I believe. My chains would rip their throats out before their tail-blades ripped mine. But the noise would be unavoidable, and the others would come running, and other guards would join in. Slave owners band together when slaves break out.

And—those miserable wights with whom I passed the days would all suffer—that was as true as Zim and Genodras rise each morning.

So I melted back into the shadows, and lay among the coffle, and we were all asleep when the commotion began. In the end, because the Katakis found it impossible to believe we cowed slaves could have performed that deed, the mischief was put down to a light-fingered rogue from an adjoining camp, and we escaped punishment.

I breathed easier.

Hunch said, "Would that I had hit the rast. He would not have got up again."

I said nothing. The sentiments he expressed were valiant enough. But he was a Tryfant and the rest of the slaves were cowed to near-imbecility. All, that is, excepting the Brokelsh, Nodgen.

Just supposing I had won free. Would Deb-Lu-Quienyin have helped me? Could he help? There was no point in approaching Phrutius. And the Hamalese—I was just an acquaintance, and, to be honest, they might not even recognize or remember me. And any debt, such as it was, outstanding from Lobur the Dagger was owed to Drax, Gray Mask—dare I own to being one and the same?

The other components of the expedition gradually became known, more or less. A Sorcerer of the Cult of Almuensis traveled in style, and everyone said the milk-white zorcas were enchanted beasts. Certainly, they were fine animals with their well-groomed close-coupled bodies and tall spindly legs. Each one's single spiral horn gleamed with polish and gold. They were almost as splendid animals as those found on the plains of the Blue Mountains. Whether or not they were real zorcas or animals of illusion no one knew or cared to find out.

This sorcerer traveled in a majestic palanquin borne by garnished krahniks, a swaying structure fabricated from silks of peach and orange and lemon, pastel colors soothing in all ordinary seeming, and yet eerily eye-watering.

His retinue of hired guards contained a dozen stout-bodied Chuliks, indomitable, fierce, inhuman, and their tusks were banded in gold.

These Chuliks were probably real—although they might well be apparitions, like the milk-white zorcas they rode. I wondered what Quienyin would have to say about this Sorcerer of the Cult of Almuensis, and his bodyguard.

There was a flying man from down south by the Shrouded Sea. His expedition was in nowise as magnificent as some of the others, and he and his friends spent most of the day winging freely ahead of the expedition. They proved of great use in spying out the way and of seeking water holes and routes that were the best way to go through the wilderness.

To an observer who was not a slave we must have made a splendid spectacle. The barbaric trappings of the warriors and the colors of the carriages and palanquins, the high-stepping saddle animals, the flying men, the glint and glitter of armor and weapons, the flicker of spoked wheels, the trailing waft of multicolored scarves—all must have presented a blaze of brilliance under the Suns of Scorpio.

Heads thrust forward, choking dry dust from the trample of hooves and the churning of wheels, we slaves in our chains blundered on. There was no high and heady sense of excitement for us.

We passed a night beside a dry gulley and the next day, early, we started on the last stretch across the badlands.

Truth to tell, all that mattered little to me. I was now determined that, with the aid of Nodgen the Brokelsh and, I hoped, of Hunch the Tryfant, I would break free the moment we hit decent water and trees to give us a chance. We'd smash our way out, and to the Ice Floes of Sicce anyone who tried to stop us.

As I had said when making my ludicrous attempt on the airboat: that was the theory.

This was the day when, toiling on and trying to make ourselves believe we could, indeed, see trees ahead through the haze, we became aware of riders pacing our progress.

Men in the long column pointed, and heads craned to look.

Off along the low ridges paralleling our course the riders swung along easily. They rode swarths, those fearsome saddle dinosaurs with four legs and snouting wedge-shaped heads, and their lances all raked into the sky, like skeletal fingers threatening our lives.

Stumbling along in my chains I tried to estimate the numbers of riders. The vakkas lined along in single file, and their looming presence, ominous and brooding, struck a chill into us all.

There must have been upwards of five hundred of them.

Occasional winks of glitter smote back from armor or weapons; but the general impression was one of dark menace, somber and foreboding, biding the time to strike.

Then someone raised a shout: "Trees! There are trees—and a river!" And we all struggled to look eagerly ahead, and when we thought once more to gaze upon those dark lines of swarth-mounted warriors—they had vanished, every one.

"I was a mercenary, once," said Nodgen. "Almost got to be a real paktun, and to wear the silver pakmort at my throat." He shook his bullet-bristle head. "Never did like fighting swarthmen. Big and clumsy; but strong. Knock you over in a twinkling, by Belzid's Belly."

Those long lines of iron riders reminded me in their frieze-like ghostly effect of some of the famous passages from *Ulbereth the Dark Reiver*. Whatever they portended, no one in the caravan could pretend it did not bode ill for us.

"A paktun?" Hunch was interested as we hurried on for the shelter of the trees. "Get into any big battles?"

"Aye, one or two."

To the best of my knowledge, Nodgen had been a cutpurse running with Lop-eared Nath's gang in his quarter of LionardDen. But, then, when a man has upward of two hundred years of life, as Kregans have, he may do many things, many things...

We were drawing near the trees and work lay ahead.

"Go on, then, Nodgen. Tell us!" Hunch was eager.

"Nothing in it—all a lot of yelling and dust and sweating and running—"

"Running? You lost?"

Nodgen's bristles quivered. The Brokelsh are recognized as an uncouth race of diffs, with deplorable manners. He made an unfavorable comment in lurid language concerning the ancestry and level of military intelligence of the general in question.

Then we were in among the first trees and instead of breaking ranks to make camp, Galid the Krevarr strode up with his whip going like a fiddler's elbow, urging us on. We stumbled on through the trees and down a long loamy slope where flowers blossomed most beautifully—although, at the moment, they meant very little to us slaves.

We burst out on the far side of the belt of trees and a most remarkable vista broke upon our eyes. Even the slaves cried out in wonder. On we were urged, down the slope. Before us spread a wide expanse extending as far as we could see under clear skies, with only the merest wisps of cloudlets.

That wide and extensive sunken plain was covered in rounded hills like tells. Hundreds of them reared from the ground as far as the eye could see. Their humps broke upward in serried ranks, in confused patterns, in haphazard clumpings. None was nearer than a dwabur or so to its neighbor. They varied in size, both as to height and extent, but each was crowned with a fantastic jumble of turreted towers, with fairy-tale battlements and spidery spires from which the mingled radiance of Antares struck sparks of fire.

Now every one of us could see why this place was called the Humped Land.

Our expedition hurried on. All this talk of gold lying about waiting to be picked up had given me the impression I would find mine workings, tailings glittering under the suns. But if these were mine workings then they were totally unlike any mine engineering I had seen on two worlds.

Any thought that by this headlong rush we had escaped the riders who had so ominously scouted us vanished as the long lines of swarthmen appeared over on both flanks, trotting out from the trees, pacing us.

Prince Nedfar and his group galloped past, their zorcas splendid, and following them rode a group of men mounted on swarths. They were led by a fierce, tall, upright man who lashed his scaly-swarth with vicious strokes of his crop. These were the purply-green scaled swarths of this part of Kregen. The jutmen of the caravan made threatening gestures. But any fool could see we were heavily outnumbered. The caravan struggled on and those dark powerful lines of riders herded us.

The swarthmen of the caravan returned, evidently attempting to protect the flanks. But no attack was made. In the period that followed before the suns sank it was made perfectly plain to us that we were being herded, were being shepherded into a predetermined course between the monumental mounds.

As we passed the nearest pile, vegetation and trees growing on the miniature mountain were clearly visible, with streams falling in cataracts, and winding paths leading up to the walls and towers at the summit.

The suns declined. One hump—for to call these impressive mounds humps does not belittle their awesome character—one hump, then, lay directly before us, and to this particular one and no other it was clear the ominous riders were directing us. When we were within running distance the riders, with no warning and acting with consummate skill, lanced their swarths upon us.

Arrows curved against the darkling air. One or two slaves screamed and fell as the shafts pierced them.

In a straggling, bolting, panicking mob, we fled for the stone gateway at the foot of the mount.

There were ugly scenes as the carriages jammed trying to force their way through the stone gateway. But the riders curveted away, and loosed as they went, Parthian shots that fell among us. Men screamed. Animals whinnied and neighed and shrieked. The dust smoked up, glinting in the slanting rays of the suns.

Tarkshur lashed his zorca alongside us, swearing foully, his black armor a blot of darkness against the last of the light.

"Wait, wait—let these craven fools press on. There is time."

He was a damned Kataki; but he was right in this. The swarths melted back into the creeping shadows. They had done what was clearly expected of them. Gradually the caravan crowded in through the gate and when we followed on last we saw the carts and coaches and beasts of burden all crammed into a wide area, bounded by high stone walls, with a dominating gateway at the far end. The gates were closed. The uproar continued.

I looked at Hunch and Nodgen and we three crept into a corner by the outer gate, out of the way of all those dangerous hooves and claws. A number of slaves were not so fortunate—or not so smartly craven—and were trampled to death.

Just what the hell would have happened then nobody could say. Over the inner portals a light bloomed, a pale corpse-green lych-light. Against it the shape of a woman showed, her hair a halo of translucent silver, her face in shadow. She lifted her arms and a voice, magnified artificially, echoed over the expedition.

"Listen to me, travelers, and be apprised."

The silence dropped as a stone drops down a well.

"Do you all enter here of your own free will?"

No single person took up the shout. A chorus spurted up at once, men and women shrieking in their fear. "Yes! Yes!"

Even as the affirmative uproar went on, I fancied that Prince Nedfar, and Lobur the Dagger, for two, would not be shouting thus.

But the clamor continued.

"Let there be no mistake. You enter here to escape the riders who await you outside with steel and fire. It is of your own free will and on your own ibs. Let it be so written."

"Yes, yes, yes!" the mob shrieked.

"By the Triple Tails of Targ the Untouchable!" Tarkshur lashed his zorca to still the animal. His lowering face filled with fury. "This is a nonsense! It is all a trick!"

The nearest people turned to look at him. They saw his imperious manner, his impatient gestures, they saw all the alive dominance of him in his black armor. He pointed at the open gate through which we had all crowded to safety.

"There is no danger. The swarthriders are gone! Roko," he bellowed at one of his Kataki mercenaries, "ride out and show these cowardly fools."

Obediently the Kataki, Roko, turned his zorca and rode back out through the opening. Now many faces turned in the last of the light to watch. Tarkshur spurred across.

Practically no time passed.

Roko's zorca sprang back through the opening. His head was up and his spiral horn was broken.

Roko sat, clamped into the saddle, his tail wrapped around the zorca's body like a second girth. Through Roko's neck above the gilt rim of his iron corselet a long barbed arrow stuck wickedly. Flaming rags wrapped about the arrow burned up into his predatory Kataki face.

The silver-haired woman's voice keened out, chillingly.

"In fire and steel will you all die outside this Moder."

"Take us in! Take us in!" The screams pitched up into frenzy. Men were beating at the closed far doors.

"Of your own free will?"

I was looking at Tarkshur the Lash. He looked sullen, vicious, crafty. There was no fear there. He shouted with the rest.

"Yes, yes! Of our own free will!"

The shrieking mob clamored to be allowed in—of their own free will. The suns sank, shafting ruby and emerald fires in brilliant dying sparkles against an inscription deeply incised in the rock above the gateway. The woman lowered her arms.

Slowly, the gates opened.

Ten

Down the Moder

"I, for one," declared Nodgen, spitting, "say I do not enter this place of my own free will."

"Nor me," said Hunch.

We were moving forward with the rabble all jostling and pushing to get through the inner door before the swarthriders roared in to shaft the laggards. It seemed important to me to say aloud that I, too, did not enter here of my own free will.

I said it.

We shuffled along, as always caring for the draught animals and beasts of burden in our care. Beyond the arched gateway stretched a wide area, shadowed with dappled trees and vines, with stone-flagged squares upon the ground, and the hint of stone-built stalls at either side. Here we halted, looking about, seeing yet another gate in the far wall.

We were simply slaves and so at intemperately bellowed orders fruitfully interlarded with that vile word "Grak!" we set about making camp, caring for the animals, preparing food for our masters. These great ones went a way apart and conferred together. There were nine expeditions in the greater expedition, nine supreme great ones to talk, one to the other as they pleased.

Nine is the sacred and magical number on Kregen.

Among the superb establishments of these masterful folk with their remudas of zorcas and totrixes and swarths, their fine coaches, their wagons and strings of pack animals, their multitude of slaves, it amused me greatly that old Deb-Lu-Quienyin with his preysany to ride, his pack calsany and his little Och slave, must be accepted on terms equal to one of the nine principals.

Against the high glitter of the stars the overreaching mass of the hill lifted above us. The Moder appeared to be moving against the star-filled night, to lean and be ready to fall upon us. The slaves did not often look up.

The hushed conference of the nine masters broke up. Tarkshur came strutting back to our camp and bellowed for Galid the Krevarr, the Jiktar of his five remaining paktuns. At least, I assumed they were mercenaries, although they might well be his retainers from his estates in unknown Klardimoin.

What Tarkshur had to say was revealed to the slaves after we had all eaten. The meal was good—very good.

Then we were paraded for the master.

He came walking down toward us, and the Maiden with the Many Smiles shone down into the stone-walled area and illuminated the scene with her fuzzy pinkish light.

He halted before the first in line, a shambling Rapa with a bent beak. To him, Tarkshur dealt a savage buffet in the midriff. The slave collapsed, puking. Tarkshur snorted his contempt and walked on to the next. This was Nodgen. Tarkshur struck him forcefully in the guts, and Nodgen grunted and reeled, and remained upright.

"Him," said Tarkshur.

Galid and the other Katakis shepherded Nodgen the Brokelsh to one side.

Along the rank Tarkshur went, striking each man. He chose nine who resisted his blow. Nine slaves, in their tattered old gray slave breechclouts, stood to one side. I was one of the nine.

"Now get your heads down. Sleep. Rest. In the morning—we go up!"

And, in the morning—we went up.

Each superior master with his retainers had chosen nine slaves—excepting the old Wizard of Loh, of course. Up the stony path we trailed, toiling up as the suns brightened.

Below us the panorama of the Humped Land spread out, hundreds of Moders rising like boils from the sunken plain.

Each slave was burdened with a piled-up mass of impedimenta. I carried an enormous coil of rope, a few picks and shovels, twisted torches, and a sack of food. Also, around my shoulders on a leathern strap dangled half a dozen water bottles. It was a puffing old climb up, I can tell you.

We were venturing into a—place—of gold and magic and it occurred to me to wonder who would return alive.

Occasionally I caught a glimpse of Deb-Lu-Quienyin struggling on. He used a massive staff to assist him. Also, he had four new slaves and I guessed he had borrowed these from one of the other expeditions and my guess—proved right—was that they came with the compliments of Prince Nedfar.

Much vegetation obscured our view but at last we came out to a cleared area at the top and saw a square-cut gateway leading into the base of the tower-pinnacled building crowning the Moder. The gates were of bronze-bound lenk and they were closed.

It was daylight, with the twin suns shining; yet the light that grew in a niche above the gate shone forth brightly. Against the glow a woman's figure showed—a woman with translucent golden hair. Her voice was deeper, mellower than her sister's who guarded the lower portal.

"You are welcome, travelers. Do you desire ingress?"

The shouts of "aye" deafened.

"Of your own free will?"

"Aye!" and "Aye!"

"Then enter, and fare you well."

The gates opened. We passed through. The moment the last person entered the hall beyond the gates, lit by torches, the gates slammed. Their closing rang a heavy and ominous clang as of prison bars upon our hearing.

I, for one, knew we wouldn't get out as easily as we had entered.

The devil of being a slave, inter alia, is that you just don't know what is going on.

The hall in which we stood was coated thickly with dust. Many footprints showed in the dust—and while most of them pointed toward the double doors at the opposite side, four or five sets angled off to the corners—and without moving from where we stood we could see the dark and rusty stains on the stone floor at the abruptly terminated ends of the footprints.

At the side of the door an inscription was incised.

Useless for me to attempt to render it into an Earthly language. The problem lay in the language itself, a kind of punning play on words. The nine superior masters conferred, and now I could get a closer look at them all. Already I had met four of them. The flying man clashed his wings in frustration, trying to work out the riddle. The Sorcerer of the Cult of Almuensis gave a sarcastic and knowing chuckle, and expounded the riddle in a breath. The other three of the nine I did not know. One was a woman. One was the tall and upright swarth rider I had seen attempting to guard our flanks. The last was an enigma, being swathed in an enveloping cloak of emerald and ruby checks, diamonds of artful color that dazzled the eyes.

"You have the right of it, San Yagno," said Prince Nedfar. At this the sorcerer preened. He looked both ludicrous in his fussy and over-elaborate clothes, and decidedly impressive to those of a superstitious mind. He had powers, that was sooth; what those powers might be I fancied would be tested very soon.

"Speak up, then, and do not keep us waiting," growled Tarkshur.

The sorcerer gathered himself, lifted his amulet of power he kept hung on a golden chain about his neck, and said, "The answer is there is no answer this side of the deepest of Cottmer's Caverns."

His words echoed to silence, and the doors opened of themselves.

We pushed through, the masters first, their retinues next, and we slaves last. For the slaves this order of precedence had suddenly become highly significant.

The next chamber, lighted by torches, contained two doors.

The obvious question was—which?

From our breakfast I had filched a helping of mergem mixed with fat and bread and orange honey, rolled into a doughy ball. Now I took a piece of this from where it snugged between me and my breechclout, rolled it around my fingers for a time, then popped it into my mouth and began to chew. Let the great ones get on with solving their riddles of the right door. That was their business—not mine.

A heated debate went on. In the end they solved whatever puzzle it was and they chose to take the left-hand door.

I didn't say, "You'll be sorry!" in a singsong voice, for I didn't know if they were right or wrong; but it would have been nice to understand a little more of what the hell was going on. We picked up our gear and trailed off through the left-hand doorway.

Shouts warned us, otherwise we would have fallen.

A steep stairway slanted down. The walls glistened with moisture and mica drops. The stairs were worn. So somebody had chosen the left-hand door and gone down here before. We descended. I began to suspect that the whole hill, the entire structure of the Moder, was honeycombed with a maze of corridors and tunnels and stairways and slopes up or down, a bewildering ants nest of a place.

At the bottom three doors confronted us. I had enjoyed my piece of mergem and felt I might take an interest in whatever the puzzle might be. There was no puzzle. Each door was opened to reveal a long corridor beyond. The three corridors ran parallel.

"The left-hand one again?" said Prince Nedfar.

"I always prefer to stick to the right," said this tall swarth-rider. He was full and fleshy, with a veined face, and his armor was trim and compact, surprising in so worldly a lord. He carried a small arsenal of weapons, in the true Kregan way, and his people were all well-equipped.

"An eminently sensible system," said Nedfar, and from where I was standing in the shuffling, goggling throng of slaves, his easy air of irony struck me as highly refreshing.

The woman said something, and then the man who wanted to go right snapped out, "I shall go alone, then—"

The way he offered no special marks of deference to the prince was immediately explained as the mysterious figure in the red and green checkered cloak spoke up.

"Best not to split up too soon, kov. There is a long way to go yet."

"If the prize is at the end—I shall go," said this kov.

Well, with seventy-five slaves all milling about and shouldering their burdens, I was pushed aside. The retinues of the great ones closed up, further obscuring my view. When it was all sorted out we went traipsing along the center corridor.

There were quite clearly other decisions that were made by the important people up front. We slaves tailed along in a long procession that wound through corridors and crossed chambers and penetrated the shadows, one after the other when the way was narrow, pushing on in a gaggle across the wider spaces. We went through open doorways following the one ahead and so had to make no heart-searching decisions. We halted at times, and then were called on, and so we knew that some one or other of the clever folk up front had solved another puzzle.

A tough-looking Fristle eased up alongside of me as we passed through a corridor wide enough for two. His cat face showed bruise marks, and he had lost fur beside his ear.

"I hope the master falls down a hole," he said, companionably.

He was not one of Tarkshur's slaves.

"Who is your master?"

"Why, that Fristle-hating Kov Loriman—Kov Loriman the Hunter, they call him. And he hunts anything that moves."

He had to be the armored swarth-rider, and he had to be the Kov Loriman the Hunter against whom I had played Execution Jikaida. A few questions elicited these facts. Loriman was renowned for hunting; it was his craze. He had visited the island of Faol many times—only, not recently. Now he was on this expedition because he had heard rumors of gold and magic and gigantic monsters, and he was anxious to test himself and his swordarm against the most horrific monsters imaginable.

"Well, dom," I said to the Fristle. "You don't have to go far on Kregen to find yourself a horrific monster."

"I agree, dom. But these ones of Moderdrin are special."

We were just passing an open door in the corridor as he spoke, and we both looked into the room beyond.

The charred body of a slave lay in the doorway, headless, and his blood still smoked.

"See?"

Eleven

Prince Tyfar

Well, I mean—where on two worlds these days can you expect to stroll along and pick up gold just lying about without something getting in the way? And—magic as well?

So there were monsters.

Hunch gave me a queasy look.

Nodgen rumbled that, by Belzid's Belly, he wished he had his spear with him.

Hitching up the coil of rope, which had an infuriating habit of slipping, I said, "I'd as lief have these chains off. They do not make for easy expeditioning."

"Galid the Krevarr has the key."

On we went until our way was halted by a press of slaves crowding back in the center of a wide and shadowed hall. Tall black drapes hung at intervals around the walls, and cressets lit the place fitfully. A monstrous stone idol reared up facing us, bloated, swag-bellied, fiery-eyed, and blocking the way ahead.

Four tables arranged in the form of a cross stood near the center of the hall, and a chain hung suspended from shadows in the roof. Each table was covered with a series of squares, and each square was marked with a symbol. In addition, the squares were colored in diagonals, slanting lines of red, green and black. The slaves formed a jostling circle about the tables as the leaders contemplated the nature of this problem.

"Judging by what has gone before," observed Prince Nedfar, "it would seem that we are to select a combination of these squares, depress them, and then pull the chain."

"Ah, but," said the fellow in the red and green checkered cloak. "If the combination is not the right one—what will pulling the chain bring?"

We slaves shivered at this.

"What do you suggest, Tyr Ungovich?" The woman spoke and I looked at her, able to see her more clearly than before. She wore a long white gown that looked incongruously out of place in these surroundings, and her yellow hair, which fell just short of her shoulders, was confined by a jeweled band. Her feet were clad in slippers. I shook my head at that. Her face—she had a high, clear face with a perfect skin of a dusky rose color, and with a sprinkling of freckles across the bridge of her nose I imagined must cause her acute embarrassment, quite needlessly. The habitual authority she held was delightfully softened by a natural charm. I could still think that, and she a slave owner and me a slave.

At her back stood two Pachaks, clearly twins, and their faces bore the hard, dedicated, no-nonsense looks of hyr-paktuns who have given their honor in the nikobi code of allegiance into good hands. At their throats the golden glitter of the pakzhan proclaimed that they were hyr-paktuns, and conscious of the high dignity within the mercenary fraternity that position conferred upon them.

"My lady?" said this Tyr Ungovich, and he did not lift the hood of his checkered cloak to speak.

"It is to you we owe our safe arrival here," said the flying man. He rustled his wings. "Your guidance has been invaluable, Tyr Ungovich—"

Yagno, the sorcerer, pushed himself forward. "The answer appears a simple progression of symbols—the alphabet reversed, or twinned—"

"Or tripled, or squared, perhaps?" The voice of Ungovich, cold and mocking from his hood, congealed in the dusty air.

Old Deb-Lu-Quienyin stood with the others and said nothing.

"Well, we must get on!" Loriman the Hunter spoke pettishly. "If there is gold here, then it keeps itself to itself. Have a slave pull the chain, anyway—"

"Yes," said Ungovich. "Why not do that?"

The backward movement among the slaves resembled the rustling withdrawal of a wave as it slips back down a shingly beach.

Kov Loriman beckoned. "You—yetch—here."

The slave to whom he pointed was one of his own, as, of course, he would have to be. The fellow shrank back. He was a Gon, and his hair was beginning to bristle out in short white spears. Loriman shouted, and one of his guards, a Rapa, stalked across and hauled the Gon out. The fellow was shaking with terror.

"Haul, slave!" said Loriman in that icy, unimpassioned voice of the man who has ordered slaves about unthinkingly since he could toddle.

Seeing there was nothing for it, the Gon took the chain in both fists. The chain was of bronze and the links were as thick as thumbs, as wide as saucers.

"Haul with a will," said Loriman, and stepped back a pace.

The Gon stretched up. His wire brush bristle of white hair glinted. He hauled.

Instantly, with an eerie shriek, the chain transformed itself into a long bronze shape of horror. Like a python it wrapped folds about the Gon, squeezed.

His eyes popped. He shrieked. And, over the shrieks, the sounds of his rib cage breaking in and crushing all within in a squelching red jelly drove everyone back in the grip of supernatural horror.

"By Sasco!" Loriman fought his panic, overcame it, gave vent to his anger.

The others reacted in their various ways. Watching, I saw this Kyr Ungovich standing, unmoved.

The lady put a laced cloth to her mouth.

Prince Nedfar said, "No more. We read the riddle."

The bronze chain dangling from the shadows became once more a bronze chain. Slaves dragged the crushed corpse into a corner. Another mark was chalked up against this great Kov Loriman the Hunter.

They tried series of patterns, pushing various symbols and trying the chain. They lost more slaves. Not all were crushed by the serpent chain. Some vanished through a trapdoor that opened with a gush of vile smoke. Others charred and then burned as the chain glowed with inner fires.

Every slave prayed that his master would not attempt to read the riddle, and having done so, pick on him to prove him right—or wrong.

A young man, just about to enter the prime of life, standing with Prince Nedfar and Princess Thefi, chewed his lower lip. I had taken scant notice of him, foolishly, as I learned. He wore simple armor, and carried as well as a rapier and main gauche, a thraxter slung around him. Also, and this I did remark, swinging from his belt hung a single-bladed, spike-headed, short-hafted axe. When he moved toward the cross of the four tables, and spoke up, I took notice of him.

His features were regular and pleasing, with dark hair and frank bold eyes which he kept veiled, as I saw, and he moved as it were diffidently, as though always hiding his light.

"Father," he said, "let me try."

Prince Nedfar gestured to the four tables.

"The riddle is yours, my son."

Princess Thefi looked at him with some concern, as though she understood more of her brother than anyone else. I did not think they were twins. He smiled reassuringly at her, and moved with his hesitant step to the tables, and looked down.

He spoke up as though he had pondered what he would say during the preceding tragedies.

"There are lines of red, green and black. No one has marked them before. The symbols have taken all attention." He looked up and gestured to the walls. "See the long black drapes, separated? Then, I think, this is the answer." And he stabbed his hand down a long row of the black squares.

"Perhaps—" said the sorcerer, almost sneering.

The others waited. Prince Nedfar motioned to a slave and this wight moved reluctantly forward. He shook uncontrollably.

"Wait!" The young prince stepped toward the chain. Before anyone could stop him he seized the links in his two fists, reached up and hauled down with a will.

"No!" Princess Thefi shrieked. "Ty! No!"

She leaped forward, her arms outstretched.

The chain rattled down from the shadows, a mere bronze chain, clinking and clanking into a puddle of bronze links on the stone floor.

And the monstrous idol moved. Groaning, spitting dust from its edges, it revolved. Beyond lay a round opening, black as the cloak of Notor Zan.

"By Havil, boy!" said Nedfar. His face expressed anger and anguish. He shook his head as though to clear away phantoms. Lobur the Dagger leaped forward. He clapped the young prince—this Ty—on the shoulder in a familiar gesture of friendship.

"Bravo, Ty! Well done! It is a Jikai—prince, my prince, a veritable Jikai!"

The shouts broke out then, of acclamation and, from us slaves, of heartfelt relief. Very soon we picked up our bundles and burdens and followed the great ones into the tunnel with flaring torches to light our going.

When the tunnel opened out into a proper stone corridor once more and we faced five doors, each of a different size, and so halted to tackle the next problem, I made it my business to edge alongside one of the slaves I knew to be the property of the Hamalese.

This slave was a Khibil, and his proud foxy face was woefully fallen away from its normal expression of hauteur, such as I was used to seeing on Pompino's face. I struck up the aimless kind of conversation that seemed fitting to these surroundings, and at my more pointed questions the Khibil grew a little more animated.

"The young prince? Prince Tyfar? Aye, he is a fair one, hard but fair. He don't have us striped unless the crime was very bad. And he stops unjust punishments, for fun, like—you know."

I nodded. Indeed, I did know. But this Hamalese Prince Tyfar was not all sweetness and light. Oh, no! He was, I was told, regarded as a bit of a ninny and, because of that, the slaves whispered, was the black sheep of the prince's family. He liked to take himself off and disappear—and not adventuring, either, as a prince should. He was often dragged out of libraries, as a youngster, kicking and screaming, and forced to go to the practice arenas for play at sterner games.

I mentioned the axe.

"Aye," said the Khibil, as the leaders wrangled over which one of the five doors to chance first. They had lost a number of slaves and were growing cautious with their supplies of human trap fodder. "I heard it said—from a big Fristle fifi who was employed by the nursemaids—that in spite of them, Prince Tyfar had himself taught the axe from axe-masters. He is very good, so they say."

I thought, idly, it might be interesting to see how he acquitted himself against an axeman—and I thought of Inch of Ng'groga—by Zair! If Inch and Seg and Balass and Oby and Korero and some other of my choice comrades were here now! We'd make a fine old rumpus of this pestiferous maze of corridors, though, wouldn't we? And then I realized I had been saying that a lot just lately, if only my friends were here. They were not. I was on my own. And I was slave.

The Khibil told me Prince Tyfar had arrived in Jikaida City in his little single-place voller only a day or so before Prince Nedfar, his father, left on the expedition. "And," went on the Khibil. "Some rasts stole our voller. Yes! Thieved our voller from the roof, right under our noses."

By Krun! But that was good news!

I could guess that Pompino, at least, had hung about waiting for me to show up. Drogo would have fretted to be gone. So, in the end, they had left—and I in the slave chundrog awaiting Execution Jikaida.

Thought of my comrades, many of whom I had not seen for far too long, made me realize that I had numbered Korero the Shield, with an irrational but instinctive grasp upon reality, instead of Turko the Shield. Ah—where was my old Khamster comrade now?

The sobering reflection struck me shrewdly that Turko did not know of the creation of the Emperor's Sword Watch. By Krun! But I could guess what his ironic comment would be!

A movement from up front heralded our onward progress and that one of the five doors had been selected. On we went and, taking the middle door, pressed forward along a wide stone-flagged corridor. One side consisted of firecrystal, that Kregan substance, almost stone, that being fireproof and transparent admits of the light from fires beyond to illuminate the darkest corners of a subterranean world. The light was bright.

The opposite wall was punctuated at regular intervals by the rectangular outlines of doors. Each door we passed was thrown open and cursory glances inside revealed bronze-bound chests broken open, bales ripped apart, costly silks and fabrics scattered about, overturned and shattered amphorae.

Also, among this debris of frantic searches lay the bodies of men. Most were hideously ripped apart, just like the bales. Not all were slaves—I saw a Rapa sprawled with his iron armor crushed in and at his throat the golden glitter of the pakzhan.

"Monsters!" whispered the Khibil. He did not look happy.

But, then, who would in this diabolical maze within the Moder, without armor and arms, chained in slavery?

And then an even more sobering thought trotted up to chill the blood. In here, in the Moder with its denizens of monsters—would even arms and armor be of any use?

Hunch was casting nervous glances about, and shivering. But Nodgen the Brokelsh had no doubts.

"By Belzid's Belly! I wish I had my spear!"

We slaves were all jostling along the corridor, and a sullen-looking

Brokelsh humped with a monstrous pile of bundles on his shoulders cursed at Nodgen.

"By Belzid is it, Brokkerim? Well, by Bakkar, you do not know how well off you are! Your Kataki has not lost any of his slaves! This great rast Loriman has lost four of us already."

"Peace, dom," said Nodgen. "We all fly the same fluttrell here."

The Brokelsh swore a resounding curse and struggled on. I was aware that just because men belong to the same race does not mean they are immediately and instinctively comrades in adversity. This is a sad thought.

"Anyway," said Hunch, with a shake of his shoulders. "He is right."

"So far," said Nodgen, and poor Hunch shook again.

And, in that moment, it seemed Hunch's worse fears were to be realized. For Tarkshur the Lash lumbered his ferocious way through the press of slaves, yelling for his idle, layabout bunch of lumops. A lumop, as you know, is an insulting way of calling a fellow a useless oaf. Now we were to prove ourselves for our Kataki master.

The room Tarkshur had elected to enter frowned upon us as we crowded up. His paktuns stood ready with drawn swords. We looked inside.

The other slaves passed along the fire-lit corridor, and the sudden spurts of action ahead were signaled by screams and the clash of weapons.

"You!" said Tarkshur, pointing at a Fristle whose cat-whiskers quivered up in anticipatory fear. "Inside!"

There was no hope in all of Kregen for that Fristle. He had to enter the room. He did so. He went in slowly, his eyes swiveling about, his body hunched over, cringing at the expected horror about to befall him.

He reached the center of the room and stood, unharmed.

Tarkshur was no fool. His baleful eyes surveyed us and saw me. "You—inside!" So, in I went, to stand beside the Fristle. Presently, one by one, we all stood within the chamber.

The walls were draped in red silk. A dais stood at the far end and on the dais lifted a golden chalice. At each side two golden candlesticks lifted their four candles, the flames burning tall and straight, unwaveringly. The air smelled of musk.

"The chalice is of gold," said Galid the Krevarr. "But it will be heavy to carry."

We all knew the Jiktar of Tarkshur's bodyguard was not thinking of the pains of the slaves, but of the speed of the party. But—gold is gold, to the eternal damnation of many a choice spirit.

"The chalice *and* the candlesticks." Tarkshur made no bones about it. "Gold is what we have come for, and gold is what I mean to have. Take it!"

Two slaves, prodded by swords, reluctantly approached the chalice. It possessed a lid carved in the semblance of a trophy of arms, crowned by a helmet of the Podian pattern, plumed and visored, and around the chalice itself glittered scenes of war. The two slaves took each a handle and lifted. The chalice did not move.

"Don't lift it!" screamed Hunch—and the decorated lid rose, lifted of its own accord, and a wisp of blue smoke emerged.

We all staggered back. In a bunch we turned for the door ignoring the massive bellows of command from Tarkshur. The door through which we had walked was gone—all four walls were uniformly clothed in scarlet silk.

"Out, out!" shrieked the slaves.

The blue mist wavered and grew. Sickly, we stared upon the gruesome sight as the smoke thickened into the semblance of a human skeleton. The skeleton was apim and in its bony fists it gripped a sword and shield, all fashioned from the blue smoke. Those blue-smoke bony jaws opened. The thing spoke.

The words were harsh and croaked out like rusty nails drawn from sodden wood. We stood, petrified, and listened. The Kregish words were full of inner meanings; but a doggerel translation will give the flavor of what the ghastly apparition spoke.

One of One and you are done.
One of Two will make you rue.
One of Three your lack you see.
One of Four will give you more.

Tarkshur laughed, suddenly, that grisly laugh of the Kataki that heralds no joy. "Give me more!" he shouted.

Nothing happened.

"But, notor, how?" said Galid.

The Katakis looked about, swishing their tails on which the strapped steel glittered. Tarkshur pushed his helmet up. Then, wise in the way of the men a slave master handles, he swung his ugly face on us. "Well, slaves?"

The answer was quite obvious; but I was in no mood to point the way for this rast Tarkshur to get more. So I said nothing. In the end a grim-faced Fristle, who had beforetimes received surreptitious favors from Galid, put his bundle down and advanced to the dais. He half-turned to face Tarkshur.

"Master—I think—the candlesticks—"

"Of course." Tarkshur swaggered forward. "It is clear."

Hunch took a great risk. He spoke out without being given permission to speak.

"Master—may I speak? More, yes. But—more of what?"

"What?"

Tarkshur was not puzzled. He even, in his good humor, did not lay his lash across Hunch's back. "More gold, you onker."

I said, "I think not. More tricks, or more monsters."

Tarkshur's tail lifted and quivered. He stared at me. Oh, I do not think he bothered to look at my face, even then. Katakis are man-managers and they treat men like objects. "Come you here."

Slowly, I walked across the room and stood before him.

"You will be flogged. Jikaider. You are slave."

"Yes, master."

I could feel the chains dragging on my legs, the weight of the bundle on my shoulders. The air smelled of musk. The slaves at my back were breathing with open mouths, their sounds made a dolorous mewling in the silk-robed room.

Tarkshur gestured to Hunch, Nodgen and the Fristle. They moved up and we four slaves positioned ourselves before the candlesticks.

"Now, slaves, pull the candlesticks. Pull all four together."

Galid the Krevarr and two of the Katakis moved up to supervise our work. Tarkshur stood by me.

"Pull!"

Nodgen, Hunch and the Fristle pulled.

I did not pull.

The screech of metal on metal as the candlesticks raked forward was followed immediately by the bellow of rage from Tarkshur and drowned instantly in the clash of stone and in the shrieks of terror as the floor fell away. We eight plunged into stygian darkness.

Twelve

The Illusion of a Krozair Longsword

We struck an unseen floor in a tumbled mass. Those damned steel tail-blades of the Katakis could do someone a nasty mischief now and I rolled up into a ball and shielded myself as much as possible with the bundles and the rope.

"Help! Help! Help!" Hunch was crying.

"By the Trip-Tails—" was followed by the scrunching wetness of a hard object squashing into a mouth.

"Belzid—"

We squirmed there in the darkness and sorted ourselves out. Tarkshur was raving. Galid was bellowing to his two men.

The musky smell increased as a tiny warm wind blew about us.

"Where is the slave? Where is he? I'll have his tripes out! I'll fry his eye-balls!" Tarkshur was frothing.

Dragging myself off and feeling ahead at every step, I eased away from the noise. The chains clanked and I cursed.

Then a long narrow slit of light abruptly sprang into existence high in the darkness. It stretched out of sight in one direction, and ended in black-ness by my head. The perspective indicated that slot of light stretched a long way down a corridor. The slit widened. The light grew. Presently we saw that bronze shutters were lowering from a wall of fire-crystal. All too soon I was revealed in the light.

The Katakis sprang up and swished their tail-blades, looking at Tarkshur. But only two rose, Galid and another. The remaining Kataki lay where he had fallen and his tail-blade thrust hard through his own throat.

At his side, twisted in death, lay the Fristle. His cat-like head twisted down at an unnatural angle.

Hunch was yelling and trying to run, and falling, and squirming about.

"Silence!" bellowed Tarkshur. He looked at me. He began to walk. He began to strut. He was going to slay me, of a certainty. You can often tell by the way a Kataki holds his tail—just so.

Galid the Krevarr yelled.

"Notor! Look! By Takroti, notor—look!"

We all swiveled.

The opposite wall shone in the light. The opposite wall led into a paradise.

For as far as we could see down the corridor the light reflected back from a profusion of precious objects, of luxuries, of the delights of the senses and of the flesh, a jostling multitude of everything a man might crave and long for. Useless to attempt to catalog that outpouring of sump-tuousness. We just stared, open-mouthed.

Tarkshur forgot all about killing me—and that, by Krun, means for any Kataki only the greatest of interests in life had supervened. Katakis love killing. It is an irony and one of their burdens that, being slave mas-ters, to indulge their pastime means to destroy their profits along with the merchandise.

At about the same time we noticed an oddity about that display of wealth and luxury. Although the wall stretched away for as far as we could see, most of it was walled by fire-crystal. There were just eight openings. Eight openings for us eight who had fallen here. And, even as we looked, so fire-crystal shutters slid down over two of the openings, shutting up the display beyond.

A beautiful Fristle fifi surrounded by the richest food and the most orna-mental of treasure chests, clearly the lack of the Fristle whose neck was broken, was thus shut up.

I will not speak of what the dead Kataki had lacked, and what was gradually walled off from us. What his comrade had lacked, likewise, I will not speak of—but that opening was clear. With a mad yell of lascivious exhilaration, the Kataki paktun leaped past the fire-crystal. In seconds he had vanished from our sight.

"Stand, Galid!" commanded Tarkshur.

Galid the Krevarr quivered.

"There is plenty of time. We have only to take our fill and make our way back. The others will assemble the key." Tarkshur swung on us three slaves. "You will not be slain—you will carry the treasure out—when we are ready."

Hunch and Nodgen stood, shaking. Hunch's fear had gone. Nodgen was still getting over the smash on the head that had dizzied him. Two of the openings showed piled up treasure, and the other things of the good life that would delight an honest Tryfant or Brokelsh. Tarkshur saw. He sneered.

"Do not think—" he began.

A demoniac scream bounced in vibrating echoes from the walls. A shape, a shape from nightmare, bounded along the corridor toward us.

With a leap, we three slaves came to life and dodged out of the way. Let the two armed men tackle this monster...

It looked like a prickly pear, bristled with brown spines, with ten tentacular arms slashing about, each tipped with a poisonous sting. It bounced. It hissed. It gave off a stink like the sewers on Saturday night.

With a snap Tarkshur hurled his helmet down and closed his shield across. Galid did likewise. They faced the monster and they fought. They were both good fighting men. And, at that, the monster was not so very fierce, not so very frightening, after all. A poor bouncing stinging bristle ball. For a naked slave, unarmed, the monster might well have spelled doom. Against two tough and agile Katakis, armed and accoutered, the monster was slashed into a dozen segments in no time, its tentacular arms splaying out pathetically. From their tips oozed a yellowish fluid. Neither Kataki saw any value in that liquid.

One moment Hunch was at my side, trembling, saying, "I do not like this place at all—I am frightened clear through." When I turned to answer him, he was gone.

"He has the right idea, our Hunch," said Nodgen.

With that he raced across the corridor and threw himself into the opening of the fire-crystal wall. Beyond him lay a Brokelsh paradise. I did not doubt that Hunch was already well into his Tryfant paradise.

The two Katakis were stepping back from the dismembered monster. The smell became worse as the fluids seeped.

Tarkshur saw that I stood alone.

"Rast! Where are—" Then he realized, and sharply turned to Galid. "Stay, Jiktar! We carry the treasure out!"

"Yes, notor—but—"

I stepped away from the wall. I dropped the bundle from my shoulders and I turned to stare into the opening that would reveal my lack.

"Slave!" Tarkshur was yelling, and I heard his voice from a long distance. He gave his orders to Galid. "Chain the cramph fast so that he cannot escape."

But I looked into the opening, and saw...

No. What I saw really centered on the object that stood just inside the opening. Farther back misty shapes swam out of my vision. Around this precious object lay a rapier and main gauche, a drexer, the cut and thrust sword we had developed in Valka, a short-hafted clansman's axe. Also there lay a folded length of scarlet cloth, of good quality, and a broad and supple lesten hide belt, with a dulled silver buckle. And, in a worn sheath a seaman's knife. Leaning against the side wall stood a tall Lohvian longbow and a quiver of arrows, each one fletched with the feathers of the zim-korf of Valka. There was, also, a jeweled shortsword like those deadly shortswords that are used with such skill by my clansmen in the melee. All these objects surrounded the central object. At this I gazed.

"Slave!" bellowed Galid's voice, from some dimension outside reality. "Hold still, you rast, while I hobble you with your own damned chains."

The object within the opening held all my attention now.

It was one of mine.

It had to be. There was the nick—it had to be!—the tiniest of nicks where I had beaten down Rog Grota, a famous Ghittawrer of Genod, in that old swifter battle on the Eye of the World. And here! It was here!

I felt a hand on my neck, forcing me down, and another hand dragging at my chains.

Slowly I returned to this other dimension from that realm of reality that had for a few heartbeats claimed me. This was the reality, this frightful expedition down into a Moder, with monsters and magic, and a foul Kataki seeking to chain me fast.

And, for the first time in a long long time, I remembered I was Dray Prescot, Lord of Strombor, Krozair of Zy.

I hit Galid. He went flying back and the look on his face was so expressive of stunned astonishment that I nearly laughed.

"Rast!" shrieked Tarkshur, and his ichor-slimed sword raked for my guts.

The chains lopped his sword down and my left hand gripped onto his tail as the bladed steel sliced for my throat. For a space we glared, eye to eye.

"You will surely die, you rast, you—"

"I have chopped off many a Kataki tail, Tarkshur the Kleesh. Be very sure, yours will not be the last."

He gobbled with fury; he struggled; but he could not move that deadly bladed tail. His shield was clamped between our bodies, trapping his left arm. His right arm was forced out and down as the chains bore remorselessly on his sword.

In his eyes I saw a nickering shadow.

Without thought I swung. We pivoted as though we were that very weathervane I had so recently been, blown hither and yon by every vagrant breeze. Galid just hauled his blow back in time, swinging his thraxter away down the side. I kicked him where it would do the most good, and shifted my grip on Tarkshur, and so wedging his sword down in the coil of chain, got a grip on his neck above the corselet rim.

I choked—only a little, enough to let him know what was happening.

"You are a Kataki," I said. "I have no great love for Katakis. I have met one and one only who had any inkling at all of what humanity means. You are not that one."

His lowering, low-browed, fierce Kataki face was slowly turning a rich plum color. His eyes started out, bulging with fury. He had no fear of me, a mere slave, who had for a moment caught him up with chains. I choked him again and he tried to butt me and I slashed at the bridge of his nose, an upward blow that rocked his head back. He glared up and over my shoulder and a fresh look, an expression of strangled surprise flashed into that ugly face.

I threw him away.

He had not hit the floor before I had leaped after him and to the side.

The damned chains tangled me up and I pitched forward.

There was, for the moment, no danger from the Katakis.

The thing that moaned down upon us breathed a more deadly menace.

White and leprous sheets and folds of some insubstantial gossamer, like swirls of smoke, like sheerest curtains in a breeze, wafted and writhed along the corridor. An aura of blue sparks sizzled and spat. It was forcefully borne in on me that a sword would be worse than useless against this monster.

Tarkshur had not lost his senses. I did not see Galid.

The Kataki slave master flung up his hand. He still gripped his ichor-smeared sword; but he did not use it. On the middle finger of his hand glistened a ring—I had noticed it as a mere foolishness of Kataki vanity—and now, as the writhing leprous-white monster approached, the ring sparked in reply.

Long flashes of blue fire sped from the stone in the ring. The stone glowed with life. The fires met and fought with the blue sparks. Gyrating and twirling in the air, the monster lashed and shrieked and so, gradually, sank fluttering nearer and nearer to the floor. As it sank so its struggles weakened.

Tarkshur was panting, and I saw the way he kept looking at the ring and then at the monster—and never at me. I understood that the power in the ring was being drawn off in proportion to the monster's own strength.

Whatever sorcery was here in play, the power of the stone in the ring proved victorious. The leprous-white monster sank, fluttering weakly, beat at the ground and then slowly dissipated into wisps of vanishing white. A few little glittering stones scattered across the flags were all that remained.

The Kataki wiped his lips with his sword hand, and then looked at me.

"I have saved your life, you ungrateful yetch—and now, for the indignity you have inflicted, I will take it."

"Where is Galid the Krevarr?"

Tarkshur lowered his head and looked about. The Jiktar of his body-guard was nowhere to be seen.

"You Katakis are a miserable bunch, contemptible cramphs. He is no doubt enjoying himself now at the expense of some poor devil's misery."

"You—" Tarkshur breathed deeply and his flaring nostrils in his damned Kataki face broadened. "I shall enjoy carving you."

The farce had gone on long enough.

"You, Tarkshur, will either go away now with your life, or you will die— here and now. The choice is yours."

He just didn't believe this. I felt—well, it is difficult to say, now, exactly what I felt. Imagine lying in a grave with a granite block on your chest pressing the air from your lungs. Then imagine you have summoned the strength to push the granite block away. You sit up in the grave. You put your hands on the sides. You heave yourself up. And, suddenly, the glory of the suns shines down. Yes, well, that expresses a tithe of the way I felt...

Something in my face must have warned him. Suddenly, he took me seriously.

"You are chained, slave. You will not be quick. I shall surely win."

"Do not try, Kataki."

But, even then, he was not afraid. And, although I do not like Katakis as a rule, there was much to be said for this evil specimen of that degenerate race. He moved across, and his helmet was down and his shield was up and his thraxter pointed.

"What, slave, can you do?" The sword gestured. "Your chains will not take me twice."

I did not answer.

I took up the Krozair longsword into my fists, and I own, I own with pride, my hands trembled as I took up that superb brand. But do not mistake me. It had not been the longsword that had caused me to rise from a long sleep. And, I half think, it was not that I was a Krozair of Zy, and had called my membership of that Mystic and Martial Order to mind that spurred me. Perhaps it was a mingling. Perhaps it was that I had, with surprise, realized that I, Dray Prescot, Lord of Strombor and Krozair of Zy, did have a responsibility to myself, that to deny my nature too long was to stunt my own growth.

So I faced this Tarkshur the Lash and in my fists the Krozair blade gleamed splendidly. I held the sword with that cunning two-handed grip, the fists spaced exactly, so that enormous leverage and tremendous speed are obtained with precision.

Tarkshur sneered.

"That lump of iron! A mere bar! You are a fool!"

"I shall not tell you again, Tarkshur. Why I do not wish to slay you passes my comprehension. But you may take your life, and depart—"

He sprang.

The fight was brief.

It was as though an explosion of released passion broke all along my muscles, driving my fists into the weaving pattern of destruction that finished with a smashed shield, a shattered thraxter, a sliced helmet—and Tarkshur the Kataki running screaming along the corridor, spilling blood as he ran.

I had kept faith with myself. I had not slain him.

The blood was a pure accident. The fellow had tried to fight for just that amount of time too long, and one of the last blows intended to shred the other side of his helmet had cropped an ear.

And, the strange thing was, he kept his tail.

Two things occurred to me.

One was that I was still chained and Galid the Krevarr had the key. But there would be an answer to that. The other was that the Whiptail would know me again.

How interesting that, as slave, I had not thought to call Katakis by their slang name, Whiptail!

Aloud, I said, "There is a thing I lack. The key to unlock these chains."

I looked into the opening of the fire-crystal wall. The key was there all right, a clumsy thing of iron. As I retrieved it, it occurred to me to wonder if this was the very same key that Galid had had in his possession, or was it a simulacrum. Was the Krozair longsword that old weapon of mine with which I had gone a-roving as a Krozair over the inner sea? The chains were unlocked and I threw them from me. Whatever the answer might be, the key worked, the longsword was real.

I was alone in the Moder with its magics and its monsters.

Well, by Zair! And didn't that suit me best?

Yes and no, I told myself. There is nothing to equal the fine free feeling of adventuring alone, and there is nothing to equal the sharing of adventures with a gallant company of good friends and doughty blade comrades.

So I took out that length of scarlet cloth and discarding the gray slave breechclout I wrapped the scarlet about me and pulled the end up and tucked it in and secured all with the broad and supple lesten hide belt. I pulled the belt in tightly and the dulled silver buckle snicked home sweetly.

Never having cared much for straps over my chest I secured the weaponry to belts around my waist, different belts each to its own weapon or pair of weapons. Equally, I do recognize the value of shoulder straps from time to time, and will use them when the necessity arises. As, now, I slung the water bottles back on. I will not tolerate dangling ends of scarves and belts and folderols. A fighting man must be trim. A ravishingly exotic dangling scarf can be grabbed by your enemy to reel you in like a fish, to be gaffed—through the guts.

Of that wonderful Kregan arsenal displayed I selected the rapier and main-gauche. Also I took the drexer, for that sword holds a place of especial affection, seeing that it is a superior refinement on the Havilfarese thraxter and the Vallian clanxer, and with elements of the Savanti sword— those we could contrive—embodied.

As to why there was not a Savanti sword among those articles I lacked— I thought about this, and came to the conclusion that whatever of sorcery and magic ran this Moder, it, he or she did not have the power to set against that of the Savanti nal Aphrasöe. This is not surprising. Those mortal but superhuman men and women of the Swinging City would go through this place as a plough goes through rich loam.

My old seaman's knife went over my right hip. When I handled it I own I gulped. I felt the awe. This was the knife I had first acquired on Kregen, seasons upon seasons ago. Could it be real? Or was it a mere semblance, fool's gold, made of dreams and moonshine?

The clansmen's shortsword I left. The drexer would serve in that weapon's office. There was a Ghittawrer longsword, also, one I had owned when I had been with Gafard, the Sea Zhantil, the King's Striker; this I did not touch. I took the Lohvian longbow and the quiver. Then I looked at the bundle I had carried as a slave, and the remnants of the two monsters slain in this magic-filled corridor.

Now it would be disingenuous of me to suggest that I took the magical properties of the Moder over seriously. In long conversations with the wise men of Valka, and various Wizards of Loh I had known, the uses and abuses of magic had afforded lively debates. Wizards of Loh have real and formidable powers, as I well knew. There are many kinds of sorcerer on Kregen, and I usually steered clear of too close an entanglement with any of them. This place reeked of magic and illusion and it was vital to take everything that happened at face value, as though it were real.

An illusion of a monster biting your head off can kill you as headless as a real one.

At the same time, an illusion is harmless if you understand the nature of the hallucination.

That remained to be discovered in this den of iniquity.

Picking up the bag of food and the coil of rope, I set myself, and thought to look into the Tryfant and Brokelsh paradises. I hollered out: "Hunch!"

417

"Nodgen!" a long time. No answers being received, and not caring to enter, decided me.

So, alone, wearing the brave old scarlet, armed with my pretty arsenal of weapons, off I set.

By Zair! But didn't doing just that bring back the hosts of memories!

Those sparkles of glitter left when the leprous-white monster had vanished drew my attention again. Our discussions of magic at home in Esser Rarioch had often dwelled on the phenomenon of power being contained within reciprocal power. I thought of the blue sparks from the stone in Tarkshur's ring. I picked up the scattered stones. Maybe, they would serve.

And that yellow liquid dripping from the poison stings of the bouncing bristle ball...

Lacking a suitable container, I stated that fact, and picked up a handy little vial from within my own opening in the fire-crystal wall. Whatever power was operating here would, I judged, not provide anyone with something they did not lack. But the parameters were wide. So, with a vial of poison ichor as well as the stones, I marched off along the corridor seeking a way out.

As I marched along in the brave old scarlet a refrain of that favorite drinking song of the swods kept going around and around in my skull. "Sogandar the Upright and the Sylvie," that notorious song is called, and the refrain goes, "No idea at all, at all, no idea at all..." And as the swods sing they fairly bust their guts laughing at the incongruous notions their lewd imaginations provide.

Well, the song fitted me, now.

I had no idea what I was getting into, no idea at all, at all, no idea at all...

Thirteen

How an Undead Chulik Kept Vigil

Just as Tarkshur's Kataki expedition had become separated from the main body, so other expeditions had gone their own ways. There were a few monsters I met, prowling about—for loose monsters seemed to prowl about the corridors the deeper we went—and there were two or three lively encounters before I was able to clear them away from the path.

I did not enter any of the rooms which lay invitingly open along the route, for I was attempting to find my way out.

Shouts ahead of me along a corridor fitfully illuminated by torches indicated I had come up with a part, at the least, of the expedition which had entered with me. Perhaps. Perhaps this place was crawling with travelers lost and desperate to find their way out.

A thing shaped like a chavonth stalked ahead. It was moving away from me and seemed unaware of my presence. Its low slung head snouted away from me; but I knew what it looked like well enough. Chavonths are feral six-legged hunting cats, and this one's head would be a mask of ferocious cunning, blazing eyes, and splinter-sharp teeth. Normal chavonths are covered in a hide patterned in fur hexagonals of blue, gray and black. This one looked dusty...

From a side door where he had evidently been looting, for his arms were filled with gold goblets and bracelets and strings of gems, a man sprang out. He was a Rapa. He saw the chavonth even as the big cat leaped.

The Rapa was quick. He evaded the first lithe spring. But his leg was struck by a sweep of the chavonth's front paw.

I blinked.

Instead of that Rapa leg being ripped by sharp talons, the limb was abruptly coated in dust. Then I saw the horror, as the Rapa screamed shrilly in shocked fear.

His leg was not covered in dust. His leg *was* dust.

He collapsed and the dust-chavonth sprang on him.

Instantly, Rapa, gold, gems, all were mere heaps of dust.

The dust-chavonth heard me then, and swiveled his head, snarling.

He leaped.

The steel with which an honest man defends himself against mortal perils would be unavailing here.

I turned to run, dodging across the corridor in jagged leaps. Dusty padding followed me in bounds.

The image of that Rapa collapsing and turning to dust hung before my eyes. And I saw... If memory did not play tricks...

Turning, I swung the Krozair brand up and with a quick prayer slashed at his hate-filled mask.

The cold steel bit.

Instantly, the dust-chavonth shrieked a high shrilling vibration of agony. He changed. The dust vanished. I was facing a real chavonth, and under those hexagons of black, gray and blue his hearts beat savagely.

But a real chavonth, savage and powerful though he might be, is not the same adversary as a dust-chavonth.

The longsword slashed and backed and the chavonth limped away, yowling, leaving a trail of blood spots, vanished into the gloom beyond the reach of the torches.

Men shouted down and I shouted back. They came up bearing torches and I saw the twin Pachaks. They looked as fierce as the chavonth.

"You are unharmed, notor?"

"Aye. The beast has gone."

419

"It was a dust-chavonth—you are lucky—"

"I saw that a poor Rapa it slew and turned to dust lost his life and his gold and gems—but his sword remained true to itself."

"A chance, notor."

They called me notor, Havilfarese for lord, without thought. Truly, I had changed from the beaten and chained slave who had entered here. I did not think anyone would recognize me.

We did not touch the heap of dust as we passed. Somehow, I did not think it would ward off a dust-chavonth. It might in all probability turn all who touched it to dust.

The lady these twin hyr-paktuns served still wore her white gown. But it was streaked with grime and was torn. Her slippers were gone. She wore a pair of white fur boots. Her rose-red face and her yellow hair looked still out of place here.

"Llahal, notor. You are most welcome—I have not seen you before?"

"Llahal, lady. I am Jak—no, that is sooth." Then I thought to convince them I had come into the Moder with another party. "You are an expedition new to these places?"

"Yes. I am Ariane nal Amklana."

She said Ariane nal Amklana. Amklana was a proud and beautiful city in Hyrklana, and because she used the word "nal" for "of" I knew she was the chief lady of that city.

"Llahal, my lady. Shall we join forces?"

The two Pachaks nodded as she turned to them. They had seen the little affray with the dust chavonth.

"The notor will be a useful addition," said one.

"Useful," agreed his twin.

"Is there anyone else with you?" I said.

"Longweill, a flying man. He is farther up the corridor."

I nodded. So these two had become separated from the others. The lady Ariane looked in nowise afraid, rather, she stared on every new thing with the rapt absorption of a child, delighted at the splendors, terrified by the horrors. I felt I could come to like her, given time.

"We must try to find our way back to the others," she explained to me as we walked on up the corridor. "I am going into no more rooms of horror. I did not come here for gold."

I forbore to ask why she had come. Again the feeling struck me that only the most dire of reasons could have forced her to come at all, given that she must have understood far more of the dangers than ever we slaves had.

Longweill, the flying man, made the pappattu in a spatter of Llahals, and then, together and with a crowd of retainers and slaves, we continued this nightmare journey.

A mere catalog of the monsters we encountered and the dangers we passed would, I feel, weary. Suffice it that as we penetrated farther into the Moder and discovered more of the maze of corridors and rooms and chambers, and riddled riddles, and fought monsters, we battled against the forces of sorcery and of death.

The flying man, Longweill, was a Thief.

He made no bones about it. There are thieves and Thieves. After all, those ruffianly Blue Mountain Boys who owe allegiance to Delia of the Blue Mountains are as bonny a bunch of reivers as you will find on Kregen.

"By Diproo the Nimble-fingered!" he said, as we gazed up at the blank ending of the corridor we had been traversing. "Now how do we get through here?"

As a Thief he was first-class, I daresay. But I had up to now not been impressed by his powers of survival in a place like this. He took good care of his own skin, and his slaves were loaded with loot. Like us all, now he wanted out.

And getting out was far more difficult than getting in.

The sensation was distinctly odd, considering what had gone before, when I was consulted as to our best course.

"If we cannot go straight on, then we must of necessity go up or down."

So we looked for a trapdoor, in floor or ceiling.

When one of the Pachaks, the indomitable twin called Logu Fre-Da, curling his tail-hand high over his head, pointing, indicated a trapdoor in the ceiling we all crowded over.

Logu Fre-Da's twin, Modo Fre-Da, looked up and shook his head. His straw-yellow hair swirled. He lifted his upper left hand and made a gesture of negation.

"We have been trending down, to escape at the bottom of this pestiferous ants nest, have we not, brother?"

"You are right, brother." Logu Fre-Da turned to his lady. "Lady—we must search for another opening."

Longweill pushed through. His wings clashed together and then parted and blew our hair streaming in the downdraught as he flew up to take a closer look at the trapdoor. "No," he called down. "Who is to say there is any way out? This whole business stinks of traps, and I am expert in those. Up is the way out, the way we came in."

"By Papachak the All Powerful," quoth Modo. "He could be right, brother."

"I do not think so, brother."

"Hai, tikshim!" called down the flying man. "Remember your place among us notors."

Now tikshim, which equates with "my man"—only in an even more condescending and insulting way—is intensely annoying to whomever it is addressed. Logu Fre-Da turned away sharply from under the trapdoor in the ceiling. Modo went with him, and they began to speak in fierce whispers, one to the other.

Longweill, the flying man, pushed the trapdoor up.

He should not have done so—of course.

The jelly-like substance that poured out in a glutinous blob enveloped him. Only his wings protruded through the transparent mass. We saw him. The blob of gluey substance fell to the floor. Longweill was consumed. The blob sucked him into its substance. His wings fell and rustled slackly on the floor.

We all crowded back.

The blob started to roll after us.

Glistening brown and umber streaks writhed within the blob as it rolled, and the oily texture of the mass picked up dust and the scattered detritus of the floor. This rubbish was ingested as the blob rolled, infolding and slipping away, to be left as a trail on the floor where the blob had passed. The blob glistened.

Well, man kept back the darkness and the creatures of darkness with his ally, fire—a chancy and often untrustworthy ally, admitted by all—and the rolling glistening blob looked oily to me.

Snatching a torch from the hand of a faltering Gon I turned and hurled the blazing brand at the rolling glistening blob.

It was oily.

It burned.

Waiting, I wondered what fresh deviltry would spew forth from this monster, as we had seen other monsters rise from their destroyed predecessors.

Smoke, in this den of deviltry, was always a menace...

The smoke from the burning glister-blob rose in a black and pungent cloud. It writhed up, coiling and twisting, and in the brilliance of the flames beneath we stood back, shielding our faces, fearfully watching and waiting for the smoke to assume a more awful form.

In a black flat ribbon the smoke poured toward us, writhing some five feet off the ground. Many of the slaves started to run in deadly earnest. Steel, against insubstantial smoke, would avail us nothing. About five paces from us—and the two Pachaks stood with me together with a numim whose lion-face bore an iron-hearted resolve—the smoke abruptly switched sideways as though caught by a powerful wind. We could hear no wind. Yet the smoke thrust a long tongue against the side of the corridor wall, and split into many probing fingers, streaming, and so passed it seemed through the wall and was gone.

Naghan the Doom, the numim, said, "A grating." He crossed to the wall and called for torches. In the glow we looked. The grating was there, right enough, man height and wide enough for even my broad shoulders; but the bars confined holes no larger than bean shoots. No amount of peering in the flung light of the torches revealed what lay beyond.

The conference was brief. Picks and sledgehammers were produced and the slaves went at the grating with a smash.

"Poor Longweill," said the lady Ariane. "He was so hot-tempered. He would never listen."

"You knew him before?"

"Oh, no. We met when Tyr Ungovich organized the expedition. In Astrashum. Expeditions from all over Havilfar are constantly arriving and departing." She laughed, more nervously than I liked. "Departing from the city to come here, I mean."

"Aye."

"And we must find the others. Prince Nedfar has already two parts of the key." This statement made her pause, and color stained up into those rosy cheeks. She turned her eyes on me, gray-green eyes, fathomless. "Notor Jak—do you have any part of the key?"

"No, my lady. Not a single part."

"Oh!" she said, and bit her lip.

The picks and sledges were smashing away the stone grating.

It occurred to me to say, "And you, my lady. Do you?"

"Why, no—more's the pity. We must find the nine parts of the key before we can unlock the door at the exit and so win free from this terrible place."

"With," I pointed out, "or without what we came for."

She searched my face, seriously, and the tip of her tongue crept out to lick her lips until she remembered, and instead of licking her lips, said briskly: "Oh, but I must have what I came for. It is vital."

Still I forbore to question her. That was her business. Mine was getting out of here with a whole skin—as I then thought.

The lion-man, Naghan the Doom, shouted across, "The way is open, my lady."

"Very good, Naghan. I will follow."

And, at that, what was revealed beyond the smashed-open grating was not particularly promising. But everyone in the Moder, I am sure, felt the desire to push on. To retrace our steps would be failure and would lead to disaster.

Narrow steps led downward, wide enough for one person at a time. The walls and roof were stained with moisture and far far away, echoing with a hollowness of enfolding distance, the sound of dripping water reached up.

The steps were slippery. Men fell, and others fell with them; but there was always one stout fellow to hold and to give the others a chance to pick themselves up each time. So we penetrated down.

"We are going from one zone to another, that is certain," said Modo Fre-Da. He half turned his head to speak to me as I followed him. The two

Pachaks and the numim surrounded the lady, and my help was relegated to the rear. That suited me.

"Zone?"

"Aye—" Then there was a slipping at our backs, and we had to brace ourselves to hold the mass of men pressing down.

My thoughtless question was thus forgotten. But, all the same, it was relatively easy to guess what Modo meant by a zone. Other considerations weighed on our minds as we came out onto a graveled floor and cast the light of the torches into a vast and hollow space, filled with the sound of running water, to see what fresh terrors confronted us.

Now there are torches and there are torches on Kregen. If you can get hold of the wood of certain of the trees, and use pitch and wax prepared in certain ways, you may build yourself a torch that is a king among torches, or you may wind up with a piece of burning wood that casts its light no more than half a dozen paces. The wizards and sorcerers have means of creating lights, magical lanterns, you might call them, that cast a mellow radiance for a considerable distance. Yagno would have one of those for sure—I wondered if old Quienyin also had one in his meager belongings.

Our torches were reasonably bright, varying in quality, and shed their lights over some seventeen or eighteen paces. Light-colored objects and movement could be picked out beyond that.

So we saw the glinting shimmering waterfall erratically revealed. We walked closer over the gravel.

The water fell from somewhere out of sight, curving to fall into a stone-faced pool in which a stone island supported a shrine. In the shrine the marble idol leered at us. I, for one, was having nothing whatsoever to do with his ruby eyeballs.

"Spread out," ordered the lady Ariane. "And see what there is to see."

We found ourselves in a cavern rather than a stone-faced corridor or hall. The water ran out an arched opening at the far end bordered by a stone-flagged path. Near a jut of rock that stretched into the stream lay the figure of a man clad in full armor, his arm outstretched. His mailed glove almost touched a small balass box, bound with gold, sitting on the ledge of rock. The water did not touch man or box.

"That box looks interesting," quoth the lady.

"Mayhap, my lady," offered Naghan the numim, "it contains the part of the key to be found in this zone."

"That we will not discover until—"

"Let me," said Logu Fre-Da, and he moved forward. He stretched out his tail-hand.

My attention had been occupied by the dead man. The armor was of the kind favored in Loh, a fashion I knew although not at that time having visited Walfarg in Loh, that mysterious continent of walled gardens and veiled women. The old Empire of Walfarg, that men called the Empire of Loh, had long since crumbled and only traces of a proud past were to be discerned in once-subject nations. This man had traveled far from the west, over the ocean to reach his end here. He was a Chulik, and his savage upthrust tusks were gilded. His skin appeared mummified, a pebbly green in configuration and color. In his left hand he gripped a weapon with a wooden haft some six feet long, and whose head of blue steel shaped like a holly leaf was by two inches short of a foot.

That cunning holly-leaf shape, with the nine sharp spikes each side set alternately forward and backward, and the lowest pair extended downward into hooks, told me the weapon was the feared strangdja of Chem.

Logu was a hyr-paktun, a man of immense experience in warfare and battle. He seized up the balass box in his tail hand and, even as that tail swished up and threw the box to his brother, his thraxter was out and just parrying in time the savage blow from the strangdja.

The dead man came to life the instant the box was moved.

He sprang up, ferocious, his Chulik-yellow face restored to its natural color, his tusks thrusting aggressively. He simply charged maniacally straight for Modo, who held the box, swinging the deadly strangdja in lethal arcs.

A single blow from that holly-leaf-blade might easily sunder through the Pachak's shield, a second rip his head clean off.

"He seeks to slay the man who holds the box!" yelled Naghan. The lion-man's own halberd slashed at the Chulik as the Undead passed, and was caught on the strangdja. For a single instant the two staved weapons clung and clashed, and then with a supple quarter-staff trick, the halberd was flung off. Naghan staggered back, raging with anger, to fling himself on again.

"Throw the box!" called Ariane in her clear voice.

The box arched up, and was caught by Logu, who waited until the Chulik advanced, madly, insensately, and then the box sailed over to me. I caught it and prepared to use the Krozair blade one-handed.

Stories of the Undead circulate as freely on Kregen as on Earth—more freely, seeing that they exist there. They are often called Kaotim, for kao is one of the many words for death, and they are to be avoided. Whether or not this example could be slain by steel I did not know, although I suspected he might well be, seeing that he had resumed his living appearance when recalled to life.

"Throw the box, Jak!" called Ariane.

I threw it—to her.

"You rast!" screeched Naghan at me, and fairly flung himself forward. But the Krozair brand flamed before him. The superb Krozair longsword is not to be bested by a polearm no matter how redoubtable its reputation or deadly its execution.

So the Chulik Kaotim sought to get past me, aiming a blow at Ariane, and I chopped him. Could one feel sorry for slaying a man who was already dead?

When the Kaotim's second leg was chopped he had to fall, for the Undead had been hopping and fighting on one. He hit the stone coping to the stream, and struggled to rise, and his stumps of legs bathed in the water and no blood gushed from their severed ends.

Finally, Naghan, with a cry of: "In the name of Numi-Hyrjiv the Golden Splendor!" brought his halberd down. The Kaotim's Chulik head rolled. No blood splashed. The gilt tusks shone in the light of the torches. The armored body lay still.

For a moment there existed a silence in which the roar of the waterfall sounded thin and distant.

I said, "If the key part is so important, as, indeed, it is, it would not have been entrusted to so feeble a charge." I turned away. "Whatever is in the box—it will not be the key."

I do not know who opened the box.

All they found was a coil of hair, and a blue silk ribbon, and a tiny pearl and silver brooch.

The lady Ariane said, "Put the things back in the box. Place it back on the ledge from whence it came."

This was done.

We stood back.

The Chulik head rolled. The legs walked. As Osiris was joined together, so that nameless Chulik adventurer resumed his full stature, legs and head once more attached to his body. Painfully, he crawled to the stone ledge and stretched out his hand toward the box—and so once more died.

His yellow skin marbled over and granulated to that death-green color. He remained, fast locked in the undying flesh, his ib forever barred from the Ice Floes of Sicce and the sunny uplands beyond.

Fourteen

Kov Loriman Mentions the Hunting Sword

The torches threw grotesque arabesques of light and shadow on the ripple-reflecting roof of the tunnel. The stream ran wide and deep at our side. We pressed on along the stone path and we took it in turns to lead, for we encountered many of the more ordinary water monsters of Kregen.

Always, the two Pachaks and the numim clustered close to their lady. There were in her retinue other powerful fighting men, and between them and me we kept the way ahead clear.

"Water runs downhill," said a Brukaj, his bulldog face savage as he drew back from slashing a lizard-form back into the water from which it had writhed, hissing. "So, at least we go in the right direction."

"May your Bruk-en-im smile on us, and prove you right," I said. "For, by Makki-Grodno's disgusting diseased tripes! I am much in need of fresh air and the sight of the suns."

After a time in which more scaly horrors were slashed and smashed back into the water, it was my turn to yield the point position. Pressing back to the very water's edge, I scanned the dark, swiftly-running stream as the people passed along.

A soft voice as Ariane passed said: "I think you fight well, Jak. You are a paktun, I think."

"Of a kind, lady." I did not turn my head. The Pachaks and the numim passed along and I stepped back from the edge to bring up the rear.

Light blossomed ahead, glowing orange and lurid through the darkness. I was still in rear as we debouched into a cavern vaster than any we had yet encountered. Here the water ran into a lake that stretched out of sight, beyond the fire-crystal walls streaming their angry orange light, past the weird structures that broke the surface of the water with promises of diabolism.

"Well, by all the Ibs of the Lily City!" said Ariane. "We will not meddle with them!"

Fastened by rusty chains and rusty rings at the stone-faced jetty lay seven ships, sunken, their superstructures alone rising above the waters. They were carved and decorated grotesquely. Many skeletons were chained to the oars. In the clear water hundreds of darting shapes sped dizzyingly. They were not fish. Their jaws gaped with needle-teeth, and their eyes blazed. We drew back from the edge with a shudder.

The gravel expanse began where the stone ended, and then more stone flags started again, some twenty paces farther on.

No one offered to step upon the gravel.

Tarkshur, Strom Phrutius, Kov Loriman and, even, Prince Nedfar, would simply have told a slave to attempt to cross. I looked at the lady Ariane nal Amklana and wondered what she would do.

"Naghan!" She spoke briskly. 'Tell some of the slaves to break a piece away from the nearest boat. Throw it on the gravel."

"Quidang, my lady!"*

No slaves fell in the water as a piece of the rotten wood, the gilding

---

* Quidang—equates with "Very Good, your orders will be carried out at once." Similar to "Aye, aye, sir." A.B.A.

peeling, was broken off. It was thrown out onto the gravel. It sank out of sight, slowly but inevitably, and a nauseating stench puffed up in black bubbles around it.

"We cannot cross there, then!"

"And we do not go back—"

"We cannot swim—"

"The boats!"

But each piece of wood we tried sank, for the stuff was heavy as lead, and rotten, and putrid with decay.

"Examine the wall for a secret door," commanded the lady.

As the slaves and retainers complied, she turned to me and bent a quizzical gaze on my harsh features.

"You say you are a paktun of a kind, Jak. And you are Jak, merely Jak and nothing else?"

Now the paktuns had called me notor, lord, without thought, and no man who is not a slave upon Kregen goes about the world with only one name. Unless he has something to hide. And anyone with an ounce of sense in his skull will invent a suitable name. I would not say I was Jak the Drang, for in Havilfar no less than Hamal, that name would be linked with the Emperor of Vallia. So, without a smile, but as graciously as I could, I said, "If it please you, my lady, I am sometimes called Jak the Sturr."

Now sturr means a fellow who is mostly silent, and a trifle boorish, and, not to put too fine a point upon it, not particularly favored by the gods in handsomeness. I picked the name out of the air, for, by Krun! I was building up a pretty head of boorish anger and resentment at the tricks and traps of this Moder. By Makki-Grodno's leprous left earlobe! Yes!

She laughed, a tinkle of silver in that gloomy torch-lit cavern.

"Then you are misnamed, I declare, by Huvon the Lightning."

I did not smile. Huvon is a popular deity in Hyrklana, and I was not going to pretend to this woman that I came from that island. If she asked where I hailed from...

"And, Jak the Unsturr—where in Kregen are you from?"

"Djanduin, my lady."

"Djanduin! But you are not a Djang!"

"No. But I have my home there. The Djangs and I get along."

"Yes." She wrinkled up her nose, considering. "Yes. I think you and they would—Obdjang and Dwadjang both."

What, I wondered, as shouts rang out along the rocky wall, would she say if I told her I was the King of Djanduin? For a start she would not believe me. And who would blame her?

We walked over to the wall and Naghan the Doom indicated an opening in the wall. I would have preferred to have found a boat and gone gliding down the stream to the outside world. But as no craft were available

428

we were in for another confounded corridor. Anyway, there were probably more waterfalls, and things with jaws that were not fish, and all kinds of blood-sucking leeches and lampreys and Opaz-alone knew what down the river...

The room into which we pressed at the end of the corridor presented us with another puzzle. I let them get on with it.

Whatever it was Ariane had come here for, the scent was growing cold as far as I was concerned. Yet every step we took could bring a horrible death, and therefore this Moder had to be taken seriously, very seriously indeed, by Vox!

The room was some hundred paces wide and broad with a fire-crystal roof from which light poured. We had entered by a square-cut opening which was the right-hand one of three. Across the room towered a throne draped in somber purple. The throne itself was fashioned from gold, and surrounded by a frieze of human skulls. Bones and skulls formed the decorations around the walls. On the throne sat the wizened body of an old woman. She had, we all judged, died of chivrel, that wasting disease that makes of Kregans old folk before their time.

Her robes were magnificent, cloth of gold and silver, studded with gems and laced with gold wire. Her skeletal fingers were smothered in jeweled rings. Her crown blazed.

A series of nine white-marble steps led up to the throne. Each side, and tethered by iron links, crouched two leems, motionless, their yellow eyes in their fierce wedge-shaped heads fastened upon us. The fangs were exposed.

On the third step up to the throne lay the armored body of a Kataki. He had been a famous warrior, one judged, a slave master, powerful, in his prime. Now he moldered away and he had not been dead for as long as most of the Undead in this fearsome place. The silence hung as an intense weight upon us.

"He is not, I judge, a Kaotim," observed Ariane. She was remarkably composed. "He was an adventurer, who failed the test."

We all nodded solemnly.

On seven tables spread with white linen down the left hand side of the chamber a feast lay spread out. The viands looked succulent, the wines superb. Not one of us was foolish enough to touch a scrap of food or a drop of drink.

Going as near as I felt sensible to the dead Kataki I saw that his face was black and his eye sockets were empty.

A small spindly-legged table to the right of the lowest step contained on its mosaic surface a golden handbell.

The lady Ariane paused before this little table, and looked down. She mused within her own thoughts before she said lightly, "To ring or not to ring?"

"To touch, or not to touch—anything," I said.

"True, Jak the Unsturr."

Mulishly, I said, "It is Jak the Sturr, my lady."

She frowned. "I do not choose to be crossed."

Well, it was a petty matter and not worth arguing about. Not here, where a ghastly death might leap upon us at any moment.

Faintly at first, and then growing steadily louder, the sounds of voices; the shuffle of feet and the clink of weapons sounded at our backs. We looked around as the noises strengthened.

"From the center door," said Naghan. "Best, my lady, we keep out of sight."

Silently, all of us, slaves fearful and retainers not much happier, we crowded behind the seven tables and crouched down. It was a jostle and we were cramped; but the fighting men positioned themselves ready to leap out if the occasion warranted.

The noises spurted into the chamber and then a voice broke out, hard, high and yet lighthearted.

"Thank Havil! There is real light ahead. Courage, my friend."

"Courage?" came a wheezing voice. "It is more a pair of strong legs, like yours, I am in dire need of at this moment."

Out into the light from the central opening stepped Deb-Lu-Quienyin and, with him and leading a small bunch of warriors and slaves, came Prince Tyfar. They stared about, much as we had done when we first entered.

The lady Ariane stood up, and smoothed her white gown.

"Lahal, prince!"

The shock was profound. Ariane laughed mischievously.

I frowned. She had risked an arrow through that pretty head of hers— the warriors with Prince Tyfar lowered their bows reluctantly. The prince smiled and walked forward, his hands outstretched.

"My lady Ariane! Lahal and Lahal. What a pleasant sight in this infernal prison!"

We all stood up from where we had hidden behind the tables and we all felt foolish, I daresay. After a space for mutual greetings, our stories were told. Very similar they were, too. As Ariane and the flying man had been separated, so the Wizard of Loh and the young prince of Hamal had been cut off from the main party by a falling block of stone. Now, together, we studied our present predicament.

Deb-Lu-Quienyin walked across to peer at the dead Kataki, and I observed how these people, like ours, had learned to do nothing foolish until everything that could be worked out had been worked out. He saw me. His face expressed surprise; but no great surprise, no shock. He smiled his old smile.

"Why, Lahal, Jak. How nice to see you again—you have had success, I trust?"

I greeted him in turn and then Ariane broke in to say, "So you two know each other? How nice!"

Prince Tyfar and I made the pappattu, and he gave me a hard look. "A lone adventurer, down here?"

"There are few people with you, prince."

"Yes, true—your party?"

I pointed up, down, and around. "Havil alone knows."

"You are welcome to join our party—"

I looked at him. He was a fine, sprightly, well-set-up young man, and the axe that dangled at his belt looked freshly cleaned. He was a prince of Hamal.

I said, "And you are at liberty to join me."

His eyebrows went up. His right hand dropped betrayingly toward his axe. Then his face creased. He threw his head back. He laughed. "By Krun! You are a jokester—and that is good, down here."

"If you two have finished?" Ariane looked cross. This was man's business and she felt a little left out—or so I judged the situation. "How do we go on?" She motioned to the three doors. "The left-hand one?"

Quienyin sighed. "That will probably take us back again where we do not wish to go. And the way is hard."

In the pause that followed we all heard the noises from the third door. There was about them a familiar ring.

Quienyin nodded. "We have all been working our way through these places and have, by different routes, converged on this chamber. That, I judge, is the rest of the party."

We all agreed and did not shelter behind the tables.

The Wizard of Loh was both right and wrong. When the newcomers walked out into the chamber we saw that they were the people belonging to Kov Loriman the Hunter. He strode ahead, swinging his sword about, enraged, looking for quarry. He had only two slaves and many of his fighting men carried bundles of loot.

The pappattu was made and he gave me a queasy look for which I did not blame him. After all, I could easily be a monster waiting the opportunity to rend him into pieces. But Quienyin's word sufficed.

"These passages writhe like a boloth's guts," Loriman said, and his full fleshy face exhibited passion. "When do we get to the real treasure house? By Spikatur Hunting Sword! I need to get my hands on—" He checked himself and then blustered on— "Gold and gems! Aye, by Sasco! That is what I came for and that is what I will have!"

So, I said to myself, this fine fleshy bucko was down the Moder for something other than gold or gems...

While the slaves and retainers wandered about the chamber seeking to read its riddles, I got hold of Quienyin and steered him to the center where we might talk. From our fascinating conversations under the stars as we rested in that caravan in which we traveled to Jikaida City, I knew him to be a pleasant old buffer—for a Wizard of Loh!—who felt the loss of his sorcerous powers most keenly. Yet I had sensed in him a groping for comradeship passing strange in a thaumaturge and not to be simply explained away merely because he had lost his arts of sorcery.

"Spikatur Hunting Sword," he said and puffed out his cheeks. "The kov let slip more—well, little enough is known of that secret order—"

"I heard rumors it was a new religion out of Pandahem—"

"You see? Stories, rumors, nothing known for certain. Whatever the truth, its members are Dedicated to Hunting. That, at least, is sure." He pushed at his turban. "And it is the least—nothing vital is known."

"I am most happy to see you alive and well, San. You seek your powers here—"

The intelligent inquisitiveness he had exhibited over this matter of Kov Loriman's secret allegiances shriveled at my words. He rode the tragedy extremely well, and showed a brave and proud face to the world. He was a Wizard of Loh. Instant obedience from ordinary mortals had been habitual to him. Sucking up, to find no easier way of saying it, from simple men who feared him had been his lot in life. But this loss had changed him greatly. He was troubled. He and I had come to an understanding out there on the Desolate Waste.

"Thank you, Jak. But, I crave your indulgence, do not tell these people I am a Wizard of Loh." His old eyes shifted to peer suspiciously at a massive Chulik, one of Loriman's bully boys, who prowled past bashing his spear against the floor. "I have told them I am a Magician of the humbler sort, whose tricks are mere sleight of hand. I do not think it would go well if they knew—"

"Rest assured. And so you have a secret. Do not we all?"

"Had I my powers, young man, I Would Read Your Secret!"

He spoke in capital letters, our San Deb-Lu-Quienyin.

He pulled his shortsword around. That betrayed him, if folk knew he was a Wizard of Loh.

"We have descended many levels within the zones. I think we are on the fifth zone now. What I seek lies on the lowest zone of all, the ninth zone. San Orien advised me."

"And is there truly a way out?"

"Yes. If you have the nine parts of the key. They fit together to unlock the outer door. But without the nine parts you will never leave."

"I hear Prince Nedfar has two."

"He had three when we were parted. His son, Prince Tyfar, has one. We must ask that boor Loriman—"

"Cautious, San, how you speak of him!"

"Aye, young man. You are Indubitably Right."

"And what of this famous sorcerer, San Yagno? Is he real?"

"He has powers. Great powers. But—he is not a Wizard of Loh, by the Seven Arcades, no!"

"And the creature—apim or diff—within the swathing red and green checkered cloak, this Tyr Ungovich?"

Quienyin looked troubled, and scratched up under his massy turban. A wisp of red hair fell; but not all men from Loh have red hair, and not all men with red hair are Wizards of Loh.

"He is an enigma. Without my powers I cannot riddle him."

"He it was, I believe, who arranged your expedition?"

"That is so."

The others were still searching around and finding nothing of use. And—no one had been messily killed, either.

"Now, San, these keys—or parts of the key. How are they recognized?"

He did look surprised now. "How is it that you venture in here and do not know that, Jak?"

I stared at him. "A secret for a secret, San?"

"Ah!"

"I came here with your expedition as a slave. I won free—from that heap of foulness, Tarkshur the Lash—"

The look that passed across the Wizard of Loh's face was not so much unreadable as amazing. I saw compassion there, and sympathy, a lively indignation.

"You are fortunate, my friend, to be alive and whole."

"So now you understand my dilemma. I must pass myself off as one of the notors—"

Now he smiled, a creasing of his face that charmed. He was no fool.

"Oh, but, Jak. On the Desolate Waste, when we played Jikaida with Pompino and Bevon—why, I knew then you were more than a paktun, more than a hyr-paktun—a notor?" He shook his head. "I shall retain a *few* powers."

"Well, for the sweet sake of Opaz—"

"Ah!" Again he smiled. "This dreadful place, to a normal man, is addling your wits, Jak. You are a prince, at the least. But, I will Keep my Own Counsel, as You will Keep Yours. We are, each of us, In the Other's Hands."

"Agreed. If we chance upon Tarkshur—"

"Then we bluff. I observed the slaves, looking at each establishment, all eight of them. Ionno the Ladle is with the main party. I did not recognize you—"

"You would not expect to see a man you knew, as slave, surely? Especially here?"

"Every man may be slave."

Before I could make some mundane acquiescent reply, Loriman walked past, ostentatiously poking at the floor the Chulik had already sounded. "Some of us," said this Loriman the Hunter, "are seeking ways of egress instead of chattering." He walked on and gave us a mean look.

He would have said more, but I called across in as cheery a voice as I could muster, "We confer on a plan."

He bridled at my lack of proper respect for his exalted rank of kov, and I heard Quienyin's wheezy chuckle. "Give us a moment more—kov."

When he had gone on with his useless floor-prodding, the Wizard of Loh said, "You do have a plan?"

"Tell me how you recognize the parts of the key."

"Each zone carries its own notification, its symbol. The three topmost ones are bronze, silver and gold, for they are the petty baubles men struggle for, and kill."

"Yes."

"The next three are named for gems. Diamond, Emerald, Ruby."

"That follows. We are in the Emerald zone now. And the lowest three?"

"Gramarye, Necromancy and—and the ninth I will not, for the moment, say."

"As it pleases you. But—what you seek lies there?"

"Yes."

"Emerald," I said. "Nothing as simple as that emerald and gold crown that poor old lady on the throne wears?"

"It might be her crown." Together, side by side, we walked across and halted before the marble steps. The dead Kataki slumbered; the four leems did not move.

The lady Ariane joined us. "You have something?"

"My lady," said Quienyin in his most bluffly gallant way, a veritable performance for a haughty Wizard of Loh. "My fine friend, Jak here, wonders if the crown...?"

"Maybe. How to reach it? No man is going up those steps. Oh," she said, cross, "if only silly Longweill had not got himself killed!"

Prince Tyfar stomped across, his right fist curled around his axe haft. "There is no way out that I can find!"

He saw the direction of our quizzical looks.

"The queen's crown?"

"There is emerald in it..."

"And," pointed out Quienyin, "bones and skulls, also."

"Well," said Tyfar, "my heart is not in it, but we will have to send someone up there."

The group of retainers and slaves who had clustered to find out what was going on suddenly became, as it were, mere wisps of smoke, vanishing into the far corners to prod and pry industriously at the solid walls.

I said, "If we attach a line to an arrow—"

"Capital!" declared Tyfar. "And I have the very man for us. He is renowned in Ruathytu as a bowman."

At Tyfar's imperious shout a bear of a man lumbered across. He was apim; but massively built and with a shock of dark hair. He wore a leather jerkin, brass-studded, and his bow was a composite reflex bow of some pull. I was quite content to let him shoot, for I judged the range demanded a flatter trajectory weapon—although I fancied Seg would argue that one.

Kov Loriman objected. He stomped up with a Fristle in tow who was holding a composite reflex bow which, although it looked much the same as the one the man from Ruathytu carried, was by its construction and the curves the product of a different philosophy. Both were good, both would do the job. They were just different tools and both equally efficient.

A wrangle ensued as to which bowman would shoot.

I did not—as you might expect—intemperately loose myself. A piece of fine thread had first to be attached to the arrow. This was done—to both shafts. Kov and prince glared at each other.

Ariane tinkled her laugh. "Let me choose—"

"This is touching honor and is not to be settled at a woman's whim," growled Loriman. "Lady."

Tyfar's face went white. But Ariane turned her brilliant eyes upon him. She checked her own words. What she was going to say, what she would have brought to the quarrel, I do not know. I do know that Prince Tyfar was set to knock the boorish kov into Kingdom Come.

Deb-Lu-Quienyin said: "Let us twirl a shaft."

Rumbling, we all agreed this was the answer and the arrow was tossed. It came down cock-feather down, and Kov Loriman, who had chosen that—unusually—smirked.

About to pass some casual comment that it was a pity all the Hamalese crossbowmen were with Prince Nedfar, I checked, almost choking. By Krun! I wasn't supposed to know anything about this expedition!

They gave me an odd look as I choked and I turned the movement into a shake of the head and a sneeze. "This dust," I said. "It gets right up my hooter, by Djan!"

The two bowmen were Professionals, no doubt of that. Loriman's Fristle drew to cheek and let fly. Now maybe it was merely the weight of the line upon the shaft, light as it was, or maybe there really did come a sudden and fierce gust of wind. Whatever caused the phenomenon—the archer missed. The shaft went skittering off a skull, caroming, and struck the ebon wall at the rear of the throne.

A blaze of crimson light devoured the arrow.

When we hauled in the line the end was charred black.

That did not encourage any of us.

Prince Tyfar's champion from Ruathytu shot next and exactly the same thing happened.

Three times each they shot, adjusting their deflection for that unpredictable wind. Six shafts burned.

"By Sasco the Wonder!" stormed Loriman. "I'll have you jikaidered! You hire yourself as a bowman and you cannot shoot as straight as a five-year old coy!"

Prince Tyfar raised his eyebrows at his bear of a man.

"My prince—there is a wind. It cannot be judged."

Loriman swung on me, his thick face flushed. "A fine idea you had!"

I said: "If a sorcerer were here he might well say the wind was an illusion."

"The arrows are blown out of true, ninny!"

Prince Tyfar's gasp was perfectly audible to us all. I ignored both that and Kov Loriman's insult. Anyway, what could he do in the way of insult and indignity to me, who had played him at Execution Jikaida?

"Then if the wind is real," I said, still in an even unimpassioned voice, "there must be holes, funnels, something from which the wind blows."

They all craned their necks to peer up into the shadows fringing the throne.

Loriman was completely unaware of his insulting behavior.

"I do not see any! Lights, you rasts, bring lights!"

Torches were brought and their light smoked up into the shadows of the throne, and a cloud of bats swooped out, red-eyed, squeaking, to fly madly away around the walls. We watched them narrowly. But they appeared harmless, and perched themselves upside down on tall crannies of rock.

I said, "And, if I am right, as it seems I am, seeing some force prevents us from toppling the crown down—what happens when we do bring it down?"

"We will meet that when it comes." Prince Tyfar spoke firmly. "And I am now convinced the part to the key is there."

"In that case," I said, "prince, call up a slinger."

"Of course, Notor Jak. Of course!"

Quickly a slinger was hauled out, a tough-bodied Brokelsh whose coarse body bristle was armored on his left side and mother naked on his right. The line was attached to one of his leaden bullets. He looked at the crown, and shrugged his shoulders, and winked his eyes, and licked his lips.

"Give me room, doms," he said, in that brokelsh way.

He swung and let fly.

The slingshot arched. The wind blew—we all knew that supernatural wind blew. The bullet flew true. He was a good slinger, that uncouth Brokelsh.

The line tightened as the leaden bullet swung about with a clatter against the crown. Prince Tyfar was among the first who took a grip and hauled.

The crown tilted. Sparks of green fire shot from it, irradiating the chamber in an eerie green glow.

"Oh, no!" cried the lady Ariane.

But the crown tilted, toppled, fell.

It crashed down onto the steps, bouncing, shedding shards of green light. It struck the Kataki corpse and rebounded high, spinning, refulgent with a glitter of gold and gems.

When it struck the bottom step a long, wailing moaning began vibrating throughout the chamber.

And the steps revolved, the throne and the drapes and the wizened crone vanished out of our sight and from the revealed black hell hole a horde of ravenous shapes from nightmare leaped full on us.

Fifteen

Of a Descent Through Monsters

The horrors skittered and hopped and flew upon us. They were hairy, squamous, warty-hided. They ran on four legs or six legs, their tails were scaled and barbed. Their eyes were red or yellow and they blazed maniacally with hate, or were smoldering green and glared with crazed venom. A whole heaping stinking gargoyle menagerie of monsters fell upon us—and not one was larger than a terrestrial cat.

We slashed away at them beating them off, seeing men fall shrieking with long orange fangs fastened through corded throats. The uproar, the stench, the sheer horror of it all beat frenziedly upon us.

Exactly how many different types of monster there were I do not know. Certainly among the hundreds that poured screeching from that hell hole there were at least twenty different sorts. And all of them, every single one, was bent upon our destruction.

The slaves did not last long.

Near naked, unarmored, weaponless, the slaves were stripped of flesh in a twinkling, and it seemed their macabre skeletons still ran, the bony jaws clacking in fear.

I saw Quienyin striking bravely about him with his shortsword, surrounded by a cloud of fluttering horrors. It was a case of wading through clutching scratching teeth and talons to reach him and assist in beating away the mind-congealing host.

"Fliktitors, Jak!" The Wizard of Loh panted as he struck. "That is what they are, Fliktitors."

The drexer in my right fist slashed and hewed. The main gauche carved a bloody path—as the saying is—and yet that was as near as you would come to the truth of the saying. For the horrors formed a tightly packed host and each blow struck them down so that I did, in truth, carve a way through them.

Prince Tyfar battled with superb fury and cunning, and his axe hissed as it clove through spiny back and leathery wing.

The two Pachaks and the numim closed up around their lady and fought as only Pachaks and numims can fight.

The outpouring of scaled horrors ceased. The warty-hided ones ran on their six legs and were crushed. The hairy ones clawed up with curved talons and were cut down.

But men were cut down also.

When, in the end—in the long bloody end—we had finished the last mewling one, the Brokelsh slinger planting a heavy and uncouth boot upon its black and squirming neck, we stood back, panting, and surveyed the carnage.

No slaves survived.

Kov Loriman was berserk with rage, and went about slashing with his sword at the putrid corpses of the Fliktitors.

The Lady Ariane's white gown shook with her panting, and it was stained and splattered with blood, red and green.

We all felt, we survivors, that we would rest and refresh ourselves before we essayed any further the mystery and terror of this haunted place.

Loud were the voices raised in argument, loud were the quarrels between diff and apim, between men of the same race, between warrior and retainer. But we all knew, every one of us, that we must stick together.

Loriman stalked over to me, livid. "So your idea was a fine idea, ninny! This is what you have brought us to!"

I picked up the tumbled crown. It was ice cold.

"Look in this, kov, and see what there is to be seen."

The leaders crowded around as Loriman snatched the crown and shook it. An oddly shaped piece of bronze tumbled out.

"Ah!" said Tyfar.

"The key!" exclaimed Ariane. "The part from the fifth zone!"

Loriman grunted and picked it up, started to stuff it away under his armor.

I said, "I think, kov, I will take care of that."

"You rast! I am a kov—I shall—"

"You will hand that over, or, kov or no kov, you will..." And then I caught myself. I breathed in deeply and slowly. Vosk-skulled onker of onkers, Dray Prescot! Quienyin stepped forward. The inflection in his voice took our attention.

"Perhaps, as she is so well guarded, the lady Ariane...?"

"I would offer to carry the part of the key," said Prince Tyfar. "But will gladly yield the honor to the lady."

Loriman was outvoted. I looked curiously at Tyfar. A bright, bonny prince, the slaves had said. But a bit of a ninny, also... The axe was pure compensation. He tended to glow a bit around the edges when confronted with women. And he regarded carrying the damned bit of key as some kind of honor. Well, given romantic notions and frames of reference, of course it was. But down here in this Moder with Monsters and Magic were, if you thought about it, fine times for chivalry and honor.

Everyone was glad of the food and rest. A round umbrella-shaped object, translucently white and shining, drifted in through the center door. It was some three feet in diameter and from its center a long thin tendril drooped twelve to fifteen feet, for it was rising and falling, and occasionally flicking about. Quienyin called out, "Don't touch the feeler!"

By this time down here no one touched anything if they hadn't given it all the tests they could think of—which made progress slow. This round umbrella was quick. From that slow drifting floating it exploded into action the instant its dangling tendril touched living organic substance.

That feeler locked around the neck of a Brokelsh who was not quick enough.

We expected, given the horror of this place, that the unfortunate man would be reeled in like a fish at the end of a line. Instead the round translucent horror reeled itself in, swooping down, positioning itself exactly above the man's head. I was irresistibly reminded of the cone of a flick-flick as the translucent circle closed over the man's head. It drew itself in like a hood over his head, tightly, tightly—his staring features were clearly outlined in the translucent material.

"It is a Suffocating Hood!" shouted Quienyin.

"Cut it off!" commanded Ariane.

Loriman lifted his sword.

"You will cut the man, also." Quienyin looked sick.

The Brokelsh was running in crazy circles, as though controlled, and his chest jerked spasmodically. He collapsed quickly enough, suffocated, and we could see the blueness of his face through the translucent material of the Suffocating Hood.

"Has anyone an atra with the symbol for air?" demanded the Wizard of Loh. "Hurry!"

Everyone—except me—began searching desperately through the amulets they wore around their necks or hidden upon their persons. Most folk of Kregen—not all—carry an atra or two to ward off various kinds of evil. A Fristle let out a yell. With marvelous speed, Quienyin had the atra in his hand, with a quick jerk breaking the leather thong around the Fristle's neck. The cat-man jumped. Quienyin started to force the atra up inside the tiniest of wrinkles in the lower edge of the Suffocating Hood as we gripped the shivering, dying Brokelsh. The atra was a simple, clumsily cast chunk of silver in the shape of a nine-sided figure, with the symbols for Fur, Lightning, Air and Milk, engraved on its dull surface.

After what seemed a long time, the Brokelsh breathed again, his blueness seeped away—but the horrific Suffocating Hood remained clamped around his head.

"How do we remove that ghastly thing?" whispered Ariane.

"Why waste time?" demanded Loriman. "He is only a Brokelsh." He strode across, lifting his sword. "Let me—"

"Loriman! Kov!" said Ariane, shocked. "No—"

But the Hunting Kov got the tip of his sword up the same fold where the atra had been forced. Perhaps it was the passage of air, perhaps it was the right thing to do, perhaps it was just luck. He started to twist his sword and cut into the thin material of the Suffocating Hood. He cut, also, the face of the Brokelsh. I did not think that man would mind.

The Hood, suddenly, like an umbrella opened violently against a rainstorm, swelled out, and skimmed away aloft, trailing its tendril. Loriman gave a vicious slash at the dangling line; but missed. I wondered if a sword would cut the line at all.

"Let us push on," growled Loriman.

Fortified wine was pressed on the Brokelsh. He looked shattered. But he was lucky still to be alive. Of course, maybe quiet suffocation would be preferable to what awaited him in the lower zones of this Moder...

Our order of march was reorganized and we plunged with uplifted torches into that black hell hole beyond the throne.

The moment the last mercenary pushed through the whole throne construction revolved. We saw the purple drapes, the throne, the frieze of skulls and bones, the four leems, all turning back to face once more into the chamber. I wondered if a new crown would appear on the dead queen's head.

At my side, his face crimson in the torchlights, Quienyin whispered, "Those leems—had we rung the bell..."

"Probably," I said. And we all hurried on into the darkness.

The way led down. Nitre glittered on the walls, and our lights reflected back from obscene carvings which appeared to writhe and cavort. I observed the way Tyfar, highly embarrassed, kept trying to engage the lady Ariane in animated conversation and her quick bird-like looks of fascination past his glowing face at those highly personal carvings. Well, one day, the youngster would learn about women... We marched on down the long slope and it was at length clear that we must have penetrated down into the next zone within the Moder.

The hall we entered was a single blazing mass of ruby walls.

The walls were studded with rubies.

Some of those hard-bitten paktuns started in at once with their daggers. No lightnings flashed, no thunders rolled, no monsters leaped upon us as the first stone broke free.

The mercenary, he was one of Loriman's powerful Chuliks, reached out with a cupped palm as the ruby popped out from the wall. The deep crimson gem fell onto his palm, fell through his palm, burned a seared black hole through flesh and bone and sinew. The Chulik let out a shout—and, knowing Chuliks, I was not at all surprised that the yell was almost all of anger and outrage and only a trifle of pain.

"The Glowing Stones!" Quienyin pulled an apim back as the next stone bounced free. It struck the floor and exploded in a shower of sparks, red and brilliant even in the massy ruby light of that devilish room.

Very cautiously we looked for the opening, and found a trapdoor in the floor which, when opened by prizing blades, revealed a hollow white radiance beneath. Tyfar said, "By Krun! White is better than red!" And he dropped down, his sword pointed before him.

Yes, well, he was a brave young man. Foolhardy, perhaps.

When we all stood on the floor at the foot of the flight of stairs down—and not before—the floor tilted. Helplessly, we were all tumbled away down a long slippery slope, the reek of thick oil in our nostrils. Down and down we shot, slipping and sliding. Above our heads the white light dwindled and was gone.

The slope down which we skidded gradually eased out and became horizontal, like a chute, and deposited us, jumbled up and swearing, in a confused mass on a normal stone floor. Fire-crystal walls shed a yellow light. We picked ourselves up. Not a drop of oil stained our garments or armor. We looked about.

In the opposite wall stood just two doors, one rounded and one pointed, both shut, and between them leaned an iron-bound skeleton of an anthromorph, grinning and grotesque.

Otherwise, the chamber was bare.

"Which?" said someone, and he spoke for us all.

"I," observed Kov Loriman, "prefer to choose the right."

That was the pointed arched doorway.

For the rest of us that confirmed our decision to choose the round-headed doorway.

Of such petty stuff are great decisions made.

I did not speak aloud; but I said to myself, "Of Roman or Gothic, either will do for me..."

The corridor beyond looked perfectly normal. Not one of us believed it was.

But—we were wrong. A simple plain straightforward stone corridor, well-lit, led on for some way within the Moder, gently inclining down. The walls were unremarkable. At length, and with something of a relief, we came to a small chamber into which we could not all press, so perforce a bunch of warriors remained outside.

In the room, within a glass case set upon a silver and balass table, we found an object upon which we gazed with great speculation. It was a key. It was fashioned from silver. It was an ordinary key.

"Not, I think," said Ariane, "one of the parts of the Key—"

"That, lady, is obvious!" snorted Kov Loriman.

"In that case, kov," pointed out Tyfar, "there should be no difficulty for you to smash the glass and take the key. Surely?"

But Loriman was a Hunter and was not to be snared like that.

"Before I tell one of my paktuns to take the key, we will look more thoroughly."

That made sense, and so we searched the chamber.

We found nothing else and Loriman told one of his men to break the glass. The Chulik polished up his tusks with a wetted thumb and started forward, and Tyfar said, "Kov! I mean you no disrespect. We are all in this together and must accept the needle. Let my slinger smash the glass while we wait outside..."

The Chulik paktun—he was a hyr-paktun—turned about at once and marched toward the door. The rest of us followed suit. Only Loriman was left in the room. He gave a disgusted snort and followed us out. Tyfar's Brokelsh slinger went through his ritual of shrugging his shoulders, winking his eyes and licking his lips. He slung.

Barkindrar, his name was, a fine slinger. From Hyrzibar's Finger. Down in the southeast of Havilfar.

The glass vanished in a welter of smashings. It tinkled to the stone floor.

A long rope-like object snapped up from the base of the shattered case and lashed, looping, around the empty space where any man must stand who had smashed the case with a sword. The diamond-backed rope, like a serpent, hissed as it coiled and lashed and, finding nothing there, collapsed limply. It hung down like a disused bell rope.

"By Krun!"

The Chulik who had been given the duty shouldered forward and hooked the key out with his dagger. The golden pakzhan glittered at his throat. The key lifted and he held it on the tip of the dagger, the point through one of the loops in the handle. He held it out to Kov Loriman, his employer.

We all tensed.

Loriman, with a coarse laugh, took from a pouch a wooden box, of a sort men use to carry cham which they chew all day, and the Chulik obediently dropped the key into the box. Loriman snapped the lid shut.

We relaxed. If Loriman had vanished in a puff of smoke we would have been sorry. He was a powerful force to have with us, and I, for one, would have wished his end to be of a more obviously useful kind.

So we went traipsing on up the corridor and left that room far in the rear. The corridor curved gently to the right, and this, I felt, must please the Hunting Kov.

Ariane and Tyfar were deep in conversation.

Quienyin and I walked side by side.

"We must make a proper camp and rest soon, Jak. I am weary and, I fear, My Limbs are Not what They Were."

"I agree. The lady Ariane bears up wonderfully well."

I told the Wizard of Loh something of what had befallen me in the Moder, and then said, "And the openings offered what men lacked. If we could find a way back there, surely, you would find what you lack—is this not so?"

He shook his head. "All is Not What it Seems. I think you will find the equipment you have will vanish when you leave this place."

"I had the thought myself. But it is real now, and serves."

"Some of the treasures these avaricious men have collected are real, others are mere fool's gold. And the magical items which the more cunning among us seek share the Same Propensities."

"We are, I suggest, in the Gramarye zone?"

"We may have descended through two zones and be in the Necromantic zone. I learned what San Orien had to tell me; but each Moder is different. Some are abandoned. We know why we are in this one..."

He told me that San Orien, the resident Wizard of Loh in Jikaida City, had advised him as far as he could. The secrets of the Moders were kept as far as possible from the poorer folk, and this explained no doubt the mystery of Nathjairn the Rovard and his slit throat. Other cities to the south also sent expeditions. "On the six upper zones of the Moder are seven hundred and twenty-nine different types of monster." He glanced up at me. "Which, as you will readily perceive, young man, is Nine Times Nine Times Nine."

"Oh, readily."

"The yellow poison you stoppered in your vial must be some form of protection to your skin—the Fliktitors did not scratch or bite you at all— or did you put that down to your superb swordsmanship?"

Deb-Lu-Quienyin had seen me fight Mefto the Kazzur.

I felt suitably chastened.

"And you suggest that the sparkling stones from the Leprous Sheet can be used as Tarkshur used the stone in his ring?"

"One was able to purchase little magics against some of the monsters, but their value is dubious. Yagno did a trade, as did that mysterious Ungovich.

Your stones I think would be effective against another Leprous Sheet. Against any of the more Fearsome Monsters Down Here..." He shook his head.

Cure-all magics were a fool's dream, anyone but a fool knew. But men might draw a little comfort from exchanging gold for magic charms.

The corridor branched and branched again and ranked doorways opened on either hand. Here Loriman demonstrated that some of his gold had not been wasted.

The inclination to look into every room we passed had still not been mastered. Quienyin and I were content merely to look; others prodded and pried in the search for treasure and magic. It would not be altogether fruitful and might weary to catalog continuously all the rooms and chambers and monsters and horrors; but Loriman's gold saved him at least twice on this level.

A warrior marched up from the shadows of a room with fluted columns of red and yellow ocher and drapes of purple and gold—very tasteful to those with that taste. The warrior wore purple armor, and carried a purple shield whereon was described a golden zygodont—all fangs and claws and membranous wings and barbed tail. His sword looked useful, yet that cunning blade, too, was fashioned from purple metal. The visor of his helmet was closed.

Loriman bristled up at once. He swelled. The veins in his nose throbbed.

"Any man who wants a fight can have one! I am a hunter—and I hunt anything that moves!" And with a yell he threw himself into the onguard position ready to smash down onto the warrior in his closed purple armor.

Quienyin shouted, "Kov! Caution! He is no man, he is a monster! A Hollow Carapace!"

Loriman heard, luckily for him, and he jerked back. The purple-accoutered warrior strode on.

"We had best run," said Quienyin, looking about.

"A Hollow Carapace! Like a fighting man!" boomed Loriman, and his voice echoed eerily in the chamber. "Aye! I have somewhat for that monster! The tricky rast!"

From his pouch he drew forth—after snicking his sword away—a narrow box such as stylors use for their pens. From this he took forth a little animal like a pencil with squat wings. At its pointed head, which spiraled sharply, glinted moisture.

Quienyin looked pleased.

"An Acid-Head Gimlet! Charming—"

"I paid gold for this," said Loriman. "If it does not work as I was promised—"

A Chulik—he was a hyr-paktun—abruptly screeched, high in his corded throat, and leaped upon the purple warrior. His sword lifted and blurred. The Hollow Carapace shifted the purple shield to deflect the blow; but the Chulik knew all about shields and swerved his blow away beautifully to hack past the side of the shield and into the purple cuirass beyond. At least, that savage and skilled blow would have hacked into a normal cuirass unless it was of superb quality.

The sword bounced. The Chulik staggered back. "By Hlo-Hli!" he shrieked. His sword was a mere mass of molten metal, dripping, and when he dropped it it shredded away his glove and the flayed skin of his palm beneath.

"Not the shield, kov," cautioned Quienyin as the Hollow Carapace advanced, sword and shield ready.

"I know, I know," snapped Loriman. He lifted the little winged animal, the Acid-Head Gimlet. It was a dart of blue and green and brown, almost like a dragonfly. The moisture at its gimlet-shaped head glittered. Loriman launched it. It flew, its wings buzzing like ripsaws, skimmed across the space between to bury its head in the visored helmet. It rotated.

Three heartbeats—three and a half, at the most—passed before the Hollow Carapace reacted. By then it was too late. From the hole drilled by the gimlet head and bitten by the acid puffed a foul odor. Whatever caused that was invisible and was, I think, not material. For the Hollow Carapace was—hollow.

It collapsed.

It fell in on itself as a vessel exhausted of air collapses under the ambient pressure.

Bits and pieces of the armor bounced on the stone floor. We tensed anew, for we were well-accustomed to the ghastly phenomenon of fresh monsters rising from the remains of the old. The golden zygodont sprang into bestial life from the shield, sprang hissing out to charge full on us. The men fell back.

"The sword!" yelled Quienyin, dancing around beside us.

The purple sword skittered among the detritus of the Hollow Carapace. Fittingly, it was Loriman who dived for the sword, got it into his fist, swung at the golden zygodont. The blade sheared through a foreleg and Loriman swung again and the next stroke half-severed the serpent-neck. The third blow decapitated the zygodont. Everyone breathed out—shakily.

"Now thank all your gods it did not resume its true size!" said Quienyin.

I went across to the Chulik hyr-paktun who was gripping his right wrist, his hand stiffly extended. As I went so the pieces of purple armor puffed into purple smoke and dissipated.

"Drop the sword, kov!"

Loriman dropped it—just in time. He would have lost his hand—at the least.

I took out the stoppered vial of yellow poison from the Bristle Ball and pressed it against that grisly flayed palm. "Hold still, Chulik!"

He went rigid with shock, and then looked down. I took the vial away. The skin of his hand was whole again, yellow and unmarked.

The hyr-paktun stared at me with his dark slit eyes.

"You have my thanks, apim—"

"We all fly the same fluttrell here."

The golden zygodont had disappeared. Dust hung in the air. We pushed on, warily. Many rooms, many chambers, many wonderful things...

And, also, many ghostly apparitions, were-creatures, ghouls from the diseased imaginings of madmen, vampires with red-dripping fangs, specters, wraiths, banshees...

We walked through a long corridor fitfully illuminated by orange torches in the yellow-brown fingers of skeletons ranged against the black walls. The oppressive atmosphere crashed down. We spoke in quiet voices—even Kov Loriman. Tyfar and Ariane walked together.

"I believe we approach something of quality," said Quienyin.

Between each skeleton stood a table carved in the form of an impossible monster. On the tables rested objects of unimaginable use mingled with treasure, arms and armor, food and drink, valuables.

Now Chuliks fear very little on Kregen and their imaginations are limited. One massive warrior, straining his armor, gazed upon an artifact that would keep him in luxury for the rest of his life. It was a single enormous yellow gem, subtly carved into the likeness of a Chulik head. It fascinated him, and, clearly, he felt himself to be the most fortunate of Chuliks to be nearest. He picked it up. I can guess he could not stop himself from picking up that magnificent gem.

He cupped it in his fist and it did not burn, he did not disappear in smoke, he was unharmed.

The skeleton at his side stretched out its empty hand, still gripping the torch in the other, and fastened those bony fingers about the Chulik's wrist.

Men yelled and stumbled away. The torches threw dizzying orange lights and shadows between writhed. The Chulik pulled his hand back sharply. He could not break that skeletal grip.

"Here, Chekumte—" said a compatriot.

"Hurry," said Chekumte. "It grips hard."

The second Chulik brought his sword down in a sweeping cunning blow against the yellowed wrist bones of that skeletal arm. The sword did not shear through. The bones sheared through the sword. The point fell onto the floor with a mocking clang.

"By Hlo-Hli!" yelled Chekumte. "Bring a blade! Strike hard!"

We sheared through four swords before I thought that, in all decency, I should try the Krozair brand.

Quienyin saw my movement as I made to unsheathe the longsword.

He shook his head. "I fear not, Notor Jak. That is a form of the Snatch-ban. The rope at the cabinet of the silver key was another. I believe they are also found in whip forms, liana forms, tentacle forms. Mortal steel will not cut them. We do not have the blade that will."

Loriman glared along the corridor. "We must push on."

The Chulik Chekumte struggled against the bony fingers. The pakmort shone a silver glint at his throat and his pakai of many rings shook. He was a paktun from Loh. "Do not leave me, comrades! I am a man, a mortal man!"

He was a Yellow Tusker, almost as lacking in humanity as a Whip-Tail. Loriman gestured to his Chulik comrade. "Do what you have to."

"Yes, yes, by Likshu the Treacherous!" cried Chekumte. He writhed again, his yellow skin sheened with the sweat of terror. "Do it!"

Prince Tyfar drew Ariane away, bending his head to her, gently.

The Chulik brand slashed down.

Chekumte from Loh staggered back, his severed wrist spouting Chulik blood.

I thought of Duhrra of the Days...

My vial of yellow poison sealed the wound but did not restore the hand. Chekumte held his stump aloft. "See, doms!" he cried. "Now you may call me Chekumte the Obhanded!"

"No," said his comrade. "Better Chekumte the Skohanded."*

The skeleton moved again. It lifted its mottled brown fingers gripping the freshly severed fleshy hand, the thick blood dripping. Its hideous jaws opened. Blood spattered. The jagged teeth crunched down. The skeleton's jaws closed with a snap. The hand vanished—forever.

We shuddered and pressed on down that skeleton-guarded corridor.

Through apparitions, through fire, through poison, we battled our way on and we realized we were—we must be!—approaching a crisis. The horrors multiplied, shrieking and clawing—and then, suddenly, fell away. In a hushed expectant silence we passed through an ebon portal. Somber drapes opened with the fetid odor of death.

A series of dusty anterooms which we treated with the utmost caution led us at length into a macabre chamber of considerable extent.

This wide and lofty hall extended about us bathed in yellow light. Quienyin perked up. We had passed through horrors and now although the threat of terrors to come existed here, plainly, we felt we had gained an important objective.

"Ah!" he said, pleased. "We must be in the penultimate hall to what San Orien called the heart and reason for being of the Moders."

The ceiling bulged low in some places, festooned with carvings of a grotesque and repulsive character. Bats swooped about high, and peered down

---

* Ob: one. Sko: left. Mon: right. *A.B.A.*

with red eyes. A faint incense stink hung on the air and slicked flat and unpleasant on the tongue. Sounds echoed.

The opening through which we had entered remained in being and did not close on us. Directly ahead at the far end of the hall the wall rose, tiered into many shelves. In each side wall openings almost as high as the ceiling led onto short passageways. Every wall was honeycombed with slots of stone. They jutted into the hall here and there forming oddly angled aisles. Above the main doorway and inscribed deeply into the marble an inscription glittered with gold.

THE HALL OF SPECTERS

"San Orien knew of the Nine Halls surrounding the mausoleum," said Quienyin. He was peering every which way, quivering with attention, seeming to shed years from his age. "This is the Hall of Specters. There is a confusing complex of halls and corridors cradled here. And the whole place is a single vast mausoleum."

Dead bodies lay everywhere.

The walls were honeycombed with the dead.

Mummified as though in life, mere heaps of dusty rag, skeletons, masses of dried corruption, the bodies lay silently upon their biers of stone. Relaxed in the sleep of eternity, the corpses lay in rank on rank, niche on niche, tomb on tomb.

In every direction nothing but corpses.

But—were they dead?

Sixteen

In the Hall of Specters

Uneasily, we stared about. The lady Ariane said, flatly, that she could not go on any farther. So we made a camp in a corner where two walls joined at not quite a right angle and where the serried ranks of crypts were empty of corpses. It was a case of cold tack until some foraging Chuliks returned with smashed coffins. These burned with an eerie blue light; but on them were cooked up a meal and brewed Kregan tea.

Just then a Specter of Mutual Loathing walked in.

He looked just like a young and lissome youth, naked, long of hair, smooth of skin. He was smiling in friendly fashion.

"Leave him alone!" called the Wizard of Loh.

But one of the Chulik mercenaries—he was not a hyr-paktun—could not resist. With a grunt of contempt and loathing he slashed his thraxter at the smiling youth. Everything down here that was not a known friend was a monster.

The sword struck against the youth's side. He went on smiling that wide zany smile.

The Chulik yelped and went smashing backwards.

"Jak!" shouted Quienyin. "Face the youth and strike yourself!"

For a single heartbeat I did not understand what he meant—and then I saw. I whipped out the drexer and gave myself a resounding blow over the head, swinging the blade fiercely. I felt nothing. But the Specter of Mutual Loathing lost his smile. He staggered back. And purple blood sprouted from a deep wound in his head. With a wailing cry of despair he ran away, ran off, shrieking and shedding spots of purple blood that smoked as they spattered the floor.

"By Huvon!" whispered Ariane.

"A devil's trick!" shouted Loriman.

"You are to be congratulated, Notor Jak," said Tyfar.

I sheathed the unbloodied sword. "Rather, prince, thank Quienyin here, who saw through the devil's trick."

The Chulik paktun came forward. His kax was deeply marked by the blow he had struck at the Specter of Mutual Loathing.

"By Likshu the Treacherous!" he panted. "I struck only with sufficient force to slice a naked man—had I struck full force..." His powerful fingers traced the ugly mark in his cuirass.

"He was but a simple monster," said Quienyin. "He must have prowled down here and lost himself."

"You do not reassure us, Master Quienyin." Tyfar drew his eyebrows down. Then he gave a small gesture with a hand that seemed to imply that what Krun brought, Krun brought. "But we are much dependent on your wisdom."

"There are much worse monsters here?" demanded Ariane.

Tyfar gave Quienyin no time to answer. "If there are," he said firmly, smiling at Ariane, "then we will meet them, aye, and best them, too!"

We set sentries and took turns to sleep. We lords—and I relished in a distant muffled way the irony of being numbered among the notors—each took a watch, acting as Guard-Hiks.*

The Hall of Specters formed one arm of a nine-armed complex of chambers, and each of these halls possessed its own resounding and macabre name. At the center, so Quienyin informed us, lay the mystery of this zone. There, we anticipated, also, we would find the eighth part of the key to get us out of here.

---

* Hik: abbreviation for Hikdar, roughly equivalent to a captain, a company commander... Its use here is correct Kregish. A.B.A.

His quota of sleep being short, Quienyin joined me as I stood my watch. We talked quietly. He told me that San Orien's explanation for the existence of the Moders seemed reasonable and to be given a due meed of credulity. Originally the mounds—low then and simple—were used as places of burial. The habit of the living to bury costly treasures with the dead brought the inevitable train of grave-robbers. So the structures grew more complex and the traps more hideous. The Undead stirred at disturbances. Illusion prevailed, for the Moders were controlled by a people who, although sadly shrunken in numbers in these latter days, retained awesome powers.

"There is more to it than that," I said.

"Assuredly. The Moder-lords—to give them a euphemistic title—discovered much about their own natures as they watched the dying struggles of would-be robbers. They discovered that not only did they enjoy the intellectual stimulation of providing ever more elaborate puzzles and traps, they found also, and to their undisguised joy, that they could feed from fear."

I nodded. "Other people have discovered that—think of the rasts who infest the Jikhorkdun and squeal at the blood in the arena. Or," I added darkly, "think of Kazz-Jikaida..."

"No, no, young man. The Moder-lords feed directly from the psyches of the frightened."

"That is possible?"

His comical turban slipped and he pushed it back; but the gesture was not the usual irritated push. "I Must Confess that many a famous Wizard of Loh shares that dark desire."

He looked not at all proud of that.

He went on after a space in which I let him gather his thoughts: "San Orien believed there was but one Moder-lord to each dark labyrinth, sitting in his battlemented towers on high and giggling and chuckling to himself as he ran the poor demented creatures below."

"They all came here of their own free will."

"You wound sorely, Jak—but it is sooth."

A guard stirred at the other side of the fire and stalked across. The firelight glinted from his armor and weapons. The smoke wafted away and was lost. We kept a sharp eye out for smoke, down here.

"So these rasts up aloft can survey our progress?"

"It would seem so—although I begin to doubt the fact."

"And there's only one of 'em to each Moder?"

"In all probability."

"Well, I just want to get out of here. I have much set to my hand in Kregen. Time wastes."

"There is, also, Much to be Won Down Here."

"As?"

"You know what I seek. The lady Ariane seeks ways to topple her fat

Queen Fahia. Loriman seeks ways to enhance his standing with and the glory of Spikatur Hunting Sword."

"And Tyfar?"

"He adventures with his father—"

"And what does Prince Nedfar seek in this dolorous place?"

"I am not sure. Mayhap it is pure adventure. He is a great Jikaida player, and will respond to any challenge."

"And Yagno, the Sorcerer of the Cult of Almuensis?"

Quienyin smiled and stretched. "It is obvious, that one. He must read his spells from a book, a hyr-lif. They are difficult to master. But they are effective. Yagno seeks ways to enhance his own sorcerous powers."

"Could he learn enough to make himself a Wizard of Loh?"

"No. By the Seven Arcades—no—I hope not!"

"Yet—you—?"

"I but seek to regain what I have lost, not to gain what I never had."

"Illusion and reality."

"Aye."

I found a stoppered jar containing a little wine and we drank companionably together. Quienyin lowered the jar and spoke reflectively. "San Orien says they go in for magical objects down here. Things that, when possessed, confer special powers."

"My jar of yellow poison—"

"Precisely, Jak."

The yellow light filled the close air with radiance and the fire burned with its eerie blue flames. The sentries prowled, alert, and our gazes kept flickering all about this mausoleum, surveying and noting the shadows in the corners, the corpses on their stone shelves.

"And Strom Phrutius," I said. "What of him?"

"Gold and gems, I think. Treasure of the worldly sort."

"Maybe he has more sense than I credited him with."

"There is a well-known spell which will cause an armband to chain the wearer to the will of the giver. When I say well-known I mean in the sense of its existence being well known. The spell itself is arcane and difficult. With its knowledge a man could spell hundreds of armbands and thus ensure the willing and total obedience of all who wore them."

"Tarkshur!" I said. "That's what he's after."

"It is very likely."

"He'll turn up again, at the exit, you'll see." I clenched a fist. "Katakis are devils at survival."

"So will your two friends, Nodgen and Hunch." Quienyin offered me the wine. I shook my head. He went on, "It is Tyr Ungovich who provokes my curiosity. He is indeed an enigma."

"What he wants," I said, guessing, "will likewise be found on the ninth zone." Then, quickly, I said, "You are confident Hunch and Nodgen will reappear? They went right merrily into their paradises."

"Illusion, as the weapons you bear. They will appear."

I touched the Krozair longsword. The metal was warm—and hard and solid to my fingers. I shook my head. Illusion...

"It is a great pity," Quienyin said, "that Longweill the Fluttrhim* was killed. His gifts would have been useful."

"He's down skating about on the Ice Floes of Sicce now," I said. "May Opaz have him in his keeping, poor Thief though he was."

Shortly after that there was a general alarm as a procession of Green-Glowing Ghoul Vampires wandered past and we had a merry set-to. They were amenable to the kiss of steel, and were driven off. Again I noticed the fine free way Prince Tyfar fought, and, foolishly, I thought of Barty Vessler, and sighed.

When all had rested we set off to explore the nooks and crannies of the various halls containing the corpses. Prowling monsters were encountered and dealt with, each to its own peculiar fashion, and we lost a few more men.

If this was the Necromantic zone, as we believed, the key we sought—the part of the key—lay somewhere hidden. Finding it would take us a long time. And, as we explored, so we drew ever nearer the central chamber and the horrors it would most certainly contain.

There would be a dozen or more cassettes to be filled with my record of the things we encountered in that nine-armed complex before we walked along and reached the place where we had camped. So we had come full circle, had found no way in or out, and must most carefully put our heads together to discover a method of forcing ingress to the center and its mystery.

"To the right, as ever," quoth Kov Loriman. "I will smash a way through the wall, by Lem, and then we will get through!"

He seized a corpse by its arm and pulled and the corpse snapped at once into hideous life and leaped for Loriman's throat. The Hunting Kov was not one whit dismayed. His sword whirled, the corpse's head flew off, and one of his Chuliks swept a broad-bladed axe around and chopped the corpse's legs away.

They kicked the bits of mummified remains of the Kaotim aside and bringing up picks and sledgehammers started smashing into the wall.

"One has," observed Tyfar, "to admire their enthusiasm."

Quienyin touched my arm and we drew a little apart.

"Have you noticed, Jak, that while the vast majority of the corpses are apim, like you and me, there are every now and then a few diffs?"

"Yes."

"There is, I think, a Pattern to be Observed."

So, leaving Loriman and his henchmen to go on smashing the wall down, the rest of us started to inspect the arrangements of the Undead.

In the end, and inevitably, it was Quienyin who spotted the significance. He smiled and pushed his turban straight.

Now, I must of necessity spell the words in English but the final result was the same as the original Kregish. The corpses lay in a pattern, as Quienyin had indicated, and their order was thus: Gon. Hoboling. Och. Undurker. Lamnia. Och. Rapa. Djang.

Be very sure I looked long and with choked feelings at the Djangs— most of them were Obdjangs, those clever, gerbil-faced people who so efficiently run Djanduin, and whom the ferocious four-armed Dwadjangs respect with reason.

"It seems," said Quienyin, "we are to find what we seek in the Hall of Ghoul. And it will be the ord* something."

We went carefully through the Hall of Vampires and the Hall of Banshees to the Hall of Ghouls. The yellow light showed us the ranked shelves of corpses. We all expected the Kaotim to stir and sit up and then leap upon us, uttering wraith-like wails.

In this Hall of Ghouls, somewhere, there were seven somethings, and the eighth something would give us the answer.

The sense of oppression enclosed us. We were entombed. Surrounding us lay mile upon mile of corridors and secret rooms, prowling monsters, darkness, and light more hideous than darkness.

The feeling that the domed ceiling would fall upon us choked us with primeval terrors we would not admit. The idea of clean fresh air, and the radiance of the suns, and the feel of an ocean breeze—all these things were gone and lost and buried in the grave. The oppression held us in iron bands. The feeling of hollowness, of dusty silence, of the abandonment of years, choked like skeletal fingers at our throats.

"I—I do not like this place," whispered Ariane.

Tyfar took her hand, and held it, and did not speak.

The tough mercenary warriors looked about with uneasy eyes, drawing together, fingering their weapons.

And then a silly Hypnotic Spider as big as a carthorse fell on his thread through a trapdoor.

"Do not look into his eyes!" yelled Quienyin.

One Fristle, shocked, was too late. The cat-man stood, petrified, ridged gristle and fur, and the gigantic spider, dripping venom, swung to take the poor fellow's head into its jaws.

Tyfar and I sprang together. His axe whirled. The Krozair longsword bit.

---

* Ord: eight.

453

The Giant Hypnotic Spider burst apart like a paper bag filled with water and dropped from a great height. The squelching stink gagged us all. The spidery arms scuttled away, singly, hairs bristling, and the gross body drooped into a flaccid puddle. The Fristle still stood, petrified.

"If that is the best they can do..." said Ariane, shaking herself. She laughed, a shrill tinny sound.

They were all laughing. The reaction after the black thoughts of a moment ago shuddered through them. But the Fristle still stood, unmoving.

"Here," said Deb-Lu-Quienyin. He shuffled up to stand before the Fristle. He did not touch him. "Jak," he said in his casual conversational voice. "Just Take a Look up through the trapdoor. There May Be More Up There..."

If I were a man who laughed easily, I would have laughed then. Obediently, I climbed up a pyramid of men and stuck a torch through the opening. The trapdoor hung down. A fetid odor broke about my head and I spat. The space beyond looked empty, full of ghosts and bones and stink.

"It appears clear, although—"

"Quite!"

Now we took greater cognizance of the configuration of the roof. The dome was broken here and there by bulging cornices, grotesquely carved. From one of these the spider had dropped, and the height, reachable by my pyramid of men, was not too great. We began to study the other bulging protuberances in the roof. The decorations particularly intrigued Prince Tyfar.

"As Hanitcha the Harrower is my witness! I do not discern any pattern! What do you see, Notor Jak?"

Before I answered I killed my automatic wince at his use of the name Hanitcha the Harrower. Ah, Hamal, Hamal, that empire had done great damage to my beloved Vallia!

"If there is a pattern, prince, we must find it."

"True, by Krun!"

"And," said his Brokelsh slinger, Barkindrar the Bullet, "My prince—beware, in the name of Kaerlan the Merciful! There may be more giant spiders..."

We all hopped back a few paces out from under the direct drop-zone in case there might be more Giant Hypnotic Spiders.

"Catch him!" suddenly shouted Quienyin's voice, and we whirled to see the Fristle who had been petrified running, head down, racing madly and with demoniac screams, racing away down past the ranked biers of corpses.

"By Krun!" exclaimed Tyfar. "It's enough to give a fellow a bad heart!"

A group of the mercenaries chased after him and brought him back, calmed him down. He still shook like the leaves of the letha tree. What he had seen in the eyes of the spider no one cared to inquire.

"And have you riddled the riddle yet?" demanded Quienyin.

"No." Ariane was short with the old Wizard of Loh.

"Well, we must see what an Old Fellow Can Do."

"Your permission, my prince," said Barkindrar. "There are nine bulges—whatever you call 'em."

The great apim bear of a man, the renowned archer from Ruathytu, craned his thick neck back, stared up. "And only one, my prince, has dropped a stinking spider, by Kuerden the Merciless!"

Quienyin smiled. "You are well served, prince."

"Yes, yes," exclaimed Ariane. "But which way do we count?"

I said, "Widdershins would seem appropriate in this place."

We all moved to the bulge to the left of the one from which the spider had dropped, and stared up, at a loss.

"This is becoming impossible!" Ariane tapped her fur boot against the floor impatiently. "Are all you famous Jikais fools?"

"I do not pretend to be a Jikai, lady," said Quienyin. He spoke quite mildly; but I, at least, caught the undercurrent in his patient voice. And, I knew, his patience was forced on him by the loss of his powers as a Wizard of Loh. I glanced across at the lady Ariane nal Amklana. She was not wearing well, of a sudden, and I could not find it in my heart to fault her for that.

She was a girl on her own with us. She had left her four handmaids and their bodyguards with the main party. No doubt she missed their loving ministration. Her rosy face stared up, deeply flushed, and her bright yellow hair tangled in disarray, uncombed, with bits of dust and detritus still matting the fine strands. Her dress was in a woeful state.

Yes, I felt sorry for her, the lady of Amklana.

As yet I had not learned her rank; but I felt absolutely certain she was a kovneva. Nothing less would explain her manner and carriage. And, she had been gracious to me.

"It seems to me," I said, and I spoke deliberately loudly, "if these Moder-lords want their fun out of us they won't have much more if we cannot get on."

This was not strictly true. But my words made no difference. Nothing happened as a result of them, unlike the occurrences in that fire-crystal-lit corridor where I had fought Tarkshur and had summoned the key to unlock my chains. Different orders of illusion were clearly operative in the Moder. And I wondered just how the damned Moder-lord watched us—as a Wizard of Loh might do, by going into lupu and observing events at a distance?

Logu Fre-Da and his twin, Modo Fre-Da, were casting worried looks at their lady. The big numim, Naghan the Doom, was looking at the two hyr-paktuns, and his mane indicated his own concern.

The twins, I had observed with some pleasure, each had the same number of trophy rings from defeated paktuns dangling on their pakais. When a paktun defeats another noted mercenary he takes the ring with which either the pakmort or the pakzhan is affixed to the silken cords at the throat. I had once been betrayed by just such a dangling pakai. But I saw the twins fingering their pakais and I realized they were reassuring themselves, seeking sustenance from their own prowess, the pakais giving them fresh confidence in their nikobi. I have a great deal of time for Pachaks, and these two, it seemed to me, were fine representatives of their fine race.

The intriguing thought occurred to me to wonder how much swag they had concealed about their persons.

An acrimonious discussion began—at least, it was acrimonious from the lady Ariane, although Quienyin and Tyfar remained exquisitely polite. We seemed to have reached a dead end, an impasse, and no one could with any equanimity contemplate going back the way we had come.

For lack of anything better we tramped off around the Nine Halls again, passing Loriman and his men still hard at work. We encountered a few prowling monsters, and lost a Rapa, and so returned to the Hall of Ghouls and stared up at the roof once more.

The answer to the riddle was either so complicated we could not solve it—and with Quienyin with us, despite that he had lost his sorcerous powers, I did not think that likely—or was of an imbecilic simplicity.

Many folk on Kregen are fond of calling me an onker, a get onker, a prince of fools...

"Make me a pyramid of men again," I said and, I own, my voice rasped out as the Emperor of Vallia's voice rasped—or the First Lieutenant of a seventy-four.

At the top of the pyramid I lifted the Krozair longsword and I smote against the roof, savage blows, eight of them, eight intemperate smashes against the prominent knob of polished jet over my head.

The echoes of those vicious blows rang and rattled away along the stone biers.

And the corpses all rose up.

Every corpse rose, and from those ghastly mouths a shrill and ghoulish screaming shattered against our nerves. Every corpse rose up, screaming, and rushed away, ran blindly from the Hall of Ghouls.

They poured in a blasphemous rout through the two side openings to the Hall. We were all gathered in the inner end of the arm, that between the two side passages and the center of the mausoleum complex.

The floor moved.

The floor revolved.

The ends of the side passages and the anteroom at our backs slid swiftly sideways—going widdershins!—and the floor on which we stood, petrified, turned and carried us around to face into the mysterious heart of the mausoleum.

A few of the mercenaries at last broke. They were not paktuns. With shrieks of fear they raced madly for the narrowing slot of yellow light, leaping off the revolving floor, screaming, tearing desperately away, rushing madly anywhere to escape the horrors of this place.

We who were left revolved with the Hall of Ghouls, swinging in to face whatever it was that had caused the Undead to rise in panic and flee.

Seventeen

Out from the Jaws of Death

We never again saw any of those mercenaries who had fled—not one, ever.

What we expected to see, Opaz alone knows. I do not.

What we did see was a solid wall of darkness. The floor revolved one hundred and eighty degrees, and halted with a shuddering lurch, as though we were suspended by chains over a fathomless gulf. The blackness smote our eyes. The yellow light within the Hall of Ghouls continued; but it remained thin and pale. The stone slabs lay empty of corpses. The detritus on the floor crackled underfoot as we moved. Cautiously, we advanced toward that ebon wall, and it resisted, and we could make no impression on its immaterial substance.

The tall rows of empty biers frowned down. The light smoked somber upon us, and the silence stunned us.

Quienyin said, "The walls. The stone slabs. I think—"

"You are right, Master Quienyin!" Tyfar rushed to the nearest wall and put his foot against the bottom slab. With a slow remorseless pressure his foot was pushed along the floor.

"The walls!" shrieked Ariane. "They are closing in upon us!"

Steadily, with small screeching sounds as of trapped animals, the walls closed one upon the other. The wall of blackness ahead narrowed.

Now we could see that there was a finger-wide gap between wall and floor. And then the full diabolical nature of these stone jaws was borne in on us.

"The stone slabs!" shouted Ariane, and she tore her hair wildly, staggering. "See—they are not opposite!"

It was true. The stone slabs in one wall were set at a higher level than in the opposite wall. When they met, the stone juttings would pass between one another. Useless to jump up and cower in a stone slot so recently vacated by a corpse. The opposite stone slab would crush into that slot and...

We looked about frenziedly for a way out. "These are the Kaochun," Quienyin informed us, although few of us were in a condition to appreciate the knowledge. "The Jaws of Death."

These Kaochun, these Death Jaws, were going to squash us flatter than an ant under a boot heel if we did not quickly discover the answer. I saw the rock chippings fallen from the stones.

Without shouting, trusting to the others to see what I was up to and follow my lead, I picked up and discarded the chunks until I found a solid wedge-shaped piece. This I pushed point first under that finger-wide slot between wall and floor. I kicked it in savagely. The two hyr-paktun twins were the first to see and copy. Soon we were all ramming wedges under the walls as hard as we could. Some ground to powder, others slipped. But some held.

The chittering noise as of trapped animals faltered, and strengthened as wedges crumbled, and then dwindled again as we went ruthlessly along ramming wedges in as fast and as hard as we could.

The walls shuddered. A thin high whine began.

The walls trembled.

Dust blew suddenly in a cloud from the discarded corpse wrappings. We flailed our arms, heads and shoulders smothered in the gritty dust. We choked and coughed. But the walls did not move in. The tremble shuddered to a stillness, the dust fell away, and the walls stopped.

That high shrilling whine passed away above the audible threshold. We shook, suddenly, each one feeling the pain drilling into his ears.

Slowly, as an iris parts, the wall of blackness opened before us.

When the harsh actinic white light rushed in I saw that we stood in a slot between the stilled walls. There was space left for us only to walk out in single file, so narrow had been our confinement and so narrow our separation from death.

Prince Tyfar was the first to march out.

Head up, sword in his fist, he stomped out onto a black marble floor and into the white light. He stopped. As we crowded out he gasped: "By all the Names!"

Difficult to describe this Mausoleum of the Moder, so many impressions crowded in like a kaleidoscope.

A place of wonder, of awe, and of horror...

The chamber stretched about us, full four hundred paces in diameter. The roof rippled oddly, hung with black insubstantiality, ever-shifting so that it was impossible to estimate the height. And that height appeared to waver and alter and to press up and down.

Positioned some fifty paces in from the walls around the chamber stood fire-crystal tanks, each with a girth of at least twenty paces. In each tank coiled and writhed a monster from nightmare, tentacled octopus-like shapes that slimed and hissed and beckoned obscenely. They would have put the shudders up the toughest of backbones.

Deb-Lu-Quienyin started to talk at once, and I guessed he sought to hold our tattered nerves together.

"We are clearly below ground level here, and I imagine this to be the heart of the Moder—"

"You said there were nine zones and this is the eighth—"

"True. But the ninth zone is not for normal men."

We walked slowly forward between two of the tanks. We did not look again at the gruesome denizens. We all sensed that Quienyin spoke the truth and here was what we had come for—all of us, that is, except the Wizard of Loh... And myself.

Ranged in a circle within the circle of tanks, and crammed close together, stood cabinet and chest, box and trunk, glassed and bound with bronze. Small alleyways led through this circle. The treasures contained within this mass of cabinets defied the imagination. We halted, greedy eyes surveying the wealth displayed there.

Quienyin looked back.

"There will be time to sample these wares—after."

No one had the hardihood to inquire of him, "After what?"

What lay in the next circle drew some of us on.

We could not look over toward the center of the chamber, because of the brilliance of the light that poured up in a wide shaft from the central floor, lifting and flooding up to be consumed in that shifting darkness of the ceiling.

Around that shaft of pure white light stood a fence, a wall, an insubstantial-seeming yet iron-hard barrier. Passing through alleyways in the circles of displayed wealth and magical equipment we stood before the iron barrier. A silver gate showed immediately ahead, and a golden gate showed to the right. To the left a bronze gate shut off ingress beyond the barrier. Somehow, we all knew there would be nine gates leading onto the shaft of fire.

"I think, my friends," quoth Quienyin, "that is our way out—after."

"Through—" squeaked Ariane. "Through the fire?"

"Yes, lady."

"Well, how do we pass the gates?"

"Climb the fence," offered Tyfar.

"No, prince." Quienyin spoke quickly. "That way lies a sure and ghastly death."

We took his word for it.

The mercenaries were jostling before the cabinets. In there lay unimaginable wealth. I saw a trunk the size of a horse trough filled to bursting with diamonds. At its side stood another, similarly filled with rubies. The glitter of gold paled to insignificance in the luster of gems.

"Touch nothing until we are sure!" commanded Tyfar.

The paktuns growled—but even their greed was tempered by our experiences. And, do not forget, these were the hardiest and the toughest of those who had entered, for they had survived.

One quickly showed us a simple way to die.

The black marble of the floor that ringed the chamber gave way to white marble and then to yellow. Where we stood before the flame the floor was broken into patterns, intricate lozenges and heart shapes, circles and half-moons of inlaid stone. This paktun, he was a Rapa, stood upon a crescent of green, without thinking anything of it.

The green crescent swallowed him.

One instant he was standing there, rubbing his wattled neck, the next he was gone, and the green crescent reappeared.

Ariane screamed.

"Test every part of the pattern before you trust it!" called Tyfar. From then on, every one of us cat-footed about like ghosts.

Remembering Quienyin's ominous words, I looked into the recesses of the chamber, alcoves past the tanks and their hideous denizens. Shadows shifted there, eye-wateringly.

Tyfar was talking, quickly and softly, to the lady Ariane.

The Wizard of Loh said, "Jak, my friend. These things are real. There is no illusion here. Your weapons...?"

Displayed in glassed cabinets stood ranked many swords, many daggers, many different weapons of quality.

"I do not think, San, I will find a longsword like this. Until it vanishes from my fists, I will keep it."

All the same, I did decide to replace the rapier and main gauche once we had the cabinets open.

But—opening the cabinets was the nub of the question.

We all knew that horror would burst upon us as we burst open this treasure.

"My prince," said the slinger, Barkindrar the Bullet. "Let us all stand well away and let me smash a cabinet."

Barkindrar had proved himself on this expedition down a Moder. Tyfar nodded. Quienyin pulled his lower lip and looked at me. I made a small gesture which meant "What else?"

A distant tapping noise that had irritated my ears for a short time now grew loud enough for me to turn, puzzled. The others heard it now. The banging echoed hollowly and sounded like devil-tinkers at work on a yellow skull.

Quickly we ascertained that the knocking noise came from a wall away to our left and we moved back, positioning ourselves, wondering what fresh horror would burst upon us.

Chips of stone facing the wall flaked off. Then a larger piece fell. The noise redoubled. Whatever was forcing its way through the wall was large and powerful. The banging bashed and boomed and rock fell and the wall split. In a jagged wedge-shaped gap the wall split from the floor to a point ten feet above and yellow light poured through with a spray of dust and rock chippings, glinting.

Dark shadows moved within the jagged opening in the wall. They looked black and evil against the streaming yellow radiance.

A form lumbered through, and stood up, and bellowed.

"Hai! I am through!"

We all stared.

More figures burst into this dread chamber, and there was Kov Loriman, smothered in dust, shoving through, a massive sledgehammer in his fist, panting, triumphant. He saw us.

"You famblys! And how many have you lost? Did I not say I would smash my way out?"

Quienyin called across, "Or, kov—in!"

To be honest, I could not understand why some horror had not carried off the Hunting kov and all his men sooner.

I could not understand that riddle then. But it was made clear to me, and, I owned, despite his despicable propensities for Execution Jikaida and other unmentionable acts of abomination, Kov Loriman materially assisted me by that bashing entrance through the wall.

We gave him warning about the green crescents, and his men were as wary as ours of the wantonly displayed wealth.

One interesting fact I noticed then was that, of these survivors of the expedition, there were more hyr-paktuns with the golden pakzhan at throat or knotted in silken cords at shoulder than there were of paktuns with the silver pakmort or of ordinary mercenaries who were not yet elevated to the degree of paktun. But, then, surely, that was to be expected?

Tyfar was your proper prince. However much of a ninny he might be in ordinary life, he was lapping up the marvels and terrors of this Moder. He was punctilious with Loriman.

"The suggestion is, kov, that my slinger puts a bullet through one of these glass cabinets while we stand back."

Loriman grunted, and glared at his Jiktar, the commander of his Chuliks. This one, a magnificent specimen of the Chulik race, impressive in armor, fiercely tusked, pondered.

"Quidang!" he roared at length.

Chuliks have about as little of humanity in them as Katakis; they have

461

given me a rough time of it on Kregen, as you know. But, at least, they are mercenaries born and bred to be paktuns, and not damned slave masters. And while their honor code in no way matches the nikobi of the Pachaks, they are loyal to their masters. And, they can be loyal even when the pay and food runs out, which is more than can be said for most mercenaries.

As we prepared for this fraught experiment, I realized that the place with all its creepy horrors was actually powerful enough to make me maudlin over Chuliks. By Zair! But doesn't that stunningly illuminate the stark and overpowering impression this Moder was making on me!

So, with Chuliks as comrades, I hunkered down with the rest as Barkindrar the Bullet went through his pre-slinging ritual.

Did he, I wondered, do this in the heat of battle?

Prince Tyfar put store by him, as he put store by his bear-like apim archer, Nath the Shaft who hailed from Ruathytu. And, I should quickly add, neither of these two retainers were mercenaries, as Ariane's numim retainer, Naghan the Doom, was not a mercenary.

As Barkindrar went through his preparation and whirled his sling another odd little thought occurred to me. As we had penetrated nearer and nearer this Mausoleum of the Moder, so Deb-Lu-Quienyin had grown in confidence. It was as though by merely approaching what he sought he took reverberations from his coming powers, sucking strength from his own future.

Barkindrar let rip. The leaden bullet flew. The glass cabinet splintered into gyrating shards. Splinters and shatters of razor-edged glass splayed out. Anyone standing nearby would have been slashed to ribbons. The smashing tinkles twittered ringingly to silence on the marble floor.

We stood up.

"Well done, Barkindrar!" said Tyfar. He beamed.

"Have a caution, prince," said Quienyin. "There may be a guardian..."

Kov Loriman hauled out his pouch and extracted a small body. It was a tiklo, a small lizard creature, and he held it by the tail gingerly.

"When we were being outfitted by Tyr Ungovich he charged me a great deal of red gold for this little fellow. By Havil, yes! Ungovich said that at the final moment he would prove his worth. Is not this the final moment of this damned maze?"

"Have a care, kov."

"What ails you, Master Quienyin?"

"I do not—rightly—know. It is passing strange."

Old Quienyin looked about, vacantly. I saw his arms begin to lift up from his sides as the arms of a Wizard of Loh rise when he is about to go into lupu. But the old mage's arms dropped and he hooked his thumbs into his belt, and he squiffled around a space before he said, "You could be right."

Loriman laughed and led off to the smashed cabinet.

Barkindrar had picked a cabinet containing crowns. They were ranked on their pegs, brilliant, redolent of power and authority, clustered with gems, shining. Each one would have bought the kingdom its owner ruled.

Loriman picked one out unceremoniously. Nothing happened. He lifted it, with some casual remark that, by Havil, it suited him. He was about to put it on when Quienyin struck it from his hands. It fell and rolled. I noticed, from the corner of my eye, the little tiklo give a twitch in Loriman's fingers.

The crown rolled across the marble. It grew smaller. Rapidly it constricted in size, shrinking, until finally, with a little plop, it vanished.

"Your head, kov, would have been inside that."

Loriman lost his smile and his color. The veins in his nose seemed to strangle into thin white lines. He shook.

"This is a place damned to Cottmer's Caverns—and beyond!"

Tyfar looked troubled and he spoke in a voice low and off key, as though what he had to say perturbed him. "You said, Master Quienyin," he remarked in that indifferent voice to our oracle, "that these treasures were real."

Quienyin coughed and wiped his lips.

"So I said, prince, and so I maintain. Watch."

Deliberately the old Wizard of Loh picked up another bejeweled crown. He lifted it high in both hands. Then, with a decisive gesture, he brought it down and placed it on his own head.

"No!" screamed Ariane, half fainting.

The crown remained on Quienyin's head. It did not shrink. Glittering, it surmounted his ridiculous turban, glowing with the divine right of kings to extort and slay.

"What does it mean, Master Quienyin?"

"Only that Kov Loriman should throw the tiklo away."

"You mean that rast Ungovich tricked me?"

"No. Only that, perhaps, at a distance, Tyr Ungovich was not aware of the true menace of this Moder and its Monsters."

"I'll have a word with him, I promise you!"

Ariane giggled. "Maybe it is your turban, Quienyin!"

"Aye!" shouted Loriman. "Try the crown without that!"

Quietly, the Wizard of Loh complied. The crown remained its true size, a real crown, resplendent with glory.

After that there was an orgy of cabinet smashing.

Some little of the menace of this deadly place seemed to be removed and yet I do not think a single one of us was lulled. We all knew that the sternest test yet remained—if we knew what it was.

Eighteen

The Mausoleum of the Flame

A price surely seemed demanded for the wanton looting going on in this awesome chamber. The restraints of reason were broken among these people, the terrors through which they had gone had boiled up insupportably and now burst forth in wild laughter, drunken staggerings, the crazed smashing of glass cabinets and the wholesale strewing of the contents about the marble floor.

The lady Ariane followed by her people was running madly from cabinet to cupboard to chest to box, eagerly searching for the lure that had brought her here. I could only wish her luck if it had to do with unseating poor pathetic fat Queen Fahia of Hyrklana.

We do not always see clearly into the motives of people whom we do not know well, and if they appear to agree with our own wishes, transfer our own desires into their actions.

Fulfilling my promise to replace the rapier and main gauche with a real set of Bladesman's weapons, I saw in the case alongside the equipment I chose a beautiful little brooch. It was in the form of a zhantil, that fierce, proud wild animal, king of the animal kingdom in many parts of Kregen, fashioned from scarrons, a gem of brilliant scarlet and precious above diamonds.

Carefully, I pulled the brooch out. It did not come to life and seek to bite my thumb off. Nor did it come to life and grow full sized and seek to chew my head off.

I put it into my pouch.

A looter, Dray Prescot. Well, I have been a paktun and a mercenary many times, and the paktun's guiding motto is grab what you can when you can. Life is short, brother...

Without discarding the drexer I buckled up a thraxter. If the drexer was going to vanish along with the other weapons of hallucination, then a real blade for rough and ready battling would be a comfort.

That brooch now—for whom else in two worlds would I have taken it?

So that reminded me that when a fellow returns from a little lonely jaunt it behooves him to bring back presents for all the family. Feeling remarkably ridiculous, I toured around the shattered displays seeking items I thought suitable as little gifts. The odd thing was, a little gift from this treasure house of the Moder was worth a fortune.

When Delia said to me, as she would, "And where have you been this time, my heart?" I would have to reply, "Oh, just a little game of Moders and Monsters." And attempt to leave it at that. Of course, I would not be allowed to. I knew full well that after what I told my Delia and after the

464

sight of these little gifts I'd have Drig's own job to prevent her from hopping into a voller and insisting I took her on a little jaunt of Moders and Monsters. By Zair, no! I said to myself, and saw Ariane, holding an ivory box to her breast, the tears pouring down her rosy cheeks, and thought—my Delia? Down here? Never!

Well, it just goes to show you that man sows and Zair reaps, that no man can riddle the secrets of Imrien, that—oh by Vox! That I was foolish to imagine what I imagined.

Quienyin walked across to me. He waved an arm about.

"Look at them, Jak!"

Certainly the place was in an uproar. People were staggering about under enormous loads of loot. These were old hands at the game of removing portable property, and the gold and silver were left untouched, the gems and the trinkets which were worth more than the gems of which they were made, these were the objects these ferocious paktuns were pocketing.

"Now, Jak," said Quienyin in a sharpish tone, "here is that which I think you may find of use."

He handed me a thin golden bracelet of linked swords.

"And, San?"

"And just this, young man. When a man wears the Blade Bracelet he is an invincible swordsman. But, wait—it holds its power for one fight and one fight only. After that—poof!"

"And you believe I need this?"

He eyed me with a sympathy I sensed was genuine. "Keep it safe. When you meet Mefto the Kazzur again."

"I give you my thanks, Deb-Lu. But—no, and I mean you no disrespect. Mefto is a great kleesh, right enough; but he is a swordsman and when I next meet him I shall beat him fair and square."

He looked at me as though I were off my head.

"What in the name of He of the Seven Arcades do you want here, then?"

"I," I said, "want to get out!"

The racket continued on about us as he looked shrewdly up at me, his eyes appearing to give forth more light than any human eyes could. "Now that is the most sensible desire in this whole place!"

"We have to get through that wall and up to the shaft of fire?"

"Yes. Look, Jak—" He pulled a belt from one of the many pockets of his robe. "Cannot I interest you in this. If you wear this in a fight your foeman's sword cannot harm you."

"Yes, and is that for one fight only?"

"It is."

"Do these folk know that the magical items they are taking work once only?"

"Oh, no, some of them work for quite a long time."

"I suppose there isn't a device here that will magically transport us out of here? That would be—nice."

"Sarcasm, young man, is cheap. And, no, there is not. At least," he pondered vaguely, "I have recognized nothing resembling such a device. And, I may add, I have felt remarkably young about my lost powers lately."

"I had noticed."

I had noticed, also, that he was not talking in capital letters for most of the time...

"Let us take a look at the wall where Loriman broke in. I am interested."

He nodded and we started for the jagged opening in the wall. The wall where the Hall of Ghouls had revolved to bring us—squashing—here was simply another wall like all the other eight. The wall from the Hall of Specters showed Loriman's gap. "The Hunting Kov is a—forthright—man."

"Oh, aye." I gave a hitch to the lesten-hide belt holding the scarlet breech-clout. That had been cut from an immense bolt of cloth here, and the belt was supple and strong. "D'you happen to know if he's found whatever it is he seeks to help him with the Spikatur Hunting Sword? D'you happen to know what it is?"

"He found a gold and ivory casket that gave him joy. Had I my powers—when I have my powers!—I must discern this Cult or Order."

"Well, if it works only once..."

"That is what is so intriguing."

Approaching the jagged opening in the wall Quienyin stumbled on a chunk of the masonry Loriman's bully boys had broken down. He put his hand against my back to steady himself, with a small cry and then a quick apology. Turning, I took his arm and supported him to the gap.

Noises spurted from the jagged wedge-shaped opening, distant and hollow, borne on a foul-tasting breeze that died the moment it reached the central chamber. Quienyin cupped his ear and listened intently.

Presently he looked up inquiringly, and I nodded.

"But how many...?"

A jag of masonry thrust against my side.

"The hole!" cried Quienyin. "It is closing!"

As a wound seeks to heal itself so the walls were growing whole again. I gave a yell at a bunch of shouting Chuliks who, loaded with loot, were making faces at the octopus-like monster in the nearby tank. They ignored me. I started bashing at the walls with a sledgehammer discarded among the rubble. Quienyin at my side helped with a pick.

I bellowed into the hole, that old foretop hailing roar.

"Hurry! The gap closes! Hurry, you famblys! Bratch!"

As I smashed away stones so they grew and pressed in. So, although I hate the word, it fitted here, by Krun! and aptly, I bellowed into the hole: "Hurry! Hurry! Grak! Grak!"

In only moments they were up to the opening and the first face to show, peering through past the glitter of a sword, was that belonging to Prince Nedfar. He looked mad clean through.

"I see you, rast!" In a twinkling he scrambled out and his sword leaped for my throat. I threw myself backwards.

Lobur the Dagger was out, and other fighting men. Quienyin yelled.

"Prince! Prince! Hold! It is us—we are here—this is Notor Jak and he is a friend. Hurry through, all of you, before the gap closes on you."

There followed a right old hullabaloo before the rest of the expedition tumbled through the opening. The last one through was Hunch, and he shivered and shook as the stones closed up at his rear with a clashing thunk, making him leap as though goosed.

He did not recognize me, for I stood talking to the prince, girded with weapons, clearly one of the lords.

"Jak? Aye—I remember you. You are well met." Nedfar possessed the princely merit of remembering faces. "If your story is as strange and horrific as ours…"

"It is, prince," said Quienyin. He explained as the newcomers with howls of glee threw themselves at the glitter of treasure.

Nodgen the Brokelsh was with Hunch. They did not know me. So it goes with the eyes of slaves. They both looked as though they had spent a continuous month of Saturday nights without a break.

I wished them well of their Tryfant and Brokelsh paradises.

Tyfar welcomed his father and sister with a seemly show of emotion. Also, I noticed the comradely way he greeted Lobur the Dagger. As for Kov Thrangulf, Tyfar welcomed him in the proper style, as befitted a young and untried prince toward a high-ranking influential noble.

The flaunting display of wealth drew the newcomers as a flame draws a moth, and the uproar redoubled in that august and eerie chamber with the Shaft of Flame illuminating all the frenzied moths.

The Sorcerer of the Cult of Almuensis pushed through and stood, feet braced, fists on hips, a glittering figure surveying the mausoleum, the circle of weird creatures in their tanks, the smashed treasure chests and scattered wealth. He nodded, sagely, as though he had planned it all.

"So this is the nadir of the Moder," he said. He puffed out his cheeks. His splendid figure glittered almost unmarked by the desperate adventures of the journey that had turned us into a rag-tail and bob-tail collection.

"Not quite, San," said Quienyin, cheerfully.

But San Yagno ignored the old mage. His eyes lighted on a chest fastened with nine locks shaped into the likenesses of risslacas. The scaled dinosaurs were prancing in bronze. Yagno advanced upon the chest, pushing people and bric-a-brac out of his way. He planted himself before the chest, which was of sturm-wood inlaid with balass and ivory, and bound in bronze.

"I recognize that sign," he said, half to himself. He reached into that sumptuous gown and pulled out a thick book, covered in lizard skin, locked with gold.

"Watch this, Jak," said Quienyin. "It is something worth the seeing."

The Chuliks of San Yagno's bodyguard—there were but five left of the original dozen—formed a ring about their master. But Quienyin and I could still see. San Yagno opened the hyr-lif, thumbed the stiff paper over, found the page he sought. He held the book close to his face and began a long incantatory mumble. Most of it concerned sunderings and breakings and smashings of one kind and another.

The first bronze lock, shaped like a risslaca, snapped open.

The second through to the ninth snapped up in turn.

San Yagno puffed his cheeks out. He was panting. He stowed the book away and motioned to the Deldar of Chuliks.

This one lifted the lid.

"A vast expenditure of thaumaturgical lore," observed the Wizard of Loh. Only the slightest tinge of irony colored his mild words.

"Had it been Kov Loriman," I said. "He would simply have taken an axe to the fastenings."

"Precisely, young man."

And, I swear it, we both laughed.

We did not stop to see what San Yagno found in the chest after the first reeking objects were revealed. But they seemed to delight the sorcerer. He was laughing away to himself and distributing his loot among his followers. I wondered if they would hurl it all away to load themselves down with gems.

Ariane's four handmaids were cooing and aahing over her and attempting to tidy her hair and prepare a quiet corner where she might change into a clean new dress, of which they had a store borne by patient slaves. That made me realize that the arrivals did have slaves with them.

I said to Lobur the Dagger, "How did you fare with the Fliktitors?"

He didn't know what I was talking about.

It turned out that Nedfar's party had followed a vastly different route from ours. Once they had branched off, the fortunes of the Moder had treated them as harshly, but had spared some of their slaves. They had lost Strom Phrutius.

"He is now being ingested in the guts of some half-invisible creature we could only see in the dark. As soon as there was light he incontinently disappeared."

"San Orien mentioned such a monster. I am sorry to hear about Strom Phrutius. It was a Laughing Shadow."

"Oh, aye, Master Quienyin. It laughed most dolefully when Tobi, a fine archer, shafted into its nothingness. It took itself off, then." Lobur pulled his lip. "Tobi is dead, now. He was engulfed by a poisonous flower that grew from a crevice in the wall at prodigious speed."

We expressed our regrets at the losses suffered by the Hamalese, and it was clear to me, as to Quienyin, that while we might be on the threshold of the heart of the matter, for this short space a sense—a damned false sense, to be sure—of release from tension eased the burdens on the minds and fears of these people. It was cat and mouse. That seemed clear. I asked Lobur the Dagger about his slaves, and he mentioned casually that they had picked up a couple of odd fellows somewhere who had almost been cut down before they managed to convince Prince Nedfar they were not demons.

And then I quelled a quick grimace which might have been misconstrued as a smile as Lobur said: "They were left over from an earlier expedition, wandering about, poor devils."

Hunch and Nodgen had hit upon the same lie as I had to explain wandering slaves without a master. As for Tarkshur—well, that must wait.

I made myself look eager. "By Zodjuin of the Gate! They might be two of my fellows!"

It was now vitally necessary for me to get to Hunch and Nodgen and browbeat them into dumb acceptance before anyone else espied their stupefied reactions when they saw me and, at last, recognized me by what I would say. It would be nip and tuck. Here, in the wider danger of the Moder, this small and social-order danger remained just as perilous.

They had dressed themselves up in finery which had been sadly ripped and stained in their struggled advance along the corridors. I found them with a bunch of other slaves, all goggling at the uproar. The slaves were nerving themselves to break constraints and join in the looting.

I took Hunch's Tryfant ear between finger and thumb of my left hand, and Nodgen's Brokelsh ear between finger and thumb of my right hand, and I ran them a way apart, yelling as I did so: "You pair of yetches! You have caused me great concern! But I forgive you! You have done exceeding well! To have remained alive!"

They almost hung on their ears, swinging, as it were, to glare up at me. I bore down on them, bellowing, and, between bellows, I rasped in a low voice, "Yes, you famblys, it's me—and a word will have your ears—no, your heads!—off. Act up. We came here before; but your memories are bad. Say nothing!"

They just looked at me as though a demon had opened his mouth and spat out all his fangs at them.

In a bull-roaring voice I said, "I promised you manumission and manumission you shall have!" I glared about and saw Lobur and Princess Thefi and Prince Tyfar looking at me with undisguised curiosity. "Witnesses!" I raved on. "There are the witnesses. When we are out of the Moder the bokkertu can be concluded, all legally—but, as of now, you are manumitted, Hunch and Nodgen, both—free!"

Had the audience broken into a small and polite round of applause it would have been perfectly proper. In this place it would have been incongruous. But the deed was done and seen to be done, and these two would—if we lived—receive their papers.

The idea of gratitude did not cross my mind. All three of us knew that Tarkshur would turn up—almost bound to—and then our deception would face a sterner task. But these two looked at me, at the continuous looting, and Hunch stood up rather taller than was his usual wont, and Nodgen bristled up in such a way that he looked fierce rather than boorish.

Curiosity touched me as to what exactly they would do. When they launched themselves at the overturned cases and shattered cabinets, I sighed, and went off to see what Nedfar would have to say about the damned nine key-bits we needed.

As Quienyin joined me and we started to move off from the area where the slaves squatted, still quaking, still not sure just how to breach the domination of the lash, we saw an odd—a pathetic—act.

One of the slaves, more bold, more hardy than his fellows, crept cautiously from that shivering group. These were slaves who had been slaves for a long time, many had been born into slavery. This tough one of them inched across to a toppled cabinet and scooped up a brass dish and then, holding it with his back curved and the bowl pressed to his belly, he scuttled back. We watched. He began to hand out chunks of the stuff in the brass bowl. The slaves stuffed it into their mouths and began to chew. It was cham, the great jaw-moving panacea of poor folk on Kregen—and a delicacy for these poor slaves. Quienyin and I exchanged looks and walked on. When the slaves, at last, broke out, would be time enough coming.

From the actions of the group of principals around Prince Nedfar, we judged most of them had found what they sought. Tyr Ungovich, still shrouded in his hooded robe of red and green checks, stood among them. We walked up and San Yagno, glittering, said, "You have a place here, Master Quienyin. But who is this fellow to come thrusting himself in where he is not invited?"

I said, "I leave you to your discussion." I took myself off. There was nothing to be gained by making an issue of this petty business yet; I felt the Wizard of Loh would inform me of the decisions reached. I went off to find Tyfar and Lobur.

Ariane's handmaids had taken her off to the shelter and they would be making her presentable. Slave labor was a mere part of her expectancy, and her handmaids were slave girls, no doubt of it.

Princess Thefi said, "You cannot know how much I am in your debt, Notor Jak! My brother has been telling me of your adventures—"

"You are fortunate to have such a brother," I said, in my best gallant way. But it was true. "And we are going to come through, safe and sound, all of us."

Lobur the Dagger said, "By Krun! I know so!"

Well, he knew more than I did then.

Kov Thrangulf hovered. Somehow, these three managed to have their backs to him. I felt awkward. But Kov Thrangulf, as though bearing a burden to which he was accustomed, went off toward the treasures again.

Presently, Prince Nedfar shouted for Kov Thrangulf, and he went gratefully off to join the conference, along with other second-in-commands. Lobur the Dagger laughed, all bronzed face and flashing teeth. "You have to feel sorry for him."

"Yes," said Thefi. "But if only he wasn't so—so—"

"Did I show you this?" said Tyfar, hauling out a pretty bauble, and thus changing the tone of the conversation.

Among the profusion of treasure and magical items there lay scattered about a vintner's dream. Some of the mercenaries, unable to resist free booze, had been drinking and had, apparently, suffered no ill effects. We four decided not to risk sampling the wines or food. Lobur, with one of his raffish smiles, produced a squat green bottle, and we drank companionably, in turn. It was a Hamalian porter, dark and brown and heavy, and went down with a rich taste.

The sensation was distinctly odd to stand thus in pleasant conversation and drink Hamalian porter in the midst of the scenes caterwauling on about us, in this horrific Moder, and know the three with whom I so companionably drank were avowed enemies of my country. Odd...

The Princess Thefi had outfitted herself in charming style, with tight black trousers and a blue shirt with a darker blue bolero jacket, all in fetching fashion, with a green cummerbund around her waist, which was delightfully slender, by Krun! She wore rapier and main gauche. She looked splendid.

I said, "Princess, my lady—did your clothes come from this place—or did you acquire them within the other zones of the Moder?"

"Oh, we found a veritable storehouse of clothes and weapons."

"Then, princess, best you had don clothes from here. Otherwise," I said, and I did not smile, "you will find yourself stark naked when we emerge onto the outside world."

"Say you so?"

"Aye!"

She gave a little amused squeal and turned her quick lively gaze on Lobur.

"I know those who would joy in that!"

"Princess!" protested Lobur, outraged. "You impugn my honor!"

Well, it was all pretty stuff. But the Moder stretched about us with its dark secrets and we must find a way out—if we could.

Talk of clothes brought other thoughts to their minds.

"You wear deuced little clothes, Jak," said Lobur. "I call to mind stories I have heard—vague, distorted—of a man, a very devil, who went everywhere clad only in a scarlet breechclout."

"Oh?" I said, injecting surprise into my tones. "Can you remember anything...?"

"Only that he was no friend to Hamal," said Prince Tyfar.

"In that case, I shall find something else. When it comes to the fluttrell's vane... Blue, would you say? Or green?"

They began to discuss this with some seriousness and Thefi went off to find clothes that would not vanish to reveal her splendor to the goggling world.

As they talked I wondered just how much they did know from hearsay of that very devil in the scarlet breechclout, that Dray Prescot who was the Emperor of Vallia and deadly foe to the Empire of Hamal, and also the same Dray Prescot who had good friends in Hamal and despaired of a country unjustly governed.

I saw Nodgen and Hunch talking to Quienyin. The two ex-slaves were clad sumptuously and garnished with a Kregan arsenal of weapons. Nodgen held a broad-bladed spear. They went off together, the three of them with Quienyin in the lead, searching among the tumbled magics.

Prince Nedfar called his son over to join the discussion with the chiefs and principals. The princess returned dressed in new clothes, tight black trousers and blue shirt as before.

Lobur looked at Thefi and then at me.

I said, "I have urgent business..." I drifted away.

The situation appeared that we might stay in this wondrous chamber—the Chamber of the Flame, it might have been called—for as long as we wished. When we made our move to break free would be the time when the horrors would pounce.

Yet the object of challenging the dangers of the Moder was to escape with the treasures one desired. Escape was the problem.

Ariane, radiant in a pure-white gown, her hair impeccable, her face rosy-red and glowing, had joined the conference.

"Well, Notor Jak—" This was Quienyin, smiling, ironic, striding up to me with Nodgen and Hunch looking sheepish. "They want you to join them. I have persuaded them that you are not a monster or a djinni or any form of ghoul." He snuffled. "It was a hard task."

"He's a right old devil," said Hunch.

I said, "Strom Phrutius may be dead, Hunch, you hulu—but his chief cook, Fat Ringo, has survived to bring his gross bulk into this place."

"I know. I have kept clear of him."

"Stick by me when we quit this place. We'll win free, have no fear."

Easy words, those—but how were they to be accomplished?

Quienyin and I walked across and joined the enlarged group around Prince Nedfar.

"You are welcome, Notor Jak. I am glad I did not cut you down when we entered through that Havil-forsaken hole."

I said, "Had you not hurried you would have had a puzzle to solve and the Jaws of Death to dare."

"I have been told. Now we need all our wits to riddle the way out of here."

Ariane had regained much of her composure. "The way lies down beside the Shaft of Flame."

"There is a wall of insubstantial iron, lady—"

"There are nine gates!"

"To which we do not have the keys."

Tyr Ungovich's shoulders moved, as though he shrugged in resignation, or laughed quietly to himself.

The red and green checkered hood did not move as Ungovich spoke in a voice like a rusty hinge: "Without the sorcerous power of San Yagno the party would never have reached here. You are fortunate, Notor Jak, that your party is still alive without the aid of so mighty a thaumaturge."

Carefully, I said, "We survived."

"Let me set one of my fellows to climb the wall!" burst out Kov Loriman.

"By all means," said Tyr Ungovich.

We remembered what had chanced the last time he had said that. Loriman hunched himself up, his face bloating with anger.

"Well, Tyr Ungovich. What do you suggest?"

"Do we have all the parts of the key?"

They were produced as though they were precious relics, and Nedfar laid them out on a table which his son quickly turned up the right way. There were eight curiously-shaped pieces of bronze. We all stared at them solemnly.

Well, and by Zair! Weren't they the most precious objects in all this Moder?

And, without the ninth part, they were valueless.

Nineteen

Of a Gate—and Honor

Much of the rampaging about and the ecstatic sorting through treasures to uncover the finest abated. The explosive release of tensions neared its own exhaustion. Men still capered about, fantastically arrayed in cloth of gold and festooned with gems, they still played stupid silly magical tricks one against another, with spurts of blue fire and whiffs of occult stinks, causing Yagno to twitch. But gradually they quieted and looked toward the group where the decisions of their fates rested.

The hood of ruby and emerald checks drew forward, shadowing all within, as I spoke to Ungovich.

"You sold Kov Loriman the Hunter magics to ward off the magics here. And the others bought trinkets of some power." As the Hunting Kov started forward, clearly about to blaspheme by Sasco over the uselessness of the tiklo, I went on in a louder voice, "Perhaps in view of your knowledge of conditions here, you have knowledge of what it is we need to open these gates."

"It is in my heart to have been with you and witnessed what went on when you were separated from us. Did any of your party find a key?"

"What we have is there on the table." Tyfar pointed.

Kov Loriman subsided, caught up in the importance we all sensed in the words of that rusty-hinge voice, consigning the matter of his tiklo to a Herrelldrin Hell.

"Nothing else?" Tyr Ungovich sounded as though he was becoming annoyed. His rusty voice grated unpleasantly.

These men had talked over and over before I had joined the group, and had settled nothing. We were going to be trapped here if one of us did not come up with the right answer.

"We found a golden key," said Ungovich. "But an oaf lost it for us."

Prince Nedfar drew in his breath. He spoke and all the quiet dignity of the man showed splendidly in that place. "Amak Rubbra, who was a just and honorable man, lost his life with that golden key."

"An oaf, I said," the rusty voice said spitefully. "And an oaf I mean."

"Without a key—" San Yagno started to amplify.

"Here," snarled Kov Loriman. He hauled out the box of a size to take a portion of cham and, opening it, proffered the contents. "A silver key we found. Is this what you want?"

"Ah!" grated Ungovich.

We all craned to look.

Ungovich reached for the silver key. It was left to Yagno to say, startled, "Tyr! Careful! It may be—"

"Quite."

"A silver key for a silver gate, notors?" said Tyfar.

We all moved across to stand before the silver gate in the insubstantial iron wall. The shaft of pure white light lifted blindingly over our heads. Shadows fled away in long fingers of darkness. A smell of ancient decay hung in the air here.

"I do not think the key will harm me," said Ungovich. He lifted it out.

Nothing happened. We all watched him as, carefully, he inserted the key in the keyhole and turned, pressing sideways as he did so. The silver gate moved inward a hand's-breadth. He paused.

A man shrieked in terror and as we whirled to look back into the Chamber of the Flame other men took up that scream of horror.

This Mausoleum of the Moder was guarded.

From the transparent tank opposite the silver gate the colossal tentacled monster rose, twining those slimy arms and clawing at the sides, lifting itself up. As its gross body climbed to the lip of the tank its eyes, red as fire, large as shields, blazed upon us, and its serrated yellow beak clashed with a champing grating sound that chilled the blood.

I reached forward, seized the handle, and slammed the gate shut.

Instantly, the octopoid monster shrank back into its tank.

"By Havil!"

"May the gods preserve us!"

"To open the gate is to release—*that!*"

Prince Nedfar said over the hubbub: "It seems a perfectly logical arrangement."

Tyr Ungovich's unpleasant voice scratched out. "Well, notors. And what do you suggest now?"

"We cannot stay down here forever!" shouted Loriman.

"Yet if we open the gate—" said Yagno.

"Cannot you spell the beast, San Yagno?"

Ungovich said, "I do not think a mortal spell will affect that beauty."

I looked at Quienyin. He had been keeping silent lately. He caught my look and, in the pause after Ungovich's conversation-stopping statement, said, "This is not a case for spells. This needs the military mind, organization, determination and decision."

Prince Nedfar, Prince Tyfar, I was pleased to see, understood at once what Quienyin meant.

Ungovich said, "I do not see—"

Loriman had grasped it, now.

"Then stand aside, Tyr, and let those who do see—do!"

"Before you begin," I said, "notors, two things." I shouted to Hunch who was standing nearby with his aptitude of overhearing likely conversations. "Did more than one monster climb up its tank?"

"Aye, notor!" shouted back Hunch, quaking.

"And, two," I drew an arrow and nocked it. "Will a shaft perhaps dissuade a monster from climbing—?"

"You delude yourself!" said Ungovich.

"I think not, Notor Jak."

"But more than one monster moves. So we must be quick."

All the same, I held the Lohvian longbow half-bent, the arrow gripped in the old archer's knack in my left fist, as we went about organizing what had to be done.

We allowed half a bur for final preparations. The Deldars—those who were left—bellowed and roared in fine Deldar style and the men formed ranks. The slaves, piled with loot, were positioned and threatened with unmentionables if they stirred too soon and did not run when told to grak. The notables arranged themselves with each party. Nedfar would lead. I offered to be the last, and Tyfar and Lobur said they would stay also, seeing that my party consisted of myself and two men only. Hunch and Nodgen, shuffling up under enormous bundles, looked at me reproachfully.

"Remember," Nedfar called, his voice ringing out for us all to hear. "There is no need for panic. Long before there is any danger we will prevent it. Do not jostle or push. Any man who disobeys me will be cut down."

There spoke your true Prince of Hamal, by Krun!

What we were about to attempt was obvious in the context of the situation. I just hoped the situation would not change. The bastard up there, the Wizard of the Moder, the Moder-lord, could so easily change the rules.

Quienyin stood beside me. "I think I will—"

"You, San, will go out with an early party—as you value my friendship!"

"But, Jak—"

"It will be a pretty skip and jump at the end, I think."

He looked at me with a worried expression. And he was a Wizard of Loh! "The Moder-lord will run us hard."

"Aye."

He nodded. "You are right. I feel strength in the—in the air. Mayhap I can do most good as you suggest."

"I am confident of it."

Prince Tyfar walked to the head of the line to bid his father luck, as I judged, and then he turned to Ariane. She nodded, once, white-faced under that rosy-red, and swung away to speak to her numim bodyguard. The Pachak twins guarded her close. Tyfar, scowling, came back to me.

"Notor Jak—my fellows will swing the gate. Agreed?"

"Agreed." Then I added, "Prince."

"You are a strange fellow—and I see you still wear the red."

"I overlooked that, prince. Still, it is the color of blood."

"Oh, no, Jak! Why, that loincloth is brilliant scarlet!"

"So it is. Well, let us swing the gate and hope it is not stained a darker red."

Ungovich came over. "Get as many through at one time as you can." As he spoke I felt an irrational desire to haul off that concealing hood and have a look at this mysterious man.

He stalked off to take his position in the line, and Quienyin rubbed his thumb under his jaw, scratching. "I think," he said, and he looked meaningfully at Tyfar and me. "I really do think you should not allow the creature to climb out of the tank."

"Once out—?" said Tyfar.

"Indubitably, my dear prince."

I turned away. Deb-Lu-Quienyin was most certainly feeling some tremor of the future, some inkling of the resurrection of his powers. I wondered what kind of a man he really was. The old buffer I knew was certainly far removed from a puissant and feared Wizard of Loh, that was for sure.

All the relaxed air had gone out of the situation. The hullabaloo as the treasures were spilled out wantonly had vanished. Now the men looked anxiously at the silver gate, and cast uneasy glances over their shoulders at the ominous writhing shapes in the tanks. That close confining breathless sensation clamped down on us.

Prince Nedfar called, "In the name of Havil the Green! Open the gate!"

Tyfar nodded to his men, chief among whom were Barkindrar and Nath the Shaft. The silver gate swung open. Nedfar stepped resolutely through, his shield and sword positioned, vanished out of my sight. I swung about, narrowly watching that coiling slimy monstrosity within the tank lifting itself up. The tentacles seemed to be signaling to me, hypnotically waving and demanding my obedience. The tentacles slid over the rim. One red eye appeared, and another. The curved serrated beak showed. Over half the bloated body lifted above the rim of the tank.

"Close the gate!" I bellowed.

Tyfar's men slammed the gate, and others held back the next in line. They halted, sullenly, looking back. The monster slowly sank down into its tank.

I watched it narrowly. Down and down it dropped behind its transparent wall. I fancied, when it stopped moving, it had not dropped as far down as it had been.

"Gate!"

The gate opened and the line began to pass through, inevitably jostling and pushing. Now that the first party had gone on through and had not reported back disaster, the second party were more confident.

When the gate was shut at my shout and we waited for the coiled monster to subside I took stock of the man who came up to stand beside me, breathing deeply. Kov Thrangulf held himself stiffly erect, and his face flushed a dark and painful red. Over in the third group, where we had thought it wisest to include the women of the expedition, Lobur was laughing and talking to the Princess Thefi, who was responding beautifully. Thrangulf bent his lowering brows upon them. Ahead of the princess, the lady Ariane and her people waited patiently.

"By Havil," said Thrangulf. "I am forced to put up with much!"

I watched the monster sinking down. When it came to rest I was convinced it was not as far down as previously.

And—one limp tentacle hung down over the rim of the tank and was not withdrawn. "Gate!"

The people pushed along. Following the women's group a column of Chuliks waited. One of them was quite clearly incapacitated from the drink and as they moved forward he toppled flat on his face. Some of his comrades were for leaving him; in the end and moving with speed, they threw his sack of booty away and a comrade hoisted him up onto his shoulder, perched precariously along with the swollen bundle of swag. "If he wants his life, we will give him that. But as for his booty—"

"He will never make paktun now," said another. They pressed on. The little check caused them to be tardy, opening up a gap into which they crowded forward smartly, leaving a gap to their rear. I eyed the monster. The tentacles writhed above the rim and a red, shield-sized eye peered balefully down. It seemed to me the damned thing was climbing up quicker each time. I would take no chances. As the serrated beak began to move forward above that gross body, surrounded in slimy coils, I bellowed, "Shut the gate!" I whirled as shouts broke out by the silver gate. Tyfar and his men were pulling the gate but three burly Chuliks struggled within the opening, effectively blocking the closure. They insisted on pushing through. The gate hung open, jammed. And the monster began to hiss. "Out of it, you cramphs!" shouted Tyfar. I ran. I sped up to the gate and gave the center Chulik such a buffet he took off headlong, his feet flying up. He vanished out of sight and his two comrades were caught, a fist around each pigtail of coiled hair, and thrust savagely on. Tyfar's men hauled the gate shut.

I stood back. I felt intensely annoyed by such stupidity.

The monster hissed and began to descend—and the thing dropped down reluctantly...

"By Krun, Notor Jak! You deal severely."

"Onkers," I said. "Get onkers."

"Next time—"

"Next time teach 'em with steel!"

And I stomped away.

Kov Thrangulf was staring at me as though I was a madman.

"That was Prince Tyfar to whom you had the honor of addressing yourself—"

"I know. And he'll be a prince in that tentacular beast's inward parts if he doesn't look lively!"

Kov Loriman stumped over. He had elected to stay with the last party, which did not surprise me. Despite all the horrors of this place I had the dark suspicion that he rather fancied getting his blade into one of those red eyes.

"The prince was given the task because he is a prince and the son of a prince. But if he cannot manage—"

"He will," I said. "Kov. Do not fret." Then I added ominously, "By the time it is our turn that beast is not going peaceably back to its tank."

He looked at my bow—I should say that I had put the bow away once I had taken up my new task—and he grunted. "I say shaft it, Notor Jak."

That was sweet politeness from the Hunting Kov.

"I think," I said, "I might try a shaft at it the next time it shoves its ugly snout out."

"Let us all try, by the Blind Archer!"

When next the gate was opened all the archers left let fly at the flaming red orb of the tentacular monster. If the shafts hit at all, it was difficult to say. They ricocheted and caromed away. When that happens to an arrow driven by a Lohvian bowstave, the archer knows he has loosed at something special.

"The thing is cased in some kind of damned armor!"

"Kov—would you care to try your sword against it?"

He took my meaning at once. The veins in his purple nose swelled. He looked meanly at me. "When the order to open the gate is given—I will..." He hesitated, and then said, "I will try."

Kov Thrangulf drew his sword. "If you will, kov, I will stand at your side and smite blow for blow."

"You are welcome, Kov. Let us stand together and smite!"

Although as usual I was amused by all these kovs this and kovs that, here was an intriguing example of etiquette functioning in ways that were universally recognized on Kregen.

The gate opened and the two kovs, positioned and ready, leaped to strike doughty blows at the writhing tentacles. Their swords rebounded. I would not have been surprised had they both been snatched up and ground to pulp in that ugly yellow beak. Kov Thrangulf went on slashing and hacking like a madman, quite uselessly. Kov Loriman dragged him back and a glistening tentacle swept past closer than any fighting man cared to see. A bright blue favor was wrenched from the shoulder plate of Thrangulf's armor.

"By Krun, kov! That was—" Thrangulf swallowed down and looked about. "You pulled me back!"

"Aye! Otherwise you'd be beak-fodder by now—kov!"

Then it was time to bellow the gate closed. The monster was now quite clearly remaining much higher in the tank, and three tentacles hung down outside the rim. As we waited a thought crossed my mind. The Krozair longsword might only be an illusion; it could cut, had cut—would it cut this monster?

I went across. The two kovs were stiltedly polite, one to the other, and it was clear Loriman's opinion of Thrangulf as a fighting man had plummeted. I lifted the Krozair brand.

Loriman said, "You are wasting your time."

"Nevertheless, it is needful I try." And I slashed.

The shock vibrated right up my arms, through my shoulders and exploded in my skull. I was swung around and staggered.

"I told you," said Loriman.

Thoroughly bad-tempered I stomped across and bellowed for them to open the gate. On that occasion we did not get above half the next waiting group through. I began to calculate the odds.

That confounded red and green checkered hood came into view and the rusty hinge voice croaked, "You cannot do it."

"We will try."

"That is the privilege of apims."

So that meant nothing. He could be apim or diff and say that, say the same words with vastly different meanings.

I went down to the gate and gave Tyfar's men a thorough talking to. Then I stalked along the waiting lines and threatened them. The threats were redundant with the looming menace writhing within the tanks. Four limp tentacles hung down outside; those within the transparent walls coiled and squirmed.

And, the tanks farther around in the circle showed their awful denizens at precisely higher stages of movement, as though they were notes in a scale—a scale of horror.

I said to the people at the tail end, "If we all move faster, and do not stumble, we will all get through—just."

Hunch looked ill. Nodgen shook his spear.

Kov Thrangulf came up to me again, puffing his cheeks out.

"They all contume me," he said. He was by way of being light-headed. "I do not have that famous ham in my name. My grandfather carved out the kovnate, and I have held it. Is not that a great thing?"

"Aye, kov." I spoke true words—for I knew of the dangers and difficulties in retaining a hold on lands and titles.

"I am a plain man. I do my best. The Empress Thyllis has turned her face from me." He sounded maudlin. I think at that moment he believed he was going to die, that he was facing certain death and not the possibilities of death that lurked in the Moder. "I am a plain man," he said again. "Not fancy. I try."

"I'm sure," I said. "Kov."

"My grandfather, the kov. He lived too long. My father never forgave him for that." He choked up and wiped his mouth. "My father showed me his displeasure, knowing I would be kov."

Another batch of fugitives went through and I narrowly surveyed those remaining, measuring the length of the lines against the height up the tank of the nearest monster. And, as I thus watched the lines and the monsters, and listened to Kov Thrangulf, I was aware of another thought itching away, a trembling suspicion that we would not get away as easily as all that, even from here.

I felt sorry for Thrangulf. What he said added up; but the urgencies of the moment supervened, so I contented myself with saying, "All men have a purpose in life, kov. Find yours."

He looked at me as though I had struck him. I stared back, and he took a step away from me as though blown by an invisible wind. I suppose my ugly old beakhead carried that demoniac look.

"Take your place in line, kov, and go through quickly..."

"I shall not forget you, Notor Jak—even if I die!"

He resumed his place in the line. The process of escape went on, a remorseless logic of attrition. Now there were a dozen tentacles hanging outside the tank. Limp when the gate was closed, they wriggled to squirming life when the gate opened, hauling up that gross body. The red eyes glared malevolently. The serrated beak clashed.

Hunch and Nodgen looked at me appealingly. I showed them a stony face. Someone had to bring up the rear. I could have wished it was someone other than them, though.

No prowling monster wandered through, gibbering. Had one done so I believe we would have roared with laughter at the inconsequentiality of such an apparition at this time.

Many of the nearer monsters hung close to the tops of their tanks, and bunches of tentacles hung down outside.

When but three groups of people remained I said to Loriman: "Let us leave the gate closed for a longer period, kov. Mayhap that beast will slip down."

"We can try..."

So we waited, apprehensively, in that gruesome chamber among the overturned treasures. The tentacles of the monster hung limp. It did not, as far as I could see, drop down an inch. We waited.

Presently, Loriman swore. He said, "By Hito the Hunter! It is no use. Open the gate and send the next one through."

We did so.

The monster balanced on the very rim of the tank, swaying and clacking its beak. That beak could grind stone to powder.

I believe the very remorselessness of the whole process, the gradual approach of the monster to escape and our destruction, the logic of it all, wore us down more than any screaming screeching monster-charge could ever do. And something of that feeling must have permeated the Moder-lord, watching us, no doubt, and giggling and mumbling soggy toothless jaws. A piece of discarded gold in the shape of a dancing Talu, beautiful and abandoned, stood up and began to dance toward a cabinet that righted itself and shuffled its legs into the position it had occupied before. The glass joined together over the Talu.

With a scraping whispering furtiveness the strewn treasures began to replace themselves within healed boxes and cupboards. Chests turned upright and refilled with spilled gems. The whole mausoleum filled with the glint of gold and the glitter of gems and the rustle of scuttering treasure. As for the magic items—ghosts, wraiths, call them what you will, the cabinets filled and resumed their accustomed places.

"The cramph of a Moder-lord considers we are finished," said Loriman. He spat and hitched up his shield and sword.

"There is still a chance," I said. "There were two men in Jikaida City reputed to have returned from the Humped Land with treasure and with magic. Can they best us?"

"It is not they who will best us—"

"No. I think the monster will climb out of the tank the next time we open the gate—"

"Agreed!"

"So we must open wide and all press through, fast—fast! It must be done."

Kov Loriman the Hunter, a rough, unpleasant slave-owning man, a player of Execution Jikaida, said, "I shall, of course, go last."

I said, "Kov, tell me. What did you say to Master Scatulo when you lost at Execution Jikaida?"

He stared. "You were there?"

"I was there."

"I told him that he had one more chance and then I would send him to take the place of the Pallan of the Blacks."

"Very good. I shall go through last."

"Do you wish to fight me for it?"

And then the incongruousness of the situation came to my rescue. I didn't give an adulterated copper Havvy for him. Did I? Whatever path his honor made him tread, my path lay in the light of the Suns of Scorpio and of the well-being of Vallia.

"Of course, of course. With my compliments—you may go last,"

"As is right and proper." And he fingered his sword and looked back with a black look at the octopoid monster.

Other intrepid adventurers had come here and gone through the gates loaded with treasure. Mayhap this Moder was different from others, and those two successful men of Jikaida City had plundered an easier tomb. For, of course, we were all grave robbers—although the stakes were raised to a rarefied level. But, still, other men had succeeded here, I felt sure. The tentacled monsters could be outwitted. That could only mean worse things awaited down the Shaft of Flame.

"Now?" said Loriman.

I couldn't say I liked him. But he had been—useful—in his uncouth way. And I didn't know from whence on Kregen he hailed. He had carefully not said.

I looked at the last men waiting. I shouted. "When the gate opens—run! If any man stumbles he must be pushed aside and tail on at the rear! So, doms—do not stumble!"

Loriman shouted, "I shall stand at the gate. If any man attempts to push out of place, him I will strike down!"

Prince Tyfar looked a trifle green about the gills. I walked across. "Prince—go out with your men first—we will close the gate."

"But—"

"Do it!"

He looked crestfallen, like a chastised child. I turned away and gave him no room to argue further.

"All set?"

"All set!"

The gate swung open. The men began to run through, quickly, plunging out of view, shooting like peas from a pod. Tyfar went. His men followed. The lines ran up, men panting, frightened, pushing on, keeping in line, shouting. Loriman stood at one side of the gate, his sword raised, his face hateful.

I prowled the other side, urging the men on, encouraging them.

With a monstrous hissing the tentacled octopoid, immense, writhing, slimy, toppled from the tank and scuttled for us.

"No brainless bunch of guts is going to beat us!" roared Loriman. "No matter that it is invulnerable to honest steel. Run, you hulus, run!"

Shrieking, a man stumbled and I seized his neck and hurled him on. Out of sight through the silver gate they crashed, two by two, hurling on. Hissing, writhing, the monster raced swiftly over the marble toward us. No treacherous pattern of that floor engulfed it. The tentacles swirled, slimy, reaching out...

Only a half dozen more... Nodgen and Hunch were through... Two more—then the last two... I swung to face Loriman.

In that moment he stood there, exalted, his face a single ruby flame, his eyes murderous. I thought he would stay and challenge the monster out of the sheer joy of hunting.

I grabbed his arm and pulled as a clansman pulls a vove up over a fire-filled trench. Together, we roared through the silver gateway and I slammed the portal shut. Its clang sounded like sweetest music.

The shaft of fire rose before us, lifting from a stone-walled pit. Men were running forward, following the one ahead and vanishing out of sight down between flame and wall.

"We've done it!" exulted Loriman. He swaggered toward the pit from which rose the Flame. "The cramph of a monster has been beaten!"

A gigantic hissing belched up behind us, like a volcano bursting. We swung about. We stared up, appalled.

Tentacles appeared over the top of the insubstantial iron wall. A gross form rose into view. Red eyes like flame, the size of shields, stared wickedly down upon us. A yellow serrated beak clacked. Deliberately, the monster lifted over the wall, balanced, fell clutching down toward us.

Twenty

The Fight over Vaol-Paol

Dread of that primeval horror exploded in my skull. Two thoughts clashed in my head. The monster was impervious to steel. And other men had escaped from this awful place.

Squirming with coiled animate energy the monster rushed swiftly across the stone toward us as we fled for the Shaft of Flame. Between that supernal white light and the lip of the stone pit a narrow opening offered the way of escape. Stone-cut steps spiraled downward within the confines of the pit. Another monster flopped over the wall and, hissing, propelled itself on those wriggling serpent-like tentacles toward us.

Men pushed on down the steps. The slot between wall and flame was perhaps just wide enough for my hulking shoulders. A man toppled. Screaming, he pitched from the steps. His body entered the flame. Spread-eagled, his pitiful bundle of loot flogging free, he drifted down as though suspended against a blast of invisible force, and as he fell he dwindled and burned. We shuddered and hurried down the stone steps, treacherous with slippery moss and slimy with fungus.

Looking back past Loriman, who thumped down with a look of ferocious distaste on his florid features, I saw the monster's red eye appear, festooned with coils of slimy writhings, saw it lash futilely down after us.

Loriman bellowed, jerking his head back. "The thing is balked! Ha! We have bested the monster!"

But the monster launched itself into the column of pure white light.

Like thistledown, it floated. It sank. Its arms writhed and its eyes glared, its beak clacked, and it dropped down and down within the Shaft of Fire.

Loriman switched up his sword.

"If we are to die," he shouted, hard and venomously. "I will strike and strike until I am dead!"

I thought of that poor devil who had fallen through the Flame. "Look!" I shrieked. "Look—the thing shrinks!"

And it was so. As we hurried down and the monster sank within that supernal radiance, so, we saw with thankfulness, it dwindled in size and shrank until it was no larger than a coiled mass of rope such as would be found on the deck of a swordship.

That shrunken bundle of horror still held menace. It drifted in to the steps and as we hurried down so it fastened upon the arm of a Rapa. He shrieked, his feathers all stiff with horror. He slashed with his sword, and the steel bounced, and the dwindling monster pulled him free of the stone steps, and he sank with his death into the shining whiteness.

Up there other monsters launched themselves into the Shaft of Flame.

As we hurried with desperate caution down those slippery steps I knew that no magics we might have found above would preserve us from this danger. And, also, I was convinced that nothing the Moder-lords with all their thaumaturgical arts could provide would prove of any use to me in my dealings with the Star Lords or the Savanti. The Moder-lords dealt in illusion and horror and fear. But they were mortals. Their reach of dread power had its limits.

Looking down the spiral stone stairs one could see only the bobbing heads of the men in front, curving away out of sight beyond the radiance of the Flame. The stairs went down widdershins. How far the pit sank into the ground, no one could tell.

To our left the shrinking monsters drifted down through the Flame. Their hissing ceased. The only sounds were of men's breathing, and the slip and slither of feet upon the stone. Down we went and then I saw the men below me turning into a low stone opening, arched in the wall at our sides. The steps down trended on and down and out of sight. Thankfully, Loriman and I ducked into the opening, to stand erect in a wide chamber and see the rest of the expedition waiting for us.

The babble of greetings and the quick question and answer as the fate of comrades was disclosed went on like a surf roar. Light of a sickly green fell from a roof away behind the dazzle.

"Thank Havil we are all safe—save for those poor unfortunates who succumbed." Prince Nedfar betrayed determination. He issued his orders in a hard voice. "We have discovered a passageway and a long corridor leading upward. This must be the way out. But—we go carefully." That, we all knew, was a remarkably redundant piece of advice and betrayed the state of our nerves no less than those of Prince Nedfar's.

"We go on in the same order." He looked meaningfully at Loriman and Tyfar and the rest of us latecomers. "It has been a long and trying wait down here."

I looked about among the people.

"Where is Master Quienyin?" I shouted, pushing through the throng.

But Quienyin, Ungovich and Yagno were missing.

"I believe they went on ahead, to spy the way," said the lady Ariane. "Let us go on!"

Her face had lost a great deal of that high color. But what she said made sense, although Nedfar might have thought differently. We started up the corridor, and all of us, from time to time, cast apprehensive glances backwards.

"By Tryflor!" panted Hunch. "This place has scared me witless." He shook with fear.

Nodgen tried to bolster his courage with a bellow. "You Tryfants are all the same. Only good for running!"

"True," moaned Hunch. "Too true!"

We pressed on and soon we recognized that the sequence of corridors and rooms matched those through which we had first passed when we entered the Moder. Nedfar shouted that this was a good sign. "The way out mirrors the way in! Courage! Onward!"

We trended upward and when we reached a chamber draped in solemn purple we stopped, dismayed. No doorway broke those somber walls.

Men rushed about pulling the purple curtains aside. All they found was a small secret door beyond which stood a lever. The lever was fashioned of ivory and bronze, and it looked ominous.

"Pull that...?" said Loriman. "It is a riddle."

"We have no time for riddles." Nedfar looked outraged.

Tyfar stood near me, and Ariane leaned on the shoulder of her numim.

"The three who went ahead," I said, "they must have riddled this riddle aright—or where are they?" I looked at Ariane. Her face flushed, bringing her color back to that rosy red. She stamped her foot. I said, slowly, "Did they go ahead, lady?"

"Yes!" she flared. Then: "No—I do not know. I did not see them. I think they went on down the stairs of the pit."

The transparency of the lie could not soften my feelings.

"I shall go back for Quienyin."

"I shall come with you, Notor Jak—" said Tyfar.

"No, prince. Better not—you should stay to take care of the lady Ariane."

He looked at me. His spirit was up. The diffidence had gone, at least, for a space.

"No, Notor Jak. I think not."

"Pull the Havil-forsaken lever," roared Loriman, "and have done!"

Nedfar snapped out, sharply, "Not until we have examined everything thoroughly, three times over!"

"There is," put in Kov Thrangulf, swallowing, "the matter of the ninth part of the Key—"

"Yes, kov," sang out Lobur the Dagger. He stood very close to the Princess Thefi. "You are right, by Krun! Now how could we have overlooked that weighty matter?"

I turned away sharply. I went back along the corridors through which we had just toiled. The scene I left was not to my liking.

Through the corridors I hurried and crossing a nine-sided room with curlicued marble floor inlaid with the symbol for vaol-paol, The Great Circle of Universal Existence, I stopped stock still. Against three of the walls stood tall glass cabinets. In each cabinet and plainly visible through the glass glowered a Kildoi warrior. On each, the four arms and tail hand grasped weapons.

Now I could have sworn those cabinets had not been there when we hurried past this nine-sided room. Then, with a resounding Makki-Grodno curse, I pushed on. Mysteries, mysteries...

The quick shuffle of footsteps in the corridor a few rooms along heralded Deb-Lu-Quienyin. He looked different. And, yet, he was the same.

We turned together to hurry back, exchanging news.

"The three mages went on down the pit of the Shaft of Flame. I warned Yagno; but he said he was a Sorcerer of the Cult of Almuensis. Well—" Quienyin sounded genuinely aggrieved. "What I saw down there, on the ninth level, I will not say, young man. It is not for ordinary mortals."

"Did you regain your powers, San?"

He gave a half-despairing, half-amused laugh. "Yes and no. I found what I sought, as San Orien had promised. The Moder-lords do not allow Wizards of Loh into their Moders. That is a fact. But I was no longer a real Wizard of Loh. So I found that which was needful."

"Wonderful—but, in this place, there is a catch?"

"There is a catch, Jak. I will only regain my full powers when I am safely outside the Moder."

"Then that is all right. They are searching for the last part of the key now. They have found a lever. We will soon be out." Then, I said, "And Yagno? And Ungovich?"

"Yagno was—no, better I do not reveal that. As for Ungovich, he disappeared, and I fear he shares the same fate as Yagno."

"So—unhappy though it is, we do not wait for them?"

"By every Queen of Pain who ever reigned in Loh," he said, and surprised me by that word, "no. It is useless to wait."

We entered the nine-sided chamber with the inlaid motif of vaol-paol in the floor. Quienyin halted. The three glass cabinets opened. The three Kildoi stepped forth. They glared at us.

No time to think. No time to understand that these three were Kildois, just as Mefto the Kazzur was a Kildoi, with four arms and a tail equipped with a fist, superb fighting men, tremendous in their strength and skill. Mefto had bested me at swordplay. No time, no time. No time even, with the flashing memory of Seg Segutorio heartening me, to bring the great Lohvian longbow into action and shaft the first of them as he rushed upon me.

Quienyin shouted something, and I caught the tailing words: "...the Kazzur!"

The Krozair longsword ripped free.

In my two fists and gripped in that cunning Krozair hold, the brand gleamed in the unwavering beams of the black candles in their golden holders... The Kildois hurled themselves on.

The first gripped thraxters in his right upper and right lower hands. His lower left hand slanted a round shield. His upper left hand wielded a spear. And in his tail hand that wicked daggered steel glittered as his tail swept in high above his head.

No time to delay. No time for fancy work. As I had fought the overlords of Magdag on the swaying deck of a swifter I would have to fight now. It was all hard, merciless, practical fighting and none of your fancy academy fencing...

The thraxters slashed for me. The Krozair brand blinded, whirling like a living bar of light, chunked through the shield, bore on to score a deep wound all down the Kildoi's chest. Before he had time to yell, before he had time to fall, I bounded away and swung into action against his fellows. They bore in from each side, cunning, clever, supreme fighters. And as these superb Kildois attacked they did not understand they faced an old Krozair Brother, a Krozair of Zy—who knew more tricks than the Krozairs, by thunder! The longsword swept dazzlingly. A thraxter scored across my right shoulder and then the first Kildoi was down, minus a tail he had flung unavailingly across to protect his throat. Tail blade, tail hand, throat, vanished in a welter of purple blood.

The second flung himself forward, shield up, spear aiming for my eye. I slid his blow, brought the Krozair brand around, quick, quick! Ah, the Krozair Disciplines teach a man how to stay alive, by Zair!

Whether they were real Kildoi retainers of the Moder-lord or whether they were illusions, I did not know. But their steel would kill.

The fight was over. Three dead Kildois lay on that inlaid representation of the symbol for vaol-paol, and their purple blood dripped thickly. I stood back. I panted only a little.

"By the Wizard of—!" said Quienyin, shaking.

"By the Black Chunkrah! Now that opened the old pores a trifle! Let us, San, hurry on—and get out of here!"

As we came up to the purple-draped chamber and the noise of the people of the expedition arguing away at the top of their voices—as usual—I said, and I admit rather slyly, to Quienyin, "San, tell me—that Bracelet of Blades you wished me to wear—how would it have worked there? For all three Kildois? Or the first one only?"

He gave me a look along his nose. "You are a hard man, Jak."

"Aye—to my sorrow."

Hunch and Nodgen appeared glad to see me and the Wizard of Loh still alive. They told us that the lever had at last been pulled, that a wailing pack of Lurking Fears had writhed out, that the warriors, although quaking with supernaturally-induced terror, had managed to slay all the Lurking Fears.

"And," shouted Hunch, "the lever did two things—"

"The ninth part of the key in a secret cavity!" shouted Nodgen.

"—and the keyhole in an onyx wall—there!"

"And now," said Nodgen, "they are fiddling about putting the bits of the key together. That is brainy work."

A triumphant shout racketed down from the far wall. Nedfar waved the completed key aloft, his face radiant. "We have it!"

Everyone felt that we must hurry. Urgency drove us on, for we were all confident that at any moment fresh horror would prowl down upon us. The purple draperies were pushed aside to reveal the onyx wall and the keyhole. It had to be a keyhole! There was no other way.

"Something dire will happen when that key is turned," said Prince Tyfar. He looked excited and wrought up in a way far different from his usual diffident manner.

Ariane shuddered and drew away from him.

Lobur the Dagger held Princess Thefi close. Retainers and paktuns held their weapons ready, a forest of steel blades. We looked about the chamber and back to Prince Nedfar and the onyx wall with the keyhole. He placed the key in the lock. He paused. Then: "In the name of Havil the Green!" He pushed the key in and turned it.

The purple draperies vanished in puffs of smoke. The odor of charred flesh gusted. The solid wall peeled back to reveal a colossal statue of Kranlil the Reaper, a full hundred feet tall, crowned, ferocious, malefic, wielding his flail.

Between the mammoth columns of his feet a narrow door groaned open; bronze bound, crimson, double-valved, the door slowly opened.

A long upward slope was revealed. And—at the far end, tiny and distant—light! Daylight! As our eyes made out the drifting shapes up there we saw clouds and the streaming mingled radiance of the Suns of Scorpio.

And then, as the first mobs broke through, shrieking their joy, a whirling darting maddening cloud of stinging insects broke down about our heads. They poured from the opened casket in the claws of Kranlil the Reaper. They tormented us as we ran, stinging and lacerating and driving us mad.

The vial of yellow poison kept my skin partly immune, so that I felt the stings as light prickles, like nettles.

Men were screaming, and flailing their arms, and running, running, tearing madly up that long narrow corridor.

Tyfar screamed and caught at his collar. I grabbed him and twitched out the little horror that was clinging to his neck. It was banded in yellow and green, gauzy-winged, and its sting was black and hard and tipped with a globule of moisture. I threw it away. I could not see Nodgen and Hunch in the bedlam.

We pushed on and Logu Fre-Da and his twin, Modo Fre-Da swiftly assisted Ariane along. Her hair was covered with insects. She screamed, trying to beat them free. Modo let out a yell and fell, clasping his legs. Both limbs crawled with the insect horrors. Logu bent to him.

"Leave him, you fool!" screamed Ariane. "Help me!"

Shrieking, Ariane stumbled. Tyfar caught her, helped her up. He was covered with the stinging insects. He choked, trying to go on, and fell. Quienyin grasped my arm, shaking, beating at the air. Tyfar was on his knees, looking up imploringly, still gripping Ariane's white dress which crawled with banded green and yellow.

"Ariane—princess—"

"Let go, you rast! I do not care a dead calsany's hide for your life! Let me go!"

She struck Prince Tyfar. She wrenched free and ran screaming and sobbing up the slot, pushing and beating at the backs of the people struggling on. The two hyr-paktuns watched her go.

Quienyin said, chokedly, "Let—let them go—the insects will follow—" He let go my arm and beat at himself. "I am on fire!" The hideous uproar persisted, a cacophony of torture.

Barkindrar the Bullet and Nath the Shaft sprang to the side of the prince. All three hummed and buzzed with insects.

"We must go on!" I shouted.

We staggered and stumbled on. We were the last. The two Pachaks struggled along side by side, helping each other.

Our little group fought a way through the swarming clouds of insects. Hunch and Nodgen, trying to shout and making mewling noises, lurched on up the slope. Up there the daylight showed, bright and welcoming. The glory of the ruby and jade light fell into the opening, and irradiated the walls, and we fell and crawled on, afire with the poisonous stings from the winged furies.

We neared the top and the way to freedom.

Slaves, paktuns, retainers, notables, passed out through the opening and faintly we heard their yells of exaltation and triumph.

We pressed on.

Almost—almost we reached the opening.

Then the slab fell clashing down, stone on stone, and the blackness descended upon us.

We were shut in, denied life, trapped within the Moder.

Twenty-one

Of the Powers of a Wizard of Loh

Trapped... And all that ghastly catacomb of the Moder as our tomb...

"Back!" I yelled, savagely. "Out between the legs of Kranlil before that door closes!"

Scrambling, shouting, we raced desperately for the lower door. We came shooting out into the purple-draped room, and the double doors, crimson, bronze bound, groaned shut at our backs.

"But it is no use!" cried Tyfar. "We are doomed—"

"The insects are gone," I said. "We have our lives still."

Quienyin looked at me and shook his head.

"It is a long way—"

"Yes. But the only way, now. We must return through the Moder and make our escape the way we came in."

We stared one at the other with frightened eyes. We knew what we had been through...

"We are a choice band," I said. "We can win through if we bear up and trust in ourselves."

"But, think of it..." whispered Hunch. Then he shouted, "I will not think of it! It is too frightening."

"It is," agreed Nodgen. "So best think of something else and just come along."

Yes, they were a choice band. Prince Tyfar and his men, Barkindrar and Nath. Nodgen and Hunch. Logu and Modo Fre-Da. And Deb-Lu-Quienyin, a Wizard of Loh whose powers would return only when he was safely out of here. A choice bunch, indeed, to venture back through this Castle of Death.

They were all scratching themselves. My vial soothed away their stings; but we still itched uncomfortably.

"It is a mortal long way," observed Barkindrar.

"Look," said Nath the Shaft. "I wager you I can shoot out the right eye of that damned statue before you can sling out the left. Is it a wager—for an amphora of best Jholaix when we sit in The Scented Sylvie?"

"Done," said Barkindrar.

Sling whirled instantly, bow bent at once—leaden bullet and steel-tipped bird flew. Both of those staring green eyes clipped out, sparking, tinkled away somewhere.

"Mine, I think—"

"Ha! Mine, of a surety!"

I said, "I am surprised they allow ruffians like you in The Scented Sylvie. By Hanitch! What Ruathytu has come to!"

They gaped, then, and Tyfar suddenly burst into a laugh.

"You know the Sacred Quarter, then, Notor Jak of Djanduin?"

Nodgen and Hunch stopped arguing to stare at us like loons. The two Pachaks gave up hunting for the fallen eyes of Kranlil.

"Well enough to know I intend to spend a pleasant evening and night there again. You may not be a Bladesman, but I wager your axe sings a sweet tune."

"And I shall share that evening and night with you!"

"Done!"

"Now we must make our way back," he said, airily. "There is a charming tavern on the Alley of Forbidden Delights—The Sybli and the Vouvray, it is called." He started to walk out of that dolorous chamber and along the corridor. We all followed. "I shall have great pleasure in taking you there, Notor Jak."

"You do me the honor," I said, walking on.

Well, at least, this was one way to anchor the mind to sanity. What we faced was like to test us to the utmost. And there was an intriguing fact I had not overlooked. As we marched on I counted us again. Yes, I was right.

Nine.

We were nine adventurers, challenging the sorcery of the Moder.

As we walked the twin Pachaks talked to each other and then, respectfully, they addressed Prince Tyfar.

"Prince, we request that you witness our formal severing of our nikobi to the lady Ariane nal Amklana."

Tyfar's face pinched in. But all he said was, "I so witness."

We went on toward that spiral stair up the pit of the Flame. I took the opportunity to say to the two hyr-paktuns, "You would do me a favor, and confer honor if you were to look out for Master Quienyin. Is this acceptable to you?"

They nodded solemnly. They did not give their nikobi—not yet. But I felt a little easier for Quienyin. We were going to need stout hearts and hard fists to get out of here. Hunch was a weak link, possibly, but I fancied Nodgen and I would handle him.

I do not propose to detail all our struggles and torments as we battled our way back up the Moder. I will say that we found Kov Loriman's discarded picks and sledgehammers and simply bashed our way out, as he had bashed in. We did take a number of magical items indicated to us by Quienyin in the spirit that we had earned them the hard way. We plodded on, encountering monsters and vanquishing them by sorcery or by steel, and so went on and up.

We found ourselves taking a different way fairly soon, and we saw no sign of the lake and the sunken ships and the quicksands.

Corridor after corridor, room after room... They blurred after a time into a continuing progression of horrors. But we went on. We were nine adventurers and if we were not hard-bitten when we began, we were hard-bitten enough at the end, by Vox!

Another interesting fact was that, going up as we were instead of down, we ran into traps from, as it were, the rear. Monsters, too, seemed a trifle put out that we did not appear from the right direction. I can say we left a trail behind us that would have done credit to a raging boloth in a potter's yard.

We came to a corridor which curved gently out of sight ahead. Low golden railings separated each side from the main passageway. Within these golden railings stood or lounged or reclined on sofas hundreds of the most beautiful women of many races. They smiled seductively. Their eyes lighted on us brilliantly. Lasciviously they beckoned to us. Some played harps and sang. The whole impression was of a single gigantic offering to passion.

Hunch and Nodgen stopped. They licked their lips.

Most of the women were half-dressed in exotic and revealing costume, attire calculated to drive a man wild with desire. I pointed at the long rows of carved skulls set back from the golden railings, each some four or five feet from the next.

"You are not in the Souk of Women now, you famblys."

"No, but—look at that one!"

"And look at her!"

"Look—that is all."

A Kaotim prowled along just then, a figure of a skeleton of a Rapa with his big beak glittering. He seemed surprised to see us. Quienyin whiffed him into ashes with a sprinkle of powder from a jeweled box taken from the Hall of the Flame. "Over a hundred pinches of powder left, friends," he reported.

The Undead drifted away in a dribble of ash.

Kao is only one word for death in Kregish, which is a language rich and colorful.

"But," said Hunch, "only to look..."

"You are in a Moder. You know what mod means, Hunch?"

He shivered, and took his longing gaze away from the sylvie who smiled lasciviously, beckoning, sweet.

"Yes. I know what mod means."

"Then let us go on."

So we went along between those wanton women and heard the mewling slobbering cries ahead. We proceeded cautiously.

A man came into view. He had clearly not heeded the warnings implicit here. The women near him were all laughing and displaying themselves and taunting him. From the mouth of one of the skulls a long, thin, pre-hensile line, like a whip, fastened about this man's tail. The two whip-tails linked and held, fast locked, knotted.

The man kept trying to pull himself away, and crying, and shrieking, and then falling to his knees. In his hand he held a knife. He was, we judged, insane.

"A Snatchban," said Quienyin. "He will never cut that."

On the floor lay two swords and a dagger, sundered into halves.

Hunch and Nodgen started forward and then, as the imprisoned man shrieked and swung his knife down and so withdrew it, they halted, as it were, on one foot, and stood staring dumbly.

"If there is one thing they fear above all else," said Tyfar, "it is to have their tail cut off."

"Yet, if he doesn't cut if off, he will perish here, miserably."

"Would you cut it off—for him?"

"Me?" I said. "Well—I might."

Quienyin did not say anything.

Nodgen and Hunch came to life. Each took out his knife.

"We will cut it off for him, notor." Then Nodgen said, "Perhaps it would be better if you went ahead a little?"

Hunch said, "He may be—violent."

I said, "We will walk on."

So we seven walked on between those beautiful women until the curve of the corridor closed in at our rear and the next chamber opened up ahead. Muffled mewling sounds drifted up from the way we had come. We entered the next chamber and set ourselves to read its riddle—backwards. Once we were through the riddle, the way out would be clear, for that was the way in. Presently Nodgen and Hunch rejoined us.

"And?" I said.

They kept their gazes down.

"We talked about it, notor. We felt it would be—undignified—for him to lose his tail. He would probably prefer death."

"You put him out of his misery?"

They shook their heads.

"Oh, no, notor. It would not be seemly for two ex-slaves to slay him."

I screwed my face up. I did not blame them. But, all the same. I started for the way we had come in, saying, "Then I will cut his damned tail off." The entrance closed with a snap.

"There is no way back to him now," observed Tyfar.

"No..."

"Poor devil," said Tyfar. "I do not like them as a rule. I wonder who he was?"

"You did not recognize him?"

"No, should I have?"

"I do not think so." He had—changed. The experience had altered him profoundly. But Hunch and Nodgen and I knew him.

Thus was Tarkshur the Lash left to his fate.

I wondered if they had left him his knife.

We were now running low on food and water; but we made a camp and rested up until we were refreshed enough to continue. How we managed our escape at the top occupied a deal of our conversation, but I found I was going beyond that in my own black thoughts. A very great deal further, by Vox!

The thought that the beautiful Krozair longsword would vanish when we reached the outside had to be faced. I was conscious of the privilege of having it in my fists once more. The Eye of the World, Grodnim and Zairian, seemed a long long way away now.

We were nine. One Tryfant. Two Brokelsh. Two Pachaks. Four apims. Nine.

Chance had brought us together. And we used chance to our own ends. We nine battled our way through the horrors until we stood in an echoing hall where the screams of lycanthropes banished away still lingered, and recognized where we were.

"Through that door, yonder," said Quienyin, pointing.

"The first thing I do," began Nodgen.

"That will be the second thing for me," quoth Hunch.

"I think, my friends," said Quienyin, "it will go something like this." He drew himself up and took a breath. In a strong voice he called, "Answer no is there."

From the room where I had last eaten a chunk of doughy mergem we walked out as the doors opened of themselves. We stood in a hall and the dust coated the floor. I studied the many sets of footprints. Then I began to walk quietly off to a corner.

"Beware, Jak!" cried Tyfar. "Look at those stains at the ends of footprints which end—abruptly!"

"Yes. But we are not the ninnies who entered here."

"That is true, by Hanitcha the Harrower!"

"I am not sure I know what you are about, Jak," said Quienyin, "and if I suspected what it was I am sure I would not want to know. But, let me see..."

He walked across and halted well before the end of the line of footprints I had chosen. The ceiling curved into a bulge here, and the shadows clustered among the cobwebs. Quienyin took a small crystal object the size of a shonage from inside his robe and turned it about. Presently in its pale depths we saw a blue-green glow and the outline of a humped shape. Quienyin turned the crystal until he had the blue-green glow responding most strongly.

He nodded his head and then pushed his turban straight.

"Yes. A Trap-Volzoid. Nasty—serrated teeth that will fasten around your neck—that explains the stains. He'll lift you straight up. He's lurking up there somewhere and spying on us."

"A Volzoid—but—"

"This is a Trap-Volzoid. He can leap for perhaps three or four paces. He is waiting for you to walk into range."

"Let him wait, notor!" called Nodgen.

Hunch said, "The door is this way." He started to walk to the portal through which we had entered—a long time ago.

I said, "Will the harpy with the golden hair open it for you?"

The torches still burned above the gates. But they were fast closed, and the iron bars and studs did not look rusty.

"Oh, by Tryflor—have mercy!"

The others went across to the door. They banged on it. It did not open. Nothing happened.

"Right," I called. "You've had your fun. Now scoop up handfuls of dust—large handfuls—and when I yell cast them up into that corner. Make the dust thick."

"You think to blind it, Jak?"

"Long enough for me to reach the corner."

"You take a terrible—"

"That is what this is all about. Now, doms, ready!"

I yelled, the gathered dust flew up in a thick black sheet, and I went hurtling forward for the corner expecting to feel a fetid breath envelop me and razor-sharp fangs encircle my neck and find my head inside the capacious mouth of the Trap-Volzoid.

The dust smothered everywhere and I crashed into the wall.

Winded, I clung to the dusty stone. After a space I could see the other's faces like full moons rising through the dust cloud. I began to feel for the catch in the wall and found the right knob after a space and pressed. The door in the wall swung inwards.

I turned back.

"The last one—"

"I will go last!" declared Prince Tyfar.

"Wait!" I said crossly. "Logu and Modo. You next. We will go up and deal with the Trap-Volzoid. Then the last will cross in safety." The two Pachaks nodded, pleased I had selected them for their superb fighting ability in confined spaces.

We went up a narrow stone stair and crept out into a hollow and stinking place filled with detritus and bones. The Trap-Volzoid crouched on the lip of the bulge, looking away from us, ready to leap the moment an unsuspecting man walked within range.

496

The Krozair longsword bit, the Pachaks swung—and the damned thing, wounded and hissing, leaped out into the dusty hall.

In the end Tyfar and his men finished it off. It lay, a leathery ball, fanged and vicious and stinking, and the men stood back and looked up at us in the bulge and shouted.

So, up the winding stair we all went, and I led over the protestations of Tyfar, and we went with naked steel in our fists.

"I am beginning to think, my dear Jak," said Quienyin as he puffed up the steep and narrow stairs, speaking over the heads of the two Pachaks who followed me—Tyfar brought up the rear—"that this may count as being Outside the Moder."

The others would not guess the significance of that. But, if he was right!

"I pray Djan you are right, San."

"Mind my foot, you fambly!" came Nodgen's indignant voice, followed at once by Hunch, saying, "This is too scary for me!"

They were good fellows... We went on and the narrow stair gave onto a tiny landing where a skeleton leered at us and an arched lenken door with its bronze studs all green shut off the way.

"This is not a case for magic, I think," said Tyfar, and Quienyin closed his mouth. Hunch stepped forward and looked at the door and the lock. He pursed up his Tryfant mouth.

"Looks normal enough. Nothing to fear there—" He started working his dagger about in the lock and, after a surprisingly short time, the catch snicked back and he pushed the door open.

When we were all inside the room, which was harmless, I said: "You showed skill in opening the lock, Hunch, but—"

"Oh, well, notor," he said, spreading his hands, "everyone has to have a trade."

"Maybe so. But, next time, do not push the door open so recklessly—else!"

Hunch the Tryfant went green.

We eased out into a passageway. It was paneled in painted wood, carpets covered the floor, there were exotic vases with flowers, and paintings and carvings against the wall. The air smelled sweet and yet there hung in the warmed air the faintest smell of tangs, as of sweet rottenness.

What followed I would prefer to pass over swiftly. But my narrative would be incomplete if I did not attempt to convey the sense of disgust which pervaded us as we investigated that palace. For it was a palace. We were prowling among the luxurious chambers of the towers perched atop the Moder. Yes—we had penetrated to the lair of the Moder-lord himself. Or—itself...

The sights we saw there made us realize that our stomachs were not as tough as perhaps we had thought.

We spoke in hushed whispers.

"I am uneasy, Quienyin. It seems to me we have gained entrance here too easily. A mere Trap-Volzoid? A skeleton that did not move?" The air carried that sweet smell of putrefaction. "We are being sucked into a trap."

"Oh, yes, my dear Jak. Indubitably."

I glanced quickly at Quienyin. He stood by tall curtains of thick dark blue damask. He looked—different. The air of being an old buffer fell away from him. Although men on Kregen do not materially alter as they age through over two hundred years of adult life, until the very end, the change in him was profound. His eye was clearer, the lines around nose and mouth fined away. He walked with an alert step.

"Your powers—?"

"Not all. Some. Enough to bring us here and not notice what the Moder-lord had spread for our destruction."

I let my breath out. I have said that the powers of the Wizards of Loh are very real and very terrible. Perhaps this very exhibition of them, unconscious as it was, chilled me most.

"What—?" said Prince Tyfar.

Quickly, on a breath, I said, "We have come far enough. We must find a way out. A normal way."

"If there be such a normal thing in this devil's cauldron," growled Nodgen.

"Bound to be," said Hunch. "Got to be—hasn't there?"

We had crossed through most of this palace from the entrance we had found and so I said, "A stairway down near the outside. There has to be one somewhere."

Walking along the corridor, warily, we entered a chamber through draped crimson curtains. The room glittered with gold. Everything, it seemed, was fabricated of gold. A golden cage stood in a corner, with a golden statue of a creature none of us had ever seen before. Then Tyfar started, pointing.

"Look, by Krun! So one of us had the same idea. Perhaps he knows the way out—?"

The figure in the red and green checked cloak turned.

The hood fell back.

We all gasped.

The head was hairless—and lipless and noseless and earless. The skin was of a gray-green marbling, deeply fissured by furrows that turned the whole head into a ghastly parody of humanity. The face looked as though decay and dissolution, well advanced, had been halted and petrified. Thick green sinews stretched between the chin and the neck of the checkered robe. And the eyes—black and red, and demoniacal in their intensity of hate!

"You are welcome," said Tyr Ungovich. "I had not expected you, but here you are—"

"You did not expect us," I said. "And, Ungovich, tell me a riddle, as you love them so. Why should you live?"

No readable expression crossed that gruesome countenance.

"Surely it is you who should answer that?"

I put my hand to the hilt of the Krozair longsword—and it was not there.

Nothing remained of what I had taken from the fire-crystal opening that provided what I lacked. But those replacements I had taken from the Mausoleum, the Hall of Flame, these remained.

I touched the hilt of the rapier.

"Steel will not harm me." The red and green checks stirred as Ungovich swung about, sharply. "And now you die!"

He put a golden whistle to his mouth and blew.

No sound issued.

He blew again, the ghastly gray-green marbling of his cheeks pulsing. Again and again he blew. He swung to face us, and the eyes blazed in unholy anger—demoniac.

"I am the Wizard of the Moder! You will die when my pets—"

Quietly, Deb-Lu-Quienyin said, "I do not think they heard your call, San."

The exquisite irony of that formal salutation of San was not lost on us—nor on the Wizard of the Moder.

He peered closely at Quienyin.

Then he moved back, sharply, and—from nowhere—a sword appeared in his left hand.

"You—" he said, and his words were a thick choke. "You are—"

"Yes."

"But none enters here! None! It is not permitted!"

This—thing—had caused us great grief. It had set traps for us, riddles, hurled occult monsters upon us, tortured us. Now it stood there, slashing a sword about, mewling, fiery-eyed, and helpless in the grip of those awesome powers of a Wizard of Loh.

"Let me shaft it and have done," said Nath.

"Let me put a bullet between its eyes," said Barkindrar.

Hunch goggled.

Nodgen hefted his spear.

The two Pachak hyr-paktuns set themselves, as ever, ready for what might befall.

I said, "We came here of our own free will. We have taken treasure from this thing. Let us not slay it."

"No?" breathed Tyfar. He was shaking.

"It protected its honored dead," said Quienyin, "and the protection turned ugly, became a game, a game of death."

"I didn't come here of my own free will," said Hunch. "By Tryflor, I said as much at the time!"

"By the Resplendent Bridzilkelsh, nor me!" quoth Nodgen.

"Nor did I," I said. "But most of us did. We agreed to this thing's terms for its abominable game. We have exposed it. I think that wounds it sorely."

"Wound it!" said Nath the Shaft. His bow lifted, the arrow nocked. "I'll wound it past the Ice Floes of Sicce!"

"Together, Nath," said Barkindrar. His sling swung suggestively.

The thing that called itself Ungovich hissed at us.

"Should we kill it?" whispered Tyfar.

"Men kill things they do not understand. Do we understand this thing, this Moder-lord? Do we descry why it does what it does?"

"You have the right of it, Jak," said Quienyin. "Let us begone!"

Silently, we left the Wizard of the Moder hissing and slashing his sword about. We left that golden room. We were perfectly confident we would find the way out.

Ungovich, green and marbled with arrested decay, slobbered after us. He sobbed in the agony of his spirit. As we reached the crimson curtains of the doorway, Nodgen turned back and spoke.

"The next time we come here, old Wizard, we may not be so magnanimous!"

"Come back!" squeaked Hunch. "Come back here! You off your head?"

And so as we went out we laughed.

But I felt again that dark sense of dread that, one day, I would return... If not to this Moder then another of the many dark death traps of the Humped Land...

We found the stairway, we found the door, we opened it with an ordinary handle.

We stepped outside.

We stepped into the clean fresh air, and into the glorious streaming lights of the Suns of Scorpio...

The dark and ominous bulk of the Moder brooded at our backs.

By Zim-Zair! But it was good to be alive, and on Kregen!

A VICTORY FOR KREGEN

A Note on Dray Prescot

Dray Prescot is a man above middle height, with brown hair and level brown eyes, brooding and dominating, an enigmatic man, with enormously broad shoulders and superbly powerful physique. There is about him an abrasive honesty and indomitable courage. He moves like a savage hunting cat, quiet and deadly. Reared in the inhumanly harsh conditions of Nelson's navy, he has been transported by the Scorpion agencies of the Star Lords, the Everoinye, and of the Savanti nal Aphrasöe, the Swinging City, to the savage and exotic world of Kregen, under the twin Suns of Scorpio, four hundred light-years from Earth.

Here, in the unforgiving yet rewarding world of Kregen, struggling through disaster and triumph, Prescot has made his home. Called on to shoulder the burden of being the Emperor of Vallia and of freeing the islands from the cruel grip of invaders, he is determined, when the country is once more united and free, to hand all over to his son Drak. But the Star Lords have dispatched him on a mission for them in the southern continent of Havilfar, and Prescot and eight comrades have barely escaped with their lives from an underground labyrinth of horror. Now Prescot must battle his way home to resume his work for Vallia.

One

Tyfar Wields his Axe

The gray-beaked fellow flourishing his bronze decapitator fondly imagined my name was written on that wicked curved blade. His one desire in life was to keep my head as a precious souvenir. He even provided himself with a wicker basket swinging at his belt all ready for the trophy.

"Hai! Apim—now you die!"

The path down the side of the artificial mountain led here under overarching branches and the mossy-trunked trees stretched about us, ancient and gnarled, patched and puddled in the light of the suns.

As is my custom in a fight, I do not waste breath replying to taunts or battle chants, unless base cunning indicates the advantage of an even more coarse taunt in return, so I bent my head beneath the horizontal slash of the decapitator. The sword in my fist thrust once. The wicker basket, the bronze-studded armor, the leather boots, and the decapitator all fell away to the side, sloughing like too-wet dough, slid off the path and away down the slope between the trees.

The fellow was not alone. Other headhunters pressed on, yelling, screeching their taunts, seeking to take the heads of us nine—who sought merely to escape off the mountain with our lives.

By chance it happened I led the descent of the mound and so these decapitating warriors met me first. They were not apim like me but those hard, gritty diffs men call Nierdriks, with coarse-skinned, high-beaked, hooded-eyed faces like killer turtles, and compact muscular bodies equipped with only two arms and two legs and no tails. Their bronze blades glimmered molten in the smoky shafts of crimson fire from the red sun, and their hides sheened muddy emerald in the fire from the green sun. With shrill yells of hatred they leaped for me.

My comrades were yelling, hullabalooing to get on along the path and at the Nierdriks. The first two attackers were seen off with no great difficulty. The shifting light and shade beneath the trees and the rutty slope of the path made the action precarious.

My foot turned on a knobby tree root snaking like a swollen vein across the path.

I pitched headlong. My sword switched up instinctively and parried the flurry of blows. The ground came up—hard. The decapitators were held off easily enough; but I was on the ground and smelling the ages-old dust puffing up into my nostrils, feeling that damned tree root gouging into my back.

With a slash measurably faster and more intemperate than those that had gone before, I slashed the nearest fellow's ankles and then had to twist aside to avoid the thwunking great blow of his comrade's head cleaver. There was no real danger. In the next instant I would be up, on my feet, and that bloodthirsty head-and-body parter would go tumbling down the slope spraying blood.

There was no real danger—but, in the instant as I gathered myself, a shadow moved over me and two firm, muscular legs straddled me, and Tyfar was yelling and swinging his blade over my head.

"Hold, Jak! I'll cover you!"

He was remarkably lucky I hadn't chopped him. He stood over me, swinging and smiting, his shield well up, his axe a silver-stained blur in the dappled shadows.

This was a new and remarkable experience. The sensation intrigued me. Here was I sprawled on the ground in the middle of a fight, and this fine young prince Tyfar stood over me battling off our foemen!

Remarkable!

Also—highly amusing.

All the same, by Zair, comical though it was it could not be allowed to go on.

I wriggled away and degutted the Nierdrik who sought to sink his brand into Tyfar's unshielded side and then sprang up and clouted the next one over the head. His big turtle nose burst and sprayed purple fluids into the shadows.

"You are unharmed, Jak?"

"Aye. Aye, I'm unharmed—Prince." And then, because he was young and vehement and very much your proper prince of honor, I said—and with warmth, "My thanks."

More Nierdriks dropped from the trees upon us and for a space we had a merry set-to. In the confusing shadows, twinned in jade and crimson, we fought. Presently the headhunters drew off and gathered in a bunch a few paces below us on the path. Many bodies strewed the ground between, and they must have realized now that they had sought to slay and take the heads of a party unwilling to allow them that liberty.

Abruptly, one of the turtle-faces spun about, silently, and collapsed.

Barkindrar the Bullet said, "They are real, then." He took out another leaden slingshot and began to fuss with his sling.

Tyfar said, "Yes. It was in my mind they were mere phantoms."

"Not phantoms," said Deb-Lu-Quienyin. "I would have known."

He would, too, not a doubt of it. The kharrna, the powers, of a Wizard of Loh would certainly have told Quienyin if we faced hallucinatory projections. He had taken no part in the combat, as was right and proper, and with a typical little hitch to his turban, setting it straight, he was visibly becoming a proper Wizard of Loh, respected and dreaded.

An arrow winged like a sliver of wrath and skewered a Nierdrik through that turtle neck.

"And," quoth Nath the Shaft, "I'll have that one back when we go past."

"You didn't see where my bullet went, Nath?"

"I did not. If you must sling lead then you must expect to lose it. If you must be a slinger then you must—"

"I'll knock the next three over before you clear your quiver, you great fambly!"

Well, that was normal. Nath the Shaft and Barkindrar the Bullet arguing over their respective skills, and wagering any and everything on the outcome of their shots, provided a never-failing source of joy and amusement to us through the horrors we had endured. The Nierdriks clustered in a rocky clearing among the trees, a dozen yards or so below us, and the radiance of the Suns of Scorpio fell about them. They provided capital targets.

Another leaden shot and another feathered shaft flew.

"Ha! Your man is only winged!"

"He'll never fly again, for sure!"

These two, archer and slinger, prepared to cast again. They were Prince Tyfar's retainers, the only two he had left to him from his father's expedition. But, for all the fun and frolic, we had to get down off this artificial mountain before nightfall, and that was not too far off...

An abrupt shriek rent the air.

Two shrieks shattered past us as the Pachak twins bounded down the trail. Ordered, methodical, intensely loyal, Pachaks, but when they loose their yellow hair and turn berserk, then it is prudent for any man to guard himself. Screaming war cries, the twins hurtled down the path. Their weapons glittered. Like maniacal savages of a primitive time before the dawn of civilization, they burst in among the astounded head-hunters.

Barkindrar and Nath held their shots, and only just in time.

"We are with you!" shouted Tyfar. He started in running down the trail after the two Pachaks, whose right arms were going in and out twinkling with fighting fervor. The Pachaks' two left arms apiece held their shields slanted expertly, and their tail hands swept razor-sharp steel in lethal slashes. The Nierdriks fell back, gabbling, some already turning to run.

So I lumbered down and saw off a man or two and, lo!, the path was clear.

"Well done!" panted Tyfar. "By Krun! That was a sight!"

The two Pachak brothers, Logu Fre-Da and Modo Fre-Da, bent to clean their weapons with methodical care on the scraps of cloth twisted around the corpses. Often it took a considerable time for a Pachak to regain normalcy from that fierce fighting frenzy; but I, like many men, considered that this berserk image of the Pachaks was carefully fostered, designed to impress and intimidate. It formed a part of their life-style only when they chose. All the same, there was no doubt that, often and often, something in that skirling onslaught got into their blood.

The Wizard of Loh, Deb-Lu Quienyin, was looking pleased. So was I. We had arranged with the two Pachaks to look out for the old wizard, and although they had not yet entered his employ and given their nikobi, which code of loyal service would have bound them, they were actively aware of their responsibility.

There were nine of us, nine adventurers seeking to escape from this artificial mound, this Moder which contained treasure and horror, and now I turned to look at my two rascals who came walking down toward us.

Nodgen, the tough Brokelsh, carried a bloodstained spear.

Hunch, the Tryfant, poked apprehensively at one of the Nierdriks, who flopped over, his arms limp.

"Are they all—?" began Hunch.

"You great fambly!" roared Nodgen, in his coarse Brokelsh way.

I did not smile. I was aware of the decline of the suns, and the lengthening jade- and ruby-tinged shadows beneath the trees.

"Let us get on."

Yes, there were nine of us, and we wended down the side of the Moder and we kept a very sharp eye out for more unpleasantness.

We had chosen to descend by a path different from the one up which the expedition had toiled to the summit, and now as we went down, the sweet scent of twining plants filled our nostrils, and the tinkling sounds of hidden brooks made a mockery of the horror contained within the Moder. Hunch kept on casting glances back up the path. Well, that was fine. That meant we had our backs covered.

To look at us as we came to the base of the descent and surveyed the belt of thorny scrub ahead would no doubt have occasioned either amusement or disdain in any splendid court of Kregen. We had outfitted ourselves with fresh clothes; but now these were ripped and torn and stained. But our weapons were sharp. I noticed with interest that Quienyin continued to carry his shortsword strapped to his waist. Perhaps his powers had not fully returned? He had lost his powers as a famed and feared Wizard of Loh, and within the lowest depths of the Moder he had regained them. But—perhaps he had not satisfied himself? It seemed to me he was not prepared to put full trust in himself or his powers just yet. That made sense, given the harsh and terrible nature of much of Kregen.

The sense of power being exercised wantonly, the crushing feeling of oppression, and the expectation of impending doom we had lived with during our time in the Moder did not magically lift the moment we stepped off the mountain. Naïve to expect it would. The Wizard of the Moder might have been tamed; now we had to face the terrors of the Humped Land, the sere and unforgiving land clustered and clumped with the artificial mounds, each containing fortune and horror.

The land ahead of us and barring our escape would test us all.

"You two," said Prince Tyfar with that habitual note of command tempered by the feelings of comradeship, "scout the entrance where we came in. It is just possible a few beasts have been left us."

"Quidang, Prince!" said Barkindrar and Nath, and they took themselves off, moving very circumspectly among the foliage.

The members of the main expedition, from whom we had been parted in the depths of the Moder, would have been long since gone. They would be spurring back to civilization bearing the loot. I looked at Tyfar and he saw my quizzical glance.

"I know, Jak, I know. But we must try."

"Yes."

"Let me bustle around and make a fire while those two are gone," said Hunch, the Tryfant. "I am famished—"

"Very well. Do I need to caution you over the fire?"

"No, no, Jak—I mean, notor—no need." And Hunch shivered and looked across at the trees where there were more shadows than the last of the suns shine.

He had taken a sack stuffed with goodies from the abode of the wizard, after we had humbled that proud and cruel man—if the thing had been a man at all—and when the fire was going well within the little dell beneath a bank we had picked, Hunch shook out his sack.

We all stood back. The stench offended.

"By Tryflor!" yelped Hunch. "The damned Moder lord—"

"The rast has tricked us!"

"The food—putrid!"

"Well," I said over the hubbub. "Maybe it is just as well. That cramph of a Moder lord might have magicked the vittles in our insides. I do not care to contemplate that, by Krun!"

"You have the right of it, Jak," observed Tyfar. "But we are hungry."

"The Humped Land will not be so sere that we cannot find aught to eat."

Tyfar made a face. He was a prince—admittedly, a prince of Hamal, which great empire was locked in deadly combat with my own land of Vallia—and the idea of chasing rodents and other lowly creatures for food did not appeal to him. Then he smiled.

"When you come to the fluttrell's vane, Jak, one must do what one must. I shall not care for it, no, by Krun. But I will eat a green lizard when my guts rumble!"

"Nodgen," I said, "do you go and see what fruits there are on those bushes."

"Aye, Jak—notor—that will be something."

These two, Hunch the Tryfant and Nodgen the Brokelsh, had been slave with me, and my trick of freeing them and giving them manumission before witnesses still had not quite overcome the old freedom of speech. It mattered nothing to me. But I fancied our deception had to pass muster, at least in the eyes of Tyfar. He was a man with high ideals, studious and yet quick with his axe; but he had been brought up in a culture in which slavery was a mere part of life. I wondered if he would ever be brought to understand what we were trying to do in Vallia, and if he shared the blind hatred of that island empire of his fellows. He thought I came from Djanduin. Well, I do, in a very real sense—but if he discovered I was a Vallian...

I brushed these tiresome thoughts away. We had to survive to cross the Humped Land. I had not forgotten the fearsome swarth riders, who infested the land between the Moders; but I forbore to mention them at that moment, for fear of what would happen to the water pot Hunch was carrying across to the fire.

We set watches and the suns sank and Barkindrar and Nath returned. They reported the compound was empty of life, not a riding animal to be seen. But they did bring a few crusts of bread and a packet of palines wrapped in leaves somewhat shriveled.

"Whoever dropped this and cursed for his loss did us a good turn, by Belzid's belly," quoth Barkindrar.

By this I understood that he and Nodgen, Brokelsh both, were compatible.

"You did not believe the Wizard of the Moder had let us get away with his food, then?" said Quienyin. He was clearly interested in Barkindrar's reasoning.

The slinger looked down, despite all his bluff toughness, discomfited by this direct interest in him by the Wizard of Loh.

"It was in my mind, San. We got away easy, like."

"We put the damned Moder Lord down," said Tyfar. "I still wonder if we did the right thing not to kill him. I see it was right and a kind of a small Jikai; but, all the same... He has played a scurvy trick on us."

"It was right not to slay him, Prince." I spoke briskly. "Now, if you agree, we will eat up this princely meal, stand our watches, and when the Twins rise we will set off."

They all gaped.

"But—Jak—"

"I do not think you will enjoy travel in the heat of the suns. And if we are to find ourselves mounts, we must look to the future. Or do you wish to remain a heap of moldering bones here?"

There was no answer on Kregen under Antares to that.

508

After our exertions and despite our hunger and the conditions in which we found ourselves, we found sleep. The watches changed, and no one felt inclined for conversation. Our thoughts, I feel sure, dwelt on the confrontations of the morrow when we could expect to be visited by the swarth riders. They had shepherded the expedition to this particular Moder out of all the hundreds dotting the Humped Land. They were mysterious, enigmatic; but they were some kind of men and therefore amendable to the argument of steel.

But, for all that, they possessed the only riding animals that we could expect to lay hands on around this desolate place.

With the rising of the Twins, the two second moons of Kregen eternally orbiting each other, we rose also and gathered our weapons and set off marching across the Humped Land.

Under the moon glitter, the dark and ominous shapes of the Moders rose from the plain about us. They stretched for mile after mile, set in patterns, and at random, some relatively small, others encompassing many miles of subterranean passages.

"D'you fancy going down another one to see what we can lay hands on, Hunch?" I overheard Nodgen speaking thus, and half-turned. Hunch spluttered a passionate protest.

"What! Has your ib decayed, Nodgen! Go down there again!"

"It was a thought," said Nodgen, and he laughed in his coarse, bristly, Brokelsh way.

The Pachak twins marched in silence, and their eyes remained alert and they scanned every inch of the way.

The slinger and the archer marched one each side of their lord, Prince Tyfar. He strode on, head up, breathing deeply and easily. Yes, I had seen much of goodness in this young man during those periods of horror; now, with our way ahead at least for the moment clear, I hauled alongside him and we fell into a conversation about—of all things—the state of theater in Ruathytu, the capital of Hamal.

"A few houses play the old pieces," he said. He sounded aggrieved. "But by far the majority play these new nonsenses, all decadence and thumping and sensation. It is the war, I suppose."

"Yes. Fighting men—"

"But, surely, Jak, a fighting man needs the sustenance of the inner spirit? Needs to have himself revitalized?"

"You mean, when he isn't trying to stop his head coming off?"

Tyfar breathed in. He eyed me meanly. "You mock me, Jak."

"Not so. I agree with you. But you are a prince—"

"I am! But—what has that to do with it?"

"Just that you have had the advantages and privileges of an education that was not primarily aimed at earning a living."

I probed deliberately here. I had opened a gambit—in Jikaida I would have been opening the files for the Deldars to link ready for the zeunting—and he was aware that I meant more than I said.

"You know no man may inherit his father's estates and titles as easily as he climbs into bed, Jak. You know that, one day, when—and I pray to all the gods it is a long and distant day—my father dies I shall be called on to fight for what is mine. You know that. The law upholds. But a man must uphold himself as well as the law. I have been trained as a fighting man, and much I detested it at the time."

I had heard how he had always been running off to the libraries as a young lad, and how he had taken up the axe as a kind of reproach to those who taught him.

The conversation at my nudging came around to his axe and he repeated what the slaves had said. He preferred the knowledge that came from books; but he had become an accomplished axeman as though to proclaim his independence from that emblem of many things, the sword. I thought I understood.

There was in this young prince an inner fire I found engaging. His diffident manner, so noticeable when in the company of his father, had all fallen away under the tutelage of the horrors of the Moder. He gave his orders with a snap; yet one was fully alive to his own estimation of himself and what he was doing, as though he saw himself acting a part on a stage of his imagination.

Our conversation wended along most comfortably, and Quienyin joined us to debate again what we had discovered and our chances of the morrow. Our voices were low-toned. And we all kept a sharp lookout.

"We must seek to move from one point of vantage to another," I said. "If we get our backs against good cover we can deal with the swarth folk. Once one of them is dismounted we will see what his mettle is on his own two feet."

"Yes," nodded Quienyin. "I fancied they did have only two legs apiece. Although, of course, you cannot be sure."

"Quite."

"I couldn't make out what kind of diff they were," said Tyfar. "There was something of the Chulik about them—"

"No tusks, though," said Quienyin.

"No tusks. But something about the jut of the head."

"We shall find out when the suns are up," I said, and that tended to end the conversation for a space.

The Moders rose from the rubbly plain something like a dwabur apart. Walking those five miles gave us an itchy feeling up the spine, traipsing as we were across relatively open ground. The trouble was, that open ground was probably safer than the areas in the immediate vicinity of the artificial mountains, the Moders, the tombs of the ancient dead and their treasurers and magics.

The rosy shadows of the next Moder enfolded us, and Hunch, for one, let go with a sigh of relief.

"Still!"

Modo's piercing voice reached us, thrown so as to tell us the position and not to reach to the danger he had spotted ahead. We stopped stock-still. A few scrubby thorn bushes threw splotchy shadows from the Twins. In this dappled shade we stood and watched the file of Nierdriks pad past.

They looked like ghostly silhouettes, animated dark dolls against the radiance of the moons. Silently they padded past, one after the other. They were walking. I, for one, was content to let them go. Had they been riding, now, straddling any of the magnificent assortment of Kregan riding animals—why, then, I do not think my companions would have let them go...

When the last had gone, vanishing into the shadows of the Moder, we resumed our progress.

And we kept even more alert, staring about even more vigilantly.

Quienyin kept up with us, struggling along without a murmur.

"Prince," I whispered quietly so that the Wizard of Loh would not overhear. "I think we must rest for a moment or two—"

"Rest, Jak? I thought the plan was to march as far as we might in the light of the moons and rest in the heat of the suns."

He saw my gaze fixed on Quienyin, who had not turned to stare back at us but was doggedly ploughing on over the rubbly surface.

"Ah—yes, of course. It is thoughtless of me."

Tyfar hurried ahead and checked the Pachaks in the vanguard.

We all rested, although of us all only Quienyin needed the break.

Again I pondered on Prince Tyfar. Many a haughty prince would simply have gone on, ignoring anyone else's discomfort. That Quienyin was a Wizard of Loh was now known to my companions; but that had not caused Tyfar to call a brief halt.

We discussed the fate of our dead fellows of the expedition, and we expressed ourselves as confident that the survivors had escaped. We had seen them emerging into the sunshine before we had been trapped within the Moder, and Tyfar, it was clear, could not countenance any thoughts that his father and sister had not escaped to safety.

"And, Jak, do not forget. Lobur the Dagger was there and he is mighty tender of my sister Thefi."

"As is Kov Thrangulf."

"Oh, yes, Kov Thrangulf."

That pretty little triangle had its explosion due, all in Zair's good time.

When we set off again Quienyin unprotestingly marched stoutly with us. Dawn was not far off. The sweet smell of the air, only faintly tinged with dust, the host of fat stars, the glistering glide of the moons, all held that special pre-dawn hollowness, that waiting silence for the new day.

I began to spy the land with more stringency, seeking a strong place where we might rest. What I needed was precise and as we dipped down into a little groove or runnel in the ground, with thorn-ivy crowned ridges each side, I felt we had come as near as I could hope for. This was not perfect; it was as precise as we would find.

"Here, I think, Tyfar."

He stared about. I watched his face, wondering if he would suffer a character change now that we were out in the fresh air.

The thorn-ivy, vicious stuff that flays the unwary, clustered thickly on the two ridgeways bordering the runnel. This was the real spiny ivy of Kregen. The Kregish for ivy is hagli. If we kept low we would be out of sight of a rider approaching at right angles. We chose a kink in the runnel so we could arrange one avenue only to watch. The clumped bushes shone a lustrous green and the thorns prickled like an army of miniature spearmen.

"You think so, Jak?" Tyfar looked uncertain.

The three principals stood together. The other six would not offer their opinions until asked, although the two Pachaks had every right to speak up.

Presently, Tyfar called, "Barkindrar, Nath. We camp here."

I nodded to myself.

That was the way it ought to be done. Confidence. The two Pachaks said nothing; silently they got on with cutting thorn-ivy and fashioning a form of boma around the open angle of the kink in the runnel. Old campaigners, these two Pachak hyr-paktuns, capital fellows to have along with you in a chancy business.

"I am quite fond of bright-leaved hagli around the door," said Quienyin. "But this stuff is murderous."

We hauled the thorn-ivy around, using sticks and weapons and not touching the stuff, and so fashioned the boma. I spied the land in the first flush of light. Jumping out, I walked a way off, turned to check the look of our hide.

It looked innocent enough.

Going back along the runnel I felt a burst of confidence.

We could hole up there all day and never be spotted unless some damned rider fell on top of us.

If that was what was in Tyfar's mind, it most certainly was not in mine. Hunch was in no doubt.

"We can hole up here all day," he said to Nodgen. "We've water to last us and we can march on to the next stream tonight." He yawned. "I think I shall sleep all day."

"The dawn wind will blow our tracks away," said Nodgen. "But you'll stand your watch like the rest of us, you skulking Tryfant."

"At least I don't always need a shave—"

"Quiet, you two," I said.

They froze.

"All of you—still!"

As the light brightened with the rising of the red sun, Zim, and the green sun, Genodras, and the shadows fleeted across the sere land, specks drifted high against the radiance. We squinted our eyes. Yes—Flutsmen. They were flutsmen up there, sky flyers sweeping across the land on the lookout for prey. True mercenaries of the skies, the flutsmen serve for pay in various armies; but they mostly enjoy reiving on their own account. And no man is safe from them.

We remained perfectly still.

High and menacing, the wings of their flyers lifting and falling in rhythm, the flutsmen circled twice, rising and falling, and then lined out and headed north.

"May the leather of their clerketers rot so they fall off and break their evil necks," said Hunch. He shut his eyes tightly. "Have they gone?"

"They've gone, you fambly—you can stop shaking."

"The trouble is," said Hunch the Tryfant, opening his eyes and looking serious. "I couldn't run away then, and you know how it upsets me not to have a clear run."

There spoke your true Tryfant. But Hunch had proved a good comrade, despite his avowed intention of running off if the going got too tough.

We composed ourselves for the day. I positioned myself so that my head was just under the lowest prickly branch of a thorn-ivy bush, where I had to be careful. The view afforded lowered down—the dusty surface, ocher and dun, blowing a little with the dawn wind, and the prospects of the Moders, massive artificial mounds that gave the Humped Land its name of Moderdrin, spotting the landscape for as far as I could see. Slowly, the Suns of Scorpio crawled across the heavens. And we waited and sweated.

The first sign came, as so often, in a patch of lifting dust.

I narrowed my eyes against the glare. The dust plumed white streamers and grew closer. A body of men rode out there. Logu Fre-Da, who was on watch, called down gently, "Swarths."

We remained still. The dust neared.

Dark shapes, fragmentary, appearing and disappearing, thickened beneath the dust. We waited.

"How many, Logu?"

An appreciable pause ensued before he replied.

"At least a dozen, notor—perhaps as many as twenty."

"They will ride nearer."

"Yes."

Perhaps twenty—twenty of those hard dark riders who had hounded our caravan toward one particular Moder. Their swarths, agile, scaled risslacas with wedged-shaped heads, fanged, terrible, would carry them in a thumping rash if they spotted us. They would have no mercy, seeing we were not an expedition but merely victims for their sport—or so it was easy to believe.

For very many of the mysterious races of Kregen that is just how it is, no matter that there are many splendid races on Kregen who regard that kind of bestial behavior with abhorrence. There was no mistake with this little lot. If they spotted us they'd seek to have sport with us before they slew us.

"Not a squeak out of you," said Prince Tyfar. "Or you'll be down among the Ice Floes of Sicce before you've finished yammering."

Not one of these men crouching with noses in the dust would make so much as a bleat. Now we could hear the soft shurr and stomp of the swarths. From their angle of approach they were making for the nearest Moder. They would pass within three hundred paces of our little thorn boma. They'd never see us. Not from where they would pass, avoiding the line of thorn-ivy. All we had to do was remain perfectly still and silent and we'd be safe.

Gently, making no fuss over it, I stood up.

I climbed out past the edge of the thorn-ivy.

"Jak!" screeched Tyfar. I heard the others cursing.

I walked a few paces forward, toward the swarth riders. I lifted my arms high. I shouted.

"Hai! Rasts! Over here! You zigging bunch of cramphs—what are you waiting for?"

Two

Of the Testing of a Wizard of Loh

Hunch's agonized wail floated up at my back.

"He's mad! Oh, may the good Tryflor save me now!"

The ground felt hard and rocky underfoot. The air tasted sweet. The brightness of the day fell about me.

"Hai! Rasts of the dunghill! Why do you tarry?"

Sharp-edged, brittle, black against the radiance, the swarth riders crowded forward. They saw me, standing clear of the thorn boma. I stood alone. The runnel led directly toward me. The vicious heads of the swarths jerked around, dragged by reins in equally vicious fists.

White dust drifted away downwind. The smell of tiny violet flowers crowning spiky bushes, shyly hiding in crevices along the crumbly sides of the runnel, reached me. The suns shone, the wind blew, the flowers blossomed—and I, Dray Prescot, Lord of Strombor and Krozair of Zy, challenged this glorious world of Kregen to do what it could against me...

As Hunch the Tryfant had said, shocked, I must be mad. Well, he was not above four foot six tall, and a Tryfant, and so there were excuses for him. I took a step forward, seeking a secure purchase for my gripping toes, and I drew forth the Lohvian longbow.

The saddle dinosaurs were coated in that white dust, but as they moved and jostled the sheen of their purply-green scales glittered against the thorn-ivy. They began to move, urged on by the riders perched on their backs. All those long, thin lances descended from the vertical, slotting into the horizontal, and lethal steel point was aimed for my heart.

Four abreast—that was all the runnel would allow. There was some jostling and cavorting for positions. Each swarth-man was determined to be in the front rank of four, knowing that those following on would have only tattered rags and blood to take as an aiming point.

I banished my comrades from my mind.

Now the Lohvian longbow mattered—the great longbow was the only thing that mattered, that and the shafts fletched with the blue feathers of the king korf of Erthyrdrin. The longbow I had found in the crystal cave that provided what I lacked and its arrows fletched with the rose-red feathers of the zim korf of Valka had vanished with all the other phantasmal artifacts of the Moder. This longbow, these shafts, came from the Mausoleum of the Flame, and they were real.

The bow drew sweetly. The first shaft sped. The second was in the air, and the third was loosed before the first struck. The fourth followed instantly.

Four honed steel bodkins drove in to a cruel depth.

The shrieks and the bedlam, the racket of crashing swarths and hurtling riders, might sound sweetly, but there was no time to contemplate them. Two more shafts sped and then I was up and through the little gap in the thorn-ivy we had made dragging bushes down for the boma. Out on the lip of the runnel I could flank those harsh riders. More shafts arched.

The dust swirled. The uproar boiled. Now Nath the Shaft, using his composite bow, joined in. Barkindrar the Bullet swung and hurled.

The dust obscured much of the tangle.

We shot into the mess.

Three swarths cleared the obstacles to their front. They raged down the runnel, heads outstretched, scales glittering between the dust streaks. The lances reached forward. The riders, heads bent in metallic helmets, short cloaks flaring, bellowed down the slot.

One I took. One Nath took. One Barkindrar took.

Nodgen was up and leaping about, waving his spear.

"Leave some for me!"

The two Pachaks were running forward, their tail hands stiff above their heads, the daggered steel brilliant.

"They run!" yelled Tyfar, beside himself, running on with his axe poised.

Four swarths galloped madly away; and one carried a dead rider lolling from the saddle, one sped with empty saddle, and the other two were being urged on with whip and spur.

These two last were shot out by Tyfar's retainers. I had thrown down the Lohvian longbow which had served so well and, ripping out the thraxter, the straight cut and thrust sword of Havilfar, leaped headlong into the dust.

It was all a bedlam of heaving scaled bodies and wicked fangs and lashing blades. Some of the Chulik-like riders attempted to claw their weapons free. They could be given no chance to fight back, of course, and we set on them with a will. We had seen what they had accomplished, and we did not wish to suffer a like fate. The fight was quick and deadly. The thraxter slimed and lifted, struck and thrust, withdrew with more ominous streaks along the dulled blade.

Tyfar fought with a wild panache, his axe blurring in short lethal strokes. The two Pachaks fought as Pachaks fight. And Nodgen's thick spear thrust with all the power of his bristle body.

And—there was Hunch, his bill cunningly slanted, cutting the legs away from the riders who attempted to smite down on him. Yes, Tryfants will put in a wild, brave, skirling charge, magnificent in attack. It is the retreat, in the withdrawal, when doubts arise, that Tryfants rout so easily.

The suddenness of the attack, the ambush that had shot them into pieces, and then the headlong rush of fighting men undid these swarthmen. None escaped. Modo Fre-Da, curling his tail cunningly out of the way, leaped astride a swarth. He seized up the reins and jammed in his heels. The animal shot ahead. Furiously, the Pachak hyr-paktun galloped after the dead rider lolling in the saddle of his fleeing swarth.

We others gathered up the reins of the surviving animals, quieting them in the dust and turmoil, sorting them out and calming them. No one was bitten, which was a thankfulness.

The saddle dinosaurs were middling-quality mounts, with two among their number of superior breed. These two had the thickened scale plating over their eyes, which were fierce and arrogant, and their tails were triple-barbed. Once you know how to handle a swarth, he is a tractable enough mount. Mind you, I would take a zorca or a vove any day of the week.

"Did you see—"

And: "That fellow bit on the shaft!"

And: "He went over backward and his head—"

We looked at the corpses of the swarth riders.

"Muzzards," said Quienyin, walking up and standing, his head on one side to balance his turban before he pushed it straight. "Ugly customers. There are a lot of them down south in the Dawn Lands."

They did look a little like Chuliks, at that. They did not have the oily yellow skin or the upthrust tusks, but their build and thickness and stance—when they were alive—suggested the Chulik morphology to our eyes.

Their skins carried a leaden hue, which had not been caused by death, and they exuded a musky stink I, for one, found unpleasant. Modo returned with the dead warrior still lolling in the saddle, and so we nine stood, looking down on the dead. The living animals clustered farther along the runnel and began tentatively to rip off the thorn-ivy, munching it up quite oblivious of the thorns. Tough, your Kregan swarth—although their trick is simply to twist their fanged mouths around to get the thorns in sideways and then get their masticating dentures at the sharp spines.

This, as I saw it, was just another example of that peculiarly Kregan marriage of convenience between conflicting demands. The omnivorous animal comes equipped with two sets of implements. At the time I was still, despite my conversations with a Savapim, unsure if these Kregan eccentricities were part of natural evolution—either on Kregen or some other world—or if they were the result of artificial interference with nature's handiwork.

"Cut-price, unsophisticated Chuliks," said Logu Fre-Da, nodding to his brother. "These Muzzards."

"They bear harness and weapons, brother."

"Aye, brother."

The Pachaks were mercenaries. I, too, have been a paktun in my time. We were not long in stripping harness and weapons and collecting the loot in a pile. The bodies we left for the carrion-eaters of the Humped Land to dispose of, in nature's way. I know I did, and I am sure some of the others must have also, said a short prayer to Zair for the well-being of these lost souls in the Ice Floes of Sicce.

Then we crawled into the shade beyond the boma and contemplated the pile of harnesses and weapons.

"Which, Jak," said Tyfar, "reminds me you never did change your scarlet breechclout."

"Why, no," I said. "But we were rather—busy."

"Yes."

"I shall keep it, as I am sure there is nothing hygienic on these Muzzards. But I admit I am not averse to a stout coat of leather, studded with bronze. And a helmet, too, although—" and here I picked one up and turned it on my hand— "they are poor specimens, of iron bands and leather filling."

"They put the wind up me, I can tell you."

"Is that all they put up you, Hunch?" Nodgen guffawed. "Then you're lucky."

Because the two Pachaks were hyr-paktuns, wearing the golden pakzhan at their throats, I knew they would be able to handle the long lances from swarthback. I said to Hunch, "Can you manipulate a lance? Or would it be a waste for you?"

"A waste, notor," he said at once, without preamble. "I like a long-staved weapon; but these are ill-balanced, as I judge."

And, by Vox, he was right.

"Let me cut an arm's length off the end," said Nodgen. "Then I'll have a capital long-spear."

"Each man to his own needs," I said, and looked at Tyfar. "Prince?"

He smiled.

"I will stay true to my axe."

In the saddlebags we found comestibles of a hardtack kind, such as a warrior would carry. There was also wine in leather bottles. Tyfar and I exchanged glances.

"Water for now," I said. "I'll answer for Nodgen and Hunch."

"And I for Barkindrar and Nath."

Quienyin said, "The brothers Fre-Da will, I think, answer for themselves, as is right and proper."

The Pachaks lifted their tail hands in acknowledgment.

"When the suns are over the yard arm," I said, although in the Kregish it was not what I said at all. We lay back, munching hardtack, sipping water sparingly, and every now and then a white gleam in Hunch's face told of his roving eyeballs gazing fondly on the wine skins.

Truly, Moderdrin is an amazing and forbidding place. The mountains stud the plain with their humps, crowned by jumbles of towers and domes and walls, smothered in vegetation, with tumbling waterfalls and bosky avenues in which, as we knew, were to be found savage denizens.

But, those denizens were nowise as monstrous as the horrors within the artificial mountains.

We dozed and kept watch, and the water remained stoppered in the bottles. Prince Tyfar showed signs of wishing to protest, after the first sips had ceased to refresh him.

"Prince," I said, and I spoke evenly, "if you drink now you will simply sweat the precious liquid away, wasting it. Wait until the worst of the heat goes."

"But my mouth is afire—"

"Suck a pebble." I nodded at the Pachaks. The cheeks on each hardy Pachak face bulged.

He did as I bid; and he had the sense to see the sense in it. I felt he was a young man, prince or no, who grasped the uses of sense in a way that would be approved, at least, by men who thought as I did. For your full-bloodied, rambunctious hell-for-leather rampant princeling, Prince Tyfar was altogether too much of an intellectual—and a superb axeman, withal.

He had gone raging into the Muzzards. There was no dilly-dallying there. I fancied he was more of a proper prince than most of that ilk in Hamal.

Three times during that day we spotted flights of flutsmen, and we stayed close. The swarths were lying down and dozing against the heat, shivering their scaly tails every now and then. We were not observed by those sky reivers.

That night we drank sparingly, mounted up on nine of the animals, and led the remaining six bundled up with all we thought necessary to take. The ground scavengers had been at work on the corpses, but our presence had deterred the warvols from swooping down on rustling wings to join in the devouring. By morning there would be left only bones.

At my insistence, Tyfar and Quienyin rode the two superior swarths. Tyfar, I noticed, just took the best one without even thinking about it. Quienyin looked across at me, and it was then I insisted he take the beast.

So, mounted up, not quite as thirsty as we had been, we set off again across the Humped Land, the Land of the Fifth Note. The strong probability was that the Moder Lords organized these Muzzard swarth riders, and agreed among themselves which mound the arriving expeditions of gold-and magic-hungry adventurers should be directed into. Well, the wizards had their fun running poor crazed folk through their tombs, torturing them and extracting the last jot of enjoyment from their anguish. As for the magic items we had taken, they had been expended in our troubled ascent to the surface and escape. There would be no spells of paralysis, no more burning drops, no more tail-shrivelers for us now. Now we must rely on steel and muscle to see us through.

That night passed and toward dawn we ventured close to one of the mounds where we filled the bottles at a stream and set up, stalked, and slew our supper. Everyone cheered up.

"If it means steering out of here from Moder to Moder—"

"Aye, Jak!" said Tyfar. He beamed. "We will be back into the grasslands in no time. And then we will hear word of my father and sister, I am sure."

I looked at the Wizard of Loh, who sat by the fire munching a leg of one of the birds brought down by Barkindrar the Bullet.

Again we had chosen a strong place for our camp, beneath a rocky outcrop where the fire was shielded by cut branches of thorn-ivy. The swarths rested after their exertions of the night, and I fancied they were well content that their new masters rode them at night and rested them by day here.

"I feel sure you are right, Tyfar. We follow their tracks, I believe, although the wind wipes them out smartly enough."

"Once I am back in Hamal—once we are both there, Jak—you do not forget my invitation to a bladesman's night out in the Sacred Quarter?"

"I do not. I anticipate it with relish."

By Vox! Did I not!

What, I wondered, would he say if I said, quite casually, "Oh, and, Prince Tyfar of Hamal, by the way, I am Dray Prescot, Emperor of Vallia, the chief of your country's sworn enemies?"

That, I felt, would repay in the glory of his face much discomfort.

But, of course, he would not believe me.

How could he?

He would think I jested with him, and in damned poor taste, into the bargain.

He knew nothing of me, save what I had told him, and that was going to have to be altered, soon. He would ask what on Kregen the Emperor of Vallia, the great rast, was doing down here in the Dawn Lands of Havilfar. That was, by Vox, a good question. Tyfar knew nothing of the Star Lords and their engaging habit of putting me into situations of peril in order to affect the future course of the world.

Well, I had done the Star Lords' bidding here and was now free to return home to Vallia. I longed to get back, to see Delia again and my comrades and what of my family deigned to show up when their grizzly old graint of a father returned from one of his wild jaunts over the world. There was so much still to be done in Vallia it defied all common-sense evaluation. The island was split by war and factions; the people had called on me, had fetched me to be their emperor, and I was in duty bound to honor that trust and that demand. The island would be united and healed. Then I would hand it all over to my fine son Drak, and with a thankful sigh shake the reins of empire from my sticky hands.

And, make no mistake, this was what I intended to do.

All the same, Drak was in Vallia now, and I had many outstanding councilors and generals. I could leave the country to get on well enough without me for a space.

For—I had other fish to fry.

Down here in the Dawn Lands I was not too far away from Migladrin, from Herrelldrin, from Djanduin. Also, in the opposite direction lay Hyrklana. In all these lands I had business.

"Jak!"

I did not jump. I realized I had been sitting brooding on the Wizard of Loh.

"By the Seven Arcades, Jak! You were far gone in your thoughts—I did not pry," he added, quickly. I did not wish to understand just what he meant, although the gist was plain enough. I did not smile; but I was aware of an easing in the graven lines on my craggy old beakhead of a face.

"Yes, Quienyin, I was thinking. Prince Tyfar would like news of his family and friends, and I do not doubt the others of us nine would, also."

"And you?"

"Yes."

He nodded, half to himself.

"You miss Hyrklana, Jak?"

Before I could open my mouth—for thus suddenly had come up the change in the story of myself that Prince Tyfar of Hamal must know—the prince spoke.

"Hyrklana? That nest of pirates? What has that to do with you, Jak of Djanduin?"

I sighed. There, displayed before me, was the reckoning for the sin of lying about one's origins and playing at cloak and dagger for the fun of it. I had told Quienyin I hailed from Hyrklana, that large and independent island kingdom off the east coast of the continent of Havilfar, and I had told Tyfar I came from Djanduin, the remote, massive peninsula in the far south and west of the continent.

And, as you know, I had not lied in saying I was from Djanduin. I never forget I am King of Djanduin.

Usually, it is not particularly helpful in maintaining a good cloak and dagger cover to say you come from a country you know nothing of and have never visited.

Dressed up in a disguise and wearing a gray mask, I had successfully convinced Lobur the Dagger, one of Tyfar's father's retinue, that I was of Hamal. Other priorities had supervened in my description of my place of origin, and I felt it high time I sorted out the tangle.

Looking about as the suns smote down, shedding their streaming mingled lights, I sighed. How we practice to deceive and then come a cropper in the nets of our own weaving!

"Well, Jak?" Tyfar, your proper prince, was a trifle tart. "Are you from Djanduin? Or Hyrklana?"

"Would it make any difference, Tyfar?"

He waved a hand. "No. I think we have been through enough together by now—I think I know you—I thought I knew you. But Hyrklana. You know what they think of the Hamalese there."

"I do. I have visited Hyrklana and I have unfinished business there."

"But," interposed Quienyin. "You are not Hyrklanian?"

"No."

"So you are from Djanduin?"

I could have left it there. Djan knew, I was well enough cognizant of all Djanduin to claim it completely as my country. As long I had fought for that beautiful land against her enemies and won.

"I have land in Djanduin," I said. "I love the place—it is unspoiled so far."

521

"So you are a notor of Djanduin, as we believe?"

"Yes."

Tyfar was continuing to stare at me. "You know that because of the war waged by the Empress Thyllis, Hamal is not much cared for in many lands of Havilfar. This is simple knowledge. Perhaps you are from a land that has been invaded by Hamal. Perhaps, Jak my friend, you conceive yourself as an enemy to me?"

I had waited on his last words in some trepidation. But I was able to relax. He had said, "enemy to me." Had he said, "enemy to my country" my reply must, in all honor, have been different.

The trouble was, Tyfar was quite right. Mad Empress Thyllis had alienated just about every country within reach of her iron legions.

And, also, I had the feeling, substantiated only by intuition and a few scraps of idle converse, that Tyfar's father, Prince Nedfar, was both not happy with Thyllis and not in her good books. And I had suggested to Lobur the Dagger that I worked secretly for Empress Thyllis. I squared my shoulders.

"I cannot tell you, Tyfar, all that I would wish to tell you. Suffice it to say that I know the Sacred Quarter, I can walk it blindfolded, I have ruffled many a night away as a bladesman. I have wide estates in the country— well, not so much wide as passing fair and rich—and I work for the good of the country."

That was true.

He was surprised.

"You are Hamalese?"

I have estates in Hamal. I am called there Hamun ham Farthytu, the Amak of Paline Valley. But I was not Hamalese. If anything, I was Vallian, not being born on Kregen.

These things I could not tell Tyfar—or Quienyin.

"I work for the good of Hamal," I said. Again, I spoke the truth, even though, perhaps, Vallia would have to put down the worst excrescences of Hamal, chief of whom was the Empress Thyllis. "I deplore what the empire is doing to neutral countries—"

"So do I, by Krun!"

That declaration, by a prince whose father was second cousin to the empress, really was nailing his colors to the mast.

I managed a smile.

"Then we see eye to eye in that, Tyfar. Do not press me further. Only remember: what I do I do for the good of Hamal and for all of Paz. For the eventual good."

"And you will not confide in me?"

"Not will not."

He frowned and then banished the scowl and replaced it with a smile, uncertain, but a smile nonetheless. "I—see."

And Deb-Lu-Quienyin, that puissant Wizard of Loh, sat looking at me, and he had stopped gnawing on his bone.

"Hyrklana, Djanduin, or Hamal," he said briskly, waving the bone, "it does not matter, not to me. I have gone through so much with Notor Jak that if he came from some hellhole in Queltar—where no man should have to exist—by the Seven Arcades, he is a man and a friend—"

"Well said, San." Tyfar stood up. Now he did smile. "I see you are about secret business, Jak. Well and good. That is your affair and none of mine. You have given me your word that you work for Hamal. I, too, work for Hamal, as does my father. I trust we do not work in opposition."

I shook my head. "Now, now, Prince. You will not worm it out of me like that!"

He laughed. Some princes I knew would have called on their retainers to spit me there and then.

So, because I did not wish to drop into a maudlin scene, I took up the thought that had been in my mind when this scene began.

"We would all like to know that our families and friends are safe." I addressed myself to Quienyin directly. "You know what I talk about, San. It is nothing new. But we have no rights to your kharrna, no claims—"

"Come now, Jak—do not belittle what we nine mean one to the other!"

I nodded. "So be it. If you go into lupu you can tell us what is happening far off. I think Tyfar would more than welcome news that his father and sister are safely out of this desolate place."

We all sat, still and silent, looking at the Wizard of Loh.

He stared at me. I could guess what he was thinking. He had sustained a nasty accident and had lost his powers and now he had recovered them, or most of them, in the lowest zone of the Moder. He had explained that the Wizard of the Moder had no real conceptualization of what awful powers he had locked up in the lowest zone. An ordinary wizard, one Yagno, a sorcerer of the Cult of Almuensis, mightily puffed up with pomp and pride in his own prowess, had ventured down into the lowest zone and had never returned. This was not so much a useful gift to us in telling us what we wanted to know. This was much more the testing moment for Quienyin himself.

And he saw that very clearly.

How strange, thus to read the riddle of a Wizard of Loh!

They are rightly feared and respected; but they are mortal, human men, and many a mighty warlord and king has his own Wizard of Loh to serve him as he sees fit. My own Wizard of Loh—although it is foolish, really, to call any Wizard of Loh as a normal retainer—had been sent back to Loh. No man unless he has other powers will willingly cross a Wizard of Loh. They are rumored to be able to do terrible things. And, in Zair's truth, I have seen wondrous deeds. And, here we were, calmly realizing that a Wizard of Loh was on trial with himself.

What other proof could be required to show how our experiences had made of us nine a special band of brothers?

Speaking with all that old bumbling hesitancy completely banished, Quienyin said, "Very well."

Very carefully, he made his preparations.

Some Wizards of Loh I have known were able to go into lupu very quickly, with a minimum of fuss, and so send a spying eye out to reveal what transpired at a distance. Others go through a rigmarole of mental agility, physical activity, and magical mumbo jumbo to achieve the same result.

Deb-Lu-Quienyin was, as it were, starting from scratch. He was like a novice wizard, seeking to insert his mind along the planes of arcane knowledge. Very sensibly, he went back to basics and set about going into lupu with all the trappings that thaumaturgical art form required.

Equally, just as Tyfar's attitude to us had been tempered from princely choler by our mutual experiences and new-found comradeship, so Quienyin's wizardly contempt for ordinary mortals had been modified. We watched him in no sense of judgment whatsoever; rather we actively sympathized with him and wished him well and in however minor a way sought to partake of his struggle. But, when all is said and done, the ways of Wizards of Loh of Kregen are passing strange...

We could only sit and stare.

Deb-Lu-Quienyin composed himself. He sat cross-legged, his head thrown back, and his eyes covered by his hands. I noticed how the veins crawled on the backs of his hands; yet his hands were plump and full-fleshed. He remained perfectly still, silent and unmoving.

Respecting Quienyin's preliminary insertion of his kharrna into unspecified but occult dimensions, we also sat still.

Quienyin began to tremble.

His whole plump body shook. His shoulders moved. He brought his hands down slowly from his face. His eyeballs were rolled up, and the whites of his eyes glared out in a sightless blasphemy of a gargoyle head. Hunch choked back in his throat. We sat, enthralled, knowing how Quienyin battled himself as he sought to hurl his kharrna through realms unguessed of by ordinary men.

Breathing almost at a standstill, Quienyin appeared to gather himself, as a zorca gathers himself at an obstacle. With a wavering cry he rose slowly to his feet. His arms lifted, rising out from his sides, lifting to the horizontal. His fingers were stiffly outthrust. Gently at first, and then faster and faster, he revolved, whirling about, his arms razoring the air.

As always, my mind conjured the vivid impression of a whirling Dervish, a maniac cyclone, a hurricane-whirled scarecrow.

Abruptly, Quienyin ceased to whirl about so madly. He sank to the ground and resumed that calm pose of contemplation. Both his hands rested flat on the ground.

And then he looked up at us and was ready to answer our questions.

Rather, he was ready to speak to Prince Tyfar.

What the Wizard of Loh had to say reassured the young prince. Had it not done so, I own, I would have found the subsequent confusion inconvenient.

Yet, even as I relate these events, I am touched by the weirdness of it all. Here Quienyin sat, and he was aware of and could tell us of events transpiring dwaburs away across the land. Just how far a Wizard of Loh can see in lupu is a matter of serious conjecture. They, for sure, give nothing of their secrets away to the casual inquirer. True, in conversation with Quienyin I had learned much. But, then, that was before he had recovered his powers. I wondered, as he spoke to Tyfar, if he would recall with displeasure what he had said, and seek in some nefarious and occult way to rob me of the knowledge.

"Is it possible, San—?" began Modo Fre-Da.

"May we crave, San—?" began Logu Fre-Da.

Both spoke together.

So Quienyin told them what they wished to know. I listened, for I needed to learn of my comrades, bearing in mind what I half-purported toward them. They asked for their mother, for their father was long dead, having met his end gallantly on an unmarked battlefield. She lived in Dolardansmot, whereaway that was I did not know, and they were very tender toward her. They made inquiry about no other person.

Nodgen and Hunch, Barkindrar and Nath, all received news, good or bad—Barkindrar's younger brother had died of a fall down a disused well, which depressed him for a space, until he reflected, half aloud, that what the Resplendent Bridzilkelsh ordained must be accepted as one accepts the needle—and they all turned to look at me.

"Well, Jak," said Quienyin, kindly, although he looked tired, "and where in the world of Kregen shall I seek for your loved ones?"

Three

The Bonds of Comradeship

Before replying, I pulled off the boot taken from a dead Muzzard and chucked it down. The boot was not so much either too tight or too loose

525

as badly fitting; it was well enough for riding, but walking in it and its mate would be agonizing. I wriggled my bare toes. The eight pairs of eyes regarded me expectantly. I scratched under my anklebone.

"Well, Jak? And is there no one in the whole wide world?"

"Without disrespect, San—you are clearly tired. Your exertions have exhausted you." I pulled off the other boot and wriggled those bare toes in turn. "And, you are quite clearly possessed of very great powers indeed, for you have been able to give us news of our relations, people you have never met or seen. This, I know, is unusual—"

"Yes, Jak. Although I do not think I am fully recovered, I am able to do more in lupu than many Wizards of Loh."

Deb-Lu-Quienyin spoke simply. There was no boasting here. Also, in the comradeship forged between us nine in the horrors through which we had successfully fought, Quienyin's own history had been, at least partially, revealed.

"Come on, Jak," spoke up Tyfar. "If San Quienyin is willing, then surely you must long to know."

Interesting how, when the Wizard of Loh displayed his supernatural abilities, we'd all resumed calling him San.

"Or is it that you do not have any blood relatives still alive?"

Again I scratched my foot.

"There is a man whose whereabouts I would like to establish. If I know him aright he will be tossing people about like split logs. He is a Khamster, A Khamorro, a high Kham. No doubt he will be in Herrelldrin now."

"And he cannot then be any kin to you."

"No. A good comrade. As we are down—"

And then I hauled myself up, all canvas flapping. By Krun! I'd been about to say, "down here in Havilfar," which was a perfectly logical thought to a Vallian, or anyone from the northern hemisphere of Kregen. But if I claimed Hamal, which was the most powerful empire in Havilfar, the southern continent, I'd hardly talk about being "down here." So I scratched my foot again and reached over for a small piece of meat clinging to a leaf platter, and said, "down not too far it will be convenient for me to go to Herrelldrin and seek him out. If he is there. If you can scan him, San."

"No blood relation?"

"No."

He sat quite still for a moment, looking on me. He had put his ridiculous turban aside after the last items of news had been passed on in lupu, and his red Lohvian hair stuck out like the feathers of the rooster with the wind up his tail. His old face had lost many of the lines and wrinkles, and had filled out, and his clear and piercing eyes looked astonishingly young. And I felt he was looking at me as though I were a glass of crystal-clear water.

Sink me! I burst out to myself. I had too much at stake in Kregen to allow a tithe of my secrets to be spilled here, even despite the special comradeship we nine felt.

"No blood relation, this fearsome Khamorro. I suggest you sleep now, Quienyin, and then we can talk on this matter later."

"You are very desirous of finding this man?"

"Yes."

"Then I will sleep for a space. Wake me at the hour of mid, when the suns burn in the zenith. I may be able... Well, no matter, Jak the Sturr. I bid you a pleasant repose."

And with that Deb-Lu-Quienyin rolled over onto his side on the spread cloths and seemed immediately to fall into a deep slumber. I chewed my morsel of meat and gazed at the Wizard of Loh. I did not mind if he read some of my riddles. And the six retainers, also, were men amenable to reason of one kind or another. But Prince Tyfar, this brave, bright, bonny princeling of Hamal, my country's bitter enemy? What would he say, what do? No. I must continue with my deceptions. And, by Krun, they were not petty deceptions, either!

Tyfar shook his head, smiling.

"I am mightily glad my father and sister are safe. I thank Havil the Green for that. The news for you will be as good, Jak—and did you notice the sudden formality of Deb-Lu-Quienyin? He called you Jak the Sturr, which you claim is your name."

"And, Tyfar, I notice you do not give a warm thanks to Havil the Green. Mayhap, Krun of the Steel Blade merits a greater gratitude?"

We trod thin ice here.

He eyed me.

"Aye, Jak the Sturr. Aye."

"So be it."

Havil the Green presided as the chief god of many lands of Havilfar. He had, in the past, represented to me all that was evil and to be destroyed. I was over those impulses now, and could even come out with a good rolling Hamalian prayer or two addressed to Havil the Green. All the same, fighting men tend toward Krun... as must be clear from the conversations peppered with his name.

"And also, Jak, the Sturr—I do not think your name can be Sturr. It does not fit."

I lifted an eyebrow. Sturr is the slang name given to a louche fellow, a morose, silent, boorish kind of chap who is all left feet and ten thumbs. "No? I thought it suited me."

"The Lady Ariane nal Amklana dubbed you Jak the Unsturr."

"She—let us not talk of her."

"Willingly."

The Lady Ariane nal Amklana, of Hyrklana, had not turned out quite as we'd expected during our recent adventures. I had thought Tyfar was inclined to become romantically attached to her. Now I knew he was not. He deserved a far finer mate than Ariane.

"Let us take up the question of your name, Jak."

"Before that, I will just say that one should not be too hard on Ariane. She was sore pressed. By Krun! But she does have fire—"

"A fire that is inwardly directed only."

"Let us talk of our plans to get out of here—"

"The Sturr—or the Unsturr?"

I just looked at him. We sat in the grateful shadow and the watch was set and the others were lying back and no doubt reviewing what Quienyin had told them and, an ob would bring a talen, wishing they were out of Moderdrin and safely back with their loved ones. Although—well, there were arguments about that, also...

Once a young man sets his feet on the mercenaries' path and seeks to become a paktun and then a hyr-paktun, he must banish foolish longings for home. He will return in the fullness of time, bearing his scars and the choicest items of his loot—if he is lucky—and take a wife and settle down and raise more fine young men to go off adventuring across Kregen. But daydreaming of home is weakening. Thanks to Opaz—men are weakened every day doing that!

"Should, Jak, I call you—" said Tyfar. He was half-laughing. "Should I dub you Muzzardjid?"*

"I think not."

"It is a fairly won name."

"Maybe. Not for me."

"I just do not like Sturr. I am a prince and empowered to confer names upon the worthy. You are—although you have not said—I guess, of a middling rank of nobility?"

The name of Hamun ham Farthytu had been conferred upon me in all honor; it was not just another alias. And the rank of Amak is at the bottom end of the higher nobility; there is the wide range of the lesser nobility, of course. But caution held me. Even in this, the old harum-scarum, riproaring Dray Prescot who would go raging into a fight without an ounce of sense in his head, would have held back. The Amak of Paline Valley was an identity, a real identity, that I did not wish to reveal as yet.

So, leaning back on an elbow, I said, "It is of no matter, Tyfar. What concerns me is the slow progress we make."

He looked as though he was going to carry on with his thought; but he must have changed his mind, for he contented himself with, "Very well, Jak. But as soon as the time is ripe I shall dub you with a name more fitting. So you have been warned." He wiped his lips with a cloth and closed his eyes

---

* jid: bane.

in the heat. "As to our making better progress, I think it still too risky to travel in daylight. But, if we must—"

"Think of Quienyin."

"I am."

"Given an opportunity, we can change our mode of travel. But it will be chancy—"

So we talked, low-voiced, and then ceased this prattling and sought the deeper shade and tried to sleep. We had ample water, thanks to the stream from the Moder, and our swarths were cared for. We had food, meat, and fruits. But we all felt the screaming need to get out of this damned place.

Promptly on the hour of mid Quienyin woke up and, reaching for his turban, looked around our little camp. He saw me. He opened his mouth and I spoke quickly, quietly.

"Tyfar is asleep. I would prefer not to awaken him."

He nodded and then caught his turban and slapped it down, hard. The blue cloth was dusty and cracked, and many of the fake pearls and brilliants had been lost. But it still gave him that aura of omniscience so necessary for the credulous folk.

"Do you wish...?"

"When the suns are gone down a little more."

"We will see what a Wizard of Loh can do, then."

"Remember, Quienyin, I do not ask this of you, do not beg or plead. I know nothing of the cost to you; but, I—"

"There is no need to go on. Of course I shall do all I can. Are not we all comrades?"

This was, truly, a most strange way for a feared Wizard of Loh to talk. But, by the insufferable aroma of Makki Grodno's left armpit—he was right.

"You have never been to Loh, Jak?"

"I paid a fleeing visit to Erthyrdrin, and—"

"Well, they are a strange, fey lot up there, and hardly call themselves Loh-vians at all."

"That is sooth. You have traveled widely?"

"Mainly in this continent of Havilfar. I, I must confess, regard travel as a means of arriving somewhere."

"As we did in that caravan across the Desolate Wastes?"

"Grim though it was, the time had its pleasant moments."

"You have been to Hamal?"

"I shall not return to that empire." His gaze twitched to the sleeping form of Tyfar, and then away. I would have to ask Deb-Lu-Quienyin what had chanced in Hamal. I felt he did not care for the place. "I did make a quick trip to Pandahem; but that was not successful."

"And Vallia?"

He glanced up at me.

Was there a special note in my voice, a tremor, an inflection, as I spoke the name of the country of which I was emperor? Did he truly see so much more than ordinary mortals?

"Vallia? No, Jak. I have never been there."

I took a breath. Tyfar slumbered. The others were either asleep, dreaming, or standing watch. I summoned my courage.

"I think, Quienyin, if you visited Vallia you would be received with proper respect. You would like it there."

"Oh? You speak with—authority—of the empire at war with the empire of Hamal."

"You remember I asked you about the Wizard of Loh called Phu-Si-Yantong?"

"I do. San Yantong is a most puissant adept—I was sorry to have missed him."

I jumped, startled. "You mean—he was there—in Jikaida City?"

"I thought so. I am not sure. His kharrna is very powerful, superb, superb. I did not press too hard."

I swallowed down. By Vox! That devil Phu-Si-Yantong, so near! Yet—could he have been and not struck a blow at me?

"When I asked you of Yantong before you said he was marked for great things. You expressed the hope that he would prosper. You also said nothing about his little difficulty." I know my old beakhead of a face had grown grim and like a leem's mask as I spoke, and I could do nothing about that. One cannot always hide emotions behind a placid countenance. I went on and the words ground out like vosk skulls being crushed in the grinders. "Do you still harbor good wishes toward Yantong? Have you learned nothing of him since we spoke?"

He was abruptly intense, concentrated. He looked at me and those lines that had been vanishing on his face deepened and grooved. The force of his power shocked out.

"You speak in a way that could offend a Wizard of Loh, Jak. I will not be offended. But it is necessary that you explain yourself."

Given the awesome powers of the Wizards of Loh, given their aloofness from the petty concerns of normal men, given that they regard others as, if not inferior beings, then beings without the same necessities of the inner life—what Deb-Lu-Quienyin said to me was perfectly rational.

Any man of Kregen would tremble if a Wizard of Loh spoke to him thus.

"By Hlo-Hli! Jak! Speak!"

"If you seek—"

"No ifs, Jak, by the Seven Arcades!"

"Seek the truth of Yantong. I promise to speak then. Although—" and I glowered down on my comrade, Deb-Lu-Quienyin "—although, my friend, my words will then be unnecessary."

"You speak now in riddles." He breathed in and then out, deliberately. This was an exercise in self-control. I waited.

Presently he said, "I will do as you suggest—and only because of our comradeship, which is something precious to me because it is something I could never fully experience as a Wizard of Loh. This is a matter I do not expect you to understand."

"I do understand something, probably more than you realize. I have had dealings with Wizards of Loh before."

"Then let me go off a ways and try my newfound kharrna."

The shadows lay very short now, mere blobs of reddish and greenish discoloration under the thorn-ivy. Everything possessed two shadows. Quienyin and his two shadows went off to crouch down by the rock face. He took up a position which, although I had no idea of its significance, I recognized to be a position of ritual. He looked exceedingly uncomfortable, too.

Four times during the course of the day skeins of flutsmen had sailed over us, high and distant, mere forbidding specks, potent with disaster. They worried me. I looked up now as Quienyin sat so uncomfortably, and up there another wedge of flutsmen winged over. Slotted like nits in a ponsho fleece as we were down here, we were not likely to be espied easily. But the worry remained. The flutsmen were active and I wondered what caused that. Something, of a surety, had stirred them up.

Common sense indicated that I should try to catch some sleep. I did doze off for a few burs. I was awakened by Nath and Barkindrar coming off watch and the two Pachaks going on. I decided not to raise a ruckus over their waking me up; I know I sleep lightly, ready to leap up almost, it seems, before the danger that stalks me would leap for my throat. It is an old sailorman's trick.

The Shaft and the Bullet were not too sleepy, and were carrying on with great vehemence the argument that had absorbed them during their watch.

"Jikaida! Now you can take your Jikaida and—"

"Now, Barkindrar! What you say against Jikaida can be said against Vajikry. Do not forget that!"

They wrangled on about the merits or otherwise of Jikaida, which is the preeminent board game of Kregen, and of Vajikry, which is of not quite so universal acceptance but which is, as I know to my sore cost, highly baffling and irritating and calculated to arouse the itch in any man or woman. Vajikry takes a special kind of twisted logic, I suppose, to make a good player.

So, with that as a starter, I found myself running an old Jikaida game through my head, move and countermove, and so I closed my eyes and, lo! I was being shaken awake and the shadows were measurably longer. Thus does abused nature force her just demands on the physique.

531

The hand shaking me, the footstep, the low voice, were all devoid of menace.

I sat up.

"Time to go on watch, Jak—notor."

I looked at Hunch.

He licked his lips. "You said—you said you would stand a watch, Jak."

"Aye. I did and I will. And I could wish you and Nodgen did not have to keep up with this notor nonsense."

Nodgen said, "We have talked about this, Jak. We were all three slave together. You escaped. You have made something of yourself and have manumitted us before Prince Tyfar. But we think you are truly a notor, a great lord."

"That's as may be. But your freedom is very real to you, because the word of Tyfar, Prince of Hamal, is worth much."

"Oh, yes, we will take the bronze tablets. But we still believe you to be a great lord, and therefore we do not mind calling you notor. Only," and here Hunch screwed his Tryfant face up, "only, sometimes, Jak, it is hard to remember."

"By the disgusting diseased tripes of Makki Grodno! I do not care. But you will have the outrage of an offended princeling if you forget in his hearing."

"Aye, that we will." They both sounded marvelously little alarmed. This special sense of comradeship developed between us, and the terror of the Moder worked on us all, paktun, retainer, escaped slave, wizard, and prince.

And, as though to underline those thoughts, the voice of Deb-Lu-Quienyin, who was privy to Hunch's and Nodgen's secret, reached us. He sounded troubled.

"Tyfar would overlook that lapse," said Quienyin. "Jak, I must speak to you—and at once—"

"Assuredly." I stood up. Quienyin stood back in the shadows, so that I could not discern his expression. He wore his turban. A fierce bellow cut the air from the thorn-ivy.

"Vakkas! Riders heading for us!"

I spun to look. Tyfar was sinking down behind the thorns and the others were flattening out, steel in their fists.

Beyond them, across the flat, and clear in the slanting rays of the suns, a party of riders broke from a clump of twisty trunks, the crinkly leaves down-drooping and unmoving in the breathless air.

The men rode totrixes, zorcas, hirvels. There was not a swarth among them. They rode hard, lashing their beasts on, and the dust rose in a flat smear behind them, hanging betrayingly in a long yellow-white streak. I looked up. Up there the flutsmen curved down, the wings of their flyers wide and stiff, and the glint and wink of weapons glittered a stark promise of destruction over the doomed party of riders below.

532

Four

Dead Men Pose Puzzles

Straight for the rocky outcrop and running at lung-bursting speed, the forlorn party rode on. They were making for the shelter we had chosen. There, it was clear, they hoped to make a stand against the reining sky mercenaries. Now the sound of the hooves beat a rattling tattoo against the hard ground.

"They'll never make it." Tyfar stared hotly through the thorn-ivy.

If that young prince decided to stand up and run out to assist those doomed jutmen, I, for one, would seek to stop him. He was become precious to me, now, as a comrade. I would not relish his death. I had seen too much of death.

"Jak—" whispered Quienyin.

"Yes?"

"I have sought out—"

"See! They shoot!" Tyfar was panting now, and his lithe body humped as though about to leap out.

I said, "We cannot allow Tyfar to throw his life away. We will do what we can, but—"

Quienyin looked vaguely through a chink in the thorns.

"Those poor people will never reach here alive." He looked back at me. "There is much we must talk about."

"I agree. But, I think, it will have to wait the outcome of this mess out here."

"You are right. But I will say I am—am shattered—"

"So you descried a little, then, and understand more?"

"Indeed! Indeed!"

"Nath the Shaft!" called Tyfar in a low, penetrating voice.

"My Prince!"

"Shaft 'em, you onker! Shaft 'em!"

"Nath," I said. My voice jerked his head around, and his reaching fingers stilled as they touched the feathers of the shaft in his quiver.

"Jak, Jak!" said Tyfar. "What? You cannot abandon them!"

"No. No, I suppose not. But they are done for—there are ten of them and twenty-five or thirty flutsmen. We can—"

"We can shaft them from cover—and we must hurry!"

His face blazed eagerness at me. I sighed. What can one do with these high and mighty princelings whose honor code rules them to death and destruction? And yet—Tyfar was a man of better mettle than mere unthinking bludgeoning.

"You don't have to let those flutsmen know we are here, do you?" said Hunch. His voice quavered.

Nodgen hefted his spear. He could throw that with skill and power, even though it was not a stux, the stout throwing spear of Havilfar. "I have four spears," he said. His voice growled. "That's four of the cramphs."

"They are too far away for you, Nodgen, you onker!"

"They'll come nearer, once the arrows fly."

"That," I said, "is true."

"I will not wait any longer." Tyfar shouted it. He started to stand up. I moved forward. What I was going to do Opaz alone knows. I was confused, knowing I ought to help those poor folk out there against those rasts of flutsmen, and knowing, also, that my responsibilities were wider by far than this mere stupid little fracas in the Humped Land.

The flutsmen swooped down.

The great Lohvian longbow snugged into my grip. The blue-fletched arrow nocked home sweetly. I lifted the bow and stood up. By Zair! The stupid things I have done in my time on Kregen! But—Kregen is a world where anything may happen and frequently does.

Together, Nath the Shaft, Barkindrar the Bullet, and I, Dray Prescot, prince of onkers, let fly.

Three flutsmen sagged and dropped from their clerketers, the leather flying thongs holding their bodies dangling from the big birds as they struggled to stay aloft with the limp, dragging weight frightening them and hauling them down.

Again we shot, and again. Someone of us missed the third time; who it was I do not know.

Now the flutsmen were veering like gale-tossed spindrift, swirling over toward our rocky outcrop. The rear ten or so fell straight down, the fluttrells settling with a flurrying uproar and updriven billows of dust about the galloping jutmen. The fight sprawled over there across the flat.

We shot again as the leading flyers chuted down toward us. The two Pachaks and Hunch brought the short bows taken from the Muzzards into action. Those damned flutsmen astride their fluttrells, all a mass of glitter and waving clumped feathers and brandished weapons, looked massive and indomitable. They looked as though they could fly right through us. That is the impression they seek to convey.

The leading flyers were close enough for Nodgen to hurl his spear. The thick shaft burst through the leather and feathered flying gear of his target, and the flutsman screeched, a thin, high wail of despair cutting through the din. He went smashing back against his wicker saddle, slipped sideways, making despairing, jerking grippings with his hands, which slid off to dangle.

"Where's the next?" raved Nodgen.

The flutsmen circled. We shot, a rolling flighting of steel birds that wreaked cruel damage on the flesh-and-blood birds aloft. Spears sliced down to rattle against the rocks. But, as so often happens when a man afoot shoots it out with a man aloft, the man on the ground has all the advantages. A barbed spear grazed past Tyfar's arm, and he cursed, and shook his axe.

We kept low, cocking our bows up steeply, using the rocks as cover, keeping in the shadows of the thorn-ivy. The fluttrells would not come near that, for they are canny birds when it comes to self-preservation.

A flung stux whipped in toward me and I flicked it away with an outthrust arm. The men up there must have loosed their crossbows against the jutmen out on the flat, and thinking to finish the thing quickly, had not reloaded. In this they were poor quality flutsmen, quite unlike the band in which I had served.

The dust smothered across the fight out on the flat and only a thin and attenuated yelling told us that men were still left to battle it out. We had taken the major part of the force attacking the vakkas and they would have to fend for themselves until we had seen off the reivers attempting to slay us. So—we fought.

Now your true-blue mercenary of the skies knows when to fight from his natural perch, astride the back of a bird or flying animal, or when to alight and get on with handstrokes on the ground. We had seen off a sizeable gang of this bunch; now the rest forced their fluttrells in to haphazard landings and leaped off their backs, swords and spears brandished. They leaped toward us over the dust between the rocks.

Nath the Shaft calmly shot two of them out even as they cocked their legs over the wicker saddles and the sheening feathers.

The rest of us shot methodically, and then we were at the tinker's work. The flutsmen they were close to proved to be a surprise. They were the usual mixture of diffs and apims, a Rapa, a Fristle, a Brokelsh. They were clearly still unaware quite of their losses. They ran in and started to fight bravely enough. But when half their number fell, screaming, with not one of us so much as scratched, they abruptly came to a realization of the situation. As I said, they were of poor quality. They were, if you will pardon the conceit, masichieri of the skies.

When this raggle-taggle band broke back for their birds, I shouted the orders it was necessary to give and see obeyed instantly.

The Pachaks raced forward first. They were, after all, hyr-paktuns, with the golden pakzhan at their throats. They were more used to what goes on in the aftermath of battles than Tyfar's two retainers, or the Tryfant Hunch. But Nodgen, who had been a mercenary in his time—almost made paktun—understood swiftly, and was out of the rocks and running after the two Pachaks.

Tyfar yelled to me. "The people out there!"

"Let us go over, by all means."

So the rest of us ran past the end of the thorn-ivy and quitted the shelter of the rocks. We ran toward the boil of dust marking the fight. Long before we reached it, the flutsmen were lifting away, the birds' wings flapping with vigorous downstrokes to gain takeoff speed.

Then I let out a roar.

"The famblys! Come back! Come back—"

But the jutmen, freed of the horror of the flutsmen all around them, simply clapped in their spurs and went haring away across the flats. They galloped in a string and they had their heads down and I do not doubt that most of them had their eyes shut, also.

So we stopped running, and stood and watched the folk we had rescued simply flee in panic.

"The stupid onkers!" said Tyfar. He breathed in, and then made a grimace of distaste, and spat. The dust drifted in, clogging our mouths, flat and unpleasant on the tongue.

Among the drift of detritus of the fight—dead animals, dead birds, dead flutsmen, dead jutmen, and a scatter of weapons—an arm lifted.

"One of them," I said, "at least is alive."

We ran across.

He had been a strong fighting man, clad in bronze-bound leather, with a neat trim of silver to the rim of his helmet. His face, heavily bearded, was waxen now, all the high color fled. His lips were ricked back. Near him lay a young man, dressed in clothes and armor of exceeding richness, and this young man's neck was twisted and ripped, and he could have looked down his own shoulder blades, had his eyes still possessed the gift of sight.

"He—is dead—the young lord," gasped the bearded, dying man. "So—best—I die, too..."

"Who was he?" said Tyfar. He spoke in a hard, contained voice.

The bearded lips opened but only a gargle sounded.

I bent closer.

"Rest easy, dom. You are safe now—"

"Flutsmen—lord, my lord—you must—" His head fell sideways, and those craggy, bearded lips gusted a last breath.

I stood up.

"I," said Tyfar, "wonder who they were."

"It does not matter. They are dead or fled."

We stared about on that unpleasant scene.

Presently, Hunch said, "Can we go back to the rocks now, please?"

"Not before you and Barkindrar and Nath have collected what is useful to us. And be quick about it. There may be other flutsmen about."

Hunch looked sick.

536

"Do we have to?"

"Assuredly you do. Now—jump!"

Tyfar nodded. "Nath, Barkindrar, set to it."

I ploughed in to help select anything we thought would be of use to us. But, as a prince, Tyfar moved a little way off. He did not help us strip the dead of the rich armor, or rake through the satchels, or lift up the blood-caked weapons. But he did not walk away. He stood nearby, and if any further flutsmen showed up, why, then he would show what being a prince involved.

The bulky, bearded man bothered me. He had given his life, and that had not been enough. His young lord was dead. I surmised they were part of an expedition out to venture down a Moder after treasure and magic, and had been separated from the main body by the Muzzard vakkas. Then the flutsmen, ever avid to pick up morsels like that, had attacked.

Twisted under a fine zorca that had been shafted—I took a single look and then looked away. The vile things that happen to faithful saddle animals at the hands of men is a sore subject with me, as with many other men on two worlds. Twisted under this poor dead zorca, as I say, lay the body of a large man who had been pitched from the saddle. His neck had broken.

I studied his face, calm, lined, filled with the remnants of a vigor that had sustained him in life and was now deserting him in death. He wore magnificent armor. It had not stopped his neck from being smashed. I sucked in my breath and went to work.

He was not the bearded servitor's young lord, and I guessed he was a lord in his own right, gone adventuring on his own account. The expedition of which we nine were the last to escape from Moderdrin had contained nine separate expeditions within our ranks. The armor came off easily, for it had been well cared for. I hoisted it on my back and took his weapons and then trailed off after the others who were hurrying back to the rocks.

I saw Prince Tyfar looking at me.

He said nothing.

I said, "When you have been adventuring out in the wild and hostile world, Tyfar—" And then I stopped myself.

He would not understand. He might learn—if he lived long enough. But I knew enough to know that his ideas of honor could not comprehend my motives.

"Just, Tyfar, one thing."

"Yes, Jak?"

"Do not think the less of me. I hazard a guess that you have never starved, never been flogged, never really wanted in all your life. These things give a man a different view of the values in life and, yes, I know I am being insufferable and almost preaching, but I value your comradeship and would not see it spoiled over so small a matter."

And, even then, that was the wrong note. The matter was not small when it touched the honor of a prince of Hamal.

Then he surprised me.

"I have a deal to learn—everything is not contained in books or the instructions of axemasters. I shall don this poor young lord's armor, which Nath and Barkindrar carry back for me—when it is necessary."

I felt, I admit, suitably chastened.

When he reached the outcrop, the others had finished up their work and had secured the surviving fluttrells. The big birds were chained down by their wing chains, and had found it suddenly restful in the shade.

I nodded. "Well done."

"And, what do we do with the swarths?"

"Cut them loose," said Tyfar. "They will fend for themselves and, eventually, find their way to fresh employment."

"Agreed."

The night would soon be upon us and although we could fly quite easily by the light of the moons, we judged it better to give the fluttrells a time to recuperate. Hunch busied himself brewing up tea, that superb Kregan tea, for a supply was discovered in the saddlebags we had taken from the dead animals. Also, we found something that told us who at least some of these folk had been.

Modo brought the package across and we opened it and read the warrant in the last of the light.

"Rolan Hamarker, Vad of Thangal—most odd." Tyfar looked up from the paper. "That is a good Hamalese name. Yet I do not know of anyone called that. Thangal has no Vad. It is a Trylonate."

"Due northwest of Ruthmayern," I said.

"Yes. This is, indeed, a curiosity."

"And this came from the effects of the young man?"

"Yes, Jak," said Modo.

"Well, there was nothing with the other lord to identify him. And that, to me, is stranger still."

"You are right, by Krun!" said Tyfar.

"Perhaps," said Quienyin in his mellow voice. "They did not wish to give their true names when they ventured into Moderdrin."

"Of course." Tyfar beamed on the Wizard of Loh. "You have the right of it."

"Probably," I said.

We now had a plethora of weapons and armor and equipment. So we could take our pick. Any good Kregan will take as many weapons along with him as the situation warrants, or the situation that might arise the day after tomorrow will warrant.

As I picked up the dead lord's sword, I looked across at Tyfar and said,

"But that warrant, made out for Rolan Hamarker, gives him authority to arrest anyone he sees fit to question. It is exceedingly wide. And, of course, you observe the signature and the seal?"

"I do. It is the seal of King Doghamrei. Although the scrawl is so bad it could have been signed by any damned slave who had stolen the seal cylinder."

"King Doghamrei," I said, and I fell silent, my mind choked with memories: of Ob-Eye, his one optic quite mad, trussing me up and stuffing me into a metal cage, of the cage being swung over the bulwarks of the massive Hamalian skyship Hirrume Warrior, of Ob-Eye thrusting the torch into the mass of combustibles piled around my bound form, of the cage being readied to drop onto the decks of the Vallian galleon Ovvend Barynth on the sea below. They'd set my pants alight, all right. Somehow, because I was a Krozair of Zy, as I truly think, and because I did not wish to be parted from Delia, I had gotten out of that scrape. But—all those vile things had been done to me not on the orders of the Empress Thyllis—Queen Thyllis as she was then—but of King Doghamrei. Oh, yes, I recalled him with some clarity.

And so, because of all those old memories ghosting up, I said, "By Krun! I've half a mind to feel sorry he's still alive."

Then I looked at Tyfar.

He smiled.

"Then in that you do not stand alone, Jak. He never did succeed in his plot to marry the empress—her poor doting husband still mopes away in some fusty tower or other—and King Doghamrei is still only a servile king in fee to the empress."

"Well, I was incautious in my sentiments. Perhaps, one day, you will understand my feelings."

"My father once fought a duel with Doghamrei—"

"Ha! Then I'll wager Prince Nedfar acted as a true horter and let the rast off—more's the pity."

"He did and it is. But that is smoke blown with the wind."

"Your father, Tyfar, is a prince for whom I cherish the most lively affection and respect. Now, why couldn't he be a king—or even an emperor?"

Tyfar drew his cheeks in. He looked suddenly grave, all the banter fled.

"You run on leem's tracks hastily, Jak."

"I will say no more. I have said too much."

"Yes. But, I think—I know—your sentiments are not yours alone."

"Ah!"

Now, of course, all this sentiment was sweet in the ears of a Vallian. Anything to discomfit Hamal until that empire was willing to talk decently to her neighbors must be to the advantage of Vallia. All the same, what I had said about Tyfar's father, Prince Nedfar, was true.

What a plot it would be to depose Thyllis and set up Nedfar as emperor of Hamal! I fancied I could talk to him, get him to see reason, see that all the countries of Paz had to unite to face the menace of the shanks, who raided and spoiled from over the curve of the world. For I felt sure their depredations, raids at the moment, would develop into a mass migration, a gigantic attempt to invade our lands. And that, we of Paz could not in honor allow. The fish heads would not be satisfied until every one of us, diff and apim, man, woman, and child, was exterminated.

We made our selections of weapons and armor and equipment and stuffed ourselves with the food in the saddlebags. Then we decided to let our meal go down and set off astride the fluttrells in exactly two burs.

Sitting with my back propped up against a folded cloak on a rock, I popped palines into my mouth, chewing the luscious berries contentedly. Quienyin sat down by my side and I offered him the yellow berries, extending the dish.

He chewed. Tyfar walked across and we passed the dish around. We felt relaxed, comfortable, perfectly confident that now that we had flying steeds we would be out of Moderdrin in no time. Quienyin coughed.

"Prince Tyfar. This war between you and your neighbors, which has extended into Vallia—"

"Yes. Vallia is recalcitrant. The Hyr Notor has the command there. But the news is—odd, to say the least. We have had to recall a number of regiments."

"So I believe. They have a new emperor up in Vallia now, do they not? Tell me, Tyfar, what are your views on this new and fearsome emperor of Vallia, this Dray Prescot?"

Five

"Dray Prescot, Vile Emperor of a Vile Empire!"

One of the tethered fluttrells let out a squawk, and Hunch gentled him with quick, sympathetic skill. A small branch broke and fell from the fire. Nath and Barkindrar suddenly laughed, and I caught a coarse reference to Vajikry. The light of the moons shone exceedingly brightly upon the dusty land.

"The Emperor of Vallia?" said Tyfar, Prince of Hamal. "Well, now. A hyr-lif might be written about that great devil."

"Tyfar," I said, "did you see this great devil Dray Prescot paraded through the streets of Ruathytu lashed to the tail of a calsany? In the Empress Thyllis's coronation procession?"

"Aye, Jak, I did."

"And, Tyfar," said Quienyin, and he looked at me as he spoke to the Prince, "your thoughts on that occasion?"

Tyfar poked at the fire with a stripped branch.

"This Emperor Dray—it was just, that he should be brought down and humbled, but the way of the doing of it..."

Quienyin took his penetrating gaze from my leem's-head of a face and stared questioningly at Tyfar.

"Yes?"

"By Krun! The rast deserved what he got, did he not?"

"He deserves all he gets," I said.

"But, all the same..." And, again, Prince Tyfar did not complete his sentence. I wondered if he was unwilling to face the consequences of his own thoughts, or unwilling to reveal them to us.

He pulled his shoulders back and threw the branch on the fire.

"Anyway, Quienyin. Why do you question me, now, about the great devil Dray Prescot?"

The nasty suspicion gathered in my mind that I knew the answer to that. But, then, why was it nasty? If Deb-Lu-Quienyin had discovered the truth about Phu-Si-Yantong, then surely he would understand the horrendous problems confronting Paz? Yantong's insane dream was to encompass all of Paz, to take over and control and dominate all of the grouping of continents and islands on our side of the world of Kregen. He had made a start with Pandahem and other places, was destroying Vallia even now, even though we Vallians fought back, and had, under the alias of the Hyr Notor, achieved much with Hamal.

If Quienyin knew all this, as I now suspected he did, then of a certainty he must see the justice of the fight being waged by those opposed to Phu-Si-Yantong.

One of the chiefs of that opposition to the maniacal Wizard of Loh was Dray Prescot, Emperor of Vallia. This, I believed, was what Quienyin was leading up to, what he was telling me in this way. And, cunning old leem-hunter that he was, he had his reasons.

"Well, Quienyin? I fly to join my people. We have been through much together, surely you can find a more enjoyable subject of conversation?" Tyfar stood up and stretched his legs. "By Krun! When Princess Thefi hears what has been going on—"

"Will you join the army of Hamal, or the Air Service, and fight in Vallia, Tyfar?"

Quienyin's question drew a down-drawn and hesitating look from Tyfar.

"We are comrades, Quienyin, and therefore—for anyone else to question me thus would touch—"

"Your honor?"

And then, characteristically, Tyfar laughed. "I do not know! My whole view of the world has changed. What is honor? It can get you killed, that is sure, certain sure."

I said, "But that knowledge would not stop you from acting in honor, Tyfar? You would not let those vakkas be hounded to death by the flutsmen without an effort to help them."

"That is true. It was foolish. But Jak, and you know it, I would do it again."

"Then," said Quienyin, "as your comrade—and thus taking full advantage of being rude or overweening to you—I would counsel you most seriously not to go to Vallia to fight." He shook his head and his turban did not so much as quiver. "No, Tyfar. I am a Wizard of Loh—and I say to you with all the force at my disposal, do not go to fight the Vallians."

"Why?"

That was your Prince Tyfar for you. Straight out, direct, to the point. It was a damned good question and a damned hard one for Quienyin to answer.

I studied their faces by the lights of the moons and the erratic flickers of ruddy light from the fire. Quienyin and I were wrapped up in what underlay our words; Tyfar was in the middle and slowly becoming aware of what was not being openly spoken of. He could become exceedingly angry, a prince being treated like a child. But he was Tyfar. He spoke evenly.

"You have no answer for me, Quienyin? I think you are being mysterious on purpose—but what is your purpose?"

"It is simple. It is to save you much grief."

Tyfar sucked in his cheeks. Then: "So it is true. You Wizards of Loh can see into the future?"

"Perhaps."

At that I smirked. No Wizard of Loh was going to reveal any of his secrets, and the worse that was thought of them the more their power and the dread they invoked in the hearts of ordinary folk.

"You spoke of Dray Prescot, the vile emperor of a vile empire. Why should I not go up there and chastise him for the evil he has wrought?"

"Do you know of this evil? Can you show it to me?"

Tyfar spread his arms. "Well—all men know—"

"All men hear tales. Dray Prescot has the yrium, he has that special power, that charisma that marks him out among men and—"

"The yrium!" Tyfar was incensed. "Rather he has the yrrum, the evil charismatic presence, the vile leading the vile, rotten clean through, decadent—" He was panting.

542

I said, and I spoke gently, "I think the Empress Thyllis would joy to hear you speak thus, Tyfar."

That sobered him.

He stared toward Quienyin and then toward me. I say toward. I don't think he saw us, not then, for he was looking with his inward eye at past events and conversations and trying to grapple with the problems he now saw more clearly than, probably, he had ever seen in his life before.

At last he said, and his words were still breathless, "So you tell me Dray Prescot has the yrium and not the yrrum, that he is not evil clean through, that he has not brought shame and misery to Hamal, that—"

"I tell you, Tyfar," interrupted Quienyin, "only to search your own ib for the truths in these things."

"And I," I said, "tell us all it is time we departed."

Whatever was going through Quienyin's mind would have to wait. He was Up To Something, as he would have said in his Capital Letter Days. But I banished all that from my own mind as we rose into the air.

Ah! To fly free on the back of a great bird, soar through the sweet air of Kregen, with the blaze of the stars and the fat, serene moons shining down! She of the Veils and the Maiden with the Many Smiles shone refulgently, pink and gold, shining down on the fleeting surface of Kregen passing swiftly below.

The windrush in my face, blowing through my hair... The feel of the rhythmic rise and fall as the fluttrell bore me on with wide pinions beating... The whole sublime sense of flight and motion and headlong movement... Yes, flying over the face of Kregen beneath the moons, there is very little in two worlds to equal that, by Zair!

And, as for the fluttrells themselves, they were the big birds with the silly head vanes that were always in the way, it seems. Well, there is a simple-minded saying among the simple folk of Kregen that sums up the magic in simple terms. Of the birds' flight through the air, they say: "They can do it because they think they can do it." A pathetic little bit of philosophy, per-haps. But it rings, all the same, it rings...

Our flying mounts skeined through the air and we drove on through the moons-washed night. When by the feel of the birds' motion and the little draggling skip to the wings we knew they had had enough, we descended in a grove of tuffa trees, for we had flown past the end of the Humped Land and left that desolate landscape astern. The fluttrells had been hard-driven by their former owners. It is the habit of flutsmen to use their mounts to the utmost. We had a distance to travel and wished to husband the flut-trells' strength.

All of us, I feel, had been touched by that night flight.

We spoke softly, doing what had to be done in the way of caring for the birds and of brewing up. Then the wine was passed around. We spoke quietly, not just because we were somewhere in Havilfar none of us knew and therefore must expect the eruption of danger at any moment. As I say, we had been impressed by that flight under the moons.

Prince Tyfar did not raise our previous subject of conversation. I, for one, by Vox, was happy to let it lie.

Nodgen, as a bristly Brokelsh, was content to dunk his head in the stream and splash water vigorously all over himself. Hunch, being a Tryfant—and you know how foppish they can be on occasion—had to go the whole hog and give himself the full treatment. Mind you, although I say I have no feelings one way or the other for Tryfants, I had seen enough of Hunch by now to have summed him up better, I fancy, than he guessed or knew himself. And Nodgen shared my opinion. Hunch was a Tryfant, sure enough, not above four foot six in height and full of quivers and quavers and always with an eye open for the nearest bolt hole—but he had gone with us through the horrors of the Moder.

"Jak," said Quienyin as I turned away from the stream, shaking myself like a collie.

"Aye," I said, blowing water. "Aye, Quienyin. What you have to say is overdue."

"Come a little way apart. Much Is To Be Said."

Those capital Capital Letters, as it were, alerted me. I followed the Wizard of Loh into the shadows of the tufa trees and we settled down, facing each other so that we might keep an eye open on each other's back.

I said, bluntly, "You have sussed Phu-Si-Yantong and you do not care for what you have found."

He rubbed his fingers through that reddish hair, shoving the turban aside, uncaring if it fell to the ground.

"We Wizards of Loh set store by certain standards. We have power and we try not to abuse it. Certainly we lust after gold and gems and suchlike baubles—or some of us—but it is the pursuit of knowledge and its manipulation that is our goal and that sustains us. We do not seek petty princely dominion."

"But..."

"But, Jak the Sturr, I have been overcome. I entertain the liveliest respect and admiration for San Yantong. He represented all that was fundamentally encouraging about us Wizards of Loh. He would make a stir in the world, we all said—"

I stared at Quienyin. "He was your tutor."

Quienyin did not flinch back. "No. We do not work on that basis in Loh, where we are trained. Not at all. And, also, we never discuss this training. But our comradeship down the Moder has—"

"It seems to me, Quienyin, there has been altogether too much talk about this comradeship. Methinks there is too much protestation going on."

He would not know my source for the adapted quote; but Nalgre ti Liancesmot expresses similar sentiments in Part Three of the Seventh Book of *The Vicissitudes of Panadian the Ibreiver*.

He nodded again; but it was not an unthinking nod. Rather, it was the expression of a man who has reached a conclusion.

"Now that I am a little aware of the quality of person I am to do business with, I agree with you."

"So you think you know who I am?"

"Certainly. You are Jak, calling himself the Sturr, claiming to hail from Hamal—or Djanduin or Hyrklana if the mood takes him—a paktun, probably a hyr-paktun. Is there any other quality you would wish me to assume you possess?"

The old devil was thrusting the gimlet right in, well enough. I warmed to him.

"I have had dealings with Wizards of Loh before. I respect their arts. I respect their integrity insofar as I have met with it. I own to a grievous debt outstanding to a Wizard in Ruathytu—"

"You refer to San Rening? Que-si-Rening who was resident and secret Wizard of Loh to Queen Thyllis?"

I shook my head in amazement. "I do. He assisted me and I promised to aid him, and I have not done so."

"Do not trouble your head over San Rening—"

"No!" I said. "He is not dead?"

"No. He effected his escape. It was prettily done. I did not know you knew him. He lives now in safety and practices at a small court in the Dawn Lands. It is not a useful thing for you to know which—"

"No. I agree. But I am glad he is a free man again."

"But San Yantong..."

"Do you also know Khe-Hi-Bjanching?"

Bjanching was that certain Wizard of Loh with whom Delia and I and others had gone through the adventure of the doors and the test—and the pit, too, by Vox!—and he had taken up residence in my home of Esser Rarioch. Now he had been banished back to Loh by superior sorcery and I wondered if he was well, as I wondered if all my friends who had been sent sorcerously packing off to their homes were well.

"I have heard the name, only. He is a new and young adept and has his name to make."

"If you contact him on whatever astral plane you go wandering in when you are in lupu, tell him he is missed."

He inclined his red-haired head.

"As you please."

"And now—about this kleesh Yantong."

He talked, slowly at first and then warming to his subject as his indignation overcame him. Yantong had been defying the sacred tenets of the Wizards of Loh. Always the Sans exercised their power from the background, from the shadows. Now Yantong wanted to strut forth and hog the limelight, to take the power and be seen to take it. slaying all who stood in his path. Quienyin was quite clearly shattered.

He told me a few things I did not know; but generally he merely recited what I knew of Yantong's sins against humanity.

"And yet," I said, "he is a man. There must be something of good in him. Surely, everything has not been thrown away?"

"I would like to think that, Jak. But if there is aught of goodness left in him, I have not descried it."

I let out a breath.

"Well. I'll put a blade through his guts if we meet, if I can; but I'll still like to think he's not all evil. Can there be such a thing as a totally evil man?"

"Theory says not. But we have to test that theory."

"Yes—and my Khamorro?"

"You mean, of course, Turko the Shield?"

I refused to be amazed.

"You know much. I accept that, and I respect your still tongue and your friendship. Yes, I mean Turko."

"He quitted Herrelldrin. You will not be surprised if I tell you he attempted to reach Vallia—"

"Attempted?"

"He is down in South Pandahem. As a Khamorro he works in a booth in a fairground—"

"My Turko!"

"It is a common occupation for the Khamsters—"

"Aye, it is. And they do not like anyone but themselves calling them Khamster."

"So I believe. He is well, and seems to be resigned to his fate. There is a girl and a man—but they veil their emotions. If you go to South Pandahem you will find him at the Sign of the Golden Prychan in Mahendrasmot."

"I've never been there. But I shall go."

Quienyin shifted around. He licked his lips. If he weren't a Wizard of Loh I'd have thought he was nerving himself to ask something. We spoke a little, then at random, waiting for the burs to pass so that we might resume our flight. At last he said, in a straight, fierce voice, "And if I went to Vallia, you believe I would be well received?"

If he wasn't going to come out with it, neither was I.

"Yes. Go to Vondium. Go to the Imperial Palace. You have the presence to gain audience of the empress. She will receive you kindly, if you tell her—certain things she will wish to know."

"Thank you—Jak. The prospect pleases me."

"You will be right royally welcome, Quienyin."

Tyfar was moving about down by the fluttrells and a general animation stirred our little camp as we prepared to carry on.

"Of course," I said. "The empress may not be in Vondium. She is often away about her own affairs. Then ask to see the Prince Majister, Drak. Or Kov Farris. You will, I am sure, know just who best to see."

"I shall—Jak."

I stood up. I stretched. Then, sharply, I said, "And my friends in Hyrklana?"

"I shall attempt to obtain news."

"Good. Now it seems we are moving on."

Six

We Fly Over the Dawn Lands

We reached Astrashum, the city from which expeditions set out for the Humped Land. In this place Hunch, Nodgen, and I had been auctioned off on the slave block. The man who had bought us, Tarkshur the Lash, a Kataki, had ventured into the Moder filled with avarice. He had been left with his tail fast gripped in the uncuttable tentacle of one horrific kind of Snatchban. The decision seemed to me sound to banish memories of the Moder from my mind.

Prince Nedfar and his party had gone on to Jikaida City. The other principals alive of our expedition had taken their leave and gone home. Kov Loriman, the Hunting Kov, was reported as being in fine fettle. Ariane nal Amklana had set off for Hyrklana with her small imperious head lifted in regal disdain.

Folk in Astrashum expressed themselves as vastly surprised there had been as many as three survivors from the original nine. Quienyin and I kept very low, and we set off at once for Jikaida City. Nedfar, Quienyin warned us, had left immediately for Hamal. Fresh airboats from Hamal had been flown in for his party. Their passage home would be swift.

"I joy that my father and sister, and all the others, are safe," said Tyfar. But he bit his lip, and added: "But I view with alarm what the empress will say. My father did not conclude the embassy with Prince Mefto and we have no great store of armies on which to call. She knows he does not see eye to eye with her war policy. I call on Krun of the Steel Blade to watch over him."

"And I, too," I said. "We follow?"

"As fast as our fluttrells can fly."

"Prince," said Nath the Shaft, respectfully, "flyers are scarce, as we all know. We must take care of them, lest they are stolen away from us. Their value is above price."

"That is the war—"

"Aye!"

"Can you tell why Thyllis entrusted your father with the task of making the alliance with Mefto?" I wanted to know.

"He is known to be above party politics, seeking only the welfare of Hamal. If we can win the war quickly, then much grievous loss will be spared us. Thyllis knew this."

Well, that made sense in a nonsensical world.

Honest men are used by the cunning of two worlds—as I know, having been used and user in my time.

Flying over the Dawn Lands of Havilfar reveals their haphazard splendor. They are like a patchwork quilt of countries. There are scores of tiny Stromnates and trylonates, larger vadvarates and kovnates, and broad princedoms and kingdoms. Here was where the first men to reach these shores settled, around the Shrouded Sea. Now all this wide land was in ferment as the looming monster of Hamal, to the north, sent tentacles of force to rip them apart and take all. Truly, the Empress of Hamal, this Thyllis, was besotted with a crazed ambition.

In this she shared the maniacal notions of Phu-Si-Yantong. Always, as you know, I wavered and hesitated over my own role in these great affairs of state. For, was not I, this new Emperor of Vallia, also caught up in these mad power politics?

To reach Hamal we flew something east of north. I was content in this, for to fly direct to South Pandahem would have occasioned flying over the Wild Lands of Northwestern Havilfar, and no man, unless he be mad, a fool, or uncaring, willingly ventures there. Once we hit Hamal I'd bid remberee to my comrades and fly on out over the sea and then take a sharp left turn along the northern shore of Havilfar, by the Southern Ocean, and skirting the island of Wan Witherm, reach Pandahem.

That was the theory, one of those famous theories I had been promulgating and failing to perform just lately.

Mind you, had I not been with this band of eight comrades, I would probably have flown westward, visited Migladrin and Djanduin, and then flown north to Pandahem up the South Lohvian Sea between Havilfar and Loh.

I am glad, now, that I did not...

Prince Tyfar was eager to press on.

"I wonder what Princess Thefi took from the Mausoleum of the Flame," he said. "As for that scamp, Lobur the Dagger—he and I will buffet each other when we meet."

"And," I said, turning the blade in the wound, "do not forget Kov Thrangulf."

"No. Who could forget him—save the entire world? He is hard put upon and there is something in the man finer than the world sees, struggling to get out. I wish Lobur was not so hard on him."

"We will soon be in Hamal and then your worries will be over. Also, it is there that our ways will part."

"I grieve for that, Jak. Cannot you stay in Hamal? After all, it is your country."

"I am under duress—well, you know I may not talk of that, save to assure you as I have."

"If ever you need a friend in Hamal—you know where they are."

"Aye. Thank Krun I do, Tyfar!"

The southern border of Hamal is marked off by the majestic River Os. This wends its regal way from the Mountains of the West which spine the center of the continent there, to the Ocean of Clouds in the east. Its mouth divides to run around the country of Ifilion, which is fiercely independent and had not been overrun by the iron legions of Hamal.

South of the Os the countries had been invaded and subjected and Clef Pesquadrin, Ystilbur, Frorkenhume, had all felt the oppression of the iron legions. And still Thyllis's ambitions were not slaked, and she sent her iron legions farther to the south still. And, down in the Dawn Lands, the opposition to her and her schemes grew.

Flyers cannot sustain the long hauls that fliers may, and we had to descend periodically to rest and feed our fluttrells. Naturally, we chose places well out of the way. We were not disturbed as we flew north. The land opened out into a broad and pleasant prospect, and although we skirted towns and hamlets, we saw them, gleaming like lilies across the green fields.

At one halt in the shade of missals, Quienyin told me that my friends in Hyrklana were alive. I felt the leap of relief. Balass the Hawk, Oby, Naghan the Gnat, and Tilly were dear to me. The Wizard of Loh struck a note of alarm when he said they were involved in the Jikhorkdun again. I frowned.

"That bloody arena of Huringa should be—"

"Not while human nature is as human nature is, Jak."

"As soon as I meet up with Turko—but, no. I have other things to do which supervene—I think." The truth was, by Zair, I was all at sea. Vallia called. Yes, yes, the country was in good hands. But—well, easy enough to sense my feelings even if they do me no credit as your cool and hard-headed adventurer. I wanted to see Delia. I wanted to know that my home was not once more a sea of flames.

Emotion and feeling rule us, whether we will it or not. "As soon as I have done what I must do, it is Hyrklana for me, and the Jikhorkdun of Huringa."

Quienyin nodded sympathetically.

"They are all perfectly safe, I assure you."

"In the Jikhorkdun?"

"Yes."

The old sayings have fallen into disrepute on Kregen as on Earth. I had to do what I had to do. There was no easy way out for me. But we all smirk when we hear the words, "A man's gotta do what a man's gotta do." They are trite, stupid, meaning nothing out of overuse and unthinking repetition. But, they do mean a great deal. I had to go back to Vallia, first, and stopping off for Turko was an indulgence to my sensibilities. By Zair! What it is to be an emperor, what it is to be a man!

"South Pandahem is a more or less direct route through to Vallia," said Quienyin. "Hyrklana is not."

I stared at him. He knew who I was all right. But we kept up the pretense. I really think—I know—he had been so profoundly shocked at his discoveries of the antics of his old friend Phu-Si-Yantong that he was still in something of a state of shock. And he had not asked me what I was doing down in the Dawn Lands. I could not tell him that, of course. He could know nothing of a power that had sent me here in the first place, a power immeasurably greater than all the powers of the Wizards of Loh combined.

From northwest to southeast the Dawn Lands stretch for something just under three thousand miles. From northeast to southwest the breadth is of the order of one thousand five hundred, reaching a little more past the Western Mountains.

The whole place is like a beehive of energy.

Kingdoms rise and fall, borders stretch and contract. Racial, religious, political differences hold the frontiers. Geography plays its part, so that rivers and mountains form natural barriers. We flew on north and east and so passed the massive lenk forests of Shirrerdrin. Ahead lay Khorundur.

"We approach areas where runs the writ of Hamal," said Tyfar. He sounded half angry and ashamed along with his pleasure.

I knew why.

So I took no notice. We made a frugal camp and decided what to do. Now you can shoot a paly and feast on succulent roast venison. You can slingshot a bird down and eat that. And you call pull fruit off trees and enjoy the succulent flesh and juices. But you cannot easily come by bread, or tea, or wine out in the wilds.

"I will go in," said Nath the Shaft. "With Barkindrar. We have money, good gold which these folk of the city will exchange for food—"

"Wine," said Hunch.

"Shall we go in, Hunch?" said Nodgen.

"Me? Why? Barkindrar and Nath offered, didn't they?"

"Buy only enough to last us over Khorundur. Beyond that kingdom we will be among friends and may ask for all we need," Tyfar told his retainers.

"Quidang, Prince!"

So the two went off and we waited and waited and when so much time had elapsed that we knew they were not coming back, Tyfar said, "They have been taken up. I shall go in after them and fetch them out. They are loyal men—and comrades."

Standing up, I looked at Tyfar, and there was no need for words.

Hunch quavered out: "You are going off and leaving me here, Jak!"

"You will be safe enough, Hunch. After all, Nodgen has his spear—and you have your bill, I see."

The two Pachaks started laughing, and then Hunch, staring around, laughed, too. But it was a dolorous sound, for all that.

The city stood beside the banks of a pretty little river which wound between wooded slopes. Built of a bright yellow brick, this little city of Khorunlad. That yellow is a fine, strong color, yet not harsh, not offensive... The yellow of just that tint is called tromp in Kregish, a fuller tone than the more subtle yellow called lay. Domes were burnished with copper, green and glowing, and the avenues opened out into stone-flagged kyros where striped awnings promised refreshment for thirsty throats.

We two, Tyfar and I, walked in past the open gates. They were stout, fabricated of bronze-bound lenk, and the watchtowers were manned. Many of the roofs of buildings uplifted landing platforms for airboats. I perked up.

We had both chosen to wear the armor taken from the dead lords destroyed by the flutsmen. We looked a resplendent pair. That was all to the good, for we had to get to Nath and Barkindrar before anything too unpleasant occurred to them.

Tyfar was all for going up to the magistrates and asking.

I pursed my lips.

"We-ell, Tyfar, we are strangers. D'you see the looks we got from the guard? And they looked handy fighting men, not your local city militia at all."

I considered it odd that we had not been questioned, were not already in some iron-barred cell charged with some nameless crime, and our weapons gone and our pockets emptied.

The armor I wore was of that superb supple mesh link manufactured in some of the countries of the Dawn Lands. Armor of the highest quality is usually made to fit the wearer. I was glad that the dead lord had been large across the shoulders. All the same, I had had to let the shoulder thongs out to their fullest extent to get the harness on. Tyfar's dead lord's armor was of the plate variety, a kax of exceptional beauty which snugged on Tyfar's brawny yet supple frame. We wore the green and yellow cloaks that came with the outfit, our helmets glittered in the suns, our weapons jutted with a fine panache, and, in short, we presented a splendid spectacle of two of the lords of the land.

Well, maybe that had not been such a good idea, after all.

Maybe had I done as I so often did, and padded in barefoot with a breechclout and weapons, I would have avoided the mischief. But, then, I would have avoided an adventure that afforded me enormous joy—even though I was not aware of it at the time.

Seven

Of a Meeting in a Hayloft

The first kyro to which we came was a plaza of pleasing proportions. The flags were uniformly arranged in blue and white hexagons. Tyfar stopped and stared at the tables beneath the bright umbrellas outside a tavern with the promising name of The Bottle and Morrow.

"Ronalines," he said, and smacked his lips. "I have a penchant for them— and with thick, clotted cream."

I sighed. People in clean and colorful clothes sitting at the tables were spooning up the ronalines smothered in thick cream. Ronalines are very much your Kregan strawberry, and highly tasty, too. Tyfar strode across and started opening his scrip ready to dole out money.

Deb-Lu-Quienyin suddenly appeared at my elbow.

A wash of coldness shriveled in the heat of the day.

"Jak—our two comrades. They are lodged in a hayloft in Blue Vosk Street. Barkindrar is injured."

I could see right through Quienyin.

One or two people at the tables were beginning to look more closely toward me. The Wizard of Loh had gone into lupu back in our camp and had thrown his astral projection to advise and warn us. How many times I had been hounded by the infernal projection of Yantong!

"Thank you, San. We will hurry. Best you—"

But Quienyin's projection moved into the shadows by the far wall of the tavern—and vanished. His going was a matter of the supernatural; I just hoped the clients spooning up their ronalines and cream would disbelieve the evidence of their eyes and believe common sense.

I started after Tyfar.

He sat down and leaned back in the wooden chair and looked around. Before the little Fristle fifi in her yellow apron could reach him I stormed up and whispered in a modulated bellow in his earhole, "Tyfar! Our comrades are in trouble and Barkindrar is injured. You'll have to forgo your ronalines."

He stood up at once, quelling the flash of fury on his face.

"That Barkindrar! Let us go, then, Jak—and mayhap we can stop here on our way back. By Krun! Ronalines and cream!"

We walked smartly off.

A Rapa slave in the gray slave breechclout stepped out of our way as we rounded the corner out of the kyro. He carried an enormous table on his back, and his beak was thrust forward. Perched on the table was a wicker basket and in the basket, wrapped in soft moss, lay two tiny Rapa babies. The Rapa lowered his eyes as he walked by.

"Rapa," I said, "tell me where is Blue Vosk Street."

He could only have been able to see our lower halves; but he could see the polished boots, and the sword scabbards, and the ends of the expensive cloaks.

"Masters," he quavered. He dare not straighten up for the babies would slide off the table. "Masters. Straight along the Avenue of a Thousand Delights, and turn left—no, masters, turn right—a hundred paces along, by the river."

I found a copper ob and pushed it into his hand.

"Thank you, Rapa."

What he said I did not know, for I went off quickly, with Tyfar tailing along.

We walked up the Avenue of a Thousand Delights, and while there might only have been nine hundred ninety-nine on display, the place warranted the trademark of a thousand. Following directions we turned a hundred paces along by the river, which here was confined by wooden stakes and a mass of overgrown foliage, and so entered Blue Vosk Street. Here, it was clear, lived the folk who catered to the customers for the thousand delights.

Tyfar put a hand to his sword hilt.

"Ignore the cutpurses," I said, "and slit the throats of the cutthroats—first."

"What a place! I did not know such a place could exist."

"You mean because it is a hundred paces or so from refinement and civilization?" The stink didn't bother me; Tyfar put a kerchief to his nose with his free hand. "No, Jak. I did not mean that."

But I fancied I knew what he did mean. He was a prince and had not rubbed shoulders with the poor of the world. Many of the shacks were simply moldering away. Those built of the soft mud, hardened by a kiss of fire, were sloughing their footings into the mud in which they were set. People moved about their business, and three-quarters of that, I'll warrant, was highly illegal. I drew my cloak around that splendid mesh mail. Tyfar saw the movement.

"Do you likewise, Tyfar. We are too brightly decked for this neighborhood. And keep your weather eye open."

"Where is this pestiferous hayloft?"

A string of calsanys blundered past, their backs obscured by swaying lashings of straw. The Rapa leading them shuffled, head down, a wisp of straw sticking out from under the vulturine beak. Farther along a pair of hirvels drew a cart which lurched over the ruts, its fragile wheels appearing as if they would burst asunder at every forward plunge. Slaves were not too much in evidence. The people here were on the breadline, no doubt, and villainy kept their stomachs apart from their backbones.

Khorundur was one of the countries of the Dawn Lands in which airboats were manufactured. These fliers were in nowise as splendid or efficient as those made in such secrecy by Hamal or Hyrklana; but they were functional, although small and oftentimes chancy of operation. No doubt the voller builders of Khorundur had not mastered all the secrets of the various ingredients contained in the silver boxes that uplifted and powered vollers.

Six taverns stood cheek by jowl, so that when a drunk was thrown out of the first, he could work his way along the rest without having to walk too far. Beyond them a cluster of stores displayed dusty goods, and then a hostelry lifted two stories. A beam and ropes jutted from a double door in the gabled front.

"There," said Tyfar, and he would have pointed had I not cautioned him swiftly. "Yes, Jak, you are right. They are a cutthroat lot down here."

"And quiet. Too quiet. Something is going on."

He did not have the ruffianly experience of an old adventurer to give him the scent of mischief. The string of calsanys had gone, the cart vanished up a dolorous side alley. The people were taking themselves off the street. Although the surface was pockmarked with potholes and rutted, this street for these people would serve as their open-air gathering place. One would expect it to be filled with chaffering throngs, and also one would be certain that we two, our expensive cloaks betraying us even though the armor was concealed, would have been subjected to more than simple horseplay. In all probability as many attacks as there were paces would have been launched against us.

So that meant just one thing.

You have to have the nose for authority if you wish to stay alive in many of the more raffish and desperate places of Kregen.

Zair knows, I'd kicked against authority enough in my time.

"Just rest a moment in the shade of this awning, Tyfar."

"But we must press on! Barkindrar—"

"Watch."

He glared at me. Something in my manner showed him I did not counsel thus without reason. More probably, although it pains me to report this, something about my manner must have told him I was in no mood to be argued with. He was a prince; but he subsided and we stood in the shadows, looking keenly out onto that doleful street.

A neighborhood gets to know when trouble is on its way.

In a tightly controlled voice, Tyfar said, "We should have gone straight away to the magistrates. Or even the king. His palace may be a moth-eaten dump; but he is a king and would have received me as a prince."

About to find a diplomatic way of reminding Tyfar of his country of origin, I closed my mouth. The tramp of iron-studded soles and the swish and clang of a party of soldiers kept us both stock still. I said in a voice that just carried, "This is the reason, Tyfar. Bide you still."

The soldiers were paktuns, clearly enough, a mixture of races, all clad in a semblance of uniform. They were a hard-bitten lot. At their head marched their Jiktar, and I can say I did not care for him at first glance. I would not like to serve as a paktun in his pastang. He had not brought his whole pastang, a company which might be eighty strong; but only three audos, three sections of eight men each. The iron-studded boots stomped the rutted road.

The mercenaries approached from the direction we had come, and I said to Tyfar, "Quickly, now! Around the back of the stables and in the rear window. Sharp!"

We ran between the wooden wall of the stables and the sagging mud wall of the nearest store. At the back a lumberyard showed with an adobe wall beyond. Thick trees cut off the view. At the back of the hostelry an aromatic yard piled with dung and straw and a few broken carts gave us access to the back of the building. There were a few calsanys in their stalls and a hirvel twitched his snout at us, his cup-shaped ears flicking forward, his tall round neck curving. The air hung unnaturally quiet, and the buzz of flies sounded like miniature ripsaws.

"In this window—quick and quiet!"

The sill was rotten and I shoved the wooden leaves open cautiously. The interior of the place stank. The floor was cumbered with shadow-shrouded impedimenta of the animal trade. Stalls lined both walls with a ladder beyond. Most of the stalls were empty. In the one nearest to the ladder a freymul, the poor man's zorca, suddenly looked splendid as he tossed his head in a shaft of the suns' light breaking in through a crack in the dilapidated walls. His fine chocolate-colored coat with those brave streaks of tromp beneath gleamed, and he showed his teeth and neighed.

"That's done it," I said. "Up the ladder!"

I sprang up the ladder four rungs at a time. If one of the treads snapped beneath my boots... But they held. I reached the landing at the top and faced a half-open door in which the light of a mineral-oil lamp glowed. Shadows moved.

In the hayloft, Quienyin had said.

Tyfar sprang up the ladder after me.

Three paces took me to the door.

My hand reached out to push the door open.

Abruptly, it was snatched back.

I stared into the oil lamp's radiance. Hay piled up to the pitch of the roof. A woman stood facing me, the bow in her hand bent and the steel head of the arrow aimed directly at my breast. The man who had flung the door open appeared. It was nicely done. In a single instant the bow could loose and the arrow drive through me.

"Hold still, dom," said the man. He was apim, strongly built and with a brown beard, trimmed to a point. His eyes were dark and his face, big-boned, powerful, held a look of such savage anger I knew I would have to treat him with the utmost caution. "One move—one—and you're spitted."

"Stand quite still," said the woman.

Her voice was mellifluous, very pleasing in other circumstances. She wore a russet tunic and russet trousers, cut tightly, and her slender waist was cinctured by a wide brown belt, and the gold buckle glittered in the light. As to her face, that lay in shadow; but I caught the impression of a firmness there, the shape conveying that sense of strength as her head half-turned to stare along the shaft. Her eyes fastened upon me, large and brown and luminous above the bar of shadow from her left arm.

"We shall all have to move very—" I began.

The man spat out a curse.

"You speak when you are spoken to, dom, not before. You are very near death."

"Oh, aye," I said. "And so are we all—"

The man lifted his fist. His nostrils pinched in.

"Kaldu!" The voice of command as the woman spoke smoked into the room. She was used to telling people what to do and seeing them do it. "Quiet, Kaldu. No chance has brought these two horters here."

"They mean us mischief, my lady. Let me—"

I said, "Stop clowning about, Kaldu. Listen to your mistress. And we must all get out of here. The watch is on the way. Where are—where is the injured man and his comrade?"

The bow was held in a grip that did not tremble by so much as an eyelash. The bow was a big, compound reflex weapon that pulled enough to let a man know he held a bow; the girl gripped it and held the arrow in such a fashion that told me she knew exactly what she was doing. One thing was sure, this mysterious woman was a superb archer.

"You know? How could you? The watch—?"

"Come on, Kaldu," I said. "Close your mouth. We must get out of here at once."

"I believe you," the woman said. She lowered the bow.

I heard Tyfar let out a shaky breath. He did not put as much trust as I did in the bowmanship of this girl. "Which way is the watch coming?"

"In the direction of the Avenue of a Thousand—"

"Very well. We must go over the roof to the bakery beyond. Kaldu, fetch Barkindrar. Tell Nath." She swung to face Tyfar and me. "I do not know who you are—yet. But if you are traitors—"

"Barkindrar and Nath are my men," spoke up Tyfar. "Lady. I trust they are not badly hurt—"

"They can run." Tyfar flinched back.

"Then," I said, "for the sake of Havil the Green, let us all run!"

The girl flashed me a look. "Havil," she said. "You are Hamalese?"

"Yes—" began Tyfar.

I said, "Havil is known over all Havilfar. Now enough shilly-shallying." Barkindrar and Nath appeared, helped along by Kaldu. He loomed over them. "Come on, you two famblys. We must run for it."

They started to speak and an enormous battering began on the door. The noise burst up from front and back of the building.

"The watch!" said Kaldu. "We are too late!"

"No!" flared the girl. She looked like an enraged zhantilla, fiery, incensed, splendid. "It's never too late, until you're dead!"

Eight

An Arrow in the Swamp

The bakery leaned against the stables for mutual support. They propped each other. The aroma of baking bread fought with the dungy whiffs from the yard at the back of the barn. As we prepared to run through the opposite door to the bakery, the woman looked at Barkindrar. The Brokelsh was clearly in pain; but in that sullen, mulish, Brokelsh way he refused to acknowledge the fact. The woman placed her hand on Barkindrar's forehead.

The hand was shapely, firm, clearly the hand of a woman and yet I knew that hand could accomplish warrior deeds. Her face relaxed for a betraying moment from her tough no-nonsense pose and revealed the compassion she felt. Then she swung back to us, hard and imperative.

"They take their time. They will never see us past the bakery."

She wore a rapier and main gauche. The bow went up on her shoulder out of the way. Her brown hair, trimmed neatly and rather too short, shone bravely in the light of the suns.

I looked past the jut of the stable roof as we went out. If some damned inquisitive mercenary took it into his head to move well out into the yard, he could not fail to see us. Once they had broken into the building they'd be up the stairs like a pack of werstings, all fangs and ravagings.

The bakery was a single-story affair and we ought to scramble down easily enough. I judged there would be no need to set a rear guard, and Nod the Straw, out on the roof, would have warned us if a mercenary did stroll out too far.

Nod the Straw, a wispy little fellow who worked in the stables, waited for us on the roof. His pop-eyes and thick-lipped mouth expressed no surprise that there were two more people suddenly appearing from the shelter of his barn. But he was savagely annoyed and kept brandishing a cut-down pitchfork.

"I know who it was," he raved. "That crop-eared, no-good kleesh of a Sorgan! He must have betrayed us—and they'll give him a dozen stripes quicker'n a dozen silver sinvers."

"Never mind about who betrayed us now, Nod," said the woman. "Help get Barkindrar down off your roof."

Tyfar said, "Do you all go on. I shall hold the roof and delay them—"

The woman threw him a glance that I, for one, would not welcome. Although, by Krun, that self-same look that says what a great ninny you are has been thrown at me in my time.

"Leave off, Nod," said Kaldu. "I will take Barkindrar on my back."

"You great dermiflon!" jibed Nod the Straw. But he desisted in his efforts, and Kaldu took Barkindrar up and bore him swiftly down over the roof of the bakery. Nath the Shaft followed with Nod the Straw.

"What are you waiting for?" said Tyfar. He drew his sword. "I can hold them off for long enough—"

"You think, then," said this woman in her imperious way, "that you are some kind of Jikai?"

Tyfar's color rose up into his cheeks.

"I think I know where honor—"

"Honor!" She laughed, and, even then, even in all that thumping racket from below, and the peril in which we stood, that laughter rose, pure and untrammeled, and exciting.

"Go on, Tyfar," I said. "There is time to get across into the shadows of the bakery."

"I shall not precede this—lady."

"Then," I said, and if you are surprised you still do not understand that old reprobate, Dray Prescot, "then I shall go at once myself and leave you two to wrangle it out between you."

And, with that, I jumped down onto the adjoining roof and crabbed deuced swiftly across to follow the others as they clawed their way down a crumbling wall to the alley. I had no compunction. I knew Tyfar's honor would make him follow me, wasting no more time. If the woman wished to be last, no doubt following some obscure honor code or discipline of her own, then we'd only hold things up by further wrangling.

Tyfar breathed down my neck as I jumped for the alley.

"That woman! Insufferable! Vosk-headed! Stubborn as a graint!"

"Charming, though, you must agree."

"Yes, yes, of course. I noticed her at once. Although I would not say charming—in fact, charming is the last word I'd use. Attractive, alluring, beautiful—yes, she's all those. But who can put up with seductiveness cloaked with superciliousness?"

I peered suspiciously at Tyfar. "Isn't that San Blarnoi? Although, to be sure, I think the quote phrases it somewhat differently from 'put up with.'"

"San Blarnoi knew what he was talking about. That woman!"

"Yes?" came that smooth mellifluous voice, sweet as honey and sharp as a rapier. "What woman would that be, horter?"

Tyfar spun about. I was facing him, and he swung back to stare accusingly at me. His whole stance, his shining face, screamed out: "You might have warned me!"

I said, "Why, some shrewish fishwife who landladied it at our last inn. Now, we had best hurry. Those paktuns looked as though they know their job. And if Sorgan did betray you they'll know we have an injured man."

"Yes," she said, instantly forgetting the pettiness of impending annoyance at Tyfar's incautious words. "We must get on. Kaldu! Make for Horter Rathon's."

"Quidang, my lady."

We all ran down the alley, and we ran away from Blue Vosk Street and headed for the thick stand of tall timber.

"There is a section of bog in here, lady," said Nod the Straw. "No one ventures here." His eyes rolled. "I do not like to go in—but—"

"Needs must when you come to the fluttrell's vane, Nod."

"Aye, my lady."

"This Rathon," I said, "to whom we are all running like a flock of ponshos. Did Sorgan know of him and his house?"

"No," said Kaldu.

Tyfar wanted to bristle up at the incivility. But I restrained him with a quiet word. How odd it is that a prince will stand for uncouthness when an arrow is aimed at his heart, and prickles up when it is not! Although, to give Tyfar his dues, he wasn't the least afraid of arrows in the normal course of things. That a beautiful and well-formed woman had been the person aiming the shaft at us—that, I think, had thrown him off balance.

The trees closed over us, a mixture of the beautiful as well as the ugly in Kregan trees. The path became distinctly moist. I looked back. Our footprints were perfectly legible to the eyes of a tracker.

"It gets a lot stickier ahead," said Nod. "Unfortunately."

"There is a boat," said the woman. She spoke briskly. "We can cross the river without trouble, and lose ourselves in the Aracloins.* Horter Rathon will give us shelter."

"Why did you not go there first, instead of to Blue Vosk Street?"

She gave me a withering look.

"That was nearest. We did not know who Barkindrar and Nath were when the watch tried to take them up. When we realized they were Hamalese, of course, we stepped in."

"You are revolutionaries?"

The moment I spoke I heard the fatuity of my question.

She said, "Kaldu! Watch your step."

He did not answer but plunged on with Barkindrar slung over his back. The Bullet had taken a nasty cut along the leg. The wound was bound—and bound expertly, too, the handiwork as I guessed of this surprising woman.

Along by the edge of the river where this boggy section was difficult to tell from river itself, we threaded along the narrow path. Nod the Straw led, and he was not at all happy. In any niksuth, any small marshy area, of Kregen you are likely to find uncooperative life. Teeth and fangs, spines and stings, they hop up out of the bog and seek to drag you down for a juicy dinner. Even in a city like Khorunlad. Aware of this delightful fact of Kregan bogs, I loosened my thraxter in the scabbard.

"If no one comes here," I said. "The watch will not think we have. There is no need to hurry, they will not know how long we have been gone from the stables."

"There was a quantity of blood spilled on the straw," she said.

"I see. Then we had best hurry."

"Jak," called Tyfar.

I swung about to look.

He was half off and half on the path, and one leg was going deeper and deeper into a foul-smelling stink of blackness. Tendriliferous vines snaked over the oozing mud. But he got a grip on a clump of weed and arrested his sucking-in.

He had been following up last. The girl at my side said, "The oaf!" She spoke tartly.

---

* Aracloins: General name for city areas of confused alleys and covered souks and bazaars, teeming with commerce and villainy. A.B.A.

Tyfar got a better grip and started to haul himself in.

A head appeared over his shoulder, one of those snouting, fanged heads of Kregen, all scale and tendrils and gape-jaws. The eyes were red slits. It hoisted itself a little free of the ooze with two broad paddle-like forefeet. In the next instant it would open and close that fearsome set of jaws, and Tyfar's head would provide the dinner the thing craved.

The girl took a single step forward. She was splendid.

The bow came from her shoulder as a skater comes off the ice. The arrow nocked, was drawn back—to the ear—and the shaft flew. Straight and strongly driven, that shaft. It pierced cleanly through one of those red slit eyes. The steel point must have gouged on, deep into the minuscule brain.

I could not watch the death throes of the beast any more. A mate to the first appeared almost soundlessly beside me and the jagged-fanged jaws thrust for the girl in her russets, who stood ready with a second shaft aimed for the monster by Tyfar.

My thraxter swept around and then straightened. Point first it drove into a red-slitted eye. The thraxter would not have cut the thing's scaly neck deeply enough. But the solid steel punched through eye and head and into brain. I jerked back. Like its mate, it thrashed and screeched.

The girl gave a single convulsive jump back.

Her bow lifted, the arrow pulled—then she summed up the picture and did not loose.

"I give you my thanks for saving Tyfar," I said.

He was off the ooze now and safely on the path. His leg sheened with the muck. He waved his sword at us and then started to run along the treacherous path to catch us up. I own I felt enormous relief knowing that he was safe.

The woman looked at me. Woman? Girl? She was young, around Tyfar's age, I judged, although men and women change so slowly over their better than two hundred or so years of life on Kregen. Sometimes she had the airs of a queen, and at others those of a roistering tavern wench, and both were nicely calculated. She was controlled in her emotions; but her emotions were real and could break out fiercely—

"By Krun, Jak! That beastie nearly had me—and you!"

"You were busy saving Tyfar, for which my thanks again."

"You are his father?"

"No, no. He is a good comrade."

"Then you have my thanks, for what they are worth, for my life—"

"Do not, I beg you, say, for what that is worth."

"Sometimes my life has meant a great deal to me, and sometimes nothing at all."

Tyfar panted up then, and started in at once thanking the girl. Then he said, "And I do not know to whom I owe my life."

"You may call me Jaezila."

561

We started off along the path again, and I felt it prudent to hang back. I did this to guard against pursuit and, also, as I realized with a sly amusement, so that they might have it out between them.

"Jaezila," said Tyfar, rolling the syllables around his mouth as though they were best Jholaix. "And is that all—my lady?"

"No. It will do for you—Jikai."

She cut him with that great word, used as she used it, in mockery of his warrior prowess.

"Jaezila," persisted Tyfar, and I own I was impressed by his refusal to become warm. After all, he was a prince. "And no more—you are Hamalese?" He sounded doubtful.

I thought I detected a wary note in Jaezila's voice.

"Hamalese—does it matter? I seek to aid you, who are Hamalese. Is not that good enough?"

"I accept that." Tyfar passed on, following her beyond the end of a screen of curly-fronded ferns where the dragonflies, as big as chickens, flitted and flurried on diamond wings. "And what brought you to Khorunlad?"

"Your breeding left much to be desired, dom."

Tyfar bridled up like a spurred zorca. To be accused of poor breeding, and a Prince of Hamal! And to be addressed so familiarly as dom, the common greeting! I watched it all, enthralled. Then I jumped forward.

My Val! We had been growing very chummy with these people, with stubborn Kaldu and this enigmatic woman styling herself Jaezila. But we did not know them. I didn't want Tyfar labeling himself a prince—particularly a Prince of Hamal—until we knew them a great deal better.

"You may be surprised to know—" Tyfar was saying with his voice as frosty as the caverns of the Ice Floes of Sicce. He was going to put Jaezila properly in her place by telling her that she had the honor of addressing a prince, I didn't doubt that. I burst in, quite rudely.

"Come on, come! Don't stand chaffering. I think there were sounds of pursuit along the path."

Tyfar immediately swung about and lifted his sword.

Jaezila simply looked at me. "You think there is pursuit?"

She missed nothing, this girl, nothing...

"And if there is not, that is still no reason to stand lollygagging about. By Krun! Let us get out of this bog and onto firmer ground."

"Fifty paces will bring us to the bank. If you can call it a bank. I scouted this area—"

I said, "You are not from Khorunlad, Jaezila. Hamalese? Maybe. But I do not inquire why you help us from Hamal."

"Do you think that the Empress Thyllis will conquer all the Dawn Lands, Jak?"

That was a confounded question!

562

It suited my purposes to be thought a Hamalese. Yet it went against the grain to have to say that, yes, mad Empress Thyllis would overrun all the Dawn Lands, one after the other.

"She might," I said. "If her throat is not cut first."

She drew her breath in. The others showed up ahead waiting under a grove of drooping missals. Beyond them the river glimmered blue as the summer sky.

"You spoke of revolution," said Jaezila. "Now, I see—"

I interrupted, swiftly but courteously: "My lady Jaezila, do not misunderstand me." Zair knew, I'd taken long enough getting myself accepted as a Hamalese, and this girl quite clearly was more than she appeared. She could go running back to Hamal with a tale that would destroy my plans. I had to dissimulate. "I spoke figuratively. We all serve the empress, do we not? Hamal is set on the road of conquest, is not this so?"

"By Jehamnet! Hamal is set on the road to conquest!"

Her voice contained emotions I couldn't fathom. She swore by Jehamnet, a spirit of harvest time associated with crop failures and similar disasters, and who is known as Jevalnet in Vallia, and Jegrodnet and Jezarnet in the Eye of the World. But she had said Jehamnet, which is Hamalian. He is known as Jehavnet in most of Havilfar. I fancied she was Hamalese and therefore, down here, out doing skullduggery for Thyllis. I held my tongue.

We gathered by the boat, a little skiff that would just about take us all and give us a hand's-breadth freeboard. The river rippled gently in a small breeze. On the opposite bank the walls and roofs of the jumbled Aracloins offered shelter. We pushed off and Kaldu and I pulled the oars, taking it gently. There were a sizeable number of other boats on the river. A low pontoon bridge spanned the river lower down, and this impediment assisted in the formation and continuance of the boggy area upstream.

So, moving cautiously but with purpose, we successfully reached the safety of Horter Rathon's questionable establishment.

Nine

We Strike a Blow for Hamal

"By Havil! I don't intend to sit here mewed up like a blind bird!"

"I agree. And I'll tell you something else, Tyfar. If we're not back at the camp before very soon, the Pachaks will come in after us. Or even, Krun forfend, Hunch might—"

"What!" And Tyfar lay back on the pallet and roared.

Horter Nath Rathon joined in the laughter, although he wasn't at all sure what the jest might be. He was like that. He was a jolly, fat, smiling, hand-washing little man, clad in a long green and red gown with a silver chain around his neck and depending from it a bunch of keys reposing on the proud jut of his belly. He had sent one of his servants out to spy the land.

This fellow, Ornol—a massive Gon whose shaven head gleamed brilliantly from the application of unguents, a fashion some of the Gons have—came back to report not the hair or hide of a Havil-forsaken mercenary to be seen.

Nath Rathon burbled and jingled his keys.

"Excellent, Ornol. Now go and keep watch."

Ornol went off, his pate glistening, and I looked carefully at Tyfar. Young Prince Tyfar was high of color, and a trifle breathless, and given to wider gestures than usual. He was not drunk. The nearness of his escape from death in the little swamp was beginning to work on him, and he was going through the shakes like a true horter. Also, I fancy the idea that he had been saved and his life preserved to him by the quick and skillful actions of a girl came as a novel surprise.

"You will assuredly have to wait until the suns set," cautioned Nath Rathon.

"That is a pesky long way off," grumbled Tyfar.

"I think," I said, "our friends will wait until nightfall." I did not add that I felt it highly unlikely they would venture into Khorunlad before Quienyin had sussed the city in lupu for us.

There might well be a period of fraught explanation if his apparition appeared, ghostlike, to scare the others half to death.

But, then, I had come to the conclusion that it would take a lot more than that, a very great deal more than that, to scare this mysterious young lady Jaezila witless.

She had tended to Barkindrar's wound, and the Bullet had declared stoutly that he was fit to walk out with us. The situation was complicated—some situations are and some are not and most times they are resolved by death but not always—and we understood that while the official policy of Khorundur toward Hamal was neutrality, factions inevitably arose. The common folk labored under the delusion that if the Empress Thyllis took over their country they would miraculously inherit a better life, with free food and rivers of wine and not a day's work in a sennight. If this is pitching the stories they believed too high, think only of the slaves that would come onto the market after a successful invasion and conquest. Hamalian gold was in this.

Rathon clinched that for me when he said to Jaezila when she walked in, smiling, "I fear, my lady, you will buy no vollers now."

She frowned, quickly, losing that smile on the instant, whereat I surmised her mission to buy vollers for Hamal was a secret one. Thyllis had been prodigal with her treasure and had given patents of nobility for gold. She had lost many fliers. Clearly, she was desirous of purchasing what she could not make.

"Why so, Horter Rathon?"

"You were seen when—these two Hamalese—it were best you left the city, my lady. It is hard enough work as it is."

He might smile and jingle his keys; but he was a man for Hamal, and if the common folk welcomed invasion, the better-off did not. That was obvious. They had hired bands of mercenaries, and because paktuns were hard to come by had had to hire men who were not of the top quality, or even of the second or third quality. I did not think the paktuns who had chased us were as low as masichieri; but I was told that masichieri, mere bandits masquerading as mercenaries when it suited them, were in the city in large numbers to keep order.

This, as you will readily perceive, placed me in a quandary.

I was opposed to Hamal, although pretending to be Hamalese. The poor folk were deluded. But those who were opposed to Hamal employed means I did not much relish. I would not strike a blow willingly against folk who stood up in opposition to mad Empress Thyllis. So, as I listened to the others debating what best to do, I felt myself to be shoved nose-first into a dilemma.

"My work must be completed," Jaezila was saying, and her composure remained. There was the hint, the merest hint, of her true feelings boiling away.

"How, my lady?" Rathon spread his hands. "You will be taken up by the watch. These mercenaries the nobles have hired, they are little better than drikingers, bandits who will slit your throat for a copper ob."

"And, my lady," put in Kaldu, "the voller manufacturers here are all rich." His brown beard tufted. "Well, that follows, by Krun, does it not? They will not welcome you."

"And it was all arranged!" said Jaezila. Her face—what a wonderful face she had! Broad-browed, subtle, perfect of curve of cheek and lip, illuminated by a passionate desire to esteem well of life—I felt myself drawn to her. As for Tyfar, he was goggling away. "Everything was going splendidly," she said. Some lesser girl would have been crying by now. "And then these people against Hamal seized the power, and the vaunted neutrality of Khorundur—where is it now?"

"I and my associates will get the common folk out into the streets," said Rathon. "But that is going to take time. And there will be a great deal of blood spilled." He lifted his keys and then let them jingle against his gut. "Well, they are common folk and so 'tis of no matter."

I turned away from him, and took my ugly, hating old beakhead of a face off out of the way. By Vox! But wasn't that the way of your maniacal, empire-puggled Hamalese bastard?

Tyfar followed me.

"What ails you, Jak? Your face—you look as though you have fallen among stampeding calsanys."

"No matter," I said. Control returned to me, and with it common sense. "I think it would be a good plan to take a few vollers for ourselves." I did not add that I would fly mine to South Pandahem and then Vallia.

"Capital!" Tyfar brisked up. "Let us make a plan."

Rathon began at once to put all manner of obstacles in the way—the sentries were alert, we had no chance of reaching a landing platform, didn't we have gold to buy a voller, it was madness. Jaezila looked fierce. "The plan is good!"

I was not so sure. This lady, if she was not Hamalese, at least worked for my enemies. I felt drawn to her and she was, in truth, splendid. But she was an enemy. Well, poof to that. Were not Chido and Rees enemies, and were they not good friends, Bladesmen, comrades? In this, at least, we could work together.

I noticed that this Jaezila had an odd little habit of suddenly turning her head, and looking slightly to her side and rear, as though expecting to find someone there.

Now, in this enterprise going forward I had to think most carefully. We were a bunch of desperadoes, yes. But we purposed taking a voller from folk who were aligned against us in the political arena, and folk who were fighting against my enemies. It was a puzzle. In the end I did the only thing I could do, and went along and placed the outcome in the hands of Zair.

Barkindrar the Bullet would have to be figured into the calculations. Eventually we persuaded Nath Rathon to apprise us of the best location for picking up vollers, and he said that the bright sparks flew in from the outlying districts and parked on the roof of The Rokveil's Head.

"They'll be inspecting the undersides of tables with Beng Dikkane* long before the hour of midnight." And he laughed.

I forced myself to be polite to him.

"Then, good Nath Rathon, you will show us this place a few burs before that."

"Me? Oh, no, dom. I will send Ornol—"

Jaezila and Tyfar looked questioningly at me.

"Oh, no, dom," I said, "you will show us."

He spluttered indignant protests. What my face looked like I do not know; but I do know I fought for control. I made myself relax. Just why I acted as I did, Zair forgive me, you may more readily perceive—now—than I did—then.

---

* Beng Dikkane: The patron saint of all the ale drinkers in Paz. A.B.A.

"I wish that you, Nath Rathon, should show us The Rokveil's Head. I do not think you will argue."

He blinked. His keys jangled. He opened his mouth, looked at me, closed his mouth. His face, fat and plump and merry, on a sudden looked amazingly long. He shut that glistening mouth. Then, weakly, he said, "As you wish. I shall lead you."

"Good," I said. And I smiled most genially.

Our preparations made, we ventured out when She of the Veils cast her rosy golden light over the nighted city. The way was not far. We walked as a party of roisterers, out for a good time, and we made no bones about singing a few ditties. There was no problem as to who was to fly the vollers. Retainers of nobles and adventurers as we were, flying air-boats was a mere matter of normal occupation.

The Rokveil's Head turned out to be an imposing place, lit up with many lanterns, pillared and porticoed, and doing a humming business. Tyfar and I, allowing our expensive cloaks to conceal our armor, had no difficulty in entering. That mark of the notor we now realized had brought us with the ease that had puzzled us into the city. The lords ran this city. And the common folk looked to Hamal for relief. Truly, that was a colossal and vile joke on innocent people, to be sure!

Nath Rathon had dressed himself in popinjay fashion, which we assumed to be normal for him. Jaezila had borrowed a demure but still devastating evening gown, all sheer peach-colored sensil. Rathon had taken it from one of the women of his establishment, and with the gown a display of gems. They were all fakes. And Kaldu wore a sober evening lounging robe of dark green. We all wore weapons—except Jaezila, outside our clothes—and this was a mere natural part of evening attire.

The flunkeys wanted to bustle about and take our wraps and cloaks; but Rathon assured them that this was not necessary as he had just happened to meet this party and they were desirous of patronizing the best establishment in the city and so he had just gone out of his way to bring them here. No, they were not friends of his and he did not know them, and now he must take himself home to his house and family in the eastern suburbs.

The majordomo thanked Rathon for bringing him the custom; but Rathon, whose hand hovered now continually at his mouth, smiled and bobbed and went off very quickly. We did not know if his deception would pass muster.

As we went up the wide balustraded stairway with the carved statues of sylvies flanking the treads, Tyfar said, "I am not sure that was a clever move, Jak. It seems to be you may have placed Rathon in some jeopardy if he is recognized."

"Oh," I said, airily, "he will get away with it."

Privately, I would have no sorrow if Rathon were discovered and thrown out of Khorundur. That would be one agent of Hamal the less. So we went on up. The halls were palatial. There were many slaves, all stupidly dressed in feathers and bangles and little else. Much wine was in evidence. The sounds of laughter and horseplay reached us from the various magnificent chambers. We passed a room in which Jikaida was in full swing, with great piles of gold wagered on the outcome. Jikalla too was being played, along with Vajikry. We saw no rooms devoted to the Game of Moons and that surprised no one.

People were staggering about, this early already the worse for wear. And so, steadily, we passed on up the wide stairways until we reached the top floor.

Sometimes I have swift attacks of nostalgia for remembered struggles. Sometimes; usually I am too bound up with the struggle going on at the moment. We found the door leading to the roof and stepped out under the stars of Kregen.

"We take three if we can," said Tyfar. "Is that agreed?"

He was brilliantly excited, keyed up. "We strike a blow for Hamal tonight! Do not forget that."

"How can we forget it?" said Jaezila.

Tyfar colored up again, and then shook himself, dark in the starlight, and we padded off in search of a suitable voller for the first of us to fly away. Our first port of call would be to pick up Barkindrar and Nath, and then we'd make for the camp and pick up the others. Then it was Hamal...

The airboats were parked neatly and the guards moved about, dim silhouettes against the stars.

Tyfar crept forward with Kaldu at his elbow.

Jaezila and I, for the moment, waited in the shadows.

"That one, I think, Jak, for me."

"Yes. A fleet craft. But you cannot trust a voller from Khorundur as you would trust one from Hamal."

"No—yes. You are right. But, I am not sure if I should go to Hamal. My work here has been spoiled—"

"You'll never obtain fliers now that the lords are against Hamal. Is there nowhere else you can try?"

"You mock me, of course. I find your manners—uncouth." She used the word sturr. I laughed. Oh, yes, I laughed.

"You have the right of it, my lady. That is my name. Jak the Sturr."

She gazed at me. And then she, too, laughed. The look of her, the way her head tilted, the star-gleam in her eyes... I felt my stupid old heart give a leap. She was magnificent, and she worked for my enemies.

Quietly, the laughter still bubbling away but held now within her poised manner, she said, "I shall not forget the way you dealt with that beastie that sought—it was quick."

"No quicker than the way you loosed to save poor Tyfar."

"Poor Tyfar! Indeed! He is a ninny, is he not?"

"No... No. He is a gallant young man a little out of his depth."

And, a ghost rising to torment me, I carried on the thought in my head—like Barty Vessler.

"Well, Jak the Sturr," she said, and there was the bite of decision in her voice, "you are not out of your depth in this midnight murder and mayhem, that is very sure."

"I hope there is no murder."

"So do I."

A low whistle cut the dimness. We moved forward. Kaldu stood over the unconscious body of a Khibil guard. A Fristle slumbered at his side. Kaldu held his sword very purposefully.

"There are two vollers, my lady. And the third for the hyr-paktun."

She looked at me, swiftly. "Kaldu dubs you a hyr-paktun and he has an eye for these things. Do you wear the pakzhan at your throat, Jak the Sturr?"

"I have done so, in my time, my lady."

"So be it. Then let us board—and woe betide the laggard!"

"Now, just a minute—" began Tyfar.

She turned on him like a zhantilla turning to meet the rush of a leem.

"Tyfar! Fambly! Get aboard and fly—the guards will not wait for your waiting."

"My lady, you treat me hard—"

"Now Krun save me from a pretty-speechifying ninny!" she said, and swung her leg over the voller's coaming. That fancy sensil robe split down and revealed her long russet-clad leg. She was in the voller in a twinkling and Kaldu at her side.

I said to Tyfar, "Take your voller, Tyfar, and let us go."

"What a—a girl!" stuttered Tyfar.

What a girl, indeed!

Ten

The Brothers Fre-Da Give Nikobi

As the three vollers touched down on the grass and then ghosted in under the trees out of chance sight from the air, I felt relief that we had carried it off successfully. Tyfar leaped down from his craft, leaving Nath to assist Barkindrar. Such is the way of unheeding princes. I was watching Tyfar.

A shadow moved under the trees and the moons' glitter caught on the blade that pressed against his breast.

I started to leap down, dragging the thraxter free, when Tyfar said, "What? What? Oh—yes, I understand, Modo."

The Pachak's tail hand quivered and the blade vanished in shadow.

I came up with them, pretty sharpish, and Modo, seeing me, said, "Jak. A word from San Quienyin. He wishes you to call him Naghan and not to let these new people know he is a Wizard of Loh."

"Very well. If it is his wish."

The others crowded forward and Hunch and Nodgen came up, and the pappattu was made, and Quienyin had forsaken his blue robes and doffed that turban, and stood forth in a simple brown tunic—admittedly, there was a touch of silver braid at throat and hem—to be introduced as Naghan.

"Naghan what?" said Jaezila in her sweet voice, not at all rudely. She smiled and charmed old Quienyin clean through.

"Naghan the Dodderer, some folk call me, my lady. But, for you, the name Naghan the Seeing is more seemly. If it pleases you, my lady."

I marveled. Such humbleness from a Wizard of Loh!

"It pleases me, Naghan the Seeing. And I am famished—"

"My lady!" And Hunch was there, grimacing away, filled with enormous desires to be of help to this imperious and lovely lady, who had appeared at our camp from the shadows.

We ate the viands we had, and none that we had brought from Khorunlad, alas.

"We rest for two burs," declared Tyfar. "And then we fly. And we will let our fluttrells go free. They will bring joy to whoever finds them."

"If they do not fly wild, Tyfar, as anyone would who had to support your—"

"Whatever happens to the fluttrells," I said, "they deserve well of us. Now, rest us all—and I shall stand the first watch."

Tyfar and Jaezila glared hotly, one at the other. I sighed. Bantam cocks— and a bantam hen, by Krun!

The Maiden with the Many Smiles shed down her fuzzy pink light as we took off into the soft night air. Tyfar expressed himself as mightily pleased that Jaezila elected to fly with me.

"For if I have to endure the barbs of her tongue," he said, "I swear by the names I shall—" And then Jaezila, climbing up beside me, smiled down, and Tyfar was struck dumb.

So we flew over the sleeping face of Kregen beneath the moons. Two of the lesser moons hurtled close by above. The night air breathed sweet and cool. The windrush in my face, my hair blowing, ah, yes—and a glorious girl at my side! Well, she was not Delia, my Delia of Delphond, my Delia of the Blue Mountains; but I felt then they would be well-matched, and that, in all soberness, by Zair, was a strange feeling for me.

She talked a little, small inconsequential matters, of her mother whom she loved dearly, and her brothers and sisters, although she did not mention their names. It would have been all too easy to slide into confidences, and to have spilled out my own near-despairing feelings about my own children. But I did not. I purported to come from Hamal, and must therefore watch my tongue.

Hunch and Nodgen sat in the body of the voller. We fleeted on our way north and east toward the empire of my enemies.

And I had to make a decision. I was going to stop by South Pandahem and drag Turko the Shield out of his fairground booth. Then I would look in on Vallia, just, I assured myself, to make sure the place was on an even keel. I felt a traitor even to think it might not be with Drak at the helm. And then it would be Hyrklana for me.

"You are pensive, Jak the Sturr."

"Aye, my lady. I am thinking that I shall have to leave you and Tyfar soon."

"Oh!" she flared. "Why link my name with that ninny's?"

"Now, young lady," I said, and I heard my voice harden, "you are altogether too harsh on Tyfar. He is a young man with high ideals and great notions of honor—"

"Like to make a laughingstock of himself—"

"That is true. But, at the least, laughingstock or no, he will not be shamed."

She cocked her head at me. The moons' light caught her hair and sheened soft brown and fuzzy pink. "No. I think you are right. But he is so—so—"

"Gallant?"

"Very well." And she laughed, her head thrown back. "A gallant ninny!"

We flew on into the blaze of dawn when the twin suns, Far and Havil, rose and the land came alive with color. Tyfar, in the lead voller, pointed down. Below us a small stream wended between wooded uplands. Some two dwaburs ahead, almost lost to sight, the towers of a city or fortress rose from the trees. Below us, by the stream, a clearing offered a landing place. Down we went.

Making camp, with the vollers pulled into the shelter of the trees, and a circumspect fire going, we surveyed our paltry rations and resigned ourselves to going hungry. The Pachaks glided into the woods to find game. Hunch brewed tea. Barkindrar, wounded leg or not, went off by the river to sling at birds.

Nath the Shaft and I stood watch.

Presently this Deb-Lu-Quienyin, whom we now called Naghan the Seeing, approached. He looked thoughtful.

"Tyfar and Jaezila and Kaldu are for Hamal. I would like very much now to go to Vallia. But—what of you, Jak?"

"You know. South Pandahem."

"Yes. I followed your adventures in Khorunlad, a little, a few quick observations in lupu to make sure you were all right. I can tell you I was heartily glad you came out safely."

I favored him with a searching look. His face that had, since he'd regained his powers, lost a deal of those lines and wrinkles, was now down-drawn in fatigue. The smudges under his eyes, bruised purple, were new.

"You are tired, Quienyin?"

"Aye, Jak. By the Seven Arcades! Since our little trip with Monsters and Moders I do think... I need to sleep in a soft bed for a whole season."

"That can be arranged in Vallia."

"So? I shall go, and, I sincerely trust, with your blessing. But you?"

"Give me a look out, from time to time," I said, lightly, thinking nothing of the words, trying to jolly him along. He was very down and I wondered why. "I shall pull out with a whole skin, never fear."

He shook his head.

"From anyone else, I would take that as boasting, Jak—"

I was dutifully repentant. "And from me, also, I confess."

"Mayhap."

I drew a breath. "I have known other Wizards of Loh. Some I account good friends and others, as you know, as foe-men. But for none have I felt... Even Khe-Hi... It is strange. I would never have believed it of a Wizard of Loh. But it is, and I joy in the gift."

He smiled. "And I, too—Jak."

Again, that hesitation before the name. A deliberate hesitation? Yes, by Vox, I said to myself. Oh, yes...

The Pachaks came back with game, and Barkindrar with a half-dozen birds, and Hunch got busy by the fire. Nodgen helped. Barkindrar stretched out with a grunt of relief, sticking his wounded leg before him like a crutch itself. Nath bent to him and Jaezila came across, imperious and commanding, ordering this and that, and mightily tender as she unwrapped the bandages to attend to the Bullet's leg. I noticed that Kaldu remained always near his lady, ready to leap instantly to her defense. As a retainer, he was invaluable. Tyfar stood by as Jaezila worked on his man, and the cooking smells began to waft up. It was a pretty scene, there in the woodland, not quite Arden, perhaps, but very much a scene as I would like it on two worlds.

Now appeared a good opportunity to inspect the vollers we had liberated. I used this euphemism quite deliberately, to cloak the mischief we might have wrought in the desperate straits of our own needs. Two of these craft would go eventually to Vallia, and only one to Hamal. The Khorundese craft bulked far more blockily than the petal-shaped vollers of comparable size manufactured in Hamal or Hyrklana. They were profusely ornamented. I had felt the handling of the example I had flown to be clumsier than I was used to, not so quick in response to the levers of control. But, more primitive though they might be, they flew.

The food was served and we ate, a quite unbalanced diet; but succulent. Then I drew the Pachak twins aside.

"Brothers Fre-Da," I addressed them seriously. "San Quienyin is for Vallia. Would you consider accompanying him?"

They looked, one at the other, each waiting a sign.

I went on, "I can assure you he will be received with honor in Vondium. As will you."

"Will there be honorable employment for us there, Jak?"

I pulled my lip. "I am told the Emperor of Vallia no longer employs mercenaries to fight for his country."

"This word," said Logu Fre-Da, "we have heard."

"With acrimony among the paktunsa," elaborated Modo Fre-Da.

"It would not be seemly to allow the San to travel alone. I think if you give your nikobi, Vallia will welcome you royally. And there are many Pachaks who now call Vallia home."

The twins looked at each other again and the looks said it all. They nodded. "This we will do."

"Good." I felt relieved. "Then that is settled."

Nodgen returned to camp then bearing two huge armfuls of paline branches, and we all fell on the yellow cherry-like fruits with delight. So the day passed. Any good Kregan likes his eight good square meals a day—six at a pinch. But, as I say, our meals were woefully unbalanced. The suns began to sink.

The ostentatious way in which Prince Tyfar and Jaezila each avoided the other's company amused me. We were given a demonstration again of her prowess with the bow, for she hauled the bow off her shoulder, nocked the shaft, and let fly, and the bird that had been fleeting across the clearing fell plump down alongside Hunch. He jumped a foot.

"By Tryflor!" He grabbed the bird by the neck and swung it about, so that the arrow whirled. "It would not surprise me if the bird descended already plucked and stuffed for the fire!"

We all laughed.

Shadows of russet and sea green lay across the clearing. The Suns of Scorpio plunged into banks of ocher and rose clouds, and the broad bulk of Kregen rolled up to enfold them once more in night. The vollers were brought out from under the trees.

Barkindrar the Bullet declared roundly that, by the Resplendent Bridzilkelsh, he could get his leg up into the voller without assistance. He climbed in awkwardly. Nath the Shaft hovered over him. Tyfar was in the cabin stowing away his armor. At the second voller the Pachaks were stowing their gear and organizing the meticulous arrangements for their new employer to whom they had given their nikobi, and Quienyin was leaning on the coaming watching me walk across to him. I made up my mind.

"Hunch! Nodgen!"

"Jak?"

"You will fly with San Quienyin."

"But—!"

"I shall see you soon. But I value the protection you, together with the twins, can afford the San."

"Oh, of course," said Hunch, crossly. "We can look after him all right."

"So long as there is somewhere to run away, eh, Hunch?" And Nodgen guffawed. But there was no malice in him. He had seen how his comrade Hunch could fight, as had I.

"Up with you," I said.

The good-byes were made. Tyfar came over with the others and we all called the Remberees... Quienyin and those four men to look after him lifted away in the voller into the darkling shadows. The suns were nearly gone.

Tyfar hurried back to finish stowing his armor. He had picked up a fine harness and cared for it. Jaezila and Kaldu stood looking over the coaming of the foredeck beside the control levers. I started for the remaining flier. Then I halted and swung back. I wanted a final word with Jaezila and Tyfar both, some jumbled notions in my old vosk skull of a head of trying to get them to see reason, one with the other. When Jaezila arrived in Ruathytu that young lady would discover that the gallant ninny Tyfar was a Prince of Hamal.

A twinge of disappointment that I would miss that entertaining spectacle afforded me resigned amusement.

From under the shadows of the trees men broke in a long savage line of twinkling steel and bared teeth. They yelled war cries as they charged. They raced for the voller where Jaezila's bow slapped into her fist. I stood halfway between the voller and the thrusting line of foemen.

"Run, Jak!" screamed Jaezila.

There was no time to reach either of the fliers.

I unlimbered the thraxter and swung about.

"Take off!" I bellowed.

The men running in with such headlong ferocity were a mix of races. I cast a swift look back. Jaezila was about to leap over the coaming to join me. There was no sign of Tyfar.

In a buffeting of wings, scores of mirvols catapulted over the trees, fell toward the voller. The flying animals bore flyers on their backs, counterparts to the footmen advancing against me. Weapons flamed in the last of the suns.

The trap had been sprung. But the cramphs were too late to take Quienyin's airboat. Just before I swung about to start hammering at the running men I saw Kaldu seize Jaezila and draw her back into the voller. Heartbeats later the voller lifted into the air, smashing through the fluttering wings of the mirvols. She turned, she lifted, two mirvols collided and fell away in a smashing clawing of wing and talon, and then the voller soared away over the trees.

I was left to face the savage onrush of naked steel.

Eleven

Vajikry

The thongs binding my wrists were not lesten hide and when the time came for me to burst them, I fancied they'd snap without too much effort. As I stood before Trylon Nath Orscop I had to check myself and realize that time had not arrived yet.

His private room was furnished with an austerity surprising in a man wielding his kind of power. He sat behind a plain desk of balass, black and shining, the walls were covered by plain silk drapes, the floor by plain carpets of some indescribable weave that scratched the feet, and his men wore plain dark harnesses of black and bronze. But they had been smart enough in knocking me over, netting me with iron links in the old way of man management on Kregen. Now I was brought before the trylon to discover what he wanted.

A trylon is four rungs down the ladder of nobility, usually. This Nath Orscop, the Trylon of Absordur, ruled a small trylonate; but it was buried in the woodlands, rich in timber and minerals, and he kept himself to himself. He had a single ruling passion, and I was to discover what that was rather sharply.

"You claim your name is Jak the Sturr?"

"Yes, notor."

I spoke with just enough neutrality in my voice to pass muster. I was prepared to humor this trylon, for the fellow intrigued me. He wore clothes of severe cut, a rusty black, with a flat, black velvet cap. His face was long and narrow, gaunt, very pale, and his gray eyes seemed filmed. Deeply indented lines grooved beside his nose and mouth. A tall oblong of pallid violence, that face, framed in the rusty black.

"You play Vajikry, of course."

"Moderately, notor. Now, if it is Jikaida—"

The guard at my side, a hulking Gon, hit me alongside the head with his bludgeon.

"My lord!" bellowed the Gon. "I heard nothing!"

"That is good," said Trylon Nath, as I put a hand to my head where the famous Bells of Beng Kishi were starting their second round of campanological mayhem. "That name, that game, is never mentioned here. Only—" And here he leered at me. "Only we flog jikaider—that is the only use for the name here in Absordur."

"As the notor pleases," I said, eyeing the Gon's bludgeon.

Many a fellow winces when Jikaida is mentioned; this cramph seemed possessed of more than a fair share of hatred for the game. But, for Vajikry, his passion was all-encompassing.

"All who enter my trylonate uninvited are given the opportunity to play Vajikry. The game is supreme here. If you win you go free and with a handful of golden deldys to go with you. If you lose..."

He didn't have to tell me, did he?

I said, "Do many men win, notor?"

He sniggered and wiped his pallid lips with a kerchief.

"Do not let that disturb you, Jak the Sturr. You will need all your concentration for the game."

I'd been playing games a lot, just lately, what with Kazz-Jikaida and Monsters and Moders—and now, Vajikry. I'm no real hand at it, and admit that. Maybe I was in a tighter spot than I had realized.

Trylon Nath stood up from behind that black balass desk. At his waist he wore a bronze-link belt, and a thick, curved dagger sheath swung from lockets. The blade of that kind of dagger, well-known in Havilfar, is often as wide as a knuckle at the hilt, and a Kregan knuckle is 4.2 inches. The blade curves very sharply to a fine point, is sharpened on both edges, and can go in your guts and burst your heart. The Havilfarese call that manner of dagger a kalider. The hilt was thick and heavy and without gems.

"Now, Jak the Sturr, you will be given refreshment. We meet here as the suns go down. You will play Vajikry with me. Whatever your gods may be you would do well to pray to them for guidance."

"Yes, notor," I said, bowing. "Thank you, notor."

He smiled.

They stuffed me into a small stone-walled chamber with a window large enough for a woflo to squirm through and gave me to eat. Rough viands: coarse bread, fatty vosk rashers, stewed cabbage, momolams too long in the tooth for tastiness, and, at the end, a clay dish with eleven palines. I know, I counted.

The water from an earthenware cup tasted of weeds and mud.

In the next cell a man was singing a nice cheerful song. His voice rose dolorously. He sang "The March of the Skeletons." This starts off by recounting how a brilliant and charming girl returned from a boat holiday, and goes on, as is the way of that inscrutable Kregan humor, to detail her story of how the skeletons all marched from the graveyard in search of their missing flesh and blood. As I say, a nice, rousing, cheerful song for the surroundings.

The spires and battlemented towers we had glimpsed as we set the vollers down crowned the very place in which I was confined. This was the palace and chief city of Trylon Nath's Absordur. I had seen little of it, being brought here festooned with iron nets. Pretty soon when the shafts of emerald and ruby from that mocking window shifted to the far wall the guards took me out and spruced me up a trifle under three buckets of water, and then we all marched off to Trylon Nath's private room.

If I felt just as those skeletons felt, marching off all clicking and bony in search of their missing flesh, I am sure you will grasp my feelings. Vajikry! That infuriating game!

I remember once, in the Fleeced Ponsho in Sanurkazz, Nath and Zolta starting on a game in all friendship with a couple of swiftermen, and how, long before the end, the bottles were flying, the fists were flying, the ale was flying, we were flying and the mobiles—well, jolly fat mobiles with their rusty swords, no, they weren't flying after us. But it was a right old punch-up—and all over a simple board game. Trouble is, Vajikry is not as simple as it looks.

Trylon Nath Orscop sat at his black balass desk and I saw his long pallid face and the way he gloated on the Vajikry board set out on the polished desk surface. The board was hexagonal, although you can have round or square boards, and a serpent or ladder-like series of hexes or squares coil inward from one edge to the center. Often there are two parallel coils, curled one within the other, and this confounded mournful-faced old buzzard would have the dual-coil variety, naturally.

The Vajikry board looks not unlike a coil of rope. If you set squares so that two squares abut onto one, giving two ways to go, you have what is in effect the same as hexagons. I am not a hexagon man, preferring eight ways to go rather than six; but the linear distance argument holds some weight. I looked at the board, and at the guards standing beside me with their bludgeons ready and their swords scabbarded. Four samphron-oil lamps shed a mellow light, a silver dish contained a piled-up display of fruits, wine stood in flasks—it looked a cosy scene, and this old vulture brooded over it like a dopa-doomed Rapa.

"Come in and sit down, Jak the Sturr. I trust you are ready for the game?"

"Notor," I said, and sat in the sturmwood chair across from Trylon Nath.

The pieces were set out, and, surmising that I had better show some interest in the confounded game, I studied them. It is not necessary to understand very much about Vajikry to follow what happened. By Vox, no!

But, all the same, the game is a tartar. You have a number of pieces of different ranks, and the irritating thing is that while the chief piece, called a Rok, of which you have two, can take the other pieces of superior rank, he cannot take the lowest ranked superior piece, called a strom. In between, the kov can take vads and trylons; vads can take trylons and Stroms; and trylons can take Stroms. This is the old scissors, stone, paper idea, or pikes, swordsmen, cavalry on a sterner field. For—a strom may capture a Rok.

The Roks cannot take the opposing Roks; but of the inferior pieces, some are called flutsmen, and when a Rok chooses to land on a square—or hex—containing a friendly flutsman he can fly right off the board and reappear during a later turn at a prescribed distance. I suppose there is a resemblance to the zeunt of Jikaida in this move. The other inferior pieces cannot be taken by their opposite numbers. Some inferior pieces are zoids, traps, and a secret mark is made on a flap of the board denominating which particular pieces are traps. When a superior piece lands on the square of a zoid, the secret mark is turned up and, lo! the superior piece is taken instead.

That, at the least, has always appealed to me.

If a superior piece is taken, not a Rok, of course, you can promote an inferior piece, not a flutsman, to his place.

So I studied the board and saw that Trylon Nath was a Vajikry fiend, all right, for he had laid out the maximum number of pieces allowed to each rank. The numbers, in varying, control the duration of the game, as well as changing its character.

We were in for a long session, until one of us had taken both the opposing Roks and then safely seated at least one of his own Roks at the spider's web center of the board.

And no flutsman may enter the final circle at the center.

"I shall, of course, allow you to go first."

"Thank you, notor."

"Play well, Jak the Sturr. I do not trouble myself over winning or losing." In that, the old buzzard lied most damnably, that was very clear. "But, for you, a lost game is a lost life."

"So I gathered—notor."

"Well, what are you waiting for? Let us get down to it, as King Naghan said to the fifi."

"Yes, notor."

So, not without some hesitation, I moved my first piece. This was a nicely carved representation of a swordsman, an inferior piece, called a hiviku. Now Hiviku the Artful is, I suppose, the Havilfarese equivalent to Vikatu the Dodger, the archetypal old sweat, the old soldier who knows all the tricks and can swing the lead furiously. And this I was now about to do. I took my time. I played cautiously, well guessing that Trylon Nath would suss me out in no time and then bore in with all his force. And his long mournful face would look more mournful still. For he might be an old reprobate; but he dearly loved his Vajikry, and longed to meet an opponent who would give him a prolonged and engrossing tussle. I knew I was in no frame of mind to concentrate. My Val! Didn't Turko, all Vallia, await me?

Well, that's as may be.

We played. I fell smack into one of his traps, and with a mournful look he turned up the secret mark and his zoid whisked one of my vads away.

I had a nice opening showing, and took a chance, and one of my fluts-men removed a Rok from the board, ready to come in hell for leather when he least expected it. He reached for the wine.

He poured himself, so I judged his temper concerning slaves.

"You will join me, Jak the Sturr?"

The wine was a green pimpim, thick and cloying, out of Loh.

"Thank you, notor. A little pale yellow, if I may...?"

He waved a negligent hand to the array of bottles and amphorae stacked on the side table and the floor on tripods.

I stood up. The guards were all looking at the board, and I judged Trylon Nath was forced to play them when he had no unsuspecting and uninvited guests. The thongs binding my wrists impeded me only a little. The chains and nets had been removed. I moved to the side table and took up a goblet. I half-turned, looking at the room, placing the positions of the guards.

Very well...

Turning my back on the Trylon so that I could break the thongs, I suddenly turned back. The old devil was in the act of lifting up the flap of the board to look at my secret mark denominating one of my hivikus as a zoid.

The yetch!

Swiftly I twisted back to the table and broke the thongs. My wrists tingled as they came free. Holding a glass, low, I swung back to face into the room. The guards were smirking away, one to the other, letting their lord see how much they admired his astuteness.

There were four strides to the desk—three if I jumped a trifle.

Three strides took me there, that wicked curved dagger came free of Trylon Nath's scabbard, and the broad, sharp blade pressed against his neck.

"Just all hold still," I said, cheerfully.

Trylon Nath was a rigid lump. He knew a single twitch from that deadly curved blade could slit his throat from ear to ear.

"Yes, trylon," I told him. "And will slit your damned throat. Now you will play my game, and not your cheating brand of damned Vajikry."

"You are a dead man, Jak the Sturr."

"And, my friend, so are you, if that be the case. Now, up with you. I am tired of games."

The guards sweated. They looked at me and I looked at them. They knew the score.

"We are going to take a little walk." I didn't care if I sounded like a cheap melodrama down on Wharf Street in Vondium. "You have a voller? Good. I shall regard that as fair quittance for unwanted hospitality." Then I wounded him sorely. "And for a damned cheating rogue who wins foul at Vajikry."

"Never!" he said, and he tried to twist that gaunt head to glare at me. The blade bit and he choked. "I had you—you know nothing of the arts of Vajikry—"

"I know enough to know when to take a dagger to your scrawny throat. Move!" And I amplified that with: "Bratch!"

He jumped.

We went out of the room and if the guards thought to stop me they saw my face and made no move. Which was the wiser course for them. We went up the stairs, and retainers and servitors shrank away as the trylon called, hoarsely: "Let us pass. This mad leem means me ill."

"Right, trylon," I said. "Absolutely right!"

"You will spare me my life? I can give you wealth—"

"A voller is all I need. And, Trylon Nath Orscop, I may return your voller to you, one day, and play another game of Vajikry with you. It is, I own, infuriating and fascinating."

A thought struck me. They had in the nature of these things stripped my splendid mesh steel from me and taken my weapons away. I am so used to padding about in the old scarlet breechclout I'd clean forgot I owned a pretty little arsenal, and fine armor.

"Oh, trylon. Bid your people bring my belongings. All of them." And the bright curved kalider twitched against his skin.

"You heard!" shrieked Nath Orscop. "Run, you nulshes! Fetch this—this man's armor and weapons!"

So, as we emerged onto a flat roof between two spires and I fastened my gaze on a chunky little voller, retainers ran up bearing the mesh steel and the armory. "Into the voller with them!" I snapped it out, and they obeyed. I wondered why no one had challenged that dagger at the throat of the lord. Surely, some one of all these folk would wish to see the trylon dead?

But I climbed into the voller gripping Orscop by the neck.

He slumped down and his gaunt face turned up, pleadingly.

"You said..."

I looked over the side. The landing chains were cast off. I moved the control levers and the voller lifted a couple of feet into the air. I nodded, satisfied.

"Over you go, Orscop. And thank whatever gods you pray to that I spare you your miserable hide."

He clawed up, gibbering, and as he went over the side I assisted him with an ungentle foot.

Then, roaring with laughter, I sent the voller skimming into the night sky, racing away under the Moons of Kregen.

Twelve

Of an Invitation at the Golden Prychan

Why is the air of one continent or island so different from that of any other? Each country's air holds its own essences and aromas. Does the air over Valka smell sweeter than the air over any other part of Vallia? I believe so—but to ask me to explain it—ah, there you should better question the Todalpheme, the wise mathematicians and meteorologists of Kregen.

I know that as I breathed in the air of the island of Pandahem, I tasted the difference, and vivid memories of Pando and Tilda rose up to torment me. Yes, at that time on Kregen I still owed dues to many people. I gave thanks that Deb-Lu-Quienyin had eased my mind on the score of Que-si-Rening. But, when I went to Hyrklana this time, I vowed, as well as seeking out Balass the Hawk, Oby, and Tilly, I would make more strenuous efforts to discover what had befallen the Princess Lilah. All the agents I had sent off to make inquiries had reported a total absence of news. All that was known then, all I had heard here and there, were merely rumors. Rumors of the "tragedy" that had overtaken Princess Lilah of Hyrklana.

So I marched down from the jungly foothills where I had hidden Trylon Nath Orscop's voller. And, of course, he had not lost on the deal. The airboat I had left in the clearing, the one of the three we had liberated in Khorunlad, was fair recompense.

The island of Pandahem, between Vallia to the north and Havilfar to the south, is divided into two halves by a massive east-west chain of mountains, variously named along their rambling length. Kingdoms divide up the northern portion of the island, lands some of which I knew well. The southern half's kingdoms were virtually unknown to me, and were mostly smothered in thick, lush, hot, and mostly inhospitable jungles.

Walking along the overgrown path toward the town of Mahendrasmot I fell into conversation with a lanky Relt. He was clad decently in loincloth and sandals, with his rolled coat over one shoulder. Looking like skinnier replicas of their distant cousins the fierce and voracious Rapas, the Relts do have beaked faces, but these are of altogether a gentler aspect. He carried a hollow bamboo filled with pens, and a scrip with paper and three bottles of ink, bamboo bottles, swung at his girdle.

He was a stylor, and so we fell into easy conversation, as I had been a stylor at one time, working for the Overlords of Magdag. He, this Relt called Ravenshal, knew nothing of the inner sea of Kregen, of course.

"The fair, Jak?" he said, striding along easily, with the deep green of the foliage each side of the path framing his eager birdlike face. "It is a dire place, dreadful, sometimes. There are a large number of seafaring folk who go there, and, well, you know how rough they are."

"Yes, Ravenshal. They lead a rough life."

"People come from a long distance to the fairground. The sailors from the swordships are almost as bad as the renders they chase."

"Do pirates frequent these coasts?"

"Naturally. Commerce is brisk."

"Of course. And do you know the Golden Prychan?"

He gave his beak a brisk rub with his fist. Then: "I would not wish to know the place. It is infamous."

Well, I commented to myself, that sounds a capital place to hoick Turko out of.

In Trylon Nath's airboat I had stumbled on a bundle of clothes, and so had selected a plain brown tunic and a short blue cloak. I had without any regrets laid aside the splendid mesh steel. That was like to get me into trouble where I was going, among wrestlers. But I carried my weapons. They, of course, would attract no undue attention.

Ravenshal told me he had been up to take a deposition from a tree-tapper who lived up in the hills. His wife had run off and he wanted the lord of Mahendrasmot to send men to find her and had offered a reward of a hundred silver dhems.

"He must care for her—" I said.

"Perhaps." Ravenshal, belittling his nervous ways, had seen most of it. "But it is lonely up in the hills."

"That's why she ran off, then. Some young spark from the city, I shouldn't wonder."

"If Notor Pergon lays hands on him, he will wish he had not seduced another man's wife away."

"Strict, is he, this Notor Pergon? And with this notorious fairground in his city?"

Ravenshal fisted his beak again. "Yes, strict. He is a strom, and proud of that. The fairground brings in money. But Notor Pergon will take the hundred silver dhems for his trouble, and take his pleasure out on the hide of the young man."

"If he catches him."

"He will, he will, if such a man exists. He runs his city as the suns cross the sky, does the notor."

So as we walked down the overgrown track to the city we talked and I learned a little something of the place my Turko passed his life away in a fairground booth.

The mild Relt stylor was anxious to get back to his wife and children, saying he lived in a pretty little house near the men's quarters of the steel works. "There is a modicum of regular work to be had there, Jak." And then, with that gracious little lift to his beak that Relts have, he said, "I do not know why you go to Mahendrasmot, but you would do me honor if you supped with me and my family this night."

Well, now...

I said with a gravity that was not assumed, "It is you who do me the honor, Stylor Ravenshal. I shall be delighted."

So that was how I, a desperado of desperadoes—as you know only too well—entered this strict city with its gutter side discreetly hidden in the fairground, in the meek company of a Relt stylor.

His house was delightful, small and cheerful, his wife was charming, and the kids splendiferous, a squeaking bunch of charming mischief. We ate well, wine was brought, the lamps were lit, and when I broached the subject of going to see about finding an inn for the night, nothing would halt them in their protestations that I must use their guest room and welcome, seeing it was now little used after Rashenka's sister had moved so far away, fully fifty dwaburs along the coast, with that husband of hers.

Rashenka brought the lamp to the guest room, neat and tidy, and fussed only a little, and Ravenshal came along to bid me a good night's sleep with Pandrite, and gently drew his wife away, and they went off full of smiles.

I slept with my usual caution, weapons at hand.

In the morning they greeted me with smiles, and a cup of superb Kregan tea, and small octagonal biscuits they call sweet Ordums. I stretched. After the toilet we sat down to a fine breakfast of crisp vosk rashers, and loloo's eggs, and more tea, and red honey and palines.

You see—there are good simple folk on Kregen, just as there are on this Earth.

The mention of payment would have been insulting.

I went out and found a tiny Banje shop in the nearest souk where they sold baubles for children, and candies and knick-knacks of that kind, and went back to Ravenshal's little house, and insisted they take the trifles I had brought. The children squealed, tiny bundles, all beak and feathers, and fell on the candies.

"And again my thanks. Remberee!"

"Remberee, Jak—and you have brought us luck. I have a commission today that will bring in at least five dhems. Five whole dhems! You have brought us good luck, praise to Pandrite."

Shaking my head and wondering about the way of the world, I took my hulking old self off to the Golden Prychan.

Had I saved Ravenshal from footpads on the road he and his wife could not have been more attentive. And they were diffs and I was apim. Truly, I thought, as I passed along the crowded streets where people shouted and jostled and the mytzer carts clattered by without thought for the unwary pedestrian, truly, that was the spirit and attitude sorely needed in all Paz to confront the menace of the Shanks.

The fact that the stylor had been able to walk down that lonely, jungly road and not be attacked by footpads also gave a good idea that this Strom Pergon, strict as he was reputed, kept an iron control on his stromnate. That could work for me, in some areas; but it was far more likely to make any mayhem more difficult. Just what had Turko got himself into here?

The notorious fairground of Mahendrasmot was not what I expected. For a start, it was fenced in by a tall lapped-wood barrier, and uniformed guards patrolled outside and stood sentry at the gates. This early in the morning the place held a lackluster look. Marquees and tents flapped a trifle in the early morning breeze; but the pennons hung limply. The ground was still soft and puddled with the marks of last night's feet. When the daily rain came drenching down only the boardwalks gave pedestrians a reasonably mud-free walk. I went in. That was not difficult. The corollary came to my mind, to be pushed away.

The Golden Prychan looked a formidable inn. It stood four square just inside the eastern gate. Many riding animals of the lesser kind stood hitched to rails; but there were three totrixes and just the one zorca.

The walls were built of baked brick. The roof was tile. The chimneys were twisted brick. And the windows were glazed. All these signs of affluence were emphasized by the sign swinging at its grandest on a tall pole. The prychan, which is the tawny-golden furred version of the black neemu, showed up there in bold style, painted by an artist of imagination. The neemu again brought my thoughts back to Hyrklana, for fat Queen Fahia loved to have her pet neemus, fierce, independent four-legged hunting cats, lolling on the steps of her throne.

Standing with my head cocked back studying the sign, I became aware of a shadow at my side and then a voice, saying: "You stare overlong at the prychan, dom. Do you wish to have your ribs crushed? Or would you prefer a broken arm—only the one, since you have only two?" I looked down.

He was big. He was burly. He smiled with his lower jaw swinging like a jib boom in a gale. He wore a pair of tights colored bright purple, and a wersting breechclout. Otherwise he was naked—naked and hairless. He was a Chulik. I drew in my breath.

"Llahal, dom. I was admiring the sign. You are a wrestler?"

"Come now, dom. Do not refuse my offer. I am sharp set, for I bested Tranko last night, and I owed him that."

This Chulik's tusks had been sawn off close to his gums. That is a cruel and horrendous thing to do. Much as I deplore the activities of Chuliks, I had grown to a better understanding of them and their ways. Trained to be mercenaries from birth, they are superb paktuns, demanding high rates of pay. With their merciless black eyes and pigtails, their oiled yellow skins, their fierce three-inch tusks thrusting up from the corners of their mouths, they earn their hire. But—this one, tuskless—a wrestler in a fairground? Oh, my Turko!

As I did not reply immediately, the Chulik said in a less friendly voice, "You are impolite. I am Kimche the Lock. I shall have to teach you manners."

"Look, Kimche the Lock, I do not wish to fight you—"

"I did not say fight. I said wrestle."

"Why should I? By the Blessed Pandrite! Why?"

"Why?" Now that really puzzled him. He shook that bald yellow head. "Why? You mock me. Me! Is this not the Golden Prychan?"

"So I believe."

"Well, then! Onker!"

So, of course, very late in the day, I fell in.

"Oh—the Golden Prychan—you are all wrestlers here—"

"Take up your guard. It is the third syple of the Hikaidish. Protect yourself!"

"I," I said, "carry weapons."

Now he was truly puzzled, puzzled and angry. His chest swelled. The yellow skin, oiled and glistening, stretched like a drum.

"You talk of weapons, here? You are decadent or mad."

If I'd had a hat I'd have taken it off and jumped on it.

By Zair!

"I am not a wrestler. I came here seeking someone—"

"If you are frightened witless to try a fall with Kimche the Lock, why, dom, you should have said so. There is no shame in fearing to grip wrists with me." His face broke into an oily smile. He clapped me on the back. "Now I understand!"

"If that is how you will have it."

"Of course!" His bad temper evaporated. "There is no shame in it, dom. By Likshu the Treacherous! I understand!" And then he stuck his thumbs into his mouth and began to massage those pathetic stumps.

I looked about. Nothing much was happening, save a couple of gyps starting an interesting friendship. Kimche took his thumbs out of his mouth, spat, and said with a wistful air, "All the same. I could have gone a fall or three with you. I am fair set for it."

"Perhaps you know the man I seek?"

"There is such a man?" He looked puzzled again and I guessed he was considering the reason he had found for himself for my lack of response to his genial challenge.

"There is. His name is Turko—"

He looked about at once, and put a finger to his lips.

"Ssh, dom! Have you no wits! Caution!"

He drew me out of the streaming mingled radiance of the Suns of Scorpio into the shadows under the eaves. He looked about again, with much eye rolling. For a Chulik he was evidencing much non-Chulik behavior.

But, then, his tusks had been sawed off, and that must profoundly change the mental attitudes of any self-respecting Chulik.

For a start, how could one call him a Yellow-Tusker now?

The dependent fronds of a brilliantly green tree, a fugitive from the jungle—or the advance guard of the jungle returning—concealed us from prying eyes out along the boardwalk. Kimche stared at me, and his tongue crept out to lick his lips.

"I did not take you for Hamalese. If you are, I shall surely fight and slay you—you do understand that?"

"I do."

One factor I had not overlooked was the simple problem of the island of Pandahem now being in the vulture-like grip of Phu-Si-Yantong. With the duped help of the iron legions of Hamal he, under his cloaking alias of the Hyr Notor, had conquered the various and separate kingdoms of the island. Queen Lush of Lome had been his tool, coming from Pandahem, and was now with us of Vallia. Other rulers had been subjugated or slain. Yantong ran the island working through human tools. If there was a resistance to Hamal, then Turko would be up to his Khamorro neck in it, that was for sure.

"I am aware of the problems you Pandaheem face—"

"Tell me your name, rank, and station, dom."

He had no fear of me or my weapons. In a twinkling he would have my back across his knee, and, snap!—one more Hamalese cramph gone to the Ice Floes of Sicce.

"I am Jak the Sturr. And I fight against Hamal."

He stared at me with those feral black Chulik eyes.

He nodded. "Very well. And Turko is in trouble. Do not think you can deceive him, for he is a man among men."

"When can I see him? Where is he?"

"Early this morning, before dawn, he went to Black Algon's marquee to reason with him once again. I do not think he was successful." Kimche screwed up his mouth. "I think Turko must take my advice and break the yetch's back."

I sighed.

Problems, problems...

"Tell me, Kimche the Lock."

The story was simple and straightforward and not at all pretty. One of the wrestlers' comrades, a young Khibil called Andrinos, was deeply in love with a Khibil maiden who was slave to Black Algon. She worked in a fire-eating and magic act. Black Algon, gloating in his own power, would not release her or sell her. Andrinos was in despair. His comrades had vowed to help him; but short of violence, gold being of no assistance, they had so far failed to secure the maiden Saenci's release.

"Trust Turko to become embroiled in an affair like this. Can nothing be done to convince Black Algon to part with the girl?"

"One thing only, by Likshu the Treacherous. Break the nulsh's back!"

Now, I had hitherto on Kregen detested Chuliks as fierce and inhuman diffs. They had caused me much pain. But, then, so had other diffs, and apims, too, by Krun! Lately, certain experiences had modified my views on the Yellow-Tuskers, and, too, I did not forget that Chulik with whom I had spoken before the Battle of the Dragon's Bones. So I could talk quite reasonably to Kimche the Lock, and treat him as a man first, discounting all my old hostile feelings toward Chuliks. Truly, life brings changes to the most flinty of characters!

"The marquee of Black Algon? And you say this fellow supports the Hamalese?"

"Aye. If you go there, take care. He has many friends among the wrestlers in the booth of Jimstye Gaptooth. He is the mortal foe of us at the Golden Prychan, who are comrades all."

One of the cardinal principles of staying alive on Kregen is to remember names. Names confer power, not power for misuse, but self-power, the knowledge to orient a life-style amid dangers. If you forget or confuse names, you can end up skewered on the end of a rapier or have your head off in the slice of a cleaver—so be warned!

I nodded. "I shall tread carefully. Tell me, Kimche, does this Jimstye Gaptooth have any Khamorros in his booth?"

"Yes."

The monosyllable shook me. The savagery with which Kimche spoke told me much. I did not press. What there was to learn I would find out. That was as certain as Zim and Genodras rose and set, by Zair!

Thirteen

Of a Few Falls with Beng Drudoj

Black Algon's marquee was tightly shut and his slaves told me he had gone into the city about important business. There was no sign of Turko. When I mentioned Saenci, the Khibil slave girl, the slaves ran off. Annoyed, I walked around the fairground, spying it out, seeing the bright booths and sideshows and all the gaudy come-ons and money-taking-offs revealed in the pitiless light of the suns. The air dried up the mud. Shortly after the hour of mid the rains would fall down in solid masses of water, and the mud would ooze again into its sticky consistency. I took myself back to the Golden Prychan.

"It is time for ale, Jak the Sturr," Kimche greeted me. He took me through the wide, sawdust-sanded floor into a back snug. The bamboo-paneled room contained about a dozen wrestlers. They looked a ripe assortment of battered humanity. The ale was brought in by Fristle fifis, and we sat to drink.

I was reminded of Dav Olmes and his penchant for stopping at the least provocation for a stoup of ale. These men were drinkers.

Food, very naturally, was brought in and no one seemed to be concerned if I would pay the reckoning. There were Khamorros among these wrestlers. Kimche wiped suds, and leaned forward, and said, "You know the story of Lallia the Slave Girl, Jak?"

"I know the story of Lallia the Slave Girl."

"Well, it is not quite like that, Kimche," put in broken-nosed Naghan the Grip.

"I know, I know. But Andrinos and Saenci worry our Turko. That is what concerns us. He is our best Khamorro and Jimstye Gaptooth has three high kham Khamorros—and what may a mortal man do against them?"

The other wrestlers, florid and bulky and coiling with muscles, grumbled and grunted, and drank. Truthfully, there are few mortal men who may go up in handgrips against a Khamorro and stand a chance in a Herrelldrin hell of winning.

I asked the obvious questions, and learned that the wagers dictated the relative powers of the contests. In catch as catch can the ordinary wrestler, with Turko available, handled his opposite number and called in Turko in the inevitable crisis. As Jimstye Gaptooth could put more Khamorros onto the canvas than the consortium operating from the Golden Prychan, Turko was called on frequently.

The smell of sweat in the bamboo-walled snug was barely noticeable, for these wrestlers were particular about themselves. But the smells of oils and liniments rose pungently. Some of the men wore bandages, tightly strapped and pasted, and two carried broken arms in slings of clean yellow cloth.

"And," said Nolro, a young Khamorro whose headband indicated he had barely begun his climb through the khams, "where is Turko, anyway?"

"And Andrinos?"

"By Morro the Muscle!" declared Nolro. "We fight tonight and if Turko is not here—"

Kimche reached for the ale. "He will be ready to step onto the canvas, Nolro. You, of all men, should know that."

"I do. But—I worry..."

When they questioned how I had come to know Turko I simply said we had met in the past and as I was passing through I thought to look him up.

I made no big thing of it, and went on to question them as to the advisability of all this ale-drinking if they fought this night. They guffawed.

"This ale gives us our strength, dom!"

Well, it might, too, given that it was brewed from top-quality Kregan barley and hops and was filled with good things. I drank and wiped my lips, and we talked of this and that. And still, Turko did not appear. He was never once referred to as Turko the Shield. A couple of times they called him Turko the Rym, and I will not advise you of what that means. So the time passed and then the note of exasperation in their voices sharpened. They were a consortium of wrestlers, and if one let the others down, his shares were forfeit. Also, his honor was smirched, that was plain. I sighed. I had no desire to step into a ring and take Turko's place. But, if I had to, I had to...

The secret disciplines under which the Khamorros train in Herrelldrin, the syples, their allegiances and their kham status, are all shown on their reed-syple, the headband with its symbols. I could read a paltry handful of those, from previous experience, and recognized none of the reed-syples of the Khamorros here.

Turko, of his own desire, wore a plain scarlet reed-syple. By this he proclaimed his allegiance, his disdain of other syple disciplines, and to hell with anyone who questioned his kham status. A bit of a rogue Khamorro, our Turko the Shield. And he had a fine mocking way with him, too!

I looked at Muvko the Breaker, who appeared to be the likeliest of the khamsters present.

"Muvko," I said, with a smile. "I mistook good Kimche's offer of a fall or three. After we have finished our bout, would you do me the honor of gripping wrists?"

He laughed good naturedly. I guessed these Khamorros were not high khamsters, lacking the refinement of skill to take them into the master class, and were happy to find employment in a fairground booth. For all that, no ordinary unskilled mortal in the arcane lore of wrestling stood a chance against them in fair combat.

"If Kimche leaves you with any bones joined together."

"By Beng Drudoj Grip and Fall!" quoth Kimche. He was mightily pleased and showing it for a Chulik. But, remember, he was minus his tusks. "You are my man, Jak, after all!"

"Then let us begin," I said, and stood up.

Their practice ring was functional. An alcove with a neat little bronze statue of Beng Drudoj, the patron saint of wrestlers, faced a broad table with medical impedimenta at hand. Most of the medical assistance, as far as I could see, consisted of bottles of liniment and unguents, bandages and slings, and copious buckets into which a man might spit his teeth. And over this table on which a defeated combatant would be laid out frowned the intolerant bronze features of Beng Drudoj Grip and Fall.

These spartan surroundings were enough to perk a flutter through the heart!

Because I have had the good fortune to go through the Disciplines of the Krozairs of Zy, which teach a man wrestling and unarmed combat tricks— all the martial arts—that leave the best syples of the Khamorros far in the shadows, I had been able, without actually fighting Turko, to convince him that I had the besting of him and many a high khamster.

So, Kimche and I stripped off and began and it was not made too swift and there was a deal of grunting and straining before he gave me best. I stood back.

"You fight well, Kimche. But—"

"By Likshu the Treacherous!" he panted, standing up and shaking himself like a dog run from the sea. "You must be a Khamorro!"

"No, Kimche. I am not a Khamorro."

"Then," said Muvko the Breaker, stepping forward, "let us see what you can avail against a true khamster."

Muvko was, as I had suspected, competent within the syples. Again I made nothing great of it, and the contest prolonged itself long past the moment when Turko, for one, would have had Muvko flat on his back. But it is foolish to puff up one's abilities if there are skullduggeries to follow.

"Now may Morro the Muscle be my witness!" declared Muvko, sitting up and staring at me. "If you are no Khamorro—what manner of man are you?"

Useless to answer, "A Krozair of Zy." So I smiled, and said, "I had luck and the knack of it, Muvko. Now, who is for ale?"

My intentions were plain to them. And, having seen me in action, they were fully in agreement.

"And when Turko returns, we will have a few words to say!"

"Aye!"

The daily downpour had come and gone outside, no doubt adding a fair quantity of fresh growth in that voracious jungle, and we started to prepare seriously for the evening's contest.

Hoping that I had not created too great an impression, I joined in. After all, ordinary wrestlers stand no real chances against Khamorros. The wagers and rules reflected this, as they would have to do. So—how could I be explained? As a freak, that seemed the only answer, and thus I was accepted. They made plain I was standing in for Turko, and could have no share of the consortium's profits on my own account. This seemed reasonable.

A smart trot across to the marquee of Black Algon revealed the place open and girding its magical loins for the night's doings. Black Algon, himself, was still not there. Neither were Saenci and Turko. And Andrinos was still missing.

Back at the Golden Prychan, Kimche expressed himself of the opinion that mischief was afoot but that, by Beng Drudoj Triceps and Biceps, he had no inkling what it might be.

"Sink me!" I burst out. "If he's got Turko and the others chained up in some infernal chundrog, I'll—"

"So would we all, Jak, if we knew if and where!"

"There is one way to find out, a very old and still reasonably efficacious way."

"If you can find any rast to question."

'True, may the black lotus-flowers of Hodan-Set breathe on the cramph!"

"Jimstye Gaptooth may know," said Nolro. "He must put in an appearance tonight when his men fight us."

"By Morro the Muscle! Could we do it?" demanded Muvko.

A hubbub ensued. Of one thing I was sure, in all the bicep-rolling, muscle-flexing, stomach-tautening going on around me, these fellows would be ugly customers to cross on a wet and windy night, by Krun!

Kimche, the Chulik, a man who had been trained from birth to bear weapons and who now, tuskless, worked as a wrestler in a fairground booth, struck a note of warning.

"Remember, doms! Jimstye Gaptooth employs swordsmen. Who among you can handle a blade?"

The reaction to this unwelcome reminder brought scowls and fists gripping wrists and twisting so the muscles jumped, and a coarse variety of oaths heating the atmosphere. But the fact remained and real; just as these wrestlers were masters of their craft, so swordsmen hired by Jimstye Gaptooth would be masters of theirs. Only Kimche could face them with steel in his fist, and only the Khamorros could hope to live against pointed and edged weapons with empty hands.

"I have a large club," shouted Fat Lorgan, and his belly shook. "With a nail in the head!"

"And I a dagger," said Sly Nath the Trivet, looking fierce.

They looked at my little arsenal stacked to hand.

"When is this expedition to be, doms?" I said.

"After the bouts, when the credulous public are all drunk and chasing women and Jimstye Gaptooth is counting his money."

"A remarkably fitting time," I observed.

Each office of the consortium was held by a wrestler, and they were punctilious in the discharge of their duties. They employed a tall and supercilious Ng'grogan to present a front to the public, and to call their titles and stations before the contests. He was not, this Abanch from Ng'groga, anything at all like Inch, Kov of the Black Mountains. In a spirit of devilment I offered Abanch a juicy portion of squish pie as we took our meal, the fifth or sixth of the day.

591

"Thank you, master Jak," he said, and took it and wolfed it down. I waited. Abanch looked around. "Is there more? For I am inordinately fond of squish pie."

Kimche handed across the rest.

I said, "I knew a man who stood on his head—"

"Ah!" said Abanch, and spluttered rich juice down his chin and crumbs onto the table. "He is your high and mighty, hoity-toity Ng'grogan, too good for the likes of me."

I did not hit him. He was like Inch in only one thing; he was tall.

But, in the public address he made as the crowds flocked into the enormous marquee where the contest would take place, Abanch earned his hire money. The public paid. They were mostly men, with a sprinkling of women, seafaring folk, and I did not doubt there were a number of renders among them, pirates who had crept in a longboat into some jungly creek and stolen ashore for a night's jaunt among the flesh-pots. As for the swordshipmen, they preened in fancy uniforms and flashed their smiles and their swords and gold lace.

Many steelworkers and city folk, of course, patronized the fairground. The place was brilliantly illuminated by mineral-oil lamps, with bits of colored glass to lend a fairyland lighting. The noise was prodigious and quite drowned out the eternal sound of the sea. Refreshments were served continually, and many a honey cake was flung in the wrath of an argument along the benches. As for drink, that flowed in a broad river of ale and wine and fermented in the brains and bloodstreams of the spectators.

The whole scene in the marquee was rough and rowdy and heated. Everyone hungered to see the fights. As for betting, that was a nicely calculated art and anyone whose skill was lacking would go home with his pocket linings hanging out—if he was not hit on the head in the firm belief that he walked thus to conceal the waist belt stuffed with gold and silver.

Before Abanch had finished two men were carried out; unconscious or dead, it did not seem to matter. The crowds yelled.

The contest began.

Well, by the offensive stink of Makki Grodno's disgusting diseased liver and lights, it went ill for the consortium from the Golden Prychan.

In the singles only two of our fellows scored outright wins.

When the tag matches began we were on to a hiding to nothing.

Four of us stood on small raised platforms outside the ring, which was fenced with a single bronze chain at waist height. The canvas covered sturmwood planking, and the whole was raised a little. Four of us stood on these platforms, and four of Jimstye Gaptooth's men stood on platforms adjacent.

One from each side leaped into the ring and started to twist each other's arms and legs off.

592

Kimche was controlling this bout. He faced me across the canvas where squirming bodies writhed. The crowd wanted blood.

Our man, it was Sly Nath the Trivet, hoicked himself on top of his opponent and started banging his head on the canvas covered sturmwood. This was highly pleasing.

The leader of the opposition bellowed, and a hulking Gon, his head a sheen of buttered baldness, leaped into the ring and caught Sly Nath around the throat and choked him back.

"Fat Lorgan!"

Fat Lorgan leaped and used his belly to knock the Gon down. He sat on his head. The first two crawled away on hands and knees. The crowd bellowed. Presently two more were at it, and then I was called in and got my man down, and was only just in time to avoid a diabolical kick in the ear. Kimche loomed up and threw that one away, and we looked about, and, lo! we of the Golden Prychan remained in the ring. Of Gaptooth's men, none remained. Two were spitting blood on the platform around the outside of the bronze chain; one was lying head down, out to the wide; and the last was being sick all over a plump gentleman in the front row of benches.

Mind you, Sly Nath had an eye that would, come the morning, be a single gigantic purple lump. And Fat Lorgan was staring at a finger that bent backward and dangled when he pushed it.

The yelling lessened by a fraction, and Kimche said, "Next foursome."

Slowly, we of the Golden Prychan overhauled the lead Jimstye Gaptooth's wrestlers had opened. A singles win counted as one, and one was scored for every man remaining in the ring after the opposition had been thrown out.

Then Muvko said to me as we sat on the participants' benches, "Now they start in earnest. Their Khamorros come on."

So I looked at the four men on their platforms, as Kimche, Muvko, and Nolro walked across to our platforms. I joined them, studying the Khamorros belonging to Gaptooth. They were all, instantly seen, of high khams. They were all deadly.

So Kimche began, for Muvko was leader of this bout. The Chulik did not last more than a few murs against the khamster and Nolro went in. Then another one from the other side was followed by me. As I jumped the bronze chain a single scarlet thought flamed across my vosk skull of a head.

What was I doing here? What on Kregen was the Emperor of Vallia doing playing tag with a bunch of bone-breaking Khamorros? In a sleazy fairground booth by the light of cheap mineral-oil lamps and surrounded by a blood-hungry mob? It was crazy.

And then, of course, all that went from my mind and I leaped on the fellow who was about to snap Kimche's arm, hauled him off, twisted him in the grips, and hurled him over the bronze chain.

After that it was a splendid blur.

I saw no reason to injure these Khamorros. They were only employees. So I caught them by an ear, or a wrist, or by some more interesting part of their anatomy, and threw them away.

The bout was over very quickly, The marquee held a complete silence for six heartbeats, and then the benches erupted.

Muvko was shaking his head.

"You are a marked man now, Jak."

"Just let us get this over with honor and then we can go and ask Jimstye Gaptooth the questions."

"May Morro the Muscle have you in his keeping."

Four more bouts took place with fresh Khamorros or the ones who had been defeated returning. That made no matter. Between us, Muvko, Nolro, Kimche, and I threw them all over the bronze chain. Yes, yes, it was petty, all sweaty men heaving and grunting; but, too, there was a panache about it.

They were shouting now, from the benches, shouting that great word that is the unarmed combatman's equivalent to the Jikai of the swordsman.

"Hikai!" they shrilled. "Hai, Hikai!"

It was quite a night.

And that night was less than a third over.

"What!" I shouted at Kimche as Abanch took his inordinate length into the ring to shout our triumph. "Not over!"

"We were the first contest of the night. There are two more to come." He saw my face. "We are not involved—"

"Thank Pandrite for that!" Then I glowered at the backs of the Khamorros as they trailed away up the aisle between the seats. "All the same, I was just getting the blood flowing nicely and freely... Perhaps it is a pity, after all."

"But the third contest will be fought by Jimstye Gaptooth's people—some he has in reserve, these who will have recovered."

I glowered. I felt the old blood climbing up inside my head and I ground down on that scarlet rage.

"I can't wait all damned night to see this cramph!"

"There he is, just come in, and passing strange it is, too, that he was not here to see his men in action." Kimche nodded his bald yellow Chulik head. I looked where he indicated.

Jimstye Gaptooth—well, yes, his two front teeth were missing. He lowered himself to a padded seat at the front reserved for principals. He wore sumptuous clothes of blue and ivory, with much gold lace. He was bulky and fatter than he ought to be, with a full-fleshed face that concentrated into a single crimson scowl. At his side sat a man who took my closer attention.

I knew this man—I had never seen him in my life before, but I knew him.

He wore gray leathers all over his body, except his head, and his face was very pale, with dark hair cropped short. His mouth, a mere thin gash, his sharp nose—and his eyes! Dark, piercing, intent, concentrating on all he saw with the power of an incisive instinct—revealed him to me. Revealed him as clearly as the rapier and main gauche he wore in the bravo-fighter's unmistakable fashion.

A bravo-fighter from the enclave city of Zenicce.

By his colors of gray and blue, worn discreetly, I knew him to belong to the noble House of Klaiton. I had no quarrel with that House. My own House, the House of Strombor, had more than once assisted in an insurance loss for young Nalgre Stahleker, Prince of the House of Klaiton, and his seductive wife, Nashta. So what was a bravo-fighter of Zenicce doing sitting next to a professional wrestling owner in South Pandahem?

Kimche told me, and my face darkened.

"And the story is true, Jak. This swordsman, Miklasu, eloped with the Princess Nashta. He was the house champion. The prince did not seek him, so we are told, because he said if his wife wished to go she would go, and if she did not she would return."

"And?"

"She chose to return. And her ship sank off the coast of Segesthes in a great storm, sent, it was said, by one of the Sea Lords, Notor Shorthush of the Waves. So Miklasu hires his sword and, it was said, he told his cronies he was well quit of the woman."

I had known Princess Nashta. Her seductiveness had destroyed her, that and the weakness of her will. And I felt for Prince Nalgre, even though I could not guess at the real reasons why his wife should leave him. Perhaps Quergey the Murgey would know, for all reports spoke well of Nalgre. Delia had said he was a fine young man. Of such puzzles is the world constructed.

"So we must wait until the end of the contests," said Kimche.

"No," I said. "I do not think so."

Whatever Jak the Sturr might do in these circumstances was one thing; but I knew what Jak the Drang would do—aye, and Dray Prescot!

The changing rooms yielded my clothes. The other wrestlers were clearing their things out. We went outside, under the stars and the fuzzy pink light of the Maiden with the Many Smiles. I had brought the kalider taken from Trylon Nath Orscop. With this naked in my hand I prowled around the outside of the marquee. The others, led by Kimche, followed.

"What, Jak—?"

"I can't lollygag about all night," I said.

The first guy rope parted under the keen steel.

I went around the marquee methodically, slicing the guy ropes asunder. The marquee began to sag. By the time I had reached three-quarters of the way the roof billowed in. The roars of excitement within changed to yells of alarm. The marquee billowed like a collapsing dermiflon, speared on the field of battle. It rippled and sagged and flapped, and the rest of the ropes parted.

The whole lot collapsed.

"There," I said, standing up with the dagger in my fist. "Now perhaps that rast will come out!"

Fourteen

The Khamorro Way

Like fish struggling upstream, the audience battled their way out beneath the collapsing folds of cloth. The uproar was just as prodigious as a sensible man would expect. By the fuzzy pink light of the Maiden with the Many Smiles we stared on that heaving scene. I stuffed the kalider away and moved across the boardwalk where mud lay in thick cakes from heedless boots.

"Watch for the rast! Spread around the marquee."

"This is not in the plan, Jak!" Kimche looked wild, gesticulating, his bald yellow head glistening in streaks of mingled color in the moons' light.

"But it will get him out, Kimche. We need to ask him, do we not?"

"Aye. Aye, Jak, that we do."

No one could believe the marquee had fallen of itself and the first conjectures, expressed with many oaths, took the view that some god or spirit inimical to Beng Drudoj Flying Alsh had wrecked the bouts out of spite. Some very watchable fights started between the pirates and the steelworkers, and drew admiring crowds. No doubt Beng Drudoj Grip and Fall took pleasure from this substitute entertainment. The light of torches splashed the scene with vivid color. The smell and mood of the crowds thickened.

The wrestlers from the Golden Prychan spread out and pretty soon Sly Nath the Trivet came arunning, pointing. His eye was beginning to look magnificent. We followed him and saw a group of men staggering out from the folds of fallen cloth. They staggered up amid much blasphemy. The guards had come running up; but the marquee was fallen and they couldn't put it up again. The wrestling was abandoned for the night. The cut guy ropes were found, and the blasphemies mounted against the night sky.

Sly Nath, eye and all, was chuckling away to himself.

Well, yes, it was funny, too, if you thought about it...

We followed Jimstye Gaptooth and the bravo-fighter Miklasu, as they went off with their people. I would not have been surprised if they stayed at an inn called The Black Neemu; but its name was The Wristy Grip, which showed how proud they were of their wrestlers.

"I," said Fat Lorgan, "do not have my club with the nail in its head with me."

"I think, Jak," said Kimche, after due consideration, "that I would like to have a sword. A Khamorro can break the bones of a swordsman, that is well known; but if the swordsman is very good, an unarmed man has no chance. It is a matter of relative skills."

I well knew that Kimche would have the skills of the sword, being a Chulik.

"I only want to talk to this Gaptooth, not fight his army of khamsters."

"But the two will of necessity go together."

"May Drig take the fellow!" I am used to going ahunting alone. I said, briskly, "Do you return to the Golden Prychan and fetch what weapons you have, and mine, also. I shall sniff around a little. Something May Turn Up." Shades of Quienyin!

The fairground formed a pulsing bubble of light and noise in the moon-lit night. The Wristy Grip reached up three imposing stories, and many windows were illuminated, and the sounds of revelry within indicated a good night was being enjoyed.

If you consider me a bash-on sort of fellow, well, you may be right in that I like to get on with it. But I fancied that it would be less than clever to go in the front door acting as an ordinary customer. I eyed the upper win-dows. It was a climb under the moons of Kregen for me...

Kimche and the others trailed off, and I sensed they were not too sure about leaving me. But I told them to get back with the naked steel and to think about the Khamorros. As they went off into the shadows I went around to the back of the inn.

Climbing into other people's houses, and inns, and palaces, is a tricky business; but one which has its own lessons. I clawed up a vine by the rear wall, and chinned myself to a ledge, and so opened a window, whose wood, while warped, did not squeak, and so dropped silently into a darkened room.

The sounds of breathing came from a bed, half-seen.

I tiptoed to the door and let myself out into a corridor.

I knew exactly what I wanted.

If Turko was being held prisoner, which seemed the only explanation for his absence, it appeared highly unlikely he would be held here in the inn. But—he might be. So I eased to the head of the stairs and had not to wait too long before a potman came puffing up. He was looking for fresh can-dles, as he was relieved to tell me. He was a Fristle. His green and yellow striped apron was bunched around his neck when he spoke to me, and my fist was tight around the cloth.

"And where is the Khamorro they hold prisoner here?"

His cat's eyes goggled. "No, notor, no—I know nothing of any prisoner!" Eventually, I believed him. I pondered.

Brown shadows lay thick in the corridor. Dust hung in the air and tickled the nostril. The sounds of revelry from below wafted up faintly, as from a distant shore. The corridor was very quiet. I knew that I could not trust this Fristle potman an inch.

Wrapping his unconscious body in his striped apron, I stowed him away in a broom cupboard. Then I started down the stairs.

The doors of the rooms of the next floor down were all closed, and from the sounds within I judged it prudent to let them remain shut. At the far end of the corridor a double door promised to reveal something more interesting. I put my ear to it. The rumbling sounds of conversation could not be interpreted into words. Again, I pondered.

It seemed most likely to me that Gaptooth and his cronies would have a private suite here, and these rooms were likely to lie beyond this double door. So, very well, then. In we go...

The double doors were locked. So I kicked them in. Beyond them lay a small anteroom and the doors at the far end opened almost instantly at the racket I had made and men crowded in. Some were Khamorros and some bore naked steel.

"I have come to see Jimstye Gaptooth," I said. "Is this the way to greet an old friend?"

That held them for the space of three heartbeats.

As soon as I spoke I realized I had been too clever for my own good. As an old friend, my story would be stupid. My story, to hold water, would demand a rueful admission of misplaced loyalty.

Why, with a glib story all ready, had I blurted out this nonsense about being an old friend?

They ushered me into the chambers beyond the anteroom. The place was furnished with a kind of tongue-licking lavishness I found not to my taste. Gaptooth bustled forward, very much the center of attention. At his shoulder hovered the bravo-fighter.

So, one story having been shot and the other about to be shot to pieces, I decided I would have to bait this Jimstye.

"Old friend? I don't know you. Who the devil are you?"

"I am Nalgre ti Hamonlad," I said, inventing on the spot with a nudge-nudge to the swordsman, Miklasu, in the use of the name Nalgre.

"But I know him, the nulsh!" spoke up a Khamorro I had thrown over the bronze chains at least three times.

"And I! Let me at him in fair fight—" Others crowded forward.

"If you choose not to recognize me, Jimstye," I said brightly, over the hubbub, "then that is your affair. I did not know you were in Mahendrasmot, otherwise I would have signed up with you instead of that mangy lot at the Golden Prychan."

So, I had blended both stories. Let him chew on the implications of his refusal to acknowledge an old friend.

He looked annoyed.

"I've never met you—but if you are the man who—"

"He is! He is, the rast!"

The fellow who spoke thus, a husky khamster, stood near enough to enable me to take his arm in a grip to pull and then push him. He staggered; but being a Khamorro, he recovered with cat-like speed and bored in, his hands razoring for me.

I sidestepped, swung back, chopped him, and then, as he went on past flailing, kicked him up the backside.

"Can't you control these idiots?" I demanded hotly. "By Havil! You always said you hated the guts of all Khamorros."

The gazes of these feared men of martial art fame fixed on Gaptooth. He looked keenly at me and lifted a hand.

"You are clever, you rast. I admire Khamorros and always have. Take him out and slice his throat—"

For a space no one made a move.

"So you don't want me to fight for you in the contests?"

He sneered. "You would?"

"Why am I here, Jimstye—even if you deny friendship?"

"Shastum! Silence!" he called over the hubbub. "Let me think."

The upshot of his thoughts was that avarice won over common sense. He knew damn well he didn't know me. But if I was the man who had bested his fighters, and I was willing to work for him—he saw much money flowing in. And perhaps that is common sense, after all, making the most of what occurs.

"I did not see you fight. Can you—"

"Let me!" And: "I'll twist his neck!"

They just did not believe, these Khamorros, and that was understandable. They were accustomed to seeing men shrink away from them unless they carried steel and knew well how to use it. The truth is, of course, that the very highest khamsters do not travel overfar from Herrelldrin, which is down in the southwest of Havilfar. These men were not out of the top drawer; but they were good. All Khamorros are good at their trade.

After half a dozen lay about the chamber I said to Jimstye, "That is enough." I had my eye on the farther door which must lead to the inner private chambers and if Turko was here, that was where he would be. "You are satisfied—old friend?"

"I am satisfied. We will discuss terms later."

He gestured to the wrestlers. "Best clear out now and take advantage of the night off. When I find who cut down the marquee I shall pull his thumbs out, for a start. Go on!"

It was clear to them as to me that he wanted to discuss terms with his new acquisition in private. That suited me. When they had gone, he said, "Wine, Nalgre ti Hamonlad?" Miklasu moistened his lips and went across to a side table. His rapier and main gauche were plain, hard-used weapons, the Jiktar and the Hikdar, the weapons of a killer.

I said, "I believe, Jimstye Gaptooth, that you know the whereabouts of a friend of mine. I am minded to see him, and at once. Perhaps you will be good enough to tell me where he is?"

He looked surprised. Miklasu turned sharply from the table, a glass of wine in each hand, the red steady as a level.

"A friend? I know we have never met before, and I see you used that to gain entrance." He frowned. "Although you pressed overhard by trying to stir up trouble between me and my Khamorros. What friend?"

"Turko."

Miklasu dropped both wine glasses. His rapier and his main gauche flamed in his fists, drawn instantly, a superb bravo-fighter's fighting draw.

Gaptooth laughed. "So it was all a fake, a trick! You are from the Golden Prychan, after all, and you are another seeking this Turko!" He turned to Miklasu. "Kill him."

The bravo-fighter moved forward, and his sword and dagger were held just so.

"I am not one to be taken by a khamster," he said. "You have no weapons. So, it follows you will surely die."

"As to that, we shall see. Klaiton, is it?"

He stared. "What—?"

"Get on with it, Miklasu, get on with it!"

"Before he starts," I said, "tell me—if I am to die it will prove of illusory comfort. Where is Turko?"

Again he laughed. "Oh, you will die. There is no swordsman in all Pandahem like unto Miklasu. And, Turko—" He jerked his thumb toward that inner door. I sighed.

Now I remembered my encounter with Mefto the Kazzur, when that superb Kildoi swordsman had bested me in fair fight. I thought it highly likely that I could beat this Miklasu; but, as always, there was the chance that he would have the beating of me. And Turko was my first concern.

I ran for the door, kicked it down, and burst through.

The three of them were in there, hung up like chickens on hooks. They were all mother naked. The room gave ingress to other bedrooms. The sound at my back heralded the vicious onslaught of Miklasu. I turned to face him.

I shouted, "I—Nalgre ti Hamonlad—caution you, Miklasu. I do not wish to slay you—" And then he ran in on me with his rapier doing all the flash and the dagger ready to rip into my guts. A pretty bravo-fighter's trick, that. I swayed, took his wrist, but he hacked back and so I ducked away. He was good.

Turko said, "I might have known..."

The two Khibils, Andrinos and Saenci, hung in their bonds, gawping. I noticed that the Khibil maiden had not been crying. Andrinos's foxy face showed determination as well as a goggling surprise at my eruption.

Miklasu foined around; but he was too canny to let me get close to him. Gaptooth appeared, shrieking for the bravo-fighter to get on with it.

Working my way around out of the reach of that sharp rapier, I came along the wall where the three captives hung. There was not much time left, for the row would surely bring the wrestlers arunning. I whipped out the kalider, slashed Turko's bonds. He fell to his knees and, for two heartbeats, his head hung down. Then he was up, flexing his superb muscles. He did not say anything. I threw him the dagger and turned to make a feint at Miklasu and so draw him away. Turko could have handled the rapier-man, I knew, but his muscles would be stiff and the blood must be giving him one hell of a time right now. He made no sound, but slashed the other two free.

When he had done that, he moved with his ferocious speed toward Jimstye Gaptooth... Long before that man could escape, Turko had his neck in one fist. He looked across at me.

"Do you remember Mungul Sidrath?"

"Aye."

"So do I."

He put Jimstye Gaptooth to sleep. Miklasu shouted, and leaped, and the rapier and dagger swirled in a twin cyclone of glittering steel and the Khibil maiden let out a tiny scream and Miklasu was suddenly upside down, his head crashing into the floor, and the rapier and main gauche were in my fists.

"And about time too," said Turko. "Nalgre, was it?"

I bent to the bravo-fighter. He was not dead, and his eyes opened and fluttered. "Nalgre Stahleker," I said. "I know him. I knew his wife, too, Princess Nashta."

Miklasu's eyes rolled up.

Disgust shook me. I stopped what I was going to say, some stupid boasting about the Lord of Strombor. I turned to Turko.

"Let us get out of this pestiferous place."

"With all my heart, Nalgre. My limbs appear to have returned to me."

"But," said Andrinos. "How?"

I ripped the cloak away from Miklasu and handed it to Saenci. She was a

601

beautifully formed girl. Turko ripped off Gaptooth's shirt-tunic and Andrinos donned that.

"We go out the way I came in," I said.

Then Turko smiled. "Hark," he said.

The uproar outside took on a new and suddenly splendid difference. We went into the main chamber and saw a very large and knobby club with a six-inch nail embedded in the head going up and down like the head of a sissingbird snapping insects. A thraxter was slicing away with all the Chulik skills. Other weapons were being used, and the Khamorros were throwing people about like ninepins. Against the high khamsters our people would have had a more tricky time; but Turko waded in with all the venom engendered by being hung up like a chicken on a meat hook, and I took my part, and in short order we broke back through the door and ran down the stairs in a shouting, laughing mob.

No one offered to stop us as we ran out of The Wristy Grip into the pink radiance of the Maiden with the Many Smiles and the rosy golden light of She of the Veils.

Fifteen

The Confidence of the Kov of Falinur

The experiences through which I had gone since escaping from the Humped Land formed a distinct pattern in my head. Finding Turko was not quite the last knot of that pattern. He was, of course, unwilling to leave the Golden Prychan and his wrestling comrades until the business of Andrinos and Saenci had been settled. But, for all that—and I warmed to the idea—he was ragingly eager to return to Vallia.

Born in Herrelldrin though he had been, trained as a Khamorro, rising to a high kham, he now made his home in Valka and regarded himself as a Vallian. Well, did not I, also?

The last knot in this chain would be, of course, Hyrklana.

And that must wait until we had returned to Vallia.

"He has had a fright, that Jimstye Gaptooth," quoth Kimche. "But if you leave us, Turko, we face a hard time of it in the contests."

This was a matter I must not interfere in and must leave to Turko.

"When I joined the consortium of the Golden Prychan," said Turko, and he spoke slowly and with gravity, "I was beholden to you. But I did warn you, fair and square—"

"Yes. You said you would have to leave us one day—"

"And that day is now. Black Algon must be made to see reason."

"I have gold," I said.

They all stared at me.

"But I will not interfere."

Andrinos, one arm about Saenci as we talked in the bamboo-lined snug, said, "If we win free, I will go with Turko." He did not know where Turko was bound. Saenci would go with him. "And for the gold—that I will earn and repay and thank you with all my heart."

I nodded.

With a lift of her Khibil head, Saenci said, "Tell Black Algon I will never return to him. If he refuses the gold, tell him I shall surely kill myself. Then he will have neither gold nor me." She made herself smile. "And he is very avaricious."

So that was the way of it. Turko said to me, "Andrinos is a lucky fellow."

And I said, "Yes."

Now Turko the Shield is an extraordinarily handsome man. With the superb athletic build of a Khamorro and that brilliant profile, he must have wreaked havoc in many a female heart. When he married and settled down, then, I judged, a shadow would come over the bright days of many and many a beauteous maid.

And, as you shall hear, I had the confounded problem of Korero the Shield to attempt to solve...

Perhaps it was just blind luck; perhaps it was fate; perhaps it was some beneficent god or spirit of Kregen taking a hand, but what fell out heartened every one of us.

On the very day Turko, Andrinos, and Saenci prepared to walk with me up that lonely, jungly path, the Khibil's gold having been paid over and her manumission processed very smoothly, three fearsome Khamorros arrived at the fairground and were immediately taken into the consortium of the Golden Prychan. Kimche rubbed a thick hand over his glistening yellow pate.

"Now may Likshu the Treacherous smile, doms! Our comrade Turko leaves us and we replace him with three of his compatriots!"

So, laughing, filled with good cheer, we set off for the flier hidden away in the jungle.

Fliers are rare craft in Pandahem. Andrinos and Saenci walked on ahead of us, close together, so I was able to have a private word with Turko as we followed. When I expressed myself as being surprised that so many Khamorros came to Mahendrasmot, he smiled that ironical, infuriating damned smile of his.

"Mahendrasmot is well known. The fairground attracts people from far away. And, Dray, as you saw, the Khamorros were not high khams."

"And you?"

He repeated what I had heard from our comrades of their shattering surprise when they had been sorcerously hurled back to their homelands. Turko had begun to work his way back to Vallia and had bogged down here, out of cash, and taking the fairground job to earn his passage money on. At this time there was no real volume of trade between Pandahem under Yantong and our sections of Vallia, apart from smuggling. He would have landed in an inhospitable section of Vallia, and he told me how concerned he had become at the rumors and stories out of Vallia.

He was avid for news. I told him of the changed circumstances in the island empire, how the old emperor was dead, and of how I had been fetched to be the new. I said we must all act as our consciences dictated, and there were new men in the world, and Vallia was most miserably divided up and many of her people cruelly mistreated by Yantong and his minions, by riffraff, flutsmen, aragorn, and by the Hamalese.

"There are stern battles ahead, Turko—"

"And I shall be there, with my shield."

"It is in my mind to make you—" And then I stopped myself. I had been going to say I would create Turko a kov, that exalted rank similar to that of duke, as a preparation for broaching the subject of Korero. I saw that as contemptible.

I said, "I have fought in a few battles since we parted, Turko. I have a fine Kildoi to guard my back with his shields. You will meet Korero the Shield."

His eyebrows lifted and he half-turned. Then, in stony silence, he walked on up the jungly path. Andrinos and Saenci were laughing. The suns burned down.

I ploughed on, my throat on fire. "Since you will have no truck with steel and edged weapons, in which you have my admiration, I think it right—"

Then he said, "So you are casting me off?"

"My Val!" I said. "Sink me! Of course not! You are a fambly to think it, let alone say it!"

"So what is in your mind for me, then, Dray? Or should I call you emperor, majister—?"

"Do you wish to try a few falls, dom? Listen, and shut that black-fanged winespout!"

Then he laughed. "You are the same, at any rate, thanks be to Morro the Muscle!"

"Seg and Inch are both kovs of Vallia. I see no reason why you should not be a kov also. I shall arrange this. And, as a kov—"

"You can get rid of me and my shield at your back in the day of battle?"

"Not so. Oh, no! When we fight the Hamalese, as we must, and the clansmen, and the riffraff tearing the heart out of our country, I shall count on you, Kov Turko, to be in the thick of it, as usual."

He kicked a jungly frond that tendriled across the path.

"And, being a kov, and high and mighty some of them are, as we both know—" He stopped speaking then and scowled.

We walked for a space in silence.

Khamorros have reflexes as quick as thought. Turko's hand whipped out and his fist cupped a sparkling fat, blue insect. It was harmless. It buzzed in the prison of Turko's fingers for a space; then he opened his hand and the fly buzzed free.

"Yes," he said. "Seg is a kov and Seg is damned unhappy with his kovnate. Oh, Thelda loves it—" He saw my face. "What? Is Thelda dead? What has chanced with Seg?"

Very firmly, I lied to him. "Thelda is reported dead, seeing no one has seen her in Vondium since we were all parted. Seg is getting over it." As I spoke I realized these were not lies, for Seg's wife, Thelda, although not dead but very happily married to Lol Polisto in all ignorance that her real husband was not dead, was generally regarded as being dead. Seg thought so. I cleared my throat. "Seg is unhappy, yes... But that does not mean you will be."

"It does not. If I am to be a kov I would like to take over Seg's kovnate of Falinur. They are a bunch of rogues who deserve to be brought into a better understanding of life."

I was astounded. Then it was my turn to laugh. "I have spoken to Seg about his kovnate. He remains a kov. But, Turko, you have the lands and the titles and are the Kov of Falinur."

"Right," he said, and I did not miss the ring in his voice. "I thank you for this, majister. There will be changes. And the first will be to alter that damned miserable ocher and umber checkerboard schturval.* Those colors for your kovnate clothes and symbols are depressing. I shall border each square with a nice thick line of cheerful red."

"Quidang!" I said, and thus mocked him in turn.

He was filled with a bubbling confidence, which both amazed and heartened me. I had been totally unsure how he would take to the idea that he was no longer to stand at my back in battle with his shield. I had wondered how he would receive the comical notion that he should be a kov, with titles and estates and cities owing allegiance to him. He seemed to be thriving on the latter idea, and I, shrewdly I suppose, surmised he had not given up on the former and would seek to stand with me in battle as always.

Korero would have to be handled, too...

So, as we found the hidden voller and all climbed aboard, I felt that the future for the midlands of Vallia looked brighter than it had for seasons.

---

* Schturval: Color-coded badge, symbol, banded sleeve, and figurative representation of animal or plant or abstract design, forming insignia denominating allegiances in Vallia.

We took off and soared away, heading for the islands of Vallia and what was left of my empire. And, at the thought, I suddenly felt a coldness, and stupidly longed to be down the Moder with all the Monsters and menace... By the Black Chunkrah! A few footling fun and games around passages and secret doors and ghoulish weirdies seemed then to be children's pastimes beside the job facing me in Vallia and all of Paz. Again and again I had tried to throw off the yoke, and always some stupidity in my own nature forced me to resume the burden. The single decisive fact impelling me to go on was simply this: that I had been called on, chosen, fetched by the people of Vallia to lead them in their way of life and their struggle for freedom.

My comrades were individual people, with strong characters and minds of their own. If, sometimes, it sounds as though I ordered them about willy-nilly, this is not so. Each one was a personality, a real living, breathing person, and if I fail to bring them vividly alive to you in these tapes, then the lack is mine, the loss yours, for, by Zair, they are a bonny bunch!

Now Turko said to me, "I see you fly due west. So you do not intend to chance the mountains?"

I shook my head.

"This voller may not let us down as those cranky rubbish heaps from Hamal so often do. But the mountains offer a risk we do not have to accept." I looked at him. "Anyway, I've a mind to fly over Rahartdrin."

I had told him how we had lost contact with so many of the outlying provinces and islands. Rahartdrin, the large island off the southwest of Vallia, was the kovnate of the Lady Katrin Rashumin. As a friend of Delia's, her welfare concerned me. No news had come out of that part of the empire, and all our spies had either reported failure or had not returned.

Turning north off the west coast of Pandahem, we soared on over the southern reaches of the Hobolings and struck out across the Sea of Opaz. The whole distance was above seven hundred dwaburs and we estimated should take us the best part of three days, as the flier was not of the fast variety. We took turns to conn the helm and stand by the levers, Saenci catered splendidly, and we bustled through the skies of Kregen in fine style.

The strategic concept of having to stop for fuel, and have coaling stations conveniently scattered across the world, was one with which I was at that time unfamiliar. Vittles and water were the limiting factors in a journey time. The silver boxes, the vaol and paol, with their mix of minerals and gas, upheld us and drove us on, so there was no need to make any halts.

Out over the Sea of Opaz, the islands of the Hobolings dropped astern; looking for the dawn and then a few burs of sunshine before we reached Rahartdrin, I stood at the controls and felt the lightness of spirits on me. I felt more free than I had for ages, and this despite the ponderous weight of the problems facing me at home. Going back to Delia; that was the answer. So I stood there and snuffed the night air and Deb-Lu-Quienyin appeared at my side.

His ghostly form glimmered spectrally against the side of the voller. I could see the canvas stitching through him.

He gestured. Commandingly, he pointed two points off the starboard bow. Darkness shrouded the sea, with the massed glitter of the stars above and the Twins fast sinking in the west. Then he stabbed his fingers into the air, five fingers, and his mouth framed the word "Bur." The Kregan bur is forty terrestrial minutes long and there are forty-eight of them to a Kregan day.

I moved the controls and the voller swung onto the heading Quienyin indicated. The Wizard of Loh smiled, and pushed his turban straight, and disappeared.

Well, I said to myself, lucky Andrinos and Saenci had not witnessed that supernatural manifestation. I felt the chill. Yet how splendidly different this apparition from those with which that egomaniacal cramph Phu-Si-Yantong favored us!

Turko came on deck at the change of course. He yawned.

"In about five burs' time, Turko, we shall see something interesting. The suns should just about be up by then."

He looked at me. "What—?"

A brief, a very brief, explanation had to suffice.

"And this Wizard of Loh. You will no doubt kick Khe-Hi-Bjanching out as you—"

"Now, Turko!"

But he was smiling, and as we sailed on he launched into a summary of his plans for his new kovnate. I listened. I fancied the recalcitrant folk of Falinur were in for a shock. Turko had seen how Seg's methods had failed to impress. As I listened I realized that Seg had attempted to do things in the way he knew I would approve, without force. Turko was prepared to bear down that much harder—well, by Vox! So was Seg; but he had genuinely attempted to apply the new principles we all wanted to bring to the hard and harsh world of Kregen. There was a lesson here. But, I knew, I would not give up my plans, even if, from time to time, they were temporarily set back.

As for Quienyin, this visit proved to me he had been accepted in Vallia, and for that I joyed.

I broke the bad news about Falinur with a little lift of that mockery subsisting between us. "Oh, and Turko. The ex-pallan, Layco Jhansi, has taken over in Falinur. We will have to send him packing first."

Turko glowered. I had told him of the treachery of Layco Jhansi, the old emperor's chief pallan. "I find it odd, to say the least, Dray. Vallia, the

607

island empire, divided up into a parcel of warring factions. Odd, damned odd."

"Odd but true. We hold Vondium and much of the south and midlands. But we must patrol these artificial frontiers, and hold strong reserves in loci where they can march instantly to any threatened point. And the flutsmen drop down anywhere, for they are returning to Vallia in increasing numbers. The world regards Vallia as doomed and as merely a fat prize to be sucked dry. Oh, and we have good friends in Hawkwa country, up in the Northeast."

"And Inch and Princess—I mean Empress—Delia? The Blue Mountain Boys, Korf Aighos, they would not take kindly to these rasts stealing from them. That is certain. And the Black Mountain Men. Inch's kovnate must have fought."

"They both did and have kept themselves relatively clear of the vermin infesting our land; but it is mighty hard."

He had received the news that our island of Valka had been cleaned up with joy. "I expect fresh regiments from Valka to join in the struggle," I told him. "The job is immense."

"Right. So between Inch and me, we can squeeze this traitorous Layco Jhansi until he squeaks."

"You have yet to win Falinur back."

"I'll do that."

He did not say that the gift of the kovnate was a poor gift, seeing it was occupied by usurpers. I felt fresh resolve in him, and knew the wise thing had been done here.

Seg Segutorio had been happy to dump Falinur. Next time around, he would run a kovnate that would be a marvel.

The voller's speed was about five db.* She was not fast, but she was a useful, chunky craft with a deal of urge in her. Neither Turko nor I could place her country of manufacture. The wise men at home would have to examine her silver boxes to learn what secrets she contained. Certainly, she was unlike the fliers with which we were familiar.

The alteration of course to starboard would bring us east of Rahartdrin. A number of small islands dot the sea off the south coast of Vallia here. Some are densely populated by reason of their fertile soil, others are barren and empty. Many are ringed by fanged rocks. As the sky lightened and the first rays of palest rose and leaf green flushed the sky we saw that a gale had broomed the sea beneath us during the night. We had been speeding faster than we thought. Down there the sea heaved in long, running swells, the breeze brushed the tops into shot-silk, it was a day for expanding the chest and avoiding a lee shore.

Turko pointed. I nodded.

---

* db: dwaburs per bur.

A ship down there, dismasted, wallowing, had not avoided a lee shore. The islands ahead reached out cruel reefs of rock and the sea spouted in climbing combs of foam. The ship was doomed, for she could never claw off the rocks and round the headland into a muddy bay opening up on the far side.

"This is what Quienyin meant," I said. "But he had more in his mind than merely to summon us to witness a shipwreck."

"She's an argenter out of one of the free cities along the Lohvian coast," said Turko. His expression remained noncommittal. What we did would be down to me, and Turko would loyally support me, for that was the way he had chosen.

"We could—" I said, and stopped and looked again, figuring angles and calculating with a seaman's quickness. "It could be done."

Turko mistook my meaning. "You'll never get them all aboard, Dray!"

The deck of the argenter was packed with men. Like any ship given the appellation of argenter, she was broad in the beam, capacious, a tubby, comfortable, not particularly weatherly vessel, and fleets of argenters formed the backbone of the merchant navies of the maritime nations—except Vallia. I noticed an odd thing about those men seething on the deck below. They had all stripped off so as to be able to swim after the impending shipwreck had pitched them into the sea; but every man carried weapons strapped to his naked body. Yes, I know I say a Kregan will not willingly walk his world without weapons; but when you must swim for your life in murderous breakers, that, surely, is one occasion when you must cast away your sword, your spear, your bow? These men were naked and armed.

Turko was quite right. Taking a quick block count I reckoned there must be a hundred fifty to two hundred men jammed on the deck, all braced for the impending impact. We'd never get them all in this flier.

"Rustle out what rope we have aft, Turko. Get Andrinos. We'll tow that argenter around the point!"

Instantly, without fussing, Turko went aft to the rope locker. We might not have enough. We could drop a line to them down there; they'd not shoot a line up to us. A pretty little calculation entered my mind as we maneuvered into position. Could even Seg Segutorio, in my view the greatest bowman of Kregen, shoot a shaft trailing a line from that ship up to us? Turko let out a yell and he waved, so I knew we had rope enough.

The trickiest part of the operation would be keeping a steady strain on the hawser. The argenter was going up and down sluggishly and rolling with that dead effect that told me she was filling. It would be touch and go. Three results were in the offing: she could strike the rocks and fly to flinders, she could be towed around the point—or she could sink before either of those events took place. The line dangled down and was seized in a forest of upraised arms and made fast to the inboard stump of the bowsprit. Gingerly, I opened up the forward control lever and the voller moved ahead.

Aft, Turko kept a watchful eye on the line.

"And get your head out of the way. If she snaps—"

"Aye, Dray. I know."

And, with his superb Khamorro reflexes, he would be moving and avoiding the deadly whiptail of broken line faster than the eye could follow.

The argenter proved a stubborn beast. Most Kregan vollers are soundless in flight; had engines been involved they would have been screaming in protest. But we moved. We moved!

Slowly, painfully, we hauled the argenter crabbing through the waves, seeing the white water bursting clean over her. Not a man was washed off. Her blunt bows rose and fell and churned the white froth in a welter of foam. Slowly she came around and we crawled for the point. The hawser sang.

This unknown voller might not be fast; but she could pull!

Gradually we saw the vital stretch of sea opening up as we hauled the ship away from the rocks. It was a maelstrom down there. The men clustered, looking up at us, and we prayed with them that all the gods of Kregen would smile on this enterprise.

As we passed clear of the spit of land dividing the cruel rock reef from the muddy bay, a small group of totrixmen galloped along the spiny ridge below. The six legs of their mounts spraddled out and their leathers glistened in the flung spray. They carried lances, and their helmets gleamed in the early light. They rode inland and were lost to view.

"Company," I shouted at Turko. "We'll have a reception committee."

"Friends?"

And then, of course, I realized that this part of Vallia was firmly in the hands of a vicious foeman, that Kataki Strom, Rosil Yasi, the Strom of Morcray, who was a tool of Phu-si-Yantong's and who would joy to see me dead. I may add that those sentiments were reciprocated in part.

"More likely to be enemies, Turko."

He did not reply; but I saw the muscles along his arms bunch and roll.

Andrinos, with his keen foxy face concerned, said, "Then this ship full of armed men could be enemies going to join their friends?"

I shook my head. "It is a possibility, and a risk we must take." I did not say that I considered Quienyin would have acted differently had this been a shipfull of enemies. Andrinos and Saenci shared the respect and caution accorded Wizards of Loh. Feeling my reply to be somewhat abrupt, and, into the bargain, hardly reassuring, I added, "I am convinced they are not friendly toward the enemies of Vallia. On the contrary, if I am right they have sailed here to fight for us."

"We pray Pandrite and Horata the Bounteous you are right, pantor,"*
said Saenci.

We were almost clear of the point. Beyond the crags the water ceased its
frantic turmoil and smoothed into placidity. Once there the argenter could
drift gently toward that muddy shore and ground without a fuss. After that,
in due course of the seasons, she could molder to ruination.

At that point the hawser snapped.

Turko moved. One instant he was checking the tension and calling to
me, the next he was flat on the deck, yelling a warning.

The end of the line snapped over our heads and came down like a sjambok, thwack, across the cabin roof.

With a frantic snatch at the control levers, I halted the mad onward leap
of the voller. She swung about and soared back over the argenter. The men
down there stared up. The seas took the ship into their grip and remorselessly pushed her down onto the rocky crags.

"There's only one thing for it, now!" I yelled at Turko. The voller swerved
and descended. We felt the force of the breeze. With finicky movements
I brought her low over the sea, to leeward of the argenter. As we passed
that high, ornate poop the name leaped up, gilded and carved, *Mancha of
Tlinganden*. Tlinganden was one of the Free Cities left after the collapse of
the old Empire of Loh, situated on the east coast opposite the country of
Yumapan in Pandahem. This ship had successfully fought her way through
the renders infesting the Hobolings. Now she was going to come to grief
with all her people, if we could not save her.

Gently I eased the voller in until we nudged the surging bulk of the
argenter. It was touchy business. I had to maintain the same rhythm as the
sea, lifting and lowering the flier, and at the same time maintain a steady
pressure against the bulky hull.

"By Morro the Muscle!" exclaimed Turko, joining me forward and cran-
ing out over the coaming. "You're going to push her free!"

"It's the only way left. Just hope we don't stove her in."

The voller rose and fell and rolled and the argenter was like a sodden
souse refusing to move along.

"Or she doesn't drag us down."

Water sluiced inboard, drenching us.

The pressure kept up. The black crags ringed with creamy foam seemed
to be racing up toward us as we went careering down, forced by wind and
sea. But the silver boxes of the voller exerted their power as I forced the
levers over. Slowly, we saw the angles widen, slowly we saw the bows creep
past the last disturbed confusion of water, slowly the argenter, *Mancha of
Tlinganden*, rolled and sagged and pitched clear of the last fangy outcrop.

---

* pantor: The Pandahem word for lord, equating with the Havilfarian notor and
the Vallian jen.

"We've done it!'" shouted Andrinos. His hands were clasped together. Saenci clung to his arm. "Never have I seen such flying!"

Spray burst over us. The argenter rolled uglily. Men clung to her, like bees on a honeypot. And we weren't done with her yet. She had to be turned, now, turned poop on to the run of the sea, so that she would ground less forcefully.

And then disaster struck. One moment I was beginning to think that we had successfully done it, the next a brute of a sea surged in, crisscrossing the current, the towering sterncastle punched at us, the poop swung shrewdly, and the voller was caught and flung and toppled end over end into the sea.

Sixteen

Homecoming

The water felt like a brick wall.

Spread-eagled, cartwheeling, I crashed into that brick wall and burst through it with all the breath knocked out of me. Water buried me.

To struggle back to the surface and to gulp air... To struggle, never to give in, to go on fighting and clawing even as they shovel the grave sods over your face. That is the way of Dray Prescot, and often and often I wonder just how far it has got him. As the sea smashed into me and water clogged my nostrils I gave a few erratic strokes with my legs, turning and twisting upright, forcing myself to rise. Up. Up I went and my head broke the silver sky and the Suns of Scorpio blazed in my face.

Light blinded me. Shimmer of wavetops, spray cutting across, all a liquid movement of colors and radiance. I spat. I shook my head. I forced my eyes to remain open. I felt, I admit, like a side of beef must feel after it has been corned and stuffed into a tin.

The situation was quite other than I had expected, for the voller floated. Amazingly, the flier sat on the water, upright, rising and falling with the motion of the sea. Just beyond her the argenter *Mancha of Tlinganden* rolled and wavered in my vision, surging on like a runaway temple to Kranlil the Reaper, shedding bits and pieces, falling apart, scattering timber as she lurched and shuddered to her doom.

A few strokes took me to the voller. I handed myself up and felt the sluggishness. The canvas had been ripped and most of her starboard side stove in. She would sink in a few murs. There was no sign of my companions.

612

Standing on the splintered deck of the voller, I looked about. The advantage of vision afforded by that little extra height proved sufficient. Two heads showed in the sea, among white splashes, and then a third. Saenci's reddish foxy hair drifted on the water and I dived in first for her. She was swimming well; but going the wrong way.

Spitting, I gasped out, "Steady, Saenci. It's all right now. Just relax and let me—"

"Where is Andrinos?"

"He's all right. We must reach the argenter."

I held her in the prescribed fashion for lifesaving and swam across to the drifting ship. Turko and Andrinos swam across. We trod water and looked up and they threw ropes down for us and helped us inboard. Like half-drowned gyps we crawled aboard.

Being your ruffianly kind of mercenary, I knew I had not much time left before the voller sank to act as any proper hyrpaktun would act now. I dived back and swam to the flier.

I left the hubbub and howls of protest. Clambering onto the warped deck and working very rapidly, very rapidly indeed, by Krun! I snatched up my weapons and that superb harness of mesh links. Swimming back with the bundle was not too difficult although not a sport I'd take up for pleasure, and once again they hauled me inboard. This time I was content to lie on the deck and let my battered old carcass recover.

"You're a right maniac, dom!" quoth a cheerful voice. I looked up.

He stood, his thick legs spread apart, his hands on his hips, stark naked but for the weapons belted to him. His face was plug-ugly, scarred, with prominent eyebrows and a mass of thick brown hair, plastered into shiny flatness by spray.

"Aye," I said. And then, "Llahal."

"Llahal, dom. I am Clardo the Clis. I thank you for saving us—" A gleam of gold at his belt caught my eye. He had taken his pakzhan, the little golden zhantil head that is the mark of the hyrpaktun, from around his neck and twisted the silken cords tightly around his belt.

About to reply that, Llahal, I was Jak, a sudden shadow fell over me as I sat up and a fierce, excited, bubbling voice burst about us and brought instant silence from everyone.

"Lahal!" said this voice. "Lahal and Lahal, Strom Drak! It's me, Torn Tomor. And you are now Emperor of Vallia. Lahal, majister, Lahal!"

I stood up and looked at him.

Yes, he had the virile toughness of his father and the slim agility of his mother, and if he had a tithe of their strengths he would be a most puissant young man. I smiled.

"Lahal, Torn Tomor. And your father and mother are well and thrive, thanks be to Opaz. And, as for you, your faith was too fragile, for the murderer confessed." He started at this, a young, eager, alive man with all his life to lead. "Yes, Torn, you ran off to be a paktun when we all knew you would not strike down a man from the shadows, with steel between his shoulder blades."

"But," he stammered, "majister—everyone said—it looked black—"

"It is black no more. Do I need to ask why you return to Vallia?"

"By Vox, no!" spoke up Clardo the Clis. "But—" And here his scarred face swung toward Torn Tomor. "—is this really the emperor, Torn? How can he be, seeing the emperor sits in Vondium and waits for us to fight and win his battles for him?"

The argenter gave a lurching heave that made us all brace ourselves to the sway of her. The muddy shore was not far off and soon the ship would splinter to flinders. Turko stood at my side. Andrinos was holding Saenci. I looked at the crowding men, hardened men, professional fighting men, tough and ruthless in combat, easy and reckless in camp. Yes, they were mercenaries, going to Vallia to find employment. A few quick words established what I had instantly guessed, and what had made Deb-Lu-Quienyin direct me here. Every man was a Vallian. Each man had gone off from his own country as a lad, seeing that Vallia had no army but employed paktuns to fight for gold. And, now the mother country was in dire danger, beset by enemies, her sons were returning home. But they were not the country bumpkins, the smart townies, who had left. Now they were paktuns and hyrpaktuns. Now they were professionals. I sighed. What I could do with a hundred thousand like this!

The voller had taken with her the secrets of her silver boxes, and I had to quell the spurt of anger. All that had chanced to me since leaving Vallia for the Dawn Lands formed a part of a pattern, that was clear. Prince Tyfar and Quienyin; well, Quienyin was actively assisting me now and Tyfar was going to have a much more prominent part to play in my plans than he dreamed of. By Zair! He had a much bigger part to play than *I* dreamed of! How fate does throw the knucklebones, and sits back, giggling. And that Vajikry fanatic, Trylon Nath Orscop, had afforded me a voller able to pull. No Vajikry, no voller. No voller, no ship of fighting men for Vallia.

Turko said, "We're going to hit any mur—and that company you spoke of. They're waiting."

Along the edge of the surf the lines of totrixmen cantered. They looked hard and sharp. They were waiting for us. As we staggered up out of the clutch of the sea they would ride forward and spear us. The Vallians in the ship were shouting and waving. They thought these riders were waiting to succor them. And that was the sensible thought to any Vallian who had left the country before the Time of Troubles.

I shouted, hard and high, in an ugly voice.

"Those jutmen are our mortal foes! They will spear us as we wade ashore through the mud. Each man must be ready to resist them. They are a parcel of the cramphs who are eating up your homeland."

Well, that changed the demeanor of the returning mercenaries wonderfully.

A staff-slinger stepped forward. "Lahal, majister. I am Larghos the Sko-handed." He spread his left hand. "My men will loose, seeing all the bowstrings will be wet."

Larghos had a long, narrow chin, and a slinger's shoulders. A squatter, fiery-faced man stepped forward, spluttering.

"Lahal, majister! I am Drill the Eye." He waved an oilskin pouch. "Give me a few murs to string our bows and we will see!"

I did not laugh. But the vivid image of Barkindrar the Bullet and Nath the Shaft flashed up before me. By Krun! But they do love a fine professional argument, these slingers and these bowmen of Kregen!

I eyed the surf. It was not too dangerous; but it would knock a fellow over unless he was well-braced and not too far out.

"Stand back, you missile men, and give the swordsmen a chance. Loose over them." Again I eyed the narrowing distance between us and the shore. "If she grounds close enough, best you remain aboard for as long as you can and shoot from here."

"Aye, majister!" they shouted. "Until she falls to pieces!"

That was the moment the keel of the argenter touched bottom. We held our breaths. Some of that luxurious stern ornamentation, all gingerbread work, fell off with a roar and a splash. She lifted up with the surge of the waves and shuddered on. Thrice more she touched and thrice more she lifted and rolled nearer the shore.

The breeze blew our hair forward and chilled our skins. The smell of brine and mud grew more pungent. Turko had found a shield—I saw him talking to a swarthy fellow who nodded and handed his shield over without a fuss. I marked him. The shield was the rectangular cylindrical shield of Havilfar. Efficient.

When a vessel marked for destruction touches the shore, always, I think, a man must mourn for another hostage lost to the implacable elements. *Mancha of Tlinganden* struck at last, and her keel scraped through slimy mud, and the black stuff swirled up in the water alongside. She shuddered on for a few more paces, and then stuck, slewing slightly, canting over, coming to her final rest with a kind of peace we had bought for her. She did not fly into flinders, as I had feared. But her doom was certain. We plunged down into the sea and struck out for the shore.

Andrinos swam with me and Turko was there also, the shield almost like a surfboard.

The surf crashed about us and men yelled and were knocked flying, and surfaced, spluttering and going doggedly on. With an increase of pace I managed to get ahead. I did not wear the mesh-link iron harness. I held the thraxter, and the sword glimmered wet with running water. Jumping the retreating waves, I crashed on up that muddy beach, feeling the gluey muck clinging and trying to haul me back. Like a mud-devil I reached forward with the water around my waist, and the muck did not wash off.

The riders on the beach turned their mounts to face us.

They rode down, the six legs of the totrixes splaying out, their heads high against the commotion of wind and water. The spear points twitched down. They cantered on, full of confidence that they would spear us poor half-drowned rats before we could stagger clear of the waterline.

Two of them came for me. I braced myself with the tug of the sea about me. The first abruptly switched from his saddle as though jerked by puppet cords. A long arrow sprouted from his neck. The second had no time to puzzle over his comrade's fate. I leaped for him, brushed the spear aside, sank the thraxter in.

After that as the paktuns roared up out of the sea, naked, shining with mud and water, half-crazed, yelling, we tore into the totrixmen. Leaden bullets flew. Shafts pierced. Swords glinted and ran red. We had the beating of them in the first half-dozen murs. We fought as men fight coming up out of their graves. Only a dozen or so survived to gallop off wildly.

Panting, the Vallians gathered, and stared balefully after the fleeing riders.

"Hai, Jikai! Emperor!" someone shouted.

I quieted the hubbub.

"I think we are on the island of Wenhartdrin. It is a rich land, and the best wines of Vallia, some say, come from here. But the whole land here is in the grip of our enemies. We are Vallians!"

"Aye!"

"Let us then see what honest Vallians may do, by Vox, and in the radiance of the Invisible Twins made manifest through the light of Opaz, let us go forward!"

And, by Vox, forward we went!

Seventeen

Emperor's Yellow Jackets

The captain and first lieutenant of the argenter had been killed in an accident, and this in part accounted for her doomed course of destruction toward the rocks. Most of the crew were Hobolings who are among the finest of topmen. These and the other deckhands had no part of our fight. I did not inquire how the arrangements for the passage had been made. We agreed to leave these folk on the island and see to it that they were repatriated.

Ashore, we busied ourselves scrubbing off the mud. The ship broke apart slowly. I marked the spot. On a more auspicious occasion I'd return here and see if I could salvage those silver boxes from the sunken voller.

Boxes and bales and barrels floated ashore, mingled with the sad detritus of a destroyed ship. There were many fat bales of a good quality cloth, all of that bright, strong, yellow color called tromp. There was food, also, that was not contaminated by sea water and we soon had fires going and tea brewing and food sizzling. To clothe our nakedness we cut up squares of the tromp cloth and made holes and so put them over our heads. We cinched our belts tight, and we looked a fine rousing rabble under the suns.

Some few remnants of the paktuns' original clothes drifted ashore, and a few pairs of boots. But, in general, we were a band of yellow brigands to all intents as we set off.

The old emperor, Delia's father, had always liked the wines from Wenhartdrin. We marched on and soon passed signs of viticulture, most of it blackened and ruined. Houses had burned. We saw no one for some time until, reaching a tumbledown village, we found a few poor people who told us the news. This was simple. Strom Rosil Yasi, being a damned Kataki and therefore by nature a slavemaster, was more interested in human merchandise. These folk were left free and alive because they were too ill, too weak, or could till just enough land to provide food for the conquering invaders. Well, by Zair, we sorted out that local problem.

The band of yellow-clad comrades fought like men possessed. As we progressed into the island and saw the evidences of what being occupied meant, they grew hard and fierce even above all their mercenary habits. We found the aragorn, slavers who occupy an area and from a strong point terrorize and suck dry everything of value, and we slew them in battle and drove them into the sea. Wenhartdrin is not above fifteen dwaburs long and ten wide, shaped rather like two triangles apex to apex. We discovered that Strom Rosil Yasi, known as the Kataki Strom, had left but two squadrons of cavalry and a half regiment of infantry to hold the island. These men were all mercenaries of various races.

Military organization varies from country to country on Kregen, that stands to reason; but hereabouts the regiment of infantry very often consisted of six pastangs of eighty or so men each, giving four hundred and eighty men to a regiment. So there were around two hundred to two hundred and forty mercenaries swanning about Wenhartdrin that we had to deal with. Cavalry regiments varied more widely in numbers and composition and we had seen off one squadron on the beach and the second squadron, some hundred or so, we caught in a pretty little ambush along a defile crowded with tufa trees. By this time a portion of our force was mounted; but what with sickness and casualties, we now numbered not much more than a hundred and seventy-five or so.

We had shaken out into a loose organization, all wearing those tromp-colored uniforms which, gradually and against all expectations, smartened up and grew into proper uniforms. Larghos the Sko-handed commanded a group of expert staff-slingers. Drill the Eye commanded his bowmen—they used the compound reflex bow, not the great Lohvian longbow. The bulk of the force consisted of swordsmen, many of them sword and shield men, churgurs, and these were handled by Clardo the Clis. Although these people had gathered together relatively recently to return to Vallia, many of them had served as groups in one war or another, and in general their names and reputations were known among themselves.

On the evening when we knew on the morrow we would have to go up against that half regiment, I stood talking quietly to Torn Tomor. The campfires burned and the viands sizzled and the wine passed around companionably. We talked of his parents, Tom Tomor ti Vulheim, the Elten of Avanar and his wife, Bibi, who were comrades of the Strom of Valka and Elders of the high assembly of Valka.

"And you will wear the orange of the high assembly in due course, Torn," I said. "Be very sure of that."

"Before that, majister, I will serve in the Strom's Sacred Life Guard."

He saw my instinctive frown, a twist of irritation to my lips I could not halt. I have mentioned before my equivocal feelings regarding these bodyguards. When we had been clearing out the island of Valka, before I was fetched to be the strom—which is grandly recorded in the famous song "The Fetching of Drak na Valka"—they had put together a devoted band of blade comrades to stand watch and ward over my person, in battle and camp and wherever the blade of an assassin might strike. They had served nobly, even though I had still managed to find a few adventures on my own account, as you have heard.

As I struggled to find the right words, a man passed us. He was, as I thought, talking to himself. Torn Tomor glanced across. The fellow's head was turned to his left shoulder and his right hand gestured vehemently as though he spoke to someone who walked at his side. He was a swordsman, with thick brown mustachios and that swagger of your true hyrpaktun.

"Oh," said Torn, "that's old Frandor the Altrak."

"He looks—" I began cautiously.

"Don't bother your head about old Frandor. He lost his twin brother in a battle seasons ago and still fancies he is with him. He talks to him all the time. Watch him at meals. He takes a phantom plate and fills it with phantom food and offers it to his brother—who lies moldering somewhere in Loh, and his ib is wandering the Ice Floes of Sicce seeking the sunny uplands beyond."

"He is not makib," I said. I guessed Frandor was not insane. He just had one of those little funny habits fighting men are prone to.

Many of the most renowned of fighting men had peculiarities that would, on this Earth, have landed them in lunatic asylums. Nath the Flim-cop, when his name was shouted out at roll call, would answer with a roar: "Gone fishing!" No punishments could break him of the habit; and now that he was a paktun he could get away with that very mild example of irrational behavior. Some of the near nut cases among seasoned fighting men would shrivel your hair. Naghan the Thumb collected the right thumbs of those he defeated and he wore a belt of the shriveled things around his waist. He had swum ashore with the thumb belt. It had grown considerably since, and he was debating how best to loop it up into a double thickness.

Talk of the Strom's Sacred Life Guard—Torn had said En Luxis Bliem Juruk, and Sacred Life Guard is a near enough translation. Kregish is particularly rich as a language, filled with colorful words. Bliem, for life, is merely one word, and the one chosen here. These fellows had fought well and loyally and I had thought the Praetorian Guard, the Imperial Guard, idea had died when I became emperor. But then, as you know, the Sword Watch had been formed. So, what with Frandor the Altrak wandering past carrying on an animated conversation with his dead twin, I was spared the embarrassment of stumbling out some words or other to Torn about my feelings on bodyguards.

And, by Vox! Bodyguards are a delightful invention when some of the cramphs trying to kill me on Kregen take action!

On the next day my seasoned veterans caught that half regiment and tumbled the three pastangs into bloody ruin. When it was all over and we turned over the loot, as all good paktuns do, sharing one with another, we were able to outfit our whole little force with armor. And, over the armor, these men wore their old yellow homemade jackets, still.

On the way back to our camp our outriders spotted a flier cruising over the island. Instantly we all faded into the bushes. Down here any air-service boats were operated by adherents of Strom Rosil. Peering up through the leaves, I studied the craft as she flitted past. She was a very small single-place job, and no doubt before the Time of Troubles had been some sporty fellow's pride and joy. Then I stared again, harder.

"Keep your heads down, you famblys!" Clardo the Clis rumbled the words. He had no need to, for these men were kampeons*; but Clardo no doubt felt the need of expressing his feelings about cowering in the bushes.

---

* kampeon: veteran who has received recognition and won renown.

I stood up. I walked out from the bushes. Lifting my arms and waving, I shouted.

"The emperor!" someone yelled from the bushes.

"Shastum!" came Clardo's irate voice. "The emperor knows what he is doing. But, by Vox, I do not!"

The flier circled and dropped down. With a sweet swoop of precise piloting she landed ten paces from me.

I knew that a score of bows were aimed for the pilot's heart.

He stepped out and threw up an arm in salute.

"Lahal, majister! Well met!"

"Lahal, Quardon," I said. "Well met indeed." I half turned and bellowed at the bushes. "Come on out. We have been found."

From the short flagstaff in the stern of the voller flew the union flag of Vallia. That yellow cross superimposed on a yellow saltire, all on a red field, had told me the airboat was friendly. Down here, she could only be looking for us on the advice of Quienyin. And, as you will readily perceive, none of these paktuns freshly returned to their native land would know that the flag they saw was their new flag of Vallia.

The splendid upshot of this meeting appeared a few burs after young Quardon, a rip-roaring lad of the Sword Watch, shot off in the voller. Soaring in over the trees, all her sails set, one of our flying ships from Vondium threw her long shadow from the suns. The paktuns gathered with me stared up and it was a wonderful sight to see their faces. The sails came in smartly and the ship let down through thin air, upheld and supported by her silver boxes that were, alas, in nowise as efficient as the silver boxes of the powered vollers.

Flags of Vondium flew from her, and men's heads dotted along the bulwarks. She was a fine craft, three-decked and with proper accommodation, and armed with varters and gros-varters. I own to a thrill, myself, as she touched down.

Well, the Lahals rang out and there was much clasping of hands and back-thumping. Many of the new Second Regiment of the Sword Watch were there. These fighting men had come ahunting me when Quienyin in lupu had sussed out our whereabouts.

"She is a fine, large craft, majister," said Torn. "Finer, I daresay, than those with which Vallia thrashed Hamal at the Battle of Jholaix."

"As good, Torn," I said. "As good. Now let us all board and catch the breeze for home."

Only two men looked glum. These were the brothers Niklaardu—for their home was Wenhartdrin itself.

"Have faith," I said, speaking the easy words, but meaning them, and demanding a response in kind. "We will free all Vallia. You will return to your home in Wenhartdrin. Believe that."

"Aye, majister. We believe it. But it will be a hard road."

Sheer common sense and the practicalities of government told me that during my absence many changes must have taken place at home. I asked questions, an endless stream of them, and digested the answers. I preferred this method to allowing my comrades to babble on haphazardly telling me what jumped into their memories. All the relevant information I will retail as and when it affects this my narrative; suffice it to say now that Vallia was still an island sundered and divided, with factions warring for power, and the capital city of Vondium, still in our hands, standing like a rock in a raging sea.

With those silver boxes we had made ourselves in Vondium uplifting the ship, we sailed on. The boxes gave us no forward motive power, as the complete boxes did for the vollers; but they extended gripping, invisible holds into what the wise men called the ethero-magnetic lines of force and thus afforded the ship a kind of keel so that we could tack and make boards against the wind. Leaving Wenhartdrin, we sailed east over the sea with the lovely coastline of Vallia passing to the northward.

One item of news gave me an itchy feeling up the spine. Delia and I had discussed the designs of Queen Lushfymi of Lome upon our splendid son Drak. Drak was our eldest, the stern, sober, competent one of our sons. Queen Lush had been sent by Phu-Si-Yantong from her country in Pandahem to seduce, suborn, and destroy the old emperor. Instead, she had turned to us Vallians, and stood at our side against the Wizard of Loh. Now that the emperor was dead, Queen Lush was set on marrying Prince Drak, well knowing that one day she would thus become Empress of Vallia. Delia and I felt that Seg's daughter, Silda, was the proper mate for Drak. Nothing openly had been said. This was one of those fractious knots of problems that bedevil men and women, whether they be puffed-up emperors or empresses, or shopkeepers with a business to care for.

By Zair! How I was looking forward to the day when I could throw down the burden of empire, and become once again plain Dray Prescot, of Esser Rarioch in Valka!

And, of course, Lord of Strombor and King of Djanduin and all manner of other splendid and sometimes mocking titles and estates.

The flutsmen circled out of the suns' glare as I pondered the problems facing me. The trumpets pealed the alarm.

How marvelous to see the Sword Watch and these new comrades in their yellow jackets work together! Shafts rose from the flying ship, leaden bullets flew. The flutsmen, screeching, their mottled clumps of feathers flying, their weapons glittering, swooped upon us. It was a pretty set to. The flying argosy was called *Challenger*, registered in Vondium, and as she coursed through thin air with all her canvas pulling and the flutsmen spun and darted in to attack, I felt that here we had a microcosm of the evils inflicting Vallia with agony, a prophecy of the struggles to come.

621

When the flutsmen saw their attacks were fruitless, what remained of them drew off. Their wings bright in the suns' light, the fluttrells swerved away. They sped in a long, defeated string northward for the coast.

"We are within a few dwaburs of Delphond, are we not?" I said to Captain Hando, the master.

A thin, razor-nosed man with a tufty chin beard, he screwed up his eyes. He had been a galleon captain, and had transferred to the new flying ships service.

"Aye, majister. Devil take the flutsmen. So near the capital! It is beyond bearing."

I learned that implacable frontiers had been drawn between Delia's province of Delphond and Venavito, just to the west. Venavito was an Imperial Province. I should say, had been an Imperial Province. The Imperial Province of Vond, just to the north of Delphond, was in our hands; but Thadelm, to the west, was a battleground. I frowned at this news. We had fought battles in that part of the country and I had hoped we had cleared the enemy out.

"It is mostly a matter of border raids, majister," I was told.

This area of action was altogether too close to the capital. Plans had been laid before I was summoned away by the Star Lords to my adventures in the Dawn Lands of Havilfar for an army to march to the southwest and liberate all that corner of the island. Why had not that been done? Why had the plans not been acted on? I could obtain no satisfactory answers to my questions on that score.

The answer that I guessed, at the time, to be near the truth, reflected my own caution and anxiety. The Lord Farris and the Presidio well knew my concern for dissipating our forces. We had the raging armies of clansmen in the northeast to deal with. We had Layco Jhansi and the Racters in the northwest. We had to pivot on a center to face all ways at once. If we committed too much in a single lone thrust, we exposed our backs. Yet, I was now convinced, we must strike, make a decisive move in one direction or another, and so begin the final campaigns.

When Captain Hando used the word "implacable" to describe the new frontier between Delphond and Venavito, I understood exactly what he meant. It was not an incongruous word. I stared after the fluttrells. But I did not give the order to swing the ship after them. *Challenger* continued on her course, sailing the sky, and the suns shone and the flutsmen vanished back to their camps and fortresses in Venavito.

Too much awaited me in Vondium. The state of the country had to be seen to first, before I could go harum-scarum after a pack of miserable sky-reivers, much as I would have liked to have done.

Even after all this time I know I have not done justice to the splendor, the beauty, the grandeur of Vondium. It is a human city, filled with warmth and light, and the brilliance of the vegetation, the silver-gleaming canals, the traceries of bridges, all the spires and towers, complement and enhance the city's welcome. At this time much of the proud city lay in ruins. Rebuilding went on spasmodically, when we could spare workmen and materials. So as *Challenger* came slanting down out of the sky and the topmen swarmed aloft to furl her canvas and Captain Hando brought her nearly in to a landing in her berth in the admiralty complex alongside the Varmondsweay Canal, I felt the shiver of appreciation for the great city despite her scars and dilapidations. Here, in the capital of the empire, was the place where I worked.

There is a word in Kregish—diashum—which I suppose can be translated as magnificent. Certainly, in those days of travail and struggle for the island empire, it was diashum to be a Vallian. And, while that was true, it was also remarkably easy to join the ranks of the diashum dead.

For me, this homecoming turned out to be dust and ashes.

Practically no one was left in the city of those to whom I wished so urgently to talk. Prince Drak and most of the army had flown and marched north to deal with a new and serious incursion of the clansmen. He had taken with him the majority of the Sword Watch, which explained, as I knew, why those who had flown for me in *Challenger* were from the Second Regiment. Seg Segutorio was already up there, locked in combat. Nath Nazabhan and the Phalanx were fully engaged. The Lord Farris had taken his air along. My son Jaidur, as usual, was missing. As for my daughters— Lela was Opaz knew where, and, likewise, Dayra was off conducting more mischief, I did not doubt. Inch sent news from the Black Mountains of violent affrays and ambushes and of a gradual clearance of his kovnate.

Filbarrka kept busy in the Filbarrka regions of the Blue Mountains. A number of my Valkan regiments had arrived in the city and had incontinently gone north. Jilian had taken her Battle Maidens off to the wars again. Many another fine comrade you have met in my narrative had gone.

So, as you can see, I felt down.

Yet, despite all this, I was fully conscious of the fact that I could not go haring up north after them. I had been accused by Tyfar of being overhasty in running on a leem's tracks. Those people up there, they could handle the problems. I was firmly convinced that all that had happened to me since I had left Vondium bore most strongly on what was afoot. Very little, if anything, had happened by chance. Everything was all a part of that master plan I now knew to be guiding my footsteps on Kregen.

Even Deb-Lu-Quienyin had gone. I was cheered to hear that Khe-Hi-Bjanching had returned, and the two Wizards of Loh, so I gathered from the palace staff, had warmed one to the other. Khe-Hi knew of Deb-Lu's reputation. They would work together.

So... In all this... Yes. Delia. Where the hell had she gone to this time?

Eighteen

Silda

The pouch containing the brooch and the baubles I had retrieved from the Moder and which I had retained through my adventures now lay on the desk before me. I sat in that small room in the imperial palace and I glowered at the brooch, at the shelves of books, and the maps that, as ever, mocked me from the walls, at the arms rack. In this room I had done a deal of work and, by Vox, was to do a damned deal more.

"Yes, yes," I said to Chuktar Naroku, "you have taken employment with the Prince Majister and I shall honor the pledge."

Chuktar Naroku rubbed his thumb along his right tusk. His three-inch-long tusks, thrusting up arrogantly from the corners of his mouth, were banded in gold. His oily yellow skin glistened in the radiance of the samphron-oil lamps. His pigtail hung down his back. He filled his armor. He sweated. He was not apim like me, he was a diff, a Chulik out of the Chulik islands off the east coast of Balintol. Reared from birth to the handling of weapons, Chuliks are justly respected and feared as mercenaries. Of humanity...? Well, they do have a modicum more of that precious commodity than, say, the damned Katakis.

The diff at Naroku's side coughed. He had a long-nosed canine face, and his air of eternal supercilious superiority was guaranteed to get up the snub nose of diff and apim alike.

"My archers, majister—" began this Chuktar Unstabi.

"The same goes for you, too," I said. I own my voice snapped a trifle pettishly. Chuktar Unstabi was an Undurker, from the Undurkor islands south of the huge promontory of Persinia. Both these Chuktars, which is a rank something like junior general, brigadier, were hyrpaktuns. They were costing my treasury good red gold.

My son, Prince Drak, had contracted to hire mercenaries to wage the war against the mercenaries hired by our enemies.

Fume though I might, I had to honor his pledge. But, by the Black Chunkrah! I said to myself. I'll have something to say to that son of mine when I see him, by Krun!

I looked sharply at the man who stood silently a little to one side of the two hyrpaktuns. He was a Vallian. He wore a fancy new uniform, all buff and red, with a solid iron breastplate. His shrewd, weather-beaten face conveyed the sense of a man of gravitas, and the brown Vallian eyes were partially hidden by down-drooping lids. He wore a rapier and main gauche. The two mercenaries also wore their weapons.

"And now you feel you are fit to march to the southwest, Kov Vodun?"

"Yes, majister, with your blessing." Kov Vodun Alloran had lost his kovnate of Kaldi, right in the toe of southwest Vallia, to that rast Strom Rosil Yasi. Kov Vodun kept up an unceasing barrage of contumely against our enemies, and lusted after returning and hanging every last one from the tallest tree branches he could find.

A number of invasions had been launched through his province. We had resisted and now, with Kov Vodun to prod us into action, we felt the time was ripe for us to return in strength and kick Yasi and his foul henchmen out of our land. The trouble was, and this trouble explained our experiences after *Mancha of Tlinganden* had been wrecked, our army had been forced to march north. The strength left in the capital was now rather too weak for my liking. But, still and all, that southwest rankled...

"If we can clear all the southwest," I said, "it will free our hands for the sterner tasks ahead."

Kov Vodun snapped erect. "Sterner tasks, majister?"

I sighed. Trust me to say the wrong thing.

"Only in matters of number, kov; not in anything else."

"I see."

A prickly customer, Kov Vodun Alloran. Very popular with the ladies, with his tales of guerrilla action from the hills. Alloran had done well at the Battle of Kanarsmot, and afterwards in that fraught action to take the fortress where Inch had rejoined us. Kov Vodun Alloran had been chosen by the Presidio, with the blessings of Prince Drak and the Lord Farris, to lead the Army of the Southwest to liberate that area of our land.

"Very well," I said. "My mind is made up. You have the nucleus of the forces earmarked for you—"

"The most of which were taken away!" said Alloran, with a prickly nastiness. He had regained a very great measure of his own self-esteem since escaping from his kovnate and fighting with us here. I nodded.

"That is true. And, no doubt, that is why the Prince Majister contracted to engage paktuns. You will have a tidy army to lead into your kovnate."

He moved his shoulders under the armor and the polished iron caught the light and glittered. "There is the matter of the Fourth Phalanx, majister. I was promised the Fourth, and one wing was taken from me and flown north. I now have only one Kerchuri, and it is in my mind I should take a Kerchuri from the Fifth."

My old blade comrade Nath Nazabhan had been busy, and besides finishing the raising of the Fourth, he had started the Fifth. Now a phalanx is a wonderful engine of destruction and the pikemen in the files, the brumbytes, of whom there are 10,368, are flanked by the axe and halberd men, the Hakkodin, of whom there are 1,728. There are also strong bodies of archers, and lads to strew caltrops and run with chevaux de frises. A whole lot of men are locked up in a phalanx.

I stirred the piece of paper on my desk. In Drak's handwriting the composition of the proposed Army of the SW stared me in the face. Drak had written down: "One Kerchuri." A Kerchuri is a wing of the phalanx, one-half. I looked up at Alloran.

"Two Kerchuris, kov?"

"Aye, majister, two."

"But the Fifth Phalanx is green raw."

"Their Ninth Kerchuri is ready. And, by Vox, by the time I have marched them a sennight or so they'll smarten up!"

"You would leave Vondium with only the Tenth Kerchuri?"

"You need, with your permission, majister, archers to defend city walls." That was only half true.

I wondered if he was going to bargain his paktun archers, these Undurkers, for the Ninth Kerchuri. It was, in my view, no bargain at all.

I said, "What do your spies report of the strength and composition of Strom Rosil's army?"

"Scattered," he said at once. "He will have time to scrape his men together before I reach him, of course, after the initial breakthrough battles. He has something of the order of thirty thousand he can concentrate with reasonable speed. Give him two of the Moons of the Twins and he will have fifty or more."

I stirred Drak's list again.

"If you move with speed, you can catch him before he concentrates his full strength."

"That is my plan."

"And the composition?"

Alloran smiled. "Mercenaries of varying quality. A normal mix of infantry and cavalry. He has also masichieri and aragorn. They hardly count."

I looked up suspiciously. "Never underrate those rasts."

"I am thinking, majister, of First Kanarsmot."

"We surprised them there."

"And I," said Kov Vodun, "shall surprise the cramphs again."

The decision I was being called on to make was your everyday, normal, ulcer-breeding decision facing emperors. If I allowed Kov Vodun to take the army as listed by Drak, less those units detached for duty in the north, plus the Ninth Kerchuri, there would be a skeletal force left in the city. I looked up. I know my face must have looked like a chunk of granite dredged from a thousand-season-old wreck.

The Southwest had to be cleared, the risk accepted. He could take a full phalanx, the Eighth and Ninth Kerchuris. The commands would mesh. Get the job done fast. I told him my decision. Then I said, "Very well. You will take upwards of forty thousand. That should suffice."

His down-drooping lids lifted, then he smiled, and nodded his satisfaction with what he had salvaged.

"The original army was to have been upwards of sixty thousand, majister. But I will do what I must with these straitened circumstances."

Just as I was thinking this was a damned boorish way of carrying on, he added, "And I give you my thanks, majister."

"May Opaz go with you and guide you in the forthcoming battles."

So off he went with his paktuns and in came Enevon Ob-Eye, my chief stylor, a man whom I trusted and who had a head for figures and lists, and the warrants were prepared.

"You leave the city perilously undefended, majis."

"Aye, Enevon. But while we attack in the north and attack in the south-west, we have the cramphs off balance. They'll be too busy defending themselves to attack us here."

The heavy atmosphere in the room during the interview with Alloran seemed to have gone with him. Enevon reported that the swarths I had ordered collected were stabled in the sleeth's stables at the merezo, and the lads of the racing track were caring for their new charges. My experiences in the Humped Land with those damned swarthmen had convinced me a few regiments of swarth-mounted cavalry would not come amiss.

So, as you will see, I was in the thick of this paperwork and caring for it only insofar as I worked for Vallia and Delia. I just could not twine my thoughts around the whereabouts and well-being of Delia. She was off with the Sisters of the Rose, doing marvelous and secret wonders, and no doubt having a tremendous time. As ever, unless I felt that peculiar sense of urgency and disaster, I would not request a Wizard of Loh to go into lupu and spy out Delia's whereabouts.

During this period both Quienyin and Bjanching paid a courtesy call on me. Oh, they were both up north; but their ghostly apparitions showed up in my room, and this comforted me considerably, as you may well imagine. Paying polite visits by these supernatural means, and taking it all as a matter of course, came with an all-standing kind of refresher to me, even if to them it was all in the day's business.

One visit gave me immense pleasure. Silda, Seg's daughter, called on me. She couldn't stop, she said; she was on her way through. I did not inquire. She was about business for the SoR, that was clear.

Silda had grown more beautiful than ever, a bright, charming, happy girl who mentioned the death of her mother just the once. She was also very strong-minded. I could see that. There was in her much of Seg's greatness of character, and also a deal of her mother's outgoing warmth which in Silda was not inevitably brought to disaster. If I had to choose a daughter-in-law—and, by Vox, I did not have to, not with Drak making up his own mind!—there was no one I could think of to surpass Silda Segutorio.

She said her brother, Dray Segutorio, was now a hyrpaktun and had only just learned of the troubles afflicting us. He was on his way home.

"The quicker he gets here the better. We need every trained professional we can lay hands on. And I'm not talking about mercenaries. Young Drak has—" And I stopped. I would not too openly criticize Drak in front of Silda. I had seen the way her eyebrows went up, and the purse to those delectable lips, the flush of color along her cheeks. Silda would fight for Drak, aye, fight against his own father! And the luck of Opaz with her!

Then she said, with an abrupt switch of mood, "Have you seen Queen Lushfymi of Lome since you got back, Uncle Dray?"

"I have not. And it's about time you stopped calling me Uncle Dray. By Zair! It makes me feel a million years old."

"I beg your pardon, majister. Of course—"

"Silda, Silda! Just knock it off."

Her eyebrows flicked up again. Damned attractive, those eyebrows, like the rest of her.

"I mean, knock off the uncle bit. As for Queen Lush—I wish she'd go home to Lome. But of course, poor woman, she can't. Not with Yantong ready to put her down if she does."

"Poor woman!" flared Silda. Then, calmly: "It must be hard for her. Aunt Delia's father meant a great deal to Queen Lushfymi. But do you really think Yantong is in Pandahem?"

"I do not know and I wonder if I really do want to know. No. No, I'd like to know. Then perhaps we could—well, all that is wishful thinking. Even Quienyin doesn't know where Yantong hides out and tries to run the world."

Then we talked of more personal matters. When she left with my good wishes and the last Remberees and her refusal of any aid in particular she might need—independent girl—I reflected that not once had she called Lushfymi Queen Lush.

What she had told me, and been at pains to tell me without acknowledging that she had told me, was that Delia was all right, was safe and well, and was chafing to get home. So I could draw a deep breath and soldier on alone. The passing on of that information, I saw, had been the reason for Silda's visit.

I wondered, with a pang, if Delia knew, or if Silda had brought me the news of her own volition. That would be like Silda.

Kov Vodun was burning to be about his business of clearing up the southwest. I rode faithful old Grumbleknees out to Voxyri Drinnik to see the advance guard off. They were flying out. They would be reinforced as fast as the ships of the air could turn around. The breeze, the Todalpheme had told us, would stay fair, giving a good stiff-sailing course to be steered out and back.

Apart from the Eighth Kerchuri of the Fourth Phalanx and the Ninth Kerchuri of the Fifth, Kov Vodun was taking five thousand churgurs, three thousand archers and five thousand kreutzin, the light infantry and skirmishers. Many of these infantry were mercenaries. For cavalry I had let him have three regiments of totrix heavies, and five divisions of a mixed force of totrix and zorca lancers and archers. He took forty varters, the efficient bal-listae of Kregen, wheeled and drawn by a variety of draught animals.

Enevon Ob-Eye rode with me and wore a gloomy face.

"All these fine men leaving the city," he said. He shook his head. "Pray Opaz nothing untoward occurs."

"Long before the enemy can even think of reacting and mounting an attack on us," I told him, "the armies will be victorious and return. You'll see."

I was thinking of the foemen we knew, up in the north and east and down in the southwest.

The life of the city roared on, even though to me the place appeared empty. There were many folk who were still civilians, going about their daily tasks and providing the sinews to keep the army moving and supplied and fed. Every day men would march in having toiled for many dwaburs out of the invaded territories. Most of them simply wanted to get into a uniform and take up a weapon and go right back and have a bash at the occupiers. We had to instill in them the notion that they must be trained and drilled and hardened before they could even think of returning.

Turko took a large hand in the hardening of the men. He might be a Khamorro and therefore far more deadly with empty hands than with a weapon; but he ran these raw recruits ragged and built them up not only in physique but in spiritual confidence.

Many men saw me every day over matters touching every part of daily life, and of these, some you have met and many there are whom I grew to know better and who feature in later episodes. And then, one day, a voller appeared over the palace. She was a large craft, and she flew the Vallian tresh, blazing under the suns, and also my own battle flag, Old Superb. I looked up and I frowned. I had a good idea of what this was all about, I had expected it, and I knew what course I was going to take and how confoundedly angry that was going to make everyone. I was not looking forward at all to the coming scene.

But, I admit, I did look with great joy upon the tough, fierce men who crowded from the voller and advanced upon me as I stood upon the high landing platform to greet them.

You know them, you know their lineaments and much of their history. These men were the Emperor's Sword Watch. They were the ruffianly spir-its of my Choice Band. Cleitar the Standard stepped forward.

"Majister!" he bellowed. "They have elected me as spokesman."

I gave him no further time. "Lahal to you all!" I know I looked fierce. These men and I had been through perilous times together. "I understood there was fighting in the north. Battles against our foemen. What? Have you deserted in the face of the foe?"

Their faces, wreathed in smiles, brilliant at seeing me again, were cast down in an instant. They looked puzzled and hurt.

"Majister!" stammered Cleitar. "Us? Run away...?"

Dorgo the Clis stepped forward, his scar a vivid slash across his face. "Majister! We return to where we belong!"

"Aye!" bellowed Targon the Tapster. "We are the Emperor's Sword Watch!"

"We stand always at your side, majister!" roared Naghan ti Lodkwara. "You cannot send us away!"

The others joined in then and the air filled with protests and lurid oaths. They were all incensed at my obtuseness. So I had to explain.

"Prince Drak, the Prince Majister, commands the Army of the Northeast. He is in the forefront of the battle. Your duty is to him at this time."

Well, as I say, I had not relished the scene and it turned out as I had gloomily suspected. In the end they saw that I meant what I said. They shuffled. They protested. But at last they all returned to the voller and observed the fantamyrrh and so took off to return to Drak. But they did not do this right away. Oh, no. We spent a raucous night drinking and singing and telling the old stories before they left bright and early and mostly hung over. That, at the least, gave me a single bright spot to put alongside the visit from Silda—and one or two other timely interruptions to the everyday slog of work.

And, in a sense, that decided me on a project I had long contemplated. The Second Regiment of the Sword Watch, mainly brave and brilliant young men still under training, were all very well. There were the paktuns from the sea in their tromp-colored uniforms. Now they were called the Emperor's Yellow Jackets. But I looked at the empty barracks and the thinness of the morning parades. So, I went to see the Chief Assassin of Vondium.

Nineteen

Of Assassins, Dynasties, and Invasions

Perhaps I had been over-hasty in sending the Sword Watch back to keep an eye on my son Drak.

"I did warn you, majister, that contracts had been placed for you. We have had to deal with two such attempts—but you were not in the city at the time, and that made it easier."

Nath the Knife, the chief of assassins, styled the Aleygyn of the Stikitches, studied me through the eyeholes of his steel mask. We both sat at the table under the arch of the Gate of Skulls this time, and there was no need for either of us to attempt to gain stature by sitting or standing.

"Have the builders been working as I promised?"

"Yes, majister." His words were plain enough; but his meaning was difficult to judge. "They work well. Our houses grow."

Drak's City, the oldest part of Vondium, was a law unto itself. Here the rascals, the scalawags, the thieves, and the disaffected lived. The aid from the rest of the city might have been aimed at preventing disease; but it was in a very real sense a humanitarian gesture. Within the walls life bustled along. Everybody scratched a living somehow. Nath the Knife had positioned his bodyguard in the Kyro of Lost Souls, as men of the Sword Watch and the Yellow Jackets waited on me on the outside.

"You will not tell me who is letting out these contracts, Aleygyn? That would be against your code of honor?"

"You know it would."

We talked for a space of the city and the rebuilding and skirted the tricky business of the payment to kill me, and then I said, "If I mention the word kreutzin, Aleygyn, you, as an educated man, will know what I mean, even if some vosk-skulls might not."

"I understand." The kreutzin are the light infantry, the voltigeurs, who skirmish ahead of the line. "I promised to send some of my young men to join your army—"

"Not my army, Aleygyn. The Army of Vallia."

"I think not. You cannot buy my young men for Vallia with bricks and mortar, or with medicines."

I looked at him and I kept the fury out of my face.

"Some idiots might call you an old warrior, Nath the Knife. I think you are—"

"I am not foresworn. My honor is a stikitche's honor!" He spoke up briskly. Damned difficult to carry on a conversation with a fellow who wears a steel mask over his face! "I will send my young men to serve you. They will serve the Emperor of Vallia. There is a difference. And, as you see, there are reasons for this nicety in our arrangements."

I could see that, all right. By the disgusting diseased right eyeball of Makki Grodno! And then I laughed. The thought struck me that if Drak sat here, in conversation with an assassin, his rectitude and composure would fight like merry hell with all his natural fighting instincts. But, he'd learn. By Krun, but he'd learn what being an emperor meant.

"You mean," I said, when I'd had my laugh out, "you are a pack of rogues in here, hulus, rascals and fools, thieves, stikitches—and the rest of respectable Vondium—"

"Precisely. They would burn us out if they could."

"They could, Nath the Knife. They could. But not while you and I talk, man to man."

That shook him. For centuries the sanctity of Drak's City as a Kingdom of Thieves had been unwritten law.

"Go on, Aleygyn. You will send your young men to serve me? I need them. We are overstrained—"

"You told me you would not hire mercenaries. Yet paktuns walk the streets of Vondium and march with the army." The steel mask glittered. "We are pleased. Their pockets are full." If he smiled that confounded mask hid all. "You changed your tune there, majister."

"Temporarily only. A matter of policy." I was not prepared to admit to this stikitche that my son Drak had done this thing.

"I have made arrangements. The young men will report to you and your Deldars at the barracks you appoint."

"My Deldars are intolerant drill masters. But your young men will rise to become Deldars, in their turn. Even kreutzin must learn drill and discipline in my army."

"Agreed. I will tell them so."

After a few more words I rose to go. Grumbleknees waited, his single spiral horn jutting proudly. I turned back, my fists gripping the reins, my booted foot in the stirrup.

"These contracts, Aleygyn. If I was in the habit of letting contracts with stikitches, I think the names of Kov Colun Mogper of Mursham, and Zankov, illegitimate son of the High Kov of Sakwara, might prove lucrative."

That steel mask went back. His gloved hand, with the ornate ring outside the glove, clenched.

I swung up into the saddle and Grumbleknees walked gently forward out of the shadow of the Gate of Skulls.

"Remberee, Aleygyn."

"Remberee, majister."

Yes, I reflected as, followed by my men, we trotted back to the palace, that laugh had been worth it. What, indeed, would Drak have made of his father the emperor talking to a damned assassin? Yet I felt sure Drak would see the difference between using Vallian assassins in our army and hiring mercenaries. I do not care over much for stikitches, having had one or two sprightly measures with them; but by the time my Deldars got through with them, they'd know they'd been punched, drilled, and bored, by Vox! Then, they'd be soldiers first, and I could hope would never return to their despicable trade—if they lived.

There are people who say, and I go some way in agreement with them, that a soldier's trade is despicable. But if your home is about to be burned down and your family butchered, a fellow tends to want to do something about that—at least on Kregen.

Despite my big talk of drill sergeants, we were still short of veterans who could train up the new armies we needed. The Emperor's Yellow Jackets were hardened professionals. They had many military skills in their ranks.

They took the newly arrived young men from Drak's City and trained them up. Many of these limber young rascals were not assassins, of course, many being thieves and swearing by Diproo the Nimble-Fingered. Many were simply poor lads with no prospects in life. We fed them and clothed them in the yellow jackets and made full use of their special skills. I didn't give a fig about training them merely as light infantry. They would learn to handle all the weapons a fighting man may manipulate, and would be employed as we saw fit. They welcomed that as a proof of their own quality.

Thankfully, my tough paktuns expressed no aversion to serving alongside these newcomers. Truth to tell, many an old friendship was renewed...

And, also, old enmities. But only three men were found dead in a ditch or in their quarters; two from Drak's City and one paktun. That seemed to let the spleen of the force out for good, thanks be to Opaz.

News was received from Alloran that he had fought a skirmish and cleared his front. I wished I had more men to dispatch to secure the rear areas; and managed to scrape up two regiments of spearmen. On the next day different news came in.

Enevon Ob-Eye walked into my room very quietly. He made no great fuss about it. He was entitled to rave and accuse.

He said, "Majister, news has just arrived of an army marching and flying south out of Vindelka. They press over the borders of Orvendel. The land is being put to the torch. The people cry out for help. Orvendel, majister," he said, and turned the blade in the wound, "is an Imperial Province. They are your people. And the southern border of Orvendel is but forty dwaburs from Vondium."

By this time I knew the map of Vallia; it was not so much engraved on my brain as burned on my heart.

Despite that, my gaze fastened on those infuriating maps adorning the walls. Oh, yes, he had worked it beautifully, the cramph.

"Layco Jhansi?"

"No, majis. We do not think so. The scouts have him located still in his own kovnate."

That made me think. Layco Jhansi, the old emperor's chief minister, had proved a traitor. Now he fought the Racters, the one-time most powerful political party, who were penned up in the northwest, north of Jhansi. But, if he had not sent this army to attack us while we were weak, who had?

"The scouts report the presence in this army of those we know. Tarek Malervo Norgoth—you remember him, majis. He headed the deputation from Jhansi you sent packing with a zorca hoof up their rumps?"

"I remember, Enevon." A Tarek is a rank of the minor nobility. I guessed this fat and pompous Norgoth with the spindly legs was bucking for an increase in his patents of nobility. But the news reassured me even as I raged at the iniquities being committed up there by Jhansi's men. Orvendel is a pretty province. Many of her sons served in the army. I could not allow the destruction to go on unchecked, could I?

When my comrades of the Sword Watch had flown in to Vondium, they had left forces still with Drak. Volodu the Lungs, the chief trumpeter, and Korero the Shield, had remained. The expected confrontation of Korero and Turko had not taken place. I suddenly felt a pang, a hunger for my blade comrades to be with me now. And—I had been on the point of going off to Hyrklana to fetch out Balass and Oby and Tilly! Just as well the Hyrklanian trip had been postponed...

These weakling thoughts must be pushed aside. What I had to do was perfectly clear to me. Even if, like King Harold of England, it led to disaster, I could not halt myself. And, anyway, the situations were not quite the same. A last voller to Drak would bring in fighting men to garrison Vondium. And I knew, as is obvious, that the time would not allow that simple a solution. I had to face up to Malervo Norgoth with what men I had, and we would fight. Win or lose we would halt this raid. After that, if we moldered in our graves, time would have been bought.

"Jhansi would not, I think, place an army into the hands of Norgoth without a general to guide him?"

Enevon nodded. "There is a Kapt with them. A Kapt Hangrol. He has the command. Naghan Vanki's spies are sure." He paused. Naghan Vanki was the empire's chief spy-master. But Enevon went on with a bite in his voice. "His name is Hangrol ham Thanoth."

I glared. I felt the fury rising. "A damned Hamalese!"

"Aye, majis."

"Well, that settles it. Write the orders. We'll call out everyone who is able to march instanter." I stabbed the map with a fierce finger. "Ovalia. Every ship that will fly will take us to Ovalia. That's the key. The city must be held."

"Quidang, majis!" Enevon grasped essentials at once.

The map glowed with color. It showed the River of Shining Spears running southeast from the Blue Mountains to join the Great River, She of the Fecundity. To the north of the fork my Imperial Province of Bryvondrin stretched broad and rich and in our hands. Northwest of Bryvondrin lay Orvendel. If Jhansi's men broke through, overwhelmed the city of Ovalia, the raid would turn into a major attack, a dagger thrust at Vondium, the proud city herself. We had to muster our forces, what we had of them, fly to Ovalia, set down, and smash the living daylights out of this Opaz-forsaken cramph of a Hamalese general and his army. As for Malervo Norgoth, he was quite obviously Jhansi's man of the spot, a kind of commissar, and we'd hang him high with his toes all adangle if we caught him...

Because the majestic canal system of Vallia is so efficient and extensive, roads in the island were atrocious at this time. We'd have to fly out with what we could. A reserve force could follow. They might be there to continue the victorious pursuit. They might have to fight a stern rearguard action.

As to the forces available... Just about everybody had gone north to fight with the Army of the Northeast. It appeared to me to be the fashionable thing, the in thing, to serve in that army alongside the Prince Majister. Some of the people up there, well, when I heard their names I had to smile my bleak old grimace that passes for a smile. By Zair! But some right popinjays had ridden off gallantly to be seen with the Prince Majister. Men who had contumed me as a hairy unwashed clansman now thronged about my son. My own pride in Drak told me that he would be level-headed enough to see through all the flattery and the flummery. At least, by Krun, I hoped so!

And, to be truthful, there was far more of trust in Drak than could be expressed by mere hope.

On the same day that the news of Layco Jhansi's raid reached us our vanguard flew off for Ovalia.

They flew in all the vollers we had. A regiment of churgurs, sword and shield men, and a regiment of archers, almost one thousand men. The swods in the ranks of these regiments were old hands, they had served with me before and would have to form one of the hard cores of the little force. The other hard core, it goes without saying, would be the Tenth Kerchuri. The pikes would have to stand, and hold, and charge, as they had been trained, and no one must allow doubt to creep in that these men, these brumbytes wielding their pikes in the files, were green, raw, and had seen no action.

Like that half-blinded man standing on the center and seeking to strike out in all directions at those who attacked him, we of Vondium had lashed out northeast and southwest. And Layco Jhansi had seized his chance to raid us from the northwest. It was perfectly clear by the presence of a Hamalese Kapt with his forces that the dirty finger of Hamal was busy stirring up this pot. The fight would be tough; we'd be facing regulars, possibly some of the iron legions of Hamal, as well as the screaming fanatical irregulars of Jhansi's cowed provinces.

The regiments from the Fifth Brigade of churgurs and the Ninth Brigade of archers who had flown off had served with me at the Battles of Kanarsmot. They were good men. The remaining two regiments of each Brigade, together with a motley bunch of spearmen, slingers, and axemen, waited transportation. The flying ships of the air gathered on Voxyri Drinnik and that broad space of open land seethed with all the commotion of an army embarking. I call it an army; well, yes, it was in spirit and composition and determination if not in numbers.

The Presidio met to deliberate, as was their wont, and I spent a couple of precious burs speaking to them from the rostrum, impressing on these grave senators the need for cool heads in this time of crisis. They ran the country and knew of my dreams of the kind of country I had been asked to bring into being by the people who had called me. There was a little of the wheeling and dealing that had characterized the reign of the old emperor still in evidence; but these men were a new breed of senator. Naghan Strandar, whom I trusted, stood up to reply, and he astonished me.

"Majister! You have made us, and we are mindful of that." The council chamber in the Villa of Vennar echoed to his words, and the rows of soberly clad men listened with composed faces. "The old emperor is dead and with him died the Valhan Dynasty. You are the first of the Prescot Dynasty of Vallia. We shall serve you and the country no matter what transpires."

I sat in the seat reserved for the emperor and listened as he went on for a short space in these terms. I own I found this idea amazing. Of course, I had begun a new dynasty in Vallia. It was something I had scarcely even acknowledged. And, as you who understand the Kregish will perceive, Valhan had a special meaning. The upshot of that was a vow of total allegiance to Vallia, and a determination to bring every last ounce of energy and will to the struggle.

Going back to see the leathery swods boarding the vessels, I reflected that great words do, very often, deserve great deeds. And, as Erithor, the great poet of Valka, would have said, the opposite holds true, also.

Two men attempted to desert and were caught and dragged before me as I sat Grumbleknees with the dust blowing and the pandemonium bellowing up all over the Drinnik.

"Let them go," I said. "Put them to work baking bread, or cleaning sewers, or forging weapons."

"But, majister!" said Chuktar Vogan, commanding the Ninth Brigade of archers. "They should be hanged up high so that all men may see the miserable cramphs!"

"Then they would be dead, Vogan. Mayhap, after a dwabur or so of sewers, they might rescind their decision to desert."

Chuktar Vogan saw only the obvious, brutal side of that. He guffawed, and slapped his thigh, and allowed the emperor was blessed with brains from Opaz himself.

I had no time to try to explain that any man had the right to feel fear at battles to come, that running away was a natural and healthy thing to do if you wanted to keep your skin intact, that simple brutal warfare was a horrendous thing which no civilized man should have to endure. He would not have grasped those concepts, not with a raging pack of Hamalese coming down to burn his home and slay his family. I could see both sides of this pathetic human problem, and sighed, and could see no way out for me other than doing what I was doing, and hoping for the best in the sweet light of the Invisible Twins.

I suppose that the agonies a woman suffers in anticipation of childbirth, and then in the birth itself, are analogous to the agonies a man suffers in the anticipation of battle, and the ghastly event itself. Something like, perhaps...

"My Val!" said Orlon Sangar ti Deliasmot. "Majister, I'm delighted to get the chance of showing you what my lads can do. By Vox, I thought I'd rot in Vondium forever."

Orlon Sangar came from Delphond. He was the Kerchurivax in command of the Tenth Kerchuri. He had risen through the ranks in the Third, and the Third was by way of being a special phalanx to Nath Nazabhan and me. I nodded.

"Your lads will do well, Orlon. I just wish we had more of you."

He made the expected reply. Well, that answer has been given many and many a time before a battle, on two worlds...

The brumbytes handed in their pikes as they boarded. These long weapons were bundled and then lashed to the ships. The men kept their shields, and they hung them on the bulwarks in fine style. There was a deal of the horseplay and raucous coarse humor inevitably surrounding the movement of green troops. These men had been trained hard; but only the faxuls of the front ranks, and not all of them, had seen active service. A wisp of nerves can be concealed beneath a huge guffaw and a practical joke.

Essential though the religious ceremony honoring and imploring Opaz most certainly was, I own—a coarse, profane, swearing kind of fellow as I am—I chafed to have it over with and get the troops airborne. When the prayers for the safekeeping of the men and for the victory were offered up and the voice of the chief priest rang to silence, a deep stillness held all Voxyri Drinnik. Absolute quiet for ten long heartbeats proved how wrong I was, how much the feelings of the soldiers had been affected, how needful this was. Then a cough, the scrape of a boot, and the Deldars yelling, the shrill notes of trumpets.

Even the flags began to rustle again.

One of the texts chosen as suitable for the service was the well-known advice from the Instructions to Novices. This says, in effect: "Be Brave, Bold, and Resourceful; Fret not on the Hazard." A fair comparison may be made with Aristophanes in The Frogs, where he uses words of similar meaning and intent. Easy to give advice and harder than keeping warm on the Ice Floes of Sicce to take it. I had accepted the risk and, in theory, should now push all thoughts of the hazard from my mind and go forward in bold confidence. But, while that might be fine for your valiant and daring prince, for me, plain Dray Prescot, the doubts and premonitions of disaster remained. Weak, of course; but in my usual fashion I put a tough face on my ugly old beakhead and concealed the torture and turmoil in my head from my comrades.

Then an event occurred which the doubter would take merely as a trifle from a Fairy Story. One of the new regiments of zorca archers was loading. The animals were being led up the gangplanks, and the cavalrymen were in the usual lather, yelling, pushing, pulling, cajoling the zorcas into the ship. A commotion greater than usual began as I cantered by. I was riding Fango, a fine bay zorca, who had lost a hand-breadth of his spiral horn at some time in his career. The imperial stables had fashioned a new horn tip for him from Chemnite ivory, neatly banded with gold. Grumbleknees and Snowy were having the day off.

"Catch him!" The shouts spurted up. "Grab the beast!"

Cavalrymen went spinning every which way, their red uniforms dusty and stained already. A monstrous black shape reared high, hooves lashing, nostrils crimson, seeming to breathe fire. His eyes glittered in the light of the suns. Down he came, roaring down the ramp, scattering folk like ninepins. Straight up to me he galloped, horn up, tail flying, mane splendid. Fango backed off, alarmed, thinking he was being attacked.

"Majister!" They were yelling. "The emperor is in danger from a wild beast! Shoot the zorca down!"

"Hold!" I bellowed. I really let go a shout that rattled the teeth in their heads. I gentled Fango and as the huge black zorca crashed alongside I laid a hand on his head.

"Shadow!" And Shadow threw up his head and whinnied, glorious in his shining splendor.

Shadow... A great-hearted zorca with whom I had built a special relationship of trust and affection, and whom I had thought lost in Vondium, and yet, and yet... Always I had known we would meet again.

That was quickly sorted out. I was told Shadow had been found in Vond, dwaburs away from Vondium, and in our eternal quest for quality zorcas had been brought into the army. He had always given trouble, being highly independent-minded. The Jiktar to whom he had been issued sighed with relief when I said, "He is my zorca, Jiktar." I dismounted. "Take Fango. He is a first-class animal and you will joy in him."

"Quidang, majister!"

The saddles were swiftly changed and I stuck my boot into the stirrup and mounted up on Shadow. He showed his pleasure. We had been through many adventures together; we would go through many more. But in the heady moment of reunion all those perils could wait.

Then another little crisis developed. Long lines of yellow-clad men marched toward the gangplanks. I frowned.

"Larghos the Sko-Handed!" I bellowed.

Larghos came over, beaming. His shoulder wings stuck out far more than regulations allowed. He looked fit and tough.

"Where, Larghos, do you think you are going with those coys?" A coy is a recruit, a greenhorn.

"Coys, majister! Are not they damned assassins? They will fight! By Vox! I will see to that!"

I sighed. What would you do with these fellows?

Nath the Knife had sent us an initial seven hundred young men. They could fight, of course. But they weren't swods.

Larghos saw my face. "You would not deny them the glory?"

About to break out into bitter invective against this stupid, shuddery, bloody idea of glory, I held my tongue. If our country was in the dire danger we all knew her to be, why should not these fine young men go off to fight? Why should they? Because it was their duty? Because they would be less than men if they did not? No—the reasons lay deeper than that...

Larghos's slingers went on boarding. Drill the Eye shouted at his bowmen to carry on and rolled over, spluttering, to join his comrade. When Clardo the Clis, his scar burning, nudged his zorca across, I knew I was beaten.

"You are taking the Sword Watch," pointed out Clardo, with consummate cunning. "They are coys, also—"

"Not quite," I said.

"Nor neither are we!"

"Very well. You'll have to skirmish forward. Your drill is not up to formed standards yet."

"Aye, majister. We'll skirmish the zigging Hamalian tripes out!"

So that was settled. The Emperor's Yellow Jackets joined the Second Regiment of the Emperor's Sword Watch aboard the flying ships. Both men and swods would be created out of the lads embarking. That is life.

The return of the vollers enabled me to send off part of a regiment of totrix heavies. They would still arrive ahead of the sailing fliers. Other units went up to the northwest. Regular reports told me Ovalia was filling up, and the locals were helping with energy.

Consigning the rest of the paperwork to Enevon, confiding the city once again to Naghan Strandar and the Presidio, I collected the last of the troops we were taking and with Turko stepped aboard the voller, observing the fantamyrrh, and took off for Ovalia and destiny.

Twenty

The Depths of Deb-Lu-Quienyin's Eyes

The messenger stood before me in the Tower of Avoxdon in Ovalia where I had set up headquarters. His flying leathers were stained and travel worn. He looked exhausted. But before he would allow himself to sit down, this merker would deliver his message from Drak.

"The armies of the Prince Majister are fully committed. He has sent a number of provisional regiments to Vondium, mostly walking wounded and invalids. A brigade of churgurs is on the way to you and is following me within a day."

Instead of saying anything I indicated the chair and the merker sat with a flummox. His bird was being cared for by the flutswods of my single squadron of flutduins. I stared at him.

"And cavalry?"

"Three squadrons of totrix javelinmen."

We were short of cavalry, of the land and of the aerial kind. Well, all commanders are always short of cavalry, unless they be barbarian chieftains of a savage host of jutmen, as admirals are always short of frigates. Most of the force sent by Jhansi on this raid into our land consisted of jutmen; many were cavalry, some were mounted infantry riding a variety of animals. The balance of his infantry was carried in airboats. He had mirvols, powerful flying animals, with experienced flutswods to fly them, as his aerial cavalry component. Kapt Hangrol ham Thanoth commanded a powerful and fast-moving force.

We had been operating out of Ovalia for three days now and our initial dispositions had been made. As I sat brooding on this travel-weary merker I thought back to that smart little dust-up Prince Tyfar, Quienyin and our comrades had gone through in the Humped Land. It all added up. Those damned swarthmen had ridden on, confidently, and we had enticed them and tricked them and dazzled them before we'd seen them off. What a fellow may do with half a dozen staunch comrades against superior numbers, surely the same fellow could do with a small army against a larger?

Sipping the wine poured by Deft-Fingered Minch, a crusty, bearded veteran who ran my field quarters, the merker answered questions and conveyed news. Kov Seg Segutorio fought in the vaward, as usual, and commanded the Second Army. His daughter had visited him and gone on to see Prince Drak, commanding the First Army. This numbering of armies was new to me, and, to my ears, smacked of magniloquence. The Presidio had dished out the numbers, following Drak's instructions. Kov Vodun Alloran had marched into the West Country with the Fifth Army. Other numbered armies guarded our other provinces and frontiers. I gathered my little lot were the Eighth Army.

All that flummery meant nothing, of course. You could call yourselves what you liked; what counted was your strength and tenacity, physical and moral.

The merker, he was a Hikdar and his name was Ortyg Lovin, an honored name in Vallia, went on with his news. Our enemies fought obsessively but we pushed them back. An assassination attempt on Prince Drak had been frustrated by the Sword Watch. At this I sat up straight and felt anger, and horror, and sickness. Zankov, the arch enemy, had not been seen in the enemy camps. Kov Inch of the Black Mountains made slow progress. Fil-barrka was in the thick of it. There was more, much more, and I looked at the maps spread on the camp table and pondered. The red tide of war engulfed Vallia. Had I not been called by the people to lead them out of these miasmic shadows, I believe I would have thrown it all in and flown off to Strombor to see Velia and Didi. As it was—we had a damned raid to see off and to see off, by Vox, with far too few men.

Ovalia was the key to campaigning hereabouts. Had we not garrisoned the city first, Kapt Hangrol would have seized it and controlled the route for his onward march. As it was, daily we had small-scale aerial combats, and my single squadron of flutduinim would be worn down before long at this rate. As for our airboats, we had a weyver, which is a wide, flat, barge-like affair and which we had adapted to carry two hundred men. We had two vollers each carrying a hundred. And we had ten which could take fifty or so at a pinch. Of them all, only four of the latter were real fighting vollers.

There were also a handful of smaller vollers for scouting and messenger duty.

When the merker left and Turko and my Chuktars came in, I pointed to the maps and very simply said, "We do it the thorn-ivy way." At their gapes of non-comprehension I explained the plan in detail. And, to say plan is to dignify the harebrained scheme. But they nodded, bright-eyed, and vowed that it would work and that, by Vox, they'd have the tripes out of these Hamalese rasts in a twinkling.

Our air component left at once to set about the enticement part of the scheme. The three squadrons of totrix javelinmen came in and their transport, under orders to return at once, I would not touch. And, as you will see, stupid parental pride and dignity came in here! I would not let Drak see how hard-pressed we were, well-knowing the complexities of the problems he faced.

There was no question in my mind of sitting tight in Ovalia and allowing Kapt Hangrol to open a formal siege. He could hold us down quite adequately with a part of his force and, collecting up the rest, fly on. But we needed him to hold still just long enough for our forces, which had to move piecemeal, to reach their start lines. After that—thorn-ivy!

And, as though the gods joined in the scheme, I was apprised of the spirit of the army. One of the wide avenues of the city with its cobblestones was being torn up. Those stones were being loaded into carts, drawn by Quoffas, and would eventually be discharged against the Hamalese. Gangs of men worked with pick and crowbar. A number of taverns were well patronized by the thirsty off-duty.

They gave me a yell as I cantered by.

One group of men attracted my attention. I knew who they were, of course. A stoutly formed, scarlet-faced man with shining black hair—

unusual in a Vallian—bellowed his lads to attention. He was smiling, his face dimpled, good-humored, sweating a little, and as he saluted with his right hand, his left still clasped his tankard.

"When do we march out, majister?"

"As soon as you lot have drunk the taverns dry, Brad."

His men chorused their appreciation of this. Brad the Berry was a publican of Vondium. But he was much more than that, by Vox! It was rumored he'd been a wizard in his time; certainly his magic tricks astonished all who witnessed them. He was also rumored to be the son of a prince, who had cleared off because he preferred the life of wizardry and pubs to that of the courts. He'd raised and equipped a regiment at his own expense, mainly recruited from the regulars of his establishment, the Hagli Bush. They were titled the Hagli Bush Irregulars. I glanced at the covered wagons parked nearby.

"And, Brad, I would take a bet that there is more beer than bows, more ale than arrows, more wine than weapons, in those carefully packed wagons."

He laughed, cheerful and happy, supping along with his men.

"We'll have 'em, you'll see, majister," he said. That was sufficiently obscure to cover the points raised. I had Brad the Berry marked out for high office. He was the Jiktar of his regiment now; he would prove of more use in other areas of life than that of going off to be a soldier. Much more use...

The Hagli Bush Irregulars diligently went about their sworn duty of drinking every tavern in Ovalia dry—in between laboring mightily to help the army along.

It ought to be said, in addition, that the uniform designed for the Hagli Bush Irregulars by Brad the Berry was a marvel of practicality and ornateness. It was rumored he had once served an apprenticeship to a goldsmith in his wizardry search for the secret of making gold out of straw. Like many and many another sorcerer and wise man, he might not have discovered that particular secret; but he could bring to anything he set his hands to, a wonderful felicity of invention. We needed men like Brad the Berry.

Riding Shadow back toward the Tower of Avoxdon I looked up and saw a magnificent scarlet and golden bird, circling in the upper air, blinding in the mingled streaming radiance of the Suns of Scorpio. I sucked in my breath. But I rode on. No one else could see that gorgeous raptor. He was the Gdoinye, the messenger and spy of the Star Lords, and I wondered if I was about to be dramatically transported to some other part of Kregen on business of the Star Lords. So I rode on and took no notice of the bird. He eyed me for a space, winging wide above my head; then he flicked a wing and soared away, vanishing in the suns' glare.

Well, now... Just keep the old cranium down and get on with the job in hand. That was the way of it, by Zair! The only way.

Jiktar Travok Ramplon, to whom I had given Fango in exchange for

Shadow, led his zorca archers out to trail his skirts before the enemy. He would raise the dust and lure Hangrol on.

We had no Battle Maidens, no Jikai Vuvushis, with us, for which I was profoundly thankful.

The local people rallied round wonderfully and scraped up a wild assortment of riding animals. These were apportioned among the infantry, for neither men nor beasts would be fit to act as cavalry against the kind of opposition we were facing.

Our two regiments of swarthmen were weak, only around three hundred each; but they were going to have to take the brunt of it when the cavalry came to handstrokes. The totrixmen were good quality, and Drak's three squadrons would help. But...

We marched out of Ovalia, heading for our start lines, and news came in that Hangrol had turned like a maddened graint to follow Jiktar Travok Ramplon and his zorca bows. Turko nodded in satisfaction. "Grapple him, Dray, like any ordinary wrestler. Then throw him and twist his neck!"

"Aye."

Very rapidly becoming accustomed to being addressed as a kov, our Turko the Shield. "Yes, kov," and, "Certainly, kov." Oh, yes, Kov Turko of Falinur—living very high on the vosk, our Turko!

The flags flew in the light of the suns, the men marched, the dust rose, and as we of the Eighth Army swung along so the swods in the ranks sang. They sang old songs and new songs, sprightly ditties and scurrilous comments on their officers. They sang sickly love ballads like "She Lived by the Lily Canal." This was the song sung almost obsessively by the men on the night before that resounding affray, the Battle of Kochwold. Of a similar sentimental nature was "Wedding Dirge of Hondor Elaina."

Then the veteran swods of the Fifth Churgurs struck up "Paktuns's Promenade" and sang their own repeatable words, and when that was done they warbled out many a ditty I have mentioned to you. At last I half-turned in the saddle and glared at the Second Regiment of the Sword Watch. In my fruity old bellow I started to yodel out "The Bowmen of Loh."

And, soon, the whole army bellowed out that brave old song and the imbalances of echoes as the words rolled down the lines sent tiny birds scurrying for shelter.

Seg Segutorio was not with me. Many of my fine Archer regiments of Valka, who used the Lohvian longbow, were with Drak. But we raggletaggle bobtail of any army sang as we marched.

Continually I rode up and down the lines, observing the men. And, in their turn, they observed me. Many were the comradely greetings flung to and fro. And, as we marched, my thoughts insisted on dwelling on Prince Tyfar and our comrades and our experiences in Moderdrin. It seemed to me I had learned something there and I did not know what it could be.

Certainly, a mere trick of thorn-ivy and its escalation into army scale could not be the reason I had found my way to the Humped Land. If Quienyin knew, I fancied he would tell me.

Marking how the Tenth Kerchuri marched, their pikes at ease, the Hakkodin with their axes or halberds over their shoulders, the attached Chodku of archers singing lustily, I thought of other times when we had marched singing into battle. Well, this time would be different and yet just the same. The differences became apparent as, wheeling to meet an attempt to flank us, I realized afresh the frightening smallness of our company. Kapt Hangrol was a seasoned campaigner, and he sought to pin and crush us. We had to work on him, out-march him—for all his aerial strength would avail him nothing if he could not put troops on the ground—and whittle away both his strength and his confidence.

We lost men in skirmishes. I raged and grieved; but we went on with the words of Clardo the Clis to sustain us.

"If one man dies for what he believes in—would you deny him that right? We all chose to be here!"

The maneuvers were complicated and pretty. We kept to good cover, making the utmost use of woods and darkness. The pace told on us and the men grew lean and hungry. The quoffa-drawn wagons caught up with us from time to time and yielded provisions and provender. Brad the Berry disgorged an amazing quantity of first-class food from his wagons, the Hagli Bush Irregulars delighting in showing how well they could provide. And we played Kapt Hangrol and his army, and in one classic attack we cut off and destroyed four full regiments of the iron legions of Hamal. With them went a shrieking collection of Layco Jhansi's hoodwinked adherents, spearmen, savage, almost barbaric fanatics.

As a few miserable and shaking prisoners were interrogated, I reached the conclusion that Jhansi must be using sorcery to control and enflame these men. Only a few seasons ago, before the Time of Troubles, these same shrieking savages had been sober, industrious citizens of Vallia. It was not just civil war and all its attendant horrors that had brought this travesty into being.

"That rast Hangrol draws near," said Turko, most cheerfully, on the day when the maps and the scouts' reports showed the raiding army to be within a day's march. All ideas of raiding farther into Orvendel had been abandoned by Layco Jhansi's men. I could guess that Kapt Hangrol and Malervo Norgoth had been exchanging acrimonious words. That cheered me up, since I was a malignant sort of fellow. We had trailed the red rag and they were bedazzled and enflamed.

"Right, Turko—or should I say, Kov Turko?"

"And I say to you —do you wish to try a few falls?"

We laughed companionably together. For all the seriousness with which

Turko took his new status as a kov, he, like my comrades and myself blessed or cursed with these noble titles, could see the ludicrousness, the pompous jackass nonsense, of putting too much store by rank and title. Estates, now—ah! That was a different matter.

These intricate maneuvers were of absorbing interest. We pivoted so as to maintain the Tenth Kerchuri with its solid mass of pikes as our fulcrum. And, of course, the local folk of Orvendel were extremely severe on any raiders who fell into their clutches.

Absorbingly interesting or not, the purely maneuvering phase had to come to an end.

"You are right, Turko. Tomorrow should see them nicely positioned."

"The spot you have chosen and worked them to is perfect. Now all that remains is for them to go in like idiot dermiflons, braying and charging full pelt."

"I think they will. Empress Thyllis has sent men up here in a desperate attempt to recover her losses in Vallia. Hangrol knows his head is forfeit if he loses."

My knowledge of mad Empress Thyllis encompassed her macabre Hall of Notor Zan where the wretches she deemed had failed her were thrown to the slavering fangs of her pet Manhounds.*

Everything was in order and to hand. The men sat around their campfires and a few songs lifted; but in the main they got their heads down and tried to sleep. I fancy that most of them did not, not being veterans. So the morning dawned. Palest rose and apple green, the Suns of Scorpio, Zim and Genodras, rose into a dappled sky. The air tanged with a morning bite. Food was eaten by those whose appetites remained. The final polish to weapons, the last adjustment to harness, the bilious shouts of the Deldars bellowing the men into their ranks—so we raggedy little bunch, so magniloquently styled the Eighth Army, fell in.

The lay of the land was simple and all important. Not being sufficiently strong to meet Hangrol in open battle, we must perforce make him attack piecemeal, which, being a skillful general, he would not do unless hoodwinked. The plain was here cut by a wide gash, the bed of an ancient stream long since lost to the Canals of Vallia. Vegetation clothed its flanks. Here were posted the archers. At the end of the depression the Tenth Kerchuri stood, formed, solid, a glittering array of crimson and bronze. They were withdrawn just enough to be out of sight of the distant end. Our cavalry waited my orders on the flanks. Scouts and skirmishers moved forward in clouds to deny the enemy clear observation. The churgurs waited just inboard of the archers. It was a simple arrangement to all seeming, and not a particularly military layout, either. I knew a fair old number of princes and generals who would blanch at the mere sight of the formations we adopted.

* See Dray Prescot #11, *Armada of Antares*.

Our total aerial force went whirling off to put into effect the final dazzlement. Even the lumbering old weyver went, with a rascally gang of cutthroats concealed behind her low bulwarks and a dozen varters ready to spew out chunks of Ovalia's fine street paving.

"You'll never dupe all that cramph Hangrol's aerial forces, Dray!" Turko rested his massive shield on his saddle. "By Morro the Muscle! We'll have the hornets around our ears—"

"Difficult to say." I spoke seriously, for this was a tactical and psychological problem. "If our fellows can draw off a goodly part, our archers can deal with the rest."

"I just wish Seg was here," said Turko, and gentled his zorca between his knees.

By Zair! And didn't I! And Inch, too, and all the others!

We watched the lads of the Tenth Kerchuri running back down the dry, ancient riverbed scattering their caltrops. If you question—if you condemn—the use of youngsters here, I sympathize. But they were born on Kregen, Vallians, and they burned to do what they could. The chevaux de frise were unloaded from the krahnik carts and carried forward ready to be run out where needed. I lifted in the stirrups to survey the scene. There was no fleet voller for me now to oversee the dispositions. Our men melted into the shadows of the bushes, and were still. A lazy breeze tufted the leaves, which was most useful and was taken by many men as a sign of the direct assistance we had from Opaz and Vox.

Into that ravine trotted Jiktar Travok Ramplon's regiment. The zorcas looked marvelous. The men had smartened themselves and their mounts up for the occasion, and wore their brightest uniforms. Red and gold glittered in the light. They rode forward and they suddenly seemed, despite their trim appearance and martial order, very small and lonely and isolated trotting up that dusty defile.

They trotted on and the hooves of the zorcas glittered through the dust, the spiral horns jutted proudly, the tails switched impatiently. Each trooper held his bow in his left hand, straight down his left leg, and his right hand gripped the nocked arrow. Jogging along in the trot, guiding their mounts with knees and body movement and voice, the swods of the zorca bows rode forward.

At the far end of the defile appeared the scouts from Hangrol's forces. Overhead a bunch of mirvols flew up ready to swoop down. I held my breath. You can see the tricky situation. Too soon and Hangrol would never follow. Too late, and that fine zorca regiment would be a mangled ruin.

With faithful Fango between his knees, confident, exalted, Jiktar Ramplon judged it to a nicety.

His men loosed at the mirvols. The flying animals swerved away, preferring to leave to the advance guard of land cavalry the sweeping away of this troublesome zorca unit. Remember, Ramplon had been baiting these adversaries for the past days. They had blood in their eye. The leading units of enemy zorcas simply let rip a yell of rage and anger and charged like leems. Jiktar Ramplon gave his orders, his trumpeter blew, the regiment pivoted and pulled back, building up their speed into a fine, free gallop.

Around that kink in the defile Ramplon sent on his regiment, for he had chosen to ride last, for which I marked him. He had the Twenty-seventh Regiment of zorca archers. They raced around that bend, and the following cavalry roared around after them. Dust smoked into the air. When the pursuing cavalry were out of sight of their following main body, our archers let fly. Ramplon's men hauled up, skidding, turned, and those bows came up and showered shafts into the abruptly huddled, terror-stricken mass.

Shot to pieces, the enemy zorcas tried to flee back, and ran full tilt into a wall of steel that closed as though on a hinge across the defile. The Tenth Kerchuri received the fleeing cavalry as though they received a charge. Perhaps half a dozen zorcamen survived to scramble around the edges and run for it—and each one of that half-dozen was brought down by a marksman.

The noise was such, I hoped, as to convince Hangrol that his advance cavalry had successfully chased off the annoying hornets who had been stinging him so unmercifully. The first elements of his main body came into sight, and I judged that Hangrol did think so. Apart from those early mirvols, there was no sign of his aerial support.

I looked back to where the 2ESW and the EYJ lay waiting in the runnels in the ground. All our men waited in concealment. Hangrol's forces advanced, led by more cavalry, with bunches of irregulars following, and backed by regiments of the iron legions of Hamal. I counted quickly. Ten regiments... They were the hard nut we had to crack. Like the other troops in Hangrol's force, the Hamalese swods were mounted up; they would dismount to go into action.

The moment approached and nothing was going to stop it now.

The Jiktars of the Archers awaited the signal. The churgurs gathered themselves. The kreutzin strained to get in among those brilliant adversaries. Close they came, nearer and nearer, riding with all the aplomb and confidence of men sure of themselves.

Any minute now...

Deb-Lu-Quienyin appeared at my side.

He was standing and leaning back, with his left hand pressed flat against thin air, as though he supported himself against an invisible wall. His clothes were filthy, torn, and tattered, and his turban was hanging over an ear. His face worked with passion and near despair, and he glared upon me with frightful meaning.

I bent from Shadow's back to peer more closely.

With an effort, Quienyin motioned.

Not understanding what he wanted, and aware that Turko was taking no notice whatsoever, I for a moment thought I was hallucinating and imagining I saw the Wizard of Loh. Hangrol's army marched on and the distance lessened. The giving of the signal could not be long delayed. I looked back at Quienyin, and he was still there, an apparition bold in the light of the suns.

He lifted his right hand with a gesture of weariness. The short sword in his fist was broken in half.

He dropped the sword. The moment it left his hand it vanished.

He pointed. He pointed with his right forefinger. He pointed at his eyes. I leaned from the zorca, staring. I stared into the eyes of the Wizard of Loh...

I was looking into a stone-walled chamber pierced by tall windows through which the suns light streamed in emerald and ruby. Silda Segutorio, half-naked, blood staining her shoulder, was staggering up distraught and trying to wield a blood-crusted rapier. Crumpled in a corner lay the body of a man in clothes splashed with blood. I stared. I felt the sickness rising. The man's fist rested on a sword, flat on the straw-covered stone.

My vision swung to the doorway. Men crowded in, fierce, bright, savage men, exulting. They were clansmen. Their weapons flickered in the brilliant light. They kicked aside the dreadful evidences of their handiwork. They trod contemptuously over the shattered corpses of men wearing the red-and-yellow uniforms of the Emperor's Sword Watch. Clansmen, savage, horrific, far more lethal than any barbarian, they jostled in to be the first to slay the Wizard and Silda and the man who lay crumpled in the corner.

I knew that man. His fist made a sudden spasmodic attempt to seize the sword, and fell away, limp. I knew the sword.

That was a great Krozair longsword.

That man was my son Drak.

Twenty-one

Victories for Vallia

Turko said, "Almost time, Dray! Another hundred paces or so, and then..."

He spoke, Turko the Shield, and I could not see him. I could hear the susurration of the breeze, hear the ominous drumroll of that advancing army; I could feel Shadow between my knees and the warmth of the suns, but I glared with awful fury into a stone chamber where some of the most ferocious warriors of all Kregen stalked down with bloodied weapons upon the helpless form of my son.

The vision's view shifted again and I saw Silda drawing herself up. Her blood-spattered body glowed through her ripped russet leathers. The rapier trembled in her fist. But she staggered up, her face pallid and distraught, her eyes fierce, her brows downbent, and I knew she would hurl herself forward. Seg's daughter would fling herself to destruction to protect my son!

The feral, bearded mouths of the clansmen opened and I knew they roared their appreciation of the gallantry of it, shouted compliments of the High Jikai; yet I could hear nothing of them, only the onward tramp of an enemy army dinning in my ears.

How could I give the signal to loose when I could not see Hangrol's forces? How could I assist Drak and Silda when I was miles away from them?

In my nostrils blew the sweet-scented breeze of Kregen. I could not smell the dust in that stone chamber or the raw stink of spilled blood. Among the refuse of swords scattered from the shattered Sword Watch lay a drexer, one of those swords we in Valka had designed and forged to make a superior weapon. It stirred.

The sword moved of itself.

Jerkily, it lifted into the air and the hilt dropped down and the blood-smeared point snouted up.

I knew. This, I had witnessed before. Gladiomancy! Swordomancy! Deb-Lu-Quienyin was exercising his powers, putting forth his kharrna, and manipulating that sword through the force of his mind. The sword trembled.

So, at once, near-instinctively, I understood what the Wizard of Loh required of me.

The clansmen hauled up. Soundless, that ghastly scene. The clanners stared at the sword floating unsupported in midair. But they did not run away. They were Clansmen of the Great Plains of Segesthes. They had little truck with sorcerers. One leaped. He was a Zorcander, one of the chiefs, and his broadsword struck like a sliver of silver fire.

"Dray! What—? What ails you?"

The drexer parried the first flashing blows.

"Nothing, Turko." Still keeping my gaze fastened on the eyes of Quienyin and through them that scene within the stone chamber, I dismounted from Shadow. I gripped the saddle. "My eyes—tell me when Hangrol's advance reaches the second down-drooping missal tree."

"Hai!" Turko started to yell, prepared to rouse our men to my aid.

"Shastum! Silence! Listen, Turko. You must be my eyes. Keep talking, tell me what goes forward, but speak quietly. Let no one know. You understand?"

"I understand. And the cramphs have reached the first missal."

"Then it will not be long delayed."

The drexer was beaten aside and the Zorcander, with a soundless yell of triumph, burst past. A discarded rapier lifted and struck and drove deeply into his side. He staggered back, and between the fingers of his left hand the bright blood seeped.

The rapier hovered in the air. And then—and then it was as though I gripped the hilt of that rapier in my fist. I could feel it, silver-wound and ridged, hard in my fingers. And I knew I gripped Shadow's saddle!

The rapier twitched up, and my body and arm did what bodies and arms with rapiers attached are accustomed to do on Kregen. The Zorcander fell, and the next clansman, leaping, silently roaring, fell also. But a rapier is no weapon with which to go up against Clansmen of Segesthes, by the Black Chunkrah, no!

Quienyin, through his kharrna, controlled the weapons. His strength had been taxed to the utmost. His skill would not avail him in swordplay against these supreme warriors. So he stretched out the powers of his mind and brought me in to wield the weapons through him. Uncanny, weird, spirit-shaking—but the only chance left in all the cruel and exotic world of Kregen for Silda and Drak.

The Wizard had to channel my skill at swordplay through his control. The rapier was a flashing blur of bloodied silver, and the broadswords beat and slashed. They had to knock that slender sliver of steel away before they could pass, and when they thrust they pierced thin air. But they drove on and I felt the shifting, sliding movement of my feet on the straw-covered stone, and yet I knew I stood braced on the ground beside my zorca and gripping onto his saddle.

The smashing power of the clansmen's blows forced me back, and the rapier slicing and thrusting unsupported in the air drew back. Had I been there in the flesh, I would have been sore wounded by now. Back and back, until I stood a few paces only before Drak and Silda. A single comprehensive glance showed me Drak sprawled unconscious and Silda crouched over him with her rapier half-lifted. She panted and her eyes were wide and wild. She would spring up at the last and fight until the end over the body of Drak.

The chamber spun about me as Quienyin turned once more to face the clansmen, for I realized I saw through his eyes. Stubbornly I tried to move back. I let go of Shadow's saddle and the dizziness caught me and I staggered. I felt Turko's Khamorro arm wrap about me and support me. But as I released my grip on the saddle so the rapier fell soundlessly on the stone.

This lack of communication baffling us infuriated me. It was like shouting into fog and receiving nothing in return. But Deb-Lu-Quienyin had been with me through the Moder where in that subterranean hellhole he had seen me battling with a longsword. The Wizard understood instantly. The Krozair brand under Drak's limp fingers twitched. It shivered. It lifted. It seemed to me I reached out with both fists and took the hilt into my grasp, and I turned in Turko's arm and so once again gripped onto Shadow's saddle. This time I gripped with both hands.

"They have reached the second missal, Dray."

"Then—loose! And Opaz have us in his keeping."

The noise of the battle I could hear; the sounds of the combat within the stone chamber remained cut off. In two places at once, I fought.

The battle I could hear and smell but not see roared on as our archers and slingers loosed and the Tenth stepped into view to block the ravine and entice Hangrol on. The combat I could see but not hear or taste flowered in the stone chamber as the clansmen smashed on to strike down the Krozair blade and have done. The battle was of vital importance to the welfare of the country. The combat was of excruciating agony for me, for through wizardly powers I sought to save the life of Drak.

"They go on! They go on!" roared Turko.

I switched the Krozair brand in a blur and chopped and sliced and thrust.

"Their cavalry, Turko?"

"Cannot maneuver for the shafts pinning them."

"Tell me when they charge—if they charge."

"The Hamalese have dismounted and are formed—the skirmishers run like rasts—our fellows are in among them now—"

A clansman dropped to a knee and brought two blades, a broadsword and a shortsword, up in a cross of glittering steel. That was a cunning and brave trick, for he sought to trap my blade in the neck of the cross and so wrench it free. With supple Krozair skill the longsword looped and hummed and the clansman fell back, silently.

Hangrol had over twice our force. We had to remain in cover and shoot and shoot. The Tenth Kerchuri did not entirely fill the width of the ravine where once a river had flowed. The Hakkodin spread out and the Chodku of archers shot with their comrades along the bushy heights each side. Turko kept up a ceaseless flow of reports and I swirled the Krozair longsword and, by the Light of Opaz, did not move a hairsbreadth!

The trumpeter of the Second Sword Watch on that day was Vardon the Cheeks. I said, "Bid Vardon stand ready."

Turko yelled, and then said, "The Hamalese are formed, their shields are up. They advance. They charge!"

"And the ground between?"

"Cumbered with dead men and fugitives still running."

"The cavalry?"

"They mill. It looks as though they will recover in a mur or so."

"And the skirmishers and their mercenaries?"

"Some press on with the Hamalese. Some wait the outcome."

Three clansmen came for that disembodied longsword together and now two of them swirled cloaks in a valiant effort to entrap that ghostly brand. I sliced and—without moving!—leaped away and so launched myself at them from the side. Quienyin's powers flowed through my arms and fists and the Krozair brand slashed in a vivid bar of light.

"The distance left?"

"Five hundred paces, no more, and narrowing all the time," Turko's voice rasped. "But the bowmen bring them down."

'Tell Vardon the Cheeks to blow the Tenth Kerchuri Prepare."

The silver notes rang out, swirling and skyrocketing in the air. And the clansmen drew back a space, panting, and their weapons glittered in the light of the slanting rays of the suns.

Two murs, three...

"Bid Vardon blow, Turko. Blow the Charge!"

"Quidang!"

And over the field and floating free and lilting with blood-quickening urgings, the Charge blew in ringing imperative.

As the clansmen came on again and the Krozair brand leaped and flashed I could imagine I saw the Tenth Kerchuri. I could see their pikes come down, down, pointing, their sharp steel heads a bristle of menace. The crimson shields would all slant together. Down would go the bronze-fitted helmets. The plumes would ruffle bravely. And then the brumbytes, formed, solid in their crimson and bronze, would charge. Blind to that sight, I could yet see it all, and hear and taste and smell the blood-thumping excitement of it.

Yet the clansmen would not leave off their attacks upon this eerie sword that floated in midair and chopped them as they charged.

"They meet!" yelled Turko. "By Morro the Muscle! You have created a veritable weapon in this phalanx, Dray!"

Very little can stand and survive in the path of a charging phalanx. We had proved that before. I had not really believed. But here, in what came to be known as the Battle of Ovalia, the pikes in their steel-crested fervor charged and overthrew the iron legions of Hamal. Raging, like a bursting dam that spills destruction in the path of its waters, the Tenth Kerchuri swept everything away before that intemperate onslaught.

And I did not see it!

Raw, green, they might be, these brumbytes wielding their pikes. But their helmets were down and their shields were slanted and their pikes went in and they rolled on and on and nothing could stand before them.

Silda was standing now, gripping her rapier. She had overcome the first tremor of horror when swords swirled with no visible hands to wield them. She stepped forward. I brought the longsword across in a vicious defending blow and smashed a clansman away.

"Stand clear, Silda!" I shouted.

"What?" Turko's voice reached me, alarmed. "What's that, Dray?"

"How goes the battle?"

"The Hakkodin are in among their cavalry and the cavalry do not like it—they run—they flee..."

"Blow for the churgurs—blow for everything! General Advance!"

The General Advance rang out over the roar of the battle.

The Tenth would be rolling down the ravine like a tidal wave of destruction, and now the sword and shield men would rage from the bushes crowning the slopes and hit the bewildered enemy from both flanks. And, all the time, I knew, the archers and staff slingers would be loosing into the huddled masses.

Kapt Hangrol had been sucked into the thorn-ivy trap. And now he was paying the price.

Many clansmen littered the stone floor. Their blood ran greasily in the cracks between the flags. And still they sought to pass that disembodied sword and slay the Prince Majister of Vallia.

The next Clanner struck at the sword seeking by main force to beat it down. The enormous leverage exercised by the Krozair two-handed grip brought the sword in a neat curve around the clansman's blade. The longsword twitched and the clansman's broadsword struck it square. I felt the shock, like liquid fire, jolt all up my arms. By Zair! Slow—slow and weak...

With a spurt of passion I slashed the clansman away and swung to the next and his blade clashed down on mine. I felt the shock, shuddering through me, and I smashed back.

I knew what was happening. Deb-Lu-Quienyin was weakening. What he had accomplished already was a miracle. But his kharrna was not limitless. The fight raging in the stone chamber became fraught with its inevitable end.

With the sounds of a greater battle ringing in my ears, I faced defeat in this contemptible little fracas, and knew it to be by far the more important, the vital, of the two—for with Quienyin's exhaustion the Krozair brand would fall, and Silda would hurl forward with her rapier blurring, and would die and then would die also my son Drak.

Still Quienyin upheld me. Still I continued to battle.

Turko yelled that the pikes rolled on like the millstones of the gods. The churgurs welted into the flanks of the foemen. Our irregulars were in there, smiting and dodging and smiting again.

Drooping now, the Krozair brand, drooping like a victim of the black lotus-flowers of Hodan-Set. Useless my exerting all the bestial and savage power pent within me by civilization. I fought only through the wizardry of gladiomancy. With the slipping away of Quienyin's powers so dropped away all the Krozair skill.

The longsword slashed and slashed again, and at every blow I could feel the lessening of force. The chamber blurred, the stones merging as though melting in some supernal heat. The stone flags of the floor pitched beneath me like the deck of a swifter. I knew I was grasping onto Shadow's saddle

653

with fists in which the knuckles ridged into skulls. Turko was yelling; but I did not hear him clearly, could see nothing in the world but the next opponent and do nothing in all Kregen but strike on.

Two clansmen battered their broadswords down on my sword, and the blade slithered. I strained of myself to bring it up, and could feel no life, no response, could feel only a deadly leaden lumpiness of total fatigue. A six-inch-long sliver of steel appeared from the floor. It was grasped in a fist. It drove smartly into the left-hand Clanner and a second, precisely similar steel blade, gripped in a fist of precisely the same nature, struck the right-hand clansman. Both fell away.

Two Pachaks raged into the fight. With them, glorious in their red and yellow, men of the Sword Watch drove on. But, ahead of them, the Pachak twins, Modo and Logu Fre-Da, smashed on in defense of the Wizard of Loh to whom they had given their nikobi in all honor.

Then I let out a harsh snort of sound, a breathy explosion that might in Cottmer's Caverns be taken for a laugh.

"What?" said Turko somewhere a million miles away.

Nodgen and Hunch pranced into the stone chamber, and Nodgen's spear was darkly stained, and Hunch's bill bore the marks of hard blows given and taken.

The First Sword Watch did not waste time on the clansmen. And, to be truthful, those clanners had fought heroically against sorcery. Very few other hardy warriors would have stood, let alone fought so determinedly, against wizardry like this. The 1ESW cleared out the clansmen, and arrows brought down those who sought to flee. But these four, the Pachak twins and Nodgen and Hunch, ran across toward me.

Their mouths were opening and closing and their eyes were popping and they were giving every indication of extreme animation. My viewpoint changed, and I was looking at the ceiling, with these four faces ringing the perimeter of vision. So I knew they were caring for Quienyin, all unknowing that Jak the Sturr stared through the wizard's eyes!

In the next instant I was staring at the polished leather of Shadow's saddle, twisting, and Turko was hauling me up, and saying, "Dray! Dray! For the sweet sake of Opaz—"

"I am all right, Turko—now. Let me see the battle."

"Your eyes—?"

"Perfectly all right now. I will explain. Are there any of our vollers in sight?"

"Not one. I trust they are all safe." He looked at me with all his old quizzical mockery; but he'd been shaken up, all right, no mistake about that!

All along that ravine of death the dead lay. The Tenth had stormed on with their pikes level and left nothing living in their wake. The rest of our little army, our Eighth Army, pushed on and Kapt Hangrol's forces fled.

"They won't come araiding over the borders again in a hurry, Dray."

"That is what I would like to think. By Vox! But it is a melancholy sight. Pull Jiktar Brad the Berry and his Hagli Bush Irregulars out and get them to tend the wounded. Brad will understand."

"Aye, he will. We are light on medical services."

A battery of krahnik-drawn varters went rumbling past. They had limbered up the ballistae in record time, and the krahniks, powerful, deep-chested, full of fire, hauled with a will. They were off to try to take up new positions and harry the rout. Their darts and rocks had wrought fearful execution in that blood-soaked ravine.

Well, the aftermath of a battle is always a messy business, and we had to make sure Hangrol kept running and did not stop to try to regroup. Our little cavalry force swept out in pursuit. The Tenth Kerchuri halted and I sent word to Kervax* Orlon Sangar telling him of my pride in his men and my congratulations. All the units involved had done well. There would be bobs** aplenty in the wake of the Battle of Ovalia...

In all decency I could not leave at once. Some reassurance could be allowed in that the Sword Watch and Quienyin's comrades had burst in to the rescue. But I vowed I wanted to know what had gone wrong over in the Northeast. By Krun, yes!

A Kerchuri of the phalanx, when arrayed in the normal formation of twelve men to a file, spreads out to cover a frontage of approximately three hundred and seventy paces. Drill movements can expand or contract this front, of course, containing as it does four hundred thirty-two pikes in each rank. The Tenth had swept up the ravine like a steel broom.

Turko and I and a few others of my officers walked slowly along the ravine. Everywhere our men were tending the wounded and carrying off the dead to be decently interred according to the rites suggested by the atras, the little amulets, the slain wore. Some of us made the usual trite observations about life and death. The scene was somber; but I did not feel—then—the chill I knew would near overwhelm me at all this waste.

I bent and picked up a shield from the phalanx. Its five-ply wooden construction was still intact, leather faced, bronze bound. The carrying strap was cinched tight; but the battle grips were broken. On the strip across the top the colors and symbols and numbers proclaimed this shield to have belonged to the Paltork—the second in command to the Relianc-hun—of the Sixty-fifth Reliach of the Eleventh Jodhri. In glowing yellow the stylized representation of the brumby, that long-horned, eight-legged, armored battering ram of destruction and an animal thought to be long extinct if not legendary, appeared on the face of the crimson shield. The brumby from which the brumbytes took their name was the symbol of the

---

* Kervax: Abbreviation for Kerchurivax.
** bobs: phalerae, medals.

entire Phalanx Force. I put my finger alongside the painted symbol of the Tenth Kerchuri of the Fifth Phalanx, a Prychan grasping Thunderbolts, and I shook my head.

Yes, the Golden Prychan, the wrestlers inn, had yielded up the means to bring back Turko. But as I stared on this shield, I realized I did not know the name of the Paltork who had carried it into battle. How could I? But this seemed to me wrong. I felt I should have known his name.

Tucked around the strap was a little cloth packet of cham. The Paltork no doubt chewed stoically as he marched forward; well, I fancied he would never return to claim his favorite chew.

The group of officers did not dwell overlong on that depressing scene. Having made sure that everything that could be done was being done, we trailed back to camp in a heavy silence. Of our voller force, nine returned. We had lost five. The flutduins had done well and had taken minimal casualties. As the returns came in I realized the thorn-ivy ambush had worked, and worked extraordinarily well. Our casualties were exceeding light.

I took Turko and Deft-Fingered Minch and one or two others, and left the Eighth Army under the command of Orlon Sangar, with orders to recoup and to clear the area, and flew direct for the northeast. No one expressed any surprise or chagrin that I should be leaving. It was taking me some time to realize that emperors could behave in this peremptory way without causing comment. After all, every man knew the emperor's concerns were wide, covering all of Vallia, and he was clearly needed elsewhere.

We caught up with the grandly named First Army at a bleak little town of Northern Jevuldrin called Ithieursmot. Its chief claim to fame until now was a mildewed mass of ruins left over from the Sunset People. Drak lay in his camp cot in his tent and fumed and swore and was in a thoroughly bad temper.

"The wound in itself was not serious," Quienyin told me as we stood looking down on the fractious Drak. The needlemen had worked well and Drak was in no pain. "But the prince had taken a savage knock on the head which Rendered Him Unconscious."

Silda sat on a low stool at the cot side, holding Drak's hand, and would not be moved. I thanked Opaz she was there, her own wound bandaged, and her ripped leathers replaced by a yellow gown. Had she not been, I think Drak would have blown up.

"Deb-Lu has explained it all to me, Father," said Drak. "It seems I owe my life to you."

"As to that, it is Deb-Lu-Quienyin in whose debt we both stand. And, Quienyin, you know my thanks is yours—aye! And I do not forget all we said in the Desolate Waste, and the Moder and the Humped Land. It is all coming together, now."

"Did I tell you," said the Wizard of Loh, "what your pair of rogues, Hunch and Nodgen said when they were apprised who you were?"

"I am not sure I wish to know that."

Drak looked suspiciously at me. He had not seen me smile overmuch when his mother was not present.

As to the fracas in the stone chamber, Drak had brought on a battle with superior forces, which was why he had been unable to spare me very many, in the complete conviction that Seg would come up with the Second Army. Seg had done so; but a flash flood had delayed his arrival by three burs. In that time Drak's army had fought devotedly, but a wing of clansmen had broken through. What I had witnessed had been the last dying attempt on the clansmen's part to slay the Prince Majister of Vallia before their whole force was broken and driven off. Seg's arrival and Quienyin's wizardry had saved us, and now the Second Army was hot-foot thrusting the minions of Zankov, cavalry, infantry, and air, farther north. The Hawkwas, a most savage bunch who were now devoted to the Emperor of Vallia, were swinging in to crush the enemy between them and Seg. Altogether, a satisfactory day's work, if you omitted to dwell too long on what might have occurred.

Then a fast voller arrived to tell us that Kov Vodun Alloran had been victorious in the southwest and was marching strongly into his own kovnate in the corner of the island.

"It seems as though we are successful in the south," said Drak. He smiled at Silda as he spoke.

"There remains the southeast," I said. "And those rasts up north. And the islands—"

"Oh!" flamed Silda. "We will do it! We have to look on the bright side."

I put a hand to my jaw and stared at her. Her bright face stared back, defiant, challenging, and I felt a poignant stab of happiness for Drak. Now, if only he had the nous to take the happiness that was his, and forget all about Queen Lush...

With my old gravel-shifting voice I said, "We will win, in the end, Silda, because defeat is unthinkable." Then, to Drak, I said, "Have you seen your mother?"

"No. Nor anyone else of the family. But they are all right." He glanced up at Quienyin. "Otherwise we would have heard."

I grumped at this. But he was right.

"I would like to go after those rasts. But we must consolidate what we have and strengthen our new frontiers. The army will have to be looked at, too." My face, I think, must have looked its usual ugly self, for Drak lost a little of his fretfulness. "And as for hiring mercenaries—"

"They fought well and earned their hire."

"Maybe. But I want Vallia to be liberated by Vallians. Is that clear?"

"Why shed our blood when—?"

"Just because it is our blood and the prize is blood-worthy. If it is not, you will never secure peace in the land."

We might have wrangled then; but the needlemen insisted Prince Drak needed rest, and we were shepherded out. Silda did not accompany us. She was the best medicine Drak could have.

My comrades in camp and I decided we ought to hold a right roaring bender that night. We had done well. There was much to do. But for this night we could forget problems and carouse around the campfires and bellow out the old songs under the Moons of Kregen. And so we did. But for all the wild singing and drinking and dancing as the campfires spurted lurid highlights against flushed faces and feverish eyes—can one ever forget problems? I do not think so. A few moments of oblivion, dearly bought, look cheap and tawdry when the problems remain, as intransigent and menacing as ever with the pallid light of the suns.

Every man contains a scorpion within him. And every man is commanded by the Star Lords. My Scorpion had materialized itself and become real; my Star Lords had revealed a glimmer of themselves. In this, surely, I was more fortunate than the unhappy people who struggle uncomprehendingly against the vagaries of their own nature and the vicissitudes of what, mistakenly, they call fate.

If it be true that men are born to rule and men are born to be slaves, then surely it is an onus placed on those who rule to command toward life and not toward death? The study of history tends to the belief that those with power abuse it because they understand only a tiny part of what power is. If individual people are as nothing before the great weight of destiny, and there is no reason in the universe, then a man has just the one single fact to which to cling: he is a man. Nothing more.

Unknown powers within and without ourselves—the Scorpion and the Everoinye—may overthrow us and we may go down to eternal ruin; but can we do any more, seeing we are but men?

We had won victories against what my people regarded as the powers of darkness, yet I knew we must all go forward together in the light of Opaz, against greater forces of evil. And who was to say that those other evil powers would not, in time, be reconciled?

"There is a magnificent golden Kildoi, there, Dray," said Turko.

"Aye." The firelight glinted from Korero's golden beard and he smiled, lifting his two right arms. His tail hand wrapped around a silver goblet, and he drank.

I made the pappattu and I made it in a certain way.

"Korero the Shield—Turko, Kov of Falinur."

A welling burst of song roared out then from the nearest group around their campfire, rollicking words that finished, "No idea at all, at all, no idea at all."

We all half-turned to look and listen, and when I turned back— lo! Turko and Korero were gone.

What transpired between those two touched me nearly, and I, fallible human being that I am, trembled as vague rumors, laced with sly chuckles, reached me. Garbled stories of a fight that sprawled away into the moon shadows, a titanic conflict that roared over kools of land, made me imagine all manner of disasters. But, when I found them, the Kildoi and the Khamorro, they were sitting together and quaffing and not a bruise or a cut on either. They stood up as I approached, lithe, limber, superb men.

"You two—" I started. Then the ridiculousness of the situation overwhelmed me. How small my faith had been! "I need you both, in different ways. You are not Vallian born—well, no more am I—but our path is set out for us. Falinur is to be won back, for one thing."

"The kov was saying—" spoke up Korero, his golden beard glinting, his tail hand curled around his jar.

"Korero expressed the view," said Turko.

They paused and looked at each other. I took the measure of that look.

"Well, that's settled, then." I spoke briskly. "We'll round up an army and no doubt Drak and the Presidio will bestow an imposing number on it, and we'll see about Falinur."

"It is in my mind, Dray, to ask Korero to march with us."

"If the Prince Majister can spare him. When it's done I'll expect Falinur to be a model kovnate. As for your taxes, Kov Turko, see they are paid promptly, and in full. And I shall call on you for a few regiments. See about raising a brigade of swarthmen."

They both looked puzzled. "But—you—?"

"When I get back we will have to think seriously about the rest of the island. This King of Urn Vallia, for example."

"Get back?" they said together.

The first pastel tints of the new day lightened the horizon, the air smelled crisp and clear with a lingering trace of woodsmoke to spice the atmosphere with promise of breakfast, She of the Veils sank slowly wreathed in roseate clouds. This was a dawn on Kregen and there cannot be any other dawns in all the worlds among the stars to compare with that, by Zair!

"Get back," I said firmly. "Much of Vallia has been freed from the maniacs who destroy all they touch. Prince Drak is fully competent to run the country. The army is in good heart with these victories under their belts. Where we have the land, the people prosper. The harvests are good. There is a spirit abroad that will not be denied. I shall not be long—at least, I trust I shall not be long."

"But—" said Turko.

"Where—?" said Korero.

"You two sound like that mythical fellow from Balintol with two heads."

"Mythical or not," said a voice from the shadows at my back, "he is a fellow who stays at home for some of the time. Just where are you off to this time?"

For two heartbeats I did not turn around. I felt all that glorious dawn of

Kregen rush together and collide and burst into my stupid vosk skull of a head. I felt the dawn colors riot and coruscate and burn through my veins. Slowly, slowly, I turned.

She half-smiled, yet her face was serious and grave, pale and with the first hints of the exhaustion brought by long journeyings and too-intensive work. I barely noticed her clothes—black silk tights, black leathers, black boots, with her rapier and dagger depending from golden lockets and the wide black belt with the golden clasp. A scarlet cape swung from her shoulders. She stared at me and I stared at her, and, like two loons, we stood, not moving, staring with unappeased hunger one upon the other.

I took a breath. The fragrance of the dawn air, the subtle pastels of apple green and rose, the distant chorus of those marvelous birds of Kregen all—all swam about me. The morning radiance touched her hair and brought alive those glorious tints of auburn, making a halo about her face. I swallowed down—hard.

It occurred to me that I might have said, "So you have come home, then?" But, instead, all I could say was, "There is still much to do. We have made a beginning—"

She took a step forward.

"Yes, there is still much to be done. You great grizzly graint! And you are flying off again!"

"Hyrklana," I said. "You know."

"I know. And you will leave today?"

I took a step forward. We moved toward each other. She raised her arms and I saw the wonder of her face.

There was nothing else in all of Kregen.

I held her, held her close, and I felt her arms clasping me.

"Delia!"

"Dray!"

"I must go to Hyrklana, as you must go about the business of your Sisters of the Rose—"

"Only for Vallia—"

"We are driven—"

"But not for much longer. It will end, one day—"

"Yes, there is light at the end of the tunnel, at last."

I held her close and I could feel the warmth of her and the tremble between us. All of Vallia, then, all of Kregen, seemed of small moment, tiny, insignificant, beside my Delia, my Delia of Delphond, my Delia of the Blue Mountains...

"And you will fly for Hyrklana today?"

I could feel the growing heat of the Suns of Scorpio burning upon me.

"No, my heart, I do not think I shall leave today."

A Glossary to the Jikaida Cycle

References to the four books of the cycle are given as:

LFK: A Life for Kregen
SFK: A Sword for Kregen
FFK: A Fortune for Kregen
VFK: A Victory for Kregen

Previous glossaries covering entries not included here will be found in *Prince of Scorpio, Arena of Antares, Armada of Antares, Krozair of Kregen* and *Golden Scorpio.*

A

Absordur: A woodland trylonate of the Dawn Lands, rich in timber and minerals.

Aeilssa: Princess.

agate-winged jutmen of Hodan-Set: A mythical host of ghostly riders who scourge the nighted plains of Kregen.

Aidrin: Country of the Dawn Lands; Jikaida City is the capital.

Alloran, Vodun, Kov of Kaldi: A shrewd man who lost his lands in Vallia's Time of Troubles and who dreamed only of returning in triumph; commanded the Fifth Army, the Army of the Southwest.

Almuensis: A cult of Sorcerers of considerable powers.

alkwoin: A valuable mineral obtained by open-cast mining.

Amklana: A province of Hyrklana and its proud and beautiful city.

Andrinos: A Khibil wrestler brought with Turko and Saenci by Dray Prescot out of Pandahem. VFK

Aracloins: City areas of confused alleys and covered souks and bazaars, teeming with commerce and villainy.

arbora trees: Called this because their flowers look like arbora feathers.

Archolax the Bones: A spare man of gravitas, appointed Pallan of the Treasury of Vallia.

Ariane nal Amklana: The chief lady of the city of Amklana who did not come too well out of her adventure down the Moder.

Astrashum: A city of the Dawn Lands from which expeditions set out for Moderdrin. Here Prescot, Nodgen, and Hunch were sold on the auction block to Tarkshur the Lash. FFK

B

Bakkar: A Brokelsh spirit or deity.

Balassmane: A superb nikvove charger ridden by Prescot at the opening of the Battle of Kochwold. LFK

Banje: A shop selling candies and trifles and trinkets for children.

Barkindrar the Bullet: A Brokelsh slinger from Hyrzibar's Finger; one of Prince Tyfar's retainers.

Battle of Irginian: In which the Army of Vondium overthrew Mogper's army under command of Kapt Hangreal. LFK

Battle of Kochwold: Traumatic fight in which the Phalanx of Vondium and other arms successfully resisted the great charge of ten divisions of Clansmen of Segesthes, and the zorcas of Filbarrka triumphed. When Prescot left, command devolved on Seg Segutorio, commanding the vaward. LFK

Battle of Ovalia: Where Prescot sprang the thorn-ivy trap on Jhansi's army led by Kapt Hangrol, the Vallian Eighth Army winning despite being outnumbered over two to one. VFK

Battles of Kanarsmot, First and Second: In which Vallian forces held and threw back raiders over the Great River. SFK

Bellendur: Kovnate of the Dawn Lands.

Belzid's Belly, By: A Brokelsh oath.

Belzur the Aphorist, Master: A new and successful playwright of Vondium.

Beng Drudoj: Patron saint of wrestlers.

Beng Lomier: Patron saint of strolling players.

Beng Teaubu: Martyr who was drawn many seasons ago in the chundrog of Jikaida City.

Bevon: A powerfully built yet gentle Brukaj, slave to Master Scatulo, who obtained freedom by acting a piece in Kazz Jikaida; good comrade to Prescot. SFK

Bilsley: A vadvarate of the Kingdom of Mandua in the Dawn Lands. Dav Olmes is vad.

Black Chunguj, By the: An oath indicating disapproval of an unjust act.

"Black is White and White is Black": A song about a Pandaheem who kissed the baker's wife and went floury white to see the sweep's wife, and so went home white and black.

Blind Archer, By the: Plea to the Bowman of Chance for a good shot when the mark is difficult and a hit uncertain.

Brad the Berry: Landlord of the Hagli Bush in Vondium, a cheerful, resourceful man around whom rumors cluster. Raised a regiment from his regulars; but marked out for high office.

Brince: Second cousin to Inch.

Brokkerim: Familiar form of address from one Brokelsh to another.

Brudstern: Sword mark shaped like open flower, whose magic is whispered rather than spoken. Usually punched on forte.

Brugheim: A kovnate of the Kingdom of Mandua in the Dawn Lands. Konec Yadivro is kov.

Brukaj: A diff with a bulldog face and powerful hunched shoulders, with somewhat short legs. They are determined and dogged.

Bruk-en-im: Brukaj spirit or deity of good will.

Brumbyte's elbow, By: A Vallian pikeman's oath.

"Brumbyte's Love Potion": Sentimental song created in Vondium out of regard for the new phalanx.

C

calsax: armored howdah containing warriors mounted on the backs of huge beasts such as dermiflons, boloths, and trompipluns.

Challenger: Flying sailing ship commanded by Captain Hando which took Prescot and the Vallian paktuns off Wenhartdrin. VFK

chavnik: A form of small pet Kregan cat.

Chodku: Archer component attached to the Kerchuri, consisting of two Lanchans each of 432 bowmen.

Chodkuvax: Commander of Chodku. Equivalent rank to Jiktar.

chundrog: dungeon.

churgur: heavy infantryman equipped with sword and shield as basic weapons.

Clardo the Clis: A Vallian hyrpaktun from Vomansoir, a pug-ugly man, scarred, with prominent eyebrows, returned to fight and joined 1EYJ in command of churgurs.

"Conundrum of the Hyrshiv": Song concerning the comical efforts of a little Och maiden and a strapping Tlochu youth to sort out the twelve limbs they possess between them.

Covinglee: Small kovnate of the Dawn Lands.

D

Deb-Lu-Quienyin: Wizard of Loh.

Deft-Fingered Minch: A crusty, bearded veteran who ran Prescot's field quarters in the Eighth Army. VFK

Desolate Wastes: Difficult area, not all barren, confining the eastern approaches to LionardDen, Jikaida City.

diashum: magnificent.

Dogansmot: Town in the vadvarate of Thadelm in SW Vallia.

Dolardansmot: Town where lived the mother of the Fre-Da twins.

"Don't dice with a four-armed fellow": Saying cautioning against taking foreseeable and unnecessary risks.

Dottle's Playhouse: A theater in Jikaida City.

drexer: Pattern of sword designed in Valka by Prescot and Naghan the Gnat sharing attributes of the thraxter and clanxer with what of the Savanti Sword Prescot could incorporate.

Drill the Eye: A Vallian hyrpaktun from Vond, a squat, fiery-faced man, returned to fight and joined 1EYJ in command of archers.

drin: land; a division, usually of thirty-six squares, of the Jikaida board.

Drogo: A Kildoi who joined Prescot and Pompino in their attempt to steal an airboat and escape from Jikaida City. Bears a grudge against Mefto the Kazzur. FFK

Dromo the Benevolent: Spirit appealed to and given thanks for assistance in the Dawn Lands.

Durheim: Kovnate north of the Mountains of the North in Vallia, south and east of Evir.

E

Emder: Acts as Prescot's valet although more of a comrade; a quiet, deft, impeccable, invaluable man.

"Empty Wine Jar, The": A song popular in Vondium during the Time of Troubles.

Ennschafften: Diffs with delightful baby faces, naive and simple, the men very strong, the women very beautiful, most often employed as house servants. The name they are generally called is Syblians.

Erthanfydd The Meticulous: Spirit of Erthyrdrin under whose intolerant eye the warriors of the Erthyrrhim pass their weapons in metaphysical inspection before battle.

ESW: Emperor's Sword Watch; at this time two regiments strong, 1ESW has comrades of the Choice Band who created this bodyguard out of affection and concern for the safety of Prescot, and 2ESW mainly promising youngsters training for commands.

EYJ: Emperor's Yellow Jackets; at this time one regiment strong, 1EYJ formed from paktuns returning to Vallia and young men from Drak's City.

Execution Jikaida: Unpleasant form of Kazz Jikaida in which the pieces are taken by condemned criminals and slain on the board, in Jikaida City.

F

Fakal the Oivon: A Vallian paktun from Meltzer, swarthy-faced; returned to fight, and lent his shield to Turko as *Mancha of Tlinganden* ran aground on Wenhartdrin. VFK

Filbarrka na Filbarrka: Nazab of the blue-grass country of the Blue Mountains, a zorcaman, created the zorca archers and lancers that discomfited the clansmen in the Battle of Kochwold.

Flame Winds of Father Tolki: In the ancient, now repudiated, religion of Father Tolki, his Flame Winds would race across the land to avenge and destroy faster than a zorca could run.

Fiona: Brilliant, beautiful girl, handmaiden to Delia.

flutduinim: collective noun for men flying flutduins.

flutswod: Soldier flying any kind of bird or animal.

Fluttrhim: Flying people of various races of winged diffs.

flyer remained unsaddled: Saying indicating a problem was left unattempted.

"Forbenard and the Rokrell": An unsophisticated ditty.

Frandu the Fanch: A Fristle who has a very high opinion of himself, hence his nickname, with a sharp tongue, a doughty fighter.

Fre-Da, Logu: Pachak, with all the Pachak virtues, gave his nikobi to Deb-Lu-Quienyin, with his twin ventured into the Moder.

Fre-Da, Modo: Pachak, twin to Logu who shared adventures.

Frelensmot: Town of Vallia in which Jilian Sweet-tooth was born.

freymul: Pleasant riding animal, often called the poor man's zorca; one breed having vivid streaks of yellow below and a chocolate-colored coat. A willing mount and serves well within abilities.

Frorkenhume: Kingdom of the Dawn Lands overrun by Hamal.

Fruningen: A small rocky island northwest of the island of Tezpor north of Rahartdrin. A harsh, inhospitable place despite the near perfect climate, home of the Wizards of Fruningen.

G

Game of Moons: A game of arguable simplicity much played by those to whom Jikaida, Jikalla, and Vajikry present problems.

Garfon the Staff: Majordomo in the palace of Vondium.

gauffrer: Diff with rodent features, usually a city-dweller.

Gertinlad: City of Dawn Lands, held by Kov Pastic.

gherimcal: Small carrying chair, sedan chair.

Gilma, Ford of: Leads to Songaslad, a town of thieves.

Glyfandrin: Kovnate of the Dawn Lands.

Gonells: Women of the Gon race of diffs, many of whom allow their beautiful silver hair to grow long, as the men all shave bald.

grascent: A risslaca of medium size, scaled, with powerful hind legs used for leaping, and a wedge-shaped head.

greesh: Term of contempt used by slaves and poor folk ripe for enslavement for slavers, aragorn, slavemasters. Formed from "grak!" and "kleesh."

GrollenDen: City of Vallia, capital of Zaphoret, east of Mountains of the North.

Grumbleknees: A fine zorca, a gray, ridden by Prescot on a number of notable occasions.

Gursrnigur: Spirit or deity used in oaths by Moltingurs.

H

hagli: ivy, not the thorn variety.

Half Moon: An old theater of Vondium, partially burned in the Time of Troubles but still in use; the audience gets wet when it rains.

Hall of Specters: One of the Nine Halls surrounding the Chamber of the Flame in the Moder of Ungovich, crammed with corpses.

Havandua the Green Wonder: A spirit of the Dawn Lands of Havilfar.

heasmons: Fragrant violet-yellow flowers.

Hikaidish: Rules and regulations of different styles of wrestling.

Himindur the Three-eyed: A Havilfarian spirit of luck and good fortune, equating with the Vallian Five-handed Eos-Bakchi.

Hiviku the Artful: The archetypal old sweat in Havilfar, equating with Vikatu the Dodger.

hiviku: one of the inferior pieces in Vajikry.

Horata the Bounteous: A Khibil female beneficent spirit.

Horato the Potent: A Khibil male beneficent spirit.

Humped Land: Colloquial name for Moderdrin, the Land of the Fifth Note.

Hunch: A Tryfant from the kovnate of Covinglee in the Dawn Lands, whose father, a brass founder, fell on evil times through spending all his time and money on Vajikry, and Hunch ended up slave. A good companion to Prescot who is not afraid to tell everyone that he is afraid. Went to Vallia with Nodgen.

Huvon the Lightning: A popular deity in Hyrklana.

Hyr Brun: Giant with straw-yellow hair, broad and bulky, seven inches taller than Prescot. Servant to Ros the Claw.

Hyr Flick: A very large variety of carnivorous flower, with green tendrils and orange cones, like enormous flick-flicks.

hyrkaida: in Jikaida, checkmate.

I

ibithses: one of the many purple flowers of Kregen.

Ibs of the Lily City: A Hyrklanian reference to the ghosts of the Lily City Klana, the ancient ruined capital of the island.

Infathon: Town of the province of Vazkardrin in NE Vallia.

Inshurfraz, the Furnace Fires of: One of the hotter legendary hells of Kregen.

Instructions to Novices: Precepts for those entering the service of Opaz, used to advise and guide all Vallians.

"In the Fair Arms of Thyllis": A Hamalian song telling of the marvelous deeds of Thyllis the Munificent. Erithor made scurrilous words and Prescot entertained his comrades from Mandua with them during a Noumjiksirn after a game of Kazz Jikaida in Jikaida City. SFK

Irginian: Place in south Vallia, scene of the battle of that name.

Ithieursmot: Bleak little town of Northern Jevuldrin in Vallia.

J

Jehamnet: Spirit of harvest time associated with crop failures and other disasters. Known as Jevalnet in Vallia, Jegrodnet and Jezarnet in the Eye of the World, Jepannet in Pandahem and Jehavnet in most of Havilfar.

jibr: Pain.

Jikaida: The premier board game of Kregen. A brief description of Poron Jikaida is published as Appendix A to *A Sword for Kregen*.

Jikaida City: LionardDen.

Jikaida Dance: One of the dances of Vallia and most other countries of Paz, but not all, in which the dancers retire as they fail to adhere to the movements called for by the songs sung to the music of the dance.

Jikaidish Lore: A hyr lif containing the history, rules, comments, and games of Jikaida over the centuries. In Jikaida City the Jikaidish also contains rules concerning weapons and relative strengths of the humans acting as pieces.

Jilian: A brilliant girl, a Jikai Vuvushi, one of six children of a Banje shop keeper who failed. She was taken in by the Little Sisters of Opaz and taught sewing, then the Sisters of the Rose sent her to Lancival. She uses a whip and a claw like Ros the Claw. Formed a regiment of Jikai Vuvushis. A good comrade to Prescot and a friend and devoted adherent of Delia.

Jögen: A favorite old play from the Fifth Book of *The Vicissitudes of Panadian the Ibreiver* by Nalgre ti Liancesmot.

jutman: A word describing anyone riding an animal, the Kregish is juttim. It follows that a riding animal must be a jut.

K

kaida: In Jikaida, check.

Kaldi: Lozenge-shaped kovnate in extreme southwest of main island of Vallia. Vodun Alloran was kov.

Kaldu: A large, powerful apim retained of Jaezila.

kalider: A dagger of Havilfar, sharply curved with a heavy hilt, the blade being very wide at the quillons, a Kregan knuckle (4.2", 106.68 mm), and curving keenly to a fine point, honed on both edges.

kampeon: A veteran who has achieved great renown and recognition.

Kanarsmot: A town of Bryvondrin on the northwest bank of the Great River opposite the boundary of Mai Makanar and Mai Yenizar to the southeast of the Great River.

kao: One of the many Kregan names for death.

kaochun: The Jaws of Death.

kaotim: The Undead, the living dead.

Karidge, Nath: A fine zorcaman and cavalry commander.

Kazz: Blood.

Kazz-Jikaida: Blood Jikaida, played with people who fight for the possession of the squares on the board.

Kervax: Abbreviation for Kerchurivax.

Khorundur: A country of the Dawn Lands of Havilfar.

Khorunlad: Capital of Khorundur.

King's Hand: Gambling game played with at least six dice.

Klaiton: Noble House of Zenicce, colors are gray and blue.

Kochwold: A sweep of moorland on the southern borders of Jevuldrin and the northern borders of Forli.

krad: A bronze coin of Vallia, newly minted and issued by the Presidio.

kraitch-ambur: Thunder.

Kranlil the Reaper: Horrific spirit of maleficent evil.

kregoinye: People employed by the Everoinye, the Star Lords, on their business about Kregen.

kreutzin: Light infantry acting as skirmishers, voltigeurs.

L

Lamdu: A form of Jikaida in which there are ninety pieces to a side.

Larghos the Sko-handed: A Vallian hyrpaktun from Gremivoh, with a long, narrow chin and slinger's shoulders, returned to fight and joined 1EYJ in command of staff slingers.

Lattice House: Decadent palace in Trakon's Pillars where Thelda Polista and her child were kept prisoner. LFK

Ling-Li-Lwingling: A Witch of Loh.

LionardDen: Known as Jikaida City, situated very near the exact center of Havilfar.

Llunyush the Juice: One of the many spirits of catering sworn on by the chefs of Paz.

Lobur the Dagger: Name used by Lobur ham Hufadet, a Hamalese horter, aide-de-camp to Prince Nedfar.

Longweill: A fluttrhim and thief, who came to a glutinous end down the Moder. FFK

Loriman the Hunter, Kov: A full, fleshy, choleric noble whose passion is hunting. In his own intemperate, bash-on, bully-boy way he was a tower of strength down the Moder. What he sought down there among the horrors and the Monsters, Prescot suggests, was of use to his cult of Spikatur Hunting Sword and far outweighed in value mere gold or gems. FFK

"Lucili the Radiant": A popular song in Vondium.

Lucrina, Yasuri, Vadni of Cremorra: The Lady Yasuri, a small woman who dressed in shiny black bombazine, employed Pompino and Prescot as paktuns, and they were bound to her protection as kregoinye on orders from the Star Lords. When she became champion in Jikaida City after Prescot fought Mefto the Kazzur she lost a deal of her sharpness, most of the lines on her face, and the razor-edged nose softened. The king of her country was slain and her vadvarate overrun. SFK, FFK

lumop: Term of abuse.

Luxis Bliem Juruk nalen Strom, En: The Strom's Sacred Life Guard. Formed in Valka when Prescot Fetched the island back to the people and was Fetched to be their strom. Known as SSLG.

lynxter: A Lohvian sword.

M

Mahendrasmot: A town of Southern Pandahem.

Mai Makanar: A kovnate on the southeast coast of Vallia.

Mai Yenizar: A kovnate on the southeast coast of Vallia.

majis: Short form of majister, used only by close intimates.

Mancha of Tlinganden: Argenter in which the returning paktuns took passage to Vallia, wrecked on Wenhartdrin. VFK

Mandanillo: A stately dance.

Mandua: Kingdom of Dawn Lands hostile to Hamal.

"March of the Skeletons": A song in which a brilliant and charming girl, just returned from a boat holiday, recounts how the skeletons marched from the graveyard in search of their missing flesh and blood. The song is an example of that inscrutable Kregan humor.

marlque: A riding animal.

669

Mausoleum of the Flame: Chamber of the Flame at the heart of the Nine Halls filled with their corpses in the Moder. FFK

Mazdo the Splandu: A superb golden numim, great-hearted and generous, deadly with all kinds of weapons.

Measure of Princesses: The Jikaida Dance.

Mefto the Kazzur: Cognomen of Mefto A'Shanofero, Prince of Shanodrin, a Kildoi. An exceptional swordsman who fought through to the princedom of Shanodrin in blood and death, devoted to Kazz-Jikaida, involved in intrigues to further the cause of Hamal in the Dawn Lands. Is now minus his tail hand, which was a left hand. SFK

Mists of Sicce: Confusing fogs circumjacent to the Ice Floes of Sicce.

Moder: A large artificial mountain, a kind of tell, containing tombs, sepulchers, and vaults, corpses, Undead, treasure, traps, and monsters and magic. FFK

Moderdrin: The Humped Land, the Land of the Fifth Note, where the Moders cover the ground as far as the eye can see.

Mogper, Colun, Kov of Mursham: A brilliant-seeming but vicious and depraved kov of a province in Menaham, marked for retribution by Jilian. He slew Barty Vessler by stabbing him in the back.

Moltingur: Diff of apim size with horny carapace across shoulders, eating proboscis, feelers, faceted eyes, a tunnel mouth with rows of needle-like teeth to tear food for proboscis to masticate and swallow. Speaks with a hiss, chillingly.

mon: Right (as distinct from left).

Mountains of Thirda: Situated on the western end of the border between Jevuldrin and Forli in eastern Vallia.

Muzzard: A diff something like a Chulik, but without tusks, with skin of a leaden hue and exuding a musky odor.

Myer, Pallan: Minister of Education, Learning, appointed by Prescot in Vondium. Walks everywhere reading a book.

"My Love is like a Moon Bloom": Popular song of Paz.

mytzer: Low-slung, ten-legged, docile draught animal, inexpensive but of excellent pulling power much used by tradesmen and poor folk who cannot afford the more expensive breeds of draught animals abounding on Kregen.

N

Naghan the Doom: One of Ariane nal Amklana's retainers, a numim.

Nath the Shaft: An apim from Ruathytu, expert archer, one of Prince Tyfar's retainers.

Neagrom: City famous for beautiful ceramic ware.

Nedfar, Prince: Prince of Hamal, second cousin to the Empress Thyllis, father of Tyfar and Thefi, a man of high courage and honor.

Nierdrik: Diff with coarse-skinned, high-beaked, hooded-eyed face like killer-turtle, hard and gritty, with compact muscular body, with two arms, two legs and no tail.

Niklaardu: Family name of twin Vallian paktuns from Wenhartdrin returned to fight and joined 1EYJ.

Ngrozyan the Axe: Spirit from myths of Ng'groga.

Nodgen: A Brokelsh who has been a mercenary, a cutpurse in Jikaida City, and much else, handy with a spear, became slave with Hunch and Prescot. Good companion to Prescot, went with Hunch to Vallia.

Norgoth, Tarek Malervo: A man with thin legs and bulky body, sent as Ambassador to Prescot from Layco Jhansi, acted as commissar in army commanded by Kapt Hangrol defeated at Battle of Ovalia. A man whose self-importance expands or recedes with the company he keeps. LFK, VFK

Norhan the Flame: A useful fellow who likes to hurl blazing pots of combustibles.

Notor Shorthush of the Waves: One of the mythical Sea Lords of Kregen who send gales to sink men's ships out of spite.

Noumjiksirn: A wake, an uproarious yet serious celebration in which warriors mourn their vanished comrades.

O

Olmes, Dav, Vad of Bilsley: A good-natured noble with long yellow hair, a round, cheerful, pugnacious face, an expert swordsman. Vad of a province in Mandua hostile to Hamal. Befriended Prescot, Bevon, and Pompino in Jikaida City. SFK

"Only Zair knows the cleanliness of a human heart": A saying from the Eye of the World suggesting that all men have secrets they do not want, and act differently from the way they would wish to act, yet make attempts to overcome their failings.

Orscop, Nath, Trylon of Absordur: A noble of the Dawn Lands whose ruling passion was Vajikry. VFK

Ortyg the Tresh: Standard Bearer with 1ESW who carries the Union flag of Vallia.

Ovalia: Town of the Imperial Province of Orvendel in Vallia.

P

Panachreem: Mythical home of the gods and spirits of Pandahem.

pantor: The word in Pandahem for the Hamalian notor and Vallian jen—lord.

Phrutius, Strom: Bought Prescot as slave from Jikaida City, was eaten by a Laughing Shadow down the Moder. FFK

Polisto, Tyr Lol, ti Sygurd: Fine, limber man who lost his farming estate during Vallia's Time of Troubles, fought back as the leader of the local guerrillas and rescued and married Thelda.

Pompino, Scauro, ti Tuscursmot: A Khibil, powerful and shrewd, with scars tracing over his body, sometimes called Pompino the Iarvin. A kregoinye. From South Pandahem. Worked with Prescot for the Star Lords protecting the Lady Yasuri. Like most Khibils somewhat contemptuous of everybody else, but a good comrade to Prescot. SFK

Prado, En: A later playwright than Nalgre ti Liancesmot whose work En Prado often comments on.

Prince Larghos and the Demons: A legend of Kregen containing the story of Gilma, a water sprite, and Nafti, the potter's son.

propt: Support; given by Deldar to swod in Jikaida.

Pypor: Deity of some clans of the Great Plains of Segesthes, and a Devil Deity to other clans.

Q

Quardon: Young voller pilot of 2ESW.

Queltar: Of Queltar, Deb-Lu-Quienyin says: "Some hellhole in Queltar where no man should have to exist."

Queyd-arn-tung!: No more need be said on the subject.

R

Ralton Daw-Erentor, Tyr: Second son of a minor noble of North Vallia, hewed to Layco Jhansi's party because of his father, a keen sleeth racer, uncomfortable over confrontation with Prescot during Norgoth's embassy, potentially a fine man. LFK

Ravenshal and Rashenka: A gentle Relt stylor and his wife of Mahendrasmot, who invited Prescot to their home and treated him with kindness, two of the ordinary nice people of Kregen. VFK

reed-laurium: Reed—headband. Laurium—rank. Any headband bedecked with symbols, feathers, colors denoting rank. In this instance worn by people in Kazz-Jikaida to indicate the pieces they represent.

Renko the Murais: A Valkan axeman, member of the SSLG, saved from being hanged for a murder he did not commit by Prescot in Vondium, subsequently joined 1ESW. LFK

Risslaca Ichor: Wine; a rosé with the addition of dopa which adulterates it or fortifies it according to taste.

Rodiflor, Kov Erclan the Critchoith: Square, hard noble, savage to his subordinates, devoted to Kazz-Jikaida, a man of harsh authority and power.

Rokveil: King.

Rorvreng the Vakka! By: A strong cavalryman's oath.

Rosala: Beautiful, brilliant girl, handmaiden to Delia.

Rovard the Murvish: An initiate of the Brotherhood of the Sorcerers of Murcroinim, an ascetic, dressed in skins and skulls, smells offensively, an adept with the morntarch.

"Run over-hastily on a leem's tracks": Presuming too early to confidences in a relationship.

Ruthmayern: A country of Hamal.

S

Saenci: Pretty Khibil girl, fiancée of Andrinos, brought safely out of Mahendrasmot by Prescot. VFK

Sakkora Stones: Ruined star-shaped buildings of the Sunset People.

Sangar, Orlon, ti Deliasmot: Kerchurivax of the Tenth Kerchuri of the Fifth Phalanx at the Battle of Ovalia. VFK

Sasco! By: An oath so far of obscure provenance used by Kov Loriman, the Hunting Kov.

Scarron Necklace, The: A new play by Master Belzur the Aphorist, produced in Vondium during the troublous times.

Scatulo, Master: A Jikaidast of repute, with too high an opinion of himself, who once owned Bevon as slave. SFK

schrafter: One of the many types of animal infesting dungeons, where they sharpen their teeth on the bones of corpses.

schturval: Any kind of badge, symbol, color, denoting allegiances.

screetz: Sword.

Shanodrin: Princedom of the Dawn Lands.

shansili: A white-flowered creeper with sweet scent grown on trellises.

"She Lived by the Lily Canal": A sentimental song, much sung by the troops on the night before the Battle of Kochwold.

sherissa: A lady's filmy veil.

Shirrerdrin: A country of the Dawn Lands heavily forested with oak trees.

Sicce's Gates: Here an eons-old crack leads down deeply into the crust of the world; place in Vallia where the Vallian Army was overthrown by clansmen. LFK

sko: Left (as distinct from right).

Skull and Crossbones: A game of Kregen.

"Smoke blown with the wind": Water under the bridge.

Sorcerers of Murcroinim: A brotherhood of thaumaturges of some real powers.

Songaslad: A town of thieves in the Dawn Lands where caravans form for the journey across the Desolate Wastes to Jikaida City.

Spag the Junc! By: The favorite oath of Dav Olmes, referring to a spirit causing confusion to honest travelers.

Spikatur Hunting Sword: A secret cult of which, at the moment, little is revealed by Prescot.

Spikatur Cycle, The: The Sixth Cycle of the Saga of Dray Prescot.

Springs of Beng Jasto: Hot mineral springs in Vallia where hides are cured to an exceeding toughness.

Spurs of Lasal the Vakka! By: A mild cavalryman's oath.

Stony Korf: A forbidding fortress in the kovnate of Falinur.

strangdja: A feared weapon of Chem, six-foot-long haft, ten-inch-long steel head of holly-leaf shape, nine spikes a side set alternately forward and back, the lowest pair curving downward into hooks.

strebe: Silver coin of Western Dawn Lands, of two kinds, the broad and the short strebe. It is important in business to know which kind you are bargaining in.

Stroxals: A race of diffs of Kregen.

sturr: A fellow who is mostly silent, a trifle boorish, not particularly favored in handsomeness, louche, maladroit.

swarth: A four-legged risslaca with a cruel, wedge-shaped head sloping into a humped scaled body, clawed feet, not very fast. Has a muscular bulk that carries his rider well and is a saddle animal that jutmen are coming to favor more in Vallia.

Sweet Ibroi: Herb; the burned twigs give off aromatic smoke which invigorates and is used to revive victims of faintness.

Sweet Ordums: Small octagonal biscuits.

Sygurd: Small farming estate in Falinur; Lol Polisto is the squire.

T

Tardalvoh: A bracing dry wine, tart and invigorating.

Tarkshur the Lash: A Kataki from Klardimoin, bought Hunch, Nodgen, and Prescot on the slave auction block, a ferocious slaver, came to a gripping end down the Moder. FFK

"Teach a Wizard to Catch a Fly": Teach your grandmother to suck eggs.

tenash: A large, blundering, grazing animal with a strong hide, which when cured becomes extraordinarily tough and light.

Tezpor: Island of Vallia due north of Rahartdrin.

Thangal: A Trylonate of Hamal northwest of Ruthmayern.

Thefi, Princess: Daughter of Prince Nedfar, a charming and strong-willed girl, with no malice in her but that occasioned by her exalted status and unthinking acceptance of service.

Thrangulf, Kov: Of Hamal, calls himself a plain man, successfully held his kovnate despite his father's animosity because the old kov, Thrangulf's grandfather, lived too long, no ham in his name, generally disliked by people who did not trouble to consider his position, loyal to the Empress Thyllis. FFK

Tipp the Thrax, Kyr: A Huringan cheldur favored by Queen Fahia but lacking the powers of a Roman lanista.

Tlinganden: Free City of the east coast of Loh.

Tlochu: A diff of Kregen with six limbs.

Tomor, Torn: Son of Tom Tomor and Bibi of Valka, a paktun, returned to fight for Vallia, joined the 1EYJ.

Trakon's niksuth: Boggy area surrounding Trakon's Pillars.

Trakon's Pillars: In Falinur, built around the hill rising from the bogs, a decadent place of many palaces with Jikaida as the most prominent architectural and decorative motif.

Trefimlad: A wealthy city of Hamal.

Trip-Tails! By the: A Kataki oath.

tromp: A bright, warm, pleasant yellow color.

Tryflor: A Tryfant spirit or deity.

Tuscursmot: A town of Southern Pandahem.

Tyfar, Prince: Son of Prince Nedfar of Hamal, studious and intelligent, a lover of books, is a superb axemen, honorable and upright, dealing fairly with all, a good comrade to Prescot down the Moder and across the Humped Land and the Dawn Lands.

U

Ungovich, Tyr: The Lord or Wizard of the Moder down which the expedition including Prescot ventured. FFK

urron: Crimson.

V

Vajikry: A board game of Kregen.

Valhan: Name of the last dynasty of Vallia; Dray Prescot began the new dynasty of Prescot.

Vardon the Cheeks: Trumpeter of the 2ESW at the Battle of Ovalia.

Varmondsweay Canal: An Admiralty yard for the flying sailing ships of the Vallian air sailing service in Vondium located by this canal.

Vazkardrin: A vadvarate of Vallia between the east coast and the Kwan Hills.

Vilaha's Tripes: An incident of legend used in oaths.

Villa of Vennar: Layco Jhansi's villa in Vondium, confiscated, used as meeting place of the Presidio in the Time of Troubles.

voinsh: Happy.

Vond: Rich Imperial Province west of Vondium.

W

Wayfarer's Drinnik: Wide, dusty area outside most cities and towns of Paz where the caravans form up or disband.

"Wedding Dirge of Hondor Elaina": A sentimental song.

Wend: A dance accompanied by popular songs, in which the singers form long lines and prance through every nook and cranny of palace, villa, kyro, and avenue of their city they can reach before either the ending of the songs or exhaustion sets in.

Wenhartdrin: Small island off south coast of Vallia, produces first-quality wines, an Imperial Province.

Werven: A small place in the kovnate of Falinur.

"When Zair crooks his finger, then up you go, my friend, and nothing will detain you on Kregen": A saying in the Eye of the World indicating that individual fate will not be balked.

Wizards of Fruningen: A small sect of religious thaumaturges, regarding Opaz as a single entity, with some claims to serious consideration.

Y

Yadivro, Konec, Kov of Brugheim: An upright, determined, not-too-brilliant kov of a province in Mandua hostile to Hamal.

Yagno, San: A Sorcerer of the Cult of Almuensis, foppish, a show-off, drew power from hyr-lifs, vanished in the lowest zone of the Moder. FFK

Yervismot: Town of Vallia taken by Prescot, where he was reunited with Seg Segutorio. LFK

Z

zeunt: The unique vault in Jikaida.

zhantilla: Female zhantil.

zoid: Trap.

zygodont: A reptile with fangs, claws, membranous wings, and barbed tail; can grow to the size of a small zorca excluding the serpent-like neck.

About the author

Alan Burt Akers was a pen name of the prolific British author Kenneth Bulmer, who died in December 2005 aged eighty-four.

Bulmer wrote over 160 novels and countless short stories, predominantly science fiction, both under his real name and numerous pseudonyms, including Alan Burt Akers, Frank Brandon, Rupert Clinton, Ernest Corley, Peter Green, Adam Hardy, Philip Kent, Bruno Krauss, Karl Maras, Manning Norvil, Chesman Scot, Nelson Sherwood, Richard Silver, H. Philip Stratford, and Tully Zetford. Kenneth Johns was a collective pseudonym used for a collaboration with author John Newman. Some of Bulmer's works were published along with the works of other authors under "house names" (collective pseudonyms) such as Ken Blake (for a series of tie-ins with the 1970s television programme The Professionals), Arthur Frazier, Neil Langholm, Charles R. Pike, and Andrew Quiller.

Bulmer was also active in science fiction fandom, and in the 1970s he edited nine issues of the New Writings in Science Fiction anthology series in succession to John Carnell, who originated the series.

More details about the author, and current links to other sources of information, can be found at www.mushroom-ebooks.com, and at wikipedia.org.

CPSIA information can be obtained at www.ICGtesting.com
Printed in the USA
BVOW09s0759120214

344722BV00001B/25/P

9 781843 198222